Also by W.E.B. Griffin

W.E.B

GRIFF

Three Complete N

W.E.B. GRIFFIN

Three Complete Novels

MEN IN BLUE

SPECIAL OPERATIONS

THE VICTIM

G. P. PUTNAM'S SONS
New York

G. P. Putnam's Sons
Publishers Since 1838
200 Madison Avenue
New York, NY 10016
Copyright © 1988, 1989, 1991 by W.E.B. Griffin

Book design by Jennifer Ann Daddio

Library of Congress Cataloging-in-Publication Data

Griffin, W.E.B.
[Selections. 1996]
Three complete novels / W.E.B. Griffin.
p. cm.
Books 1–3 of the Badge of honor.
Contents: Men in blue—Special operations—The victim.
ISBN 0-399-14152-9
1. Detective and mystery stories, American. 2. Police—Pennsylvania—
Philadelphia—Fiction. 3. Philadelphia (Pa.)—Fiction. I. Title.
PS3557.R489137A6   1996   95-39351 CIP
813'.54—dc20

Printed in the United States of America
1   3   5   7   9   10   8   6   4   2

CONTENTS

MEN
IN BLUE

1 *I think I am,* the long-haired, long-legged blonde thought, torn between excitement and alarm, *about to have my first affair with a married man.*

Her name was Louise Dutton, and she pursed her lips thoughtfully and cocked her head unconsciously to one side as she considered that improbable likelihood.

She was at the wheel of a yellow, six-year-old, 1967 Cadillac convertible, the roof down, moving fifteen miles over the posted forty-five-miles-per-hour speed limit northward in the center lane of Roosevelt Boulevard, which runs through the center of Northeast Philadelphia, from Broad Street to the Bucks County line.

Louise Dutton was twenty-five years old, weighed 115 pounds, and her blond hair was real—a genetic gift from her father. She had graduated three years before (BA, English) from the University of Chicago. She had worked a year as a general-assignment reporter on the Cedar Rapids, Iowa, *Clarion;* six months as a newswriter for KLOS-TV (Channel 10), Los Angeles, California; and for eleven months as an on-camera reporter for WNOG-TV (Channel 7), New Orleans, Louisiana. For the past five weeks Louise Dutton had been co-anchor of "Nine's News," over WCBL-TV (Channel 9), Philadelphia: thirty minutes of local news telecast at six P.M., preceding the 6:30 national news, and again at 11 P.M.

A crazy scenario entered her mind.

She would get arrested for speeding. Preferably by one of the hotshot Highway Patrolmen. He would swagger over to the car, in his shiny leather jacket and his gun and holster with all the bullets showing.

"Where's the fire, honey?" Mr. Macho, with a gun and a badge, would demand.

"Actually," she would say, batting her eyelashes at him, "I'm on my way to meet Captain Moffitt."

Captain Richard C. "Dutch" Moffitt was the commanding officer of the Philadelphia Highway Patrol.

And the cop who stopped her for speeding would either believe her, and leave her properly awed, or he would not believe her, and ask her where she was supposed to meet the captain, and she would tell him, and maybe he would follow her there to see if she was telling the truth. That would be even better. Maybe it would embarrass Dutch Moffitt to have one of his men learn that he was meeting a blonde in a restaurant.

It would not, she decided. He'd love it. The cop would wink at Captain Big Dutch Moffitt and Dutch would modestly shrug his shoulders. Dutch expected to have blond young women running after him.

I am losing my mind.

Is this what happened to my mother? One day my father appeared, and she went crazy?

Is that why I'm going where I'm going, and in this circumstance? Because Dutch Moffitt reminds me of my father?

Is it true that all little girls harbor a shameful secret desire to go to bed with their fathers? Is that what this is, "Dutch Moffitt, in loco parentis"?

Ahead, on the left, she spotted the site of their rendezvous. Or was it assignation?

The Waikiki Diner, to judge from the outside decor, was not going to be the Philadelphia equivalent of Arnaud's, or for that matter, even Brennan's; more like the Golden Kettle in Cedar Rapids.

She turned into the U-turn lane, jammed the accelerator to the floor to move her ahead of an oncoming wave of traffic, and then turned off Roosevelt Boulevard, too fast. Louise winced when she felt the Cadillac bottom going over the curb.

The Cadillac was her college graduation gift. Or one of them. Her father had handed her a check and told her to pick herself out a car.

"I'd rather have yours," she said. "If I could."

He had looked at her, confused, for a moment, and then understood. "The yellow convertible? It's three years old. I was about to get rid of it."

"Then I can have it?" she'd said. "It's hardly used."

He had looked at her for a moment, understanding, she thought, before replying.

"Of course," he said. "I'll have someone bring it here."

She had leaned forward and kissed him and said, "Thank you, Daddy," and he'd hugged her.

Louise Dutton's father was not, and never had been, married to her mother. She was illegitimate, a bastard; but the reality hadn't been—wasn't—as bad as most people, when they heard the facts, presumed it was.

She had been presented with the facts when she was a little girl, matter-of-factly told there were reasons her father and mother could not be married, that he could not live with them, or see her as often as he would like. That was the way things were, and it wasn't going to change. She didn't even hate her father's wife, or her half-brothers and -sisters.

It wasn't as if her father considered her an embarrassment, wished she had never happened. The older she got, the more she saw of him. He spent his Christmases with his family, and she spent hers with her mother and her mother's husband, and she called both men "Daddy." So far as she knew, they had never met, and she had never seen her father's family, even across a room.

Her father had always, from the time she was nine or ten, found a couple of days to spend with her before or after Christmas, and he sent for her several times during the year, and she spent several days or a week with him, and he always introduced her as "my daughter."

She had been a freshman in college when he'd taken her deep-sea fishing for ten days in Baja, California. She'd flown to Los Angeles, and spent the night in his beach house in Malibu, and then driven, in the yellow convertible, to Baja. A wonderful ten days. And he knew why she wanted the convertible.

She had wondered what his wife, and her half-brothers and -sisters thought about her, and finally realized they were in the same position she was. Stanford Fortner Wells III, chairman of the board of Wells Newspapers, Inc., did what he damned well pleased. They were just lucky that what he damned well pleased to do was almost invariably kind, and thoughtful, and ethical.

Maybe that was easier if you had inherited that kind of money, and maybe he wouldn't have been so kind, thoughtful, or ethical if he was a life insurance salesman or an automobile dealer, *but he wasn't*. He had inherited seventeen newspapers and three radio stations from his father, and turned that into thirty-one newspapers, four television stations, and four (larger) radio stations.

The only thing that Louise could discover that her father had done wrong was, as a married man, impregnate a woman to whom he was not married. He had sown *her* seed in a forbidden field. But even then, he had done the decent thing. He had not abandoned his wife and children for the greener fields of a much younger woman, and he had not abandoned *her.* He could very easily have made "appropriate financial arrangements" and never shown his face.

She loved and admired her father, and if people didn't understand that, fuck 'em.

Louise found a place to park the yellow convertible, and then walked to the Waikiki Diner. There were no cars in the parking lot that looked like unmarked police cars, which meant that he had either come in his own car, or that he wasn't here yet.

She pushed open the door to the Waikiki Diner and stepped inside. It was larger inside than it looked to be from the outside. It was shaped like an L. The shorter leg, which was what she had seen from the street, held a counter, with padded seats on stools, and one row of banquettes against the wall. Beside the door, which was at the juncture of the legs, was the cashier's glass counter and a bar with a couple of stools, but obviously primarily a service bar. The longer leg was also wider, and was a dining room. There were probably forty tables in there, Louise judged, plus banquettes against the walls.

He wasn't in there.

She thought: *Captain Richard C. "Dutch" Moffitt, commanding officer of the Philadelphia Police Department's Highway Patrol, has not yet found time to grace the Waikiki Diner with his patronage.*

"Help you, doll?" a waitress asked. She was slight, had orange hair, too much makeup, and was pushing sixty.

"I'm supposed to meet someone here," Louise said.

"Why'ncha take a table?" the waitress asked, and led Louise into the dining room. Lousie saw that one of the banquettes against the wall, in a position where she could see the door beside the cash register, was empty, and she slipped into it. The waitress went thirty feet farther before she realized that she wasn't being followed.

Then she turned and, obviously miffed, laid an enormous menu in front of Louise.

"You want a cocktail or something while you're waiting?" she asked.

"Coffee, please, black," Louise said.

She didn't want alcohol to cloud her reasoning any more than it was already clouded.

She looked around the dining room. It was arguably, she decided, the ugliest dining room she had ever been in. Fake Tiffany lamps, with enormous rotating fans hanging from them, in turn hung from plastic replicas of wooden ceiling beams. The banquettes were upholstered in diamond-embossed purple vinyl. The wall across the room was a really awful mural of lasses in flowing dresses and lads in what looked like diapers dancing around what was probably supposed to be the Parthenon.

The coffee was delivered in a thick china mug decorated with a pair of leaning palm trees and the legend, *"Waikiki Diner Roosevelt Blvd Phila Penna."*

Captain Richard C. "Dutch" Moffitt came in as Louise had removed, in shock and surprise, the scalding hot mug from her burned lips.

He had no sooner come through the door by the cashier than a small, slight man with a large mustache, wearing a tight, prominently pin-striped suit, came up to him and offered his hand, his smile revealing a lot of goldwork.

Dutch smiled back at him, revealing his own mouthful of large, white, even teeth. And then he saw Louise, and the smile brightened, and his eyebrows rose and he headed toward the table.

"Hello," Dutch said to her, sliding into the chair facing her.

"Hi!" Louise said.

"This is our host," Dutch said, nodding at the mustached man. "Teddy Galanapoulos."

"A pleasure, I'm sure. Any friend of Captain Moffitt's . . ."

"Hello," Louise said. There was a slight Greek accent, and the gowned lasses and the lads in diapers dancing around the Parthenon were now explained.

"You're beautiful," Dutch said.

"Thank you," Louise said, mortified when she felt her face flush. She stood up. "Will you excuse me, please?"

When she came back from the ladies' room, where she had, furious with herself, checked her hair and her lipstick, Dutch had changed places. He was now sitting on the purple vinyl banquette seat. His left hand, which was enormous, was curled around a squat glass of whiskey. There was a wide gold wedding band on the proper finger.

He started to get up when he saw her.

It was the first time she had ever seen him in civilian clothing. He was wearing a blue blazer over a yellow knit shirt. The shirt was tight against his large chest, and there wasn't, she thought, a lot of excess room in the shoulders of the blazer either.

"Keep your seat," Louise said, "since you seem to like that one better."

"I'm a cop," he said. "Cops don't like to sit with their backs to the door."

"Really?" she asked, not sure if he was pulling her leg or not.

"Really," he said, then added: "I didn't know what you drink."

"I'm surprised," she said.

She had first met him two days before.

His Honor, Mayor Jerry Carlucci, who never passed up an opportunity to get his face in the newspapers or on television, reopened a repaired stretch of the Schuylkill Expressway with a ribbon-cutting ceremony. Louise, having nothing better to do at the time, had gone along with the regular crew of cameraman/producer and reporter, originally intending to do the on-camera bit herself.

But when she got there, and saw what it was, much ado about nothing, she had decided not to usurp the reporter. But instead of leaving, she decided to hang around in case the mayor ran off at the mouth again. Mayor Carlucci had a tendency to do that (in the most recent incident, he had referred to a city councilman as "an ignorant coon") and *that* would make a story.

She told the cameraman to shoot the mayor from the time he arrived until he left.

The mayor usually moved around the city in style, in a black Cadillac limousine, preceded by two unmarked police cars carrying his plainclothes bodyguards.

A third car had stopped right where Louise had been standing. The driver's door had opened, and Captain Richard C. "Dutch" Moffitt had erupted from it. He was a large man, and he had been in uniform. The Highway Patrol wore different uniforms than the rest of the Philadelphia Police Department.

The Highway Patrol had begun, years before, as a traffic-control force, and had been mounted on motorcycles. They had kept their motorcyclist outfits—leather jackets and breeches and black leather puttees—even though, except for mostly ceremonial occasions, they had given up their motorcycles for patrol cars; and had, in fact become an elite force within the police department, deployed city-wide in high-crime areas.

In the Channel 9 newsroom, the Philadelphia Highway Patrol was referred to as "Carlucci's Commandos." But, not, Louise had noticed, without a not-insignificant tone of respect, however grudging.

Louise Dutton had found herself standing so close to Captain Richard C. Moffitt that she could smell his leather jacket, and that he had been chewing Sen-Sen. Her eyes were on the level of his badge, above which was pinned a blue, gold-striped ribbon, on which were half a dozen stars. It was, Louise correctly guessed, some kind of a citation. Citations, plural, with the stars representing multiple awards.

He winked at her, and then, putting his hand on the car door, rose on his toes to look back at Mayor Carlucci's limousine. Louise saw that he wore a wedding ring, and then turned to see what he was looking at. Two plainclothesmen were shouldering a path for His Honor the Mayor through the crowd to the flag-bedecked sawhorses where the ribbon would be cut.

Then he looked down at her.

"I've seen you on the tube," he said. "I'm Dutch Moffitt."

She gave him her hand and her name.

"You look better in real life, Louise Dutton," he said.

"May I ask you a question, Captain Moffitt?" she had said.

"Sure."

"Some of the people I know refer to the Highway Patrol as 'Carlucci's Commandos.' What's your reaction to that?"

"Fuck 'em," he said immediately, matter-of-factly.

"Can I quote you?" she flared.

"You can, but I don't think you could say that on TV," he said, smiling down at her.

"You arrogant bastard!"

"I'd be happy, since you just came to town, to explain what the Highway Patrol does," he said. "And why that annoys the punks and the faggots."

She gave him what she hoped was her most disdainful look.

"I'll even throw in a couple of drinks and dinner," he said.

"Why don't you call me?" Louise had asked, flashing him her most dazzling smile. "At home, of course. I wouldn't want it to get around the station that I was having drinks and dinner with one of Carlucci's Commandos. Especially a married one. So *nice* to talk to you, Captain."

She did not get the response she expected.

"You're really full of piss and vinegar, aren't you?" he said, approvingly.

She had stormed furiously away. She first decided that he was arrogant enough to call her, even if her sarcasm had flown six feet over his head. She took what she later recognized was childish solace in the telephone arrangements at the studios. With all the kooks and nuts out there in TV Land, you just couldn't call Channel 9 and get put through to Louise Dutton. But they might put a police captain through, and then what?

When she went back to the studio, she went to the head telephone operator and told her that for reasons she couldn't go into, if a police captain named Moffitt called, she didn't want to talk to him; tell him she was out.

The arrogant bastard would sooner or later get the message.

And there was no way he could call her at home. The studio wouldn't tell him where she lived, and the number was unlisted.

Today, three hours before, the telephone had rung in her apartment, just as she had stepped into the shower.

She knew it wasn't her father; he had called at ten, waking her up, asking her how it was going. Anybody else could wait. If they'd dropped the atomic bomb, she would have heard it go off.

The phone had not stopped ringing, and finally, torn between gross annoyance and a growing concern that some big story had developed, she walked, dripping water, to the telephone beside her bed.

"Hello?"

"Are you all right?"

There was genuine concern in Captain Dutch Moffitt's voice, but she realized this only after she had snapped at him.

"Why shouldn't I be all right?"

"People have been robbed, and worse, in there before," he said.

"How did you get this number?" Louise demanded, and then thought of another question. "How did you know I was home?"

"I sent a car by," he said. "They told me the yellow convertible was in the garage."

She raised her eyes and saw the reflection of her starkers body in the mirror doors of her closet. She wondered what Captain Dutch Moffitt would think if he could see her.

She shook her head, and felt her face flush.

"What do you want?" she asked.

"I want to see you," he said.

"That's absurd," she said.

"Yeah, I know," he said. "I can take off early at four. There's a diner on Roosevelt Boulevard, at Harbison, called the Waikiki. Meet me there, say four-fifteen."

"Impossible," she said.

"Why impossible?"

"I have to work," she said.

"No, you don't. Don't lie to me, Louise."

"Oh, hell, Dutch!"

"Four-fifteen," he said, and hung up.

And she had looked at her naked body in the mirror again and known that at four o'clock, she would be in the Waikiki Diner.

And here she was, looking into this married man's eyes and suddenly aware that the last thing she wanted in the world was to get involved with him, in bed, or in any other way.

What the hell was I thinking of? I was absolutely out of my mind to come here!

"I'm a cop," he said. "Finding out where you lived and getting your phone number wasn't hard."

"I think I will have a scotch and soda," Louise said. "Johnnie Walker Black."

He pushed his glass to her.

"I'll get another," he said.

It was rude and certainly unsanitary but she picked it up and sipped from it as he gestured toward the bar for another.

Why the hell did I do that? she wondered, and then the answer came to her: *Because I don't know what to do to keep myself from making more of a fool of myself than I already have. How am I going to get out of this?*

The mustached Greek proprietor delivered the drink immediately himself.

"We seem to have at least one thing in common," Dutch Moffitt said.

"Wow!" she said.

"Relax, Louise," he said. "I'm not going to hurt you."

She looked at him again, met his eyes for a moment, and then looked away.

"I don't know why I came here," she said. "But just to clear the air, I now realize it was a mistake."

Dutch Moffitt opened his mouth to reply, but before the words came out, he was interrupted by a male voice.

"Good afternoon, Captain Moffitt, nice to see you."

The sleeve of a glen-plaid suit passed in front of Louise's face.

"Hello, Angelo," Moffitt said.

Louise, once the arm was withdrawn, looked up. A pleasant-looking, olive-skinned man—Italian to judge by the "Angelo"—well barbered, smelling of some expensive cologne, was standing by the table.

"My father was asking about you just this morning," the man said.

"How's your mother, Angelo?" Moffitt asked.

"Very well, thank you," Angelo said.

"Give her my regards," Moffitt said.

Angelo smiled at Louise, and then looked at Moffitt.

"Are you going to introduce me to this charming lady?"

"Nice to see you, Angelo," Moffitt said.

Angelo colored, and then walked away.

"What was that," Louise demanded. "Simply bad manners? Or—"

"That was Angelo Turpino," Moffitt said. "You don't want to know him."

"Why?"

"He's a thug," Moffitt said. "No. Correction. He's a made man. Their standards are slipping. A couple of years ago, that slimy little turd wouldn't have made a pimple on a made man's ass."

"What's a 'made man'?"

He looked at her, into her eyes again.

"When one commences on a career in organized crime, one's highest aspiration is to become a made man," Moffitt said, mockingly. "A made man, so to speak, is one who is accepted, one who enjoys all the rights and privileges of acknowledged master craftsmanship in his chosen trade. Analogous, one might say, to the designation of an individual as a doctor of medicine."

"You're saying that he's in the Mafia?"

"The 'family,' we call it," Moffitt said.

"What did he do to become 'made'?"

"About six weeks ago, Vito Poltaro, sometimes known—from his initials, you see—as 'the vice president,' was found in the trunk of his car in a parking garage downtown, behind the Bellevue-Stratford Hotel. Poor Vito had two .22 holes in the back of his head. Five-dollar bills were found in his mouth, his ears, his nostrils, and other body orifices. This signifies greed. I think that Angelo did it. A week after Organized Crime found Vito, they heard that Angelo had been to New York and had come back a made man."

There was no question in Louise's mind that what he was telling her was true.

"What about Organized Crime finding the body?" she asked. "I didn't understand that."

"There's a unit, called Organized Crime, because what it does is try to keep tabs on people like Angelo," he said.

They were looking into each other's eyes again. Louise averted hers.

"You don't really want to talk about the mob, do you?" he asked.

"No," she said. "I don't."

"Then what shall we talk about?"

"What about your wife?" Louise blurted.

He lowered his head, and shrugged and then looked at her.

And then he said, "Oh, *shit!*"

He was, she saw, looking over her shoulder.

She started to turn around.

"Don't turn around!" he said, quietly but very firmly.

He slipped off the banquette and started toward the door, moving on the balls of his feet, like a cat.

She wanted desperately to look, and started to turn, and then couldn't, because he had said not to. And then she could see him, faintly, in the mirrored side surface of a service table. She saw him brush the flap of his blazer aside with his hand, and then she saw that he had a gun.

Then she turned, chilled.

He was holding the gun with the muzzle pointed down, beside his leg. And he was walking to the cash register.

There was a young man at the cash register, skinny, with long blond hair. He was wearing a zipper jacket, and he had a brown paper bag in his hand, extended toward the cashier as if he was handing it to her.

And then Dutch Moffitt was five feet away from him, and the pistol came up.

She could hear him, even over the sounds of the Waikiki Diner.

"Lay the gun on the counter, son," Dutch said. "I'm a police officer. I don't want to have to kill you."

The kid looked at him, his face turned even more pale. He licked his lips, and he seemed to be lowering the paper bag.

And then there were pops, one after the other, five or six of them, sounding like Chinese firecrackers.

"Oh, shit!" Dutch Moffitt said, more sadly than angrily.

The glass front of the cashier's stand slid with a crash to the floor, and there was an eruption of liquid and falling glass in the rows of liquor bottles in the service bar.

Dutch grabbed the skinny blond kid by the collar of his zipper jacket and threw him violently across the room. Then he took three steps to the door of the diner. He pushed it open with his shoulder, and went through it; and then he was holding his pistol in both hands, taking aim; and then he fired, and again and again.

The noise from his pistol was deafening, shocking, and Louise heard a woman yelp, and someone swore.

The skinny blond boy came running down the aisle. She got a good look at his face. He looked sick.

Louise pushed herself off her chair and ran down the aisle to the cash register.

Dutch was outside, on his knees beside a form on the ground. Louise thought it was another blond boy, but then Dutch turned the body over on its back and she saw lipstick and red, round-framed women's eyeglasses.

"He ran into the restaurant," Louise screamed. When there was no response from Dutch she screamed his name, and got his attention, and, pointing, repeated, "He ran into the restaurant. The blond boy."

He got up and walked quickly past her. She followed him.

The Greek proprietor came up.

"He ran through the kitchen, the sonofabitch," he reported.

Dutch nodded.

He put his pistol back in its holster and fished the cashier's telephone from where it had fallen, onto the cigars and foil-wrapped chocolates, when the glass counter had shattered.

He dialed a number.

"This is Captain Moffitt, Highway Patrol," he said. "I'm at Harbison and the Boulevard, the Waikiki Diner. Give me an assist. I have a robbery and a police shooting and a hospital case. I'm hit. One male fled on foot, direction unknown, white, in his twenties. Long blond hair, brown zipper jacket. No! God*damn* it. *Harbison* and the Boulevard."

He put the phone back in the cradle, smiled reassuringly at Louise, and raised his voice.

"It's all over, folks," he said. "Nothing else to worry about. You just sit there and finish your meals."

He turned and looked at Louise again.

"Dutch, are you all right?" Louise asked.

"Fine," he said. "I'm fine."

And then he staggered, moving backward until he encountered the wall.

His face was now very white.

"It was a goddamned girl!" he said, surprised, barely audibly.

And then he just crumpled to the floor.

"Dutch!" Louise cried, and went to him.

He's fainted! That's all it is, he's fainted!

And then she saw his eyes, and there was no life in them.

"Oh, Dutch!" Louise wailed. "Oh, damn you, Dutch!"

Philadelphia, in 1973 the fourth-largest city of the United States, lies in the center of the New York–Washington corridor, one of the most densely populated areas in the country.

A one-hundred-mile-radius circle drawn from William Penn's statue atop City Hall at Broad and Market streets in downtown Philadelphia takes in Harrisburg to the west; skirts Washington, D.C., to the south; takes in almost all of Delaware and the New Jersey shore to the southeast and east; touches the tip of Manhattan Island to the northeast; and just misses Scranton, Pennsylvania, to the north.

Within that one-hundred-mile-radius circle are major cities: Baltimore, Maryland; Camden, Trenton, Elizabeth, Newark, and Jersey City, New Jersey; plus a long list of somewhat smaller cities, such as Atlantic City, New Jersey; Wilkes-Barre, Pennsylvania; Wilmington, Delaware, and New Brunswick, New Jersey; York, Lancaster, Reading, Allentown, Bethlehem, and Hazleton, Pennsylvania; plus the boroughs of Manhattan, Brooklyn, and Richmond (Staten Island) of New York City.

There are more than four million people in the "standard metropolitan statistical area" of Philadelphia and its environs, and something over two million people within the city limits, which covers 129 square miles. In 1973, there were approximately eight thousand policemen keeping the peace in the City of Brotherly Love.

The Police Administration Building on Vine Street in downtown Philadelphia is what in another city would be called "police headquarters." In Philadelphia it is known to the police and public as "the Roundhouse."

The architect who envisioned the building managed to pass on his enthusiasm for the curve to those city officials charged with approving its design. There are no straight corridors; the interior and exterior walls, even those of the elevators, are curved.

The Radio Room of the Philadelphia Police Department is on the second floor of the Roundhouse. Within the Radio Room are rows of civilian employees, leavened with a few sworn police officers, who sit at telephone and radio consoles receiving calls from the public, and from police vehicles "on the street" and relaying official orders to police vehicles.

There are twenty-two police districts in Philadelphia, each charged with maintaining the peace in its area. Each has its complement of radio-equipped police cars and vans. Additionally, there are seven divisions of detectives, occupying office space in district buildings, but answering to a detective hierarchy, rather than to the district commander. They have their own, radio-equipped, police cars.

Radio communication is also maintained with the vehicles of the Philadelphia Highway Patrol, which has its own headquarters; with the vehicles of the Traffic, Accident, and Juvenile divisions; with the fleet of police tow trucks; and with the vehicles of the various special-purpose units, such as the K-9 Unit, the Marine Unit, the Vice, Narcotics, Organized Crime units, and others.

And on top of this, of course, is the necessity to maintain communications with the vehicles of the senior command hierarchy of the police department, the commissioner, and his staff; the deputy commissioners and their staffs; the chief inspectors and their staffs; and a plethora of other senior police officers.

With more than a thousand police vehicles "on the street" at any one time, it was necessary to develop, both by careful planning and by trial and error, a system permitting instant contact with the right vehicle at the right time. The police commissioner is not really interested to learn instantly of every automobile accident in Philadelphia, nor is a request from the airport police for a paddy wagon to haul off three drunks from the airport of much interest to a detective looking for a murder suspect in an alley off North Broad Street.

So far as the police were concerned, Philadelphia was broken down into seven geographical divisions, each headed by an inspector. Each division contained from two to four districts, each headed by a captain. Each division was assigned its own radio frequency. Detectives' cars and those assigned to other investigative units (Narcotics, Intelligence, Organized Crime, et cetera) had radios operating on the H-Band. *All* police car radios could be switched to an all-purpose emergency and utility frequency called the J-Band.

For example, a police car in the Sixteenth District would routinely have his switch set to F-1, which would permit him to communicate with his (the West) division. Switching to F-2 would put him on the universal J-Band. A car assigned to South Philadelphia with his switch set to F-1 would be in contact with the South Division. A detective operating anywhere with his switch set to F-1 would be on the (Detectives') H-Band, but he too, by switching to F-2, would be on the J-Band.

Senior police brass are able to communicate with other senior police brass, and most often on the detective frequency or on the frequency of some other service in which he has a personal interest. Ordinary police cars are required to communicate through the dispatcher, and forbidden to talk car-to-car. Car-to-car communication is authorized on the J- and H-bands.

"Communications discipline" is strictly enforced. Otherwise, there would be communications chaos.

By throwing the appropriate switch, a Radio Room dispatcher may send a radio message to every radio-equipped vehicle, from a police boat making its way against the current of the Delaware River, through the hundreds of police cars on patrol, to the commissioner's car.

It happens when a light flashes on a console and an operator throws a switch and says, "Police Radio," and the party calling says, "Officer needs assistance. Shots fired."

Not every call making such an announcement is legitimate. The wise guys have watched cop movies on television, and know the cant; and ten or twelve times every day they decide that watching a flock of police cars, lights flashing and sirens screaming, descend on a particular street corner would be a good way to liven up an otherwise dull afternoon.

The people who answer the telephones didn't come to work yesterday, however, and sometimes they *know,* by the timbre of the caller's voice possibly, or the assurance with which the caller raises the alarm, that *this* call is legitimate.

The dispatcher who took Captain Richard C. "Dutch" Moffitt's call from the Waikiki Diner was Mrs. Leander Polk, forty-eight, a more than pleasantly plump black lady who had been on the job for nineteen years.

"Lieutenant!" she called, raising her voice, just to get his attention, not to ask his permission. Then she threw the appropriate switch.

Two beeps, signifying an emergency message, were broadcast to every police radio in Philadelphia.

"Roosevelt Boulevard and Harbison," Mrs. Polk said clearly. "The Waikiki Diner. Assist officer. Police by phone."

She repeated that message once again, and then went on: "Report of a robbery, shooting, and hospital case." She repeated that, and then, quickly, to the lieutenant who had come to her station: "Captain Moffitt called it in."

And then she broadcast: "All cars going in on the assist, Harbison and the Boulevard, flash information on a robbery at that location. Be on the lookout for white male, long blond hair, brown jacket, direction taken unknown, armed with a gun."

And then she repeated that.

 Highway Two-B was a Philadelphia Highway Patrol vehicle moving southward on Roosevelt Boulevard, just entering Oxford Circle. It was occupied by Sergeant Alexander W. Dannelly, and driven by Police Officer David N. Waldron. Sergeant Dannelly and Officer Waldron had moments before seen Captain Dutch Moffitt going into the Waikiki Diner, dressed to kill in civvies.

It was four in the afternoon, and Captain Dutch Moffitt usually worked until half-past five, and often longer. And in uniform.

"The captain is obviously engaged in a very secret undercover investigation," Sergeant Dannelly said.

"Under-the-covers, you said, Sergeant?" Officer Waldron asked, grinning.

"You have an evil mind, Officer Waldron," Sergeant Dannelly said, grinning back. "Shame on you!"

"How about a cup of coffee, Sergeant?" Waldron asked. "The Waikiki serves a fine cup of coffee."

"You also have a suicidal tendency," Sergeant Dannelly said. "I ever tell you that?"

Two beeps on the radio cut off the conversation.

"Roosevelt Boulevard and Harbison," the dispatcher's voice said. "The Waikiki Diner. Assist officer. Police by phone. Roosevelt Boulevard and Harbison. The Waikiki Diner. Assist officer. Police by phone."

"Jesus Christ!" Officer Waldron said.

"That's got to be the captain," Dannelly said.

"Report of a robbery, shooting, and hospital case," the dispatcher said. "All cars going in on the assist, Harbison and the Boulevard, flash information on a robbery at that location. Be on the lookout for Caucasian male, long blond hair, brown jacket, direction taken unknown, armed with a gun."

As Sergeant Dannelly reached for the microphone, without waiting for orders, Officer Waldron had dropped the transmission shift lever into D-2, and flipped the switches activating the flashing light assembly and the siren, and then shoved his foot to the floor.

"Highway Two-B in on that," Sergeant Dannelly said into the microphone.

The Ford, its engine screaming in protest, tires squealing, accelerated the rest of the way around Oxford Circle and back down Roosevelt Boulevard toward the Waikiki Diner.

The second response came on the heels of Highway Two B's: "Two-Oh-One in on that Waikiki Diner."

It was not the truth, the whole truth, and nothing but the truth. Two-Oh-One was not that *instant* responding to the call.

The Waikiki Diner was in the territory of the Second Police District. Two-Oh-One was a Second Police District patrol wagon, a Ford van.

Philadelphia police, unlike those of every other major city, respond to all calls for any kind of assistance.

If you break a leg, *call the cops!* If Uncle Harry has a heart attack, *call the cops!* If you get your fingers in the Waring blender, *call the cops!*

A paddy wagon will respond, and haul you to the hospital. Not in great comfort, for the back of the van holds only a stretcher, and there is no array of high-tech life-saving apparatus. But it will cart you to the hospital as fast as humanly possible.

Paddy wagons are police vehicles, driven by armed sworn police officers, normally young muscular officers without much time on the job. Young muscles are often needed to carry large citizens down three flights of stairs, and to restrain bellicose drunks, for the paddy wagon also still performs the function it did when it was pulled by horses, and "paddy" was a pejorative term for those of Irish heritage. Paddy wagon duty is recognized to be a good way to introduce young police officers to what it's really like on the streets.

When the "assist officer" call came over the radio, Two-Oh-One was parked outside Sid's Steak Sandwiches & Hamburgers on the corner of Cottman and Summerdale avenues, across from Northeast High School. Officer Francis Mason was at the wheel and Officer Patrick Foley was inside Sid's, where he had ordered a couple of cheese steaks and two large Cokes to go, and then visited the gentlemen's rest facility. He and Francis had attended a function of the Fraternal Order of Police the night before, and he had taken advantage of the free beer bar. He'd had the runs all day.

Officer Mason, when he got the call, picked up the microphone and said Two-Oh-One was responding, flicked up the siren and lights, and reached over and pushed open the passenger side door. It was ninety seconds, but seemed much longer, before Officer Foley appeared, on the run, a pained look on his face, fastening his gun belt, and jumped in the van.

Officer Mason made a U-turn on Summerdale Avenue; skidded to a stop at Cottman; waited until there was a break in the traffic; and then turned onto Cottman, running on the left side of the avenue, against oncoming traffic, until he was finally able to force himself into the inside right lane.

"I think I shit my pants," Officer Foley said.

The broadcast was also received by a vehicle parked in the parking lot of LaSalle College at Twentieth Street and Olney Avenue, where a crew from WCBL-TV had just finished taping yet another student protest over yet another tuition increase. After a moment's indecision, Miss Penny Bakersfield, the reporter, told the driver that there might be something in the car for "Nine's News," if he thought he could get there in a hurry.

Highway Two-B made a wide sweeping U-turn, its tires screeching, from the northbound center lane of Roosevelt Boulevard into the southbound right lane and then into the parking lot of the Waikiki Diner.

There were no police cars evident in the parking lot; that made it almost certain that the "assist officer, shots fired" call had come from Captain Dutch Moffitt, who had either been in his unmarked car, or his own car.

Sergeant Dannelly had the door open before Highway Two-B lurched to a stop in front of the diner. Pistol drawn, he ran into the building, with Waldron on his heels.

A blond woman was on her knees beside Dutch Moffitt, who seemed to be sitting on the floor with his back against the wall. Dannelly pushed her out of the way, saw the blank look in Moffitt's eyes, and then felt for a pulse.

"He ran out the back," the woman said, very softly.

"Go after him!" Dannelly ordered Waldron. "I'll go around outside."

He pushed himself to his feet and ran back out of the diner. He recognized the signs of fury in himself—*some miserable fucking pissant shit had shot Dutch, the best goddamn captain in the department*—and told himself to take it easy.

He stopped and took two deep breaths and then started to run around the diner building. Then he changed his mind. He ran to the car, whose doors were still open, switched the radio to the J-Band, and picked up the microphone.

"Highway Two-B to radio. Will you have all Highway cars switch to J-Band, please."

He waited a moment, to give radio time to relay the message, and to give everybody time to switch frequencies, and then put the mike to his lips again.

"Highway Two-B to all Highway cars. We have a police shooting at Boulevard and Harbison involving Highway One. All Highway units respond and survey the area for suspect. Radio, will you rebroadcast the description of the suspect?"

He threw the microphone on the seat and started to run to the rear of the Waikiki Diner. He knew that all over the city, every Highway Patrol car had turned on its siren and flashing lights and was heading for the Waikiki Diner.

"Highway takes care of its own," Sergeant Dannelly said firmly, although there was nobody around to hear him.

The third response to the "assist officer, shots fired" call came from a new, light tan 1973 Ford LTD Brougham, which was proceeding northward on Roosevelt Boulevard, just past Adams Avenue and the huge, red brick regional offices of Sears, Roebuck & Company.

There was nothing to indicate the LTD was a police vehicle. It even had whitewall tires. When the driver, Peter F. Wohl, a tall man in his very early thirties, wearing a well-cut glen-plaid suit, decided to respond, he had to lean over and open the glove compartment to take the microphone out.

"Isaac Twenty-three," he said to the microphone, "put me in on that assist."

He pushed in the button on the steering wheel that caused all the lights on the LTD to flash on and off (what Ford called "the emergency flasher system") and started methodically sounding his horn. The LTD had neither a siren nor a flashing light.

"Isaac" was the call sign for "Inspector." Peter F. Wohl was a Staff Inspector. On those very rare occasions when he wore a uniform, it carried a gold leaf insignia, identical to the U.S. military's insignia for a major.

A Staff Inspector ranked immediately above a captain, and immediately below an inspector, who wore the rank insignia of a lieutenant colonel. There were eighteen of them, and Peter F. Wohl was the youngest. Staff inspectors thought of themselves as, and were generally regarded, by those who knew what they really did, to be, some of the best cops around.

They were charged with investigating police corruption, but that was not all they did, and they didn't even do that the way most people thought they did. They were not interested in some cop taking an Easter ham from a butcher, but their ears did pick up when the word started going around that a captain somewhere had taken a blonde not his wife to Jersey to play the horses in a new Buick.

As they thought of it, they investigated corruption in the city administration; fraud against the city; bribery and extortion; crimes with a political connection; the more interesting endeavors of organized crime; a number of other interesting things; and only way down at the bottom of the list, crooked cops.

Peter (no one had ever called him "Pete," not even as a kid; even then he had had a quiet dignity) Wohl did not look much the popular image of a cop. People would guess that he was a stockbroker, or maybe an engineer or lawyer. A *professional,* in other words. But he was a cop. He'd done his time walking a beat, and he'd even been a corporal in the Highway Patrol. But when he'd made sergeant, young, not quite six years on the force, they'd assigned him to the Civil Disobedience Squad, in plain clothes, and he'd been in plain clothes ever since.

It was said that Peter Wohl would certainly make it up toward the top, maybe all the way. He had the smarts and he worked hard, and he seldom made mistakes. Equally important, he came from a long line of cops. His father had retired as a Chief Inspector, and the line went back far behind him.

The roots of the Wohl family were in Hesse. Friedrich Wohl had been a farmer from a small village near Kassel, pressed into service as a Grenadier in the Landgrave of Hesse-Kassel's Regiment of Light Foot. Primarily to finance a university he had founded (and named after himself) in buildings he confiscated from the Roman Catholic Church at Marburg an der Lahn, Landgrave Philip had rented out his soldiers to His Most Britannic Majesty, George III of England, who had a rebellion on his hands in his North American colonies.

Some predecessor of William Casey (some say it was Baron von Steuben, others think it was the Marquis de Lafayette) pointed out to the founding fathers that the Landgrave of Hesse-Kassel's Regiment of Light Foot (known, because of their uniforms, as "the Redcoats") were first-class soldiers, sure to cause the Continental Army a good deal of trouble. But they also pointed out that many of them were conscripted, and not very fond of the Landgrave for conscripting them. And, further, that a number of them were Roman Catholic, who considered the Landgrave's expulsion of the Church and his confiscation of Church property an unspeakable outrage against Holy Mother Church.

It was theorized that an offer of 160 acres of land, a small amount of gold, and a horse might induce a number of the Redcoats to desert. The theory was put into practice and at least one hundred Redcoats took advantage of the offer. Among them, although he was not a Roman Catholic and had entered the service of the Landgrave voluntarily, was Grenadier Friedrich Wohl.

Friedrich Wohl's farm, near what is now Media, prospered. When the War of 1812 came along, he borrowed heavily against it, and used the money to invest in a privateer, which would prey upon British shipping and make him a fortune. The *Determination* sailed down the Delaware with all flags flying and was never heard from again.

Wohl lost his farm and was reduced to hiring himself and his sons out as farm laborers.

The sons moved to Philadelphia, where they practiced, without notable success, various trades and opened several small businesses, all of which failed. In 1854, following the Act of Consolidation, which saw the area of Philadelphia grow from 360 acres to 83,000 by the consolidation of all the tiny political entities in the area into a city, Karl-Heinz Wohl, Friedrich Wohl's youngest grandson, managed to have himself appointed to the new police department.

There had been at least one Wohl on the rolls of the Philadelphia Police Department ever since. When Peter Wohl graduated from the police academy, a captain, two lieutenants, and a detective who were either his uncles or cousins sat with Chief Inspector August Wohl on folding chairs in the auditorium watching Peter take the oath.

There was a long line of cars slowing to enter Oxford Circle ahead of him, a line that was not likely to make room for him, no matter how his lights flashed, or he sounded the horn. He fumed until his path was cleared, then floored the accelerator, racing through the circle, and leaving in his wake a half dozen citizens wondering where the cops were when they were needed to protect people from idiots like the one in the tan Ford.

He reached the intersection on Roosevelt Boulevard, at the 6600 block, where Harbison and Magee come together to cross it, and then separate again on the other side. The light was orange and then red, but he thought he could beat the first car starting up, and floored it and got across to the far lane, and then had to brake hard to keep from getting broadsided by a paddy wagon that had come down Bustleton Avenue.

The cop at the wheel of the wagon gave him a look of absolute contempt and fury as it raced past him.

Wohl followed it into the Waikiki Diner parking lot, and stopped behind it.

There was a Highway Patrol car, both doors open, nose against the entrance; and Wohl caught a glimpse of a Highway Patrolman running like hell, pistol pointing to the sky next to his ear, obviously headed for the rear of the building.

Wohl got out of his car and started toward the diner.

"Hey, you!" a voice called.

It was the driver of the wagon. He had his pistol out, too, with the muzzle pointed to the sky.

"Police officer," Wohl said, and then, when he saw a faint glimmer of disbelief on the young cop's face, added, "Inspector Wohl."

The cop nodded.

Wohl started again toward the diner entrance and almost stepped on the body of a young person lying in a growing pool of blood. Wohl quickly felt for a pulse, and as he decided there was none, became aware that the body was that of a young woman.

He stood up and took his pistol, a Smith & Wesson "Chief's Special" snub-nosed .38 Special, from its shoulder holster. There was no question now that shots had been fired.

"In here, Officer!" a voice called, and when Wohl saw that it was Teddy Galanapoulos, who owned the Waikiki, he pushed his jacket out of the way, and reholstered his pistol. Whatever had happened here was over.

Teddy hadn't been calling to him, and when he ran up looked at him curiously, even suspiciously, until he recognized him.

"Lieutenant Wohl," he said.

It was not the right place or time to correct him.

"Hello, Mr. Galanapoulos," Wohl said. "What's going on?"

"Fucking kid killed Captain Moffitt," Teddy said, and pointed.

Dutch Moffitt, in civilian clothes, was slumped against the wall. A woman was kneeling beside him. She was sobbing, and as Wohl watched, she put a hand out very gingerly and very tenderly and pulled Dutch's eyelids closed.

Wohl turned to the door. The cop from the paddy wagon was coming in, and the parking lot was filling with police cars, which screeched to a halt and from which uniformed police erupted.

"Put your gun away," Wohl ordered, "and go get your stretcher. The woman in the parking lot is dead."

A look of disappointment on his face, the young cop did as he was ordered.

A Highway Patrol sergeant, one Wohl didn't recognize, walked quickly through the restaurant, holstering his pistol. He looked curiously at Wohl.

"I'm Inspector Wohl," Wohl said.

"Yes, sir," Sergeant Alex Dannelly said. "There was two of them, sir. Dutch got the one that shot him. The other one, a white male twenty to twenty-five years old, blond hair, ran through the restaurant and out the kitchen."

"You get it on the air?"

"No, sir," Dannelly said.

"Do it, then," Wohl ordered. "And then seal this place up, make sure nobody leaves, keep the people in their seats, make sure nothing gets disturbed . . ."

"Got it," the Highway Patrol sergeant said, and went to the door and waved three policemen inside.

Wohl dropped to his knees beside the woman, and laid a gentle hand on her back.

"My name is Wohl," he said. "I'm a police officer."

She turned to look at him. There was horror in her eyes, and tears running down her cheeks had left a path through her face powder. She looked familiar. And she was not Mrs. Richard C. Moffitt.

"Let me help you to your feet," Wohl said, gently.

"Get a blanket or something," Louise Dutton said, in nearly a whisper. "Cover him up, goddamn it!"

"Teddy," Wohl ordered. "Get a tablecloth or something."

He helped the woman to her feet.

Officer Francis Mason and Officer Patrick Foley ran in, with the stretcher from the back of Two-Oh-One. They quickly snapped the stretcher open and unceremoniously heaved Dutch Moffitt onto it. Wohl started for the door to open it for them, but a uniform beat him to it.

The sound of sirens outside was now deafening. He looked through the plate-glass door of the diner and saw there were police cars all over it. As he watched, a white van with WCBL-TV CHANNEL 9 painted on its side pulled to the curb, a sliding door opened, and a man with a camera resting on his shoulders jumped out.

Wohl turned to the blonde. "You were a friend of Captain Moffitt's?"

She nodded.

Where the hell do I know her from? What was she up to with Dutch?

"Why are they doing that?" she asked. "He's dead, isn't he?"

I don't know why they're doing that, Wohl thought. *The dead are left where they have fallen, for the convenience of the Homicide Detectives. But, I guess maybe no one wants to admit that a fellow cop is really dead.*

"Yes, I'm afraid he is," Wohl said. "Can you tell me what happened?"

"He was trying to stop a holdup," Louise said. "And somebody shot him. A girl, he said."

A portly, red-faced policeman in a white shirt with captain's bars pinned to the epaulets of his white shirt came into the Waikiki.

His name was Jack McGovern, and he was the commanding officer of the Second District. He had been a lieutenant in Highway Patrol when Peter Wohl had been a corporal. He had made captain on the promotion list before Peter Wohl had made captain, and they had sat across the room from each other when they'd sat for the Staff Inspector's examination. Peter Wohl had been first on the list; Jack McGovern hadn't made it.

McGovern's eyebrows rose when he saw Wohl.

"What the hell happened?" he asked. "Was that Dutch Moffitt they just carried out of here?" he asked.

"That was Dutch," Wohl confirmed. "He walked in on a holdup."

McGovern's eyebrows rose in question.

"He's gone, Jack," Wohl said.

"Jesus," McGovern said, and crossed himself.

"I think it would be better if you took care of the parking lot," Wohl said. "You're in uniform. You see the woman's body?"

McGovern shook his head. "A woman? A woman shot Dutch?"

"There were two of them," Wohl said. "One ran. Dutch got the other one. I don't know who shot Dutch."

"He said it was a woman," Louise Dutton said, softly.

Captain McGovern looked at her, his eyebrows raising, and then at Wohl.

"This lady was with Captain Moffitt at the time," Wohl said, evenly. He turned to Louise. "I've got to make a telephone call," he said. "It won't take a moment."

She nodded.

Wohl looked around for a telephone, saw the cashier's phone lying on the floor off the hook, and went to a pay phone on the wall. He dropped a dime in it and dialed a number from memory.

"Commissioner's office, Sergeant Jankowitz."

"Peter Wohl, Jank. Let me talk to him. It's important."

"Peter?" Commissioner Thaddeu Czernich said when he came on the line a moment later. "What's up?"

"Commissioner, Dutch Moffitt walked into a holdup at the Waikiki Diner on Roosevelt Boulevard. He was shot to death. He put down one of them; the other got away."

"Jesus H. Christ!" Commissioner Czernich replied. "The one he got is dead?"

"Yes, sir. It's a woman, and a witness says she's the one that shot him. She said Dutch said a woman got him. I just got here."

"Who else is there?"

"Captain McGovern."

"Jesus Christ, Dutch's brother got himself killed too," the commissioner said. "You remember that?"

"I heard that, sir." And then, delicately, he added: "Commissioner, the witness, a woman, was with Dutch."

There was a perceptible pause.

"So?" Commissioner Czernich asked.

"I don't know, sir," Wohl said.

"That was the other phone, Peter. We just got notification from radio," Commissioner Czernich said. "Who's the woman?"

"I don't know. She looks familiar. Young, blond, good-looking."

"Goddamn!"

"I thought I had better call, sir."

"You stay there, Peter," the commissioner ordered. "I'll call the mayor, and get out there as soon as I can. Do what you think has to be done about the woman."

"Yes, sir," Wohl said.

The commissioner hung up without saying anything else.

Wohl put the phone back in its cradle, and without thinking about it, ran his fingers in the coin return slot. He was surprised when his fingers touched coins. He took them out and looked at them, and then went to Louise Dutton.

"Are you all right?"

Louise shrugged.

"A real tragedy," Wohl said. "He has three young children."

"I know he was married," Louise said, coldly.

"Would you mind telling me how you happened to be here with him?" Wohl asked.

"I'm with WCBL-TV," she said.

"I knew your face was familiar," Wohl said.

"He was going to tell me what he thinks about people calling the Highway Patrol 'Carlucci's Commandos,' " Louise said, carefully.

That's bullshit, Wohl decided. *There was something between them.*

As if that was a cue, the Channel 9 cameraman appeared at the door. A policeman blocked his way.

"Christ, if she's in there, why can't I go in?" the cameraman protested.

Wohl stepped to the door, spotted McGovern, and raised his voice. "Jack, would you get up some barricades, please? And keep people out of our way?"

He saw from the look on McGovern's face that the television cameraman had slipped around the policemen McGovern had already put in place.

"Get that guy out of there," McGovern said, sharply, to a sergeant. "The TV guy."

Wohl turned back to Louise.

"It would be very unpleasant for Mrs. Moffitt, or the children," he said, "if they heard about this over the television, or the radio."

Louise looked at him without real comprehension for a minute.

"I don't know about Philadelphia," she said. "But most places, there's an unwritten rule that nothing, no names anyway, about something like this gets on the air until the next of kin are notified."

"That's true here, too," Wohl said. "But I always like to be double sure."

"Okay," she said. "I suppose I could call."

"That would be very much appreciated," Wohl said. He extended his hand to her, palm upward, offering her change for the telephone.

Louise dialed the "Nine's News" newsroom, and Leonard Cohen, the news director, answered.

"Leonard, this is Louise Dutton. A policeman has been killed—"

"At the Waikiki Diner on Roosevelt Boulevard?" Cohen interrupted. "You there?"

"Yes," Louise said. "Leonard, the police don't want his wife to hear about it over the air."

"You know who it was?"

"I was with him," Louise said.

"You saw it?"

"I don't want his wife to find out over the air," Louise said.

"Hey, no problem. Of course not. Have the public affairs guy call us when we can use it, like usual."

"All right," Louise said.

"Tell the crew to get what they can, at an absolute minimum, some location shots, and then you come in, and we can put it together here," Cohen said. "We'll probably use it for the lead-in and the major piece. Nothing else much has happened. And you *saw* it?"

"I saw it," Louise said. "I'll be in."

She hung up the phone.

"I just spoke with the news director," she said. "He said he won't use it until your public affairs officer clears it. He wants him to call."

"I'll take care of it," Wohl said. "Thank you very much, Miss Dutton."

She shrugged, bitterly. "For what?" she asked, and then: "How will she find out? Who tells her?"

Wohl hesitated a moment, and then told her: "There's a routine, a procedure, we follow in a situation like this. The captain in charge of the district where Captain Moffitt lived was notified right away. He will go to Captain Moffitt's house and drive Mrs. Moffitt to the hospital. By the time they get there, the mayor, and probably the commissioner and the chief of Special Patrol, will be there. And probably Captain Moffitt's parish priest, or the department Catholic chaplain. They will tell her. They're friends. Captain Moffitt is from an old police family."

She nodded.

"While that's been going on," Wohl said, wondering why, since he hadn't been asked, he was telling her all this, "radio will have notified Homicide, and the Crime Lab, and the Northeast Detectives. They'll be here in a few minutes. Probably, since Captain Moffitt was a senior police officer, the chief inspector in charge of homicide will roll on this, too."

"And she gets to ride to the hospital, while the police radio is talking about what happened here, right? God, that's brutal!"

"The police radio in the car will be turned off," Wohl said.

She looked at him.

"We learn from our mistakes," Wohl said. "Policemen get killed. Captain Moffitt's brother was killed in the line of duty, too."

She met his eyes, and her eyebrows rose questioningly, but she didn't say anything.

"The homicide detectives will want to interview you," Wohl said. "I suppose you understand that you're a sort of special witness, a trained observer. The way that's ordinarily done is to transport you downtown, to the Homicide Division in the Roundhouse . . ."

"Oh, God!" Louise Dutton said. "Do I have to go through that?"

"I said 'ordinarily,' " Wohl said. "There's always an exception."

"Because I was with him? Or because I'm with WCBL-TV?"

"How about a little bit of both?" Wohl replied evenly. "In this case, what I'm going to do is have an officer drive you home."

I have the authority to let her get away from here, to send *her away,* Wohl thought. *The commissioner said,* "Do what you have to do about the woman," *but I didn't have to. I wonder why I did?*

"I'm not going home," she said. "I'm going to the studio."

"Yes, of course," he said. "Then to the studio, and then home. Then, in an hour or so, when things have settled down a little, I'll arrange to have some officers come to the station, or your house, and take you to the Roundhouse for your statement."

"I don't need anybody to drive me anywhere," Louise said, almost defiantly.

"I think maybe you do," Wohl said. "You've gone through an awful experience, and I really don't think you should be driving. And we owe you one, anyway."

She looked at him, *as if she's seeing me for the first time,* Wohl thought.

"I didn't get your name," she said.

"Wohl, Peter Wohl," he said.

"And you're a policeman?"

"I'm a Staff Inspector," he said.

"I don't know what that is," she said. "But I saw you ordering that captain around."

"I didn't mean to do that," he said. "But right now, I'm the senior officer on the scene."

She exhaled audibly.

"All right," she said. "Thank you. All of a sudden I feel a little woozy. Maybe I shouldn't be driving."

"It always pays to be careful," Wohl said, and took her arm and went to the door and caught Captain McGovern's attention and motioned him over.

"Jack, this is Miss Louise Dutton, of Channel 9. She's been very cooperative. Can you get me a couple of officers and a car, to drive her to the studio, drive her car, too, and then take her home?"

"I recognize Miss Dutton, now," McGovern said. "Sure, Inspector. No problem. You got it. Glad to be able to be of help, Miss Dutton."

"Have you caught the other one, the boy?" Louise asked.

"Not yet," Captain McGovern said. "But we'll get him."

"And the other one, the one who shot Captain Moffitt, was it a girl?"

"Yes, ma'am, it was a girl," Captain McGovern said, and nodded with his head.

Louise followed the nod. A man in civilian clothing, but with a pistol on his hip, and therefore certainly a cop, was stepping around the body, taking pictures of it from all angles. And then he finished. When he did, another policeman (a *detective,* Louise corrected herself) bent over and with a thick chunk of yellow chalk, outlined the body on the parking lot's macadam.

"Where's your car, Miss Dutton?" Wohl asked.

Louise could not remember where she had left it. She looked around until she found it, and then pointed to it.

"Over there," she said, "the yellow one."

"Would you like to ride in your car, or in the police car?" Wohl asked.

Louise thought that over for a moment before replying, "I think my car."

"These officers will take you to the studio and then home, Miss Dutton," Wohl said. "Please don't go anywhere else until we've taken care of your interview with Homicide. Thank you very much for your cooperation."

He offered his hand, and she took it.

The first thing Wohl thought was professional. Her hand was a little clammy, often a symptom of stress. Getting a cop to drive her had been a good idea, beyond hoping that it would make her think well of the police department. Then he thought that it was a very nice hand, indeed. Soft and smooth skinned.

There was little question what Dutch saw in her, he thought. But what did she see in him? This was a tough, well-educated young woman, not some secretary likely to be awed by a big, strong policeman.

A black Oldsmobile with red lights flashing from behind the grille pulled into the parking lot as Louise Dutton's yellow convertible, following a blue-and-white, turned onto Roosevelt Boulevard.

Chief Inspector of Detectives Matt Lowenstein, a large, florid-faced, silver-haired man in his fifties, got out the passenger side and walked purposefully over to McGovern and Wohl.

"Goddamned shame," he said. "Goddamned shame. They pick up the one that got away?"

"Not yet, sir," McGovern said. "But we will."

"Every male east of Broad Street with a zipper jacket and blond hair has been stopped for questioning," Wohl said, dryly. Lowenstein looked at him, waiting for an explanation. "A Highway Patrol sergeant went on the J-Band and ordered every Highway vehicle to respond."

Lowenstein shook his head. He agreed with Wohl that had been unnecessary, even unwise. But the Highway Patrol was the Highway Patrol, and when one of their own was involved in a police shooting, they could be expected to act that way. And, anyway, it was too late now, water under the dam, to change anything.

"I understand we got an eyewitness," he said.

"I just sent her home," Wohl said.

"They interviewed her here? Already?"

"No. I told her that someone would pick her up for the interview at her home in about an hour," Wohl said.

Captain McGovern's eyes grew wide. Wohl had overstepped his authority, and it was clear to him that he was about to get his ass eaten out by Chief Inspector Lowenstein.

But Chief Inspector Lowenstein didn't even comment.

"Jank Jankowitz tried to reach you on the radio, Peter," he said. "When he couldn't, he got on the horn to me. The commissioner thinks it would be a good idea for you to go by the hospital. . . . Where did they take him?"

"I don't know, Chief. I can find out," Wohl replied.

Lowenstein nodded. "If you miss him there, he's going by the Moffitt house. Meet him there."

"Yes, sir," Peter said.

3 Leonard Cohen, before he had become the news director of WCBL-TV, had been what he thought of as a bona fide journalist. That is, he had worked for newspapers before they were somewhat condescendingly referred to as "the print media."

He privately thought that the trouble with most of the people he knew in "electronic journalism" was that few of them had started out working for a newspaper, and consequently were incapable of recognizing the iceberg tip of a genuine story, unless they happened to fall over it on their way to the mirror to touch up their makeup, and sometimes not then.

The phone wasn't even back in its cradle after Louise Dutton had called to make sure they wouldn't put the name of the cop who got himself shot on the air before the cops could inform his widow when he sensed there was more to what was going on than Louise Dutton had told him. He was a little embarrassed that he hadn't picked up on it while he had her on the telephone.

He went quickly to the engineering room.

"Are we in touch with the van at the Waikiki Diner?" he asked.

"I dunno," the technician said. "Sometimes it works, and sometimes it don't."

"Find out, goddamn it!"

Penny Bakersfield's voice, clipped and metallic because of the shortwave radio's modulation limitations, came clearly over the loudspeaker.

"Yes, Leonard?"

"Penny, can you see what Louise Dutton is doing out there?"

"At the moment, she's walking toward her car. There are a couple of cops with her."

"Tell Whatsisname—"

"Ned," she furnished.

"Tell Ned to shoot it," he ordered. "Tell him to shoot whatever he can of her out there. If you can get the cops in the shot, so much the better."

"May I ask why?"

"Goddamn it, Penny, do what you're told. And then the two of you get back here as soon as you can."

"You don't have to snip at me, Leonard!" Penny said.

Officer Mason, once he and Officer Foley had slid the stretcher with Captain Richard C. Moffitt on it into the back of Two-Oh-One, had been faced with the decision of which hospital the "wounded" Highway Patrol officer should be transported to.

There had been really no doubt in his mind that Moffitt was dead; in the year and a half he'd been assigned to wagon duty, he'd seen enough dead and nearly dead people to tell the difference. But Moffitt was a cop, and no matter what, "wounded" and "injured" cops were hauled to a hospital.

"Tell Radio Nazareth," Officer Mason had said to Officer Foley as he flicked on the siren and lights.

Nazareth Hospital, at Roosevelt Boulevard and Pennypack Circle, was not the nearest hospital, but it was, in Officer Mason's opinion, the best choice of the several available to him. Maybe Dutch Moffitt *wasn't* dead.

They had been waiting for him at Nazareth Emergency, nurses and doctors and everything else, but Dutch Moffitt was dead, period.

Police Commissioner Thaddeu Czernich had arrived a few minutes later, and on his heels came cars bearing Mayor Jerry Carlucci, Chief Inspector Dennis V. Coughlin, and Captain Charley Gaft of the Civil Disobedience Squad. Officer Mason heard Captain Gaft explain his presence to Chief Inspector Coughlin: Until last month, he had been Dutch Moffitt's home district commander, and he thought he should come; he knew Jeannie Moffitt pretty good.

And then Captain Paul Mowery, Dutch Moffitt's new home district commander, appeared. He held open the glass door from the Emergency parking lot for Jeannie Moffitt. She was a tall, healthy-looking, white-skinned woman with reddish brown hair. She was wearing a faded cotton housedress and a gray, unbuttoned cardigan.

"Be strong, Jeannie," Chief Inspector Coughlin said. "Dutch's gone."

"I knew it," Jean Moffitt said, almost matter-of-factly. "I knew it." And then she fumbled in her purse for a handkerchief, and then started to sob. "Oh, God, Denny! What am I going to tell the kids?"

Coughlin wrapped his arms around her, and Mayor Carlucci and Commissioner Czernich stepped close to the two of them, their faces mirroring their emotions. They desperately wanted to do something, anything, to help, and there was nothing in their power that could.

Jean Moffitt got control of herself, in a faint voice asked if she could see him, and the three of them led her into the curtained-off cubicle where the doctors had officially decreed that Dutch Moffitt was dead.

A moment later, Jean Moffitt was led out of the cubicle, and out of the Emergency Room by Commissioner Czernich and Captain Mowery.

Chief Inspector Coughlin and the mayor, who was blowing his nose, watched her leave.

"Get the sonofabitch who did this, Denny," the mayor said.

"Yes, sir," Coughlin said, almost fervently. "We'll get him."

The mayor and Chief Inspector Coughlin waited until Captain Mowery's car had gone, and then left the Emergency Room.

As the mayor's Cadillac left the parking lot, it had to brake abruptly twice, as first a plain and battered Chevrolet, and then moments later a police car festooned with lights and sirens, turned off the street. Homicide, in the person of Lieutenant Louis Natali, and the Highway Patrol, in the person of Lieutenant Mike Sabara, had arrived.

When Staff Inspector Peter Wohl drove into the Emergency entrance at Nazareth, five minutes later, he was not surprised to find three other police cars there, plus the Second District wagon. One of the cars, except that it was light blue, was identical to his. One was a well-worn green Chevrolet, and one was a black Ford.

When he went inside, it was easy to assign the cars to the people there. The blue LTD belonged to Captain Charley Gaft of the Civil Disobedience Squad. New, unmarked cars worked their way down the hierarchy of the police department, first assigned to officers in the grades of inspector and above, and then turned over, when newer cars came in, to captains, who turned their cars over to lieutenants. Exceptions were made for staff inspectors and for some captains with unusual jobs, like Gaft's assignment, who got new cars.

Wohl wasn't sure what the exact function of the Civil Disobedience Squad was. It was new, one of Thaddeu Czernich's ideas, and Gaft had been named as its first commander. Wohl thought that whatever it did, it was inaptly named (everything, from murder to spitting on the sidewalk, was really "civil disobedience") and he wasn't sure whether Gaft had been given the job because he was a bright officer, or whether it had been a tactful way of getting him out of his district.

The well-worn, unmarked Chevrolet belonged to Lieutenant Louis Natali of Homicide, and the black Ford with the outsized high-speed tires and two extra shortwave antennae sticking up from the trunk deck was obviously that of Lieutenant Mike Sabara of the Highway Patrol. Now that Dutch was dead, Sabara, the ranking officer on the Highway Patrol, was, at least until a permanent decision was made, its commanding officer.

Lieutenant Sabara's face showed that he was surprised and not particularly happy to see Staff Inspector Wohl. He was a Lebanese with dark, acne-scarred skin. He was heavy, and short, a smart, tough cop. He was in uniform, and the leather jacket and puttees added to his menacing appearance.

"Hello, Peter," Captain Gaft said.

"Charley," Wohl said, and smiled at the others. "Mike. Lou."

They nodded and murmured, "Inspector."

"You just missed the mayor, the commissioner, and Chief Coughlin," Captain Gaft said. "Plus, of course, poor Jeannie Moffitt."

The conversation was interrupted as Officers Foley and Mason rolled a cart with a sheet-covered body toward them.

"Just a minute please," Wohl said. "Where are Captain Moffitt's personal things? And his pistol?"

Natali tapped his briefcase.

"What's on your mind, Inspector?" Lieutenant Sabara asked.

"Natali," Wohl asked. "May I have a look, please?"

"What does that mean?" Sabara asked.

"It means I want me to have a look at what Dutch had in his pockets," Wohl said.

"Why?" Sabara pursued.

"Because I want to, Lieutenant," Wohl said.

"It sounds as if you're looking for something wrong," Sabara said.

"I don't care what it sounds like, Mike," Wohl said. "What it *means* is that I want to see what Dutch had in his pockets. Dutch and I were friends. I want to make sure he had nothing in his wallet that his wife shouldn't see. Let me have it, Natali."

Natali opened the briefcase, took out several plastic envelopes, and laid them on a narrow table against the wall. Wohl picked up one of them, which held a wallet, keys, change, and other small items, dumped the contents on the table and went through them carefully. He found nothing that made a connection with Miss Louise Dutton. There were three phone numbers without names, one written on the back of a Strawbridge & Clothier furniture salesman's business card, and two inside matchbooks.

Wohl handed the card and the matchbooks to Natali.

"I don't suppose you've had the time to check those numbers out, Natali?" he said.

"I was going to turn them over to the assigned detective," Natali said. "But it wouldn't be any trouble to do it now."

"Would you, please?" Wohl asked.

Natali nodded and went looking for a phone.

Wohl met Sabara's eyes.

"What about the bimbo, Peter?" he asked. "Is that what this is all about?"

"What 'bimbo,' Mike?" Wohl replied, a hint of ice in his voice.

And then he felt a cramp. He urgently had to move his bowels.

"Excuse me," he said, and went looking for a men's room.

He wondered if it was something he had eaten, or whether he had caught another goddamned flu bug, and then realized it was most probably a reaction to what had happened to Dutch at the Waikiki Diner.

When he returned to the corridor, Lieutenant Natali was there, but the cart with Dutch Moffitt's body on it was gone. Through the plate-glass door Wohl saw the wagon men loading it into the wagon.

"The furniture salesman's number is his home phone," Lieutenant Natali reported. "One of the others is the rectory of St. Aloysius, and the last one is a pay phone in 30th Street Station."

Wohl nodded and picked up another of the plastic bags. In it was a Smith & Wesson Model 36, five-shot "Chief's Special." There were also four fired cartridge casings in the bag.

"Just four casings?" Wohl asked.

Natali looked at Captain Gaft before replying.

"That's all that was in it, Inspector," he said. "I removed those from Captain Moffitt's weapon at the scene."

Wohl met his eyes.

There was no question in Wohl's mind that he was lying. There had been a fifth, unfired cartridge, and it was probably in Natali's pocket, or Mike Sabara's. Thirty minutes from now, if it wasn't already, it would be in the Delaware, or the Schuylkill.

The Philadelphia Police Department prescribed the weaponry with which its officers would be armed. Uniformed personnel were issued Smith & Wesson Model 10 "Military & Police" six-shot revolvers, chambered to fire the .38 Special cartridge through a four-inch barrel. Detectives were issued Colt "Detective Special" six-shot revolvers, also chambered for the .38 Special cartridge, which have two-inch barrels. They are smaller, and thus more readily concealable, weapons.

Senior officers, officers on plainclothes duty, and off-duty policemen were permitted to carry whatever pistol they wished, either their issue weapon, or one they had purchased with their own money, provided it was chambered for the .38 Special cartridge. Those who purchased their own weapons usually bought the Colt "Detective Special" or the Smith & Wesson Model 36 "Chief's Special," a five-shot, two-inch-barrel revolver, or the Smith & Wesson Model 37, which was an aluminum-framed version of the Chief's Special. There were some Model 38's around, "the Bodyguard," a variation of the Chief's Special which encloses the hammer in a shroud.

All the Smith & Wesson snub-noses were slightly smaller, and thus slightly more concealable, than the Colts. Aside from that, Colt revolvers for all practical purposes differed from the Smith & Wessons only in that their cylinders revolved clockwise and the S&W's counterclockwise. And there were some Ruger revolvers coming into use, and even recently, some Colt and S&W copies made in Brazil.

The regulation gave policemen no choice of ammunition. On duty or off, they would load their pistols with issue ammunition. The prescribed ammunition was the standard .38 Special cartridge, firing a round-nose lead bullet weighing 158 grains. Fired through a four-inch barrel at approximately 850 feet per second, it produces approximately 250 foot pounds of energy at the muzzle.

The .38 Special cartridges made by Remington, Winchester, and Federal are virtually identical, and what brand of cartridges are issued by the Philadelphia Police Department depends on who among the three major manufacturers offered the best price when the annual bids were let.

That particular cartridge is as old as the .38 Special pistol itself, dating back to the turn of the century. The U.S. Army found .38 Special cartridges inadequate to kill or immobilize the enemy, and turned to the .45 caliber automatic Colt pistol and cartridge long before the First World War.

In 1937, the .357 Magnum cartridge was developed. Despite the name, the .38 barrel has a diameter of .357 inch, and the new round fired the same bullet as the .38 Special. The difference was that the .357 cartridge case was a few thousandths of an inch longer, so that it would not fit into a .38 Special chamber, and that it fired the same 158-grain bullet at about fourteen hundred feet per second, and produced about 845 foot pounds of energy, or more than three times that of the .38 Special.

There was some hyperbole. The .357 Magnum would go through an automobile engine block as through a sheet of paper. It would fell an elephant with one shot. It would not; but it was, literally, three times as effective as a .38 Special in immobilizing people who were shot with it. It was, many policemen decided, the ideal police cartridge. There was only one thing wrong with it, as far as they were concerned: The heat generated when firing a lead bullet at the higher velocity was such that the outer surface of the bullet actually melted going down the barrel, leaving a thin coating of lead against the grooves and rifling.

It was a bitch to get out, and unless you promptly got it out after firing, not only would it adversely affect accuracy, but it would cause the barrel to become rusted and pitted. That problem was solved with the introduction of the jacketed bullet, which encased a quarter of an inch at the rear of the bullet in a copper alloy cup. This essentially eliminated "leading," and had another, bonus, characteristic. When the bullet hit something, the jacket kept the rear of the bullet together, which made the front of the bullet expand, causing a larger wound.

The .357 Magnum cartridge was, as many civil libertarians promptly decided, far too awesome a tool of death to be put into the hands of the police. Ideally, the civil libertarians reasoned, firearms should be used only as a last resort, and then to *wound* the malefactor, preferably in the arm or shoulder, so that he could be brought to trial, and then sent to prison to be rehabilitated for return to society. If a societal misfit, venting his frustration at his inability to cope with a cruel world by robbing a bank, were shot in the shoulder with a .357, capable of felling an elephant with one shot, it would blow the shoulder off, and the societal misfit's Constitutional entitlement to rehabilitation would be denied him.

The civil libertarians of Philadelphia prevailed. Philadelphia police were flatly forbidden to arm themselves with the .357 Magnum, or any cartridge but the issued,

158-grain round-nose bullet .38 Special. To ensure compliance, Philadelphia police were flatly forbidden to carry a pistol that would even chamber the .357 Magnum. Doing so was cause for disciplinary action.

But it was possible for a skilled reloader to make, using .38 Special casings, cartridges that produced velocity and foot pounds of energy very close to those of the .357 Magnum, using jacketed .357 bullets. The trick was to put the right amount of gunpowder (Bull's-eye powder was the usual choice) into the case, enough to increase velocity, but not too much, so that the cylinder would not let go when it was fired. The cartridges were tough on small ("J" Frame) Smith & Wesson snub noses, but you weren't going to put a couple of hundred rounds through one.

Just a cylinderful, when it was important.

Captain Richard C. Moffitt was not only a skilled reloader, but he had given Staff Inspector Peter Wohl a box of such cartridges.

"Don't tell anybody where you got these, Peter."

There was no question in Peter Wohl's mind now that—when it was important, when the left ventrical of his aorta was already ruptured and his life's blood was pumping away—Dutch Moffitt had fired four homemade hot .38's at his assailant, and put her down.

Neither was there any question in his mind that, when Lieutenant Natali had examined Dutch's Chief's Special at the Waikiki Diner, there had been one unfired cartridge in the cylinder, and that the bullet in that cartridge had been jacketed and hollow-pointed, as had been the bullets in the cartridges Dutch had given him, as were the cartridges in his own Smith & Wesson "Bodyguard."

It was possible that no one "would notice" that the bullets that would be removed from the body of Unknown White Female Suspect were jacketed. It was unlikely that anyone could have missed the hollow-nosed jacketed bullet in the unfired casing. There would have been trouble.

"What about the female suspect?" Wohl asked. He could almost hear Natali's relief that he hadn't pressed him about a fifth cartridge.

"She's a junkie, Inspector," Natali said. "I talked to Sergeant Hobbs, who's at the Medical Examiner's. He said they found needle marks all over her. I called Narcotics and they're going to run people by over there, to see if they can identify her."

"Well, I don't suppose there's any point in hanging around here," Wohl said.

Both Lieutenant Sabara and Captain Gaft shook hands with him formally. They had been worried, Wohl knew. He had a reputation for being a straight arrow, and sometimes a prick. Lieutenant Natali just nodded at him.

The van with Penny Bakersfield and the tape reached WCBL-TV fifteen minutes after Louise Dutton had walked in, trailed by two cops. There was time enough for News Director Leonard Cohen to get the story out of her, and to decide what he was going to do about it, before they put the tape up on a monitor, and he got a good look at it. It was even better than he hoped. There was a sequence, just long enough, thirty-odd seconds, for what he wanted. It showed Louise being put into her car, driven by a cop, and then following a police car out of the Waikiki Diner parking lot.

Cohen edited it himself, down to twenty seconds exactly, and then he sat down at his typewriter and wrote the voice-over himself for Penny to read.

"This is a special 'Nine's News' bulletin. A Philadelphia police captain gave his life this afternoon foiling a holdup. 'Nine's News' co-anchor Louise Dutton was an eyewitness. Full details on 'Nine's News' at six."

He got the station manager into the control room, ran the tape for him, and with less trouble than he thought he would have, got him to agree to run the thirty-second spot during every hourly and half-hourly break until six. They would lose some advertising revenue, but what they had was what, in the olden days, was called a "scoop," or an "exclusive."

And then he went to help Louise prepare her segment for the six o'clock news. He thought he would have to write that, too, but she had already written it, and handed it to him when he walked up to her. It was good stuff. She had looked kind of flaky, which was understandable, considering the cop had been killed in front of her, but she was apparently tougher than she looked.

And when they made her up, and lit the set and put her on camera, she got it right the first time. Perfect. Her voice had started to break twice, but she hadn't lost it, and the teary eyes were perfect.

"You want me to do that again?" she asked. "I broke up."

"It's fine the way it is," Leonard Cohen said; and he went to her, and repeated that she had done fine, and that what he wanted—what he *insisted*—was for her to go home and have a stiff drink, and if she needed anything to call.

Then he sat down at the typewriter again, and personally wrote what he was going to have Barton Ellison open with, fading to a shot of Louise getting into her car with the cop to go home.

"Louise Dutton isn't here with me tonight," Barton Ellison would solemnly intone. "She wanted to be. But she was an eyewitness to the gun-battle in which Philadelphia Highway Patrol Captain Richard C. Moffitt gave his life this afternoon. She knows the face of the bandit that is, at this moment, still free. Louise Dutton is under police protection. Full details, and exclusive 'Nine's News at Six' film after these messages."

What I should have done, Leonard Cohen thought, *was go to Hollywood and be a press agent for the movies.*

Stanford Fortner Wells III did not own either a newspaper or a radio or television station in Philadelphia, Pennsylvania. It might be closed on Sunday, as the comedian had quipped, but it was the nation's fourth-largest city. It was also a "good market," in media parlance, which meant that newspapers and radio and television stations were making a lot of money. Since Wells had been in a position to be interested, none of the City of Brotherly Love's five newspapers (the *Bulletin,* the *Ledger,* the *Herald,* the *Inquirer,* and the *Daily News*) had come on the market, and only one of its five television stations had. The price they wanted for that didn't seem worth it.

When Louise called and told him she had accepted an offer to go with WCBL-TV in Philadelphia, therefore, there was not one of his people instantly available on the scene to deliver a report on what his daughter would encounter when she got there.

In his neat, methodical hand, "Fort" Wells prepared a list of the questions he wished answered, and handed it to his secretary to be telexed to the publisher of the Binghamton, New York, *Call-Chronicle,* not because it was the newspaper he owned closest to Philadelphia (it was not) but because he knew that Karl Kruger knew his relationship to Louise Dutton. Karl would handle the last question on the list *("Availability adequate, convenient to WCBL-TV,* safe, *apartment for single, 25-year-old fe-*

male") with both discretion and awareness of that question's especial importance to the chairman of the board and chief executive officer of Wells Newspapers, Inc.

Karl Kruger's report on Philadelphia, telexed three days later, would not have pleased the Greater Philadelphia and Delaware Valley Chamber of Commerce. Mr. Kruger suspected, correctly, that Stanford Fortner Wells III wanted to know what was wrong with Philadelphia, not get a listing of its many cultural and industrial assets.

Mr. Wells's first reaction to the report would not have pleased the chamber of commerce either. He judged, from what he read, that Philadelphia was no worse, certainly not as bad as New York City, than other major American cities, and a lot better than most. But in people's minds, it was something like Phoenix, Arizona, or Saint Louis, Missouri, not the Cradle of the American Republic and the nation's fourth-largest city. Mr. Wells thought that if he was in Philadelphia (that is, if he owned a newspaper or a television station there), the first thing he would do would be clean out the chamber of commerce from the executive director downward, and hire some people who knew how to blow a city's horn properly.

Mr. Kruger's report had nothing to say about an apartment. Mr. Wells instructed his secretary to get Mr. Kruger on the horn.

"I thought maybe you'd be calling, Fort," Mr. Kruger said. "How've you been?"

"You didn't mention anything about housing, Kurt. Still working on that, are you?"

"I found, I think, just the place, but I thought it would be easier to talk about it than write it down," Mr. Kruger said. "You got a minute?"

"Sure. Shoot."

"How well do you know Philadelphia?"

"I went there to chase girls when I was at Princeton; I know it."

"It's changed a lot, I would suppose, from your time," Kruger said. "You know the area near Market Street from City Hall to the bridge over the Delaware?"

"Around Independence Hall?"

"Right. Well, that whole section, which they call 'Society Hill,' is pretty much a slum. Been going downhill since Ben Franklin moved away, so to speak."

"Can you get to the point of this anytime soon?"

"It's being rehabilitated; they're gutting buildings to the exterior walls, if necessary, and doing them over. Luxuriously. Among the people doing this, you might be interested to know, is the Daye-Nelson Corporation."

The Daye-Nelson Corporation was something like Wells Newspapers, Inc. Stanford Fortner Wells III was aware that in Philadelphia, Daye-Nelson owned the *Philadelphia Ledger,* WGHA-TV, and, he thought he remembered, a couple of suburban weeklies.

"Come on, Kurt," Fort Wells said, impatiently.

"They put together a couple of blocks of Society Hill," Kruger explained. "Knocked all the interior walls out, and made apartments. It looks like a row of Revolutionary-era houses, but they are now divided horizontally, instead of vertically. Three one-floor apartments, instead of narrow three-floor houses. You follow me?"

"Keep going," Wells said.

"Both sides of this street, twelve houses on a side, are all redone that way. And their title people did their homework, and found out that the street between the blocks had never been deeded to the city. It's a private street, in other words. It's more of an alley, actually, but they can, and do, bar the public. They hung a chain across it, and they've got a rent-a-cop there that lowers it only if you live, or have business, there. If you live there, they give you a sticker for your windshield; no sticker and the rent-a-cop won't let you in without you proving you've got business, or are expected. Sort of a doorman on the street."

"Secure, in other words?"

"Yeah," Kruger went on. "And they leveled an old warehouse, and made a park out of it, and made a driveway into what used to be the basement for a garage. It's ten, twelve blocks from WCBL, Fort. It would be ideal for your—"

"*Daughter*'s the word, Kurt," Wells said. "How much?"

"Not how much, but who," Kruger said. "What Daye-Nelson wants is long-term leases. And I don't think they would want to lease one to a single female."

"So?"

"The real estate guy told me they've leased a dozen of them to corporations, where the bosses can spend the night when they have to stay in the city, where they can put up important customers . . . there's maid service, and a couple of restaurants nearby that deliver."

"How much, Kurt?"

"Nine hundred a month, on a five-year lease, with an annual increase tied to inflation. That includes two spaces in the garage."

"You've seen them, I guess?"

"Very nice, Fort. There's one on a third floor available, that's really nice. You can see the river out the front window, and Independence Hall, at least the roof, out the back."

"Call the real estate man, Kurt; tell him Wells Newspapers will take it. I'll have Charley Davis handle it from there. Do it now."

"And what if Louise doesn't like it?"

"She's a dutiful daughter, Kurt," Wells said, and laughed, "who will recognize a bargain when she sees one."

The barrier to Stockton Place consisted of a black-painted aluminum pole, hinged at one end. A neatly lettered sign reading STOCKTON PLACE—PRIVATE PROPERTY—NO THOROUGHFARE hung on short lengths of chain from the pole. A switch in the Colonial-style red-brick guard shack caused electric motors to raise and lower it.

The Wackenhut Private Security officer flipped the switch when he saw the yellow Cadillac convertible coming. It was too far away to see the Stockton Place bumper sticker, but there weren't all that many yellow Cadillac convertibles, and he was reasonably certain this had to be the good-looking blonde from the TV, whom he thought of as "6-A."

The barrier rose smoothly into the air. It was only when the car passed him, moving onto the carefully relaid cobblestones of Stockton Place, that he saw she was not driving, but that a cop was. And that the convertible was being followed by a police car.

He was retired from the Philadelphia Police Department, and it automatically registered on him that the numbers on the car identified it as being from the Second District, way the hell and gone across town, in the northeast.

The first thing he thought was that they'd busted her for driving under the influence, and the lieutenant or whoever had decided it was good public relations, her being on the TV, to warn her and let her go, have her driven home, instead of writing her up and sending her to the Roundhouse to make bail.

But when the convertible stopped in front of Number Six and she got out, she didn't look drunk, and she walked back to the police car and shook hands with the cop driving it. And 6-A didn't look like the kind of girl who would get drunk, anyway.

He stepped out of the guard shack and stood by the curb, hoping that when the police car came back out, they would stop and say hello, and he could ask what was going on.

But the cops just waved at him, and didn't stop.

Louise Dutton closed the door of 6-A behind her by bumping it with her rear end, and sighed, and then went into her bedroom, and to the bathroom. She saw her brassiere and panties where she'd tossed them on the bed. A plain and ordinary cotton *underwear* bra and panties, she thought, which she'd taken off to replace with black, filmy, damned-near transparent *lingerie* bra and panties after Captain Dutch Moffitt had called and she had gone to meet him.

She leaned close to the mirror. She had not removed her makeup before leaving the studio, and there were streaks on her face, where tears had marred the makeup. She dipped a Kleenex into a jar of cold cream and started wiping at the makeup.

The door chimes sounded, and she swore.

Who the hell can that be?

It was 6-B, who occupied the apartment immediately beneath hers.

Six-B was male, at least anatomically. He was in his middle twenties, stood about five feet seven, weighed no more than 120 pounds. He paid a great deal of attention to his appearance, and wore, she suspected, Chanel Number Five. His name was Jerome Nelson.

"I was going to bark," Jerome Nelson said, waving a bottle of Beefeater's gin and one of Johnnie Walker Black Label scotch at her. "It's your friendly neighborhood Saint Bernard on a mission of mercy."

Louise didn't want to see anyone, but it was impossible for her to cut Jerome Nelson off rudely. He wasn't much of a Saint Bernard, Louise thought, but had puppylike eyes, and you don't kick puppies.

"Hello, Jerome," she said. "Come on in."

"Gin or scotch?" he asked.

"I would like a stiff scotch," she said. "Thank you very much. Straight up."

"You don't have to tell me, of course," he called over his shoulder as he made for her bar. "And I wouldn't think of prying. I will just expire right here on your carpet of terminal curiosity."

She had to smile.

"I gather you saw the cops bringing me home?" she asked. "Let me finish getting this crap off my face."

He came into the bathroom as she was cleaning off what she thought was the last of the makeup, and leaned on the doorjamb.

"You missed some on your ear," he said, delicately setting two glasses down. "Jerome will fix it."

He dipped a Kleenex in cold cream and wiped at her ear.

"There!" he said. "Now tell Mother everything!"

She smiled her thanks at him and picked up her drink and took a good swallow.

"Whatever it was, it was better than the alternative," Jerome said.

"What?"

"The cops come and haul you off, rather than vice versa," he said.

"I was a witness to a shooting," Louise said. "A policeman tried to stop a holdup, and was shot. And killed."

"How *awful* for you!" Jerome Nelson said.

"Worse for him," Louise said. "And for his wife and kids."

"You sound as if you knew him?"

"Yes," Louise said, "I knew him."

She took another swallow of her drink, and felt the warmth in her belly.

He waited for her to go on.

Fuck him!

She pushed past him and went into the living room, and leaned on the wall beside a window looking toward the river.

He floated into the room.

"Actually, I was going to come calling anyway," he said.

"Anyway?" she asked, not particularly pleasantly.

"To tell you that I have discovered we have something in common," he said.

What, that we both like men? she thought, and was ashamed of herself.

"Actually," Jerome said. "I'm just a teensy bit ashamed of myself."

"Oh?" She wished he would go away.

"It will probably come as a surprise to you, but I am what could be called the neighborhood busybody," Jerome said.

The reason I can't get, or at least, stay, mad at him is because he's always putting himself down; he arouses the maternal instinct in me.

"Really?" Louise said, mockingly.

"I'm afraid so," he said. "And I really thought I was onto something with you, when you moved in, I mean."

"Why was that, Jerome?"

"Because I know this apartment is leased to Wells Newspapers, Inc.," he said. "And because you are really a beautiful woman."

I've had enough of this guy.

"Get to the point," Louise said, coldly.

"So I went to Daddy, and I said, 'Daddy, guess what? Stanford F. Wells has an absolutely gorgeous blonde stashed in 6-A.' "

"What the hell is this all about, Jerome?" Louise demanded, angrily.

"And Daddy asked me to describe you, and I did, and he told me," Jerome said.

"Told you what?"

"What we have in common," Jerome said.

"Which is?"

"That both our daddies own newspapers, and television stations, and are legends in their own times, et cetera et cetera," Jerome said. "My daddy, in case I didn't get to that, is Arthur J. Nelson, as in Daye hyphen Nelson."

She looked at him, but said nothing.

"The difference, of course, is that your daddy is very proud of you, and mine is just the opposite," Jerome said.

"Why do you say that?"

"Why do you think? *My* daddy knows the odds are rather long against his becoming a grandfather."

"Oh, Christ, Jerome," Louise said.

"I haven't, and won't, of course, say a word to anyone," Jerome said. "But I thought it might give us a basis to be friends. But I can tell by the look on your face that you are not pleased, and I have offended, so now I will take my tent and steal away, with appropriate apologies."

"I wish you wouldn't," Louise heard herself say.

"Pissed off I can take," Jerome said. "Pity is something else."

"I knew the cop who got shot," Louise blurted. "More than just knew him."

"You were *very good friends,* in other words?" Jerome said, sympathetically.

"Yes," she said, then immediately corrected herself. "No. But I went there, to meet him, thinking that something like that could happen."

"Oh, my," Jerome said. "Oh, my darling girl, how awful for you!"

"Please don't go," Louise said. "Right now, I need a friend."

4 Brewster C. (for Cortland) Payne II, a senior partner in the Philadelphia law firm of Mawson, Payne, Stockton, McAdoo & Lester, had raised his family, now nearly all grown and gone, in a large house on four acres on Providence Road in Wallingford.

Wallingford is a small Philadelphia suburb, between Media (through which U.S. 1, known locally as the "Baltimore Pike," runs) and Chester, which is on the Delaware River. It is not large enough to be placed on most road maps, although it has its own post office and railroad station. It is a residential community, housing families whom sociologists would categorize as upper-middle income, upper-income, and wealthy, in separate dwellings, some very old and some designed to look that way.

What was now the kitchen and the sewing room had been the whole house, when it had been built of fieldstone before the Revolution. Additions and modifications over two centuries had turned it into a large rambling structure which fit no specific architectural category, although a real estate saleswoman had once remarked in the hearing of Patricia (Mrs. Brewster C.) Payne that "the Payne place just *looked* like old, old money."

The house was comfortable, even luxurious, but not ostentatious. There was neither a swimming pool nor a tennis court, but there was, in what a century before had been a stable, a four-car garage. The Payne family swam, as well as rode, at the Rose Tree Hunt Club. They had a summer house in Cape May, New Jersey, which did have a tennis court, as well as a berth for their boat, a 38-foot Hatteras, called *Final Tort IV.*

When Mrs. Payne, at the wheel of a Mercury station wagon, came down Pennsylvania Route 252 and approached her driveway, she looked carefully in the rearview mirror before applying the brake. Two-Fifty-Two was lined with large, old pine trees on that stretch, and the drives leading off it were not readily visible. She did not want to be rear-ended; there had been many close calls.

She made it safely into the drive, and saw, as she approached the house, that the yard men were there, early for once. The back of the station wagon was piled high with large plastic-wrapped packages of peat moss.

She smiled at the yard man and his two sons, pointed out the peat moss to them, and said she would be with them in a minute.

Patricia Payne was older than she looked at first glance. She was trim, for one thing, despite four children (the youngest just turned eighteen and a senior at Dartmouth); and she had a luxuriant head of dark brown, almost reddish hair. There were chicken tracks on her face, and she thought her skin looked old; but she was aware that she looked much better, if younger meant better, than her peers the same age.

The housekeeper—the new one, a tall, dignified Jamaican—was on the telephone as Patricia Payne entered her kitchen and headed directly and quickly for the small toilet off the passageway to the dining room.

"There is no one at this number by that name, madam," the new housekeeper said. "I am sorry."

Ordinarily Pat Payne would have stopped and asked, but incredibly there had been *no* peat moss in Media, and she'd had to drive into Swarthmore to get some and her back teeth were floating.

But she asked when she came out.

"What was that call, Mrs. Newman?"

"It was the wrong number, madam. The party was looking for a Mrs. Moffitt."

"Oh, hell," Patricia Payne said. "Did she leave her name?"

"No, she did not," Mrs. Newman said.

"Mrs. Newman, I should have told you," Patricia Payne said, "before I married Mr. Payne, I was a widow. I was once Mrs. Moffitt—"

The phone rang again. Patricia Payne answered it.

"Hello?"

"Mrs. John Moffitt, please," a familiar voice asked.

"This is Patricia, Mother Moffitt," Pat Payne said. "How are you?"

"My son Richard was shot and killed an hour ago," the woman said.

"Oh, my *God!*" Patricia said. "I'm so sorry. How did it happen?"

"In the line of duty," Gertrude Moffitt said. "Like his brother, God rest his soul, before him. He came up on a robbery in progress."

"I'm so terribly sorry," Pat Payne said. "Is there anything I can do?"

"I can't think of a thing, thank you," Gertrude Moffitt said. "I simply thought you should know, and that Matthew should hear it from you, rather than the newspapers or the TV."

"I'll tell him right away, of course," Patricia said. "Poor Jeannie. Oh, my God, that's just awful."

"He'll be given a departmental funeral, of course, and at Saint Dominic's. We hope the cardinal will be free to offer the mass. You would be welcome to come, of course."

"Come? Of course I'll come."

"I thought I had the duty to tell you," Gertrude Moffitt said, and hung up.

Patricia Payne, her eyes full of tears, pushed the handset against her mouth.

"You old *bitch!*" she said bitterly, her voice on the edge of breaking.

Mrs. Newman's eyebrows rose, but she said nothing.

• • •

When Karl and Christina Mauhfehrt, of Kreis Braunfels, Hesse-Kassel, debarked from
the North German Lloyd Steamer *Hanover* in New York in the spring of 1876,
Christina was heavy with child. They were processed through Ellis Island, where Karl
told the Immigration and Naturalization officer, one Sean O'Mallory, that his name
was Mauhfehrt and that he was an *uhrmacher* by trade. Inspector O'Mallory had been
on the job long enough to know that an *uhrmacher* was a watchmaker, and he wrote
that in the appropriate blank on the form. He had considerably more trouble with
Mauhfehrt, and after a moment's indecision entered "Moffitt" as the surname on the
form, and "Charles" as the given name.

Charles and Christina Moffitt spent the next three days on the Lower East Side of
New York, in a room in a dark, cold, and filthy "railroad" flat. On their fourth morn-
ing in the United States, they took the ferry across the Hudson River to Hoboken,
New Jersey, where they boarded a train of the Pennsylvania Railroad. Three hours
later they emerged from the Pennsylvania Station at Fifteenth and Market streets in
Philadelphia.

An enormous building was under construction before their eyes. Within a few
days, Charles Moffitt was to learn that it would be the City Hall, and that it was intended to top it off with a statue of William Penn, an Englishman, for whom the state
of Pennsylvania was named. Many years later, he was to learn that the design was
patterned after a wing of the Louvre Palace in Paris, France.

He and Christina walked the cobblestone streets, and within a matter of hours
found a room down by the river. He spent the next six days walking the streets, finding clock- and watchmakers and offering his services and being rejected. Finally,
hired because he was young and large and strong, he found work at the City Hall construction site, as a carpenter's helper, building and then tearing down and then building again the scaffolding up which the granite blocks for the City Hall were hauled.

Their first child, Anna, was born when they had been in Philadelphia two months.
Their first son, Charles, Jr., was born almost to the day a year later. By then, he had
enough English to converse in what probably should be called pidgin English with his
Italian, Polish, and Irish coworkers, and had been promoted to a position which was
de facto, but not de jure, foreman. He made, in other words, no more money than the
men he supervised, and he was hired by the day, which meant that if he didn't work,
he didn't get paid.

It was steady work, however, and it was enough for him to rent a flat in an old
building on what was called Society Hill, not far from the run-down building in which
the Constitution of the United States had been written.

And he picked up a little extra money fixing clocks for people he worked with, and
in the neighborhood, but he came to understand that his dream of becoming a watchmaker with his own store in the United States just wasn't going to happen.

When Charles, Jr., turned sixteen, in 1893, he was able to find work with his father, who by then was officially a foreman in the employ of Jos. Sullivan & Sons,
Building Contractors. But by then, the job was coming to an end. The City Hall building itself was up, needing only interior completion. Italian master masons and stone-
cutters had that trade pretty well sewn up, and the Charles Moffitts, *pere et fils,* were
construction carpenters, not stonemasons.

When Charles, Jr., was twenty-two, in 1899, he went off to the Spanish-American

War, arriving in Cuba just before hostilities were over, and returning to Philadelphia a corporal of cavalry, and just in time to take advantage of the politicians' fervor to do something for Philadelphia's Heroic Soldier Boys.

Specifically, he was appointed to the police department, and assigned to the ninety-three-horse-strong mounted patrol, which had been formed just ten years previously. Officer Moffitt was on crowd-control duty on his horse when the City Hall was officially opened in 1901.

He had been a policeman four years when his father fell to his death from a wharf under construction into the Delaware River in 1903. He was at that time still living at home, and with his father gone, he had little choice but to continue to do so; there was not enough money to maintain two houses.

Nor did he take a wife, so long as his mother was alive, partly because of economics and partly because no woman would take him with his mother part of the bargain. Consequently, Charles Moffitt, Jr., married late in life, eighteen months after his mother had gone to her final reward.

He married a German Catholic woman, Gertrude Haffner, who some people said, although she was nearly twenty years younger than her husband, bore a remarkable resemblance to his mother, and certainly manifested the same kind of devout, strong-willed character.

He and Gertrude had two sons, John Xavier, born in 1924, and, as something of a surprise to both of them, Richard Charles, who came along eight years later in 1932.

Charles Moffitt was a sergeant when he retired from the mounted patrol of the police department in 1937 at the age of sixty. He lived to be seventy-two, despite at least two packages of cigarettes and at least two quarts of beer a day, finally passing of a cerebral hemorrhage in 1949. By then his son John was on the police force, and his son Richard about to graduate from high school.

Patricia Payne leaned her head against the wall and put her hand on the hook of the wall-mounted telephone, without realizing what she was doing.

A moment later, the phone rang again. Pat Payne handed the handset to Mrs. Newman.

"The Payne residence," Mrs. Newman said, and then a moment later: "I'm not sure if Mrs. Payne is at home. I will inquire."

She covered the mouthpiece with her hand.

"A gentleman who says he is Chief Inspector Coughlin of the Philadelphia Police Department," Mrs. Newman said.

Patricia Payne finished blowing her nose, and then reached for the telephone.

"Hello, Denny," Patricia Payne said. "I think I know why you're calling."

"Who called?"

"Who else? Mother Moffitt. She called out here and asked for Mrs. Moffitt, and told me Dutch is dead, and then she said I would be welcome at the funeral."

"I'm sorry, Patty," Dennis V. Coughlin said. "I'm not surprised, but I'm sorry."

She was trying not to cry and didn't reply.

"Patty, people would understand if you didn't go to the funeral," he said.

"Of course I'll go to the funeral," Patricia Payne said, furiously. "*And* the wake. Dutch didn't think I'm a godless whore, and I don't think Jeannie does either."

"Nobody thinks that of you," he said, comfortingly. "Come on, Patty!"

"That old bitch does, and she lets me know it whenever she has the chance," she said.

Now Dennis V. Coughlin couldn't think of anything to say.

"I'm sorry, Denny," Patricia Payne said, contritely. "I shouldn't have said that. The poor woman has just lost her second, her remaining son."

Dennis V. Coughlin and John X. Moffitt had gone through the police academy together. Patricia Payne still had the photograph somewhere, of all those bright young men in their brand-new uniforms, intending to give it to Matt someday.

There was another photograph of John X. Moffitt around. It and his badge hung on a wall in the Roundhouse lobby. Under the photograph there was a now somewhat faded typewritten line that said "Sergeant John X. Moffitt, Killed in the Line of Duty, November 10, 1952."

Staff Sergeant John Moffitt, USMCR, had survived Inchon and the Yalu and come home only to be shot down in a West Philadelphia gas station, answering a silent burglar alarm.

They'd buried him in Holy Sepulchre Cemetery, following a high mass of requiem celebrated by the cardinal archbishop of Philadelphia at Saint Dominic's. Sergeant Dennis V. Coughlin had been one of the pallbearers. Three months later, John Xavier Moffitt's first, and only, child had been born, a son, christened Matthew Mark after his father's wishes, in Saint Dominic's.

"Patty?" Chief Inspector Coughlin asked. "You all right, dear?"

"I was thinking," she said, "of Johnny."

"It'll be on the TV at six," Denny Coughlin said. "Worst luck, there was a Channel 9 woman in the Waikiki Diner."

"Is that where it happened? A *diner?*"

"On Roosevelt Boulevard. He walked up on a stick-up. There was two of them. Dutch got one of them, the one that shot him, a woman. Patty, what I'm saying is that I wouldn't like Matt to hear it over the TV. You say the word, and I'll go up there and tell him for you."

"You're a good man, Denny," Patricia said. "But no, I'll tell him."

"Whatever you say, dear."

"But would you do something else for me? If you don't want to, just say so."

"You tell me," he said.

"Meet me at Matt's fraternity house—"

"And be with you, sure," he interrupted.

"And go with me when I, when Matt and I, go see Jeannie."

"Sure," he said.

"I'll leave right now," she said. "It'll take me twenty-five, thirty minutes."

"I'll be waiting for you," Chief Inspector Coughlin said.

Patricia hung up, and then dialed the number of Matt's fraternity house. She told the kid who answered, and who said Matt was in class, to tell him that something important had come up and he was to wait for her there, period, no excuses, until she got there.

Then she went upstairs and stripped out of her skirt and sweater and put on a black slip and a black dress, and a simple strand of pearls. She looked at the telephone and considered calling her husband, and decided against it, although he would be hurt.

Brewster Payne was a good man, and she didn't want to run him up against Mother Moffitt if it could be avoided.

After ten months of widowhood, Patricia Stevens Moffitt had arranged with her sister Dorothy to care for the baby during the day and went to work as a typist, with the intention eventually of becoming a legal secretary, for the law firm of Lowerie, Tant, Foster, Pedigill and Payne, which occupied an entire floor in the Philadelphia Savings Fund Society Building on Market Street.

Two months after entering Lowerie, Tant, Foster, Pedigill and Payne's employ, while pushing Matthew Mark Moffitt near the Franklin Institute in a stroller, Patricia Moffitt ran into Brewster Payne II, grandson of one of the founding partners, and son of a senior partner, who was then in his seventh year with the firm and about to be named a partner himself.

Young Mr. Brewster, as he was then known, was pushing a stroller himself, in which sat a two-year-old boy, and holding a four-and-a-half-year-old girl at the end of a leash, connected to a leather harness. They walked along together. Within the hour, she learned that Mrs. Brewster Payne II had eight months before skidded out of control coming down into Stroudsburg from their cabin in the Poconos, leaving him, as he put it, "in rather much the same position as yourself, Mrs. Moffitt."

Patricia Stevens Moffitt and Brewster Payne II were united in matrimony three months later. The simple ceremony was performed by the Hon. J. Edward Davison, judge of the Court of Common Pleas in his chambers. Mr. Payne, Senior, did not attend the ceremony, although his wife did. Mr. Gerald Stevens, Patricia's father, was there, but her mother was not.

There was no wedding trip, and the day after the wedding, Brewster Payne II resigned from Lowerie, Tant, Foster, Pedigill and Payne, although, through a bequest from his grandfather, he owned a substantial block of its common stock.

Shortly thereafter, the legal partnership of Mawson & Payne was formed.

John D. Mawson had been two years ahead of Brewster Payne II at the University of Pennsylvania Law School. They had been acquaintances but not friends. Mawson was a veteran (he had been an air corps captain, a fighter pilot) and Brew Payne had not been in the service. Further, Payne thought Mawson was a little pushy. It was Jack Mawson's announced intention to become a professor of law at Pennsylvania, specializing in Constitutional law. Jack Mawson was not, as Brewster Payne II thought of it, the sort of fellow you cultivated.

Mawson had exchanged his air corps lapel pins for those of the judge advocate general's corps reserve when he passed his bar examination, and three months later had gone off to the Korean War as a major. He had returned as Lieutenant Colonel J. Dunlop Mawson, with a war bride (a White Russian girl he had met in Tokyo) and slightly less lofty, if more practical, plans for the resumption of his civilian law practice.

He had earned the approval of his superiors in the army with his skill as a prosecutor of military offenders. He had liked what he had been doing, but was honest enough with himself to realize that his success was in large part due to the ineptitude of opposing counsel. Very often, he was very much aware that if he had been defending the accused, the accused would have walked out of the courtroom a free man.

Odette Mawson had already shown that she had expensive tastes, which ruled out his staying in the army. He would have been reduced in grade in the peacetime army to captain, and captains did not make much money. About, J. Dunlop Mawson thought, what a district attorney in Philadelphia made. District attorneys do not grow rich honestly.

That ruled out transferring his prosecutorial skills to civilian practice.

But it did not rule out a career in criminal law. While ordinary criminal lawyers, dealing as they generally do with the lower strata of society, seldom make large amounts of money, extraordinary criminal lawyers sometimes do. And they increase their earning potential as the socioeconomic class of their clientele rises. An attorney representing someone accused of embezzling two hundred thousand dollars from a bank can expect to be compensated for his services more generously than if he defended someone accused of stealing that much money from the same bank at the point of a gun.

When J. Dunlop Mawson, who had made it subtly if quickly plain that he liked to be addressed as "Colonel," heard that Brewster Payne had had a falling-out with his father over his having married a Roman Catholic cop's widow with a baby, a girl who had been a typist for the firm, he thought he saw in him the perfect partner.

First of all, of course, Brewster Payne II was a good lawyer, and he had acquired seven years' experience with a law firm that was good as well as prestigious. And he was also Episcopal Academy and Princeton, Rose Tree Hunt Club and the Merion Country Club—without question a member of the Philadelphia Establishment.

Brewster Payne II was not a fool. He knew exactly what Jack Mawson wanted from him. And he had no desire whatever to practice criminal law. But Mawson's arguments made sense. Times had changed. Perfectly respectable people were getting divorced. And the division of the property of the affluent that went with a divorce was worthy, in direct ratio to the value and complexity of the property involved, of the talents of a skilled trust and estate lawyer. He would handle the crooks, Jack Mawson told Brewster Payne, and Payne would handle the cuckolded.

Payne added one nonnegotiable caveat: Jack could handle anything from embezzlers to ax murderers, so long as they were, so to speak, amateurs. There would be no connection, however indirect, with Organized Crime. If they were to become partners, Payne would have to have the privilege of client rejection, and they had better write that down, so there would be no possibility of misunderstanding, down the pike.

Five months after Mawson & Payne opened offices for the practice of law in the First National Bank Building, across from the Bellevue-Stratford Hotel and the Union League on South Broad Street, Patricia Stevens Payne found herself with child.

Brew Payne, ever the lawyer, first asked if she was sure, and when she said there was no question, nodded his head as if she had just given him the time of day.

"Well, then," he said, "we'll have to do something about Matthew."

"I don't know what you mean, honey," Patricia said, uneasily.

"I'd planned to bring it up before," he said. "But there hasn't seemed to be the right moment. I don't at all like the notion of his growing up with any question in his mind of not being one of us. What I would like to do, if you're agreeable, is enter a plea for adoption. And if you're agreeable, Patricia, to enter the appropriate pleas in your behalf with regard to Amelia and Foster."

When she didn't immediately respond, Brewster Payne misunderstood her silence for reluctance.

"Well, please don't say no with any finality now," he said. "I'm afraid you're going to have to face the fact that both Amy and Foster do think of you as their mother."

"Brewster," Patricia said, finding her voice, "sometimes you're a damned fool."

"So I have been told," he said. "As recently as this afternoon, by the colonel."

"But you are warm and kind and I love you very much," she said.

"I hear that sort of thing rather less than the other," he said. "I take it you're agreeable?"

"Why did Jack Mawson say you were a damned fool?"

"I told him I thought we should decline a certain client," he said. "You haven't answered my question."

"Would you like a sworn deposition? *'Now comes Patricia Payne who being duly sworn states that the only thing she loves more than her unborn child, and her husband's children, and her son, is her husband'?"*

"A simple yes will suffice," Brew Payne said, and put his arms around her. "Thank you very much."

That was her sin, which had made her a godless whore, in the eyes of Gertrude Moffitt: marrying outside the church, living in sin, bearing Brewster's child, and allowing that good man to give his name and his love to a fatherless boy.

Patricia was worried about her son. There had been, over the past two or three weeks, something wrong. Brewster sensed it too, and suggested that Matt was suffering from the Bee Syndrome, which was rampant among young men Matt's age. Matt was driven, Brewster said, to spread pollen, and sometimes there just was not an adequate number, or even one, Philadelphia blossom on which to spread it.

Brewster was probably right—he usually was—but Patricia wasn't sure. From what she had reliably heard about what took place on the University of Pennsylvania campus, and particularly along Fraternity Row, there was a large garden of flowering blossoms just waiting to be pollinated. Matt could be in love, of course, with some girl immune to his charms, which would explain a good deal about his behavior, but Patricia had a gut feeling that it was something else.

And whatever was bothering him, the murder of his uncle Dutch was going to make things worse.

The traffic into Philadelphia was heavy, and it took Patricia Payne longer than thirty minutes to get into town, and then when she got to the University of Pennsylvania campus, there was a tie-up on Walnut Street by the Delta Phi Omicron house, an old and stately brownstone mansion. A car had broken down, against the curb, forcing the cars in the other lane to merge with those in the inner; they were backed up for two blocks, waiting their turn.

And then she drew close and saw that the car blocking the outside lane, directly in front of the fraternity house, was a black Oldsmobile. There was an extra radio antenna, a short one, mounted on the inside shelf by the rear window. It was Denny Coughlin's car.

When you are a chief inspector of the Philadelphia Police Department, Patricia Payne thought wryly, *you park any place you damned well please.*

She pulled in behind the Oldsmobile, slid across the seat, and got out the passenger side. Denny was already out of the Oldsmobile, and another man got out of the driver's side and stepped onto the sidewalk.

She kissed Denny, noticing both that he was picking up some girth, and that he still apparently bought his cologne depending on what was cheapest when he walked into Walgreen's Drugstore.

"By God, you're a good-looking woman," Denny said. "Patty, you remember Sergeant Tom Lenihan?"

"Yes, of course," Pat said. "How are you, Sergeant?"

"Tom, you think you remember how to direct traffic?" Coughlin said, pointing at the backed-up cars.

"Yes, sir," Lenihan said.

"We won't be long in here," Coughlin said, and took Pat's arm in his large hand and walked her up the steep, wide stone stairs to the fraternity house.

"Can I help you?" a young man asked, when they had pushed open the heavy oak door with frosted glass inserts and were in the foyer of the building.

"I'm Mrs. Payne," Pat said. "I'm looking for my son."

The young man went to the foot of the curving staircase.

"Mr. Payne, sir," he called. "You have visitors, sir. It's your *mommy!*"

Denny Coughlin gave him a frosty glance.

Matthew Mark Payne appeared a moment later at the head of the stairs. He was a tall, lithe young man, with dark, thick hair. He was twenty-one, and he would graduate next month, and follow his father into the marines. He had taken the Platoon Leader's Course, and was going to be a distinguished graduate, which meant that he could have a regular marine commission, if he wanted it, and another of Patricia Payne's worries was that he would take it.

His eyes were dark and intelligent, and they flashed between his mother and Coughlin. Then he started down the stairs, not smiling. He was wearing gray flannel slacks, a button-down collared blue shirt, open, and a light gray sweater.

Coughlin turned his back to him, and said, softly. "He's a ringer for Johnny, isn't he?"

"And as hardheaded," Pat Payne said.

Matt Payne kissed his mother without embarrassment, and offered his hand to Coughlin.

"Uncle Denny," he said. "What's all this? Has something happened? Is it Dad?"

"It's your uncle Dick," Patricia Payne told her son, watching his face carefully. "Dutch is dead, Matt."

"What happened?" he asked, tightly.

"He walked up on a holdup," Denny Coughlin said. "He was shot."

"Oh, *shit!*" Matt Payne said. His lips worked, and then he put his arms around his mother.

I don't know, she thought, *whether he's seeking comfort or trying to give it.*

"Goddamn it," Matt said, letting his mother go.

"I'm sorry, son," Denny Coughlin said.

"Did they get who did it?" Matt asked. Now, Coughlin saw, he was angry.

"Dutch put the one who shot him down," Coughlin said. "The other one got away. They'll find him, Matt."

"Did he kill the one who shot him?" Matt asked.

"Yes," Coughlin said. "It was a woman, Matt, a girl."

"Jesus!"

"We're going to see your aunt Jean," Patricia Payne said. "I thought you might want to come along."

"Let me get a coat and tie," he said, and then, "Jesus! The kids!"

"It's a bitch, all right," Coughlin said.

Matt turned and went up the stairway, taking the steps two at a time.

"He's a nice boy," Denny Coughlin said.

"He's about to go off to that damned war," Patricia Payne said.

"What would you rather, Patty? That he go to Canada and dodge the draft?"

"But as a *marine.*"

"I wouldn't worry about him; that boy can take care of himself," Coughlin said.

"Like Dutch, right? Like his father?"

"Come on, Patty," Coughlin said, and put his arm around her shoulder and hugged her.

"Oh, *hell*, Denny," Patricia Payne said.

When Matt Payne came down the stairs, he was wearing a gray flannel suit.

Denny's right, Patricia Payne thought, *he looks just like Johnny.*

They went down the stairs. Matt got behind the wheel of the Mercury station wagon.

"It must be nice to be a cop," Matt said. "Park where you damned well please. A guy in the house stopped here last week, left the motor running, ran in to get some books. By the time he came out, the tow truck was hauling his car off. Cost him forty bucks for the tow truck, after he'd paid a twenty-five-dollar fine for double parking."

She looked at him, but didn't reply.

The Oldsmobile moved off.

"Here we go," Matt said, as he stepped on the accelerator. "Want to bet whether or not we break the speed limit?"

"I'm not in the mood for your wit, Matt," Patricia said.

"Just trying to brighten up an otherwise lousy afternoon," Matt said.

Sergeant Lenihan turned right onto North Thirty-third Street, cut over to North Thirty-fourth at Mantua, and led the Mercury past the Philadelphia Zoological Gardens; turned left again onto Girard for a block, and finally right onto the Schuylkill Expressway, which parallels the West Bank of the river. He drove fast, well over the posted speed limit, but not recklessly. Matt had no trouble keeping up with him. He glanced at the speedometer from time to time, but did not mention the speed to his mother.

When they crossed the Schuylkill on the Twin Bridges their pace slowed, but not much. Going past Fern Hill Park, Matt saw a police car parked off the road, watching traffic. And he saw the eyes of the policeman driving follow him as they zipped past. But the car didn't move.

Lenihan slowed the Oldsmobile then, to a precise forty-five miles an hour. They had to stop for the red light at Ninth Street, but for no others. The lights were supposed to be set, Matt recalled, for forty-five. That they didn't have to stop seemed to prove it.

"There it is," his mother said.

"There what is?"

"The Waikiki Diner," she replied. "That's where Denny said it happened."

He turned to look, but couldn't see what she was talking about.

Lenihan turned to the right at Pennypack Circle, onto Holme Avenue, and into the Torresdale section of Philadelphia.

There was a traffic jam, complete to a cop directing traffic, at the intersection of Academy Road and Outlook Avenue. The cop waved the Oldsmobile through, but then gestured vigorously for the Mercury to keep going down Academy.

Matt stopped and shook his head, and pointed down Outlook. The white-capped traffic cop walked up to the car. Matt lowered the window.

"Captain Moffitt was my uncle," Matt said.

"Sorry," the cop said, and waved him through.

There were more cars than Matt could easily count before the house overlooking the fenced-in fairway of the Torresdale Golf Course. Among them was His Honor the Mayor Jerry Carlucci's Cadillac limousine.

Matt saw that there was at least one TV camera crew set up on the golf course, on the other side of the fence that separated it from Outlook Avenue. And there were people with still cameras.

"Park the car, Tom, please," Chief Inspector Coughlin said to his aide, "and then come back and take care of their car, too."

He got out of the Oldsmobile and stood in the street, waiting for Matt and Patty to drive up.

Staff Inspector Peter Wohl walked up to him.

"Can't we run those fucking ghouls off, Peter?" Coughlin said, nodding toward the press behind the golf course fence.

"I wish we could, sir," Wohl said. "If you've got a minute, Chief?"

Matt stopped the Mercury at Coughlin's signal. Patty lowered the window, and Coughlin leaned down to it.

"Just leave the keys, Matt," he said. "Lenihan will park it, and then catch up with us." He opened Patty's door, and she got out. "I'll be with you in just a minute, dear. I gotta talk to a guy."

He walked Wohl twenty feet down the sidewalk.

"Shoot," he said. "I gotta get inside. That's Dutch's sister-in-law. *Ex*-sister-in-law. And his nephew."

"The commissioner said if I saw you before he did, I should tell you what's going on."

"He here?"

"Yes, sir," Wohl said. "There was an eyewitness, Chief, Miss Louise Dutton, of Channel Nine."

"The blonde?" Coughlin asked.

"Right," Wohl said. "She was with Captain Moffitt at the time of the shooting," he added, evenly.

"Doing what?"

"I don't know, sir," Wohl said.

"You don't know?" Coughlin asked, on the edge of sarcasm.

"She said that she was meeting him to get his reaction to people calling the High-way Patrol 'Carlucci's Commandos,' " Wohl said. "She was very upset, sir, when I got there. She was kneeling over Captain Moffitt, weeping."

"Where is she?" Coughlin asked.

"She went from the diner to Channel Nine—"

"They didn't take her to the Roundhouse?" Coughlin interrupted. "Who let her go?"

"The commissioner . . . I was a couple of blocks from the Waikiki Diner, and responded to the call, and I was the first supervisor on the scene, and I called him. The commissioner said I should do what had to be done. I didn't think sending her to the Roundhouse was the thing to do. So I borrowed two uniforms from the Second District, and sent them with her. I told them to stay with her, to see that she got home safely. Homicide will send somebody to talk to her at her apartment."

Coughlin grunted. "McGovern say anything to her?" he asked.

"I don't think Mac saw the situation as I did, Chief."

"Probably just as well," Coughlin said. "Mac is not too big on tact. Is there anything I should be doing?"

"I don't think so, sir. The commissioner knows how close you were to Dutch . . ."

"Is there . . . is this going to develop into something awkward, Peter?"

"I hope not," Wohl said. "I don't think so."

"Jesus H. Christ," Coughlin said. "This is going to be tough enough on Jeannie without it being all over the papers and on the TV that Dutch was fooling around with some bimbo . . ."

"I think we can keep that from happening, Chief," Wohl said; and then surprised himself by adding, "She's not a bimbo. I like her. And she seems to understand the situation."

Coughlin looked at him with his eyebrows raised.

"The commissioner asked me to make sure nothing awkward develops, Chief," Wohl said. "To find out for sure what Captain Moffitt's relationship with Miss Dutton was . . ."

"I went through the academy with Dutch's brother," Coughlin interrupted. "Dutch was then, what, sixteen, seventeen, and he was screwing his way through the cheerleaders at Northeast High. He never, as long as I knew him, gave his pecker a rest. I've got a damned good idea what his *relationship* with Miss—whatsername?—was."

"Dutton, Chief," Wohl furnished, and then added: "We don't *know* that, Chief."

"You want to give me odds, Peter?" Coughlin asked.

Mrs. Patricia Payne and Matthew Payne walked up to them.

"Patty, do you know Inspector Wohl?" Coughlin asked.

"No, I don't think so," Patricia Payne said, and offered her hand. "This is my son Matt, Inspector. Dutch's nephew."

"I'm very sorry about this, Mrs. Payne," Wohl said. "Dutch and I were old friends." He offered his hand to Matt Payne.

"*Inspector* Wohl, did he say?" Matt asked.

"*Staff Inspector* Wohl," Coughlin furnished, understanding Matt's surprise that Wohl, who didn't look much older than Matt, held such a high rank. "He's a very good cop, Matt. He went up very quickly; the brass found out that when they gave him a difficult job, they could count on him to handle it."

There's something behind that remark, Patricia Payne thought. *I wonder what?*

"It was nice to meet you, Mrs. Payne, Matt," Wohl said. "I just regret the circumstances. I've got to get back on the job."

Chief Inspector Coughlin nodded, and then turned and took Mrs. Patricia Payne's arm and led her to Dutch Moffitt's front door.

5 With some difficulty, Staff Inspector Peter Wohl extricated his car from the cars jammed together on the streets, driveways, and alleys near the residence of Captain Richard C. Moffitt. He turned onto Holme Avenue, in the direction of Pennypack Circle.

When he was safely into the flow of traffic, he leaned over and took the microphone from the glove compartment.

"Isaac Twenty-three," he said into it, and when they came back at him, he said he needed a location on Two-Eleven, which was the Second District blue-and-white he'd commandeered from Mac McGovern to escort Miss Louise Dutton.

"I have him out of service at WCBL-TV at Seventeenth and Locust, Inspector," the radio operator finally told him. "Thirty-five minutes ago."

"Thank you," Wohl said, and put the microphone back inside the glove compartment and slammed the door.

There would be time, he decided, to see what the medical examiner had turned up about the female doer. There was no question that there would be other questions directed at him by his boss, Chief Inspector Coughlin, and very possibly by Commissioner Czernich or even the mayor. Peter Wohl believed the Boy Scouts were right; it paid to be prepared.

A battered Ford van pulled to a stop in the parking lot of the medical examiner's office at Civic Center Boulevard and University Avenue. The faded yellow van had a cracked windshield. On the sides were still legible vestiges of a BUDGET RENT-A-CAR logotype. The chrome grille was missing, as was the right headlight and its housing. The passenger-side door had apparently encountered something hard and sharp enough to slice the door skin like a knife. There was a deep, but not penetrating, dent on the body on the same side. The body was rusted through at the bottom of the doors, and above the left-rear fender well.

The vehicle had forty-two unanswered traffic citations against it, most for illegal parking, but including a half dozen or so for the missing headlight, the cracked windshield, an illegible license plate, and similar misdemeanor violations of the Motor Vehicle Code.

Two men got out of the van. One of them was young, very large, and bearded. He was wearing greasy blue jeans, and a leather band around his forehead to keep his long, unkempt hair out of his eyes. After he got out of the passenger's side, the driver, a small, smooth-shaven, somewhat weasel-faced individual wearing a battered gray sweatshirt with the legend SUPPORT YOUR LOCAL SHERIFF printed on it slid over and got out after him. They walked into the building.

Staff Inspector Peter Wohl and Sergeant Zachary Hobbs of Homicide were standing by a coffee vending machine in the basement, drinking from Styrofoam cups. Wohl shook his head when he saw them.

"Hello, Inspector," the weasel-faced small man, who was Lieutenant David Pekach of the Narcotics Squad, said.

"Pekach, does your mother know what you do for a living?" Wohl replied, offering his hand.

Pekach chuckled. "God, I hope not." He looked at Hobbs. "You're Sergeant Hobbs?"

"Yes, sir," Hobbs said.

"You know Officer McFadden?" Pekach asked, and both Wohl and Hobbs shook their heads, no.

"Charley, this is Staff Inspector Wohl," the weasel-faced man said, "and Sergeant Hobbs. Officer Charley McFadden."

"How do you do, sir?" Officer McFadden asked, respectfully, to Wohl and Hobbs each in turn.

"Where is she?" Pekach asked.

"In there," Wohl said, nodding at double metal doors. "He's not through with her."

"Don't tell me you have a queasy stomach, Inspector?" Pekach asked, innocently.

"You bet your ass, I do," Wohl said.

Pekach walked in. McFadden followed him.

Unidentified White Female Suspect was on a stainless steel table. She was naked, her legs spread, one arm lying beside her, the other over her head. Body fluids dripped from a corner drain on the table into a stainless steel bucket on the tile floor.

A bald-headed man wearing a plastic apron over surgical blues stopped what he was doing and looked up curiously and unpleasantly at Pekach and McFadden. What he was doing was removing Unidentified White Female Suspect's heart from the opening he had made in her chest.

"I'm Lieutenant Pekach, Doctor," Pekach said. "We just want to get a look at her face."

The medical examiner shrugged, and went on with what he was doing.

"Jesus," Pekach said. "What did he shoot her with?"

"I presume," the medical examiner said dryly, not looking up, "that the weapon used was the standard service revolver."

Pekach snorted.

"She shot Captain Moffitt the way she was shot up like that?" Pekach asked.

"Before," the medical examiner replied. "What I think happened is that she shot Moffitt before he shot her."

"I don't understand," Pekach said.

The medical examiner pointed with his scalpel at a small plastic bag. Pekach picked it up.

It held a misshapen piece of lead, thinner than a pencil and about a quarter of an inch long.

"Twenty-two," the medical examiner said. "Probably a long rifle. It entered his chest just below the armpit." He took Unidentified White Female Suspect's hand, raised it in the air, and pointed. "From the side, almost from the back. The bullet hit the left ventricle of the aorta. Then he bled to death, internally. The heart just kept pumping, and when he ran out of blood, he died."

"Jesus Christ!" Pekach said.

The medical examiner let Unidentified White Female Suspect's arm fall, and then pointed to another plastic envelope.

"Show these to Peter Wohl," he said. "I think it's what he's looking for. I just took those out of her."

The envelope contained three misshapen pieces of lead. Each was larger and thicker than the .22 projectile removed from the body of Captain Moffitt. The ends of all the bullets had expanded, "mushroomed," on striking something hard, so that they actually looked something like mushrooms. The other end of each bullet was covered by a quarter-inch-high copper-colored cup. There were clear rifling marks on the cups; it would not be at all difficult to match these jacketed bullets to the pistol that had fired them.

The very large young man looked carefully at the face of Unidentified White Female Suspect and changed her status.

"Schmeltzer, Dorothy Ann," he said. "Twenty-four, five feet five, one-hundred twenty-five pounds. Last known address . . . somewhere on Vine, just east of Broad. I'd have to check."

"You're sure?"

"That's Dorothy Ann," McFadden said. "I thought she was still in jail."

"What was she in for?"

"Solicitation for prostitution," McFadden said. "I think the judge put her in to see if they couldn't dry her out."

"She's got needle marks all over," the medical examiner said, "in places you wouldn't believe. No identification on her? Is that what this is all about?"

"Lieutenant Natali told me all she had on her was a joint and a .22 pistol," Pekach said. "And the needle marks. He thought we might be able to make her as a junkie. Thank you, Doctor."

He left the room.

Wohl and Hobbs were no longer alone. Lieutenant Natali and Lieutenant Sabara of the Highway Patrol had come to the medical examiner's office. Sabara looked askance at the Narcotics Division officers.

Natali saw it. "I like your sweatshirt, Pekach," he said dryly.

"Could you identify her?" Hobbs asked.

"Officer McFadden was able to identify her, Sergeant," Pekach said, formally. "Her name was Schmeltzer, Dorothy Ann Schmeltzer. A known drug addict, who McFadden thinks was only recently released from prison."

"Any known associates, McFadden?" Hobbs asked.

"Sir, I can't recall any names. It'd be on her record."

"If I can borrow him for a while, I'd like to take McFadden with me to the Round-house," Hobbs said.

"Sure," Pekach said.

"I guess you can call off the rest of your people, then," Hobbs said. "And thank you, Lieutenant."

"Now that I've got her name, maybe I can find out something," Pekach said. "I'll get on the radio."

"Appreciate it," Hobbs said. "If you do come up with something, give me or Lieutenant Natali a call."

"Sure," Pekach said. "Inspector, the medical examiner said to show you these. He said he thought that's what you were waiting for."

Wohl took the bag Pekach handed him and held it up to the light. He was not surprised to see that the bullets were jacketed, and from the way they had mushroomed, almost certainly had been hollow pointed.

"What's that? The projectiles?" Sergeant Hobbs asked.

Wohl handed the envelope to Sergeant Hobbs. They met each other's eyes, but Hobbs didn't say anything.

"Don't lose those," Wohl said.

"What do you think they are, Inspector?" Hobbs asked, in transparent innocence.

"I'm not a firearms expert," Wohl said. "What I see is four bullets removed from the body of the woman suspected of shooting Captain Moffitt. They're what they call evidence, Sergeant, in the chain of evidence."

"They're jacketed hollow points," Hobbs said. "Is that what this is all about?"

"What the hell is the difference?" Pekach said. "Dutch is dead. The Department can't do anything to him now for using prohibited ammunition."

"And maybe we'll get lucky," Hobbs said, "and get an assistant DA six months out of law school who thinks bullets are bullets are bullets."

"Yeah, and maybe we won't," Wohl said. "Maybe we'll get some assistant DA six months out of law school who knows the difference, and would like to get his name in the newspapers as the guy who caught the cops using illegal ammunition, again, in yet another example of police brutality."

"Jesus," Pekach said, disgustedly. "And I know just the prick who would do that." He paused and added, "Two or three pricks, now that I think about it."

"Get those to Firearms Identification, Hobbs," Wohl said. "Get a match. Keep your fingers crossed. Maybe we will be lucky."

"Yes, Sir," Hobbs said.

"I don't think there is anything else to be done here," Wohl said. "Or am I missing something?" He looked at Sabara as he spoke.

"I thought I'd escort the hearse to the funeral home," Sabara said. "You know, what the hell. It seems little enough . . ."

"I think Dutch would like that," Wohl said.

"Well, I expect I had better pay my respects to Chief Lowenstein," Wohl said. "I'll probably see you fellows in the Roundhouse."

"If you don't mind my asking, Inspector," Hobbs said. "Are you going to be in on this?"

"No," Wohl said. "Not the way you mean. But the eyewitness is that blonde from Channel 9. That could cause problems. The commissioner asked me to make sure it doesn't. I want to explain that to Chief Lowenstein. That's all."

"Good luck, Inspector," Hobbs said, chuckling. Chief Inspector of Detectives Matt Lowenstein, a heavyset, cigar-chewing man in his fifties, had a legendary temper, which was frequently triggered when he suspected someone was treading on sacred Detective Turf.

"Why do I think I'll need it?" Wohl said, also chuckling, and left.

There was a Cadillac hearse with a casket in it in the parking lot. The driver was leaning on the fender. Chrome-plated letters outside the frosted glass read MARSHUTZ & SONS.

Dutch was apparently going to be buried from a funeral home three blocks from his house. As soon as the medical examiner released the body, it would be put in the casket, and in the hearse, and taken there.

Wohl thought that Sabara showing up here, just so he could lead the hearse to Marshutz & Sons, was a rather touching gesture. It wasn't called for by regulations, and he hadn't thought that Dutch and Sabara had been that close. But probably, he decided, he was wrong. Sabara wasn't really as tough as he acted (and looked), and he probably had been, in his way, fond of Dutch.

He got in the LTD and got on the radio.

"Isaac Twenty-Three. Have Two-Eleven contact me on the J-Band."

Two-Eleven was the Second District car he had sent with Louise Dutton.

He had to wait a moment before Two-Eleven called him.

"Two-Eleven to Isaac Twenty-Three."

"What's your location, Two-Eleven?"

"We just dropped the lady at Six Stockton Place."

Where the hell is that? The only Stockton Place I can think of is a slum down by the river.

"Where?"

"Isaac Twenty-Three, that's Apartment A, Six Stockton Place."

"Two-Eleven, where does that come in?"

"It's off Arch Street in the one-hundred block."

"Okay. Two-Eleven, thank you," he said, and put the microphone back in the glove box.

He was surprised. That was really a crummy address, not one where you would expect a classy blonde like Louise Dutton to live. Then he remembered that there had been conversion, renovation, whatever it was called, of the old buildings in that area.

When Lieutenant David Pekach came out of the medical examiner's office, he found a white-cap Traffic Division officer standing next to the battered van, writing out a ticket.

"Is there some trouble, Officer?" Pekach asked, innocently.

The Traffic Division officer, who had intended to ticket the van only for a missing headlight, took a look at the legend on Pekach's T-shirt, and with an effort, restrained himself from commenting.

What he would have *liked* to have done is kick the fucking hippie queer junkie's ass from there to the river, and there drown the sonofabitch, and in the old days, when he'd first come on the job, he could have done just that. But things had changed, and he was coming up on his twenty years for retirement, and it wasn't worth risking his pension, even if somebody walking around with something insulting to the police like that—*Support Your Local Sheriff* my ass, that *wasn't* what it meant—printed on his sweatshirt and walking around on the streets really deserved to get his ass kicked.

Instead, he cited the vehicle for a number of additional offenses against the Motor Vehicle Code: cracked windshield, smooth tires, non-functioning turn indicators, and illegible license plate, which was all he could think of. He was disappointed when the fucking hippy had a valid driver's license.

Half a block from the medical examiner's office, Lieutenant Pekach put his copy of the citation between his teeth, ripped it in half, and then threw both halves out the van's window.

• • •

When Wohl got to the Roundhouse, he parked in the space reserved for Chief Inspector Coughlin. Coughlin was very close to the Moffitt family; more than likely he would be at the Moffitt house for a while. As he walked into the building, he saw Hobbs's car turn into the parking lot.

He was not surprised to find Chief Inspector of Detectives Matt Lowenstein in Homicide. Lowenstein was in the main room, sitting on a desk, a fresh, very large cigar in the corner of his mouth.

"Well, Inspector Wohl," Lowenstein greeted him with mock cordiality, "I was hoping I'd run into you. How are you, Peter?"

"Good afternoon, Chief," Wohl said.

"Do you think you could find a moment for me?" Lowenstein asked. "I've got a little something on my mind."

"My time is your time, Chief," Wohl said.

"Why don't we just go in here a moment?" Lowenstein said, gesturing toward the door of an office on whose door was lettered CAPTAIN HENRY C. QUAIRE COMMANDING OFFICER.

Chief Inspector Lowenstein opened the door without knocking. Captain Quaire, a stocky, balding man in his late forties, was sitting in his shirtsleeves at his desk, talking on the telephone. When he saw Lowenstein, he covered the mouthpiece with his hand.

"Henry, why don't you get a cup of coffee or something?" Lowenstein suggested.

Captain Quaire, as he rose to his feet, said "I'll call you right back" to the telephone and hung it up. When he passed Peter Wohl, he shook his head. Wohl wasn't sure if it was a gesture of sympathy, or whether it meant that Quaire too was shocked, and pissed, by what he had done.

"Peter," Lowenstein said, as he closed the door after Quaire, "it's not that I don't think that you are one of the brightest young officers in the department, a credit to the department and your father, but when I want your assistance, the way I would prefer to do that is to call Denny Coughlin and ask for it. Not have you shoved down my throat by the Polack."

"Frankly, Chief," Wohl said, smiling, "I sort of expected you would ask me in here, thank me for my services, and tell me not to let the doorknob hit me in the ass on my way out."

"Don't be a wiseass, Peter," Lowenstein said.

"Chief, I hope you understand that what I did at the diner was at the commissioner's orders," Wohl said. He saw that Lowenstein was still angry.

"The implication, of course, is that everybody in Homicide is a fucking barbarian, too dumb to figure out for themselves how to handle a woman like that," Lowenstein said.

"I don't think he meant that, Chief," Wohl said. "I think what it was was just that I was the senior supervisor at the Waikiki Diner. I think he would have given the same orders, would have preferred to give the same orders, to anyone from Homicide."

"The difference, Peter, is that nobody from Homicide would have called the Polack. They would have followed procedure. Why did you call him?"

"A couple of reasons," Wohl said, deciding to stand his ground. "Primarily because he and Dutch were close."

"And the woman?"

"And the woman," Peter said. "I'm sorry if you're angry, but I don't see where what I did was wrong."

"Was Dutch fucking her?"

"I don't know," Peter said. "I thought it was possible when I called the commissioner, and that if they had something going on between them, what I should do was try to keep anybody from finding out."

"Maybe the Polack was already onto it," Lowenstein said.

"Excuse me?"

"Just before you came in, Peter, I talked with the Polack," Lowenstein said. "I was going to call him anyway, but he called me. And what he told me was that he wants you in on this, to deal with the Dutton woman from here on in."

"I don't understand," Wohl said.

"It's simple English," Lowenstein said. "Whatever Homicide has to do with that woman, they'll do it through you. I told the Polack I didn't like that one damned bit, and he said he was sorry, but it wasn't a suggestion. He also said that I shouldn't bother complaining to the mayor, the mayor thought it was a good idea, too. I guess that Wop sonofabitch is as afraid of the goddamned TV as the Polack is."

"Well, it wasn't my idea," Wohl said, aware that he was embarrassed. "I went to Nazareth, and went through Dutch's personal possessions, and then I went to the medical examiner's office. I was going to come here to tell you what I found—which is nothing—and then I was going to call the commissioner and tell him."

Lowenstein looked intently at him for a moment.

"And go back to where I belong," Peter added.

"Yeah, well, that's not going to happen," Lowenstein said. "I was going to give you a little talk, Peter, to make it clear that *all* you're authorized to do is keep the TV lady happy; that you're *not* to get involved in the investigation itself. But I don't think I have to do that, do I?"

"No, sir," Wohl said. "Of course you don't."

"And I don't think I have to ask you to make sure that I hear anything the Polack hears, do I?"

"No, sir."

"The trouble with you, Peter, you sonofabitch, is that I can't stay mad at you," Lowenstein said.

"I'm glad to hear that," Wohl said, smiling. "What do you think I should do now?"

"I suspect that just maybe the assigned detective would like to talk to the witness," Lowenstein said. "Why don't you find him and ask him? Where's the dame?"

"At her apartment," Peter said. "Who's got the job?"

"Jason Washington," Chief Inspector Lowenstein said. "I expect you'll find him outside, just atitter with excitement that he'll now be able to work real close to a real staff inspector."

"There's a rumor going around, Chief," Wohl said, "that some people think staff inspectors are real cops."

"Get your ass out of here, Peter," Lowenstein said, but he was smiling.

There were twenty-one active homicide investigations underway by the Homicide Division of the Philadelphia Police Department, including that of Captain Richard C. Moffitt. An active homicide investigation being defined unofficially as one where there was a reasonable chance to determine who had unlawfully caused the death of another human being, and to develop sufficient evidence to convince the Philadelphia district attorney that he would not be wasting his time and the taxpayers' money by seeking a grand jury indictment and ultimately bringing the accused to trial.

Very nearly at the bottom of the priority list to expend investigatory resources (the time and overtime of the homicide detectives, primarily, but also including certain forensic techniques, some of which were very expensive) were the cases, sometimes occurring once or twice a week, involving vagrants or junkies done to death by beating, or stabbing. The perpetrator of these types of murders often had no motive beyond taking possession of the victim's alcohol or narcotics, and if questioned about it eight hours later might really have no memory of what had taken place.

There were finite resources. Decisions have to be made as to where they can best be spent in protecting the public, generally, or sometimes an individual. Most murders involve people who know each other, and many involve close relatives, and most murders are not hard to solve. The perpetrator of a murder is often on the scene when the police arrive, or if he has fled the scene, is immediately identified by witnesses who also have a pretty good idea where he or she might be found.

What many homicide detectives privately (certainly not for public consumption) think of as a *good* case is a death illegally caused during the execution of a felony. A holdup man shoots a convenience-store cashier, for example, or a bank messenger is shot and killed while being held up.

That sort of a perpetrator is not going to be found sitting in the toilet, head between his hands, sick to his stomach with remorse, asking to see his parish priest. The sonofabitch is going to run, and if run to earth is going to deny ever having been near the scene of the crime in his life.

It is necessary to make the case against him. Find his gun, wherever he hid it or threw it, and have the crime lab make it as the murder weapon. Find witnesses who saw him at the scene of the crime, or with the loot. Break the stories of witnesses who at first are willing to swear on a stack of Bibles that the accused was twenty miles from the scene of the crime.

This is proper detective work, worthy of homicide detectives, who believe they are the best detectives in the department. It requires brains and skills in a dozen facets of the investigative profession.

And every once in a great while, there is a case just like cop stories on the TV, where some dame does in her husband, or some guy does in his business partner, on purpose, planning it carefully, so that it looks as if he fell down the cellar stairs, or that the partner got done in by a burglar, or a mugger, or a hit-and-run driver.

But something about it smells, and a good homicide detective starts nosing around, finding out if the done-in husband had a girl on the side, or a lot of insurance, or had a lot of insurance and the *wife* was running around.

Very near the top of the priority list are the homicides of children, and other sorts of specially protected individuals, such as nuns, or priests.

And at the absolute top of the priority list is the murder of a police officer. There are a number of reasons for this, some visceral *(that could be me lying there with a hole in the back of my head)* and some very practical: *You can't enforce the law if the bad guys think they can shoot a cop and get away with it. If the bad guys can laugh at the cops, they win.*

Technically, the investigation of the murder of Captain Richard C. Moffitt would be handled exactly like the murder of any other citizen. The case would be assigned to a homicide detective. It would be his case. He would conduct the investigation, asking for whatever assistance he needed. He would be supervised by his sergeant, who would keep himself advised on where the investigation was leading. And the sergeant's lieutenant would keep an eye on the investigation through the sergeant. Both would provide any assistance to the homicide detective who had the case that he asked for.

That was the procedure, and it would be followed in the case of Captain Richard C. Moffitt.

Captain Henry C. Quaire, commanding officer of the Homicide Division, had assigned the investigation of the murder of Captain Richard C. Moffitt to Detective Jason F. Washington, Sr., almost immediately upon learning that Captain Moffitt had been shot to death.

Detective Washington was thirty-nine years old, a large, heavyset Afro-American who had been a police officer for sixteen years, a detective for eleven, and assigned to Homicide for five. Washington had a reputation as a highly skilled interrogator, a self-taught master psychologist who seemed to know not only when someone being interviewed was lying, but how to get the person being interviewed to tell the truth. He was quite an actor, doing this, being able convincingly to portray any one of a number of characters, from the kindly understanding father figure who fully understood how something tragic like this could happen to the meanest sonofabitch east of the Mississippi River.

Washington had a fine mind, an eagle's eye when discovering minor discrepancies in a story, and a skill rare among his peers. He was a fine typist. He could type with great accuracy at about eighty words per minute. This skill, coupled with Detective Washington's flair for writing, made his official reports the standard to which his peers aspired. Detective Washington was never summoned to the captain's office to be asked, "What the hell is this supposed to mean?"

Detective Washington and Captain Moffitt had been friends, too. Washington had been (briefly, until he had been injured in a serious wreck, during a high-speed pursuit) then-Sergeant Moffitt's partner in the Highway Patrol.

None of this had anything to with the case of Captain Richard C. Moffitt being assigned to Detective Jason F. Washington, Sr. He was given the job because he was "up on the wheel." The wheel (which was actually a sheet of cardboard) was the device by which jobs were assigned to the detectives of the Homicide Division. Each shift had its own wheel. When a job came in, the detective whose name was at the head of the list was given the assignment, whereupon his name went to the bottom of the wheel. He would not be given another job until every other homicide detective, in turn, had been given one.

The system was not unlike that used in automobile showrooms, where to keep a prospective customer, an "up," from being swarmed over by a dozen commission-hungry salesmen, they were forced to take their turn.

Jason F. Washington, Sr., knew, however, as did everybody else in Homicide, that while Dutch's shooting might be his job, he was going to be given a higher level of supervision and assistance than he would have gotten had Richard C. Moffitt been a civilian when he stopped the bullet in the Waikiki Diner.

There was no suggestion at all that there was any question in anyone's mind that Washington could not handle the job. What it was was that the commissioner was going to keep an eye on the case through Chief Inspector of Detectives Matt Lowenstein, who was going to lean on Captain Quaire to make sure everything possible was being done, who was going to lean on Lieutenant Lou Natali who was going to lean on Sergeant Zachary Hobbs, who was going to lean on Detective Jason F. Washington, Sr.

And now Peter Wohl had been added to the equation, and Jason Washington wasn't sure what that would mean. He had found that out when he'd asked Captain Quaire why the witness hadn't been brought to the Roundhouse. Quaire had told him, off the record, that Wohl had stuck his nose in where it didn't belong, and that Lowenstein was about to chop it off for him. But an hour after that, Quaire had come out of his office to tell him that was changed. He was not to do anything about the witness at all, without checking with Staff Inspector Wohl. Staff Inspector Wohl was presently at the medical examiner's office and might, and then again might not, soon grace Homicide with his exalted presence.

Quaire had thrown up his hands.

"Don't look at me, Jason. I just work here. We are now involved in bullshit among the upper-level brass."

Detective Jason Washington had seen Staff Inspector Peter Wohl come into Homicide, and had seen Matt Lowenstein take him into Captain Quaire's office, throwing Quaire out as he did so. He was not surprised when Wohl appeared at his desk, five minutes later, although he had not seen, or sensed, him walking over.

"Hello, Jason," Wohl said.

Washington stood up and offered his hand.

"Inspector," he said. "How goes it?"

"I'm all right," Wohl said. "How've you been?"

"Aside from the normal ravages of middle age, no real complaints. Something on your mind?"

"I've been assigned to stroke WCBL-TV generally and Miss Louise Dutton specifically," Wohl said. "I guess you heard?"

Washington smiled. "I heard about that." He pointed at the wooden chair beside his desk.

Wohl smiled his thanks and sat down and stretched his legs out.

"You ever read *Animal Farm?*" Wohl asked.

Washington chuckled.

"I wouldn't compare a pretty lady like that with a pig," he said.

"Let's just say then that she's more equal than some other pretty lady," Wohl said. "If you're ready for her, I'll go get her."

"Anytime it's convenient," Washington said. "But an hour ago would be better than tomorrow."

"Jason, all I'm going to do is stroke her feathers," Wohl said. "Did I have to tell you that?"

"No, but I'm glad you did," Washington said. "Thank you."

"But for personal curiosity, has anything turned up?" Wohl asked.

"Not yet, but if I was a white boy with long hair and a zipper jacket, I don't think I would leave the house today. I guess you heard what the Highway Patrol is up to?"

"I'm not sure how effective that will be, but you can't blame them. They liked Dutch."

"So did I. We were partners, once. Hell, Highway may even catch him."

"What's your gut feeling, Jason?"

"Well, he's either under a rock somewhere in Philadelphia, or he's long gone. But gut feeling? He's either here or in Atlantic City."

Wohl nodded and made a little grunting noise.

"An undercover guy from Narcotics thinks he identified the woman—"

"Sergeant Hobbs called me," Washington interrupted him. "If they can come up with a name . . ."

"I have a feeling they will," Wohl said. "Okay. So long as you understand where I fit in this, Jason, I'll go fetch the eyewitness."

He stood up.

Detective Jason F. Washington, Sr., extended something to Staff Inspector Peter Wohl.

"What's that?"

"Miracle of modern medicine," Washington said. "It's supposed to prevent ulcers."

"Are you suggesting I'm going to need it?" Wohl asked with a smile.

"*Somebody* thinks that TV lady is going to be trouble," Washington said.

Wohl popped the antacid in his mouth, and then turned and walked out of Homicide.

6   When Sergeant Hobbs and Officer McFadden got to the Roundhouse, and McFadden started to open the passenger-side door, Hobbs touched his arm.

"Wait a minute," he said. He then got out of the car, walked to the passenger side, motioned for McFadden to get out, and when he had, put his hand on his arm, and then marched him into the building. It looked for all the world as if McFadden was in custody and being led into the Roundhouse, which is exactly what Hobbs had in mind.

The Roundhouse is a public building, but it is not open to the public to the degree, for example, that City Hall is. It is the nerve center of the police department, and while there are always a number of ordinary, decent, law-abiding citizens in the building, the overwhelming majority of private citizens in the Roundhouse are there as nonvoluntary guests of the police, or are relatives and friends of the nonvoluntary guests who have come to see what can be done about getting them out, either by posting bail, or in some other way.

There are almost always a number of people in this latter category standing just outside, or just inside, the door leading into the Roundhouse from the parking lot out back. Immediately inside the door is a small foyer. To the right a corridor leads to an area from which the friends and relatives of those arrested can watch preliminary arraignments before a magistrate, who either sets bail or orders the accused confined until trial.

To the left is a door leading to the main lobby of the building, which is not open to the general public. It is operated by a solenoid controlled by a police officer who sits behind a shatterproof plastic window directly across the corridor from the door to the parking lot.

Hobbs didn't want anyone with whom McFadden might now, or eventually, have a professional relationship to remember later having seen the large young man with the forehead band walking into the place and being passed without question, as if he was a cop, into the main lobby.

Still holding on to Officer McFadden's arm, Hobbs flashed his badge at the corporal on duty behind the window, who took a good look at it, and then pushed the button operating the solenoid. The door lock buzzed as Hobbs reached it. He pushed it open, and went through it, and marched McFadden to the elevator doors.

There was a sign on the gray steel first-floor door reading CRIMINAL RECORDS, AUTHORIZED PERSONNEL ONLY. Hobbs pushed it open, and eventually the door opened. A corporal looked at Officer McFadden very dubiously.

"This is McFadden, Narcotics," Hobbs said. The room held half a dozen enormous gray rotary files, each twelve feet long. Electric motors rotated rows of files, thousands of them, each containing the arrest and criminal records of one individual who had at one time come to the official attention of the police. The files were tended by civilian employees, mostly women, under the supervision of sworn officers.

Hobbs saw the sergeant on duty, Salvatore V. DeConti, a short, balding, plump, very natty man in his middle thirties, in a crisply starched shirt and perfectly creased uniform trousers, sitting at his desk. He saw that DeConti was unable to keep from examining, and finding wanting, the fat bearded large young man he had brought with him into records.

Amused, Hobbs walked McFadden over to him and introduced him: "Sergeant DeConti, this is Officer McFadden. He's identified the woman who shot Captain Moffitt."

It was an effort, but DeConti managed it, to offer his hand to the fat, bearded young man with the leather band around his forehead.

"How are you?" he said, then freed his hand, and called to the corporal. When he came over, he said, "Officer McFadden's got a name on the girl Captain Moffitt shot."

"I guess the fingerprint guy from Identification ought to be back from the medical examiner's about now with her prints," the corporal said. "What's the name?"

"Schmeltzer, Dorothy Ann," McFadden said. "And I got a name, Sergeant, for the guy who got away from the diner." He gestured with his hand, a circular movement near his head, indicating that he didn't actually *have* a name, for sure, but that he knew there was one floating around somewhere in his head. That he was, in other words, working intuitively.

"Florian will help you, if he can," Sergeant DeConti said.

"Gallagher, Grady, something Irish," McFadden said.

"There's only three or four thousand Gallaghers in there, I'm sure," Corporal Florian said. "But we can look."

"Help yourself to some coffee, Sergeant," DeConti said. Then, "Damned shame about Dutch."

"A rotten shame," Hobbs agreed. "Three kids." Then he looked at DeConti. "I'm sure McFadden is right," he said. "Lieutenant Pekach said he's smart, a good cop. Even if he doesn't look much like one."

"I'm just glad I never got an assignment like that," DeConti said. "Some of it has to rub off. The scum he has to be with, I mean."

Hobbs had the unkind thought that Sergeant DeConti would never be asked to undertake an undercover assignment unless it became necessary to infiltrate a group of hotel desk clerks, or maybe the Archdiocese of Philadelphia. If you put a white collar on DeConti, Hobbs thought, he could easily pass for a priest.

Across the room, McFadden, a look of satisfaction on his face, was writing on a yellow, lined pad. He ripped off a sheet and handed it to Corporal Florian. Then he walked across the room to Hobbs and DeConti.

"Gerald Vincent Gallagher," he announced. "I remembered the moment I saw her sheet. He got ripped off about six months ago by some Afro-American gentlemen, near the East Park Reservoir in Fairmount Park. They really did a job on him. She came to see him in the hospital."

"Good man, McFadden," DeConti said. "Florian's getting his record?"

"Yes, sir. Her family lives in Holmesburg," McFadden went on. "I went looking for her there one time. Her father runs a grocery store around Lincoln High School. Nice people."

"This ought to brighten their day," Hobbs said.

Corporal Florian walked over with a card, and handed it, a little uneasily, to McFadden. DeConti and Hobbs leaned over to get a look.

"That's him. He's just out on parole, too," McFadden said.

"He fits the description," Hobbs said, and then went on: "If you were Gerald Vincent Gallagher, McFadden, where do you think you would be right now?"

McFadden's heavily bearded face screwed up in thought.

"I don't think I'd have any money, since I didn't get to pull off the robbery," he said. "So I don't think I would be on a bus or train out of town. And I wouldn't go back where I lived, in case I had been recognized, so I would probably be holed up someplace, probably in North Philly, if I got that far. Maybe downtown. I can think of a couple of places."

"Make up a list," Hobbs ordered.

"I'd sort of like to look for this guy myself, Sergeant," McFadden said.

Hobbs looked at him dubiously.

"I don't want to blow my cover, Sergeant," McFadden went on. "I could look for him without doing that."

"You can tell Lieutenant Pekach that I said that if he thinks you could be spared from your regular job for a while, that you could probably be useful to Detective Washington," Hobbs said. "*If* Washington wants you."

"Thank you," McFadden said. "I'll ask him as soon as I get back to the office."

"Jason Washington's got the job?" Sergeant DeConti asked.

"Uh-huh," Hobbs said. He picked up the telephone and dialed it.

"Detention Unit, Corporal Delzinski."

"This is Sergeant Hobbs, Homicide, Corporal. The next time a wagon from the Sixth District—"

"There's one just come in, Sergeant," Delzinski interrupted.

"As soon as they drop off their prisoner, send them up to Criminal Records," Hobbs said. "I've got a prisoner that has to be transported to Narcotics. They'll probably have to fumigate the wagon, afterward, but that can't be helped."

DeConti laughed.

"We have a lot of time and money invested in making you a credible turd, McFadden," Hobbs said. "I would hate to see it all wasted."

"I understand, sir," McFadden said. "Thank you."

A civilian employee from the photo lab, a very thin woman, walked up with three four-by-five photographs of Gerald Vincent Gallagher.

"I wiped them," she said. "But they're still wet. I don't know about putting them in an envelope."

"I'll just carry them the way they are," Hobbs said. "McFadden, you make up your list. When the Sixth District wagon gets here, Sergeant DeConti will tell them to transport you to Narcotics. I'll send somebody up to get the list from you."

"Yes, sir," McFadden said.

"Thank you, Brother DeConti," Hobbs said. "It's always a pleasure doing business with you."

"I just hope you catch the bastard," DeConti said.

The Wackenhut Private Security officer did not raise the barrier when the blue Ford LTD nosed up to it, nor even when the driver tapped the horn. He let the bastard wait a minute, and then walked slowly over to the car.

"May I help you, sir?"

"Raise the barrier," Wohl said.

"Stockton Place is not a public thoroughfare, sir," the security officer said.

Wohl showed him his badge.

"What's going on, Inspector?" the security officer said.

"Nothing particular," Wohl said. "You want to raise that thing?"

Louise Dutton's old yellow Cadillac convertible, the roof now up, was parked three-quarters of the way down the cobblestone street.

When the barrier was raised, Wohl drove slowly down the street and pulled in behind the convertible. Wohl looked around curiously. He hadn't even known this place was here, although his office was less than a dozen blocks away.

Stockton Place looked, he thought, except for the cars on the street, as it must have looked two hundred years ago, when these buildings had been built.

He got out of the car, then crossed to the nearest doorway. There was no doorbell that he could see, and after a moment, he saw that the doorway was not intended to open; that it was a facade. He backed up, smiled more in amusement than embarrassment, and looked at the doorways to the right and left. There were doorbells beside the doorway on the left.

There were three of them, and one of them read DUTTON.

He saw that the door was slightly ajar, and tried it, and then pushed it open.

There was a small lobby inside. To the right was a shiny mailbox, and more doorbell buttons, these accompanied by a telephone. Beside the mailboxes was a door with a large brass "C" fixed to it, and a holder for a name card. Jerome Nelson.

There were three identical doors against the other wall. They each had identifying signs on them: STAIRWAY, ELEVATOR, SERVICE.

If "C" was the ground floor, Wohl reasoned, "A" would be the top floor. He opened the door marked ELEVATOR and found an open elevator behind it. He pushed "A". A door closed silently, faint music started to play, and the elevator started upward. It stopped, and the door opened and the music stopped. There was another door in front of him, with a lock and a peephole, and a doorbell button. He pushed it and heard the faint ponging of chimes.

"Whoever that is, Jerome," Louise Dutton said, "send them away."

Jerome walked quickly and delicately to the elevator door, rose on his toes, and put his eye to the peephole. It was a handsome, rather well dressed, man.

Jerome pulled the door open.

"I'm very sorry," he said, "but Miss Dutton is not receiving callers."

"Please tell Miss Dutton that Peter Wohl would like to see her," Wohl said.

"Just one moment, please," Jerome said.

He walked into the apartment.

"It's a very good-looking man named Peter Wohl," he told Louise Dutton, loud enough for Wohl to hear him. A smile flickered on and off Wohl's face.

"He's a policeman," Louise said, and walked toward the door.

Louise Dutton was wearing a bathrobe, Wohl saw, and then corrected himself, *a dressing gown,* and holding both a cigarette and a drink.

"Oh, you," she said. "Hi! Come on in."

"Good afternoon, Miss Dutton," Wohl said, politely.

She was half in the bag, Wohl decided. There was something erotic about the way she looked, he realized. Part of that was obviously because he could see her nipples holding the thin material of her dressing gown up like tent poles—it was probably silk, he decided—but there was more to it than that.

"I'm glad that you got home all right," Wohl said.

"Thank you for that," Louise said. "I was more upset than I realized, and I shouldn't have been driving."

"I just made her take a long soak in a hot tub," Jerome said. "And I prescribed a *stiff* drink." He put out his hand. "I'm Jerome Nelson, a friend of the family."

"I'm Inspector Peter Wohl," Wohl said, taking the hand. "How do you do, Mr. Nelson?"

"You certainly, if you don't mind me saying so, don't look like a policeman," Jerome Nelson said.

"That's nice, if you're a detective," Wohl said. "What would you say I *do* look like?"

Jerome laid a finger against his cheek, cocked his head, and studied Wohl.

"I just *don't know,"* he said. "Maybe a stockbroker. A *successful* stockbroker. I *love* your suit."

"Miss Dutton, they're ready for you at the Roundhouse," Wohl said.

"Meaning what?"

"Meaning, I'd like you to come down there with me. They want your statement, and I think they'll have some photographs to show you. And then I'll see that you're brought back here."

"Will whatever it is wait five minutes?" Louise said. "I want to see what Cohen's going to put on."

"I beg your pardon?" Wohl asked.

"It's time for 'Nine's News,' " she said.

"Oh," he said.

"Can I offer you a drink?" Jerome asked.

"Yes, thank you," Wohl said. "I'd like a drink. Scotch?"

"Absolutely," Jerome said, happily.

Louise opened the door of a maple cabinet, revealing a large color television screen. She turned it on and, still bent over it, so that Wohl had a clear view of her naked breast, looked at him as she waited for it to come on.

"The guy on 'Dragnet,' " Louise Dutton said, "Sergeant Joe Friday, would say, 'No ma'am, I'm on duty.' "

"I'm not Sergeant Friday," Wohl said, with a faint smile.

She's bombed, and unaware her dressing gown is open. Or is it the to-be-expected casualness about nudity of a hooker?

That's an interesting possibility. She's obviously not walking the streets asking men if they want a date, but I don't think she's making half enough money smiling on television to afford this place. Is she somebody's mistress, some middle-aged big shot's extracurricular activity, who was taking a bus driver's holiday with Dutch?

And who's Jerome? The friend of the family?

The picture suddenly came on, and the sound. Louise turned the volume up, and stepped back as Jerome touched Wohl's shoulder and handed him a squarish glass of whiskey.

The screen showed Louise Dutton's old convertible with a cop at the wheel leaving the Waikiki Diner parking lot.

A female voice said, "This is a special 'Nine's News' bulletin. A Philadelphia police captain gave his life this afternoon foiling a holdup. 'Nine's News' co-anchor Louise Dutton was an eyewitness. Full details on 'Nine's News' at six."

The Channel Nine logo came on the screen. A male voice said, "WCBL-TV, Channel 9, Philadelphia. It's six o'clock."

Another male voice said, as the "Nine's News" set appeared on the screen, " 'Nine's News' at six is next."

The "Nine's News" logo appeared on the screen, and then dissolved into a close-up shot of Barton Ellison, a tanned, handsome, craggy-faced former actor, who had abandoned the stage and screen for television journalism, primarily because he hadn't worked in over two years.

"Louise Dutton isn't here with me tonight," Barton Ellison said, in his deep, trained actor's voice, looking directly into the camera. "She wanted to be. But she was an eyewitness to the gun battle in which Philadelphia Highway Patrol Captain Richard C. Moffitt gave his life this afternoon. She knows the face of the bandit that is, at this moment, still free. Louise Dutton is under police protection. Full details, and exclusive 'Nine's News' film, after these messages."

There followed twenty seconds of Louise being escorted to her car at the Waikiki Diner, and of the car, with a policeman at the wheel, following a police car out of the parking lot. Then there was a smiling baby on the screen, as a disposable-diaper commercial began.

"That *sonofabitch!*" Louise Dutton exploded. She looked at Wohl. "I had nothing to do with that."

"I don't understand," Wohl said.

"I never told him I was under police protection," Louise said.

"Oh," Wohl said. He could not understand why she was upset. He took a sip of his scotch. He couldn't tell what brand it was, only that it was expensive.

The diaper commercial was followed by one for a new motion picture to be shown later that night for the very first time on television, and then for one for a linoleum floor wax which apparently had an aphrodisiacal effect on generally disinterested husbands.

Then Louise reappeared. She looked into the camera.

"Moments before he was fatally wounded," she said, "Police Captain Richard C. Moffitt said, 'Put the gun down, son. I don't want to have to kill you. I'm a police officer.'

"Moffitt was meeting with this reporter over coffee in the Waikiki Diner in the sixty-five-hundred block of Roosevelt Boulevard early this afternoon. He was concerned with the image his beloved Highway Patrol has in some people's eyes . . . 'Carlucci's Commandos' is just one derogatory term for them.

"He had just started to explain what they do, and why, and how, when he spotted a pale-faced blond young man police have yet to identify holding a gun on the diner's cashier.

"Captain Moffitt was off duty, and in civilian clothing, but he was a policeman, and a robbery was in progress, and it was his duty to do something about it.

"There was a good thirty-second period, maybe longer, during which Captain Moffitt could have shot the bandit where he stood. But he decided to give the bandit a break, a chance to save his life: 'Put the gun down, son. I don't want to have to kill you.'

"That humanitarian gesture cost Richard C. Moffitt his life. And Moffitt's three children their father, and Moffitt's wife her husband.

"The bandit had an accomplice, a woman. She opened fire on Moffitt. Her bullets struck all over the interior of the diner. Except for one, which entered Richard C. Moffitt's chest.

"He returned fire then, and killed his assailant.

"And then, a look of wonderment on his face, he slumped against a wall, and slid down to the floor, killed in the line of duty.

"Police are looking for the pale-faced blond young man, who escaped during the gun battle. I don't think it will take them long to arrest him, and the moment they do, 'Nine's News' will let you know they have."

A formal portrait of Dutch Moffitt in uniform came on the screen.

"Captain Richard C. Moffitt," Louise said, softly, "thirty-six years old. Killed . . . shot down, cold-bloodedly murdered . . . in the line of duty.

"My name is Louise Dutton. Barton?"

She took three steps forward and turned the television off before Barton Ellison could respond. Peter Wohl took advantage of the visual opportunity offered.

"That was just beautiful," Jerome Nelson said, softly. "I wanted to cry."

I'll be goddamned, Peter Wohl thought, *so did I.*

He looked at Louise, and saw her eyes were teary.

"That bullshit about me being under police protection cheapened the whole thing," she said. "That cheap sonofabitch!"

She looked at Wohl as if looking for a response.

He said, "That was quite touching, Miss Dutton."

"It won't do Dutch a whole fucking lot of good, will it? Or his wife and kids?" Louise said.

"Do you always swear that much?" Wohl asked, astounding himself. He rarely said anything he hadn't carefully considered first.

She smiled. "Only when I'm pissed off," she said, and walked out of the room.

"God only knows how long that will take," Jerome Nelson said. "Won't you sit down, Inspector?" He waved Wohl delicately into one of four identical white leather upholstered armchairs surrounding a coffee table that was a huge chunk of marble.

It did not, despite what Jerome Nelson said, take Louise Dutton long to get dressed. When she came back in the room Wohl stood up. She waved him back into his chair.

"If you don't mind," she said, "I'll finish my drink."

"Not at all," Wohl said.

She sat down in one across from them, and then reached for a cigarette. Wohl stole another glance down her neckline.

"What's your first name?" Louise Dutton asked, when she had slumped back into the chair.

"Peter," he said, wondering why she had asked.

"Tell me, Peter, does your wife know of this uncontrollable urge of yours to look down women's necklines?"

He felt his face redden.

"It's probably very dangerous," Louise went on. "The last time I felt sexual vibrations from a cop, somebody shot him."

With a very great effort, which he felt sure failed, Staff Inspector Peter Wohl picked up his glass and took a sip with as much savoir faire as he could muster.

The telephone was ringing when Peter Wohl walked into his apartment. He lived in West Philadelphia, on Montgomery Avenue, in a one-bedroom apartment over a four-car garage. It had once been the chauffeur's apartment when the large (sixteen-room) brownstone house on an acre and a half had been a single-family dwelling. There were now six apartments, described as "luxury," in the house, whose new owner, a corporation, restricted its tenants to those who had neither children nor domestic pets weighing more than twenty-five pounds.

Peter nodded and smiled at some of his fellow tenants, but he wasn't friendly with any of them. He had rebuffed friendly overtures for a number of reasons, among them the problems he saw in associating socially with bright young couples who smoked *cannabis sativa,* and probably ingested by one means or another other prohibited substances.

To bust, or not to bust, that is the question! Whether 'tis nobler to apprehend (which probably would result in a stern warning, plus a slap on the wrist) or look the other way.

Or, better yet, not to know about it, by politely rejecting invitations to drop by for a couple of drinks, and maybe some laughs, and who knows what else. They believed, he thought, what he had told them: that he worked for the city. They probably believed that he was a middle-level functionary in the Department of Public Property, or something like that. He was reasonably sure that his neighbors did not associate him with the fuzz, the pigs, or whatever pejorative term was being applied to the cops by the chicly liberal this week.

And then there was the matter of his having two of the four garages, which meant that some of his fellow tenants had to park their cars on the street, or in the driveway, or find another garage someplace else. He had been approached by three of his fellow tenants at different times to give up one of his two garages, if not for fairness, then for money.

He had politely rejected those overtures, too, which had been visibly disappointing and annoying to those asking.

The apartment looked as if it had been decorated by an expensive interior decorator. The walls were white; there was a shaggy white carpet; the furniture was stylish, lots of glass and white leather and chrome. He had been going with an interior decorator at the time he'd taken the apartment, and willing to acknowledge that he knew next to nothing about decorating. Dorothea had decorated it for him, free of charge, and got the furniture and carpet for him at her professional discount.

Dorothea was long gone, they having mutually agreed that the mature and civilized thing to do in their particular circumstance was to turn him in on a lawyer, and so was much of what she had called the *"unity of ambience."*

A men's club downtown had gone under, and auctioned off the furnishings. Peter had bought a small mahogany service bar; two red overstuffed leather armchairs with matching footstools; and a six-by-ten-foot oil painting of a voluptuous nude reclining on a couch that had for fifty-odd years decorated the men's bar of the defunct club. That had replaced a nearly as large modern work of art on the living room wall. The artwork replaced had had a title *(!! Number Three.),* but Peter had taken to referring to it as "The Smear," even before Love in Bloom had started to wither.

Dorothea, very pregnant, had come to see him, bringing the lawyer with her. The purpose of the visit was to see if Peter could "do anything" for a client of the lawyer, who was also a dear friend, who had a son found in possession of just over a pound of Acapulco Gold brand of *cannabis sativa.* Dorothea had been even more upset about the bar, the chairs, and the painting than she had been at his announcement that he couldn't be of help.

"You've *raped* the ambience, Peter," Dorothea had said. "If you want my opinion."

When Peter went into the bedroom, the red light was blinking on his telephone answering device. He snapped it off and picked up the telephone.

"Hello?"

"We're just going out for supper," Chief Inspector (Retired) August Wohl announced, without any preliminary greeting, in his deep, rasping voice, "and afterward, we're going to see Jeannie and Gertrude Moffitt. Your mother thought you might want to eat with us."

"I was over there earlier, Dad," Peter said. "Right after it happened."

"You were?" Chief Inspector Wohl sounded surprised.

"I went in on the call, Dad," Peter said.

"How come?"

"I was on Roosevelt Boulevard. I was the first senior guy on the scene. I just missed Jeannie at Nazareth Hospital, but then I saw her at the house."

"But that was on the job," August Wohl argued. "Tonight's for close friends. The wake's tomorrow. You and Dutch were friends."

"It won't look right, if you don't go to the house tonight." Mrs. Olga Wohl came on the extension. "We've known the Moffitts all our lives. And, tomorrow, at the wake, there will be so many people there . . ."

"I'll try to get by later, Mother," Peter said. "I'm going out to dinner."

"With who, if you don't mind my asking?"

He didn't reply.

"You hear anything, Peter?" Chief Inspector Wohl asked.

"The woman who shot Dutch is a junkie. They have an ID on her, and on the guy, another junkie, who was involved. I think they'll pick him up in a couple of days; I wouldn't be surprised if they already have him. My phone answerer is blinking. A Homicide detective named Jason Washington's got the job—"

"I know him," August Wohl interrupted.

"I asked him to keep me advised. As soon as I hear something, I'll let you know."

"Why should he keep you advised?" August Wohl asked.

"Because the commissioner, for the good of the department, has assigned me to charm the lady from TV."

"I saw the TV," Wohl's father said. "The blonde really was an eyewitness?"

"Yes, she was. She just made the identification, of the dead girl, and the guy who ran. Positive. I was there when she made it. The guy's name is Gerald Vincent Gallagher."

"White guy?"

"Yeah. The woman, too. Her name is Schmeltzer. Her father has a grocery store over by Lincoln High."

"Jesus, I know him," August Wohl said.

"Dad, I better see who called," Peter said.

"He's going to be at Marshutz & Sons, for the wake, I mean. They're going to lay him out in the Green Room; I talked to Gertrude Moffitt," Peter's mother said.

"I'll be at the wake, of course, Mother," Peter said.

"Peter," Chief Inspector Wohl, retired, said thoughtfully, "maybe it would be a good idea for you to wear your uniform to the funeral."

"What?" Peter asked, surprised. Staff inspectors almost never wore uniforms.

"There will be talk, if you're not at the house tonight—"

"You bet, there will be," Peter's mother interjected.

"People like to gossip," Chief Inspector Wohl went on. "Instead of letting them gossip about maybe why you didn't come to the house, let them gossip about you being in uniform."

"That sounds pretty devious, Dad."

"Either the house tonight, with his other close friends, or the uniform at the wake," Chief Inspector Wohl said. "A gesture of respect, one way or the other."

"I don't know, Dad," Peter said.

"Do what you like," his father said, abruptly, and the line went dead.

He's mad. He offered advice and I rejected it. And he's probably right, too. You don't get to be a chief inspector unless you are a master practitioner of the secret rites of the police department.

There was only one recorded message on the telephone answerer tape:

"Dennis Coughlin, Peter. You've done one hell of a job with that TV woman. That was very touching, what she said on the TV. The commissioner saw it, too. I guess you know—Matt Lowenstein told me he saw you—that the commissioner wants you to stay on top of this. None of us wants anything embarrassing to anyone to happen. Call me, at the house, if necessary, when you learn something."

While the tape was rewinding, Peter glanced at his watch.

"Damn!" he said.

He tore off his jacket and his shoulder holster and started to unbutton his shirt. There was no time for a shower. He was late already. He went into the bathroom and splashed Jamaica Bay lime cologne from a bottle onto his hands, and then onto his face. He sniffed his underarms, wet his hands again, and mopped them under his arms.

He stripped to his shorts and socks, and then dressed quickly. He pulled on a pale blue turtleneck knit shirt, and then a darker blue pair of Daks trousers. He slipped his feet into loafers, put his arms through the straps of the shoulder holster, and then into a maroon blazer. He reached on a closet shelf for a snap-brim straw hat and put that on. He examined himself in the full-length mirrors that covered the sliding doors to the bedroom closet.

"My, don't you look splendid, you handsome devil, you!" he said.

And then he ran down the stairs and put a key to the padlock on one of the garage doors, and pulled them open. He went inside. There came the sound of a starter grinding, and then an engine caught.

A British racing green 1950 Jaguar XK-120 roadster emerged slowly and carefully from the garage. It looked new, rather than twenty-three years old. It had been a mess when Peter bought it, soon after he had been promoted to lieutenant. He'd since put a lot of money and a lot of time into it. Even his mother appreciated what he had done; it was now his "cute little sporty car" rather than "that disgraceful old junky rattletrap."

He drove at considerably in excess of the speed limit down Lancaster Avenue to Belmont, and then to the Pennsylvania Psychiatric Institute. Barbara Crowley, R.N., a tall, lithe young woman of, he guessed, twenty-six, twenty-seven, who wore her blond hair in a pageboy, was waiting for him, and smiled when the open convertible pulled up to her.

But she was pissed, he knew, both that he was late, and that he was driving the Jaguar. She contained her annoyance because she was trying as hard as he was to find someone.

"We're being sporty tonight, I see," Barbara said as she got in the car.

"I'm sorry I'm late," he said. "I will prove that, if you give me a chance."

"It's all right," she said.

Impulsively, and although he knew he wasn't, in the turtleneck, dressed for it, he decided on the Ristorante Alfredo. He could count, he thought, on having some snotty Wop waiter, six months out of a Neapolitan slum, look haughtily down his nose at him.

It started going bad before he got that far.

An acne-faced punk in the parking garage gave him trouble about parking the Jaguar himself. It had taken him, literally, a year to find an unblemished, rust-free right front fender for the XK-120, and no sooner had he got it on, and had, finally, the whole car lacquered (20 coats) properly than a parking valet who looked like this one's idiot uncle scraped it along a concrete block wall.

He had since parked his car himself.

The scene annoyed Barbara further, although he resolved it with money, to get it over with.

7 When she saw that Peter Wohl was leading her to Ristorante Alfredo, Barbara Crowley protested.

"Peter, it's so expensive!"

She sounds like my mother, Peter thought.

"Well, I'll just stiff my ex-wife on her alimony," he said, as he opened the door to Ristorante Alfredo. "Tell her to have the kids get a job, too."

Barbara, visibly, did not think that was funny. There was no ex-wife and no kids, but it was not the sort of thing Barbara thought you should joke about, particularly when there was someone who could hear and might not understand. She hadn't thought it was funny the last time he'd made his little joke, and, to judge by her face, it had not improved with age.

The headwaiter was a tall, silver-haired man, who had heard.

"Have you a reservation, sir?" he asked.

"No, but it doesn't look like you have many, either," Peter said, waving in the general direction of the half-empty dining room.

The headwaiter looked toward the bar, where a stout man in his early thirties sat at the bar. He was wearing an expensive suit, and his black hair was expensively cut and arranged, almost successfully, to conceal a rapidly receding hairline.

His name was Ricco Baltazari, and the restaurant and bar licenses had been issued in his name. It was actually owned by a man named Vincenzo Savarese, who, for tax purposes, and because it's hard for a convicted felon to get a liquor license, had Baltazari stand in for him.

Ricco Baltazari had taken in the whole confrontation. There was nothing he would have liked better than to have the fucking cop thrown the fuck out—what a hell of a nerve, coming to a class joint like this with no tie—but instead, with barely visible moves of his massive head, he signaled that Wohl was to be given a table. It's always better to back away from a confrontation with a fucking cop, and this fucking cop was an inspector, and Mr. Savarese was in the back, having dinner with his wife and her sister, and it was better not to risk doing anything that would cause a disturbance.

Besides, he had seen in *Gentlemen's Quarterly* where turtlenecks were making a comeback. It wasn't like the fucking cop was wearing a fucking *shirt* and no necktie. A turtleneck was *different.*

"Spaghetti and meatballs?" Peter Wohl asked, when they had been shown to a table covered with crisp linen and an impressive array of crystal and silverware, and handed large menus. "Or maybe some lasagna? Or would you like me to slip the waiter a couple of bucks and have him sing 'Santa Lucia' while you make up your mind?"

Barbara didn't think that was witty, either.

"I don't know why you come to these places, if you really don't like them."

"The mob serves the best food in Philadelphia," Peter said. "I thought everybody knew that."

Barbara decided to let it drop.

"Well, everything on here looks good," she said, with a determined smile.

Wohl looked at her, rather than at the menu. He knew what he was going to eat: First some cherrystone clams, and then veal Marsala.

She is a good-looking girl. She's intelligent. She's got a good job. She even tolerates me, which means she probably understands me. On a scale of one to ten, she's an eight in bed. What I should do is marry her, and buy a house somewhere and start raising babies. But I don't want to.

She asked him what he was going to have, and he told her, and she said that sounded fine, she would have the same thing.

"Let's have a bottle of wine," Peter said, and opened the wine list and selected an Italian wine whose name he remembered. He pointed out the label to Barbara and asked if that was all right with her. It was fine with her.

Maybe what she needs to turn me on is a little streak of bitchiness, a little streak of not-so-tolerant-and-understanding.

He was nearly through the bottle of wine, and halfway through the veal Marsala, when he looked up and saw Vincenzo Savarese approaching the table.

Vincenzo Savarese was sixty-three years old. What was left of his hair was silver and combed straight back over his ears. His face bore marks of childhood acne. He was wearing a double-breasted brown pin-striped suit, and there was a diamond stickpin in his necktie. He was trailed by two almost identical women in black dresses, his wife and her sister.

Vincenzo Savarese's photo was mounted, very near the top, on the wall chart of known organized crime members the Philadelphia Police Department maintained in the Organized Crime unit.

"I don't mean to disturb your dinner, Inspector," Vincenzo Savarese said. "Keep your seat."

Wohl stood up, but said nothing.

"I just wanted to tell you we heard about what happened to Captain Moffitt, and we're sorry," Vincenzo Savarese said.

"My heart goes out to his mother," one of the women said.

Wohl wasn't absolutely sure whether it was Savarese's wife, or his sister-in-law. Looking at the woman, he said, "Thank you."

"I was on a retreat with Mrs. Moffitt, the mother," the woman went on. "At Blessed Sacrament."

Wohl nodded.

Savarese nodded, and took the woman's arm and led them out of the dining room.

"Who was that?" Barbara Crowley asked.

"His name is Vincenzo Savarese," Wohl said, evenly. "He owns this place."

"I thought you said the mob owns it."

"It does," Wohl said.

"Then why? Why did he do that?"

"He probably meant it, in his own perverse way," Wohl said. "He probably thought Dutch was a fellow man of honor. The mob is big on honor."

"I saw that on TV," Barbara said.

He looked at her.

"About Captain Moffitt. I wasn't going to bring it up unless you did," Barbara said. "But I suppose that's what's wrong, isn't it?"

"I didn't know anything was wrong," Wohl said.

"Have it your way, Peter," Barbara said.

"No, you tell me, what's wrong?"

"You're wearing a turtleneck sweater, and you're driving the Jaguar," she said. "You always do that when something went wrong at work; it's as if—as if it's a *symbol,* that you don't want to be a cop. At least then. And then you got into it with the kid who wanted to park your car, and then the headwaiter here . . ."

"That's very interesting," he said.

"Now, I'm sorry I said it," Barbara said.

"No, I mean it. I didn't know I was that transparent."

"I know you pretty well, Peter," she said.

"You want to know what's really bothering me?" Wohl asked.

"Only if you want to tell me," she said.

"My parents called, just before I went to pick you up," he said. "They told me I should go by Jeannie Moffitt's house tonight. Tonight's for close friends. Tomorrow, they'll have the wake. And they're right, of course. I should, but I didn't want to go, and I didn't."

"You were a friend of Dutch Moffitt's," Barbara said. "Why don't you want to go?"

"Did I tell you that I went in on the assist?"

"You were there?" she asked. She seemed more sympathetic than surprised.

He nodded. "I was a couple of blocks away. When I got there, Dutch was still slumped against the wall of the Waikiki Diner."

"You didn't tell me anything," Barbara said. It was, he decided, a statement of fact, rather than a reproof.

"There's an eyewitness, that woman from Channel Nine, Louise Dutton," Wohl said.

"I saw her," Barbara said. "When she was on TV talking about it."

"I think she had something going with Dutch," Wohl said. "I'll bet on it, as a matter of fact."

"Oh, my!" Barbara said. "And is it going to come out? Will his wife find out?"

"No, I don't think so," Wohl said. "The commissioner has assigned that splendid police officer, Staff Inspector Peter Wohl, to see that 'nothing awkward develops.' "

"You mean, the commissioner knows about Captain Moffitt and that woman?"

"Staff Inspector Peter Wohl, with the good of the department ever foremost in his mind, told him," Wohl said.

Barbara Crowley laid her hand on his.

"I probably shouldn't tell you this," she said. "But one of the main reasons I like you is that you are really a moral man, Peter. You really think about right and wrong."

"And all this time, I thought it was my Jaguar," he said.

"I hate your Jaguar," she said.

"The reason, more or less subconsciously, that I wore the turtleneck and drove the Jaguar, was that I can't go play the role of the bereaved close friend of the family wearing a turtleneck and driving the Jaguar."

"I thought that maybe it was because you didn't want to take me with you," Barbara said.

"You didn't want to go over there," Peter said.

"No, but you didn't know that," Barbara said. When he looked at her in surprise, she went on: "You could go home and change. I'll go over there with you, if you would like. If you think I would be welcome."

"Don't be silly, of course you'd be welcome," he said.

"People might get the idea that if I went there with you, I was your girlfriend."

"I don't think that's much of a secret, is it?" Peter said. "But I'm not really up to going there. I suppose this makes me a moral coward, but I don't want to look at Jeannie's face, or the kids'," he said. "But thank you, Barbara."

"What it makes you is honest," Barbara said, and laid her hand on his. Then she added, "We could go to my place."

Barbara lived in a three-room apartment on the top floor of one of the red-brick buildings at the hospital. It was roomy and comfortable.

She really thought the reason I wasn't going over to the house was because taking her there would be one more reluctant step on our slow but inexorable march to the altar. I squirmed out of that, and now she is offering me comfort, in the way women have comforted men since they came home with dinosaur bites.

"What I think I will do is take you home, apologize for my lousy attitude—"

"Don't be silly, Peter," Barbara interrupted.

"And then go home and get my uniform out of the bag so that I will remember to get it pressed in the morning."

"Your uniform?"

"Dutch was killed in the line of duty," Peter said. "There will be, the day after tomorrow, a splendiferous ceremony at Saint Dominic's. I will be there, in uniform, which, my mother and dad hope, will be accepted as a gesture of my respect overwhelming my bad manners for not joining the other close friends at the house tonight."

He saw a question forming in her eyes, but she didn't, after a just perceptible hesitation, ask it. Instead, she said, "I don't think I've ever seen you in your uniform."

"Very spiffy," he said. "When I wear my uniform, I have to fight to preserve my virtue. It drives the girls wild."

"I'll bet you look very nice in a uniform," Barbara said.

He looked for and found the waiter and waved him over and called for the check.

There would be no check, the waiter said. It was Mr. Savarese's pleasure.

Barbara insisted on going home in a cab. She wasn't mad, she assured him, but she was tired and he was tired, and they both had had bad days and a lot to do tomorrow, and a cab was easier, and made sense.

She kissed him quickly, and got in a cab and was gone. He went to the parking garage and reclaimed the Jaguar.

As soon as he got behind the wheel, Peter Wohl began to regret not having gone to her apartment with Barbara. For one thing, he had learned that turning down an offer of sexual favors was not a good way to maintain a good relationship with a female. *They* could have headaches, or for other reasons be temporarily out of action, but the privilege was not reciprocal. He had probably hurt her feelings, or angered her (even if she didn't let it show), or both, by leaving her. He was sorry to have done that, for Barbara was a good woman.

Less nobly, he realized that a piece of ass would probably be just what the doctor would order for what ailed him. Seeing Dutch slumped dead against the wall had affected him more than he liked to admit. And looking down Louise Dutton's dressing gown, even if she had caught him at it, and made an ass of him, had aroused him. Whatever else could or would be said about the TV lady, she really had a set of perfect teats.

He had been driving without thinking about where he was going. When he oriented himself, he saw he was on Market Street, west of the Schuylkill River, just past Thirtieth Street Station. That wasn't far from Barbara's place.

What the hell am I doing? I really don't want to see her any more tonight.

He was also, he realized, just a couple of blocks away from the Adelphia Hotel.

There was a bar off the lobby of the Adelphia Hotel, in which, from time to time, he had found females sitting who were amenable to a dalliance; often guests of the hotel who, he supposed, were more prone to fool around while in Philadelphia than they would back in Pittsburgh; and sometimes what he thought of as *Strawbridge & Clothier* women, the upper crust of Philadelphia and the Main Line, who, if the moon was right, could as easily be talked out of their fashionable clothing.

And even if there were no females, the bar was dark, and he was not known to the bartenders as a cop, and there was a guy who played the piano.

He would see what developed naturally. The worst possible scenario would be no available women. In which case, he would have a couple drinks and listen to the guy play the piano and then do what he probably should have done anyway, go home. He really did have to remember to get his uniform out of the zipper bag in the closet and get it pressed tomorrow.

His eyes had barely adjusted to the darkness of the bar when a male voice spoke in his ear.

"Can I buy you a drink?"

He turned to see who had made the offer. The face was familiar, but he couldn't immediately put a name, or an identification, to it.

"It is you, Inspector? I mean . . . you *are* Inspector Wohl, aren't you?"

It came together. Dutch's nephew. He had met the kid that afternoon, outside Dutch's house.

"Let me buy you one," Wohl said, smiling and offering his hand. "Matt Moffitt, right?"

"Matt Payne," the boy said. "I was adopted."

"Yeah, I heard something about that," Wohl said. "Sorry."

"No problem," Matt said.

The bartender appeared.

"I don't know what he wants," Wohl said, "but Johnnie Red and soda for me."

"The same," Matt said.

"You old enough?" the bartender challenged. "You got a driver's license?"

Matt handed it over. The bartender eyed it dubiously, then asked Matt for his birth date. Finally he shrugged, and went to make the drinks.

"They lose their licenses," Wohl said. "You can't blame them."

When the drinks came, Matt laid a twenty on the bar.

"Hey, I'll get these," Wohl said.

"My pleasure," Matt Payne said. He picked up his glass, raised it, and said, "Dutch."

"Dutch," Wohl repeated, and raised his glass.

"I just came from the Moffitts'," Matt said. "After that, I needed this."

"I was supposed to be there. But I got tied up," Wohl said. "I couldn't get away. I'll go by Marshutz & Sons, to the wake, tomorrow."

"It was pretty awful," Matt said.

"Why do you say that?" Wohl asked.

"The kids, for one thing, my cousins," Matt said. "Losing their father is really tough on them. And my grandmother was a flaming pain in the ass, for another. She was a real bitch toward my mother."

"What?" Wohl asked. "Why?"

"My grandmother thinks what my mother should have done when my father got killed was turn into a professional widow, like she is. Instead, she married my stepfather."

"What's wrong with that?"

"Out of the church," Matt said. "Mother married one of those heathen Protestant Episcopals. And then Mother converted herself, and took me with her. And then let my stepfather adopt me."

"German Catholic mothers of that generation have very positive ideas," Wohl said. "I know, I've got one of them. She and Gertrude Moffitt are old pals."

"You weren't at the house," Matt said, and Wohl wasn't sure if it was a question or a challenge.

"I also have a German Lutheran father," Wohl said, "who went along with her until he suspected, correctly, that a priest at Saint Joseph's Prep was trying to recruit me for the Jesuits. Then he pulled me out of Good Ol' Saint Joe's and moved me into Northeast High. She still has high hopes that I will meet some good Catholic girl, who will lead me back into the fold."

I wonder why I told him that?

"Then you do know," Matt said.

"The reason I didn't go to see Jeannie Moffitt tonight was because I didn't want to," Wohl said. "And I figured if Dutch is really looking down from his cloud, he would understand."

Matt chuckled. "You were pretty close?"

"I knew him pretty well, all our lives, but we weren't close. Dutch was Highway Patrol, and that's a way of life. They don't think anybody else really is a cop. Maybe Organized Crime, or Intelligence, but certainly not a staff inspector. I guess, really, that Dutch tolerated me. I'd been in the Highway Patrol, even if I later went wrong."

"You were there, where he was shot, I mean. I heard that."

"I was nearby when I heard the call. I responded."

"I don't understand what really happened," Matt said. "He didn't *know* he was shot?"

"The adrenaline was flowing," Wohl said. "The minute he went to work, his system was all charged up. I'm sure he knew he was hit, but I don't think he had any idea how bad."

"You ever been shot?" Matt asked.

"Yes," Wohl said, and changed the subject. "How come you're in here? As opposed to some saloon around the campus, for example?"

"I heard they're going to close it and tear it down," Matt said, "so I thought I'd come in for a drink for auld lang syne."

"They're going to tear it down? I hadn't heard that."

"They are, but that wasn't a straight answer," Matt said.

"Oh?"

"When I left the Moffitt house," Matt said, "I had two choices. My fraternity house, or a saloon near the fraternity house. There would be two kinds of people in both, those who felt sorry for me—"

"That's understandable," Wohl said.

"Not because of my uncle Dutch," Matt said. "They didn't know about that. Because I failed my precommissioning physical examination, and am now officially exempt from military service. I didn't want sympathy on one hand, and if one more of those sonsofbitches had told me how lucky I was, I think I would have punched him out."

"Why'd you flunk the physical? Did they tell you?"

"Something with my eyes. Probably, they said, I'll never have a moment's trouble with them, but on the other hand, the United States Marine Corps can't take the chance that something will."

"I guess I'm with those who think you were probably lucky," Wohl said. "I did a hitch in the army when I finished high school. *I* wasn't going to be a cop like my old man. So I joined the army and they made me an MP. You didn't miss anything."

"I wanted to go," Matt said. "My father was a marine. My real father."

"He was also a cop," Wohl said.

"I've been thinking about that, too," Matt said. "I've seen the ads in the papers."

"The reason those ads are in the paper is because they don't pay a starting-off police officer a living wage," Wohl said. "A guy just out of high school can go to work for Budd, someplace like that, and make a lot more money. So they have to actively recruit to find a guy who meets the standards, and who really wants to be a cop, even if it means waiting for the city council to come across with long-overdue pay raises."

"I don't need money," Matt said.

"Everybody needs money," Wohl said, surprised at the remark; it sounded stupid.

"I mean, I have more than enough," Matt said. "When my father . . . I think of him as my father. My *real* father was killed before I was born. When my *stepfather* adopted me, he started investing the money my real father had left, the insurance money, the rest of it, for me. My father is a very clever guy. He turned it into a lot of money, and when I turned twenty-one, he handed it over to me."

"What would he say if you joined the police department? What would your mother say?"

"Oh, they wouldn't like it at all," Matt said. "My father wants me to go to law school. But I don't think they would say anything. I think he would sort of understand."

The booze is talking, Peter Wohl decided. *The kid lost his uncle. His father got killed on the job. He just came from Dutch's house, where Denny Coughlin and my father, and maybe the commissioner and maybe even the mayor, plus a dozen other cops were standing around, half in the bag, recounting the heroic exploits of Dutch*

Moffitt. And this kid's father. In the morning, if he remembers this conversation, this kid will be embarrassed.

I am not fall-down drunk, Peter Wohl thought, as he put the key in his apartment door. *If I were fall-down drunk, I would have tried to put the Jaguar in the garage. I am still sober enough to realize that I am too drunk to try to thread that narrow needle with the nose of the Jaguar.*

He had stayed at the bar in the Hotel Adelphia nightclub far longer than he had intended to stay, and he had far more to drink than he usually did. He had all of a sudden realized that he was drunk, shaken Matt Payne's hand, collected his change, reclaimed the Jaguar, and driven home.

A shrink would say that he had gotten drunk as a delayed reaction to seeing Dutch Moffitt slumped dead against the wall of the Waikiki Diner. So, for that matter, would his boss, Chief Inspector Dennis V. Coughlin. And so, he realized, would his father. His father had known he would not be at the wake, and why.

There was no way either Denny Coughlin or his father would hear about it. There had been no other cops in the Hotel Adelphia, and he had managed to get home without running over a covey of nuns or into a fire hydrant.

God, Peter Wohl thought, *takes care of fools and drunks, and I certainly qualify on both counts.*

The red light on his telephone answering machine was glowing a steady red. If there had been calls, it would have been blinking on and off.

He went into the kitchen, opened the refrigerator, and drank most of a twelve-ounce bottle of soda water from the neck, which produced a booming belch.

Then he went to his bedroom, and remembered (which pleased him) about getting his uniform out of the zipper bag so that he could have it pressed in the morning. He had just laid the bag on an upholstered chair and started to work the zipper when the phone rang.

He looked at his watch. It was almost two in the morning. Neither his mother nor Barbara would be calling at this hour; it was therefore safe to answer the phone.

He picked up the phone beside the bed.

"Wohl," he said.

"I hope I didn't wake you, Inspector." Wohl recognized the voice of Lieutenant Louis Natali of Homicide.

"I just walked in, Lou," Wohl said.

"Well, if you heard it over the radio, I'm sorry, but I thought you would want to know."

"I didn't have a radio," Wohl said. "What didn't I hear?"

He's calling to tell me they caught the little shit who killed Dutch; that was nice of him.

"I'll try to give it to you quick," Natali said. "Hobbs and I were down in the Third District . . . checking out a report that Gerald Vincent Gallagher had been seen. About one o'clock, we heard a radio call of a stabbing and hospital case at Six-C Stockton Place. A little while later, I called Homicide and found we had a job there. Lieutenant DelRaye is on the scene. The deceased is a guy named Jerome Nelson."

"Christ, I met him this afternoon," Wohl said. "Nice little . . ." He stopped himself and ended, "Guy."

"The female who called it in is your friend Louise Dutton."

"I'll be damned," Wohl said. "She lives upstairs."

"I was told she was hysterical and locked herself in her apartment. DelRaye just called for a wagon to transport her to Homicide. I think he's talking about taking her door if she doesn't come out."

"Jesus!"

"You didn't get this from me, Peter," Natali said.

"I owe you," Wohl said, broke the connection with his finger, and dialed from memory the number of the Homicide Division. A detective answered.

"This is Inspector Wohl," he said. "Lieutenant DelRaye is at a homicide scene on Stockton Place. Please get word to him that I am en route, and he is not to, not to, take the door until I get there."

At 2:03 A.M., One-Ninety-Four, a patrol car assigned to the Nineteenth District, went on the air and reported that he was in pursuit of an English sports car proceeding eastward on Lancaster Avenue just past Girard Avenue at a high rate of speed.

At 2:05 A.M. One-Ninety-Four went back on the air:

"One-Ninety-Four. Disregard the pursuit. It was a Three-Six-Nine."

Three-Six-Nine is the radio code used to identify a police officer.

The officer in One-Ninety-Four was naturally curious why a man carrying the tin of a staff inspector was going hell-for-leather down Lancaster Avenue in an English sports car at two in the morning, but he had been on the job long enough to understand that patrol officers were wise not to ask staff inspectors what the hell they thought they were doing.

Stockton Place was crowded with police vehicles when Peter Wohl, holding his badge in one hand, weaved the Jaguar through them to the door of Number Six.

There were two cars from the Sixth District, what looked to Wohl to be three unmarked detective cars, the crime lab van, and a Sixth District wagon.

And the press was there, on foot behind the crime scene barriers, and on the roofs of two vans bearing television station logotypes.

Wohl had put his identification away when he'd passed the last uniform barring his way to Number Six Stockton Place, but he had to take it out again to get past another uniform keeping people out of the building itself.

"Where's Lieutenant DelRaye?" he asked.

"Ground-floor apartment," the uniform told him.

Jerome Nelson was lying on his stomach on an outsize bed in his mirrored bedroom. He was, save for a sleeveless undershirt, naked. There were more wounds than Wohl could conveniently count on his back, his buttocks and legs, and the bed was soaked with darkening blood. There was the sweet smell of blood in the air, competing with the smell of perfume.

Lieutenant Edward M. DelRaye, a large, balding man who showed vestiges of having been a very handsome man in his twenties and thirties, was standing with his arms folded on his chest, watching a photographer from the crime lab taking pictures of the body with a 35-mm camera.

"DelRaye," Wohl said, and DelRaye turned around and looked at him. He didn't say anything.

"Radio relay my message to you?" Wohl asked.

DelRaye nodded. "What's going on, Inspector?" he asked.

Edward M. DelRaye had been a detective when Peter Wohl had entered the academy. He had not liked Peter Wohl from the time they had met, when Wohl had been a plainclothes patrolman in Civil Disobedience. He had still been a detective when Wohl made corporal, equivalent in rank to a detective, and they'd had a couple of run-ins, jurisdictional disputes, when Wohl had been a Highway Patrol corporal and then sergeant. When Wohl had been assigned to Internal Affairs, DelRaye had run off at the mouth more than once about how nice it must be to have a Chief Inspector for a father, who could arrange your career for you, see that you got good jobs.

DelRaye had made sergeant about the time Peter Wohl had made captain, and had only recently been promoted to lieutenant, long after Wohl had become a staff inspector. He was a good detective, from what Wohl had heard, and which seemed to be proved by his longtime assignment to Homicide, but he was also a loudmouthed, crude sonofabitch whom Wohl disliked, and whom he avoided whenever possible.

"You want to tell me what you have, Lieutenant?" Wohl said.

"Somebody carved up the fag," DelRaye said, jerking his thumb toward the bed.

"I'm interested in the witness," Wohl said.

"Are you really, now?"

"Take it from the top, DelRaye," Wohl said, evenly, but coldly.

"Well, in case you didn't know, her name is Louise Dutton. The same one that was with Dutch Moffitt this afternoon when he got blown away. She come home from work about half past twelve, quarter to one, and found the door, his door, open. So she went in, and found the faggot in here, and called it in. I was up, so when the radio notified us, I rolled on it. I heard what she had to say, and told her I was going to take her to the Roundhouse for her statement, and to let her look at some mug shots, and she told me to go fuck myself, she wasn't going anywhere."

"You were, I'm sure, your usual tactful, charming self, DelRaye," Wohl said.

"I don't like drunken women, and I especially don't like dirty-mouthed ones," DelRaye said.

"Then what happened?" Wohl asked.

"I turned around, and she was gone, and the Sixth District cop in the foyer, or the lobby, outside the apartment, said she went up in the elevator. So I went upstairs, and knocked on her door, and told her who I was, and she told me to go fuck myself again. Then I called for a wagon. I was going to have her door forced. She's acting like she could be the doer, Wohl."

That's bullshit, DelRaye. You know as well as I do she didn't do it. But there is now a Staff Inspector on the scene, who knows that while you can batter down the door of a suspect, you can't go around busting open witnesses' doors without a better reason than she told you to go fuck yourself.

"You really think she could be the doer, Lieutenant?" Wohl asked, dryly sarcastic, and then, without waiting for an answer, asked, "She's still upstairs? You didn't enter her apartment?"

"I got your message, Inspector," DelRaye said. "She can't go anywhere. I got two cops trying to talk sense to her through the door."

"I know her," Wohl said. "I'll try to talk to her."

"I know," DelRaye said. "When she's not screaming at me to go fuck myself, she's screaming that she demands to see Inspector Wohl."

"Really?" Wohl asked, surprised.

"Her exact words were, *'Get that sonofabitch down here!'* " DelRaye said. "Don't you think you ought to tell me what's going on with you and her?"

"I was in on the assist when Dutch Moffitt was shot," Wohl said. "When the commissioner heard that the eyewitness was Miss Dutton, and who she was, he decided it was in the best interest of the department to treat her with kid gloves, and since I was there, told me to take care of it."

"Something going on between her and Dutch? Is that what you're saying?"

"I'm saying that when a woman goes on television twice a day, it doesn't hurt to have her think kindly of the police department," Wohl said.

"Yeah, sure."

"And that's what I'm going to do now," Wohl said. "I'm going to go charm the hell out of her, if I can, and apologize for you, if it seemed to her you weren't as understanding as you could have been."

"Fuck understanding," DelRaye said. "My job is to catch the guys who done in the faggot."

"And my job is to do what the commissioner tells me to do," Wohl said. "I'm going to go talk to her. You make sure there's a car outside when, if, I bring her down the stairs. Get those TV people, and the other reporters, away from the door."

"How'm I going to do that, Inspector?" DelRaye asked sarcastically. "It's a public street."

"No, it's not, Lieutenant," Wohl said. "It's a *private* street. Technically, anybody on Stockton Place who hasn't been invited is trespassing. Now get them away from the door, if you have to do it yourself."

"Yes, sir, Inspector," DelRaye said, his tone of voice leaving no question what he thought about the order, about Staff Inspector Peter Wohl, or Peter Wohl *being* a Staff Inspector.

 Wohl walked out of Jerome Nelson's apartment and rode the elevator to the upper floor. There were two uniformed policemen there, a portly, red-faced man in his late thirties, and a pleasant-faced young man. He had his head against Louise Dutton's door and was trying, without success, to get her to talk back to him.

"What can I do for you?" the young one challenged when the elevator door opened.

"That's Inspector Wohl," the older one said.

"Hello," Peter said, and smiled. "I know Miss Dutton. I think I can get her to come out of there. Lieutenant DelRaye is going to move the press away, and have a car waiting downstairs. I'd like you guys to see that Miss Dutton gets in it without being hassled."

"Yes, sir," the young cop said.

"She's got a mouth, that one," the older one offered. "Even considering she's had too much to drink, and is upset by what she saw downstairs, you wouldn't think a woman would use language like that."

"Haven't you heard? That's what women's lib is all about," Peter said. "The right to cuss like a man."

The younger cop shook his head and smiled at him.

He waited until they had gone down in the elevator, and then knocked on the door.

"Go the fuck away!" Louise called angrily.

"Miss Dutton, it's Peter Wohl," he called.

There was no response for a long moment, and Peter was just about to raise his cigarette lighter to knock on the door when it opened to the width its burglar chain would permit; wide enough for Louise Dutton to look out and see Peter, and that he was alone.

Then it closed and he heard the chain rattle, and then the door opened completely.

"I wasn't sure you would come," she said, and pulled him into the apartment and closed the door again.

She was wearing a blue skirt and a high-ruffle-collared blouse. The body of the blouse was so thin as to be virtually transparent. Through it he could see quite clearly that she wore no slip, only a brassiere, and that the brassiere was no more substantial than the blouse; he could see her nipples.

Her eyes looked more frightened than drunk, he thought, and there was something about her it took him a moment to think he recognized, an aura of sexuality.

She looks horny, Peter Wohl thought.

"Here I am," Peter said.

She put a smile on her face; grew, he thought, determinedly bright.

"And what did Mrs. Wohl say when you were summoned from your bed at two in the morning, when the crazy lady from TV called for you?" Louise Dutton asked.

I know what it is. She hasn't really been going around in a transparent shirt, baring her breasts. That skirt is part of a suit; there's a jacket, and when she wears that, only the ruffles show at the neck. That's what she wore when she was on TV.

"Nobody summoned me," Peter Wohl said. "I heard about it, and came. And the only Mrs. Wohl is my mother."

"They didn't send for you?" Louise asked, surprised. "Then why did you come?"

"I don't know," he said. "Why did you ask for me?"

"I'm scared, and a little drunk," she said.

"So'm I," he said. "A little drunk, I mean. There's nothing to be afraid of."

"*Bullshit!* Have you been downstairs? Did you see what those . . . *maniacs* . . . did to that poor, pathetic little man?"

"There's nothing for you to be afraid of," Peter said.

"The cops are here, right? My knight in shining armor has just ridden up in his prowl car?"

"Actually, I came in my Jaguar," Peter said. "My department car was in the garage and I wasn't sure I was sober enough to back it out."

"A *Jaguar?*" she asked, starting to giggle. "To go with that ridiculous turtleneck? I'll bet you even have got one of those silly little caps with the buttons in the front."

"I had one, but it blew off on the Schuylkill Expressway," he said.

She snorted, and then suddenly stopped. She looked at him, and bit her lower lip, and then she walked to him.

"*Goddamn,* I'm glad you're here," she said, and put her hand to his cheek. "Thank you."

And then, without either of them knowing exactly how it happened, he had his arms around her, and she was sobbing against his chest. He heard himself soothing her, and became aware that he was stroking her head, and that her arms were around him, holding him.

He could not remember, later, how long they had stayed like that. What he was to remember was that as he became aware of the warmth of her body against him, the pressure of her breasts against his abdomen, he had felt himself stirring. And when what had happened to him became evident to her, she pushed herself away from him.

"Well," she said, looking into his eyes, "this has been a bitch of a day, Peter Wohl, hasn't it? For both of us."

"I've had better," he said.

"What happens now?" Louise asked.

"There's a car waiting downstairs," Peter said. "It'll take you down to the Round-house, where you can make your statement, and then they'll type it up, and you can sign it, and then they'll bring you back here."

She looked at him, on the verge, he decided, of saying something, but not speaking.

"I'll go with you, if you'd like me to."

"I told that faded matinee idol everything I know," she said.

He chuckled, and she smiled back at him.

"I did the 'Nine's News' at eleven," Louise said. "And then I went with the pro-ducer for a drink. Okay, drinks. Three or four. Then I came home. I went into the lobby to check the mailbox. Jerome's door was open. I went in. I . . . saw what was in the bedroom. So I called the cops. That's all I know, Peter. And I told him."

"There's a procedure that has to be followed," Peter said. "The police department is a bureaucracy, Miss Dutton."

" 'Miss Dutton'?" she quoted mockingly. "A moment ago, I thought we were at least on a first-name basis."

"Louise," Peter said, aware that his face was flushing.

"I'll be damned," she said. "A blushing cop!"

"Jesus Christ!" Peter said. "Do you always think out loud?"

"No," she said. "For some mysterious reason, I seem to be a little upset right now. But thinking out loud, I don't seem to be the only one around here who's a little off balance. Do you always calm down hysterical witnesses that way, Inspector?"

"Jesus H. Christ!" Wohl said, shaking his head.

"Don't misunderstand me," she said. "That wasn't a complaint. I just wondered if it was standard bureaucratic procedure."

"You know better than that," Peter said.

"Get me out of here, Peter," Louise said, softly, entreatingly.

"Where do you want to go?"

"I'm not that far yet," she said. "All I know is that I don't want to run the gauntlet of my professional associates outside, and that I can't, *won't,* spend the night here. I'm *afraid,* Peter."

"I told you, there's nothing to be afraid of," he said. "And I sent two officers downstairs to make sure you weren't hassled when you get in the car."

"There's an Arch Street entrance to the garage," she said. "I don't think the press knows about it."

"But you'd have to get past them to get to the garage," he said.

"There's a passage in the basement," she said. "A tunnel. And even if they were on Arch Street, I could get down on the seat, or on the floor in the back, and they wouldn't see me."

"Take your car, you mean?" he asked.

"Please, Peter," she said.

Why not? She's calmed down. You can't blame her for wanting to avoid those press and TV bastards. I'll take her someplace and buy her a cup of coffee and then I'll go with her to the Roundhouse.

"Okay," he said. "Get your jacket."

"My jacket?" she asked, surprised, and then looked down at herself. "Oh, Christ!" She crossed her arms over her breasts and looked at him. "I wasn't expecting visitors."

"I'll be damned," he said. "A blushing TV lady."

"Fuck you, Peter," she flared.

"Promises, promises," he heard himself blurt.

"You *bastard!*" she said, but she chuckled. She went farther into the apartment, and returned in a moment, shrugging into the jacket of her suit.

He waited until she had buttoned it, and then opened the door to the foyer. There was no one there. He pushed the elevator button, and he heard the faint whine of the electric motor. She stood very close to him, and her shoulder touched his. He put his arm around her shoulders.

"You're going to be all right, Louise," he said.

There was a uniform cop sitting on a wooden folding chair outside the elevator door in the basement. He got up quickly when he saw Wohl and Louise.

"I'm Inspector Wohl," Peter said. "I'm taking Miss Dutton out this way. Are you alone down here?"

"No, sir, a couple of guys are in the garage."

"Thank you," Peter said. He put his hand on Louise's arm and led her down the corridor. Halfway down the tunnel, she put a set of keys in his hand.

Two uniform cops walked quickly across the underground garage when they saw them. The eyes of one of them widened—a cop Wohl recognized, a bright guy named Aquila—when he recognized them.

"Hello, Inspector," Officer Aquila said.

"I'm going to take Miss Dutton out this way," Wohl said. "The press is all over the street."

"There's a couple of them outside, too," Aquila said. "But only a couple. You can probably get past them before they know what's happening. You want to use my car?"

"We'll take Miss Dutton's car," Wohl said. "When we're gone, would you tell Lieutenant DelRaye we've gone, and that I'm taking Miss Dutton to the Roundhouse?"

"Yes, sir," Office Aquila said. It was obvious that he approved of Wohl's tactics. He had certainly heard that DelRaye had sent for a wagon to haul a drunken and belligerent Louise Dutton off. This would be one more proof that Staff Inspector Peter Wohl knew how to turn an unpleasant situation into a manageable one.

They got in Louise's Cadillac.

"There's a thing in the floor that you run over, and the door opens," Louise said, and then, "What are you looking for?"

"How do you get the parking brake off?"

"It comes off automatically when you put it in gear," she said.

"Oh," he said.

As they approached the exit, she lay down on the seat with her head on his lap. The door opened as she said it would, and he drove through. A reporter and a couple of photographers moved toward the car, but without great interest. And then he was past them, heading up Arch Street.

"We're safe," Wohl said. "You can sit up."

She pushed herself erect.

"I am not going to the 'Roundhouse'!" Louise said. "Not tonight."

She had not moved away from him. When she spoke, he could feel and smell her warm breath.

"We can go somewhere and get a cup of coffee," Wohl said.

"Hey, Knight in Shining Armor, when I say something, I can't be talked out of it," Louise said.

"Where would you like to go, then?" Peter asked.

There was a perceptible pause before she replied.

"I don't want to go to a hotel," she said. "They smirk, when you check in without luggage. What would your mother say if you brought me home with you, Peter?"

"I don't live with my mother," he said, quickly.

"Oh, you don't? Then I guess you have an apartment?"

"I'm not so sure that would be a good idea," he said.

"I don't have designs on your body, if that's what you're thinking. I'm wide open to other suggestions."

"I'll make you some coffee," Peter said.

"I don't want coffee," she said.

"Okay, no coffee," Peter said.

Ten minutes later, as they drove up Lancaster Avenue, she said, "Where the hell do you live, in Pittsburgh?"

"It's not far."

"All of my life, my daddy told me, 'If you're ever in trouble, you call me, day or night,' so tonight, for the first time, after the matinee idol told me he was sending for a battering ram, I called him. And his wife told me he's in London."

"Your stepmother?"

"No, his wife," Louise Dutton said, as if annoyed at his denseness. He didn't press the question.

"But you came, didn't you?" Louise asked, rhetorically. "Even if you didn't know I'd sent for you?"

Peter Wohl couldn't think of a reply. She half turned on the seat and held on to his arm with both hands.

"Why did they do that to him? Keep stabbing him, I mean? My God, they *hacked* him!"

"That's not unusual with murders involving sexual deviates," Peter Wohl said. "There's often a viciousness, I guess is the word, in what they do to each other."

She shuddered.

"He was such a *nice* little man," she said. She sighed and shuddered, and added, "Bad things are supposed to come in threes. God, I hope that isn't true. I can't take anything else!"

"You're going to be all right," Peter said.

When they were inside the apartment, he turned the radio on, to WFLN-FM, the classical music station, and then smiled at her.

"I won't ask you if I can take your jacket," he said. "How do you like your coffee?"

"Made in the highlands of Scotland," she said.

"All right," he said. "I'll be right with you."

He went in the kitchen, got ice, and carried it to the bar. He took his jacket off without thinking about it, and made drinks. He carried them to her.

"Until tonight, I always thought there was something menacing about a man carrying a gun," she said. "Now I find it pleasantly reassuring."

"The theory is that a policeman is never really off duty," he said.

"Like Dutch?" she said.

"You want to talk about Dutch?" he asked.

"Quickly changing the subject," Louise said. "This is not what I would have expected, apartment-wise, for a policeman," she said, gesturing around the apartment. "Or even for Peter Wohl, private citizen."

"It was professionally decorated," he said. "I once had a girlfriend who was an interior decorator."

"Had?"

"Had."

"Then I suppose it's safe to say I like the naked lady and the red leather chairs, but I think the white rug and most of the furniture looks like it belongs in a whorehouse."

He laughed delightedly.

She looked at her drink.

"I don't really want this," she said. "What I really would like is something to eat."

"How about a world-famous Peter Wohl Taylor ham and egg sandwich?"

"Hold the egg," Louise said.

He went into the kitchen and took a roll of Taylor ham from the refrigerator and put it on his cutting board and began to slice it.

He fried the Taylor ham, made toast, and spread it with Durkee's Dressing.

"Coffee?" he asked.

"Milk?" she asked.

"Milk," he replied. He put the sandwiches on plates, and set places at his tiny kitchen table, then filled two glasses with milk and put them on the table.

Louise ate hungrily, and nodded her head in thanks when he gave her half of his sandwich.

She drained her glass of milk, then wiped her lips with a gesture Peter thought was exquisitely feminine.

"Aren't you going to ask me about me and Dutch?"

"Dutch is dead," Peter said.

"I never slept with him," Louise said. "But I thought about it."

"You didn't have to tell me that," he said.

"No," she said, thoughtfully. "I didn't. I wonder why I did?"

"I'm your friendly father figure," he said, chuckling.

"The hell you are," she said. "Now what?"

"Now we see if we can find you a pair of pajamas or something—"

"Have you a spare T-shirt?"

"Sure, if that would do."

"And then we debate who gets the couch, right? And who gets the bed?"

"You get the bed," he said.

"Why are you being so nice to me?"

"I don't know," he said.

"No pass, Peter?" she asked, looking into his eyes.

"Not tonight," he said. "Maybe later."

He walked into his bedroom, took sheets and a blanket from a chest of drawers, carried them into the living room, and tossed them on the couch. Then he went back into the bedroom, found a T-shirt and handed it to her, wondering what she would look like wearing it.

"I'll brush my teeth," he said. "And then the place is yours. I shower in the morning."

Brushing his teeth was not his major priority in the bathroom, with all he'd had to drink, and as he stood over the toilet trying to relieve his bladder as quietly as possible, the interesting fantasy that he would return to the bedroom and find her naked in his bed, smiling invitingly at him, ran through his head.

When he went back in the bedroom, she was fully dressed, and standing by the door, as if she wanted to close it, and lock it, after him as soon as possible.

"Good night," he said. "If you need anything, yell."

"Thank you," she said, almost formally.

As if, he thought, *I am the bellhop being rushed out of the hotel room.*

He heard the lock in the door slide home, and remembered that both Dorothea and Barbara were always careful to make sure the door was locked; as if they expected to have someone burst in and catch them screwing.

He took off his outer clothing, folded it neatly, and laid it on the armchairs.

Then he remembered that he had told the cop in the basement garage to tell Lieutenant DelRaye that he was taking her to the Roundhouse. He would have to do something about that.

He tiptoed around the living room in his underwear until he found the phone book. He had not called Homicide in so long that he had forgotten the number. He found the book, and then sat down on the leather couch and dialed the number. The leather was sticky against his skin and he wondered if it was dirty, or if that's the way leather was; he had never sat on his couch in his underwear before.

"Homicide, Detective Mulvaney."

"This is Inspector Wohl," Peter said.

"Yes, sir?"

"Would you please tell Lieutenant DelRaye that I will bring Miss Dutton there, to Homicide, at eight in the morning?"

"Yes, sir. Is there any place Lieutenant DelRaye can reach you?"

Wohl hung up, and then stood up, and started to spread sheets over the leather cushions.

The telephone rang. He watched it. On the third ring, there was a click, and he could faintly hear the recorded message: "You can leave a message for Peter Wohl after the beep."

The machine beeped.

"Inspector, this is Lieutenant DelRaye. Will you please call me as soon as you can? I'm at the Roundhouse."

It was evident from the tone of Lieutenant DelRaye's voice that he was more than a little annoyed, and that leaving a polite message had required some effort.

Peter finished making a bed of the couch, took off his shoes and socks, and lay down on it. He turned off the light, and went to sleep listening to the sound of the water running in his shower, his mind's eye filled with the images of Louise Dutton's body as she showered.

When Police Commissioner Thaddeu Czernich, trailed by Sergeant Jank Jankowitz, walked briskly across the lobby of the Roundhouse toward the elevator, it was quarter past eight. He was surprised therefore to see Colonel J. Dunlop Mawson hurrying to catch up with him. He would have laid odds that Colonel J. Dunlop Mawson never cracked an eyelid before half past nine in the morning.

"How are you, Colonel?" Czernich said, smiling and offering his hand. "What gets you out of bed at this unholy hour?"

"Actually, Ted," J. Dunlop Mawson said, "I'm here to see you."

They were at the elevator; there was nothing Commissioner Czernich could do to keep Mawson from getting on with him.

"Colonel," Czernich said, smiling and touching Mawson's arm, "you have *really* caught me at a bad time."

"This is important, or else I wouldn't bother you," Mawson said.

"I just came from seeing Arthur Nelson," Commissioner Czernich said. "You heard what happened to his son?"

"Yes, indeed," Mawson said. "Tragic, shocking."

"I wanted to both offer my personal condolences," Commissioner Czernich said, and then interrupted himself, as the elevator door opened. "After you, Colonel."

They walked down the curving corridor together. There were smiles and murmurs of "Commissioner" from people in the corridor. They reached the commissioner's private door. Jankowitz quickly put a key to it, and opened it and held it open.

Commissioner Czernich looked at Mawson.

"I can give you two minutes, right now, Colonel," he said. "You understand the situation, I'm sure. Maybe later today? Or, better yet, what about lunch tomorrow? I'll even buy."

"Two minutes will be fine," Mawson said.

Czernich smiled. "Then come in. I'll really give you five," he said. "You can hardly drink a cup of coffee in two minutes. Black, right?"

"Thank you, black."

"Doughnut?"

"Please."

Commissioner Czernich nodded at Sergeant Jankowitz and he went to fetch the coffee.

"I have been retained to represent Miss Louise Dutton," Colonel J. Dunlop Mawson said.

"I don't understand," Czernich said. "You mean by WCBL-TV? Has something happened I haven't heard about?"

"Ted, that seems to be the most likely answer," Mawson said.

"Take it from the beginning," Czernich said. "The last I heard, we had arranged to have Miss Dutton taken home from the Waikiki Diner, so that she wouldn't have to drive. Later, as I understand it, we picked her up at her home, brought her here for the interview, and then took her home again."

"You didn't know she was the one who found young Nelson's body?" Mawson asked.

Jankowitz handed him a cup of coffee and two doughnuts on a saucer.

"Thank you," Mawson said.

"No, I didn't," Commissioner Czernich said. "Or if somebody told me, it went in one ear and out the other. At half past six this morning, they called me and told me what had happened to Arthur Nelson's boy. I went directly from my house to Arthur Nelson's place. I offered my condolences, and told him we would turn the earth upside down to find who did it. Then I came here. As soon as we're through, Colonel, I'm going to be briefed on what happened, and where the investigation is at this moment."

"Well, when that happens, I'm sure they'll tell you that Miss Louise Dutton was the one who found the body, and called the police," Mawson said.

"I don't know where we're going, Colonel. I don't understand your role in all this. Or why WCBL-TV is so concerned."

"I've been retained to represent Miss Dutton," Mawson said. "But not by WCBL. I've been told that the police intended to bring her here, to interview her—"

"Well, if she found Nelson's body, Colonel, that would be standard procedure, as I'm sure you know."

"No one seems to know where she is," Mawson said. "She's not at her apartment, and she's not here. And I've been getting sort of a runaround from the people in Homicide."

" 'A runaround'?" Czernich asked. "Come on, Colonel. We don't operate that way, and you know we don't."

"Well, then, where is she?" Mawson asked.

"I don't know, but I'll damned sure find out," Czernich said. He pulled one of the telephones on his desk to him and dialed a number from memory.

"Homicide, Lieutenant DelRaye."

"This is the commissioner, Lieutenant," Thaddeu Czernich said. "I understand that Miss Louise Dutton is the citizen who reported finding Mr. Nelson's body."

"Yes, sir, that's true."

"Do you know where Miss Dutton is at this moment?"

"Yes, sir. She's here. Inspector Wohl just brought her in. We've just started to take her statement."

"Well, hold off on that a minute," Czernich said. "Miss Dutton's legal counsel, Colonel J. Dunlop Mawson, is here with me in my office. He wants to be present during any questioning of his client. He'll be right down."

"Yes, sir," DelRaye said.

Commissioner Czernich hung up and looked up at Colonel J. Dunlop Mawson.

"You heard that?" he asked, and Mawson nodded. "Not only is she right here in the building, but Staff Inspector Peter Wohl is with her. You know Wohl?"

Mawson shook his head no.

"Very bright, very young for his rank," Czernich said. "When I heard that Miss Dutton was a witness to Captain Moffitt's shooting, I asked Wohl to make sure that she was treated properly. We don't want WCBL-TV's anchor lady sore at the police department, Colonel. I'm sure that Wohl showed her every possible courtesy."

"Then where the hell has she been? Why haven't I been able to see her, even find out where she is, until you got on the phone?"

"I'm sure she'll tell you where she's been," Czernich said. "There's been some crossed wire someplace, but whatever has been done, I'll bet you a dime to a dough-nut, has been *in* your client's best interest, not against it."

Mawson looked at him, and decided he was telling the truth.

"We still friends, Colonel?" Commissioner Czernich asked.

"Don't be silly," Mawson said. "Of course we are."

"Then can I ask you a question?" Czernich asked, and went ahead without waiting for a response. "Why is Philadelphia's most distinguished practitioner of criminal law involved with the routine interview of a witness to a homicide?"

"Homicides," Mawson said. "Plural. Two cases of murder in the first degree."

"Homicides," Commissioner Czernich agreed.

"Okay, Ted," Mawson said. "We're friends. At half past three this morning, I had a telephone call. From London. From Stanford Fortner Wells III."

Commissioner Czernich shrugged. He didn't know the name.

"Wells Newspapers?" Mawson asked.

"Okay," Czernich said. "Sure."

"He told me he had just been on the telephone to Jack Tone, of McNeel, Tone, Schwartzenberger and Cohan, and that Jack had been kind enough to describe me as the ... what he said was 'the dean of the Philadelphia criminal bar.' "

"That seems to be a fair description," Commissioner Czernich said, smiling. He was familiar with the Washington, D.C., law firm of McNeel, Tone, Schwartzenberger and Cohan. They were heavyweights, representing the largest of the *Fortune* 500 companies, their staff larded with former cabinet-level government officials.

"Mr. Wells said that he had just learned his daughter was in some kind of trouble with the police, and that he wanted me to take care of whatever it was, and get back to him. And he told me his daughter's name was Louise Dutton."

"Well, that's interesting, isn't it?" Czernich said. "Dutton must be a TV name."

"We're friends, Ted," Mawson said. "That goes no farther than these office walls, right?"

"Positively," Commissioner Czernich said.

"Presuming your Inspector Wohl hasn't had her up at the House of Correction, working her over with a rubber hose, Ted," Mawson said, "asking him to look after her was probably a very good idea."

Commissioner Czernich laughed, heartily, and shook his head, and walked to Mawson and put his hand on his arm. "Can you find Homicide all right, Colonel? Or would you like me to have Sergeant Jankowitz show you the way?"

"I can find it all right," Mawson said. "Thank you for seeing me, Commissioner."

"Anytime, Colonel," Czernich said. "My door's always open to you. You know that."

The moment Colonel J. Dunlop Mawson was out the door, Commissioner Czernich went to the telephone, dialed the Homicide number, and asked for Inspector Wohl.

When Wohl came on the line, Commissioner Czernich asked, "Anything going on down there that you can't leave for five minutes?"

"No, sir."

"Then will you please come up here, Peter?"

There are four interview rooms in the first-floor Roundhouse offices of the Homicide Division of the Philadelphia Police Department. They are small windowless cubicles furnished with a table and several chairs. One of the chairs is constructed of steel and is firmly bolted to the floor. There is a hole in the seat through which handcuffs can be locked, when a suspect is judged likely to require this kind of restraint.

There is a one-way mirror on one wall, through which the interviewee and his interrogators can be observed without being seen. No real attempt is made to conceal its purpose. Very few people ever sit in an interview room who have not seen cop movies, or otherwise have acquired sometimes rather extensive knowledge of police interrogative techniques and equipment.

When Colonel J. Dunlop Mawson walked into Homicide, Miss Louise Dutton was in one of the interview rooms. Mawson recognized her from television. She was wearing a suit, with lace at the neck. She was better-looking than he remembered.

With her were three people, one of whom, Lieutenant DelRaye, Mawson had once had on the witness stand for a day and a half, enough time for them both to have acquired an enduring distaste for the other. There was a police stenographer, a gray-haired woman, and a young man in blue blazer and gray flannel slacks who looked like a successful automobile dealer, but who had to be, Mawson decided, Staff Inspector Wohl, "very bright; very young for his rank."

"Miss Dutton, I'm J. Dunlop Mawson," he said, and handed her his card. She glanced at it and handed it to Inspector Wohl, who looked at it, and handed it to Lieutenant DelRaye, who put it in his pocket.

"Lieutenant, I intended that for Miss Dutton," Mawson said.

"Sorry," DelRaye said, and retrieved the card and handed it to Louise.

"The station sent you, I suppose, Mr. Mawson?" Louise Dutton asked.

"Actually, it was your father," Mawson said.

"Okay," Louise Dutton said, obviously pleased. She looked at Inspector Wohl and smiled.

"Gentlemen, may I have a moment with my client?" Mawson asked.

"You're coming back?" Louise Dutton asked Inspector Wohl.

"Absolutely," Wohl said. "I'll just be a couple of minutes."

"Let's step out in the corridor a moment, Miss Dutton, shall we?" Mawson asked.

"What's wrong with here?"

"I meant alone," he said, gesturing at the one-way mirror. "And I wouldn't be at all surprised if there was a microphone in here that someone might inadvertently turn on."

She got up and followed him out of the room, and out of the Homicide office into the curved corridor. Mawson saw her eyes following Inspector Wohl as he walked down the corridor.

"How far did the interview get?" Mawson asked.

"Nowhere," she said. "The stenographer just got there."

"Good," he said. "I've been looking for you since four this morning, Miss Dutton. Where have they had you?"

"Since four?"

"Your father called from London at half past three," Mawson said.

"Okay," she said.

"I went to your apartment, and they said you had been taken here, and when I came here, no one seemed to know anything about you. Where did they have you?"

"What exactly are you going to do for me here and now, Mr. Mawson?" Louise replied.

"Well, I'll be present to advise you during their interview, of course. To protect your rights. You didn't answer my question, Miss Dutton."

"You can't take the hint? That I didn't want to answer it? *They* didn't have me anywhere. Where I was, I don't think is any of your business."

"Your father is going to be curious, I'm sure of that."

"It's none of his business, either," Louise said.

"We seem to have somehow gotten off on the wrong foot, Miss Dutton," Mawson said. "I'm really sorry. Let's try to start again. I'm here to protect your interests, your rights. To defend you, in other words. I'm on your side."

"My side? The cops are the bad guys? You've got that wrong, Mr. Mawson. I'm on their side. I'll tell the cops anything they want to know. I want them to catch whoever butchered Jerome Nelson."

"You misunderstand me," Mawson said.

"I want to be as helpful and cooperative as I can," Louise said. "I just wasn't up to it last night . . . or early this morning, and that's what that flap was all about. But I've had some rest, and now I'm willing to do whatever they want me to."

"What 'flap'?"

"There was some disagreement last night about when I was to come here," she said. "But Inspector Wohl took care of that."

"All I want to do, Miss Dutton, is protect your rights," Mawson said. "I'd like to be there when they question you."

"I can take care of my own rights," she said.

"Your father asked me to come here, Miss Dutton," Mawson said.

"Yeah, you said that," Louise said. She looked at him thoughtfully, obviously making up her mind. "Okay. So long as you understand how I feel."

"I understand," Mawson said. "You were close to Mr. Nelson?"

She didn't respond immediately.

"He was a friend when I needed one," she said, finally.

Mawson nodded. "Well, why don't we go back in there and get it over with?"

The door from the curving third-floor corridor to the commissioner's office opened onto a small anteroom, crowded with desks. The commissioner's private office was to the right; directly ahead was the commissioner's conference room, equipped with a long, rather ornate table. Its windows overlooked the just-completed Metropolitan Hospital on Race Street.

When Peter Wohl walked into the outer office, he saw the conference room was crowded with people. He recognized Deputy Commissioner Howell, Chief Inspector Dennis V. Coughlin, Captain Henry C. Quaire, commanding officer of the Homicide Bureau, Captain Charley Gaft of the Civil Disobedience Squad, Captain Jack McGovern of the Second District, and Chief Inspector of Detectives Matt Lowenstein before someone closed the door.

"He's waiting for you, Inspector," Sergeant Jank Jankowitz said, gesturing toward the commissioner's office door.

"Thank you," Peter said, and walked to the open door and put his head in.

"Come on in, Peter," Commissioner Czernich said. "And close the door."

"Good morning, sir," Peter said.

"I've got a meeting waiting. This will have to be quick," Czernich said. "I want to know what happened with that TV girl from the time I asked you to keep a lid on things. If something went wrong, start there."

"Nothing went wrong, sir," Peter said. "I had her taken from the scene by two cops I borrowed from Jack McGovern. She went to WCBL, and the cops stayed with her until she was finished. Then they took her home. I later went to her apartment and brought her to Homicide." He smiled, and went on: "Jason Washington put on his kindly uncle suit, and the interview went very well. She told me afterward she thought he was a really nice fellow."

Commissioner Czernich smiled, and went on: "But you did get involved with what happened later? With the Nelson murder?"

"Yes, sir. I was on my way home from dinner—"

"Did you go by the Moffitt house? I didn't see you. I saw your dad and mother."

"No, I didn't," Peter said. "I'm going to go to the wake. I went and had dinner . . . damn!"

"Something wrong?"

"I had dinner in Alfredo's," Peter said. "Vincenzo Savarese came by the table, with his wife and sister, and said he was sorry to hear about Dutch Moffitt, and left. When I called for the bill, they told me he'd picked up the tab. I forgot about that. I want to send a memo to Internal Affairs."

"Who were you with?"

"A girl named Barbara Crowley. She's a nurse at the Psychiatric Institute."

"That's the girl you took to Herman Webb's retirement party?"

"Yes, sir."

"I admire your taste, Peter," Commissioner Czernich said. "She seems to be a very fine young woman."

"So my mother keeps telling me," Wohl said.

"You should listen to your mother," Czernich said, smiling.

"When I got home, I called Homicide to see if anything had happened, if they'd found Gerald Vincent Gallagher, and they told me what had happened at Stockton Place, and I figured I'd better go, and I did."

That, Peter thought, *wasn't the truth, the whole truth, and nothing but the truth, but it wasn't a lie. So why do I feel uncomfortable?*

"What happened there?"

"Can I go off the record?" Wohl asked.

The commissioner looked at him with surprise, thought that over, and then nodded.

"Lieutenant DelRaye had rolled on the job, and with his usual tact, he'd rubbed Louise Dutton the wrong way. When I got there, she was locked in her apartment, and DelRaye was about to take down her door. He had a wagon waiting to bring her over here."

"Jesus!" Czernich said. "So what happened?"

"I talked to her. She'd found the body, and was understandably pretty upset. She said she was not going to come over here, period. And she meant it. She asked me to take her out of there, and I did."

"Where did you take her?"

"To my place," Peter said. "She said she didn't want to go to a hotel. I'm sure she felt she would be recognized. Anyway, it was half past two in the morning, and it seemed like the thing to do."

"You better hope your girlfriend doesn't find out," Czernich said.

"So I calmed her down, and gave her something to eat, and at eight o'clock, I brought her in. I just got to Homicide when you called down there."

"How do you think she feels about the police department?" Czernich asked.

"DelRaye aside, I think she likes us," Peter said.

"She going to file a complaint about DelRaye?" Czernich asked.

"No, sir."

"You see Colonel Mawson downstairs?"

"Yes, sir. I guess WCBL sent him over?"

"No," Czernich said. "The name Stanford Fortner Wells mean anything to you, Peter?"

Wohl shook his head no.

"Wells Newspapers?" Czernich pursued.

"Oh, yeah. Sure."

"He sent the colonel," Czernich said.

Peter suddenly recalled, very clearly, what he'd thought when he'd first seen Louise Dutton's apartment; that she couldn't afford it; that she might be a high-class hooker on the side, or some rich man's "good friend." That certainly would explain a lot.

"He's her father," Czernich went on. "So it seems the extra courtesies we have been giving Miss Dutton were the thing to do."

"She told me she had tried to call her father, but that he was out of the country," Peter said. "London, she said. She didn't tell me who he was."

He realized that he had just experienced an emotional shock, several emotions all at once. He was ashamed that he had been so willing to accept that Louise was someone's mistress, which would have neatly explained how she could afford that expensive apartment. His relief at learning that Stanford Wells was her father, not her lover, was startling. And immediately replaced with disappointment, even chagrin. Whatever slim chance there could be that something might develop between him and Louise had just been blown out of the water. The daughter of a newspaper empire was not about to even dally with a cop, much less move with him into a vine-covered cottage by the side of the road.

"Peter, I want you to stay with this," Commissioner Czernich said. "I'm going to tell J. Arthur Nelson that I've assigned you to oversee the case and that you'll report to him at least daily where the investigation is leading."

"Yes, sir," Peter said.

"Find out where things stand, and then you call him. Better yet, go see him."

"Yes, sir."

"Make sure that he understands what you're telling him is for him personally, not for the *Ledger.* Tell him as much as you think you can. I don't want the *Ledger* screaming about police ineptitude. And stay with the Dutton woman, too. I don't want the Philadelphia Police Department's federal grants cut because Stanford Fortner Wells III tells his politicians to cut them. Which I think he damned sure would have done if we had brought his daughter here handcuffed in the back of a wagon."

"Yes, sir," Peter said.

"That's it, Peter," Commissioner Czernich said. "Keep me advised."

9 Mr. and Mrs. Kevin McFadden, who lived in a row house on Fitzgerald Street, not far from Methodist Hospital in South Philadelphia, were not entirely pleased with their son Charles's choice of a career as a policeman. Kevin McFadden had been an employee of the Philadelphia Gas Works since he had left high school, and Mrs. McFadden (Agnes) had just naturally assumed that Charley would follow in his father's footsteps. By and large the gas works had treated Kevin McFadden all right for twenty-seven years, and when he turned sixty, he would have a nice pension, based on (by then) forty-one years of service to the company.

Mrs. Agnes McFadden could not understand why Charley, whom his father had got on as a helper with the gas works after his graduation from Bishop Newman High School, had thrown that over to become a cop. Her primary concern was for her son's safety. Being a policeman was a dangerous job. Whenever she went in Charley's room and saw his gun and the boxes of ammunition for it, on the closet shelf, it made her shudder.

And it wasn't as if he would have been a helper forever. You can't start at the top, you have to work your way up. Kevin had worked his way up. He was now a lead foreman, and the money was good, and with his seniority, he got all of his weekends and most holidays off.

Kevin hadn't been a lot of help when Agnes McFadden had tried to talk Charley out of quitting the gas works and going on the cops. He had taken Charley's side, agreeing with him that a pension when you were forty-five was a hell of a lot better than a pension you got only when you were sixty, if you lived that long.

"Christ," he said, "Charley could retire at *forty-five years old,* still a young man, and go get another job, and every month there would be a check from the city for as long as he lived."

And he added that if Charley didn't want to work for the gas works, that was his business.

Mr. and Mrs. McFadden, however, were in agreement concerning Charley's duties within the police department. They didn't like that one damned bit, even if they tried (with not much success) to keep it to themselves.

He went around looking like a goddamned bum. Facts are facts. Agnes hadn't let Kevin go to work in clothes like that, even way back when he didn't have much seniority and was working underground. God only knew what people in the neighborhood thought Charley was doing for a living.

Not that he was around the neighborhood much. They hardly ever saw him, they couldn't remember the last time he had gone to church with them, and he never even went to Flo & Danny's Bar & Grill with his father anymore.

They understood, of course, when he told them he had been assigned to the Narcotics Squad, in a "plainclothes" assignment, and that the reason he dressed like a bum was you couldn't expect to catch drug guys unless you looked like them. It wasn't like arresting somebody for speeding. And they believed him when he said it was an opportunity, that if he did good, he could get promoted quickly, and that there was practically unlimited overtime right now.

So far as Agnes McFadden was concerned, overtime was fine, but there was also such a thing as too much of a good thing. Charley had had his own phone put in; and two, three, and sometimes even more nights a week, he would no sooner get home, usually at some ungodly hour after they had gone to bed, than it would ring, and it would be his partner calling; and she would hear him running down the stairs and slamming the front door (he'd been doing that since he was five years old) and then she would hear him starting up the battered old car—a Volkswagen—he drove and tearing off down the street.

Maybe, Agnes McFadden thought, if he was a *real* cop, and wore a uniform, and shaved, and had his hair cut; and rode around in a prowl car giving out tickets, going to accidents, and doing *real cop-type* things; it wouldn't be so bad; but she didn't like it at all, now, and if he wouldn't admit it, neither did his father.

Charley was twenty-five, and it was time for him to be thinking about getting married and starting a family. No decent girl would want to be seen with him in public, the way he looked (and sometimes smelled) and no girl in her right mind would marry somebody she couldn't count on to come home for supper, or who would jump out of bed in the middle of the night every time the phone rang. Not to mention being in constant danger of getting shot or stabbed or run over with a car by some nigger or spic or dago full of some kind of drug.

Officer Charles McFadden, who had been engaged in dipping a piece of toast into the yolk of his fried eggs, looked up at his father.

"Pop, ask me how many stars are in the sky?"

His father, who had been checking the basketball scores in the sports section of the *Philadelphia Daily News,* eyed him suspiciously, and took another forkful of his own eggs.

"It's not dirty," Charley McFadden said, reading his father's mind.

"Okay," Kevin McFadden said. "How many stars are in the sky?"

"All of them," Charley McFadden said, pleased with himself.

It took Kevin a moment, but finally he caught on, and laughed.

"Wiseass," he said.

"Chip off the old block," Charley said.

"I don't understand," Agnes McFadden said.

"The only place, Mom, stars is, is in the sky," Charley explained.

"Oh," she said, not quite sure why that was funny. "There's some more home fries in the pan, if you want some."

Charley had come in in the wee hours, and slept until, probably, he smelled the coffee and the bacon, and then come down. It was now quarter after nine.

"No, thanks, Mom," Charley said. "I got to get on my horse."

"You goin' somewhere?" Agnes McFadden asked when Charley stood up and carried his plate to the sink. "Here, give me that. Neither you or your father can be trusted around a sink with dishes."

"I got to change the oil in the car," Kevin McFadden said. "And I bought some stuff that's supposed to clean out the carburetor. Afterward, I thought maybe you and me could go to Flo and Danny's and hoist one."

"I can't, Pop," Charley said. "I got to go to work."

"You didn't get in until four this morning—" Agnes McFadden said.

"Three, Mom," Charley interrupted. "It was ten after three when I walked in the door."

"*Three*, then," she granted. "And you got to go back? Your father has the day off, and it would be good for you to spend some time together. And fun, too. You go down to Flo and Danny's and when I finish cleaning up around here, I'll come down and have a glass of beer with the two of you."

"Mom, I got to go to work."

"Why?" Agnes McFadden flared. "What I would like to know is what's so important that it can't wait for a couple of hours, so that you can spend a little time with your family."

She was more hurt, Charley saw, than angry.

"Mom, you see on the TV where the police officer, Captain Moffitt, got shot?"

"Sure. Of course I did. What's that got to do with you?"

"There was two of them," Charley said. "Captain Moffitt shot one of them, and the other got away."

"I asked, so what's that got to do with you?"

"I think I know where I can catch him," Charley said.

"Mr. Big Shot," his mother said, heavily sarcastic. "There's eight thousand cops—I know 'cause I seen it in the newspaper—there's eight thousand cops, and you, you been on the force two years, and all you are is a patrolman, though you'd never know it to look at you, and *you're* going to catch him!"

Charley's face colored.

"Well, let me just tell *you* something, Mom, if you don't mind," he said, angrily. "*I'm* the officer who made the identification of the girl who shot Captain Moffitt, and those eight thousand cops you're talking about are *all* looking for a guy named Gerald Vincent Gallagher, because I was able to identify him as a known associate of the girl."

"No shit?" Kevin McFadden asked, impressed.

"Watch your tongue," Agnes McFadden snapped. "Just because you work in a sewer doesn't mean you have to sound like one!"

"You bet your ass," Charley said to his father. "And I got a pretty good idea where the slimy little bastard's liable to be!"

"I won't tolerate that kind of dirty talk from either one of you, I just won't put up with it," Agnes said.

"Agnes, shut up!" Kevin McFadden said. "Charley, you're not going to do anything dumb, are you? I mean, what the hell, why take a chance on anything if you don't have to?"

"What I'm going to do, Pop, is find him. If I can. Hang around where I think he might be, or will show up. If I see him, or if he shows up there, I'll get Hay-zus to go with me."

Officer Jesus Martinez, a twenty-three-year-old Puerto Rican, was Officer Charley McFadden's partner. He pronounced his Christian name as it was pronounced in Spanish, and Charley McFadden had taken to using that pronunciation when discussing him with his mother. Agnes McFadden had made it plain that she was uncomfortable with Jesus as somebody's first name. Hay-zus was all right. It was like Juan or Alberto or some other strange spic name.

"I wish *you* wore a uniform," Agnes McFadden said.

"Yeah, sure," Charley said. "Maybe be a traffic cop, right? So I can stand in the middle of the street downtown somewhere, and freeze to death in winter and boil my brains in the summer? Breathing diesel exhaust all the time?"

"It would be better than what you're doing," his mother said.

"Mom, you don't get promoted guarding school crossings," Charley said. "Or riding around some district in a car on the last out shift."

"I don't see you getting promoted," Agnes McFadden said.

"Leave him alone, Agnes," Kevin McFadden said. "He hasn't been with the cops long enough to get promoted."

"The detective's examination is next month, and I'm going to take it," Charley said. "And for your information, I think I'm going to pass it. If I can arrest this Gallagher punk, I *know* I'd make it."

"You're getting too big for your britches," Agnes McFadden replied, aware that she was angry and wondering why.

"Yeah? Yeah? My lieutenant, Lieutenant Pekach, you know how old *he* is? He's *thirty* years old, that's all how old he is. And he's a lieutenant, and he's eligible to take the captain's examination."

"That's young for a lieutenant," Kevin McFadden said. "I suppose they do all right on payday."

"You can do it," Charley said. "Pop, when I went to identify the girl who shot Captain Moffitt, down to the medical examiner's, where they were autopsying her, Lieutenant Pekach introduced me to Staff Inspector Wohl."

"Who's he? Am I supposed to know what that means?" Kevin McFadden asked.

"A staff inspector is higher than a captain," Charley explained. "All they do is the *important* investigations."

"So?" Agnes McFadden said.

"So, Mom, so here is this Staff Inspector Wohl, wearing a suit that must have cost him two hundred bucks, and driving this brand-new Ford LTD, and he ain't hardly any older than Lieutenant Pekach, that's what!"

"He must have pull, then," Agnes McFadden said. "He must know somebody."

"Ah, Jesus Christ, Mom!" Charley said, and stormed out of the kitchen.

"You shouldn't have said that, Agnes," Kevin McFadden said. "Charley's ambitious, there's nothing wrong with that."

The front door slammed, and a moment later, they could hear the whine of the Volkswagen starter.

"Talk to me about ambition," Agnes replied, "when they call up and tell you they're sorry, some bum shot him. Or stuck a knife in him."

Peter Wohl started the LTD and looked across the seat at Louise Dutton.

"You okay?" he asked.

"I'm fine," she said. "I *have* seen faster typists."

He chuckled. The typist who had typed up her statement had been a young black woman, obviously as new to the typewriter as she was determined to do a good, accurate, no strikeover, job.

"Where to now?" he asked.

"I've got to go to work, of course," Louise said. "But I think I had better get my car, first. On the way, you can drop off your uniform."

"Not that I don't want your company," he said, "but I could drop you at the station, and we could get your car later. For that matter, I could bring it to the station."

"I thought about that," she said. "And decided that since you live in Timbuktu, I'd rather get it now. On the long way back downtown, I'll have time to think, to come up with a credible reason why I was such a disgrace to journalism last night."

"Huh? Oh, you mean they expected you to come in and—what's the term?—*write up* what happened to Nelson?"

"Yes, they did," Louise said. "And when I didn't, I confirmed all of Leonard Cohen's male chauvinist theories about the emotional instability of female reporters. Real reporters, *men* reporters, don't get hysterical."

"You weren't hysterical," Peter said. "You were upset, but you had every right to be."

They were now passing City Hall, and heading out John F. Kennedy Boulevard, past the construction sites of what the developers said would be *Downtown Philadelphia Reborn.*

Louise turned and looked at him.

"You're a really nice guy, Peter Wohl," she said. "Anyone ever tell you that?"

"All the time," he said.

She laughed, and changed the subject: "When we get to your place, I have to go inside."

"Why?"

"Because my underwear was still wet, and I couldn't put it on," she said.

The logical conclusion to be drawn from that statement, Peter thought, *is that she is at this moment, underwearless. Phrased another way, she is naked under her dress.*

"You should have seen your face just now," Louise said.

"What are you talking about?" he asked.

"Your eyes grew wide," she said. "Does that turn you on, Peter Wohl? A woman not wearing underwear?"

"Get off my back," he flared.

"It does!" she said, delighted. "It does!"

He turned and glared at her. She wasn't fazed. She smiled at him.

He returned his attention to the road. Louise noticed that he was gripping the steering wheel so tightly that his knuckles were white.

They said nothing else to each other until they reached his apartment. He pulled the nose of the Ford against the garage door, turned off the ignition, handed her the apartment key, and laid his arm on the back of the seat.

"I would just run along," he said. "But I'm going to need my key back. I'll wait here."

"I'll throw it out the window," she said.

"Fine," he said.

She went up the stairs and he leaned on the fender of the Ford LTD. A minute or so later, he heard the window in his bathroom grate open. He turned and looked up at the window. All he could see was her head; she had to be kneeling on the toilet seat.

"Can you come up here a minute?" she said. "I've got a little trouble."

He went up the stairs and into the apartment.

Louise's head peered at him around his nearly closed bedroom door.

"What's the trouble?" he asked.

"I don't want to go to work," Louise said. "Not right now."

"Then don't go," he said. "Stay here as long as you like."

"You really are a very sweet guy, Peter," Louise said.

"You seem to be a little ambiguous about that," Peter said.

"You're sore about the way I teased you in the car, aren't you?"

"You enjoy humiliating people, go ahead," he said.

"I was just *teasing*," she said. "If I didn't *like* you, I wouldn't tease you."

"I understand," he said. "I don't think you're half as clever, or as sophisticated as you do, but I understand you."

"Oh, damn you," she said, and opened the door all the way. "You don't understand me at all."

She walked within six feet of him and stopped, and looked into his eyes.

"Come on, Peter," she said. "Loosen up."

"Is there anything else I can get you?" Peter asked.

Louise unbuttoned her jacket, and then shrugged out of it.

She raised her eyes to his.

"What do I have to do, Peter?" she asked, very softly. "Throw you on the white couch and rip your clothes off?"

Officer Charley McFadden pulled into a gas station and called Jesus Martinez and told him what he had in mind. Hay-zus's mother answered the phone and with obvious reluctance, after she told him Hay-zus was asleep, got him on the phone.

"You want to help me catch Gerald Vincent Gallagher?"

"I thought you were working with Homicide," Hay-zus said.

"The detective with the job let me very politely know that he didn't need my help, thank you very much."

There was a long pause.

"Where do you think he is?" Hay-zus asked.

"I want to look for him at the Bridge Street Terminal," McFadden said.

The Bridge Street Terminal, which is the end of the line for the Market Street Elevated, a major transfer point for people traveling to and from Center City and West Philadelphia.

"In other words, you don't have the first fucking idea where he is," Martinez said.

"I got a feeling, Hay-zus," Charley McFadden said.

Gerald Vincent Gallagher, Charley McFadden had reasoned, would have hidden someplace for a while. Then he would want to get out of the Northeast. He didn't have a car—few junkies did—but he would have the price of bus or subway fare, if he had to panhandle for it.

There was a long pause.

"Ah, shit," Jesus Martinez said. "I'll meet you there."

And then he hung up.

McFadden parked his Volkswagen fifty feet from the intersection of Frankford and Bridge Streets. He went to a candy store across the street and bought two large 7-Ups to go (lots of ice); two Hershey bars; two Mounds bars; two bags of Planters peanuts; and a pack of Chesterfields.

He carried everything back to the Volkswagen, and arranged it and himself on and around the front seat. He slumped down on the seat, and lit a cigarette.

It was liable to be a long wait for Gerald Vincent Gallagher. And, of course, he might not show.

If he didn't show, McFadden decided, he would not put in for overtime. Nobody had told him to stake out the terminal.

But he might. And he would really like to catch the despicable shit, so he would wait.

He had been there ten minutes when a trackless trolley pulled in. A slight, dark, young-appearing man wearing blue jeans and a T-shirt got off. He looked around until he spotted the Volkswagen and then walked to it, and got in.

"I just thought," he said. "Since nobody told us to do this, we can't put in for overtime, right?"

"When we catch him, we can," McFadden said.

"I'll bet you believe in the Easter Bunny, too, huh?" Jesus Martinez said. Then he looked at the supplies McFadden had laid in. "No wonder you're fat," he said. "That shit's no good for you."

He reached for one of the 7-Ups, and they settled down to wait.

Mawson, Payne, Stockton, McAdoo & Lester maintained law offices on the eleventh floor of the Philadelphia Savings Fund Society Building on Market Street, east of Broad. It was convenient to both the federal courthouse and the financial district.

Colonel J. Dunlop Mawson and Brewster Cortland Payne II, the founding partners of the firm, occupied offices on either side of the Large Conference Room. They shared a secretary, Mrs. Irene Craig, a tall, dignified, silver-haired woman in her fifties. Mrs. Craig had two secretaries of her own, set up in an office off her own tastefully furnished office. Although she could, if necessary, type nearly one hundred words per minute on her state-of-the-art IBM typewriter, Mrs. Craig rarely typed anything on it except Memoranda of Incoming Calls.

Her function, she had once told her husband, was to serve as sort of a traffic cop, offering, and barring, entrance to the attention, either in person or on the phone, of her bosses. Their time was valuable, and it was her job to see that it was not wasted.

She was very good at her job, and although it was a secret between them, she brought home more money than did her husband, who worked for the Prudential Insurance Company.

When she came to work, at her ritual time of 8:45, fifteen minutes before the business day actually began, she was surprised to see the colonel's office door open. Colonel J. Dunlop Mawson rarely appeared before ten, or ten-thirty. She went into his office. He wasn't there, but there was evidence that he had been.

There were cigarettes in his ashtray; two cardboard coffee containers from the machine way down the hall by the typists' pool; and crumpled paper in his wastebasket. The colonel's leather-framed doodle pad was covered with triangles, stars, a setting sun, and a multidigit telephone number Mrs. Craig recognized from the prefix to be one in London, England.

Mrs. Craig retrieved the crumpled paper from the wastebasket, unfolded it, and read it. There were names on it: *Louise Dutton, Lt. DelRaye, Insp. Wohl (Wall?),* and, underlined, *Stanford Fortner Wells III.* There was an address, *6 Stockton Place,* and several telephone numbers, none of which Mrs. Craig recognized. And then she remembered that Stanford Fortner Wells III had something to do with newspapers; what, exactly, she couldn't recall.

She dumped the contents of the ashtray in the wastebasket, added the cardboard coffee containers, and then carried it outside and dumped it in her own wastebasket. Then she went to the smaller office where her assistants worked and started the coffee machine. That was for her. She liked a cup of coffee to begin the day, and sometimes Mr. Payne came in wanting a cup.

Colonel J. Dunlop Mawson came in the office at ten past nine, smiled at her, and asked if Mr. Payne was in.

"Not yet, any minute," she said.

"Let me know the minute he does, will you, please? And could you get me a cup of coffee?"

He went in his office, and as she went to fetch the coffee, she saw him go to the window of his office that gave a view of Market Street down to the river and stand, with his hands on his hips, as if he was mad at something, looking out.

Brewster Cortland Payne II came into her office as she was carrying a cup of coffee, with two envelopes of saccharin and a spoon on the saucer across it to the colonel's office.

"Good morning," Brewster Payne said, with a nod and a smile. He was a tall and thin, almost skinny, man wearing a single-breasted vested gray suit, a subdued necktie, and black shoes. Yet there was something, an air of authority and wisdom, Mrs. Craig knew, that made people look at him in a crowd. He looked, she thought, like what a successful attorney should look like. Sometimes, especially when she was annoyed with him, the colonel didn't look that way to her.

"Good morning," she said. "He asked me to let him know the minute you came in." Brewster Payne's face registered amused surprise.

"Do you think he is annoyed that I'm a little late?" he asked, and added: "I would be grateful for some coffee myself."

"Here," Mrs. Craig said, handing him the cup and saucer. "Tell him I'm getting his."

When she delivered the coffee, Brewster Payne was sprawled on the colonel's red leather couch, his long legs stretched out in front of him, balancing his coffee on his stomach. The colonel was standing beside his desk. When she handed him the coffee, he gave her an absent smile and set it down on the desk.

Mrs. Craig left, closing the door after her. There was someone new in the outer office.

"Hello, Matt," she said. She liked Matt Payne, thought that he was a really handsome, and more important, *nice* young man. She liked the way he smiled.

"Good morning, Mrs. Craig," he said, and then blurted: "Is there any chance I could see him this morning? He doesn't expect me, but . . ."

"He's in with the colonel," she said. "I don't know how long they'll be."

"I think this was a bad idea," Matt said.

"Don't be silly. Sit down, I'll get you some coffee."

"You're sure?"

"Positive."

He was enormously relieved, Mrs. Craig saw, and was glad that she had insisted that he stay, even though it would delay the morning's schedule by fifteen minutes or more. Fifteen minutes, plus however long the colonel and Mr. Payne were in the colonel's office.

Louise Dutton came out of the bathroom wearing Peter's bathrobe. It hung loosely on her but even in the dim light, he could see the imprint of her nipples. He thought she looked incredibly appealing.

She walked across the bedroom to the bed, looked down at Peter a moment, and then sat down on the bed.

"Well," she said. "Look who woke up."

"I wasn't asleep, Delilah," he said. "I watched you get out of bed."

"Delilah?"

"I never really thought she rendered Samson helpless by giving him a *haircut,*" Peter said. "That was the edited-for-children version."

"You Samson"—she chuckled—"me Delilah?"

"And as soon as I get my strength back, I'll tear the temple down," Peter said. "Actually, what I have to do is face the dragon in his lair."

"Now I'm the dragon? The dragon lady?"

"I was referring to Chief Inspector Matt Lowenstein, our beloved chief of detectives," Wohl said. He reached to his right, away from her, and took his wristwatch from the bedside table. He glanced at it, strapped it on, and said, "I've got to see how the Nelson investigation is going, and then go see Arthur J. Nelson. I'm late now."

"Then why aren't you out of bed, getting dressed?" she asked.

He held his arms out, and she came into them. He kissed the top of her head.

She purred, "Nice."

"I wasn't sure you would like me to do that," he said, her face against his chest.

"Why not?"

"It's *after,*" Peter said. "Women have been known to regret a moment of passion."

"I was afraid when I came back in here, you would be all dressed and ready to leave," she said. "Because it's *after.*"

He laughed, and pulled his head back so that he could look at her face.

"Wham, bam, thank you, ma'am?" he asked.

"You're the type, Peter," she said.

"You like this better?"

"Much better," she said.

"Blow in my ear, and the world is yours," he said.

She giggled and kissed his chest.

"There's no small voice of reason in the back of your mind sending up an alarm?" she asked. " 'What am I getting myself into with this crazy lady?' "

"What the small voice of reason is asking is, 'What happens when she realizes what she's done? The TV Lady and the Cop?' "

"That would seem to suggest there was more for you in what happened than one more notch on your gun," Louise said.

"If I wasn't afraid it would trigger one of your smart-ass replies, I would tell you it's never been that way for me before," Peter said.

She pushed herself into a sitting position and looked down at him.

"For me, either," she said. "I mean, really, I had to ask you."

"Oh, come on," he said.

"Yes, I did," she said. "And that suggests the possibility that I'm queer for cops. What do they call those pathetic little girls who chase the bands around? 'Groupies'? Maybe I'm a cop groupie."

"This is what I was afraid of," Peter said. "That you would start thinking."

"Why shouldn't I think?"

"Because if you do, sure as Christ made little apples, you'll come up with some good excuse to cut it off between us."

"Maybe that would be best, in the long run," she said.

"Not for me, it wouldn't," he said.

" 'He said, with finality,' " Louise said. "Why do you say that, Peter? So . . . With such finality?"

"I told you before, it was never that way for me, before," Peter said.

"You don't think that might be because you saw a friend of yours slumped dead against the wall of a diner yesterday afternoon? That sort of thing would tend, I would suppose, to excite the emotions. Or that I might be at a high emotional peak myself? I was there, too, not to mention poor little Jerome?"

"I don't give a damn what caused it, all I know is how I feel about what happened," Peter said. "I gather this is not what they call a reciprocal emotion?"

"I didn't say that," Louise said quickly. "Jesus Christ, Peter, I didn't know you existed this time yesterday!" she said. "What do you expect from me?"

He shrugged.

She looked into his eyes for a long moment. "So where does that leave us? Where do we go from here?"

"How would you react to a suggestion that it's a little warm in here, and you would probably be more comfortable if you took the robe off?"

"I was hoping you would ask," she said.

"Where the hell have you been?" Leonard Cohen demanded of Louise Dutton when she walked into the WCBL-TV newsroom. "I called all over, looking for you."

"I was a little upset, Leonard," Louise said. "I can't imagine why. I mean, why should something unimportant like walking into a room and finding someone you knew and liked hacked up like . . . I can't think of a metaphor—hacked up?"

"It was a story, Lou," Cohen said.

She glared at him, her eyebrows raised in contempt, her eyes icy.

"It was pretty bad, huh?" he said, backing down.

"Yes, it was."

"What I would like to do, Lou," he said, "is open the news at six by having Barton interview you. Nothing formal, you understand; he would just turn to you and say something like, 'Mr. Nelson lived in your apartment building, didn't he, Louise?' and then you would come back with, 'Yes, and I found the body.' "

"Fuck you, Leonard," Louise said.

He just looked at her.

"For Christ's sake," she said. "The address has been in the papers . . ."

"And so has your name," he countered.

"I've seen the papers," she said. "There must be ten Louise Duttons in the phone book, and none of the papers I saw made the connection between me and here. If it is made, every creepy-crawly in Philadelphia, including, probably, the animals who killed that poor little man, will come out of the woodwork looking for me."

"Why should that bother you? Aren't you under police protection?"

"What does that mean?"

"Just what it sounded like. I called the Homicide guy, DelRaye, Lieutenant DelRaye, when I couldn't find you, and he said that I would have to talk to Inspector Wohl, that Wohl was 'taking care of you.' "

"I am not under police protection," she said, evenly. "I'll tell you what I will do, Leonard. I'll look at what you have on tape, and if there's anything there that makes it worthwhile, I'll do a voice-over. But I am not going to chat pleasantly with Barton Ellison about it on camera."

"Okay," Leonard Cohen replied. "Thank you *ever* so much. Your dedication to journalism touches me deeply. Who's Wohl?"

"He's a cop. He's a friend of mine. He's a nice guy," Louise said.

"He's the youngest staff inspector in the police department," Cohen said. "He was also the youngest captain. His father is a retired chief inspector, which may or may not have had something to do with his being the youngest captain and staff inspector. What he usually does is investigate corruption in high places. He put the head of the plumber's local, two fairly important Mafiosi, *and* the director of the Housing Authority in the pokey just before you came to town."

She looked at him, her eyebrows raised again.

"Very bright young man," Cohen went on. "He normally doesn't schmooze people. I'm sure, you being a professional journalist and all, that you have considered the police department may have a reason for assigning an attractive young bachelor to schmooze you."

"You find him attractive, Leonard, is that what you're saying?" Louise asked innocently. "I'll have to tell him."

His lips tightened momentarily, but he didn't back off.

"You're going to see him again, huh?"

"Oh, God, Leonard, I hope so," Louise said. "He's absolutely marvelous in the sack!" She waited until his eyes widened. "Put that in your file, too, why don't you?" she added, and then walked away.

10 Colonel J. Dunlop Mawson was sitting on the sill of a wall of windows that provided a view of lower Market Street, the Delaware River, and the bridge to New Jersey.

"So, I went down to Homicide," he said, nearing the end of his story, "and finally got to meet Miss Wells, also known as Dutton."

"Where had she been?" Brewster Payne asked. Mawson had aroused his curiosity. Through the entire recital of having been given a runaround by the police, and the gory details of the brutal murder of Jerome Nelson, he had not been able to guess why Mawson was telling it all to him.

"She wouldn't tell me," Mawson said. "She's a very feisty young woman, Brewster. I think she was on the edge of telling me to butt out."

"How extraordinary," Payne said, dryly, "that she would even consider refusing the services of 'Philadelphia's most distinguished practitioner of criminal law.' "

"I knew damned well I made a mistake telling you that," Mawson said. "Now I'll never hear the end of it."

"Probably not," Payne agreed.

"I have an interesting theory," Mawson said, "that she spent the night with the cop."

"Miss Dutton? And which cop would that be, Mawson?" Payne asked.

"Inspector Wohl," Mawson said. "He took her away from the apartment, and then he brought her in in the morning."

"I thought, for a moment, that you were suggesting there was something romantic, or whatever, between them," Payne said.

"That's exactly what I'm suggesting," Mawson said. "He's not what comes to mind when you say 'cop.' Or 'inspector.' For one thing he's young, and very bright, and well dressed . . . *polished* if you take my meaning."

"Perhaps they're friends," Payne said. "When he heard what had happened, he came to be a friend."

"She doesn't look at him like he's a friend," Mawson insisted, "and unless Czernich is still playing games with me, he didn't even know her until yesterday. According to Czernich, he assigned him to the Wells/Dutton girl to make sure she was treated with the appropriate kid gloves for a TV anchorwoman."

"I don't know where you're going, I'm afraid," Payne said.

"Just file that away as a wild card," Mawson said. "Let me finish."

"Please do," Payne said.

"So, after she signed her statement, and she rode off into the sunrise with this Wohl fellow, I came here and put in a call to Wells in London. He wasn't there. But he left a message for me. Delivered with the snotty arrogance that only the English can manage. Mr. Wells is on board British Caledonian Airways Flight 419 to New York, and 'would be quite grateful if I could make myself available to him imm-ee-jut-ly on his arrival at Philadelphia.' "

"Philadelphia?" Payne asked, smiling. Mawson's mimicry of an upper-class British accent was quite good. "Does British Caledonian fly into here?"

"No, they don't. I asked the snotty Englishman the same question. He said, he 'raw-ther doubted it. What Mr. Wells has done is shed-yule a helicopter to meet the British Caledonian air-crawft in New York, don't you see? To take him from New York to Philadelphia.' "

Payne set his coffee cup on the end table beside the couch.

"You're really very good at that," he said, chuckling. "So you're going to meet him at the airport here?"

Mawson hesitated, started to reply, and then stopped.

"Okay," Brewster Payne said. "So that's the other question."

"I don't like being summoned like an errand boy," Mawson said. "But on the other hand, Stanford Fortner Wells is Wells Newspapers, and there—"

"Is a certain potential, for the future," Payne filled in for him. "If he had counsel in Philadelphia, he would have called them."

"Exactly."

"We could send one of our bright young men to the airport with a limousine," Payne said, "to take Mr. Wells either here, to see you, or to a suite which we have reserved for him in the ... what about the Warwick? ... where you will attend him the moment your very busy schedule—*shed-yule*—permits."

"Good show!" Mawson said. "Raw-ther! Quite! I knew I could count on you, old boy, in this sticky wicket."

Payne chuckled.

"You said 'the other question,' Brewster," Mawson said.

"What, if anything, you should say to Mr. Wells about where his daughter was when you couldn't find her, and more specifically, how much, if at all, of your suspicions regarding Inspector Wall—"

"Wohl. Double-U Oh Aitch Ell," Mawson interrupted.

"Wohl," Payne went on. "And his possibly lewd and carnal relationship with his daughter."

"Okay. Tell me."

"Nothing, if you're asking my advice."

"I thought it might show how bright and clever we are to find that out so soon," Mawson said.

"No father, Mawson, wants to hear from a stranger that his daughter is not as innocent as he would like to believe she is."

Mawson laughed.

"You're right, Brewster," he said. He walked to the door and opened it. "Irene, would you ask Mr. Fengler to come over, please? And tell him to clear his schedule for the rest of the day? And then reserve a *good* suite at the Warwick, billing to us, for Mr. Stanford Fortner Wells? And finally, call that limousine service and have them send one over, to park in our garage? And tell them I would be very grateful if it was clean, and not just back from a funeral?"

"Yes, sir," she said, smiling.

"Hello, Matt," Mawson said. "How are you?"

"Morning, Colonel," Matt said. "I was hoping to see Dad."

"Having just solved all the world's problems, he's available for yours," Mawson said, and turned to Brewster Payne. "Matt's waiting for you."

"I'll be damned," Payne said, and got up from the couch. "I wonder what's on his mind?"

He had, in fact, been expecting to see Matt, or at least to have him telephone. He had heard from Matt's mother how awkward it had been at the Moffitt home, and later at the funeral home, making the senseless death of Matt's uncle even more difficult for him. He had half expected Matt to come out to Wallingford last night, and, disappointed that he hadn't, had considered calling him. In the end he had decided that it would be best if Matt came to him, as he felt sure he would, in his own good time.

He went in the outer office and resisted the temptation to put his arms around Matt.

"Well, good morning," he said.

"If I'm throwing your schedule in disarray, Dad—" Matt said.

"There's nothing on my schedule, is there, Irene?"

"Nothing that won't wait," she said.

"Go on in, Matt," Payne said, gesturing toward his office. "I've got to step down the corridor a moment, and then I'll be with you."

He waited until Matt was inside and then told Irene Craig that she was to hold all calls. "It's important. You heard about Captain Moffitt?"

"I didn't know what to say to him," she said. "So I said nothing."

"I think a word of condolence would be in order when he comes out," Payne said, and then went in his office and closed the door.

Matt was sitting on the edge of an antique cherrywood chair, resting his elbows on his knees.

"I'm very sorry about your uncle Dick, Matt," Brewster Payne said. "He was a fine man, and I know how close you were. Aside from that, I have no comforting words. It was senseless, brutal, unspeakable."

Matt looked at him, started to say something, changed his mind, and said something else: "I just joined the police department."

My God! He's not joking!

"That was rather sudden, wasn't it?" Brewster Payne said. "What about the Marine Corps? I thought you were under a four-year obligation to them?"

"I busted the physical," Matt said. "The marines don't want me."

"When did that happen?"

"A week or so ago," Matt said. "My fault. When I went to the naval hospital, the doctor asked me why didn't I take the flight physical, I never knew when I might want to try for flight school. So I took it, and the eye examination was more thorough than it would have been for a grunt commission, and they found it."

"Found what?"

"It had some Latin name, of course," Matt said. "And it will probably never bother me, but the United States Marine Corps can't take any chances. I'm out."

"You didn't say anything," Brewster Payne said.

"I'm not exactly proud of being a 4-F," Matt said. "I just . . . didn't want to."

"Perhaps the army or the air force wouldn't be so particular," Brewster Payne said.

"It doesn't work that way, Dad," Matt said. "I already have a brand-new 4-F draft card."

"Think that through, Matt," Brewster Payne said. "You should be embarrassed, or ashamed, only of things over which you have control. There is no reason at all that you should feel in any way diminished by this."

"I'll get over it," Matt said.

"It is not really a good reason to act impulsively," Brewster Payne said.

"Nor, he hesitates to add, but is thinking, is the fact that Uncle Dick got himself shot a really good reason to act impulsively; for example, joining the police force."

"The defense rests," Brewster Payne said, softly.

"Actually, I was thinking about it before Uncle Dick was killed," Matt said. "From the time I busted the physical. The first thing I thought was that it was too late to apply for law school."

"Not necessarily," Brewster Payne said. "There is always an exception to the rule, Matt."

"And then, with sudden clarity, I realized that I didn't *want* to go to law school," Matt went on. "Not right away, anyway. Not in the fall. And then I saw the ads in the newspaper, heard them on the radio . . . the police department, if not the Marine Corps, is looking for a few good men."

"I've noticed the advertisements," Brewster Payne said. "And they aroused my curiosity to the point where I asked about them. The reason they are actively recruiting people is that the salary is quite low—"

"Thanks to you," Matt said, "that really isn't a problem for me."

"Yes, I suppose that's true," Payne said.

"I went out and got drunk with a cop last night."

"After you left the Moffitts', you mean? I thought maybe you would come home."

"I wanted to be alone, so I went to the bar in the Hotel Adelphia. It's a great place to be alone."

"And there you met the policeman? And he talked you into the police?"

"No. I'd met him the afternoon before. At Uncle Dick's house. Mr. Coughlin introduced us. Staff Inspector Wohl. He was wounded, too. He was a friend of Uncle Dick's, and he was there . . . at the Waikiki Diner. I think he was probably in the Adelphia bar to be alone, too. I spoke to him at the bar."

"Wohl?" Brewster Payne parroted.

"Peter Wohl," Matt said. "You know him?"

"I think I've heard the colonel mention him," Payne said. "Younger man? The word the colonel used was 'polished.' "

"He would fit in with your bright young men," Matt said. "If that's what you mean."

"I don't know how you manage to make 'bright young men' sound like a pejorative," Brewster Payne said, "but you do."

"I know why you like them," Matt said. "Imitation is the most sincere form of flattery. If you started chewing tobacco this morning, they'd all be chawin' 'n' spitting by noon."

Payne chuckled. "Is it that bad?"

"Yes, it is," Matt said.

"You said you drank with Inspector Wohl?"

"Yeah. He's a very nice guy."

"And you discussed your joining the police department?"

"Briefly," Matt said. "I am sure I gave him the impression I was drunk, or stupid, or burning with a childish desire to avenge Uncle Dutch. Or all of the above."

"But you're still thinking about it?" Payne asked, and then went on without waiting for a reply. "It would be a very important decision, Matt. Deserving of a good deal of careful thought. Pluses and minuses. Long-term ramifications . . ."

He stopped when he saw the look on Matt's face.

"I have joined the police department," Matt said. *"Fait accompli,* or nearly so."

"How did you manage to do that, since last night? You can't just walk in and join, can you? Or can you?"

"I got to bed about two last night," Matt said. "And at half past five this morning, I was wide awake. So I went for a long walk. At five minutes after eight, I found myself downtown, in front of Wanamaker's. And I was hungry. There's a place in Suburban Station that serves absolutely awful hot dogs and really terrible 'orange drink' twenty-four hours a day. Just what I had to have, so I cut through City Hall, and that was my undoing."

"I don't understand," Payne said.

"The cops have a little recruiting booth set up there," Matt said, "presumably to catch the going-to-work crowd. So I saw it, and figured what the hell, it wouldn't hurt to get some real information. Five minutes later, I was upstairs in City Hall, taking the examination."

"That quickly?"

"I was a live one," Matt said. "Anyway, there are several requirements to get in the police department. From what I saw, aside from not having a police record, the most important is having resided within the city limits for a year. I passed that with flying colors, since I gave the Deke house as my address for my new driver's license, and that was more than a year ago. Next came the examination itself, with which I had some difficulty, since I had to answer serious posers like how many eggs would I have if I divided a dozen eggs by six. But I got through that, too. At eleven, I'm supposed to be in the Municipal Services Building, across from City Hall, for a physical, and, I think, some kind of an interview with a shrink."

"That's all there is to it?"

"Well, they took my fingerprints, and are going to check me out with the FBI, and there's some kind of background investigation they'll conduct here, but for all practical purposes, yes, that's it."

"I wonder how your mother is going to react to this?"

"I don't know," Matt said.

"She lost a husband who was a policeman," Brewster Payne said. "That's going to be on her mind."

Matt grunted.

"I want to do it, Dad, at least to try it."

"You've considered, of course, that you might not like it? I don't know what they do with rookie policemen, of course, but I would suspect it's like anything else, that you start out doing the unpleasant things."

"I didn't really want to go in the marines, Dad," Matt said. "Not until after they told me they didn't want me, anyway. It was just something you did, like go to college. But I really *want* to be a cop."

Brewster Payne cocked his head thoughtfully and made a grunting noise.

"Well, I don't like it, and I won't be a hypocrite and say I do," Brewster Payne said.

"I didn't think you would," Matt said. "I sort of hoped you would understand."

"The terms are not mutually exclusive," Payne said. "I do understand, and I don't like it. Would you like to hear what I really think?"

"Please."

"I think that you will become a police officer, and because this is your nature, you will do the very best you can. And I think in . . . say a year . . . that you will conclude you don't really want to spend the rest of your life that way. If that happens, and you do decide to go to law school, or do something entirely different—"

"Then it wouldn't be wasted, is that what you mean?" Matt interrupted.

"I was about to say the year would be *very valuable* to you," Brewster Payne said. "Now that I think about it, far more valuable than a year in Europe, which was a carrot I was considering dangling in front of your nose to talk you out of this."

"That's a very tempting carrot," Matt said.

"The offer remains open," Payne said. "But to tell you the truth, I would be disappointed in you if you took it. It remains open because of your mother."

"Yeah," Matt said, exhaling.

"And also for my benefit," Brewster Payne said. "When your brothers and sister come to me, and they will, crying 'Dad, how could you let him do that?' I will be able to respond that I did my best to talk you out of it, even including a bribe of a year in Europe."

"I hadn't even thought about them," Matt said.

"I suggest you had better. You can count, I'm sure, on your sister trying to reason with you, and when that fails, screaming and breaking things."

Matt chuckled.

"I will advance the proposition, which I happen to believe, that what you're doing is both understandable, and with a little bit of luck, might turn out to be a very profitable thing for you to do."

"Thank you," Matt said.

Brewster Payne stood up and offered his hand to Matt.

Matt started to take it, but stopped. They looked at each other, and then Brewster Payne opened his arms, and Matt stepped into them, and they hugged each other.

"Dad, you're great," Matt said.

"I know," Brewster Payne said. He thought, *I don't care who his father was; this is my own, beloved, son.*

When Peter Wohl walked into Homicide, Detective Jason Washington signaled that Captain Henry C. Quaire, commanding officer of the Homicide Division, was in his office and wordlessly asked if he should tell him Wohl was outside.

Wohl shook his head, no, and mimed drinking a cup of coffee. Washington went to a Mr. Coffee machine, poured coffee, and then, still without speaking, made gestures asking Wohl if he wanted cream or sugar. Wohl shook his head again, no, and Washington carried the coffee to him. Wohl nodded his thanks, and Washington bowed solemnly.

"We should paint our faces white," Wohl said, chuckling, "and set up on the sidewalk."

"Well, we'd probably make more money doing that than we do on the job," Washington said. "Mimes probably take more home in their begging baskets every day than we do in a week."

Wohl chuckled, and then asked, "Who's in there with him?"

"Mitell," Washington said. "You hear about that job? The old Italian guy?"

Wohl shook his head no.

"Well, he died. We just found out—Mitell told me as he went in that he just got the medical examiner's report—of natural causes. But his wife was broke, and didn't have enough money to bury him the way she thought he was entitled to be buried. So she dragged him into the basement, wrapped him in Saran Wrap, and waited for the money to come in. That was three months ago. A guy from the gas works smelled him, and called the cops."

"Jesus Christ!" Wohl said.

"The old lady can't understand why everybody's so upset," Washington said. "After all, it was *her* basement and *her* husband."

"Oh, God." Wohl laughed, and Washington joined him, and then Washington said what had just popped into Wohl's mind.

"Why are we laughing?"

"Otherwise, we'd go crazy," Wohl said.

"How did I do with the TV lady?" Washington asked.

"She told me she thought you were a very nice man, Jason," Wohl said.

"I thought she was a very nice lady," Washington said. "She looks even better in real life than she does on the tube."

"I don't suppose anything has happened?" Wohl asked.

"Gerald Vincent Gallagher's under a rock someplace," Washington said. "He'll have to come out sooner or later. I'll let you know the minute I get anything."

"Who's got the Nelson job?" Wohl asked.

"Tony Harris," Washington said. "Know him?"

Wohl nodded.

Detective Jason Washington thought that he was far better off, the turn of the wheel, so to speak, than was Detective Tony Harris, to whom the wheel had given the faggot hacking job.

The same special conditions prevailed, the close supervision from above, though for different reasons. The special interest in the Moffitt job came because Dutch was a cop, and it came from within the department. If Dutch hadn't been a cop, and the TV lady hadn't been there when he got shot, the press wouldn't really have given a damn. It would have been a thirty-second story on the local TV news, and the story would probably have been buried in the back pages of the newspapers.

But the Nelson job had everything in it that would keep it on the TV and in the newspapers for a long time. For one thing, it was gory. Whoever had done in Nelson had been over the edge; they'd really chopped up the poor sonofabitch. That in itself would have been enough to make a big story about it; the public likes to read about "brutal murders." But Nelson was rich, the son of a big shot. He lived in a luxurious apartment. And there was the (interesting coincidence) tie-in with the TV lady. She'd found the body, and since everybody figured they knew her from the TV, it was as if someone they knew personally had found it.

And so far, they didn't know who did it. Everybody could take a vicarious chill from the idea of having somebody break into an apartment and chop somebody up with knives. And if it came out that Jerome Nelson was homosexual, that would make it an even bigger story. Jason Washington didn't think it would come out (the father owned a newspaper and a TV station, and it seemed logical that out of respect for him, the other newspapers and TV stations would soft-pedal that); but if it did, what the papers would have was sexual perversion as well as a brutal murder among the aristocracy, and they would milk that for all they could get out of it.

But that wasn't Tony Harris's real problem, as Jason Washington saw it. Harris's real problem was his sergeant, Bill Chedister, who spent most of his time with his nose up Lieutenant Ed DelRaye's ass, and, more important, DelRaye himself. So far as Washington was concerned, DelRaye was an ignorant loudmouth, who was going to take the credit for whatever Tony Harris did right, and see that Harris got the blame for the investigation not going as fast as the brass thought it should go.

Washington thought that what happened between DelRaye and the TV woman was dumb, for a number of reasons, starting with the basic one that you learn more from witnesses if you don't piss them off. Threatening to break down her door and calling for a wagon to haul her to the Roundhouse was even dumber.

In a way, Washington was sorry that Peter Wohl had shown up and calmed things down. DelRaye thus escaped the wrath that would have been dumped on him by everybody from the commissioner down for getting the TV station justifiably pissed off at the cops.

Washington also thought that it was interesting that DelRaye had let it get around that Wohl had been "half-drunk" when he had shown up. Jason Washington had known Wohl ten, fifteen years, and he had never seen him drunk in all that time. But accusing Wohl of having been drunk was just the sort of thing a prick like DelRaye would do, especially if he himself had been. And if DelRaye had been drunk, that would explain his pissing off the TV woman.

Washington admired Wohl, for a number of reasons. He liked the way he dressed, for one thing, but, far more important, he thought Wohl was smart. Jason Washington habitually studied the promotion lists, not only to see who was on them, but to see who had done well. Peter Wohl had been second on his sergeant's list, first on his lieutenant's list, third on his captain's list, and first again on the staff inspector's list. That was proof enough that Wohl was about as smart a cop as they came, but also that he had kept his party politics in order, which sometimes wasn't easy for someone who was an absolutely straight arrow, as Washington believed Wohl to be.

Peter Wohl was Jason Washington's idea of what a good senior police officer should be; there was no question that Wohl (and quickly, because the senior ranks of the Department would soon be thinned out by retirement) would rise to chief inspector, and probably even higher.

As Wohl put his coffee cup to his lips, Captain Quaire's office door opened. Detective Mitell, a slight, wiry young man, came out, and Quaire, a stocky, muscular man of about forty, appeared in it. He spotted Wohl.

"Good morning, Inspector," he said. "I expect you want to see me?"

"When you get a free minute, Henry," Wohl said.

"Let me get a cup of coffee," Captain Quaire said, "and I'll be right with you."

Wohl waited until Quaire had carried his coffee mug into his office and then followed him in. Quaire put his mug on his desk, and then went to the door and closed it.

"I was told you would be around, Peter," he said, waving toward a battered chair. "But before we start that, let me thank you for last night."

"Thank me for what last night?" Wohl asked.

"I understand a situation developed on the Nelson job that could have been awkward."

"Where'd you hear that?"

Quaire didn't reply directly.

"My cousin Paul's with the Crime Lab. He was there," he said. "I had a word with Lieutenant DelRaye. I tried to make the point that knocking down witnesses' doors and hauling them away in a wagon is not what we of the modern enlightened law-enforcement community think of as good public relations."

Wohl chuckled, relieved that Quaire had heard about the incident from his own sources; after telling the commissioner what he had told him was off the record, he would have been disappointed if the commissioner had gone right to DelRaye's commanding officer with it.

"The lady was a little upset, but nothing got out of control."

"Was he drunk, Peter?"

I wonder if he got that, too, from his cousin Paul? And is Cousin Paul a snitch, or did Quaire tell him to keep his eye on DelRaye?

"No, I don't think so," Wohl replied, and added a moment later, "No, I'm sure he wasn't."

But I was. How hypocritical I am, in that circumstance. I wonder if anybody saw it, and turned me in?

"Okay," Quaire said. "That's good enough for me, Peter. Now what can I do for you to keep the commissioner off *your* back and Chief Lowenstein off mine?"

"Lowenstein said something to you about me? You said you expected me?" Wohl asked.

"Lowenstein said, quote, by order of the commissioner, you would be keeping an eye on things," Quaire said.

"*Only* as a spectator," Wohl said. "I'm to finesse both Miss Dutton and Mr. Nelson. I'm to keep Nelson up to date on how that job is going, and to make sure Miss Dutton is treated with all the courtesy an ordinary citizen of Philadelphia, who also happens to be on TV twice a day, can expect."

Quaire smiled. "That, the girl, might be very interesting," he said. "She's a looker, Peter. Nelson may be difficult. He's supposed to be a real sonofabitch."

"Do you think the Commissioner would rather have him mad at Peter Wohl than at Ted Czernich?" Wohl said. "I fell into this, Henry. I responded to the call at the Waikiki. My bad luck, I was on Roosevelt Boulevard."

"Well, what do you need?"

"I'm going from here to see Nelson," Wohl said. "I'd like to talk to the detective who has the job."

"Sure."

"If it's all right with you, Henry, I'd like to ask him to tell me when they need Miss Dutton in here. I don't want anybody saying, 'Get in the car, honey.' "

"Tony Harris got the Nelson job," Quaire said.

"I heard. Good man, from what I hear," Wohl said.

"Tony Harris is at the Nelson apartment," Quaire said. "You want me to get him in here?"

"I really have to talk to him before I see Nelson. Maybe the thing for me to do is meet him over there."

"You want to do that, I'll call him and tell him to wait for you."

"Please, Henry," Wohl said.

Staff Inspector Peter Wohl's first reaction when he saw Detective Anthony C. Harris was anger.

Tony Harris was in his early thirties, a slight and wiry man already starting to bald, the smooth youthful skin on his face already starting to crease and line. He was wearing a shirt and tie, and a sports coat and slacks that had probably come from the racks of some discount clothier several years before.

It was a pleasant spring day and Detective Harris had elected to wait for Inspector Wohl outside the crime scene, which had already begun to stink sickeningly of blood, on the street. Specifically, when Wohl passed through the Stockton Place barrier, Harris was sitting on the hood of Wohl's Jaguar XK-120, which was parked, top down, where he had left it last night.

There were twenty coats of hand-rubbed lacquer on the XK-120's hood, applied, one coat at a time, with a laborious rubdown between each coat, by Peter Wohl himself. *Only an ignorant asshole, with no appreciation of the finer things of life, would plant his gritty ass on twenty coats of hand-rubbed lacquer.*

Wohl screeched to a stop by the Jaguar, leaned across the seat, rolled down the window, and returned Tony Harris's pleasant smile by snapping, "Get your ass off my hood!"

Then he drove twenty feet farther down the cobblestoned street and stopped the LTD.

Looking a little sheepish, Harris walked to the LTD as Wohl got out.

"Jesus Christ, Tony!" Wohl fumed, still angry. "There's twenty coats of lacquer on there!"

"Sorry," Harris mumbled. "I didn't think."

"Obviously," Wohl said.

Wohl's anger died as quickly as it had flared. Tony Harris looked beat and worn down. Without consciously calling it up from his memory, what Wohl knew about Harris came into his mind. First came the important impression he had filed away, which was that Harris was a good cop, more important, one of the brighter Homicide detectives. Then he remembered hearing that after nine years of marriage and four kids, Mrs. Harris had caught Tony straying from the marital bed and run him before a judge who had awarded her both ears and the tail.

If I were Tony Harris, Peter Wohl thought, *who has to put in sixty, sixty-five hours a week to make enough money to pay child support with enough left over to pay for an "efficiency" apartment for myself, and some staff inspector, no older than I am, pulls rank and jumps my ass for scratching the precious paint on his precious sports car, I would be pissed. And rightly so.*

"Hell, Tony, I'm sorry," Wohl said, offering his hand. "But I painted that sonofabitch by myself. All twenty coats."

"I was wrong," Harris said. "I just wasn't thinking. Or I wasn't thinking about a paint job."

"I guess what I was really pissed about was my own stupidity," Wohl said. "I know better than using my own car on the job. Right after I saw you, I asked myself, 'Christ, what if it had rained last night?' "

"You took that TV woman out through the basement in her own car?" Harris asked.

"Yeah."

"It took DelRaye some time to figure that out," Harris said. "Talk about pissed."

"Well, I'm sorry he was," Wohl said. "But it was a vicious circle, the more pissed he got at her, the more pissed she got at him. I had to break it, and that seemed to be the best way to do it. The whole department would have paid for it for a long time."

"I think maybe he was pissed because he knew his ass was showing," Harris said. "You can't push a dame like that around. She file a complaint?"

"No," Wohl said.

Harris shrugged.

"Did Captain Quaire say anything to you about me?" Wohl asked.

"He said it came from upstairs that you were to be in on it," Harris said.

"I've been temporarily transferred to the Charm Squad," Wohl said. "I'm to keep Miss Dutton happy, and to report daily to Mr. Nelson's father on the progress of your investigation."

Harris chuckled.

"What have you got, Tony?"

"He was a fag, I guess you know?"

"I met him," Wohl said.

"I want to talk to his boyfriend," Harris said. "We're looking for him. Very large black guy, big enough, strong enough, to cut up Nelson the way he was. His name, we think, is Pierre St. Maury. His birth certificate probably says John Jones, but that's what he called himself."

"You think he's the doer?"

"That's where I am now," Harris said. "The rent-a-cops told me that he spent the night here a lot; drove Nelson's car—cars—and probably had a key. There are no signs of forcible entry. And there's a burglar alarm. One of Nelson's cars is missing. A *Jaguar,* by the way, Inspector," Harris said, a naughty look in his eyes. "I put the Jag in NCIC."

The FBI's National Crime Information Center operated a massive computer listing details of crimes nationwide. If the Jaguar was found somewhere, or even stopped for a traffic violation, the information that it was connected with a crime in Philadelphia would be immediately available to the police officers involved.

"Screw you, Tony," Wohl said, and laughed.

"A new one," Harris went on. "An 'XJ6'?"

"Four-door sedan," Wohl furnished. "A work of art. Twenty-five, thirty thousand dollars."

Harris's face registered surprise at the price.

"Police radio is broadcasting the description every half hour," he went on. "I also ordered a subsector search. Nelson's other car is a Ford Fairlane convertible. That's in the garage."

"Lover's quarrel?" Wohl asked.

Harris held both palms upward in front of him, and made a gesture, like a scale in balance.

"Maybe," he said. "That would explain what he did to the victim. I think we have the weapons. They used one of those Chinese knives, you know, looks like a cleaver, but sharp as a razor?"

Wohl nodded.

"And another knife, a regular one, a butcher knife with a bone handle, which is probably what he used to stab him."

"You said 'maybe,' Tony," Wohl said.

"I'm just guessing, Inspector," Harris said.

"Go ahead," Wohl said.

"There was a lot of stuff stolen, or I think so. There's no jewelry to speak of in the apartment . . . some ordinary cuff links, tie clasps, but nothing worth any money. The victim wore rings, they're gone, we know that. No money in the wallet, or anywhere else that anybody could find. He probably had a watch, or watches, and there's none in there. And there was marks on the bedside table, probably a portable TV, that's gone."

"Leading up to what?"

"When two homosexuals get into something like this, they usually don't steal anything, too. I mean, not the boyfriend. They work off the anger and run. So maybe it wasn't the boyfriend."

"Or the boyfriend might be a cold-blooded sonofabitch," Wohl said.

"Yeah," Harris said, and made the balancing gestures again. "We got people looking for Mr. St. Maury," he went on. "And for the Jaguar. We're trying to find if he had any jewelry that was good enough to be insured, which would give us a description. Captain Quaire said you were going to see his father?"

"I'm going there as soon as I leave here," Wohl said. "I'll ask."

"I'd like to talk to him, too," Harris said.

"I think I'd better see him alone," Wohl thought out loud. "I'll tell him you'll want to see him. Maybe he can come up with some kind of a list of jewelry, expensive stuff in the apartment."

"You'll get the list?"

"No. I'll ask him to get it for you. This is your job, Tony. I'm not going to stick my nose in where it doesn't belong."

Harris nodded.

"But I would like to look around the apartment," Wohl said. "So when I see him, I'll know what I'm talking about."

"Sure," Harris said. He started toward the door. "I'm really sorry, Inspector, about sitting on your car."

"Forget it," Wohl said.

11 The building housing the Philadelphia *Ledger* and the studios of WGHA-TV and WGHA-FM was on Market Street, near the Thirtieth Street Station, and built, Wohl recalled as he drove up to it, about the same time. It wasn't quite the marble Greek palace the Thirtieth Street Station was, but it was a large and imposing building.

He had been in it once before, as a freshman at St. Joseph's Prep, on a field trip.

As he walked up to the entrance, he remembered that very clearly, a busload of boisterous boys, horsing around, getting whacked with a finger behind the ear by the
priests when their decorum didn't meet the standards of Young Catholic Gentlemen.

There was a rent-a-cop standing by the revolving door, a receptionist behind a marble counter in the marble-floored lobby, and two more rent-a-cops standing behind
her.

Wohl gave her his business card. It carried the seal of the City of Philadelphia in
the upper left-hand corner, the legend POLICE DEPARTMENT CITY OF PHILADELPHIA in
the lower left, and in the center his name, and below that, in slightly smaller letters,
STAFF INSPECTOR. In the lower right-hand corner, it said INTERNAL SECURITY DIVISION
FRANKLIN SQUARE and listed two telephone numbers.

It was an impressive card, and usually opened doors to wherever he wanted to go
very quickly.

It made absolutely no impression on the receptionist in the Ledger Building.

"Do you have an appointment with Mr. Nelson, sir?" she asked, with massive
condescension.

"I believe Mr. Nelson expects me," Wohl said.

She smiled thinly at him and dialed a number.

"There's a Mr. Wohl at Reception who says Mr. Nelson expects him."

There was a pause, then a reply, and she hung up the telephone.

"I'm sorry, sir, but you don't seem to be on Mr. Nelson's appointment schedule,"
the receptionist said. "He's a very busy man, as I'm sure—"

"Call whoever that was back and tell her *Inspector* Wohl, of the police department," Peter Wohl interrupted her.

She thought that over a moment, and finally shrugged and dialed the phone again.

This time, there was a longer pause before she hung up. She took a clipboard from
a drawer, and a plastic-coated "Visitor" badge.

"Sign on the first blank line, please," she said, and turned to one of the rent-a-cops.
"Take this gentleman to the tenth floor, please."

There was another entrance foyer when the elevator door was opened, behind a
massive mahogany desk, and for a moment, Wohl thought he was going to have to
go through the whole routine again, but a door opened, and a well-dressed, slim, gray-
haired woman came through it and smiled at him.

"I'm Mr. Nelson's secretary, Inspector," she said. "Will you come this way,
please?"

The rent-a-cop slipped into a chair beside the elevator door.

"I'm sorry about that downstairs," the woman said, smiling at him over her shoulder. "I think maybe you should have told her you were from the police."

"No problem," Peter said. It would accomplish nothing to tell her he'd given her
his card with that information all over it.

Arthur J. Nelson's outer office, his secretary's office, was furnished with gleaming
antiques, a Persian carpet, an oil portrait of President Theodore Roosevelt, and a startlingly lifelike stuffed carcass of a tiger, very skillfully mounted, so that, snarling, it
appeared ready to pounce.

"He'll be with you just as soon as he can," his secretary said. "May I offer you
a cup of coffee?"

"Thank you, no," Peter said, and then his mouth ran away with him. "I like your pussycat."

"Mr. Nelson took that when he was just out of college," she said, and pointed to a framed photograph on the wall. Wohl went and looked at it. It was of a young man, in sweat-soaked khakis, cradling his rifle in his arm, and resting his foot on a dead tiger, presumably the one now stuffed and mounted.

"Bengal," the secretary said. "That's a Bengal tiger."

"Very impressive," Wohl said.

He examined the tiger, idly curious about how they actually mounted and stuffed something like this.

What's inside? A wooden frame? A wire one? A plaster casting? Is that red tongue the real thing, preserved somehow? Or what?

Then he walked across the room and looked through the curtained windows. He could see the roof of Thirtieth Street Station, its classic Greek lines from that angle diluted somewhat by air-conditioning machinery and a surprising forest of radio antennae. He could see the Schuylkill River, with the expressway on this side and the boathouses on the far bank.

The left of the paneled double doors to Arthur J. Nelson's office opened, and four men filed out. They all seemed determined to smile, Wohl thought idly, and then he thought they had probably just had their asses eaten out.

A handsome man wearing a blue blazer and gray trousers appeared in the door. He was much older, of course, than the young man in the tiger photograph, and heavier, and there was now a perfectly trimmed, snow-white mustache on his lip, but Wohl had no doubt that it was Arthur J. Nelson.

Formidable, Wohl thought.

Arthur J. Nelson studied Wohl for a moment, carefully.

"Sorry to keep you waiting, Inspector," he said. "Won't you please come in?"

He waited at the door for Wohl and put out his hand. It was firm.

"Thank you for seeing me, Mr. Nelson," Wohl said. "May I offer my condolences?"

"Yes, you can, and that's very kind of you," Nelson said, as he led Wohl into his office. "But frankly, what I would prefer is a report that you found proof positive who the animal was who killed my son, and that he resisted arrest and is no longer among the living."

Wohl was taken momentarily aback.

What the hell. Any father would feel that way. This man is accustomed to saying exactly what he's thinking.

"I'm about to have a drink," Nelson said. "Will you join me? Or is that against the rules?"

"I'd like a drink," Peter said. "Thank you."

"I drink single-malt scotch with a touch of water," Nelson said. "But there is, of course, anything else."

"That would be fine, sir," Peter said.

Nelson went to a bar set into the bookcases lining one wall of his office. Peter looked around the room. A second wall was glass, offering the same view of the Schuylkill he had seen outside. The other walls were covered with mounted animal heads and photographs of Arthur J. Nelson with various distinguished and/or famous people, including the sitting president of the United States. There was one of Nelson with the governor of Pennsylvania, but not, Peter noticed, one of His Honor the Mayor Carlucci.

Nelson crossed the room to where Peter stood and handed him a squat, octagonal crystal glass. There was no ice.

"Some people don't like it," Nelson said. "Take a sip. If you don't like it, say so."

Wohl sipped. It was heavy, but pleasant.

"Very nice," he said. "I like it. Thank you."

"I was shooting stag in Scotland, what, ten years ago. The gillie drank it. I asked him, and he told me about it. Now I have them ship it to me. All the scotch you get here, you know, is a blend."

"It's nice," Peter said.

"Here's to vigilante justice, Inspector," Nelson said.

"I'm not sure I can drink to that, sir," Peter said.

"You can't, but I can," Nelson said. "I didn't mean to put you on a spot."

"If I wasn't here officially," Peter said, "maybe I would."

"If you had lost your only son, Inspector, like I lost mine, you *certainly* would. When something like this happens, terms like 'justice' and 'due process' seem abstract. What you want is vengeance."

"I was about to say I know how you feel," Peter said. "But of course, I don't. I can't. All I can say is that we'll do everything humanly possible to find whoever took your son's life."

"If I ask a straight question, will I get a straight answer?"

"I'll try, sir."

"How do you cops handle it psychologically when you do catch somebody you *know* is guilty of doing something horrible, obscene, unhuman like this, only to see him walk out of a courtroom a free man because of some minor point of law, or some bleeding heart on the bench?"

"The whole thing is a system, sir," Peter said, after a moment. "The police, catching the doer, the perpetrator, are only part of the system. We do the best we can. It's not our fault when another part of the system fails to do what it should."

"I have every confidence that you'll find whoever it was who hacked my son to death," Nelson said. "And then we both know what will happen. It will, after a long while, get into a courtroom, where some asshole of a lawyer will try every trick in the business to get him off. And if he doesn't, if the jury finds him guilty, and the judge has the balls to sentence him to the electric chair, he'll appeal, for ten years or so, and the odds are some yellow-livered sonofabitch of a governor will commute his sentence to life. I'm sure you know what it costs to keep a man in jail. About twice what it costs to send a kid to an Ivy League college. The taxpayers will provide this animal with three meals a day, and a warm place to sleep for the rest of his life."

Wohl didn't reply. Nelson drained his drink and walked to the bar to make another, then returned.

"Have you ever been involved in the arrest of someone who did something really terrible, something like what happened to my son?"

"Yes, sir."

"And were you tempted to put a .38 between his eyes right then and there, to save the taxpayers the cost of a trial, and/or lifelong imprisonment?"

"No, sir."

"Why not?"

"Straight answer?" Peter asked. Nelson nodded. "I could say because you realize that you would lower yourself to his level," Peter said, "but the truth is that you don't do it because it would cost you. They investigate all shootings, and—"

"Vigilante justice," Nelson interrupted, raising his glass. "Right now, it seems like a splendid idea to me."

He is not suggesting that I go out and shoot whoever killed his son. He is in shock, as well as grief, and as a newspaperman, he knows the way the system works, and now that he's going to be involved with the system himself, doesn't like it at all.

"It gets out of hand almost immediately," Peter said.

"Yes, of course," Nelson said. "Please excuse me, Inspector, for subjecting you to this. I probably should not have come to work, in my mental condition. But the alternative was sitting at home, looking out the window . . ."

"I understand perfectly, sir," Peter said.

"Have there been any developments?" Nelson asked.

"I came here directly from Stockton Place," Peter said, "where I spoke to the detective to whom the case has been assigned—"

"I thought it had been assigned to you," Nelson interrupted.

"No, sir," Peter said. "Detective Harris of the Homicide Division has been assigned to the case."

"Then what's your role in this? Ted Czernich led me to believe that you would be in charge."

"Commissioner Czernich has asked me to keep him advised, to keep you advised, and to make sure that Detective Harris has all the assistance he asks for," Wohl said.

"I was pleased," Nelson interrupted again. "I checked you out. You're in Internal Security, that sounds important whatever it means, and you're the man who caught the Honorable Mr. Housing Director Weaver and that Friend of Labor, J. Francis Donleavy, with both of their hands in the municipal cookie jar. And now you're telling me you're not on the case . . ."

"Sir, what it means is that Commissioner Czernich assigned the best available *Homicide* detective to the case. That's a special skill, sir. Harris is better equipped than I am to conduct the investigation—"

"That's why he's a detective, right, and you're an inspector?"

"And then the commissioner called me in and told me to drop whatever else I was doing, so that I could keep both you and him advised of developments, and so that I could provide Detective Harris with whatever help he needs," Wohl plunged on doggedly.

Arthur J. Nelson looked at Wohl suspiciously for a moment.

"I had the other idea," he said, finally. "All right, so what has Mr. Harris come up with so far?"

"Harris believes that a number of valuables have been stolen from the apartment, Mr. Nelson."

"He figured that out himself, did he?" Nelson said, angrily sarcastic. "What other reason could there possibly be than a robbery? My son came home and found his apartment being burglarized, and the burglar killed him. All I can say is that, thank God, his girlfriend wasn't with him. Or she would be dead, too."

Girlfriend? Jesus!

"Detective Harris, who will want to talk to you himself, Mr. Nelson, asked me if you could come up with a list of valuables, jewelry, that sort of thing, that were in the apartment."

"I'll have my secretary get in touch with the insurance company," Nelson said. "There must be an inventory around someplace."

"Your son's car, one of them, the Jaguar, is missing from the garage."

"Well, by now, it's either on a boat to Mexico, or gone through a dismantler's," Nelson snapped. "All you're going to find is the license plate, if you find that."

"Sometimes we get lucky," Peter said. "We're looking for it, of course, here and all up and down the Eastern Seaboard."

"I suppose you've asked his girlfriend? It's unlikely, but possible that she might have it. Or for that matter, that it might be in the dealer's garage."

"You mentioned his girlfriend a moment ago, Mr. Nelson," Wohl said, carefully, suspecting he was on thin ice. "Can you give me her name?"

"Dutton, Louise Dutton," Nelson said. "You *are* aware that she found Jerry? That she went into his bedroom, and found him like that?"

"I wasn't aware of a relationship between them, Mr. Nelson," Peter said. "But I do know that Miss Dutton does not have Mr. Nelson's car."

"Miss Dutton is a prominent television personality," Nelson said. "It would not be good for her public image were it to become widely know that she and her gentleman friend lived in the same apartment building. I would have thought, however, that you would have been able to put two and two together."

Jesus Christ! Does he expect me to believe that? Does he believe it himself?

He looked at Nelson's face, and then understood: *He knows what his son was, and he probably knows that I know. I have just been given the official cover story. Arthur J. Nelson wants the fact that his son was homosexual swept under the rug. For his own ego, or maybe, even more likely, because there's a mother around. What the hell, my father would do the same thing.*

"Insofar as the *Ledger* is concerned," Nelson said, meeting Wohl's eyes, "every effort will be made to spare Miss Dutton any embarrassment. I can only hope my competition will be as understanding."

He obviously feels he can get to Louise, somehow, and get her to stand still for being identified as Jerome's girlfriend. Well, why not? "Scratch my back and I'll scratch yours" works at all echelons.

"I understand, sir," Peter said.

"Thank you for coming to see me, Inspector," Arthur J. Nelson said, putting out his hand. "When I see Ted Czernich, I will tell him how much I appreciate your courtesy and understanding."

The translation of which is "Do what you're told, or I'll lower the boom on you."

Peter Wohl called Detective Tony Harris from a pay phone in the lobby of the Ledger Building and told him that Arthur J. Nelson's secretary was going to come up with a list of jewelry and other valuables that probably had been in the apartment, and that it would probably be ready by the time Harris could come to the Ledger Building.

And then he told Harris what Nelson had said about Louise Dutton being Jerome Nelson's girlfriend, and warned him not to get into Jerome's sexual preference if there was any way it could be avoided. Somewhat surprising Wohl, Harris didn't seem surprised.

"Thanks for the warning," he said. "I can handle that."

"He also suggested that by now the Jaguar has been stripped," Wohl said.

"Could well be. They haven't found it yet, and Jaguars are pretty easy to spot; there aren't that many of them. Either stripped, or on a dock in New York or Baltimore waiting to get loaded on a boat for South America. I think we should keep looking."

Wohl did not mention to Harris Nelson's toast to vigilante justice, or his remark about what he really wanted to hear was that the doer had been killed resisting arrest. It was, more than likely, just talk.

When he hung up, he considered, and decided against, reporting to Commissioner Czernich about his meeting with Nelson. He really didn't have anything important to say.

Instead, he found the number in the phone book, dropped a dime in the slot, and called WCBL-TV.

He had nearly as much trouble getting Louise on the line as he had getting in to see Arthur J. Nelson, but finally her voice came over the line.

"Dutton."

Peter could hear voices and sounds in the background. Wherever she was, it wasn't a private office.

"Hi," Peter said.

"Hi," she breathed happily. "I hoped you would call!"

"You all right?"

"Ginger-peachy, now," she said. "What are you doing?"

"I just left Arthur J. Nelson," he said.

"Rough?"

"He told me you were Jerome's girlfriend," Peter said.

"Oh, the poor man!" she said. "You didn't say anything?"

"No."

"So?"

"So?" he parroted.

"So why did you call?"

"I dunno," he said.

"What are you going to do now?" she asked.

"I've got to go by my office, and then figure out some way to get my car from where it's parked in front of your house," he said.

"I forgot about that," she said. "Why don't you pick me up here after I do the news at six? I could drive it to your place, or wherever."

"Where would I meet you?"

"Come on in," Louise said. "I'll tell them at reception."

"Okay," he said. "Thank you."

"Don't be silly," she said, and then added, "Peter, don't forget to pick up your uniform at the cleaners."

"Okay," he said, and chuckled, and the line went dead.

He realized, as he hung the telephone up, that he was smiling. More than that, he was very happy. There was something very touching, very intimate, in her concern that he not forget to pick up his uniform. Then he thought that if he had called Barbara Crowley and *she* had reminded him of it, he would have been annoyed.

Is this what being in love is like?

He went out of his way to get the uniform before he drove downtown, so that he really would not forget it.

He had not been at his desk in his office three minutes when Chief Inspector Dennis V. Coughlin slipped into the chair beside it.

"Jeannie was asking where you were last night, Peter," Coughlin said. "At the house."

"I wasn't up to it," Peter said. "And you know what happened later."

"You feel up to being a pallbearer?" Coughlin asked, evenly.

"If Jeannie wants me to, sure," Peter said.

"That's what I told her," Coughlin said. "Be at Marshutz & Sons about half past nine. The funeral's at eleven."

"I'll be there," Peter said. "Chief, my dad suggested I wear my uniform."

Chief Inspector Coughlin thought that over a moment.

"What did you decide about it?"

"Until I heard about being a pallbearer, I was going to wear it."

"I think it would nice, Peter, if we carried Dutch to his rest in uniform," Chief Inspector Coughlin said. "I'll call the wife and make sure mine's pressed."

Officer Anthony F. Caragiola, who was headed for the job on the four-to-midnight watch, glanced at his wristwatch, and walked into Gene & Jerry's Restaurant & Sandwiches across the street from the Bridge Street Terminal. There would be time for a cup of coffee and a sweet roll before he climbed the stairs to catch the elevated and go to work.

Officer Caragiola, who wore the white cap of the Traffic Division, had been a policeman for eleven years, and was now thirty-four years old. He was a large and swarthy man, whose skin showed the ravages of being outside day after day in heat and cold, rain and shine.

He eased his bulk onto one of the round stools at the counter, waved his fingers in greeting at the waitress, a stout, blond woman, and helped himself to a sweet roll from the glass case. He had lived three blocks away, now with his wife and four kids, for most of his life. When there was a problem at Gene & Jerry's, if one of the waitresses took sick, or one of the cooks, and his wife, Maria, could get somebody to watch the kids, she came and filled in.

The waitress put a china mug of coffee and three half-and-half containers in front of him.

"So how's it going?"

"Can't complain," Officer Caragiola said. "Yourself?"

She shrugged and smiled and walked away. Tony Caragiola carefully opened the three tubs of half-and-half and carefully poured them into his coffee, and then stirred it.

He heard a hissing noise, and looked at the black swinging doors leading to the kitchen. Gene was standing there, wiggling her fingers at him. Gene was Eugenia Santalvaria, a stout, black-haired woman in her fifties who had six months before buried her husband, Gerimino, after thirty-three years of marriage.

Caragiola slipped off the stool and, carrying his coffee with him, stepped behind the counter and walked to the doors to the kitchen.

"Tony, maybe it's something, maybe it ain't," Gene Santalvaria said, in English, and then switched to Italian. There were two bums outside, a big fat slob and a little guy that looked like a spic, she told him. They had been there for hours, sitting in an old Volkswagen. Maybe they were going to stick up the check-cashing place down the block, or maybe they were selling dope or something; every once in a while, one of them got out of the car and went up the stairs to the elevated, and then a couple of minutes later came back down the stairs and got back in the car. She didn't want to call the district, 'cause maybe it wasn't nothing, but since he had come in, she thought it was better she tell him.

"I'll have a look," Officer Caragiola said.

He left the kitchen and walked to the front of the restaurant and, sipping on his coffee, looked for a Volkswagen. There was two guys in it, one of them, a big fat slob with one of them hippie bands around his forehead, behind the wheel, slumped down in the seat as if he was asleep. And then the passenger door opened, and a little guy—she was right, he looked like a spic—got out and looked for traffic, and then walked across the street to the stairs to the elevated. Looked like a mean little fucker.

Officer Caragiola set his coffee on the counter and walked quickly out of Gene & Jerry's, and across the street, and up the stairs after him.

He got to the platform just as a train arrived. Everybody on the platform got on it but the little spic. He acted as if he was waiting for somebody who might have ridden the elevated to the end of the line and just stayed on. If he did that, he would just go back downtown. If somebody like that was either buying or selling dope, that would be the way to do it.

Officer Caragiola ducked behind a stairwell so the little spic couldn't see him, and waited. People started coming up the stairs, filling up the platform, and then a train arrived from downtown and left, and then five minutes later reappeared on the downtown track. Everybody on the platform got on the train but the little spic.

Tony Caragiola came out from behind the stairwell and walked over to the little spic.

"Speak to you a minute, buddy?" he said.

"What about?"

Tony saw that the little spic was pissed. He probably knew all the civil rights laws about cops not being supposed to ask questions without reasonable cause.

"You want to tell me what you and your friend in the Volkswagen are doing?"

"Narcotics," the little spic said. "I'd rather not show you my I.D. Not here."

"Who's your lieutenant?" Tony asked.

"Lieutenant Pekach."

It was a name Officer Caragiola did not recognize.

"I think you better show me your ID," he said.

"Shit," the little spic said. He reached in his back pocket and came out with a plastic identity card. "Okay?" he said.

"The lady in the restaurant said you were acting suspicious," Tony Caragiola said.

"Yeah, I'll bet."

Officer Jesus Martinez put his ID back in his pocket and walked down the stairs. Officer Anthony Caragiola walked twenty feet behind him. He went back in Gene & Jerry's and told Gene everything was all right, not to worry about it. Then he went back across the street and climbed the stairs to catch the elevated to go to work.

Officer Martinez got back into the Volkswagen. He glowered for a full minute at Officer Charley McFadden, who was asleep and snoring. Then he jabbed him, hard, with his fingers, in his ribs. McFadden sat up, a look of confusion on his face.

"What's up?"

"I thought you would like to know, asshole, that the lady in the restaurant called the cops on us. Said we look suspicious."

At quarter to five, Peter Wohl drove to Marshutz & Sons. As he walked up the wide steps to the Victorian-style building, the Moffitts—Jean, the kids, and Dutch's mother—came out.

Jean Moffitt was wearing a black dress and a hat with a veil. The kids were in suits. Gertrude Moffitt was in a black dress and hat, but no veil.

"Hello, Peter," Jean Moffitt said, and offered a gloved hand.

"Jeannie," Peter said.

"You know Mother Moffitt, don't you?"

"Yes, of course," Peter said. "Good afternoon, Mrs. Moffitt."

"We're going out for a bite to eat," Gertrude Moffitt said. "Before people start coming after work."

"I'm very sorry, Mrs. Moffitt, about Dick," Peter said.

"His close personal friends, some of who I didn't even know," Gertrude Moffitt went on, "were at the house last night."

It was a rebuke.

"I'm sorry I couldn't come by last night, Jeannie," Peter said.

"Your mother explained," Jeannie Moffitt said. "Did Denny Coughlin ask you?"

"About being a pallbearer?" Peter asked, and when she nodded, went on: "Yes, and I'm honored."

"Dennis Coughlin was a sergeant when he carried my John, God rest his soul, to his grave," Gertrude Moffitt said. "And now, as a chief inspector, he'll be doing the same for my Richard."

"Mother, would you please put the kids in the car?" Jean Moffitt said. "I want a word with Inspector Wohl."

That earned Jeannie a dirty look from Mother Moffitt, but it didn't seem to faze her. She returned the older woman's look, staring her down until she led the boys down the stairs.

"Tell me about the TV lady, Peter," Jeannie Moffitt said.

"I beg your pardon?"

"Isn't that why you didn't come by the house last night? You were afraid I'd ask you?"

"I don't know what you're talking about, Jeannie," Wohl said.

"I'm talking about Louise Dutton of Channel Nine," she said. "Was there something between her and Dutch? I have to know."

"Where did you hear that?"

"It's going around," she said. "I heard it."

"Well, you heard wrong," Peter said.

"You sound pretty sure," Jeannie Moffitt accused sarcastically.

"I know for sure," Peter said.

"Peter, don't lie to me," Jeannie said.

"Louise Dutton and me, as my mother would put it, if she knew, and doesn't, are 'keeping company,' " Wohl said. "That's how I know."

Her eyes widened in surprise.

"Really?" she said, and he knew she believed him.

"Not for public consumption," Peter said. "The gossips got their facts wrong. Wrong cop."

"I thought you were seeing that nurse, what's her name, Barbara—"

"Crowley," Peter furnished. "I was."

"Your mother doesn't know?"

"And, for the time being, I would like to keep it that way," Peter said.

She looked in his eyes, and then stood on her toes and kissed his cheek.

"Oh, I'm glad I ran into you," she said.

"Dutch liked being married to you, Jeannie," Wohl said.

"Oh, God, I hope so," she said.

She turned and ran down the stairs.

Wohl entered the funeral home. The corridors were crowded with people, a third of the men in uniform. And, Peter thought, two-thirds of the men in civilian clothing were cops, too.

He waited in line, signed the guest book, and then made his way to the Green Room.

Dutch's casket was nearly hidden by flowers, and there was a uniformed Highway Patrolman standing at parade rest at each end of the coffin. Wohl waited in line again, until it was his turn to drop to his knees at the prie-dieu in front of the casket.

Without thinking about it, he crossed himself. Dutch was in uniform. *He looks,* Wohl thought, *as if he just came from the barber's.*

And then he had another irreverent thought: *I just covered your ass again, Dutch. One last time.*

And then, surprising him, his throat grew very tight, and he felt his eyes start to tear.

He stayed there, with his head bent, until he was sure he was in control of himself, and then got up.

12 Karl August Fenstermacher had immigrated to the United States in 1837, at the age of two. His father had indentured himself for a period of four years to Fritz W. Diehl, who had gone to the United States from the same village, Mochsdorf, in the Kingdom of Bavaria, twenty years previously. Mr. Diehl had entered the sausage business in Philadelphia, and prospered to the point where he needed good reliable help. His brother Adolph, back in Mochsdorf, had recommended Johann Fenstermacher to him, and the deal was struck:

Diehl would provide passage money for Fenstermacher and his wife and three children, provide living quarters for them over the shop, and see that they were clothed and fed. At the end of four years, provided Fenstermacher proved to be a faithful, hardworking employee, he would either offer young Fenstermacher a position with the firm, or give him one hundred dollars, so that he could make his way in life somewhere else.

At the end of two years, instead of the called-for four, Fritz released Johann Fenstermacher from his indenture, coinciding with the opening of Fritz's stall (Fritz Diehl Fine Wurstware & Fresh Meats) at the Twelfth Street Market. In 1860, when Diehl opened an abbatoir just outside the city limits, the firm was Diehl & Fenstermacher, Meat Purveyors to the Trade. Both men believed that God had been as good to them as he could be.

They were wrong. The Civil War came, and with it a limitless demand for smoked and tinned meats and hides. They became wealthy. Fritz Diehl took a North German Lloyd steamer from Philadelphia to Bremen, and went back to Mochsdorf, where he presented St. Johann's Lutheran Church with a stained-glass window. He died of a stroke in Mochsdorf ten days before the window was to be officially consecrated.

His widow elected to remain in Germany. From that day until her death, Johann Fenstermacher scrupulously sent her half the profits from the firm, although, after several years, he changed the name to J. Fenstermacher & Sons. The name was retained on the Old Man's death, just before the Spanish-American War, by Karl Fenstermacher, who bought out his brother's interest, and formed J. Fenstermacher & Sons, Incorporated.

He turned over the business to his son Fritz in 1910, when he was seventy-five. He lived six more years. In early 1916, when it was clear that his father was failing, Fritz Fenstermacher went to Francisco Scalamandre, whose firm was to stonecutting in Philadelphia what J. Fenstermacher & Sons, Inc., was to the meat trade, and ordered the construction of a suitable monument where his mother and father could lie together for eternity.

It was erected in Cedar Hill Cemetery on Cheltenham Avenue in Northeast Philadelphia, of the finest Barre, Vermont, granite. Mr. Scalamandre's elder son Guigliemo himself sculpted the ten-foot-tall statue of the Angel Gabriel, arms spread, which was mounted on the roof of the tomb, and personally supervised the installation of both the stained glass windows and the solid bronze doors.

Karl Fenstermacher was laid to his last rest there on December 11, 1916, in a snowstorm. His wife followed him in death, and into the tomb, eight months later.

They lay there together, undisturbed, in bronze caskets in a marble tomb behind the solid bronze doors until several months before the shooting in the Waikiki Diner, when Gerald Vincent Gallagher, running away from both the police and an Afro-American dealer in heroin, found himself leaning against the solid bronze doors.

It wasn't safe to leave the cemetery yet, Gerald Vincent Gallagher had decided; then both the cops and the jigaboo were really after his ass, but unless he could get inside somewhere, out of the fucking wind and snow, he was going to freeze to fucking death.

Gerald Vincent Gallagher had managed, without much effort at all, to pick the solid bronze lock mechanism on the solid brass door with a sharpened screwdriver he just happened to have with him; and he had spent the next four hours sitting, shivering but not freezing, and out of the snow, on top of Karl Fenstermacher's tomb.

The next time he went back to Cedar Hill Cemetery, he was prepared. He had cans of Sterno with him, and a dozen big, thick, white, pure beeswax candles he had lifted from St. George's Greek Orthodox Church. Both burned without smoke, and it was amazing how much heat that jelly alcohol, or whatever the fuck it was, made.

And the first thing Gerald Vincent Gallagher had thought when he ran out of the Waikiki Diner was that if he could only make it to the fucking cemetery, he would be all right. It was not the first, or the fifth, time he had run from the cops and hidden in the cemetery until things cooled off.

When he was in Karl and Maria Fenstermacher's mausoleum, and the fear was mostly gone, and he got his breath back, and he had time to think things over, the first thing he thought was that when he got together with Dorothy Ann again, he really should kick the dumb bitch's ass. All she was supposed to do was stay outside and look out for the cops. Now she'd really gotten their ass in a crack. All the charge would have been was robbery. There was nothing like that on his record. Any public defender with half the brains he was born with could have plea-bargained that down to something that would have meant no more than a year in Holmesburg Prison, and with a little bit of luck, maybe even probation.

But the minute she had fired that fucking gun, she had really got them in fucking trouble. About the dumbest fucking thing she could have done was take a shot at a cop. That made it attempted murder, and the goddamned cops would pull every string they could to get them sent before Judge Mitchell "Hanging Mitch" Roberts, who thought that taking a poke, much less a shot, at a cop was worse than blowing up the Vatican with the pope in it.

Thank Christ, she had missed. The last thing he saw when he ran through the Waikiki Diner was the cop, or the detective, whatever the sonofabitch was, was him shooting Dorothy Ann. If she had hit the sonofabitch, that would be the goddamned end. He would be an old man before they let him out.

Another thought entered his mind. Maybe the cop had hit her and killed her when he shot back. It would serve the dumb bitch right, and if she was dead, she couldn't identify him. The cashier had been scared shitless; she wouldn't be able to remember him, much less identify him. The best thing that could have happened was that both Dorothy Ann and the cop was both dead. Then nobody could identify him.

The trouble with that was there was *another* fucking law that said if anybody got killed during a robbery, or some other felony, even somebody doing the robbery, it was just as if they had shot him theirselves. So if the cop had killed Dorothy Ann, they could hang a murder rap on him.

In the times he had been in the mausoleum before (almost for a way to pass the time), Gerald Vincent Gallagher had taken his screwdriver and worked on the lead that held the little pieces of stained glass in place, so that he could remove a little piece of glass and have a look around. There was stained glass in all four walls of the place.

He hadn't been in the mausoleum half an hour before he saw, through the hole where he'd taken a piece of stained glass out, a police car driving slowly through Cedar Hill Cemetery. Not just a police car, but a Highway Patrol car, he could tell that because there was two cops in it, and regular cop cars had only one cop in them. Those Highway Patrol cops was real mean motherfuckers, who would as soon shoot you as not.

He told himself that there was really nothing to worry about, that it wasn't the first time a cop car had driven through the cemetery looking for him, and they wouldn't find him this time any more than they had before. They were thinking he might be hiding behind a tombstone, or a tree, or something. They wouldn't think he was inside one of the marble houses, or whatever the fuck they were called. They would drive through once, or maybe twice, or maybe a couple of cop cars would drive through. But they would give up sooner or later.

Everybody would give up sooner or later. This wasn't the only robbery that had happened in Philadelphia. There would be other robberies and auto accidents on Roosevelt Boulevard and Frankford Avenue, or some guy beating up on his wife, and they would go put their noses into that and ease off on looking for him.

The thing to do was sit tight until they did ease off, and then get the fuck out of town. He had money, 380 bucks. The reason they had stuck up the Waikiki Diner in the first place was to come up with another lousy 120 bucks. The connection had shit, good shit, but he wanted 500 bucks, and wasn't about to trust them for the 120 they was short, until they sold enough of it on the street to pay him back.

If the cocksucker had only been reasonable, none of this would have happened!

Gerald Vincent Gallagher began to suspect, although he tried not to think about it, that he was really in the deep shit when not only did more cop cars, Highway Patrol and regular District ones, keep driving through the cemetery, but cops on foot came walking through. That had never happened before.

There was no place he could run to, so he put the little pieces of stained glass back into the holes, and sat down on the floor with his back against the wall and just hoped no one would come looking for him inside.

It grew dark, and that made things a little better, but he decided that the best thing to do was play it cool, and not light one of the Greek candles. If there was a cop looking, he would maybe see the light.

He took off his jacket and made a pillow of it, and lay down on the floor of the mausoleum and went to sleep.

Sometime in the middle of the night, he woke up, and looked out, and saw headlights coming into the cemetery. Then the car stopped and the headlights went out. A couple of minutes later, while he was still figuring out what the first car was doing, there were more headlights, and another car drove in. He saw that the first car was a cop car, and now he could see they were both cop cars. And a few minutes after that, a third cop car came in and parked beside the other two.

And then he understood what was going on. *The cops were fucking off, that's what they were doing! They were supposed to be out patrolling the streets, looking for crooks, and instead they were in the goddamned cemetery, taking a fucking nap!*

Gerald Vincent Gallagher was outraged at this blatant example of dereliction of duty.

In the morning, he woke up hungry, but it would be a goddamned fool thing to do to try to leave just yet, so he just waited. At noon, there was a funeral about a hundred yards away. Actually, they started getting ready for the funeral a little after eight, digging the hole, and then lowering a concrete vault in it, and then putting the phony grass over the pile of dirt they'd taken out of the hole, and then putting up a tent, and the whatever it was called they used to lower the casket into the hole.

Gerald Vincent Gallagher had never seen anything like that before, and it was interesting, and it helped to pass the time. So did the funeral. It was some kind of cockamamie Protestant funeral, and the minister prayed a lot, and loud, and then when that was finally over, everybody who had come to the funeral just stayed around the hole, kissing and shaking hands, and talking and smiling, like they was at a party, instead of a funeral.

Finally, they left, and the people from the funeral home put some kind of a lever into the machine with the casket sitting on it, and the casket started dropping into the hole. When it was all the way in, they unhitched one end of the green web belts that had held the casket up, and pulled them free from under the casket.

A truck appeared and they put the machine on it, and then the folding chairs, and then took down the tent and loaded that on, and finally picked up the phony grass and put that on the truck. Then that truck left, and the one that had lowered the concrete vault into the hole appeared again. A guy got out and mixed cement or something in a plastic bucket, and then got into the hole with the bucket and a trowel and spread the cement on the bottom of the vault. Then they lowered the lid on the vault, jumped up and down on the lid, and then they left.

Next came a couple of old men from the cemetery who shoveled the dirt into the hole, wetting it down with a hose so that it would all go back in, and finally putting the real grass on top of that and watering *that* down. There was still a lot of dirt left over, and Gerald Vincent Gallagher supposed they would come back and cart that off somewhere.

By then it was four o'clock, and he was fucking *starved!*

He was just about to leave the mausoleum when a car drove up, and three people got out. It looked to him like a father and his two sons. They walked over to the grave and the old man stood there for a minute and started to cry. Then the younger ones started to cry. Finally, the younger ones put their arms around the older one, the one who was probably the father, and led him back to the car and drove off.

Gerald Vincent Gallagher waited until he was sure they wouldn't change their minds and come back, and looked carefully in all four directions to make sure there wasn't a cop car making another slow trip through Cedar Hill, and then, after first carefully replacing all the stained glass, and bending the lead over it so the wind wouldn't blow it out, quickly opened the bronze doors, grunting with the effort, grunted again as he pushed them closed, and then started walking to the narrow macadam road that led to the exit.

He passed the grave he had watched filled. There were what he guessed must be a thousand bucks' worth of flowers on it, and around it, just waiting to rot. He thought that was a hell of a lot of money to be just thrown away like that.

Five minutes later he was at the Bridge & Pratt Streets Terminal. A clock in a store window said ten minutes after five. This had worked out okay. The terminal, and the subway itself, would be crowded with people coming from work, or going downtown. He could hide in the crowd. He would be careful, when the train pulled into the station, to look for any cop that might be on it, and make sure he didn't get on that car.

Then he would ride downtown to Market Street, walk underground to the Suburban Station, and ride from there to Thirtieth Street Station. There he would buy a ticket on the Pennsylvania Railroad to Baltimore. He would find out when it left, and then go to the men's crapper, where he would stay until it was time for the train to leave. Then a quick trip up to the platform, onto the train, and he would be home free.

In Baltimore, he knew a couple of connections, if they were still in business, and he could get a little something to straighten him out. He was getting a little edgy, that way, and that would be the first thing to do, get himself straightened out. And then he would decide what to do next.

He walked past a place called Tates, where the smell of pizza made his stomach turn. He stopped and went to the window and ordered a slice of pizza and a Coke. When the Coke came, he drank it down. He hadn't realized he had been that thirsty.

"Do that again," he said, pushing the container toward the kid behind the counter, and laying another dollar bill on the counter. There was a newsstand right beside Tates called—somebody thought he was a fucking wit—Your Newsstand.

Gerald Vincent Gallagher drank some of the second Coke, then set the container down on the top of a garbage can and, taking a bite of the pizza, stepped to a newspaper rack offering the *Philadelphia Daily News,* to get a quick look at the headline, maybe there would be something about the Waikiki Diner in it.

There was. There were two photographs on the front page. One was of some cop in uniform, and the other was of Gerald Vincent Gallagher. The headline, in great big letters, asked, "COP KILLER?"

Under the photographs was a story that began, *"A massive citywide search is on for Gerald Vincent Gallagher, suspected of being the bandit who got away when Police Captain Richard C. Moffitt was shot to death in the Waikiki Diner yesterday."*

Gerald Vincent Gallagher's stomach tied in a painful knot. He felt a cold chill, and as if the hair on his neck was crawling. He spit out the piece of pizza he had been chewing, and carefully laid the piece in his hand on the garbage can beside the Coke container.

Then he started walking past Your Newsstand. At the end of the building was a glass door leading to a bingo parlor upstairs, and then the covered stairs to the subway platform.

Gerald Vincent Gallagher looked at the door and saw in it a reflection of the street. And something caught his eye. A big, fat sonofabitch was looking right at him as he came running across the street. The fat guy looked familiar and for a moment, Gerald Vincent Gallagher thought he was a guy he had done business with, but then the fat guy sort of kneeled down, and jerked up his pants leg, and pulled a gun from an ankle holster.

Then, as he started running again, he shouted, "Hold it right there, Gallagher, or I'll blow your ass away!"

Fuck him, Gerald Vincent Gallagher thought. *That fucking narc isn't going to shoot that gun with all these people around!*

He ran up the stairs toward the subway platform. With a little bit of luck, there would be a train there and he could get on it, and away.

The Bridge & Pratt Streets Terminal is the end of the line for the subway. The tracks are elevated, above Frankford Avenue, and widen as they reach the station. There is a center passenger platform, with stairs leading down to the lower level of the terminal, between the tracks, and a second passenger platform, to the right of the center platform. That way, passengers can exit incoming from downtown trains through doors on both sides of the car. Passengers heading downtown all have to board trains from the center platform.

After incoming trains from downtown Philadelphia off-load their passengers from the right (in direction of movement) track, they move several hundred yards farther on, where they stop, the crews move to the rear end of the train (which now becomes the front end), and move back, now on the left track, to the station, where they pick up downtown-bound passengers.

The lower level of the terminal contains ticket booths, and two stairwells, one descending to the ground on either side of Frankford Avenue.

When Officer Charley McFadden spotted Gerald Vincent Gallagher shoving pizza in his face in front of Your Newsstand, he was sitting in his Volkswagen, which was parked in front of Gene & Jerry's Restaurant & Sandwiches on Pratt Street, fifty feet to the north of Frankford Avenue.

Officer Jesus Martinez was inside Gene & Jerry's sitting at the counter eating a ham and cheese sandwich, no mayonnaise or mustard or butter, just the ham and cheese and maybe a little piece of lettuce on whole wheat bread.

He had his mouth full of ham and cheese when he saw Charley erupt from the Volkswagen.

He swore, in Spanish, and spit out the sandwich, and jumped up and ran toward the door. As soon as he was through it, he dropped to his knees and drew his pistol from his ankle holster.

He had not seen Gerald Vincent Gallagher, but he knew that Charley McFadden must have seen him, for Charley, moving with speed remarkable for his bulk, was now headed up the stairs to the subway station.

Two cars and a truck, going like the hammers of hell, delayed Officer Martinez's passage across Pratt Street by thirty seconds. By the time he made it across, Charley McFadden was nowhere in sight. All he could see was people with wide eyes wondering what the fuck was going on.

"Police! Police!" Officer Martinez shouted as he forced his way through a crowd of people trying to leave the station.

He jumped over the turnstile, and then was forced to make a choice between stairs leading to the tracks for trains arriving *from* downtown and tracks for trains *headed* downtown. Deciding that it would be far more likely that McFadden and whoever it was he was chasing—almost certainly, Gerald Vincent Gallagher—would be on the downtown platform, he ran up those stairs.

Officer McFadden, who had lost sight of Gerald Vincent Gallagher as he ran up the stairs from Pratt Street, had made the same decision. Already starting to puff a little, he ran onto the platform. A downtown train had just pulled into the station; the platform was crowded with people in the process of boarding it.

Holding his pistol at the level of his head, muzzle pointed toward the sky, Charley McFadden ran down the train looking for Gallagher. He had reached the last car, and hadn't seen him, and had just about decided the little fucker was on the train, that he had missed him, and would have to start at the first car and work his way back through it when he did see him.

Gallagher was in the middle of the tracks, the other tracks, the incoming from downtown tracks. As McFadden ran to the side of the center platform, Gerald Vincent Gallagher boosted himself up on the platform on the far side.

It had been his intention to run back down the stairs and get onto Frankford Avenue, where he could lose himself in the crowd. The narc, Gerald Vincent Gallagher reasoned, would not dare use his pistol because of all the fucking people on the lower level of the terminal and on Frankford Avenue.

But Gallagher had spotted him, and there was no way he could run back toward the station, because there were no people on that platform, and the goddamned narc would feel free to shoot at him. He turned, instead, and ran down the platform in the other direction, to the end, and jumped over a yellow painted barrier with a sign on it reading DANGER! KEEP OFF!

Beyond the barrier was a narrow workman's walkway. It ran as far as the next station, but Gerald Vincent Gallagher wasn't planning on running that far, just maybe two, three, blocks where he knew there was a stairway, more of a ladder, really, he could climb down to Frankford Avenue.

He looked over his shoulder and saw that the fucking narc was doing what he had done, crossing the tracks and then boosting himself up onto the passenger platform. The big fat sonofabitch had trouble hauling all that lard onto the platform, and for a moment, the way the fucking narc was flailing around with his legs trying to get up on the platform, Gerald Vincent Gallagher thought he might get lucky and the narc's legs would touch the third rail, and the cocksucker would fry himself.

But that didn't happen.

Officer McFadden got first to his knees, and then stood up. Holding his pistol in both hands, he took aim at Gerald Vincent Gallagher.

But he didn't pull the trigger. Heaving and panting the way he was, there was little chance that he could hit the little sonofabitch as far away as he was, and Christ only knew where the bullet would go after he fired. Probably get some nun between the eyes.

"You little sonofabitch! I'm going to get your ass!" he screamed in fury, and started racing after him again.

Officer Jesus Martinez reached the center platform at this time. He knew from the direction people were looking where the action was, and ran down the center platform to the end.

He saw Officer McFadden first, and then, fifty, sixty yards ahead of him, a slight white male that almost certainly had to be Gerald Vincent Gallagher. They were running, carefully, along the walkway next to the rail.

The reason they were running carefully was that the walkway was over the third rail. The walkway was built of short lengths, about five feet long, of prefabricated pieces. Some of them, the real old ones, were heavy wooden planking. Some of the newer ones were pierced steel, and the most modern were of exposed aggregate cement. They provided a precarious perch in any event, and they were not designed to be foot-racing paths.

Officer Martinez made another snap decision. There was no way he could catch up with them, and even to try would mean that he would have to jump down and cross the tracks, and risk electrocuting himself on the third rail. But he could catch the departing train, ride to the next station, and then start walking back. That would put Gerald Vincent Gallagher between them.

He ran for the train and jumped inside, just as the doors closed.

He scared hell, with his pistol drawn, out of the people on the car, and they backed away from him as if he was on fire.

"I'm a police officer," he said, not very loudly because he was out of breath. "Nothing to worry about."

When the train passed Charley McFadden and Gerald Vincent Gallagher, they were both still running very carefully, watching their feet.

Jesus Christ, Charley, shoot the sonofabitch!

The same thought had occurred to Charley McFadden at just about that moment, and even as he ran, he wondered why he didn't stop running, drop to his knees, and, using a two-handed hold, try to put Gerald Vincent Gallagher down.

There were several reasons, and they all came to him. For one thing, he wasn't at all sure that he could hit him. For another, he was worried about where the bullet, the bullets, plural, would go if he missed. People lived close to the tracks here. He didn't want to kill one of them.

And then he realized the real reason. He didn't *want* to kill Gerald Vincent Gallagher. The little shit might deserve it, and it might mean that Officer Charley McFadden didn't have the balls to be a cop, but the facts were that Gerald Vincent Gallagher didn't have a gun—if he had, the little shit would have used it, he had nothing to lose from a second charge of murder—and wasn't posing, right now, any real threat to anybody but himself, running down the tracks like this.

Hay-zus must have figured out what was going on by now, and got on the radio and called for help. In a couple of minutes, there would be cops responding from all over. All he had to do was keep Gerald Vincent Gallagher in sight, and keep him from hurting himself or somebody else, and everything would be all right.

Eighteen hundred and fifty-three feet (as was later measured with great care) south of the Bridge & Pratt Streets Terminal, Gerald Vincent Gallagher realized that he could not run another ten feet. His chest hurt so much he wanted to cry from the pain. And that big, fat, fucking narc was still on his tail.

Gerald Vincent Gallagher stopped running, and turned around and grabbed the railing beside the walkway, and dropped to his knees.

"I give up," he said. "For Christ's sake, don't shoot me!"

Officer Charley McFadden could understand what he said, even the way he said it puffing and out of breath.

Unable to speak himself, he walked up the walkway, heaving with the exertion.

And then he raised his arm, the left one, without the pistol, and pointed down the track, and tried to find his voice. What he wanted to say was "Watch out, there's a train coming!"

He couldn't find his voice, but Gerald Vincent Gallagher took his meaning. He looked over his shoulder at the approaching train. And tried to get to his feet, so that he would be able to hold on to the railing good and tight as the train passed.

And he slipped.

And he fell onto the tracks.

And he put his hand out as a reflex motion, to break his fall, and his wrist found the third rail and Gerald Vincent Gallagher fried.

And then the train came, and all four cars rolled over him.

When Officer Jesus Martinez came down the walkway, he found Officer Charley McFadden bent over the railing, sick white in the face, and covered with vomitus.

Michael J. "Mickey" O'Hara had worked, at one time or another, for all the newspapers in Philadelphia, and had ventured as far afield as New York City and Washington, D.C.

He was an "old-time" reporter, and even something of a legend, although he was just past forty. He looked older than forty. Mickey liked a drop of the grape whenever he could get his hands on one, and that was the usual reason his employment had been terminated; for in his cups Mickey O'Hara was prone not only to describing the character flaws and ancestry of his superiors in picaresque profanity worthy of a cavalry sergeant, but also, depending on the imagined level of provocation and the amount of alcohol in his system, to punch them out.

But on the other hand, Mickey O'Hara was, when off the sauce, one hell of a reporter. He had what some believe to be the genetic Irish talent for storytelling. He could breathe life into a story that otherwise really wouldn't deserve repeating. He was also a master practitioner of his craft, which was journalism generally and the police beat specifically. His car was equipped with a very elaborate shortwave receiver permitting Mickey to listen in to police communications.

Mickey had come to know a lot of cops in twenty years, and although he was technically not a member of either organization, if there was an affair of the Emerald Society or the Fraternal Order of Police and Mickey O'Hara was not there, people wondered, with concern, if he was sick or something.

Mickey liked most cops and most cops liked Mickey. Mickey, however, considered few cops above the grade of sergeant as *cops*. The cant of the law-enforcement community gets in the way here. All policemen are police officers, which means they are executing an office for the government.

There is a rank structure in the police department, paralleling that of the army, even to the insignia of rank. So far as Mickey was concerned, anybody in the rank of lieutenant or higher (a *white-shirt*) was not really a cop, but a brass hat, a member of the establishment. There were exceptions to this, of course. Mickey was very fond of Chief Inspector Matt Lowenstein, for example, and had used his considerable influence with the managing editor to see that when Lowenstein's boys were bar mitzvahed, those socioreligious events had been prominently featured in the paper.

And he had liked Dutch Moffitt. There were a few others, a captain here, a lieutenant there, whom Mickey liked, even including Staff Inspector Peter Wohl, but by and large he considered anyone who wore a white shirt with his uniform to be much like the officers he had known and actively disliked in the army.

He liked the guys—the ordinary patrolmen and the corporals and detectives and sergeants—on the street, and they liked him. He got their pictures in the paper, with their names spelled right, and he never violated a confidence.

Mickey O'Hara had just gone to work when he heard the call, *"man with a gun at the El terminal at Frankford and Pratt."* That is to say, he had just left Mulvaney's Tap Room at Tabor and Rising Sun Avenues, where he had had two beers and nobly refused the offer of a third, and gotten in his car to drive downtown, where he planned to begin the day by dropping by the Ninth District police station.

Almost immediately, there were other calls. Another Fifteenth District car was ordered to the Margaret-Orthodox Station, which was the next station, headed downtown, from Bridge and Pratt Streets, and then right after that came an *"assist officer"* call, and then a warning that plainclothes officers were on the scene. Finally, there was a call for the rescue squad and the fire department.

Mickey O'Hara decided that whatever was happening between the Pratt & Bridge Streets Terminal and the Margaret-Orthodox Station might be worthy of his professional attention.

He went down to Roosevelt Boulevard, turned left, and entered the center lane. He drove fast, but not recklessly, weaving skillfully through traffic, cursing and being cursed in turn by the drivers of more slowly moving vehicles. He went around the bend at Friends' Hospital, slipped into the outside lane, and made a right turn, through a red light, onto Bridge Street.

When Mickey O'Hara got to the Bridge & Pratt Streets Terminal, he found a crowd of people who were being kept from going up the stairs to the El station by four or five cops under the supervision of a sergeant.

He caught the eye of the sergeant, winked, and shrugged his shoulders in a "what's up?" gesture.

A moment later, the sergeant shouldered his way through the crowd.

"Undercover Narcotics guy spotted the kid who shot Dutch Moffitt," the sergeant said instead of a greeting when they shook hands. "He took off down the tracks, with the undercover chasing him, and fell off the walkway, fried himself on the third rail, and then got himself run over by a train."

"Jesus!" Mickey O'Hara said.

"They're still up there," the sergeant said.

"Is there anyway I can get up there?" Mickey asked.

"Watch out for the third rail, Mick," the sergeant said.

 Ward V. Fengler, who had three months before been named a partner of Mawson, Payne, Stockton, McAdoo & Lester (there were seventeen partners, in addition to the five senior partners), pushed open the glass door from the Butler Aviation waiting room at Philadelphia International Airport and walked onto the tarmac as the Bell Ranger helicopter touched down.

Fengler was very tall and very thin and, at thirty-two, already evidencing male pattern baldness. He had spent most of the day, from ten o'clock onward, waiting around the airport for Mr. Wells.

Stanford Fortner Wells III got out of the helicopter, and then turned to reach for his luggage. He was a small man, intense, graying, superbly tailored. The temple piece of a set of horn-rimmed glasses hung outside the pocket of his glen plaid suit.

"Mr. Wells, I'm Ward Fengler of Mawson, Payne, Stockton, McAdoo and Lester," Fengler said. "Colonel Mawson asked me to meet you."

Wells examined him quickly but carefully and put out his hand.

"Sorry to have kept you waiting like this," he said. "First, we had to land in New-foundland, and then when we got to New York, the goddamned airport, I suppose predictably, was stacked to heaven's basement."

"I hope you had a good flight," Fengler said.

"I hate airplanes," Wells said, matter-of-factly.

"We have a car," Fengler said. "And Colonel Mawson has put you up in the War-wick. I hope that's all right."

"Fine," Wells said. "Has Mawson talked to Kruger?"

"I don't know, sir."

"The reason I asked is that someone is to meet me at the Warwick."

"I don't know anything about that, sir."

"Then maybe something is finally breaking right," Wells said. "The Warwick's fine."

The only thing Stanford Fortner Wells III said on the ride downtown was to make the announcement that he used to come to Philadelphia when he was at Princeton.

"And I went from Philadelphia to Princeton," Fengler said.

Wells grunted, and smiled.

When they reached the hotel, Wells got quickly out of the limousine and hurried across the sidewalk, up the stairs, and through the door to the lobby. Fengler scurried after him.

There was a television monitor mounted on the wall above the receptionist's desk at WCBL-TV when Peter Wohl walked in. "Nine's News" at six was on, and Louise Dutton was looking right into the camera.

My God, she's good-looking!

"May I help you?" the receptionist asked.

"My name is Wohl," Peter said. "I'm here to see Miss Dutton."

The receptionist smiled at him, and picked up a light blue telephone.

"Sharon," she said. "Inspector Wohl is here." Then she looked at Wohl. "She'll be right with you, Inspector."

Sharon turned out to be a startlingly good-looking young woman, with dark eyes and long dark hair, and a marvelous set of knockers. Her smile was dazzling.

"Right this way, Inspector," she said, offering her hand. "I'm Sharon Feldman."

She led him into the building, down a corridor, and through a door marked STU-DIO C. It was crowded with people and cameras, and what he supposed were sets, one of which was used for "Nine's News." He was surprised when Louise saw him and waved happily at him, understanding only after a moment that she was not at the mo-ment being telecast, or televised, or whatever they called it.

Sharon Feldman led him through another door, and he found himself in a control room.

"There's coffee, Inspector," Sharon Feldman said. "Help yourself. See you!"

"Roll the Wonder Bread," an intense young woman in horn-rimmed glasses, sitting in the rear of two rows of chairs behind a control console, said; and Peter saw, on one of a dozen monitors, one marked AIR, the beginning of a Wonder Bread commercial.

"Funny," a man said to Peter Wohl, "you don't look like a cop."

Peter looked at him icily.

"Leonard Cohen," the man said. "I'm the news director."

"Good for you," Peter said.

"No offense, Wohl," Cohen said. "But you really don't, you know, look like what the word 'cop' calls to mind."

"You don't look much like Walter Cronkite yourself," Peter said.

"I don't make as much money, either," Cohen said, disarmingly.

"Neither, I suppose, does the president of the United States," Wohl said.

"At least that we know about," Cohen said. "Did you catch the guy who got away from the Waikiki Diner?"

"Not as far as I know," Peter said.

"But you will?"

"I think so," Peter said. "It's a question of time."

"What about the party or parties unknown who hacked up the fairy?"

"What fairy is that?"

"Come on," Cohen said. "Nelson."

"Was he a fairy?" Peter asked, innocently.

"Wasn't he?"

"I didn't know him that well," Peter said. "Did you?"

Cohen smiled at Wohl approvingly.

"Maybe the princess has met her match," he said. "I knew there had to be some kind of an attraction."

"Leonard, for Christ's sake, will you shut up?" the intense young woman snapped, and then, "Two, you're out of focus, for Christ's sake!"

Cohen shrugged.

"Good night, Louise," Barton Ellison said to Louise Dutton.

"See you at eleven, Barton," Louise said, "when we should have film of the fire at the Navy Yard."

"It should be spectacular," Barton Ellison replied. "A real four-alarm blaze."

"Roll the logo," the intense young woman said.

Through the plate-glass window, Peter saw a man step behind Louise. She took something from her ear and handed it to him, and then stood up. Then she unclipped what he realized after a moment must be a microphone, and tugged at a cord, pulling it down and out of her sleeve.

Then she walked across the studio to the control room, entered it, walked up to him, said "Hi!"; stood on her toes, and kissed him quickly on the lips.

The intense young woman applauded.

"You're just jealous, that's all," Louise said.

"You got it, baby," the intense young woman said. "Has he got a friend?"

Louise chuckled, and then took Peter's arm and led him out of the control room, through another door, and into a corridor.

"Since we'll be at my place," she said, "and I want to change anyway, I can wipe this crap off there." She touched the heavy makeup on her face. "Where are you parked?"

"Out in front," he said.

She looked at him in surprise.

"Right in front?" she asked. He nodded.

She started to say something, and then laughed. She had, Peter thought, absolutely perfect teeth.

"I was about to say, 'My God, the cops will tow your car away,' " she said. "But I guess not, huh?"

"There are fringe benefits in my line of work," he said. "Not many, but some."

"How do they know it's a cop car?"

"Most of the time, they can tell by the kind of car, or they see the radio," he replied. "Or you just have the ticket canceled. But if you have a car like mine, with the radio in the glove compartment, and you don't want it towed away, you put a little sign on the dash. Or sometimes on the seat."

"Can you get me a sign?"

"No."

"Fink," she said, and took his arm and led him out of the building through the lobby.

At Stockton Place, he parked the LTD behind the Jaguar and walked with her into the foyer of Number Six.

There was an eight-by-ten-inch white cardboard sign on the door of Apartment A. Red letters spelled out, POLICE DEPARTMENT, CITY OF PHILADELPHIA. CRIME SCENE. DO NOT ENTER.

Louise looked at Peter but didn't say anything. But when the elevator door opened and he started to follow her in, she put up her hand to stop him.

"You wait down here," she said. "What I have on my mind now is dinner."

"That's all?"

"Dinner first," she said. "No. Car first, then dinner. Then who knows?"

"I'm easy to please," Peter said. "I'll settle for that."

He walked back out onto the street and to the Jaguar, and examined the hood where Tony Harris had sat on it.

Louise came down much sooner than he expected her to. She had removed all her makeup and changed into a sweater and pleated skirt.

"That was quick," he said.

"It was also a mistake," Louise said, and got behind the wheel of the Jaguar.

"What?"

"I'll tell you later," she said. Then she said, "Kind of low to the ground, isn't it?"

"I guess," Peter said.

"Well, first I need the keys," she said, and as he fished for them, added, "and then you can explain how that little stick works, and we'll be off."

"What little stick?"

"That one," she said, pointing to the gearshift, "with all the numbers on it."

"You do know how to drive a car with a clutch and gearshift?"

"Actually, no," she said. "But I'm willing to learn."

"Oh, God!"

"Just teasing, Peter," Louise said. "You really love this car, don't you?"

"You're the first person to ever drive it since I rebuilt it," he said.

"I'm flattered," she said. "Want to race to your house?"

"No," he said, smiling and shaking his head.

"Chicken." She started the engine, put it in gear, and made a U-turn.

He quickly got in the LTD and followed her, which proved difficult. She drove fast and skillfully, and the Jaguar was more nimble in traffic than the LTD.

On Lancaster Avenue, just before it was time to turn off, she put her arm up and vigorously signaled for him to pass her, to lead her. She smiled at him as he did so, and his heart jumped.

At the apartment, as he was taking his uniform from the backseat to carry it upstairs, she came to him, and put her arms around him from the back.

"How would you feel about an indecent proposal?" she asked.

"Come into my parlor, said the spider to the fly," he said.

"What I was thinking was that you would put the uniform back in your car, and go upstairs and pack a few little things in a bag for tomorrow," Louise said.

He freed himself and turned to look at her.

"When I was in my place, alone . . ." Louise said. "Remember what I said about a mistake? I was frightened. I don't want to be alone there, tonight."

"You could stay here," he said.

"I thought about that," she said. "But I have to do the eleven o'clock news, which means I would have to come all the way out here again. *Please,* Peter." Then she smiled, and offered, "I'll blow in your ear."

"Sure, why not?" Peter said. *Sure, why not? Jesus, the most beautiful girl you have ever known asks you to spend the night and you say "Sure, why not?"*

"It won't take me a minute," he said. "You want to come up?"

"No," she said. "You're obviously the kind of man who would take advantage of an innocent girl like me."

He went in the apartment, put underwear and a white uniform shirt, his uniform cap, and his toilet things in a bag. Then, as an afterthought, he added his good bathrobe (a gift from his mother, which he seldom wore) and bottle of cologne in with it.

When he went back downstairs, she was behind the wheel of the Jaguar.

"The idea was to leave this car here," he said.

"We'll come back before we go downtown," she said. "What I want to do is go out in the country with the wind blowing my hair and eat in some romantic country inn."

"Where are you going to find one of those?"

"How about a Burger King?" she said. "Get in, Peter."

He got in beside her, and she drove off, spinning the wheels as she made a sweeping turn.

She headed out of town, driving, he decided, too fast.

"Take it easy," he said.

"If you don't complain about my driving," she said, "I won't say anything about you looking hungrily at my knees."

He felt his face color.

"My God!" he said.

She pulled her skirt farther up her legs.

"Better?" she asked.

As Stanford F. Wells III crossed the marble-floored, high-ceilinged, tastefully furnished lobby of the Warwick Hotel toward the reception desk, two men rose from a couch and intercepted him.

"How are you, boss?" the older of them said. He was short and stocky, with a very full head of curly pepper-and-salt hair.

"Who's minding the store, Kurt?" Wells asked, smiling, obviously pleased to see Kurt Kruger.

"Well, since I was here, I thought I'd wait and say hello and then go home," Kurt Kruger said. "Stan, this is Richard Dye. He's on the *Chronicle*. He used to work for the *Ledger* here. I thought he could be helpful, and he was. He's one hell of a leg man."

Wells gave the younger man his hand.

"This is Mr. Fengler," Wells said, "of Mawson, Payne, Stockton, McAdoo and Lester. Are we going to need all of them? Or just one or two?"

Kruger chuckled. "We probably won't need any of them," he said. "No offense, Mr. Fengler, but it's not nearly as bad—a legal problem, anyway—as I was afraid it would be when you called."

"My wife said she sounded very frightened on the telephone," Wells challenged.

"There's a reason for that," Kruger said. "But I think you can relax. Why don't we get out of the lobby? I got a suite for you."

"So did Mr. Fengler," Wells said. "I guess that means I have two. Let's hope there's whiskey in one of them."

When they got to the suite, Stanford Fortner Wells III disappeared into the bathroom and emerged ten minutes later pink from a shower and wearing only a towel.

"I now feel a lot better," he said, as he poured whiskey into a glass and added a very little water. "I offer the philosophical observation that not only did God not intend man to fly, but that whoever designed the crappers on airplanes should be forced to use them himself through all eternity."

There were polite "the boss is always witty" chuckles, and then Wells turned to Richard Dye.

"Okay, Dick, what have you come up with?"

Dye took a small notebook from his pocket, and glanced at it.

"Miss Dutton . . . or should I call her 'Miss Wells'?"

"Her name is Dutton," Wells said, matter-of-factly. "I already had a wife when I met Louise's mother."

Ward V. Fengler hoped that his surprise at that announcement didn't register on his face.

"Miss Dutton was interviewing a cop, a captain named Richard Moffitt, in a diner on Roosevelt Boulevard. Are you familiar with the diners in Philly, Mr. Wells?"

"Yeah."

"This was a big one, with a bigger restaurant than a counter, if you follow me." Wells nodded. "They were in the restaurant. The cop, who was the commanding officer of the Highway Patrol . . . you know about them?"

Wells thought that over and shook his head no.

"They patrol the highways, but there's more. They're sort of an elite force, and they use them in high-crime areas. They wear uniforms like they were still riding motorcycles. Some people call them 'Carlucci's Commandos.' "

"Carlucci being the mayor?" Wells asked. Dye nodded. "I get the picture," Wells said.

"Well, apparently what happened was that somebody tried to stick up the diner. The cop saw it, and tried to stop it, and there were two robbers, one of them a girl.

She let fly at him with a .22 pistol, and hit him. He got his gun out and blew her away. From what I heard, he didn't even know he was shot until he dropped dead."

"I don't understand that," Wells said.

"According to my source—who is a police reporter named Mickey O'Hara—the bullet severed an artery, and he bled to death internally."

"Right in front of my daughter?"

"Yes, sir, she was right there."

"That's awful," Wells said.

"If I didn't mention this, the guy who was doing the stickup got away in the confusion. They're still looking for him."

"Do they know who he is?"

Dye dropped his eyes to his notebook.

"The guy's name is Gerald Vincent Gallagher, white male, twenty-four. The girl who shot the cop was a junkie—so is Gallagher, by the way—named Dorothy Ann Schmeltzer. High-class folks, both of them."

"Go on," Wells said.

"Of course, every cop in Philadelphia was there in two minutes," Dye went on. "One of them was smart enough to figure out who Miss Dutton was—"

"Got a name?"

"Wohl," Dye said. "He's a staff inspector. According to O'Hara he's one of the brighter ones. He's the youngest staff inspector; he just sent the city housing director to the slammer, him and a union big shot—"

Wells made a "go on" gesture with his hands, and then took underwear from a suitcase and pulled a T-shirt over his head.

"So Wohl treated her very well. He sent her home in a police car, and had another cop drive her car," Dye went on. "Half, O'Hara said, because she's on the tube, and half because he's a nice guy. So she went to work, and did the news at six, and again at eleven, and then she went out and had a couple of drinks with the news director, a guy named Leonard Cohen, and a couple of other people. Then she went home. The door to the apartment on the ground floor—I was there, she had to walk past it to get to the elevator—was open, and she went in, and found Jerome Nelson in his bedroom. Party or parties unknown had hacked him up with a Chinese cleaver."

"What's a Chinese cleaver?" Wells asked.

"Looks like a regular cleaver, but it's thinner, and sharper," Dye explained.

Wells, in the act of buttoning a shirt, nodded.

"What was my daughter's relationship with the murdered man?" Wells asked. "I mean, why did she walk into his apartment?"

"They were friends, I guess. He was a nice little guy. Funny."

"There was nothing between them?"

"He was homosexual, Mr. Wells," Dye said.

"I see," Wells said.

"And, Stan," Kurt Kruger said, evenly, "he's—he *was*—Arthur Nelson's son."

"Poor Arthur," Wells said. "He knew?"

"I don't see how he couldn't know," Dye said.

"And I suppose that's all over the front pages, too?"

"No," Dye said. "Not so far. Professional courtesy, I suppose."

"Interesting question, Kurt," Wells said, thoughtfully. "What would we have done? Shown the same 'professional courtesy'?"

"I don't know," Kruger said. "Was his . . . sexual inclination . . . germane to the story?"

"Was it?"

"Nobody knows yet," Kruger said. "Until it comes out, my inclination would be not to mention the homosexuality. If it comes out there is a connection, then I think I'd have to print it. One definition of news is that it's anything people would be interested to hear."

"Another, some cynics have said," Wells said dryly, "is that news is what the publisher says it is. That's one more argument against having only one newspaper in a town."

"Would you print it, Stan?" Kruger asked.

"That's what I have all those high-priced editors for," Wells said. "To make painful decisions like that." He paused. "I'd go with what you said, Kurt. If it's just a sidebar, don't use it. If it's germane, I think you would have to."

Kruger grunted.

"Go on, Dick," Wells said to Richard Dye.

"Miss We— Miss Dutton—"

"Try 'your daughter,' Dick," Wells said, adding, "if there's some confusion in your mind."

"*Your daughter* called the cops. They came, including the Homicide lieutenant on duty, a real horse's ass named DelRaye. They had words."

"About what?"

"He told her she had to go to the Roundhouse—the police headquarters, downtown—and she said she had told him everything she knew, and wasn't going anywhere. Then she went upstairs to her apartment. DelRaye told her unless she came out, he was going to knock the door down, and have her taken to the Roundhouse in a paddy wagon."

"Why do I have the feeling you're tactfully leaving something out, Dick? I want all of it."

"Okay," Dye said, meeting his eyes. "She'd had a couple of drinks. Maybe a couple too many. And she used a couple of choice words on DelRaye."

"You have a quote?"

" 'Go fuck yourself,' " Dye quoted.

"Did she really?" Wells said. "How to win friends and influence people."

"So she must have called Inspector Wohl, and he showed up, and got her away from the apartment through the basement," Dye said. "In the morning, he brought her to the Roundhouse. There was a lawyer, Colonel Mawson, waiting for her there."

"She must have called me while she was in the apartment waiting for the good cop to show up," Wells said. "Either my wife couldn't tell Louise was drinking, or didn't want to say anything. She said she was afraid."

"I saw pictures of the murdered guy, Mr. Wells. Enough to make you throw up. She had every reason to be frightened."

"Where was she from the time—what was the time?—the good cop took her away from the apartment, and the time he brought her to the police station?"

"After one in the morning," Dye said. "He probably took her to a girlfriend's house, or something."

"Or boyfriend's house?" Wells said. "You are a good leg man, Dick. What did you turn up about a boyfriend?"

"No one in particular," Dye said. "Couple of guys, none of whom seem to have been involved."

"Mr. Wells," Ward V. Fengler said, "if I may interject, Colonel Mawson asked Miss Dutton where she had been all night, and she declined to tell him."

"That spells boyfriend," Wells said. "And, maybe guessing I would show up here, she didn't want me to know she'd spent the night with him. Now my curiosity's aroused. Can you get me some more on that subject, Dick?"

"I'll give it a shot, sir," Dye said.

"Has she gone back to work?" Wells asked, and then, looking at his watch, answered his own question. "The best way to find that out is to look at the tube, isn't it?"

It was six-fifteen. As Stanford Fortner Wells III finished dressing, he watched his daughter do her telecast.

"She's tough," he said, admiringly.

"I'd forgotten how pretty she was," Kurt Kruger said.

"That, too." Wells chuckled. "Okay. I'm going to see her. Mr. Fengler, there's no point that I can see in taking any more of your time. I'd like to keep the car, if I may, and I would be grateful if you would get in touch with Colonel Mawson and tell him I'll be in touch in the morning."

"I'm at your disposal, Mr. Wells, if you think I could be of any assistance," Fengler said.

"I can handle it, I think, from here on in. If I need some help, I've got Mawson's number, office and home. Thank you for all your courtesy."

Fengler knew that he had been dismissed.

"I'd like to have dinner with you, Kurt, but that's not going to be possible. Thank you. Again."

"Aw, hell, Stan."

"You, Dick, I would like you to stick around. I may need a leg man to do more than find out who my daughter has been seeing. You came, I hope, prepared to stay a couple of days?"

"Yes, sir," Dye said.

"Whose suite is this?" Wells asked.

Fengler and Kruger looked at each other and shrugged, and smiled.

"Well, find out. And then see if you can turn the other one in on a room for Dick," Wells said. "Make sure he stays here in the hotel, in any case."

Then he walked quickly among them, shook their hands, and left the suite.

There was a Ford pulling away from the front door of WCBL-TV when the limousine arrived. The limousine took that place.

Wells walked up to the receptionist.

"My name is Stanford Wells," he said. "I would like to see Miss Louise Dutton."

The name Stanford Wells meant nothing whatever to the receptionist, but she thought that the nicely dressed man standing before her didn't look like a kook.

"Does Miss Dutton expect you?" she asked with a smile.

"No, but I bet if you tell her her father is out here, she'll come out and get me."

"Oh, I'm so sorry," the receptionist said. "You *just* missed her! I'm surprised you didn't see her. She just this minute left."

"Do you have any idea where she went?"

"No," the receptionist said. "But she was with Inspector Wohl, if that's any help."

"Thank you very much," Stanford Fortner Wells III said, and went out and got back in the limousine. He fished in his pockets and then swore.

"Something wrong, sir?" the chauffeur asked.

"Take me back to the hotel. I left my daughter's address on the goddamned dresser."

Mickey O'Hara sat virtually motionless for three minutes before the computer terminal on his desk in the city room of the *Philadelphia Bulletin*. The only thing that moved was his tongue behind his lower lip.

Then, all of a sudden, his bushy eyebrows rose, his eyes lit up, his lips reflected satisfaction, and his fingers began to fly over the keys. He had been searching for his lead, and he had found it.

SLUG: FRIED THUG
By Michael J. O'Hara

Gerald Vincent Gallagher, 24, was electrocuted and dismembered at 4:28 this afternoon, ending a massive, citywide, twenty-four-hour manhunt by eight thousand Philadelphia policemen.

Gallagher, of a West Lindley Avenue address, had been sought by police on murder charges since he eluded capture following a foiled robbery at the Waikiki Diner on Roosevelt Boulevard yesterday afternoon. Highway Patrol Captain Richard C. "Dutch" Moffitt happened to be in the restaurant, in civilian clothes, with WCBL-TV anchorwoman Louise Dutton. Police say Captain Moffitt was shot to death in a gun battle with Dorothy Ann Schmeltzer, who police say was Gallagher's accomplice, when he attempted to arrest Gallagher.

At 4:24 p.m. Charles McFadden, a 22-year-old Narcotics plainclothesman, spotted Gallagher, at the Bridge & Pratt Streets Terminal in Northeast Philadelphia. Gallagher attempted escape by running down a narrow workman's platform alongside the elevated tracks toward the Margaret-Orthodox Station. Just as McFadden caught up with him, he slipped, fell to the tracks, touched the third rail; and moments later was run over by four cars of a northbound elevated train.

Mickey O'Hara stopped typing, looked at the screen, and read what he had written. The thoughtful look came back on his face. He typed MORETOCOME MORETOCOME, then punched the SEND key.

Then he stood up and walked across the city room to the city editor's desk, and then stepped behind it. When the city editor was finished with what he was doing, he looked up and over his shoulder at Mickey O'Hara.

"Punch up 'fried thug,' " Mickey said.

The city editor did so, by pressing keys on one of his terminals that called up the story from the central computer memory and displayed it on his monitor.

As the city editor read Mickey's first 'graphs, O'Hara leaned over and dialed the number of the photo lab.

"Bobby, this is Mickey. Did they come out?"

"Nice," the city editor said. "How much more is there?"

"How much space can I have?"

"Pictures?"

"Two good ones for sure," Mickey said. "I got a lovely shot of the severed head."

"I mean ones we can print, Mickey," the city editor said. He pointed to the telephone in Mickey's hand. "That the lab?" Mickey nodded, and the city editor gestured for the phone. "Print one of each, right away," he said, and hung up.

"I asked how much space I can have," Mickey O'Hara said.

"Everybody else was there, I guess?"

"Nobody else has pictures of the cop," Mickey said. "For that matter, of the tracks when anything was still going on."

"And you're sure this is the guy?"

"One of the Fifteenth District cops recognized the head," Mickey said.

"Give me a thousand, twelve hundred words," the city editor said. "Things are a little slow. Nothing but wars."

Mickey O'Hara nodded and walked back to his desk and sat down before the computer terminal. He pushed the *compose* key, and typed,

SLUG: FRIED THUG
By Michael J. O'Hara
Add One

Sergeant Tom Lenihan stepped into the doorway of the office of Chief Inspector Dennis V. Coughlin, who commanded the Special Investigations Bureau, and stood waiting until he had Coughlin's attention.

"What is it, Tom?"

"They just got Gerald Vincent Gallagher, Chief," Lenihan said.

"Good," Coughlin said. "Where? How?"

"Lieutenant Pekach just phoned," Lenihan said. "Two of his guys—one of them that young plainclothes guy who identified the girl—went looking for him on their own. They spotted him at the Bridge Street Terminal. He ran. Officer McFadden chased him down the elevated tracks. Gallagher slipped, fell onto the third rail, and then a train ran over him."

Denny Coughlin's face froze. His eyes were on Lenihan, but Lenihan knew that he wasn't seeing him, that he was thinking.

Dennis V. Coughlin was only one of eleven chief inspectors of the Police Department of the City of Philadelphia. But it could be argued that he was first among equals. Under his command (among others) were the Narcotics Unit; the Vice Unit; the Internal Affairs Division; the Staff Investigation Unit; and the Organized Crime Intelligence Unit.

The other ten chief inspectors reported to either the deputy commissioner (Operations) or the deputy commissioner (Administration), who reported to the first deputy commissioner, who reported to the commissioner. Denny Coughlin reported directly to the first deputy commissioner.

Phrased very simply, there were only two people in the department who could tell Denny Coughlin what to do, or ask him what he was doing: the first deputy commissioner and the commissioner himself. On the other hand, without any arrogance at all, Denny Coughlin believed that what happened anywhere in the police department was his business.

"Tom, is Inspector Kegley out there?"

"Yes, sir, I think so."

"Would you tell him, please, unless there is a good reason he can't, I would like him to find out exactly what happened?"

"Yes, sir."

"I mean right now, Tom," Coughlin said. "He doesn't have to give me a white paper, just get the information to me." Coughlin looked at his watch. "I'll be at Dutch's wake, say from six o'clock until it's over. Are you going over there with me?"

"Yes, sir," Lenihan said, and departed.

Two minutes later, Lenihan was back.

"Inspector Kegley's on his way, sir. He said he'd see you at Marshutz & Sons," he reported.

"Good, Tom. Thank you," Coughlin said. Staff Inspector George Kegley had come up through the Detective Bureau, and had done some time in Homicide. He was a quiet, phlegmatic, soft-eyed man who missed very little once he turned his attention to something. If there was something not quite right about the pursuit and death of Gerald Vincent Gallagher, Kegley would soon sniff it out.

Coughlin returned his attention to the file on his desk. It was a report from Internal Affairs involving two officers of the Northwest Police Division. There had been a party. Officer A had paid uncalled-for personal attention to Mrs. B. Mrs. B had not, in Officer B's (her husband's) judgment, declined the attention with the proper outraged indignation. She had, in fact, seemed to like it. Whereupon Officer B had belted his wife in the chops, and taken off after Officer A, pistol drawn, threatening to kill the sonofabitch. No real harm had been done, but the whole matter was now official, and something would have to be done.

"I don't want to deal with this now," Dennis V. Coughlin said, although there was no one in his office to hear him.

He stood up, took his pistol from his left desk drawer, slipped it into his holster, and walked out of his office.

"Come on, Tom," he said to Sergeant Lenihan, "let's go."

14 Patrick Coughlin, a second-generation Irish-American (his father had been born in Philadelphia three months after his parents had immigrated from County Kildare in 1896), had spent his working life as a truck diver, and had been determined that his son Dennis would have the benefits of a college education.

But in 1946, despite an excellent record at Roman Catholic High School, Dennis

V. Coughlin had been suspended from LaSalle College for academic inadequacy after his second semester. He had been on academic probation after the first semester.

Once Denny Coughlin had flunked out of LaSalle, life at home had been difficult, and he had enlisted in the navy for four years, in exchange for a navy promise to train him as an electronics technician. He was no more successful in the navy electronics school than he had been at LaSalle, and the navy found itself wondering what to do with a very large young man for the forty-two months remaining on his enlistment.

Shortly after reporting aboard the aircraft carrier U.S.S. *Coral Sea* as an engineman striker, the *Coral Sea*'s master at arms had offered him a chance to become what was in effect a shipboard policeman. That had far more appeal than long days in the hot and greasy bowels of the ship, and Denny jumped at it.

It wasn't what he thought it would be, marching into waterfront bars and hauling drunken sailors back to the ship, after beating them on the head with a nightstick. There was some of that, to be sure, and once or twice Denny Coughlin did have to use his nightstick. But not often. A sailor had to be both foolhardy as well as drunk to take on someone the size of Coughlin. And Denny learned that a kind word of understanding and reason was almost always more effective than the nightstick.

He found, too, that often the sailors were the aggrieved party to a dispute, that the saloonkeepers were in the wrong. And he found that he could deal with the saloonkeepers as well as he could with sailors. He sensed, long before he could put it into words, that the cowboys really had used the right word. He was a *peace* officer, and he was good at it.

After eighteen months of sea duty aboard the *Coral Sea,* he was assigned as a shore patrolman attached to the U.S. Naval Hospital, Philadelphia. He worked with the Philadelphia police, and came to the attention of several senior officers, who saw in him just what the department was looking for in its recruits: a large, healthy, bright, pleasant hometown boy with an imposing presence. The police department was suggested to him as a suitable civilian career when his navy hitch was up. With his navy veteran's preference, he had no trouble with the civil service exam. Once that was out of the way, Captain Francis X. Halloran had a word with the Honorable Lawrence Sheen, M.C., and shortly after that Bosun's Mate Third Class Dennis V. Coughlin was honorably discharged from the U.S. Navy for the convenience of the government to accept essential civilian employment—law enforcement.

Three weeks after taking off his navy blues, Dennis V. Coughlin reported to the police academy for training.

On his first day there, he met John X. Moffitt, just back from a three-year hitch in the marines. They were of an age, they had much in common, and they became buddies. When they graduated from the academy, they were both assigned downtown, Denny Coughlin to the Ninth District, Jack Moffitt to the Sixth. Without much trouble, they managed to have their duty schedules coincide, so they spent their off-duty time together, drinking beer and chasing girls, except for Tuesday nights, when Jack Moffitt went to meetings of the marine corps reserve.

He needed the money, Jack Moffitt argued, and there wasn't going to be a war anyway; Denny should join up too. Denny did not. Jack was called back to the Marines on seventy-two hours' notice, a week after they had both learned they had passed the detective's exam, in August 1950.

Jack was back in just over a year, medically retired as a staff sergeant for wounds received in the vicinity of Hangun-Ri, North Korea, where he also earned the Silver Star. He went back to work in the West Detective Division; Denny Coughlin was then in the Central Detective Division.

But things weren't the same between them, primarily because of Patricia Stevens, whom Jack had met when she went with the girls from Saint Agnes's to entertain the boys in the navy hospital. Denny was best man at their wedding, and Patty used to have him to supper a lot, and she helped the both of them prepare for the sergeant's examination.

A month after Jack Moffitt died of gunshot wounds suffered in the line of duty, a month before Matt was born, Denny Coughlin had made a rare visit to his parish rectory, for a private conversation with Monsignor Finn. It took some time before Finn realized what Denny Coughlin really wanted to talk about, and it was not his immortal soul.

"You don't want to marry the girl, Denny," Monsignor Finn said, "because you feel sorry for her, or because she's your friend's wife; nor even to take care of the baby when it comes. And you sure don't want her to marry you because she needs someone to support her and the baby. Now you'll notice that I didn't say you don't want to marry the girl. What I'm saying to you is, have a little patience. Time heals. And it wouldn't surprise me at all if Patty Moffitt saw in you the same things she saw in Jack, God rest his soul. But you want to be sure, son. Marriage is forever. You don't want to be jumping into it. What I'm saying is just keep being what you are, a good friend, until Patty gets over both her grief and the baby. Then if you still feel the same way . . ."

Dennis V. Coughlin had still felt the same way six months later, and a year later, but before he could bring himself to say anything, Patty Moffitt had gone to work, trying to work her way up to be a legal secretary, and then she'd taken Matt for a walk in his stroller, and she'd run into Brewster Cortland Payne II taking his motherless kids for a walk, and then it had been too late.

Chief Inspector Dennis V. Coughlin had been at Dutch Moffitt's wake at the Marshutz & Sons Funeral Home for about an hour when he saw Matt Payne, standing alone, and called him over. He shook his hand, and then put his arm around his shoulders.

"I'd like you to meet these fellows, Matt," he said. "Gentlemen, this is Matt Payne, Dutch's nephew."

Matt was introduced to two chief inspectors, three inspectors, two captains, and a corporal who had gone through the academy with Dutch Moffitt and was being tolerated by the brass for being a little drunk, and just a shade too friendly.

"When you get a moment, Uncle Denny, could I talk to you?"

"You bet you can," Denny Coughlin said. "Excuse us, fellows." He took Matt's arm and led him far down a wide corridor in the funeral home. Finally, they found an empty corner.

"I joined the police department," Matt announced.

"How's that again?"

"I said I'm going to be a policeman," Matt repeated.

"And when did this happen?"

"Today."

"I'll be damned," Dennis V. Coughlin said. "Let me get adjusted to that, Matt."

"So far only my dad knows," Matt said.

"Your dad is dead," Coughlin said, and was immediately contrite. "Ah, Christ, why did I say that? I'm proud to claim Brewster Payne as a friend, and you couldn't have had a better father."

"I understand," Matt said. "I have trouble with my real father, too. Keeping them separate, I mean."

"Matt, I'm going to say something to you and I don't want you to take offense, son, but I have to say it—"

"I flunked the marine corps physical," Matt said. "I was thinking about becoming a cop before Uncle Dick was killed."

"If you flunked the marine corps physical, what makes you think you can pass the police department physical?"

"I passed it," Matt said. "And I even had a talk with the shrink. Today."

"Jesus, Mary, and Joseph! What's your mother going to say?"

"Why am I getting the feeling that you're a long way from yelling 'Whoopee, good for you!'?"

"Because I'm not entirely sure it's a good idea, for you, or the department," Coughlin said, evenly.

"Why not?"

"I don't know," Coughlin said. "Gut feeling, maybe. Or maybe because I buried your father, and we're about to bury your uncle. Or maybe I'm afraid your mother will think I talked you into it."

"My father, my *adoptive* father, understands," Matt said.

"Then he's one up on me," Coughlin said. "Matt, you're not doing this because of what you think the police are like, from watching them on TV, are you?"

"No, I'm not," Matt said, simply.

"But you will admit that you have no idea what you're getting into?"

"I was going into the marines, and I had no idea what I was getting into there, either."

Sergeant Tom Lenihan and Staff Inspector George Kegley appeared in the corridor, waiting for Coughlin's attention. Coughlin saw them, and motioned them over.

"You met Sergeant Lenihan yesterday," Coughlin said. "And this is Staff Inspector Kegley. George, this is Matt Payne. He's Dutch's nephew."

They all shook hands.

"What have you got, George?" Coughlin asked.

Kegley seemed momentarily surprised that Coughlin was asking for a report to be delivered before what he thought of as a "civilian relative," but he delivered a concise, but thorough report of what had transpired at the Bridge & Pratt Streets Terminal, including the details of Gerald Vincent Gallagher's death and dismemberment.

"Did they get in touch with Peter Wohl?" Coughlin asked. "Matt Lowenstein said they wanted him to get an identification of Gallagher as the man in the diner from that TV woman."

"Nobody seems to know where either of them are, Chief," Kegley said.

Coughlin snorted, and then his face stiffened in thought.

"Thank you, George," Coughlin said. "I appreciate this. Tom, get the car, we're going for a ride."

"Yes, sir," Sergeant Lenihan said.

"You're coming," Dennis Coughlin said to Matt Payne.

"Are you all right, Matthew?" Chief Inspector Dennis V. Coughlin asked when Sergeant Tom Lenihan had eased the Oldsmobile up on the curb before the row house on Fitzgerald Street in South Philadelphia.

Matt had thrown up at the medical examiner's, not when Coughlin expected him to, when they pulled the sheet off the remains of Gerald Vincent Gallagher, but several minutes later, outside, just before they got back into the Oldsmobile. Tom Lenihan had disappeared at that point for a couple of minutes, and Coughlin wasn't sure if he had done that to spare Matt embarrassment, or whether Lenihan had gone behind a row of cars to throw up himself.

"I'm all right," Matt said.

His face was white.

"Sure?"

"I'm fine, thank you," Matt said, firmly.

"You want me to come along, Chief?" Lenihan asked.

"I think maybe you better," Coughlin said, and opened the door.

The door to the McFadden house had a doorbell, an old-fashioned, cast-iron device mounted in the center of the door. You twisted it, and it rang. Coughlin remembered one just like it on the door of the row house where he had grown up. Somebody, he thought, had probably made a million making those bells; there was one on just about every row house in Philly.

Agnes McFadden opened the door, and looked at them in surprise as Coughlin whipped off his snap-brimmed straw hat.

" 'Evening, ma'am," he said. "I'm Chief Inspector Coughlin. I'd like to see Officer McFadden, if that would be convenient."

"What?" Agnes McFadden said.

"We'd like to see Charley, if we can," Lenihan said. "I'm Sergeant Lenihan and this is Chief Inspector Coughlin."

"He's in the kitchen, with his lieutenant," she said. "Lieutenant Pekach. And Mr. McFadden."

"Could we see him, do you think?" Coughlin asked.

"Sure, of course, I don't know what I was thinking of, please come in."

They followed her down a dark corridor to the kitchen, where the three men sat at the kitchen table. There was a bottle of Seagram's 7-Crown and quart bottles of Coke and beer on the table.

Pekach's eyes widened when he saw them. He started to get up.

"Keep your seat, David," Coughlin said.

Officer Charley McFadden, who was sitting slumped straight out in the chair, supporting a Kraft cheese glass of liquor on his stomach, finally realized that something was happening. He looked at the three strangers in his kitchen without recognition.

Coughlin crossed the small room to him with his hand extended.

"McFadden, I apologize for barging into your home like this, but I wanted to congratulate you personally on a job well done. I'm sure your parents are very proud of you. The police department is."

Matt saw that McFadden had no idea who was shaking his hand.

Charley's father put that in words. "Who're you?" he asked.

"Mr. McFadden," Lieutenant Pekach said, "this is Chief Inspector Coughlin. And that's Sergeant Lenihan. I'm afraid I don't know the other gentleman."

"My name is Matthew Payne," Matt said, putting out his hand.

"Matt is ... Captain Moffitt was Matt's uncle," Coughlin said.

"I'm sorry about your uncle," Charley McFadden said. Then he realized that he should be standing, and got up. He looked at Coughlin. "You're Chief Inspector Coughlin," he said, but there was a question, or disbelief, in his voice.

"That's right," Coughlin said.

"Could I offer you gentlemen a little something to drink?" Mrs. McFadden asked.

"All I got, I'm afraid, is the Seagram's Seven," Mr. McFadden said.

"Well, we're all off duty," Coughlin said. "I think a little Seagram's Seven would go down very nicely."

More cheese glasses were produced, and filled three-quarters full of whiskey.

"I'm afraid the house is a terrible mess," Agnes McFadden said.

"Looks fine to me," Dennis Coughlin said. He raised his glass. "To Officer McFadden, of whom we're all very proud."

"I didn't want that to happen to him," Charley McFadden said, very slowly. "Jesus Christ, that shouldn't happen to anybody."

"Charley," Coughlin said, firmly. "What happened to Gallagher, he brought on himself."

Charley looked at him, and finally said, "Yes, sir."

"Lieutenant Pekach, may I see you a moment?" Coughlin said, and signaled Matt to come along.

They went to the vestibule.

"Where's his partner?" Coughlin asked.

"He was here, Chief. His doctor gave him something to calm him down, and it didn't mix with the booze. I sent him home."

"McFadden on anything?"

"No, sir," Pekach said. "He's got a thing about pills. He won't even take an aspirin."

"How long are you going to stay?"

"As long as necessary," Pekach said. "The booze will get to him, sooner or later."

"Had you planned to write him up?"

"A commendation?" Pekach asked. "I hadn't thought about that. But yes, sure."

"Not only 'at great risk to his life,' " Coughlin said. "But 'exercising great restraint,' et cetera, et cetera. You follow me?"

"Yes, sir."

"This is going to be all over the papers," Coughlin said. "George Kegley tells me that Mickey O'Hara was even up on the elevated tracks. What's that going to do to McFadden on the streets?"

"Well, he won't be much use, not what he's been doing," Pekach said.

"I'll find something else for him to do." Coughlin said. "When you're that age, working plainclothes, and they put you back in a uniform, you think you did something wrong. I don't want that to happen."

"I'll find something for him, Chief," Pekach said.

When they went back in the kitchen, Officer McFadden was being nauseous in the sink. Coughlin put out his hand and stopped Matt from going in, then gestured for Sergeant Lenihan to come along with them.

When they were in the car, moving north on South Broad Street, Coughlin reached forward and touched Matt Payne's shoulder. Matt turned and looked at him.

"Still think you want to be a cop, Matt?" he asked.

"I was just wondering how I would react in a situation like that," Matt said, softly.

"And?"

"I don't know," Matt said. "I was wondering. But to answer your question, yes, I still want to be a cop."

Coughlin made a grunting noise.

"Tom," he ordered, "when you get to a phone, call Pekach and tell him I want that boy and his partner at the funeral tomorrow. And then find out who's in charge of the seating arrangements and make sure they have seats in Saint Dominic's."

"Uniform or plainclothes?"

Coughlin thought that over a moment. "Uniforms," he said. "I think uniforms. Tell Pekach to make sure they get haircuts and are cleaned up."

"I've got to check my machine," Peter said, when he and Louise had returned from dinner and put the Jaguar into the garage. "It won't take a minute."

"I'll go with you," she said, and caught his hand and held it as they walked up the stairs. Inside the apartment, as he snapped on the lights, he saw that she was standing very close, looking at him.

She wants to be kissed, he realized. *Jesus, that's nice.*

But when he put his arms around her, and she pressed her body against his, and he tried to kiss her, she averted her face.

"I've got some Lavoris," Peter said.

She chuckled.

"No," she said. "That's not it. But I'll be on the air at eleven, and I don't want everybody in the Delaware Valley thinking, 'That dame looks like she just got out of bed.' "

"You really think it shows?" he asked, smelling her hair.

"Once might not," she said. "But we seem to have a certain tendency to keep going back for seconds."

"God, you feel good," Peter said, giving in to an urge to hug her tightly.

"Duty calls," Louise said, freeing herself. "Yours and mine. See what your machine says."

There were a number of messages.

Barbara Crowley had called.

"Peter, your mother called and asked me if I was going to the wake. I told her that I expected to hear from you. Please call me. I'll go over there with you, if you want me to."

And Detective Jason Washington had called:

"This is Jason Washington, Inspector," his recorded voice reported tinnily. "It's five-thirty. In a manner of speaking, we have Gerald Vincent Gallagher. McFadden, the kid from Narcotics who identified the girl, went looking for him, and found him at the Bridge Street Terminal. The reason I say 'in a manner of speaking' is that Gallagher got himself run over by a subway train. After he hit the third rail. Hell of a mess. McFadden knew Gallagher, of course, and so did a couple of guys from the Fifteenth District. But under the circumstances, I think, and so does Lieutenant Natali, that they'll probably want Miss Dutton to identify the body as that of the man she saw in the Waikiki. They just took the body to the medical examiner's. Do you think you could get in touch with her, and take her down there around seven, seven-thirty? I'd appreciate it if you could call me. I'll either be here at the office, or at the M.E.'s, or maybe home. Thank you."

And Lieutenant Louis Natali had called:

"Inspector, this is Lou Natali. Jason Washington said he called and left a message on your machine about an hour ago. It's now quarter to seven. Anyway, it's now official. Captain Quaire requests that you get in touch with Miss Dutton, and bring her by the M.E.'s to identify Gallagher as the guy she saw in the diner. You better warn her he's in pieces. The wheels cut his head off, intact, I mean. I'll try to have them cover the rest of him with a sheet, but it's pretty rough. And would you call me, please, when you get this? Thank you."

And Chief Inspector Matt Lowenstein had called:

"Peter, what the hell is going on? I need that woman to identify Gallagher. Nobody seems to know where you are, so I called the TV station. I was going to very politely ask her if I could take her to the M.E.'s myself, and they tell me they don't know where she is, only that she left there with you. Jesus, it's half past eight, and I've got to get over to Marshutz & Sons for the damned wake."

That message ended abruptly. Peter was quite sure that Chief Inspector of Detectives Matt Lowenstein had glanced at his watch toward the end, seen the time, thought out loud, and then slammed the phone down.

The machine reached the end of the recorded messages and started to rewind.

"What was that all about?" Louise asked.

"Well, apparently an undercover cop spotted—"

"Who was she?" Louise interrupted.

It took him a moment to frame his reply.

"Three days ago, I would have said she was my girlfriend," he said.

"Nice girl?"

"Very nice," he said. "Her name is Barbara Crowley, and she's a psychiatric nurse."

"That must come in handy," Louise said.

"Everybody who knows us, except one, thinks that Barbara and I make a lovely couple and should get married," Peter said.

"Who's the dissenter? Her father?"

"Me," Peter said. "She's a nice girl, but I don't love her."

"As of when?"

"As of always," Peter said. "I never felt that way about her."

"What way is that?"

"The way I feel about you," Peter said.

"I suppose it has occurred to you that about the only thing we have going for us is that we screw good?"

"That's a good starting place," Peter said. "We can build on that."

She met his eyes for a long moment, then said: "I'm not going to go look at a headless corpse tonight."

"Okay," he said. "But you will have to eventually."

"What if I just refuse?"

"You don't want to do that," Peter said.

"What if I do?"

"They'll get a court order. If you refuse the order, they'll hold you in contempt, put you in the House of Correction until you change your mind. You wouldn't like it in the House of Correction. They're really not your kind of people."

She just looked at him.

"I'll call Jason Washington and tell him to meet us at the medical examiner's tomorrow morning. Say, eight o'clock," Peter said.

"I've got to work in the morning," she said.

"We'll go there before you go to work," Peter said, and then added: "I thought you told me you went to work at two o'clock?"

"I usually do," she said. "But tomorrow, I've got to cover a funeral."

"You didn't tell me that," he said.

"It's my story," she said. "I was there when it started, remember?"

He nodded. They looked at each other without speaking for a moment.

"Why are you looking at me that way?" Louise asked. "What are you thinking?"

"That you are incredibly beautiful, and that I love you," Peter said.

"I know," she said. "I mean, that you love me. And I think that scares me more than going to go look at a headless body . . . or a bodyless head."

"Why does it scare you?"

"I'm afraid I'll wake up," she said. "Or, maybe, that I won't."

"I don't think I follow that," he said.

"I think we better get out of here," she said. "Before we wind up in the playroom again."

"Let me call Washington," Peter said.

"Call him from my apartment," she said. "What we're going to do is go there, whereupon I will pick up my car and go to work. You will go to my apartment."

"Is that what I *will* do?" he asked, smiling.

"Uh-huh," she said. "Where you will do the dishes, and dust, and then make yourself pretty for me when I come home tired from work."

"If you're going to be tired, you can do your own dishes."

"I won't be that tired, Peter, if that's what you're thinking, and I'm sure you are."

"I don't mind waiting around the studio for you," he said.

"But I do. I saw you looking at Sharon's boobs. And, although I know I shouldn't tell you this, I saw the way she was looking at you."

"That sounds jealous, I hope."

"Let's go, Peter," she said, and walked to the door.

Mickey O'Hara sat at the bar in the Holiday Inn at Fourth and Arch streets, sipping on his third John Jamison's.

It had happened to him often enough for him to recognize what was happening. He was doing something a reporter should not do any more than a doctor or a lawyer, letting the troubles of people he was dealing with professionally get to him personally. And it had happened to him often enough for him to know that he was dealing with it in exactly the worst possible way, with a double John Jamison's straight up and a beer on the side.

He had started out feeling sorry for the young undercover Narcotics cop, Charley McFadden. The McFadden kid had gone out to play the Lone Ranger, even to the faithful brown companion Hay-zus whateverthefuck his name was, at his side. He was going to bring the bad man to justice. Then he would kiss his horse and ride off into the sunset.

But it hadn't happened that way. He had not been able to get the bad man to repent and come quietly by shooting a pistol out of his hand with a silver bullet.

The bad man had first been fried and then chopped into pieces, and at that point he had stopped being a bad man and become another guy from Philadelphia, one of the kids down the block, another Charley McFadden. Gerald Vincent Gallagher had died with his eyes open, and when his head had finished rolling around between the tracks it had come to rest against a tie, looking upward. When Charley McFadden looked down at the tracks, Gerald Vincent Gallagher had looked right back at him.

There hadn't been much blood. The stainless steel wheels of subway cars get so hot that as they roll over throats and limbs, severing them neatly, they also cauterize them. What Charley McFadden saw was Gerald Vincent Gallagher's head, and parts of his arms and legs and his torso, as if they were parts of some enormous plastic doll somebody had pulled apart and then had thrown down between the tracks.

And then as Charley McFadden was shamed before God, his parish priests, and all the good priests at Bishop Newman High School, and his mother, of course, for violating the "thou shalt not kill" commandment, the cavalry came riding up, late as usual, and he was shamed before them.

Big strong tough 225-pound plainclothes Narc tossing his cookies like a fucking fourteen-year-old because he did what all the other cops would have loved to do, fry the fucking cop killer, and saving the city the expense of a trial in the process.

By the time he ordered his third double John Jamison's with a beer on the side, Mickey O'Hara had begun to consider the tragedy of the life of Gerald Vincent Gallagher, deceased. How did a nice Irish Catholic boy wind up a junkie, on the run after a bungled stickup? What about *his* poor, heartbroken, good, mass-every-morning mother? What had she done to deserve, or produce, a miserable shit like Gerald Vincent Gallagher?

Mickey O'Hara was deep in his fourth double John Jamison's with a beer on the side and even deeper into a philosophical exploration of the injustice of life and man's inhumanity to man when he sensed someone slipping onto the stool beside him at the bar, and turned to look, and found himself faced with Lieutenant Edward M. DelRaye of the Homicide Division of the Philadelphia Police Department.

"Well, as I live and breathe," Lieutenant DelRaye said, "if it isn't Mrs. O'Hara's little boy Mickey."

"Hello, DelRaye," Mickey said.

Lieutenant DelRaye was not one of Mickey O'Hara's favorite police officers.

"Give my friend another of what he's having," DelRaye said to the bartender.

Mickey O'Hara had his first unkind thought: *I could be the last of the big spenders myself, if I put the drinks I bought people on a tab I had no intention of paying.*

"And what have you been up to, dressed to kill as you are?" Mickey asked.

"I was to the wake," DelRaye said. "I'm surprised you're not there."

"I paid my respects," Mickey said. "I liked Dutch."

"You heard we got the turd who got away from the diner?"

Mickey O'Hara nodded. And had his second unkind thought: *We? We got the turd? In a pig's ass, we did. A nice lad named Charley McFadden got him, and is sick about getting him, and you didn't have a fucking thing to do with it, Ed DelRaye. Not that it's out of character for you to take credit for something the boys on the street did.*

"So I heard," Mickey replied. "You were in on that, were you?"

"I made my little contribution," DelRaye said.

"Is that so?"

"A plainclothesman from Narcotics actually ran him down; I'm trying to think of his name—"

"How are you doing with the Nelson murder?" Mickey O'Hara asked, as his John Jamison's with beer on the side was delivered.

"You wouldn't believe how many nigger faggots there are in Philly," DelRaye said.

"What's that got to do with anything?"

"Off the record, Mickey?" DelRaye asked.

"No," Mickey said. "Let's keep this on the record, Ed. Or change the subject."

"I think we better change the subject, then," DelRaye said. He raised his glass. "Mud in your eye."

"I'm working on that story, is what it is," Mickey said. "And if we go off the record, and you tell me something, and then I find it out on my own and use it, then you would be pissed, and I wouldn't blame you. You understand?"

"Sure, I understand perfectly. I was just trying to be helpful."

"I know that, and I appreciate it," Mickey said. "And I know what kind of pressure there must be on you to come up with something, his father being who he is and all."

"You better believe it," DelRaye said.

"What can you tell me about Nelson and the TV lady?" Mickey asked. "On the record, Ed."

"Well, she came home from work, half in the bag, and walked in and found him," DelRaye said.

"She was his girlfriend?"

DelRaye snorted derisively.

"I take it that's a no?"

"That's neither a no or anything else, if we're still on the record," DelRaye said.

"I could, I suppose, call you an 'unnamed senior police officer involved in the investigation,' " Mickey offered.

"I wouldn't want you quoting me as saying Nelson was a faggot," DelRaye said. "Because I didn't say that."

"Jesus Christ, was he?"

"If we're still on the record, no comment," DelRaye said. "We're still on the record?"

"Yeah. Sorry," Mickey O'Hara said, and then went for the jugular. "If I asked you, on the record, but as an 'unnamed senior police officer involved in the investigation' if you are looking for a Negro homosexual for questioning in the Nelson murder investigation, what would you say?"

"You're not going to use my name?"

"Scout's honor."

"Then I would say 'that's true.' "

"And if I asked you how come you can't find him, what would you say?"

"There are a number of suspects, and we believe that the name we have, Pierre St. Maury—"

"Who's he?"

"He's the one we want to question most. He lived with Nelson. We don't think that's his real name."

"Colored guy?"

"Big black guy. That description fits a lot of people in Philadelphia. It fits a lot of people who call themselves 'gay.' But we'll get him."

"But he's not the only one you're looking for?"

"There are others who meet the same description. The rent-a-cops on Stockton Place told us that Nelson had a lot of large black men friends."

"And you think one of them did it?"

"When people like that do each other in, they usually do it with a vengeance," DelRaye said.

"The way Nelson was done in, you mean?"

DelRaye did not reply. He suspected that he had gone too far.

"Mickey," he said, "I'm getting a little uncomfortable with this. Let's get off it, huh?"

"Sure," Mickey O'Hara said. "I got to get out of here anyway."

Ten minutes later, Mickey O'Hara walked back into the city room, walked with elaborate erectness to his desk, where he sat down at his computer terminal, belched, and pushed the COMPOSE button.

SLUG: FAIRY AXMAN?
By Michael J. O'Hara

According to a senior police officer involved in the investigation of the brutal murder of Jerome Nelson, a "large black male," in his twenties, going by the name of Pierre St. Maury, and who reportedly shared the luxurious apartment at 6 Stockton Place, is being sought for questioning.

The police official, who spoke with this reporter only on condition of anonymity, said that it was believed the name Pierre St. Maury was assumed, and suggested this was common practice among what he described as Philadelphia's "large 'gay' black community."

Mickey stopped typing, found a cigarette and lit it, and then read what he had written.

Then he typed, "Do you have the balls to run this, or am I wasting my time?"

Then he moved the cursor to the top of the story and entered FLASH FLASH. This would cause a red light to blink on the city editor's monitor, informing him there was a story, either from the wire services, or from a reporter in the newsroom, that he considered important enough to demand the city editor's immediate attention. Then he pushed the SEND key.

Less than a minute later, the city editor crossed the city room to Mickey's desk.
"Jesus, Mickey," he said.

"Yes, or no?"

"I don't suppose you want to tell me who the cop who gave you this is?"

"I always protect my sources," Mickey said, and burped.

"It's for real?"

"The gentleman in question is a horse's ass, but he knows what he's talking about."

"The cops will know who talked to you," the city editor said.

"That thought had run through my mind," Mickey O'Hara said.

"You're going to put his ass in a crack," the city editor said.

"I have the strength of ten because in my heart, I'm pure," Mickey O'Hara said. "I made it perfectly clear that we were on the record."

"It will be tough on Mr. Nelson," the city editor said.

"Would we give a shit if he didn't own the *Ledger?*" Mickey countered.

The city editor exhaled audibly.

"This'll give you two by-lines on the front page," he said.

"Modesty is not my strong suit," Mickey said. "Yes, or no?"

"Go ahead, O'Hara," the city editor said.

15 It had been the intention of Lieutenant Robert McGrory, commanding officer of Troop G (Atlantic City) of the New Jersey State Police, to take off early, say a little after eight, which would have put him in Philly a little after nine-thirty, in plenty of time to go by the Marshutz & Sons Funeral Home for Dutch Moffitt's wake.

But that hadn't proved possible. One of his troopers, in pursuit of a speeder on U.S. 9, had blown a tire and slammed into a culvert. It wasn't as bad as it could have been; he could have killed himself, and the way the car looked it was really surprising he hadn't. But all he had was a broken arm, a dislocated shoulder, and some bad cuts on his face. But by the time he had that all sorted out (the trooper's wife was eight and a half months gone, and had gotten hysterical when he went by the house to tell her and to take her to the hospital, and he had been afraid that she was going to have the kid right there and then) it was almost nine.

By then, the other senior officers going to Captain Dutch Moffitt's funeral had not elected to wait for him; a major and two captains could not be expected to wait for a lieutenant. Major Bill Knotts left word at the barracks for Lieutenant McGrory that Sergeant Alfred Mant (who was coming from Troop D, in Toms River, bringing people from there and farther north) had been directed to swing by Atlantic City and wait at the Troop G Barracks for McGrory, however long it took for him to get free.

The senior state police officers in Knotts's car were all large men. They all had small suitcases; and they were, of course, in uniform, with all the regalia. The trunk of Knotts's Ford carried the usual assortment of special equipment, and there was no room in it for two of the three suitcases; they had to be carried in the backseat. When they were all finally in it, the Ford was crowded and sat low on its springs.

"I think you'd probably make better time on Three Twenty-two," Knotts said, as he settled into the front seat, beside Captain Gerry Kozniski, who was driving.

"Whatever you say, Major," Captain Kozniski said, aware that he had just been given authority, within reason, to "make good time" between Atlantic City and Philadelphia. There were two major routes, 322 and 30, between the two cities. U.S. 30 was four-laned nearly all the way, from Atlantic City to Interstate 295, just outside Camden. Only some sections of U.S. 322 were four-laned. Consequently, 30 got most of the traffic; there would be little traffic on 322 and it would be safer to drive faster on that road.

Captain Kozniski hit sixty-five, and then seventy, and then seventy-five. The Ford seemed to find its cruising speed just under eighty. They would still be late, but unless something happened, they could still at least put in an appearance at the wake.

"Word is," Captain Kozniski said, "that Bob McGrory's going to be a pallbearer."

"Yeah. Mrs. Moffitt asked for him," Knotts said. "Dutch Moffitt and he went way back.They went to the FBI National Academy together."

He did not add, wondering why he didn't, that the Moffitts and McGrorys, having made friends at the FBI Academy in Quantico, had kept it up. They visited each other, the Moffitts and their kids staying at the McGrory house in Absecon for the beach in the summer, and the McGrorys and their house apes staying with the Moffitts in Philly for, for example, the Mummers' parades, or just because they wanted to go visit.

The wives got on well. Lieutenant Bob McGrory had told Knotts he had heard from his weeping wife that Dutch had stopped a bullet before he heard officially. Dutch's Jeannie had called McGrory's Mary-Ellen the minute she got back from the hospital. Mary-Ellen had parked the kids with her mother and gone right to Philly.

"I met him a couple of times," Captain Stu Simons, riding alone in the backseat, said. "VIP protection details, stuff like that. He was a nice guy. It's a fucking shame, what happened to him."

"You said it," Bill Knotts said.

"They catch him yet, the one that got away?"

"I think so," Captain Simons said. "I think I heard something. They canceled the GRM (General Radio Message) for him."

"I didn't hear anything," Knotts said. "It was a busy night."

"I hope they fry the sonofabitch," Captain Kozniski said.

"Don't hold your breath," Captain Simons said. "He'll get some bleeding-heart lawyer to defend him, and they'll wind up suing Moffitt's estate for violation of the bastard's civil rights."

Major Bill Knotts suddenly shifted very quickly on his seat, and looked out the window.

Captain Kozniski looked at him curiously.

"That shouldn't be there," Knotts said, aloud, but as if to himself.

"Whatever it was, I missed it," Captain Kozniski said.

"There was a Jaguar back there, on a dirt road."

"Somebody taking a piss," Captain Kozniski said.

"Or getting a little," Simons said.

"You want me to call it in, Major?" Captain Kozniski said.

"We're here," Knotts said simply.

Captain Kozniski eased slowly off on the accelerator, and when the car had slowed to sixty, began tapping the brakes. The highway was divided here by a median, and he looked for a place to cross it. The Ford bottomed out as they bounced across the median.

"Jesus Christ, Gerry!" Simons called out. "All we need is to wipe the muffler off!"

Captain Kozniski ignored him. "Where was it, Major?" he asked.

"Farther down," Knotts said. "Where the hell are we? Anybody notice?"

"We're three, four miles east of State Fifty-four," Captain Kozniski replied with certainty.

It took them five minutes to find the car, and then another two minutes to find another place to cross the median again.

"Stay on the shoulder," Knotts ordered, as they approached the dirt road.

Captain Kozniski stopped the car, and Knotts got out. Kozniski followed him, and then Simons. There was the sudden glare of a flashlight, and then Simons walked back to the car and got in the front seat and turned on the radio.

Knotts, carefully keeping out of the grass-free part of the road so as not to disturb tire tracks, approached the car, which was stopped, headed away from the highway, in the middle of the road.

"Give me a flashlight, please," he said, and put his hand out. Kozniski handed him his flashlight. Knotts flashed the light inside the car. It was empty. He moved the beam of the light very slowly around the front of the car.

"Major!" Captain Simons called. "It's a hit on the NCIC computer. NCIC says it was reported stolen in Philadelphia."

"Bingo," Captain Kozniski said.

"Get on the radio, please, Stu," Knotts said, "and have a car meet us here. And see if Philadelphia has any more on it."

"There was another car," Kozniski said. "You can see where they turned around." He used his flashlight as a pointer.

"If it was a couple of kids who 'borrowed' it, and then had second thoughts," Knotts said, "why get rid of it out here in the sticks?"

Kozniski went to the bumper and carefully examined it with his flashlight.

"It wasn't pushed in here, either," he said. "That rubber stuff on the bumper doesn't have a mark on it. I mean, I was thinking maybe it broke down, and they had to leave it."

"If they were going to dismantle it, there wouldn't be anything left by now but the license plate," Knotts said.

Captain Simons walked up to them.

"If the driver is apprehended," he said, formally, "he is to be held for questioning about a homicide."

"Double bingo," Captain Kozniski said. "You telepathic, Major?"

"Absolutely," Major Bill Knotts said. "You mean you didn't know?"

He walked to the Ford, switched the radio frequency to the statewide frequency, established communication with state police headquarters in Trenton; and, after identifying himself and reporting they had located a car NCIC said was hot, and which the Philadelphia police were interested in for a homicide investigation, asked for the dispatch of the state police mobile crime lab van.

"And first thing in the morning, I think we had better get enough people out here to have a good look at the woods," he said. "In the meantime, I'll need somebody to guard the site. I pulled a car off patrol, but I'd like to get him released as soon as possible."

They all got back in the Ford and waited for the patrol car to come to the scene.

Captain Kozniski, without really being aware he had done it, switched on the radar. A minute or so later, it came to life, and a car headed for Atlantic City came down the highway twenty-five miles an hour faster than the posted limit.

"You want to ticket him, Major?" Kozniski asked.

"God no, if we pulled him over and a major and two captains got out of the car, we'd give him a heart attack," Knotts said.

The car was filled with chuckles and laughter.

Two minutes later, Kozniski saw in his rearview mirror the flashing lights on top of a patrol car.

"Here comes the car," he said. Knotts got out of the Ford, explained the situation to the trooper, and then got back in.

He looked at his watch as Kozniski got the Ford moving.

"Christ, we're going to be late for the wake," he said. "You better step on it, Gerry."

The Wackenhut rent-a-cop on the Arch Street entrance to the Stockton Place underground garage stooped over and looked into the Ford LTD. Recognizing Louise Dutton, he smiled, went back to his little cubicle, and pushed the button raising the barrier.

Once inside the garage, Peter Wohl parked the LTD beside her yellow Cadillac convertible, and they got out.

She met him at the back of the LTD.

"If you find the time, dear, you might do the ironing," Louise said as she dropped the keys to her apartment in his hand. "But don't wear yourself out."

"What I think I'll do is call Sharon," Peter said.

"You bastard!" she said, and kissed him quickly and got in her Cadillac convertible.

He waited until she had driven out of the underground garage and then walked through the tunnel to the elevators. The call button for the elevator required a key to function, and he had to work his way through half a dozen before he found the right one. And then he had trouble getting into the apartment itself.

He felt strange, once he was inside and had snapped on the lights, and wasn't sure if he was uncomfortable or excited. There was something very personal, very intimate, in being here alone. He took off his jacket and threw it on an overstuffed chair, and then changed his mind and hung it in a closet by the door. There were two fur coats in there, a long one, and one so short it was almost a cape.

That reminded him that his uniform and other things were still in the LTD, so he retraced his steps and carried them up. He carried everything into the bedroom. The bedroom smelled of Louise. There was a display of perfume bottles on her dressing table and he walked to them and squirted a bulb, and then it really smelled like her.

He found the bathroom, voided his bladder, and then took a good look around. The bathtub looked like a small black marble swimming pool. He wondered if it contained a Jacuzzi, and looked for controls, but found none.

What he needed, he decided, was a drink. He went back in the living room and opened doors and found her liquor supply. He carried a bottle of scotch into the kitchen and found ice cubes and made himself a drink. Then he said aloud, "You god-damned voyeur, Wohl," and went back in the bedroom and opened the drawers of her dresser, one at a time. He found the array of underwear erotic; but a rather diligent—one might say professional—search of the premises failed to come up with a photo-graph or any other evidence, of any other male, young, old, handsome, ugly, or otherwise.

He was pleased. He went to make himself another drink, and then changed his mind. This was a momentous occasion; the most beautiful girl in the world, the love, finally, of his life, was going to welcome him into her bed, and the worst thing he could arrange would be for him to be shit-faced when she came home. No more booze.

Christ! Washington!

Five minutes later, he had relayed the information to Detective Jason Washington that he would have Miss Louise Dutton at the medical examiner's office at eight o'clock the following morning.

Champagne! Why didn't I think of that before? I'll have a couple of bottles on ice when she walks in the door.

He put his coat back on and went out in search of champagne. He bought three bottles, instead of two, and two plastic bags of ice, and returned to the apartment. He couldn't find a champagne bucket, so he put the champagne and the ice in the kitchen sink and covered it with a dishcloth. That raised the question of champagne glasses, and a further diligent search came up with some, which apparently had not been washed for years. He washed and rinsed two of them and then polished them with a paper towel.

He was ready. But she would not be here for an hour, an hour and fifteen min-utes.

An idea, so ridiculous and absurd on its face that he laughed out loud, popped into his mind.

What the hell, why not?

He went into the bathroom and turned the taps on to fill the marble swimming pool. He saw a glass container with BUBBLE BATH printed on it. If half a cupful of de-tergent was the proper amount to use for a washerful of dirty clothes, that measure would probably work for a bubble bath. He poured what he estimated to be a half cupful into the tub.

Next, he looked for and found a razor. He examined it carefully. It was a ladies' razor, with a gold-plated head, and a long, pink, curved handle. But the working part of it, the gold-plated device, seemed to be identical to a regular razor. He decided it would do.

He took the cover from the bed, folded it neatly, and then turned a corner of the sheet and blanket down, and finally returned to the bathroom. The swimming pool was now overflowing with bubbles. There were more bubbles than he would have imagined possible.

There was nothing to do about it now, obviously, so he slipped into the water. There were so many bubbles that he had to push them away from his mouth with his hand.

There's room in here for both of us. I wonder how she would react to that suggestion?

There came the sound of a door opening against a lock chain.

Oh, Christ, she came home early! And I put the goddamned chain on the goddamned door!

He erupted from the swimming pool, called "Wait a minute, I'll be right there!" and dried himself hastily. He grabbed his bathrobe from where he had left it on the bed, and ran through the apartment to the door.

"Sorry," he said, as he pushed the door closed so that he could unfasten the chain lock. "I was taking a goddamned bath."

He pulled the door open.

He found himself looking at a smallish, dapper, intense, middle-aged man.

"I'll just bet," Stanford Fortner Wells III said, "that your name is Peter Wohl."

Louise Dutton let herself into her apartment, and then turned to fasten the dead-bolt lock and door chain.

"Peter, don't tell me you're asleep," she called, and then walked into her living room, where she found her father and Staff Inspector Peter Wohl standing by the couches and coffee table. There were glasses; a bottle of scotch; a cheap glass bowl half-full of ice; and an open box of Ritz crackers on the table. They were both smoking cigars.

"Hello, baby," her father said.

"Oh, *God!*" Louise said.

"You called," Stanford Fortner Wells III said, "and I came."

"So I see," Louise said, and then ran across the room to him, and threw herself in his arms. "Oh, Daddy!"

When she let him go, she took a handkerchief from her purse and blew her nose loudly in it.

She looked at Peter. "Is my mascara running?"

He shook his head no.

She walked to him, and took the glass from his hand and took a large swallow.

"Peter and I have been having a pleasant chat," Wells said.

"I'll bet you have," Louise said, as she handed the glass back. She pointed to the bowl of ice. "What's with that?"

"It's a bowl, with ice in it," Peter said.

"What do you think that is?" she said, pointing to a large, square heavy crystal bowl on a sideboard.

Both Peter and her father shrugged.

"That's" an ice bowl," she said. "I paid two hundred dollars for it. Where did you get that one?"

"Under the sink in the kitchen," her father said.

"That figures," she said. She went to the crystal bowl, moved it to the coffee table, dumped the ice from the cheap bowl into it, and then carried it into the kitchen. She returned in a moment with a small silver bowl full of cashews and a glass.

"Where were they?" her father asked. "All we could find was the crackers."

"In the kitchen," she said. She made herself a drink and then looked at them. "Gentlemen, be seated," she said.

They sat down, Wells on the couch, Peter Wohl in an armchair.

"Well," Louise said. "Now that we're all here, what should we talk about?"

Wohl and her father chuckled.

"I thought the standard scenario in a situation like this was that the father was supposed to thrash the boyfriend within an inch of his life," Louise said. "What happened, Daddy, did you see his gun?"

"No," Wells said. "I just decided that a man who takes bubble baths can't be all bad."

"Bubble baths?" Louise asked.

"Oh, shit," Peter said.

"When he answered the door, he had bubbles in his ears, all over his head," Wells said. "You really don't want to thrash a man with bubbles on him."

Peter, grimacing, laughed deep in his throat. Wells grinned at him.

They like each other, Louise realized, and it pleased her.

"Tell me about the champagne in the sink," Louise said.

Her father threw up his hands, signaling his innocence about that.

"I'm a scotch drinker, myself," he said.

"Ooooh," Louise cooed, "champagne for little ol' me, Peter?"

"At the time, it seemed like a splendid idea," Peter said.

"That was before he answered the door," Wells said.

"Surprise! Surprise!" Peter said.

The two men laughed.

"You should have seen his face," Wells said.

"How long have you been here, in Philadelphia, I mean?" Louise asked.

"Since late this afternoon," Wells said. "I just missed you at WCBL."

The telephone rang.

"I wonder who that can be?" Louise said. "Oh, God! My mother?"

"For your sake, Peter, I hope not," Wells said.

"Jesus!" Wohl said, as Louise went to the telephone.

"Hello?" Louise said to the telephone. Then her face stiffened. "How did you get this number? Who is this?"

Then she offered the telephone to Wohl.

"Lieutenant DelRaye for you, *Inspector Wohl,*" she said, just a little nastily.

As Wohl got up and crossed the room, Wells asked, "DelRaye? Is that the cop you had trouble with?"

"Yes, indeed," Louise said.

"This is Peter Wohl," Wohl said to the telephone. Then he listened, asked a few cryptic questions, then finally said, "Thank you, Lieutenant. If anything else comes up, I'll either be at this number or at home."

He hung up.

" '*I'll either be at this number or at home,*' " Louise parroted. "What did you do, Peter, thumbtack my number, my *unlisted* number, to the bulletin board?"

"I don't even know your number," Peter said, just a little sharply. "He must have gotten it from Jason Washington."

"What did he want?" Louise asked quickly. She had seen her father's eyebrows raise in surprise to learn that Peter didn't know her number.

"They found Jerome Nelson's car," Wohl said. "Actually, a New Jersey state trooper major found it as he was driving here for Dutch's wake. In the middle of New Jersey, on a dirt road off U.S. Three Twenty-two."

"What does that mean?" Wells asked.

"One of Nelson's cars, a Jaguar, was missing from the garage downstairs," Peter said. "It's possible that the doer took it."

"The *'doer'?"* Wells asked.

"Whoever chopped him up," Wohl said.

"I love your delicate choice of language," Louise said. "Really, Peter!"

"Does finding the car mean anything?" Wells asked.

"Only, so far, to reinforce the theory that the doer took it. As opposed to an ordinary, run-of-the-mill car thief," Wohl said. "The New Jersey State Police sent their mobile crime lab to where they found the car, and, in the morning, they'll search the area. With a little luck, they may turn up something."

"Such as?" Wells pursued.

Wohl threw his hands up. "You never know."

"Why do you look so worried, Peter?" Louise asked.

"Do I look worried?" he asked, and then went on before anyone could reply: "I'm trying to make up my mind whether or not I should call Arthur Nelson. Now, I mean, rather than in the morning."

"Why would you call him?" Wells asked.

"Commissioner Czernich has assigned me to stroke him," Peter said. "To keep him abreast of where the investigation is going."

"Until just now, I thought they liked you on the police department," Wells said. "How did you get stuck with that?"

"He can be difficult," Peter said, chuckling. "You know him?"

"Sure," Wells said. "Which is not the same thing as saying he's a friend of mine."

"He's not willing to face the facts about his son," Peter said. "I don't know whether he expected me to believe it or not, but he suggested very strongly that Louise was his son's girlfriend."

"Obviously not knowing about you and Louise," Wells said.

"Nobody, with your exception, knows about Louise and me," Wohl said.

"The two of you have developed the infuriating habit of talking about me as if I'm not here," Louise said.

"Sorry," her father said. "Are you going to call him—now, I mean?"

"Yeah," Peter said. "I think I'd better."

"I was going to suggest that," Wells said. "Better to have him annoyed by a late-night call than sore that you didn't tell him something as soon as you could."

They like each other, Louise thought again. *Because they think alike? Because they are alike? Is that what's going on with me and Peter? That I like him because he's so much like my father? Even more so than Dutch?*

Peter dialed information and asked for Arthur J. Nelson's residence number. There was a reply, and then he said, obviously annoyed, "Thank you."

He sensed Louise's eyes on him, and met hers for a moment, and then smiled mischievously.

"He's got an unlisted number, too."

He dialed another number, identified himself as Inspector Wohl, and asked for a residence phone number for Arthur J. Nelson.

He wrote the number down, and put his finger on the telephone switch.

"That's it?" Louise asked. "You can get an unlisted number from the phone company that easily?"

"That wasn't the information operator," Wohl said, as he dialed the telephone. "I was talking to the detective on duty in Intelligence. The phone company won't pass out numbers."

There was the faint sound of a telephone ringing.

"Mr. Arthur J. Nelson, please," he said. "This is Inspector Peter Wohl of the Philadelphia Police Department."

Neither Louise nor her father could hear both sides of the conversation, but it was evident that the call was not going well. The proof came when Peter exhaled audibly and shook his head after he hung up.

"Arthur was being his usual, obnoxious self, I gather?" Wells asked.

"He wanted to know precisely where the car was found, where it is. I told him I didn't know. He made it plain he didn't believe me. I was on the verge of telling him that if I knew, I wouldn't tell him. I don't want a dozen members of the goddamned press mucking around by the car until the lab people are through with it."

"Thank you very much, you goddamned policeman," Louise said.

"You're welcome," Peter said, and Wells laughed.

"God*damn* you, Peter!"

"*I* didn't teach her to swear like that," Wells said. "She learn that from you?"

"I'd hate to tell you what she said to Lieutenant DelRaye," Peter said.

"I know what she said," Wells said. "If she was a little younger, I'd wash her mouth out with soap."

"I may get to that," Peter said.

"What the hell is it with you two?" Louise demanded. "A mutual-admiration society? A mutual-male-chauvinist-admiration society?"

"Could be," Wells said. "I don't know how he feels about me, baby, but I like Peter very much."

Louise saw happiness and perhaps relief in Peter's eyes. Their eyes met for a moment.

"Then can I have him, Daddy?" Louise said, in a credible mimicry of a small girl's voice. "I promise to feed him, and housebreak him, and walk him, and all that stuff. Please, Daddy?"

Wohl chuckled. Wells grew serious.

"I think he'd have even more trouble housebreaking you than you would him," he said. "You come from very different kennels. My unsolicited advice—to both of you—is to take full advantage of the trial period."

"I thought you said you liked him," Louise said, trying, and not quite succeeding, to sound light and bright.

"I do. But you were talking about marriage, and I think that would be a lousy idea."

"But if we love each other?" Louise asked, now almost plaintively.

"I have long believed that if it were as difficult to get married as it is to get divorced, society would be a hell of a lot better off," Wells said.

"You're speaking from personal experience, no doubt?" Louise flared.

"Cheap shot, baby," Wells said, getting up. "I've had a long day. I'm going to bed. I'll see you tomorrow before I go."

"Don't go, Daddy," Louise said. "I'm sorry. I didn't mean what I said."

"Sure, you did. And I don't blame you. But just for the record, if I had married your mother, that would have been even a greater mistake than marrying the one I did. I don't expect you to pay a bit of attention to what I've said, but I felt obliged to say it anyway."

He crossed the room to Peter Wohl and put out his hand.

"It was good to meet you, Peter," he said. "And I meant what I said, I do like you. Having said that, be warned that I'm going to do everything I can to keep her from marrying you."

"Fair enough," Peter said.

"You understand why, I think," Wells said.

"Yes, sir," Peter said. "I think I do."

"And you think I'm wrong?"

"I don't know, Mr. Wells," Peter Wohl said.

Wells snorted, looked into Wohl's eyes for a moment, and then turned to his daughter.

"Breakfast? Could you come to the Warwick at, say, nine?"

"No," she said.

"Come on, baby," he said.

"I have a busy schedule tomorrow," she said. "I begin the day at eight by looking at a severed head, and then at ten, I have to go to a funeral. It would have to be in the afternoon. Can you stay that long?"

"I'll stay as long as necessary," he said. "We are going to have a very serious conversation, baby, you and I."

"Can I drop you at your hotel, Mr. Wells?" Peter asked. "It's on my way."

"Come on, Peter," Wells said. "Don't ruin a fine first impression by being a hypocrite now. Anyway, there's a limo waiting for me."

He kissed Louise's cheek, waved at Wohl, and walked out of the apartment.

16 Arthur J. Nelson did not like pills. There were several reasons for this, starting with a gut feeling that there was something basically wrong with chemically fooling around with the natural functions of the body, but primarily it was because he had seen what pills had done to his wife.

Sally was always bitching about his drinking, and maybe there was a little something to that; maybe every once in a while he *did* take a couple of belts that he really didn't need; but the truth was that, so far as *intoxication* was concerned, she had been floating around on a chemical cloud for years.

It had been going on for years. Sally had been nervous when he married her, and once a month, before that time of the month, she had been like a coiled spring, just waiting for a small excuse to blow up. She'd started taking pills then, a little something to help her cope. That had worked, and when she'd gotten pregnant, the need for them had seemed to pass.

But even before she'd had Jerome, she'd started on pills again, to calm her down. Tranquilizers, they called them. Then, after Jerome was born, when he was still a baby, she'd kept taking them whenever, as she put it, things just *"made her want to scream."*

She hadn't taken them steadily then, just when there was some kind of stress. Over the years, it had just slipped up on her. There seemed to be more and more stress, which she coped with by popping a couple of whatever the latest miracle of medicine was.

In the last five years, it had really gotten worse. Jerome had had a lot to do with that. It had been bad when he was still living at home, and had grown worse when he'd moved out. It had gotten so bad that he'd finally put her in Menninger's, where they put a name to it, "chemical dependency," and had weaned her from what she was taking and put her on something else, which was supposed to be harmless.

Maybe it was, but Sally hadn't given it a real try. The minute she got back to Philadelphia, she'd changed doctors again, finding a new one who would prescribe whatever she had been taking in the first place that helped her cope. The real result of her five months in Menninger's was that she was now on two kinds of pills, instead of just one.

Now, probably, three kinds of pills. What she had been taking, plus a new bottle of tiny oblong blue ones provided by the doctors when she'd gone over the edge when he'd had to tell her what happened to Jerome.

They would, the doctor said, help her cope. And the doctor added, it would probably be a good idea if Arthur Nelson took a couple of them before going to bed. It would help him sleep.

No fucking way. He had no intention of turning himself into a zombie, walking around in a daze smiling at nothing. Not so long as there was liquor, specifically cognac. Booze might be bad for you, but all it left you with was a hangover in the morning. And he had read somewhere that cognac was different from, say, scotch. They made scotch from grain, and cognac was made from wine. It was different chemically, and it understandably affected people differently than whiskey did.

Arthur J. Nelson had come to believe that if he didn't make a pig of himself, if he didn't gulp it down, if he just sipped slowly at a glass of cognac, or put half a shot in his coffee, it was possible to reach a sort of equilibrium. The right amount of cognac in his system served to deaden the pain, to keep him from painful thought, but not to make him drunk. He could still think clearly, was still very much aware of what was going on. The only thing he had to do, he believed, was exercise the necessary willpower, and resist the temptation to pour another glass before it was really safe to do so. And there was no question in his mind that he had, in the last twenty-four hours, been doing just that. A lesser man would have broken down and wept, or gotten falling-down drunk, or both, and he had done neither.

When Staff Inspector Peter Wohl had telephoned, Arthur J. Nelson had been a third of the way through a bottle of Hennessey V.S.O.P., one delicate sip at a time, except of course for the couple of hookers he had splashed into his coffee.

And he took a pretty good sip, draining the snifter, when he hung up after talking to Staff Inspector Peter Wohl, that miserable arrogant sonofabitch.

He poured the snifter a third full, and then, carrying it with him, walked upstairs from his den to his bedroom on the second floor. He quietly opened the door and walked in.

Sally was in the bed, flat on her back, asleep. She looked, he thought, old and tired and pale. Although he hated what the fucking pills had done to her, he was glad, for her sake, that she had them now. And then she snored. It was amazing, he thought, how noisily she snored. It sounded as if she were a 250-pound man, and he supposed she didn't weigh 100 pounds, if that much.

He remembered the first time he had seen her naked, held her naked in his arms. She had been so small and delicate he had been afraid that he was going to break her. And he remembered when she was large with Jerome. That had been almost impossible to believe, even looking right at it.

A tear ran down his cheek, and he brushed at it, forgetting that that hand held the snifter. He spilled a couple of drops on his shirt, and swore, loud enough for it to get through to Sally, who sort of groaned.

He held himself motionless for a moment, until her regular, slow, heavy breathing pattern returned. Then he left the room as carefully and quietly as he entered it.

He stood at the top of the stairs. He was hungry. He hadn't eaten. The house had been full of people, and although Mrs. Dawberg, the housekeeper, had seen to it that there had been a large buffet of cold cuts, he just hadn't gotten around to eating.

And now all the help was in bed, and he hated to get them out of bed in any case; and especially now, when they would need all the rest they could get to get ready for tomorrow, when the house, all day, would be like goddamn Suburban Station at half past five.

He walked down the wide staircase, wondering if he really wanted to go into the kitchen and fix himself an egg sandwich or something. He went back in his den and drained what was left in the snifter after he—Jesus, what a dumb thing to do!!!—had spilled it on his shirt, and then poured a little more in.

To hell with going in the kitchen, he decided. *What I'll do is just get in a car and go find a fast-food joint.*

The idea had a sudden appeal. He realized that what he really wanted was junk food. Hamburgers and french fries. Not what they served these days in McDonald's or Burger King, but the little tiny ones they used to sell for a dime, the kind they sort of steamed on the grill over chopped onions. In those white tile buildings with no booths, just round-seat stools by a counter, where everything was stainless steel. He could practically smell the damned things.

He had a little trouble finding where they kept the keys to the cars. He supposed they took them from the ignition last thing when they locked up for the night. He finally found a rack of keys in a little cupboard in the pantry off the garage. They were all in little numbered leather cases, except the key to the Rolls, which had a Rolls insignia on it.

Which was which?

He didn't want to take the Rolls. He was going to go to a hamburger joint and sit on a round stool and eat cheap little hamburgers and french fries, and you don't take a Rolls-Royce to do that.

He took one key and worked his way through a Cadillac coupe and a Buick station wagon before it worked in the ignition switch of an Oldsmobile sedan he didn't remember ever having seen before. He remembered vaguely that Sally had said something about having to get Mrs. Dawberg a new car, and that he'd told her to go ahead and do it.

He thought he remembered a White Palace or a Crystal Palace or whatever the hell they called those joints about a mile away, but when he got there, there was a Sunoco gas station, so he drove on. When he stopped at a red light, he decided it had been some time since he'd last had a little sip, and pulled the cork from the Hennessey bottle and took a little nip.

Thirty minutes later, not having found what he wanted, he decided to hell with it. What he would do was go by the *Ledger.* It wouldn't be a cheap little White Palace hamburger, but the cafeteria operated twenty-four hours a day, and he could at least get a hamburger, or something else. And it was always a good idea to drop in unannounced on the city room. Keep them on their toes.

He drove to the back of the building and pulled the nose of the Oldsmobile in against a loading dock, and took another little sip. He could hardly walk into the city room carrying a bottle of cognac, and there was no telling how long he would be in there.

There was a tap on his window, and he looked out and saw a security officer frowning at him. With some difficulty, Arthur J. Nelson managed to find the window switch and lower the window.

"Hey, buddy," the security officer said, "you can't park there."

"Let me tell *you* something, *buddy,*" Arthur J. Nelson said. "I own this goddamned newspaper and I can park any goddamned place I please!"

The security officer's eyes widened, and then there was recognition.

"Sorry, Mr. Nelson, I didn't recognize you."

"Goddamned right," Arthur Nelson said, and got out of the car. "Keep up the good work!" he called after the retreating security officer.

He entered the building and walked down the tile-lined corridor to the elevator bank. Windows opened on the presses in the basement. They were still, although he saw pressmen standing around. He glanced at his watch.

It was not quite one A.M. The first (One Star) edition started rolling at two-fifteen. Christ alone knew what it was costing him to have all those pressmen standing around for an hour or more with their fingers up their asses at $19.50 an hour. He'd have to look into that. Goddamned unions would bankrupt you if you didn't keep your eye on them.

He got in the elevator and rode it up to the fifth, editorial, floor, and went into the city room.

He felt eyes on him as he walked across the room to the city desk.

Well, why the hell not? I don't come in here at this time nearly often enough.

There were half a dozen men and two women at the city desk. The city editor got to his feet when he saw him.

"Good evening, Mr. Nelson," he said. "How are you, sir?"

"How the hell do you think I am?" Nelson snapped.

"I'd like to offer my condolences, sir," the city editor said.

"Very kind of you," Arthur Nelson said, automatically, and then he remembered that goddamned cop, whatsisname, *Wohl.*

"I've got something for you," Nelson said. "The cops have found my son's car. It was stolen from the garage at his apartment when ... it was stolen from his apartment."

"Yes, sir?"

"You haven't heard about it?"

"No, sir."

"Well, I'm telling you," Nelson said. "And they're giving me the goddamned runaround. Somewhere in Jersey is where they found it. Some Jersey state trooper found it, but he wouldn't tell me where."

"I'm sure we could find out, sir," the city editor said. "If that's what you're suggesting."

"Goddamn right," Nelson said. "Get somebody on it. It's news, wouldn't you say?"

"Yes, sir, of course it is. I'll get right on it."

"I think that would be a good idea," Nelson said.

"I was about to go to Composing, Mr. Nelson," the city editor said. "We're just about pasted up. Would you like to go with me?"

"Why not?" Nelson said. "Have you got somebody around here you could send to the cafeteria for me?"

"What would you like?"

"I'd like a hamburger and french fries," Nelson said. "Hamburger with onions. Fried, not raw. And a cup of black coffee."

"Coming right up," the city editor said.

Nelson walked across the city room to Composing. The *Ledger* had, the year before, gone to a cold-type process, replacing the Linotype system. The upcoming One Star edition was spread out on slanting boards, in "camera-ready" form. Here and there, compositors were pasting up.

Nelson went to the front page. The lead story, under the headline "Man Sought In Police Murder Killed Eluding Capture" caught his eye, and he read it with interest.

If all the goddamned cops in the goddamned city hadn't all been looking for that guy, they probably could have caught the bastards who killed my Jerome. They don't give a shit about me, or any other ordinary citizen, but when one of their own gets it, that's a horse of a different color. That sonofabitch Wohl wouldn't even tell me where Jerome's car was found.

The city editor appeared.

"Now that the cops have found that pathetic sonofabitch," Arthur J. Nelson said, "maybe, just maybe, they'll have time to look for the murderer of my son."

"Yes, sir," the city editor said, uncomfortably. "Mr. Nelson, I think you better have a look at this."

He thrust the Early Bird edition of the *Bulletin* at him.

"What's this?" Nelson said. And then his eye fell on the headline, "Police Seek 'Gay' Black Lover In Nelson Murder" and the story below it by Michael J. O'Hara.

"I thought O'Hara worked for us," Arthur J. Nelson said, very calmly.

"We had to let him go about eighteen months ago," the city editor said.

"Oh?" Arthur J. Nelson asked.

"Yes, sir. He had a bottle problem," the city editor said.

"And a nice sense of revenge, wouldn't you say?" Nelson said. He didn't wait for a reply. He turned and walked down the line of paste-ups until he found the editorial page.

He pointed to it. "Hold this," he said. "There will be a new editorial."

"Sir?"

"I'm not going to let the goddamned cops get away with this," Arthur J. Nelson said. "Not on your goddamned life."

Louise Dutton slipped out of her robe, draped it over the water closet, and then slid open the glass door to her shower stall. She giggled at what she saw.

"What the hell are you doing?" she asked.

Peter Wohl, who had been shaving with Louise's pink, long-handled ladies' razor, heard her voice, but not what she had said, and opened his eyes and looked at her.

"What?"

"What are you doing?"

"Shaving."

"In the shower? With your eyes closed?"

"Why not?"

"You look ridiculous doing that," she said.

"On the other hand," he said, leering at her nakedness, "you look great. Why don't you step into my office and we can fool around a little?"

"There's not room for the both of us in there," she said.

"That would depend on how close we stood," he said.

"Hurry up, Peter," she said, and closed the door.

She wiped the condensation from the mirror and bent forward to examine her face closely. She looked into the reflection of her eyes. She felt a sense of sadness, and wondered why.

Peter came out of the shower.

"I left it running," he said, as he reached for a towel.

Louise gave in to the impulse and wrapped her arms around him, resting her face on his back.

"The offer to fool around is still open," Peter said.

"What's this?" she asked, tracing what looked like a dimple on his back.

"Nothing," he said.

"What *is* it, Peter?" she demanded.

"It's what they call an entrance wound," he said.

"You were *shot?*" she asked, letting him go, and then turning him around so she could look into his face.

"Years ago," he said.

"You're not old enough for it to be 'years ago,'" she said. "Tell me!"

"Not much to tell," he said. "I was working the Ninth District as a patrolman, and a lady called the cops and said her husband was drunk and violent and beating her and the kids up; and when I got there, he was, so I put the cuffs on him, and as I was putting him in the backseat of the car, she shot me."

"Why?"

"She wanted the cops to make her husband stop beating up on her," Peter said, "but *arresting* the love of her life and father of her children was something else."

"She could have killed you," Louise said.

"I think that's what she had in mind," Peter said.

"Did you shoot her?" Louise asked.

"I don't even remember getting shot ... I remember what felt like somebody whacking me with a baseball bat, and the next thing I know, I'm being wheeled into a hospital emergency room."

"How long were you in the hospital?"

"About two weeks."

"But you're all right? I mean, there was no permanent damage?"

"All the important parts are working just fine," Peter said. He moved his midsection six inches closer to Louise to demonstrate. "See?"

"Why, you dirty old man, you!" Louise said, and turned and went into the shower.

When she came out of the shower, she could smell both frying bacon and coffee, and smiled.

Peter Wohl, she thought, *the compleat lover, as skilled in the kitchen as the bedroom.*

Then she went into her bedroom, and saw that he had left his uniform tunic, and his uniform cap, and his gun, on the bed.

She walked to the bed and picked up the hat first and looked at it, and the insignia on it, and then laid it down again. Then she leaned on the bed and examined the badge pinned to the uniform tunic. And finally, she looked at the gun.

It was in a shoulder holster, of leather and stretch elastic that showed signs of much use. The elastic was wrinkled, and the leather sweat-stained and creased. She tugged the pistol loose and held it up to the level of her face by holding the grip between her thumb and index finger.

It was not a new pistol. The finish had been worn through to the white metal beneath at the muzzle and at the front of the cylinder. The little diamonds of the checkering on the grips were worn smooth. She sniffed it, and smelled the oil.

It's a tool, she thought, *like a carpenter's hammer, or a mechanic's wrench. It's the tool he carries to work. The difference is that the function of his tool is to shoot people, not drive nails or fix engines.*

She put the pistol back into the holster, and then wiped her hands on the sheet.

Then she got dressed.

He had made bacon and eggs. He was mopping the remaining yolk from his plate with an English muffin; her eggs and bacon were waiting for her.

"Your eggs are probably cold," Peter said.

"I had to take a shower," she said, a shade snappishly.

"Not for me you didn't," he said. "You smelled great to me."

"Don't be silly," she snapped, and this time the snappishness registered.

"Coffee?" he asked, a little coldly.

"Please," she said.

He went to the stove and returned with a pot.

"Did you ever kill anyone, Peter?"

His eyebrows went up.

"Did you?"

"Yes," he said. "Lovely subject for breakfast conversation."

"Why?"

"Because I think otherwise he would have shot me," Peter said. "Lovely weather we've been having, isn't it?"

"An interesting scenario popped into my mind in the bedroom," Louise said.

"That happens to me all the time," he said. "You really thought of something we haven't done?"

He smiled, and she knew he was pleased that he thought she had changed the subject, but she knew she couldn't stop now.

"There I am, sitting in my rocking chair, knitting little booties, in our little rose-covered cottage by the side of the road," Louise said, "while our three adorable children . . . You get the picture."

"Sounds fine to me," Peter said.

"And the doorbell rings, and I go to answer it, and there stands Hizzoner the Mayor Carlucci. 'Sorry, Mrs. Wohl,' Hizzoner says. 'But your fine husband, the late Inspector Wohl, was just shot by an angry housewife. Or was it a bandit? Doesn't really matter. He's dead. Gone to that Great Roundhouse in the Sky.' "

It took Peter a moment to reply, but finally he said, "Are you always this cheerful in the morning?"

"Only when I'm on my way to see a severed head while en route to a funeral," Louise said. "But I'm serious, Peter."

"Then I'll answer you seriously," he said. "I *am* a Staff Inspector. I don't respond to calls. Supervisors supervise. The guys on the street are the ones that have to deal with the public. That's for openers. And most police officers who do their twenty years on the street never fire their pistols except on the range."

"That's why you carry a gun all the time, right?" Louise countered.

"I can't remember the last time I took it out of the holster except to clean it," Peter said.

"I can," Louise said. "The very first time I saw you, Peter, you were jumping out of a car with your gun in your hand."

"That was an anomaly," Peter said. "Dutch getting shot was an anomaly. He's probably the first captain who fired his weapon in the line of duty in twenty years."

"That may be, but Dutch got shot," Louise said. "Got shot and killed. And there you were, with your gun in your hand, rushing to the gun battle at the OK Corral."

"What did you think when you saw me getting out of my car?"

" 'Where did that good-looking man come from?' "

"How about 'Thank God, it's the cops'?" Peter asked, softly.

She met his eyes for a long moment.

"Touché," she said, finally.

"That's what I do, baby," Peter said. "I'm a cop. And I'm good at what I do. And, actuarially speaking, I'm in probably no more of a risky occupation than a, hell, I don't know, an airline pilot or a stockbroker."

"Tell that to Mrs. Moffitt," Louise said.

"Eat your eggs before they get cold, baby," Peter said.

"I don't think so," she said, pushing the plate away. "I think I would rather get something to eat *after* I look at the head."

"I'm sorry, but that is necessary," Peter said.

"Peter, I don't know if I could spend the rest of my life wondering if I'm going to be a widow by the end of the day," Louise said.

"You're exaggerating the risk," he said.

"Is it graven on stone somewhere that you have to spend the rest of your life as a cop?"

"It's what I do, Louise. And I like it."

"I was afraid you'd say that," she said, and got to her feet. "Go put on your policeman's suit, and take me to see the severed head," she said.

"We can talk this out," Peter said.

"I think everything that can be said on the subject has been said," Louise said. "It was what Daddy was talking about when he said the idea of us getting married was a lousy one."

"Come on, baby," Peter said. "I understand why you're upset, but—"

"Just shut up, Peter," Louise said. "Just please shut up."

Antonio V. "Big Tony" Amarazzo, proprietor of Tony's Barbershop, stood behind the barber chair, swinging it from side to side so that the man in the chair could admire his handiwork. He had given the large man under the striped bib his very first haircut, twenty years before, the day before he started kindergarten.

Officer Charles McFadden looked into the mirror. The mirror was partly covered by the front page of the Four Star Edition of the *Bulletin,* with his picture on it, which had been taped to the mirror below the legend (lettered with shoe whitener) "OUR NEIGHBORHOOD HERO CHARLEY MCFADDEN."

"Looks fine, Mr. Amarazzo," Charley said. "Thank you."

" *'Mister* Amarazzo'?" Big Tony replied. "You sore at me or what? We haven't been friends since God only knows how long?"

Charley, who could not think of a response, smiled at Big Tony's reflection in the mirror.

"And now we're gonna give you a shave that'll turn your chin into a baby's bottom," Big Tony said.

"Oh, I don't want a shave," Charley protested.

"You can't go to Saint Dominic's needing a shave," Big Tony said, as he pushed Charley back in the chair and draped his face in a hot towel, "and don't worry, it's on the house. My privilege."

Ninety seconds later, as Charley wondered how long (he had never had a barbershop shave before) Big Tony was going to keep the towels on his face, someone else came into the barbershop.

"You know who's in the chair, under the towels?" Charley heard Big Tony say. "Charley McFadden, that's who. You seen the *Bulletin?*"

"I seen it," an unfamiliar voice said. "I'll be goddamned."

Charley had folded his hands over his stomach. He was startled when his right hand was picked up, and vigorously shaken by two hands.

"Good for you, Charley," the voice said. "I was just telling the wife, when we seen the paper, that if there was more cops like you, and more shitasses killed like the one you killed, Philly'd be a hell of a lot better off. We're all proud of you, boy."

"I knew all along," Charley heard Big Tony say, "that Charley was a cop. I couldn't say anything, of course."

When Big Tony pulled the hot towel off, and started to lather Charley's face, there

were three other men from the neighborhood standing behind the chair, waiting to
shake his hand.

It was a pleasant spring morning, and the Payne family was having breakfast outside,
on a flagstone patio. The whole family, for the first time in a long time, was all home
at once. Foster J. Payne, twenty-five, who looked very much like his father, had come
home from Cambridge, where he had just completed his second year at Harvard Law;
and Amelia Alice "Amy" Payne, twenty-seven, who had three years before—the
youngest in her Johns Hopkins class—earned the right to append "M.D." after her
name, had just completed her residency in psychiatry at the Louisiana State University
Medical Center, and had come home to find a place for herself in Philadelphia. Brewster C. Payne III, eighteen, who had just graduated from Episcopal Academy, had
commuted to school; but he was, after spending the summer in Europe (his graduation
present), going to Dartmouth; and Patricia Payne was very aware that the nest would
then be forever empty.

Amy was petite and intense, not a pretty girl, but an attractive, natural one. In
judging his children intellectually (and of course, privately) Brewster Payne had rated
his daughter first, then Matt, then Foster, and finally Brewster, who was known as
"B.C." Just as privately, Patricia Payne had done the same thing, with the same result,
except that she had rated B.C. ahead of Foster.

Amy was very smart, perhaps even brilliant. She had been astonishingly preco-
cious, and as astonishingly determined from the time she had been a little girl. Patricia
worried that it might cause her trouble when she married, until she learned to adapt
to her husband, or perhaps to the more general principle that it is sometimes far wiser
to keep your mouth shut than to persist in trying to correct someone else's erroneous
notions.

Matt was bright. He had never had any trouble in school, and there had been at
least a dozen letters from teachers and headmasters saying essentially the same thing,
that if he applied himself, he could be an A student. He never applied himself
(Patricia was convinced he had never done an hour's honest homework in his life) and
he had never been an A student.

Foster was, but Foster had to work at it. By definition, Foster was the only student
among the three of them. Amy rarely had to crack a book, Matt was never willing to,
and Foster seldom had his nose out of one. B.C. had been a 3.5 average student at
Episcopal without ever having brought a book home from school.

The patio was furnished with a long, wrought-iron, mottled-glass-topped table,
with eight cushioned wrought-iron chairs. Two smaller matching tables sat against the
fieldstone, slate-topped patio wall. Two electric frying pans had been set up on one
of them, and it also held a bowl of eggs and a plate with bacon and Taylor ham. The
other held an electric percolator, a pitcher of milk, a toaster, bread and muffins, and
a pitcher of orange juice.

Patricia Payne had decided, when the kids were growing up, that the solution to
everybody's sauntering down to breakfast in their own good time was, rather than
shouted entreaties and threats up the kitchen stairwell, a cafeteria-style buffet. The
kids came down when they wanted, and cooked their own eggs. In the old days, too,
there had been two newspapers, which at least partially solved the question of who
got what section when.

There was something bittersweet about today's breakfast, Patricia thought: fond memories of breakfasts past, pleasure that everyone was once again having breakfast together again, and a disquieting fear that today, or at least the next week or so, might be the very last time it would happen.

"That's absolute *bullshit!*" Matthew Payne said, furiously.

Everybody looked at him. He was on the right side of the far end of the table, bent over a folded copy of the *Ledger.*

"Matt!" Patricia Payne said.

"Did you see this?" Matt asked, rhetorically.

"Actually, no," Brewster Payne said, dryly. "When I came down, all that was left of the paper was the real estate ads."

"Tell us what the goddamn liberals have done this time, Matty," Amy said.

"You watch your language, too, *Doctor,*" Patricia Payne said.

Matt got up and walked down the table to Brewster Payne and laid the editorial page on the table before him. He pointed.

" 'No Room In Philadelphia For Vigilante Justice,' " Matt quoted. "Just read that garbage!"

Brewster Payne read the editorial, then pushed the paper to his wife.

"Maybe they know something you don't, Matt," he said.

"I met that cop yesterday," Matt said.

"You met him?" Amy said.

"Denny Coughlin took me to meet him," Matt said. "First he took me to the medical examiner's and showed me the body, and then he took me to South Philadelphia to meet the cop."

"Why did he do that?" Amy asked.

"He shares your opinion, *Doctor,* that I shouldn't join the police," Matt said. "He was trying to scare me off."

"I suppose even a policeman can spot obvious insanity when he sees it," Amy said.

"Amy!" Patricia Payne said.

Foster Payne got up and stood behind Patricia Payne and read the editorial.

"Whoever wrote this," he said, "is one careful step the safe side of libel," he said.

"It's bullshit," Matt said. "It's . . . vicious. I saw that cop. He was damned near in shock. He was so shook up he didn't even know who Denny Coughlin was. He's a nice, simple Irish Catholic guy who could no more throw somebody in front of an elevated train than Mom could."

"But it doesn't *say* that, Matthew," Foster Payne explained patiently. "It doesn't *say* he pushed that man onto the tracks. What it *says* is that that allegation has been raised, and that having been raised, the city has a clear duty to investigate. Historically, police have overreacted when one of their own has been harmed."

Matthew glared at him; said, with infinite disgust, "Oh, Jesus!" and then looked at Brewster Payne. "Now that Harvard Law has been heard from, Dad, what do you say?"

"I don't really know enough about what really happened to make a judgment," Brewster Payne said. "But I think it reasonable to suggest that Arthur J. Nelson, having lost his son the way he did, is not very happy with the police."

"Daddy, you saw where the police are looking for the Nelson boy's homosexual lover?" Amy asked. "His *Negro* homosexual lover?"

"Oh, no!" Patricia Payne said. "How awful!"

"No, I didn't," Brewster Payne said. "But if that's true, that would lend a little weight to my argument, wouldn't it?"

"You're not suggesting, Brew, that Mr. Nelson would allow something like that to be published; something untrue, as Matt says it is, simply to . . . get back at the police."

"Welcome to the real world, Mother," Amy said.

17 Jason Washington was waiting for them at the medical examiner's office. His expressive face showed both surprise and, Peter Wohl thought, just a touch of amusement when he saw that Wohl was in uniform.

"Good morning, Miss Dutton," Washington said. "I'm sorry to have to put you through this."

"It's all right," Louise said.

"They're installing a closed-circuit television system, to make this sort of identification a little easier on people," Washington said. "But it's not working yet."

"I can come back in a month," Louise said.

They chuckled. Washington smiled at Wohl.

"And may I say, Inspector, how spiffy you look today?" he said.

"I'm going to be a pallbearer," Wohl said.

"Can we get on with this?" Louise asked.

"Yes, ma'am," Washington said. "Miss Dutton, I'm going to take you inside, and show you some remains. I will then ask you if you have ever seen that individual, and if so, where, when, and the circumstances."

"All right," Louise said.

"You want me to come with you?" Peter asked.

"Only if you want to," Louise said.

Louise stepped back involuntarily when Jason Washington lifted the sheet covering the remains of Gerald Vincent Gallagher, but she did not faint, nor did she become nauseous. When Peter Wohl tried to steady her by putting his hands on her arms, she shook free impatiently.

"I don't know his name," she said, levelly. "But I have seen that man before. In the Waikiki Diner. He's the man who was holding the diner up when Captain Moffitt tried to stop him."

"There is no question in your mind?" Washington asked.

"For some reason, it stuck in my mind," Louise said, sarcastically, and then turned and walked quickly out of the room.

Wohl caught up with her.

"You all right?" he asked.

"I'm fine," she said.

"You want a cup of coffee? Something else?"

"No, thank you," she said.

"You want to go get some breakfast?"

"No, thank you."

"You have to eat, Louise," Wohl said.

"He said, ever practical," she said, mockingly.

"You do," he said.

"All right, then," she said.

They went to a small restaurant crowded with office workers on the way to work. They were the subject of a good deal of curiosity. People recognized Louise, Wohl realized. They might not be able to recognize her as the TV lady, but they knew they had seen her someplace.

She ate French toast and bacon, but said very little.

"I have the feeling that I've done something wrong," Peter said.

"Don't be silly," she said.

As they walked back to his car, they passed a Traffic Division cop, who saluted Peter, who, not expecting it, returned it somewhat awkwardly. Then he noticed that the cop was wearing the mourning band over his badge. He had completely forgotten about that. The mourning bands were sliced from the elastic cloth around the bottom of old uniform caps. He didn't have an old uniform cap. He had no idea what had happened to either his old regular patrolman's cap, or the crushed-crown cap he had worn as a Highway Patrol sergeant. And there never had been cause to replace his senior officer's cap; he hadn't worn it twenty times.

He wondered if someone would have one at Marshutz & Sons, predicting that someone like him would show up without one. And if that didn't happen, what he would do about it.

He drove Louise back to Stockton Place and pulled to the curb before Number Six.

"What about later?" he asked.

"What about later?" she parroted.

"When am I going to see you?"

"I have to work, and then I have to see my father, and then I have to go back to work. I'll call you."

"Don't call me, I'll call you?"

"Don't press me, Peter," she said, and got out of the car. And then she walked around the front and to his window and motioned for him to lower it. She bent down and kissed him. It started as a quick kiss, but it quickly became intimate.

Not passionate, he thought, *intimate.*

"That may not have been smart," Louise said, looking into his eyes for a moment, and then walking quickly into the building, not looking back.

Intimate, Peter Wohl thought, *and a little sad, as in a farewell kiss.*

He looked at her closed door for a moment, and then made a U-turn on the cobblestones, and drove away.

He had headed, without thinking, for Marshutz & Sons, but changed his mind and instead drove to the Roundhouse. There might have been another development, something turned up around Jerome Nelson's car, maybe, or something else. If there was something concrete, maybe it would placate Arthur J. Nelson. His orders had been to stroke him, not antagonize him.

And somewhere in the Roundhouse he could probably find someone who could give him a mourning band; he didn't want to take the chance that he could get one at the funeral home.

He went directly to Homicide.

Captain Henry C. Quaire was sitting on one of the desks, talking on the telephone, and seemed to expect him; when he saw Wohl he pointed to one of the rooms adjacent to one of the interrogation rooms. Then he covered the phone with his hand and said, "Be right with you."

Wohl nodded and went into the room. Through the one-way mirror, he could see three people in the interrogation room. One was Detective Tony Harris. There was another man, a tall, rather aesthetic-looking black man in his twenties or thirties whom Wohl didn't recognize but who, to judge by the handcuffs hanging over his belt in the small of his back, was a detective. The third man was a very large, very black, visibly uncomfortable man handcuffed to the interrogation chair. He fit the description of Pierre St. Maury.

As Peter reached for the switch that would activate the microphone hidden in the light fixture, and permit him to hear what was being said, Captain Quaire came into the room. Peter took his hand away from the switch.

"What's going on?" Peter asked. "Is that Pierre St. Maury?"

"No," Quaire said. "His name is Kostmayer. But Porterfield thought he was, and brought him in."

"Porterfield is the other guy?"

Quaire nodded and grunted. "Narcotics. Good cop. He's high on the detective's list and wants to come over here when he gets promoted."

"So what's going on?"

"This guy was so upset that Porterfield thought he was Maury that Porterfield thinks he knows something about the Nelson job."

"Does he?" Wohl asked.

"We are about to find out," Quaire said, throwing the microphone switch. "He already gave us Mr. Pierre St. Maury's real name—Errol F. Watson—and address. I already sent people to see if they can pick him up at home."

Wohl watched the interrogation for fifteen minutes. Admiringly. Tony Harris and Porterfield worked well together, as if they had done so before. He wondered if they had. They pulled one little thing at a time from Kostmayer, sometimes sternly calling him by his last name, sometimes, kindly, calling him "Peter," one picking up the questioning when the other stopped.

It was slow. Kostmayer was reluctant to talk. It was obvious he was more afraid of other people than his own troubles with the law.

"What have you got on him?" Wohl asked.

"Couple of minor arrests," Quaire said. "He's a male prostitute. The usual stuff. Possession of controlled substances. Rolling people."

Kostmayer finally said something interesting.

"Well, I heard *this,*" he said, seemingly on the edge of tears. "I only *heard* it; I don't know if it's *true* or not."

"We understand, Peter," Tony Harris said, kindly. "What did you hear?"

"Well, there was talk, and you know people just talk, that a certain two men who knew Pierre, and knew that he was, you know, *friends,* with Jerome Nelson, were going to get the key to the apartment—you know, the Nelson apartment—from him."

"Why were they going to do that, Peter?" Tony Harris asked.

"What certain two people, Kostmayer?" Detective Porterfield demanded.

"Well, they were, you know, going to *take* things," Kostmayer said.

"What were their names, Kostmayer?" Porterfield said, walking to him and lowering his face to his. "I'm losing my patience with you."

"I don't know their names," Kostmayer said.

He's lying, Peter Wohl thought, at the exact moment Porterfield put that thought in words: "Bullshit!"

Wohl looked at Quaire, who had his lower lip protruding thoughtfully.

Then Wohl looked at his watch.

"Hell, I have to get out of here," he said. "I'm due at Marshutz & Sons in fifteen minutes."

"You going to be a pallbearer? Is that why you're wearing your uniform?"

"Yeah. And Henry, I need a mourning strip for my badge. Where can I get one?"

"I've got one," Quaire said, taking Wohl's arm and leading him to his office. There, he took a small piece of black elastic hatband material from an envelope and stretched it over Wohl's badge.

"I appreciate it, Henry. I'll get it back to you."

"Why don't you?" Quaire said. "Then the next time, God forbid, we need one, you'll know where to find one."

Wohl nodded.

"I'll let you know whatever else they find out, Peter," Quaire said.

"As soon as you get it, please. Even at Dutch's funeral."

"Sure," Quaire said.

Wohl shook Quaire's hand and left.

Brewster Cortland Payne II had had some difficulty persuading Amy, Foster, and B.C. to attend the funeral of Captain Richard C. Moffitt.

Amy had caved in more quickly, when her father told her that her mother felt the loss more than she was showing, and that while she wouldn't ask, would really appreciate having another female along.

Foster and B.C. were a little more difficult. When Brewster Payne raised the subject, he saw his sons were desperately searching for a reason not to go.

Finally, B.C. protested, truthfully, that he had "seen the man only once or twice in my life."

"He was your brother's uncle, Brew," Brewster Payne said, "and your mother's brother-in-law."

"You know," Foster said, thoughtfully, "the only time I ever think that Mother isn't my—what's the word?— *natural* mother is when something like this comes up."

"I'm sure she would accept that as a compliment," Brewster Payne said.

"Or that Matt isn't really my brother," Foster went on. "I presume you did try to talk him out of this becoming-a-policeman nonsense?"

"First things first," Brewster Payne said. "Matt is your brother, de facto and de jure, and I'm sure you won't say anything about something like that to him."

"Of course not," Foster said.

"I already told him," B.C. said, "that I thought he was nuts."

Out of the mouth of the babe, Brewster C. Payne thought. He said: "To answer your second question, no, I didn't really try to talk Matt out of becoming a policeman. For one thing, I learned of it after the fact, and for another, he's your mother's son, and as you have learned there are times when neither of them can be dissuaded from what they want to do. And, finally, son, I don't agree that it's nonsense. I told him, and I believe, that it can be a very valuable learning experience for him."

"Amy says that he was psychologically castrated when he failed the marine corps physical, and is becoming a policeman to prove his manhood," B.C. said.

"She talks to you like that? When I was a boy—"

"All the girls you knew were virgins who didn't even know what 'castrated' meant," Foster said, laughing. "But Amy has a point, and she's really concerned."

"I don't think I quite understand," Brewster Payne said.

"What if Matt can't make it as a policeman? He really doesn't know what he's letting himself in for. What if he fails? Double castration, so to speak."

"I have confidence that Matt can do anything he sets his mind to do," Brewster Payne said. "And I'm beginning to wonder if sending your sister to medical school was such a good idea. I'm afraid that we can expect henceforth that she will ascribe a Freudian motive to everything any one of us does, from entering a tennis tournament to getting married."

Patricia and Amelia Payne came down the wide staircase from the second floor. They were dressed almost identically, in simple black dresses, strings of pearls, black hats, and gloves.

Brewster Payne had what he thought a moment later was an unkind thought. He wondered how many men were lucky enough to have wives who were better looking than their daughters.

"Where's Matt?" Patricia Payne asked.

The two men shrugged.

Amelia Payne turned and shouted up the stairs.

"Matty, for God's sake, will you come?"

"Keep your goddamned pants on, Amy," Matt's voice replied.

"It is such a joy for a father to see what refined and well-mannered children he has raised," Brewster C. Payne II said.

Matt came down the stairs two at a time, a moment later, shrugging into a jacket; his tie, untied, hanging loosely around his neck. He looked, Brewster Payne thought, about eighteen years old. And he wondered if Matt really understood what he was getting into with the police, if he could indeed cope with it.

"Since there's so many of us," Patricia said, "I guess we had better go in the station wagon."

"I asked Newt to get the black car out," Brewster Payne said, meeting his wife's eyes. "And to drive us."

"Oh, Brew!" she said.

"I considered the station wagon," Brewster Payne said. "And finally decided the black car was the best solution to the problem."

"What problem?" Matt asked.

"How to avoid anything that could possibly upset your grandmother," Patricia Payne said. "All right, Brew. If you think so, then let's go."

They collected Foster and B.C. from the patio, and then filed outside. Newt, the handyman, who was rarely seen in anything but ancient paint-splattered clothing, was standing, freshly shaved and dressed in a suit, and holding a gray chauffeur's cap in his hand by the open rear door of a black Cadillac Fleetwood.

• • •

When Peter Wohl reached the Marshutz & Sons Funeral Home, there were six Highway Patrol motorcycles in the driveway, their riders standing together. Behind them
was Chief Inspector Dennis V. Coughlin's Oldsmobile. Behind that was a Cadillac
limousine with a "FUNERAL" flag on its right fender, then a Cadillac hearse, then
finally two Ford Highway Patrol cars.

When Peter drove in, Sergeant Tom Lenihan, Denny Coughlin's aide, got out of
the Olds and held up his hand for Peter to stop.

"They're waiting for you inside, Inspector," he said. "Park your car. After the funeral, there will be cars to bring you all back here."

Peter parked the car behind the building beside other police cars, marked and unmarked, and a few privately owned cars, and then walked into the funeral home. The
corridor was crowded with uniformed police officers, one of them a New Jersey state
trooper lieutenant in a blue-and-gray uniform. Wohl wondered who he was.

As he walked toward them, Wohl saw that the Blue Room, where Dutch had been
laid out for the wake, and which had been full of flowers, was now virtually empty
except for the casket itself, which was now closed, and covered with an American
flag.

"We were getting worried about you, Peter," Chief Inspector Dennis V. Coughlin
said to him. "The Moffitts left just a couple of minutes ago. I think Jeannie maybe
expected you to be here when they closed the coffin."

"I took Miss Dutton to identify Gallagher," Peter replied. "And I just left Homicide. Vice turned up a suspect who seems to know something about why Nelson was
killed."

"I thought maybe you'd run into the commissioner," Coughlin said.

He's pissed that I'm late. Well, to hell with it. I couldn't help it.

"Was the commissioner looking for me?" Peter asked.

"I think you could say that, yes," Coughlin said, sarcastically.

"Chief, I'm missing something here," Wohl said. "If I've held things up here, I'm
really sorry."

Coughlin looked at him for a long moment.

"You really don't know what I'm talking about, do you?"

"No, sir."

"You haven't seen the *Ledger?* Nobody's shown it to you? Said anything about
it?"

"The *Ledger?* No, sir."

"When was the last time you saw Mickey O'Hara? Or talked to him?"

"I saw him a week, ten days ago," Peter said, after some thought. "I ran into him
in Wanamaker's."

"Not in the last two, three days? You haven't seen him, or talked to him?"

"No, sir," Peter said, and then started to ask, "Chief—"

"Now that we're all here," an impeccably suited representative of Marshutz &
Sons interrupted him, "I'd like to say a few words about what we're all going to do
taking our part in the ceremonies."

"You ride from here to Saint Dominic's with me," Chief Inspector Coughlin ordered, earning himself a look of annoyance from the funeral director.

"With one exception," the man from Marshutz began, "pallbearer positions will reflect the rank of the pallbearer. Chief Inspector Coughlin will be at the right front of the casket, with Staff Inspector Wohl on the left. Immediately behind Chief Inspector Coughlin, the one exception I mentioned, will be Lieutenant McGrory of the New Jersey State Police. From then on, left, right, left, right, positions are assigned by rank. I have had a list typed up . . ."

Patrol cars from the Seventh District were on hand to block intersections between Marshutz & Sons and Saint Dominic's Roman Catholic Church.

When Dutch Moffitt's flag-draped casket had been rolled into the hearse, Dennis Coughlin and Peter Wohl walked forward to Coughlin's Oldsmobile. The Highway Patrol motorcycle men kicked their machines into life and turned on the flashing lights. Then, very slowly, the small convoy pulled away from the funeral home.

The officers from the Seventh District cars saluted as the hearse rolled past them.

"Tom, have you got the *Ledger* up there with you?" Denny Coughlin asked, from the backseat of the Oldsmobile.

"Yes, sir. And the *Bulletin.*"

"Pass them back to Inspector Wohl, would you please, Tom? He hasn't seen them."

When Sergeant Lenihan held the papers up, Wohl leaned forward and took them.

"You never saw any of that before, Peter?" Coughlin asked, when Wohl had read Mickey O'Hara's story in the *Bulletin* and the editorial in the *Ledger.*

"No, sir," Peter said. "Is there anything to it? Did Gallagher get pushed in front of the train?"

"No, and there are witnesses who saw the whole thing," Coughlin said. "Unfortunately, they are one cop—Martinez, McFadden's partner—and the engineer of the elevated train. Both of whom could be expected to lie to protect a cop."

"Then what the hell is the *Ledger* printing crap like that for?"

"Commissioner Czernich believes it is because Staff Inspector Peter Wohl first had diarrhea of the mouth—that's a direct quote, Peter—when speaking with Mr. Michael J. O'Hara—"

"I haven't spoken to Mickey O'Hara—"

"Let me finish, Peter," Coughlin interrupted. "First you had diarrhea of the mouth with Mr. O'Hara, and then you compounded your—another direct quote—incredible stupidity—by antagonizing Arthur J. Nelson, when you were under orders to charm him. Anything to that?"

"Once again, I haven't seen Mickey O'Hara, or talked to him, in ten days, maybe more."

"But maybe you did piss off Arthur J. Nelson?"

"I called him late last night to tell him the Jaguar had been found. He asked me where, and I told him—truthfully—that I didn't know. He was a little sore about that, but I don't think *antagonize* is the word."

"You didn't—and for God's sake tell me if you did—make any cracks about homosexuality, 'your son the fag,' something like that?"

"Sir, I don't deserve that," Peter said.

"That's how it looks to the commissioner, Peter," Coughlin said. "And to the mayor, which is worse. He's going to run again, of course, and when he does, he wants the *Ledger* to support him."

Peter looked out the window. They were still some distance from Saint Dominic's, but the street was lined with parked police cars.

Dutch, Peter thought, *is going to be buried in style.*

"Chief," Peter said, "all I can do is repeat what I said. I haven't seen, or spoken to, Mickey O'Hara for more than a week. And I didn't say anything to Arthur Nelson that I shouldn't have."

Coughlin grunted.

"For Christ's sake, I even kept my mouth shut when he tried to tell me his son was Louise's boyfriend."

" 'Louise's boyfriend'?" Coughlin parroted. "When did you get on a first-name basis with her?"

Peter turned and met Coughlin's eyes.

"We've become friends, Chief," he said. "Maybe a little more."

"You didn't say anything to her about the Nelson boy being queer, did you? Could that have got back to Nelson?"

"She knew about him," Peter said. "I met him in her apartment."

"When was that?"

"When I went there to bring her to the Roundhouse," Peter said. "The day Dutch was killed."

Out the side window, Peter saw that the lines of police cars were now double-parked. When he looked through the windshield, he could see they were approaching Saint Dominic's. There was a lot of activity there, although the funeral mass wouldn't start for nearly an hour.

"All I know, Peter," Coughlin said, "is that right now, you're in the deep shit. You may be—and I think you are—lily white, but the problem is going to be to convince Czernich and the mayor. Right now, you're at the top of their shit list."

The small convoy drove past the church, and then into the church cemetery, and through the cemetery back to the church, finally stopping beside a side door. The pallbearers got out of the limousine and went to the hearse. Coughlin and Wohl joined them, and took Dutch Moffitt's casket from the hearse and carried it through the side door into the church. Under the direction of the man from Marshutz & Sons, they set it up in the aisle.

The ornate, Victorian-style church already held a number of people. Peter saw Jeannie Moffitt and Dutch's kids and Dutch's mother, and three rows behind them his own mother and father. Ushers—policemen—were escorting more people down the aisles.

"About—face," Chief Inspector Dennis V. Coughlin ordered softly, and the pallbearers standing beside the casket turned around. "For-ward, march," Coughlin said, and they marched back toward the altar, and then turned left, leaving Saint Dominic's as they had entered it. They would reenter the church as the mass started, as part of the processional, and take places in the first row of pews on the left.

The nave of the church was full of flowers.

Peter wondered how much they had all cost, and whether there wasn't something really sinful in all that money being spent on flowers.

Newt Gladstone pulled the Payne Cadillac to the curb in front of Saint Dominic's. A young police officer with a mourning band crossing his badge opened the door, and

Brewster, Patricia, and Foster Payne got out of the backseat as Amy and Matt got out of the front.

The young policeman leaned in the open front door.

"Take the first right," he ordered Newt. "Someone there will assign you a place in the procession."

Patricia Payne took Matt's arm and they walked up the short walk to the church door. Both sides of the flagstone walk were lined with policemen.

A lieutenant standing near the door with a clipboard in his hands approached them.

"May I have your invitations, please?" he asked.

"We don't have any invitations," Matt said.

"Our name is Payne," Patricia said. "This is my son, Matthew. He is Captain Moffitt's nephew."

"Yes, ma'am," the lieutenant said. "Family."

He flipped sheets of paper on his clipboard, and ran his fingers down a list of type-written names. His face grew troubled.

"Ma'am," he said, uncomfortably, "I've only got one Payne on my list."

"Then your list is wrong," Matt said, bluntly.

"Let me see," Patricia said, and looked at the clipboard. Her name was not on the list headed "FAMILY—Pews 2 through 6, Right Side." Nor were Brewster's, or Foster's, or B.C.'s, or Amy's. Just Matt's.

"Well, no problem," Patricia said. "Matt, you go sit with your aunt Jean and your grandmother, and we'll sit somewhere else."

"You're as much family as I am," Matt said.

"No, Matt, not really," Patricia Payne said.

"Is there some problem?" Brewster Payne asked, as he stepped closer.

"No," Patricia said. "They just have Matt sitting with the Moffitts. We'll sit somewhere else."

The lieutenant looked even more uncomfortable.

"Ma'am, I'm afraid that all the seats are reserved."

"What does that mean?" Patricia asked, calmly.

"Ma'am, they're reserved for people with invitations," he said.

"Mother," Amy said. "Let's just go!"

"Perhaps that would be best, Pat," Brewster Payne said.

"Be quiet, the both of you," Patricia snapped. "Lieutenant, is Chief Inspector Coughlin around here somewhere?"

"Yes, ma'am," the lieutenant said. "He's a pallbearer. I'm sure he's here somewhere."

"Get him," Patricia said, flatly.

"Ma'am?"

"I said, go get him, tell him I'm here and I want to see him," Patricia said, her voice raised just a little.

"Pat . . ." Brewster said.

"Brewster, shut up!" Patricia said. "Do what I say, Lieutenant. Matt, I told you to go inside and sit with your aunt Jean."

"Do what she says, Matt," Brewster Payne ordered.

Matt looked at him, then shrugged, and went inside.

"Would you please stand to the side?" the lieutenant said. "I'm afraid we're holding things up."

"This is humiliating," Amy said, softly.

The lieutenant caught the eye of a sergeant, and motioned him over.

"See if you can find Chief Coughlin," the lieutenant ordered. "Tell him that a Mrs. Payne wants to see him, here."

Four other mourners filed into Saint Dominic's after giving their invitations to the lieutenant.

Then two stout, gray-haired women, dressed completely in black, with black lace shawls over their heads, walked slowly up the flagstones, accompanied by an expensively dressed muscular young man with long, elaborately combed hair.

"May I have your invitations, please?" the lieutenant asked politely.

"No invitations," the muscular young man said. "Friends of the family. This is Mrs. Turpino, and this is Mrs. Savarese."

The lieutenant now took a good look at the expensively dressed young man.

"And you're Angelo Turpino, right?"

"That's right, Lieutenant," Turpino said. "I saw Captain Moffitt just minutes before this terrible thing happened, and I've come to pay my last respects."

The lieutenant, with an almost visible effort to keep control of himself, went through the sheets on his clipboard.

"You're on here," he said. "Won't you please go inside? Tell the usher 'friends of the family.' "

"Thank you very much," Angelo Turpino said. He took the women's arms. "Come on, Mama," he said. He led them into Saint Dominic's.

The sergeant whom the lieutenant had sent after Chief Inspector Coughlin came back. "He'll be right here, Lieutenant," he said. "He's on the phone."

The lieutenant nodded.

"Was that who I thought it was just going in?" the sergeant asked.

"That was Angelo Turpino," the lieutenant said. "And his mother. And a Mrs. Savarese. 'Friends of the family.' "

"Probably Vincenzo's wife," the sergeant said. "They was on the list?"

"Yes, they were," the lieutenant said.

"I'll be damned," the sergeant said.

"*Mother,*" Amy Payne, who had heard all this, and who was fully aware that Vincenzo Savarese was almost universally recognized to be the head of the mob in Philadelphia, exploded, "I refuse to stand here and see you humiliated like this . . ."

Chief Inspector Dennis V. Coughlin came around the corner of the church. He kissed Patricia as he offered his hand to Brewster Payne.

"What can I do for you, darling?" he asked.

"You can get us into the church," Patricia Payne said. "I am not on the family list, nor do we have invitations."

"My God!" Coughlin said, and turned to the lieutenant, who handed him his clipboard.

"You keep that," Coughlin said. "And you personally usher the Paynes inside and seat them wherever they want to sit."

"Yes, sir. Chief . . ."

"Just do it, Lieutenant," Coughlin said. "Brewster, I'm sorry . . ."

"We know what happened, Dennis," Brewster Payne said. "Thank you for your courtesy."

The pallbearers waited to be summoned behind Saint Dominic's, in a small grassy area between the church and the fence of the church cemetery.

Wohl took the opportunity to speak to the Jersey trooper lieutenant.

"I'm Peter Wohl," he said, walking up to him and extending his hand.

"Bob McGrory," the lieutenant said. "I heard Dutch talk about you."

"All bad?"

"He said you had all the makings of a good Highway Patrolman, and then went bad and took the examination for lieutenant."

"Dutch really liked Highway," Wohl said. "And they liked him. One of his sergeants rolled on the 'assist officer' call, found out that Dutch was involved, and called in every Highway Patrol car in the city."

"Dutch was a good guy. Goddamned shame, this," McGrory said.

"Yeah," Wohl agreed. "Mind if I ask you something else?"

"Go ahead."

"We've got a homicide. Son of a very important man. His car, a Jaguar, turned up missing. Then I heard they found it in Jersey. You know anything about that?"

"Major Knotts found it," McGrory said. "On his way over here last night. It was on a dirt road off Three Twenty-two."

"Do you know if they turned up anything? Besides the car?" Wohl asked.

"Knotts told me that when they got the NCIC hit, and then heard from you guys, he ordered the mobile crime lab in. And they were supposed to have people out there this morning, when it was light, to have a look around the area."

"You usually do that when you find a hot car?"

"No, but the word was 'homicide,' " McGrory said. Then he added, "Inspector, if they found anything interesting, I'm sure they would have passed it on to you. And probably to me, too. I mean, they knew Dutch and I were close."

"Yeah, I'm sure they would have," Wohl said, and started to say something else when someone spoke his name.

He turned and saw Sergeant Jankowitz, Commissioner Czernich's aide.

"Hello, Jank," Wohl said. "This is Lieutenant McGrory. Sergeant Jankowitz, Commissioner Czernich's indispensable right-hand man."

The two shook hands.

"Inspector Wohl," Jankowitz said, formally, "Commissioner Czernich would like to see you in his office at two this afternoon."

"Okay," Wohl said. "I'll be there."

Jankowitz started to say something, then changed his mind. He smiled, nodded at McGrory, and walked away.

Watching him go, Wohl's eyes focused on the street. He saw a roped-off area in which a number of television camera crew trucks were parked. And he saw Louise. She was standing on a truck, and looking at the area through binoculars. When they seemed to be pointed in his direction, he raised his hand to shoulder level and waved. He wondered if she saw him.

A hand touched his shoulder. He turned and saw his father. And then his mother and Barbara Crowley.

"Hello, Dad," Peter said. "Lieutenant McGrory, this is my father, Chief Inspector Wohl, Retired. And my mother, and Miss Crowley."

Barbara surprised him by kissing him.

"When we heard you were going to be a pallbearer," Peter's mother said, "I asked Barbara if she wanted to come. Gertrude Moffitt, before she knew you were going to be a pallbearer, told me she'd given us three family seats, and since you wouldn't need one now, I asked Barbara. I mean she's almost family, you know what I mean."

"That was a good idea," Peter said.

"Got a minute, Peter?" Chief Inspector August Wohl, Retired, said, and took Peter's arm and led him out of hearing.

"You're in trouble," Peter's father said. "You want to tell me about it?"

"I'm not in trouble, Dad," Peter said. "I didn't do anything wrong."

"What's that got to do with being in trouble? The word is around that both the Polack and the mayor are after your scalp."

"They think I talked to Mickey O'Hara and said something I shouldn't. I haven't seen O'Hara in ten days. I don't know who ran off at the mouth, but it wasn't me. And I can't help it if Nelson is pissed at me. I didn't say anything to him, either, that I shouldn't."

"The mayor will throw you to the fish if he thinks he will get the *Ledger* off his back. And so will the Polack. You better get this straightened out, Peter, and quick."

There was a burst of organ music from Saint Dominic's. The man from Marshutz & Sons began to collect the pallbearers.

When he was formed in ranks beside Chief Inspector Dennis V. Coughlin, Staff Inspector Peter Wohl glanced at the street again, at the TV trucks. He saw Louise again, and was sure that she was looking at him, and that she had seen Barbara kiss him.

She was waving her hand slowly back and forth, as if she knew he was watching her, and wanted to wave good-bye.

18 One of their own had died in the line of duty, and police officers from virtually every police department in a one-hundred-mile circle around Philadelphia had come to honor him. They had come in uniform, and driving their patrol cars, and the result was a monumental traffic jam, despite the best efforts of more than twenty Philadelphia Traffic Division officers to maintain order.

When Chief Inspector Dennis V. Coughlin and Staff Inspector Peter Wohl made their careful way down the brownstone steps of Saint Dominic's Church (Dutch Moffitt's casket was surprisingly heavy) toward the hearse waiting at the curb, there were three lines of cars, parked bumper to bumper, prepared to escort Captain Moffitt to his last resting place.

Their path to the curb was lined with Highway Patrol officers, saluting. There was an additional formation of policemen on the street, and the police band, and the color guard. To the right, behind barriers, was the press. Peter looked for, but did not see, Louise Dutton.

Both Peter and Dennis Coughlin grunted with the effort as they raised the end of the casket to the level of the hearse bed, and set it gently on the chrome-plated rollers in the floor. They pushed it inside, and a man from Marshutz & Sons flipped levers that would keep it from moving on the way to the cemetery.

The hearse would be preceded now by the limousine of the archbishop of Philadelphia and his entourage of lesser clerics, including Dutch's parish priest, the rector of Saint Dominic's, and the police chaplain. Ahead of the hearse was a police car carrying a captain of the Traffic Division, sort of an en route command car. And out in front were twenty Highway Patrol motorcycles.

Next came Dennis V. Coughlin's Oldsmobile, with the limousine carrying the rest of the pallbearers behind it. Then came the flower cars. There had been so many flowers that the available supply of flower cars in Philadelphia and Camden had been exhausted. It had been decided that half a dozen vans would be loaded with flowers and sent to Holy Sepulchre Cemetery ahead of the procession, both to cut down the length of the line of flower cars, and so that there would be flowers in place when the procession got there.

The flower vans would travel with other vehicles, mostly buses, preceding the funeral procession, the band, the honor guard, the firing squad, and the police officers who would line the path the pallbearers would take from the cemetery road to the grave site.

Behind the flower cars in the funeral procession were the limousines carrying the family, followed by the mayor's Cadillac, two cars full of official dignitaries, and then the police commissioner's car, and those of chief inspectors. Next came the cars of "official" friends (those on the invitation list), then the cars of other friends, and finally the cars of the police officers who had come to pay their respects.

It would take a long time just to load the family, dignitaries, and official friends. As soon as the last official-friends car had been loaded, the procession would start to move away from the church.

"Tom," Chief Inspector Coughlin ordered from the backseat of the Oldsmobile, "anything on the radio?"

"I'll check, sir," Sergeant Lenihan said. He took the microphone from the glove compartment.

"C-Charlie One," he said.

"C-Charlie One," radio replied.

"We're at Saint Dominic's, about to leave for Holy Sepulchre," Lenihan said. "Anything for us?"

"Nothing, C-Charlie One," radio said.

"Check for me, please, Tom," Wohl said. "Seventeen."

"Anything for Isaac Seventeen?" Lenihan said.

"Yes, wait a minute. They were trying to reach him a couple of minutes ago."

Wohl leaned forward on the seat to better hear the speaker.

"Isaac Seventeen is to contact Homicide," the radio said.

"Thank you," Lenihan said.

"There's a phone over there," Coughlin said, pointing to a pay phone on the wall of a florist's shop across the street. "You've got time."

Peter trotted to the phone, fed it a dime, and called Homicide.

"This is Inspector Wohl," he said, when a Homicide detective answered.

"Oh, yeah, Inspector. Wait just a second." There was a pause, and then the detective, obviously reading a note, went on: "The New Jersey state police have advised us of the discovery of a murder victim meeting the description of Pierre St. Maury, also known as Errol F. Watson. The body was found near the recovered stolen Jaguar automobile. The identification is not confirmed. Photographs and fingerprints of St. Maury are being sent to New Jersey. Got that?"

"Read it again," Wohl asked, and when it had been, said, "If there's anything else in the next hour or so, I'm with C-Charlie One."

He hung up without waiting for a reply and ran back to Chief Inspector Coughlin's Oldsmobile.

"They found—the Jersey state troopers—found a body that's probably St. Maury near Nelson's car," he reported.

"Interesting," Coughlin said.

"The suspect they had in Homicide said there was talk on the street that two guys were going to get the key to Nelson's apartment from his boyfriend," Wohl said. "To see what they could steal."

There was no response from Coughlin except a grunt.

The Oldsmobile started to move.

As they passed the cordoned-off area for the press, Wohl saw Louise. She was talking into a microphone, not on camera, but as if she were taking notes.

Or, Peter thought, *she didn't want to see me.*

More than three hundred police cars formed the tail of Captain Richard C. Moffitt's funeral procession. They all had their flashing lights turned on. By the time the last visiting mourner dropped his gearshift lever in "D" and started moving, the head of the procession was well over a mile and a half ahead of him.

The long line of limousines and flower cars and police cars followed the hearse and His Eminence the Archbishop down Torresdale Avenue to Rhawn Street, out Rhawn to Oxford Avenue, turned right onto Hasbrook, right again onto Central Avenue, and then down Central to Tookany Creek Parkway, and then down the parkway to Cheltenham Avenue, and then out Cheltenham to the main entrance to Holy Sepulchre Cemetery at Cheltenham and Easton Road.

Each intersection along the route was blocked for the procession, and it stayed blocked until the last car (another Philadelphia Traffic Division car) had passed. Then the officers blocking that intersection jumped in their cars (or, later, in Cheltenham Township, on their motorcycles) and raced alongside, and past, the slow-moving procession to block another intersection.

Dennis V. Coughlin lit a cigar in the backseat of the Oldsmobile almost as soon as they started moving, and sat puffing thoughtfully on it, slumped down in the seat.

He didn't say a word until the fence of Holy Sepulchre Cemetery could be seen, in other words for over half an hour. Then he reached forward and stubbed out the cigar in the ashtray on the back of the front seat.

"Peter, as I understand this," he said, "we put Dutch on whatever they call that thing that lowers the casket into the hole. Then we march off and take up position far enough away from the head of the casket to make room for the archbishop and the other priests."

"Yes, sir," Peter agreed.

"From the time we get there, we don't have anything else to do, right? I mean, when it's all over, we'll walk by and say something to Jeannie and Gertrude Moffitt, but there's nothing else we have to do as pallbearers, right?"

"I think that's right, Chief," Peter said.

"The minute we get there, Peter, I mean when we march away from the grave site, and are standing there, you take off."

"Sir?"

"You take off. You go to the first patrol car that can move, and you tell them to take you back to Marshutz & Sons. Then you get in your car, whose radio is out of service, and you go home and you throw some stuff in a bag, and you go to Jersey in connection with the murder of the suspect in the Nelson killing. And you stay there, Peter, until I tell you to come home."

"Commissioner Czernich sent Sergeant Jankowitz to tell me the commissioner wants me in his office at two this afternoon," Peter said.

"I'll handle Czernich," Coughlin said. "You do what I tell you, Peter. If nothing else, I can buy you some time for him to cool down. Sometimes, Czernich lets his temper get in the way of his common sense. Once he's done something dumb, like swearing to put you in uniform, assigned to Night Command, permanently, on the 'last out' shift—"

"My God, is it that bad?" Peter said.

"If Carlucci loses the election, the new mayor will want a new police commissioner," Coughlin said. "If the *Ledger* doesn't support Carlucci, he may lose the election. You're expendable, Peter. What I was saying was that once Czernich has done something dumb, and then realized it was a mistake, he's got too hard a head to admit he was wrong. And he doesn't have to really worry about the cops lining up behind you for getting screwed. *I* think you're a good cop. Hell, I *know* you're a good cop. But there are a lot of forty-five- and fifty-year-old lieutenants and captains around who think the reason *they* didn't get promoted when *you* did is because *their* father wasn't a chief inspector."

"I won't resign," Peter said. "Night Command, back in uniform . . . no matter what."

"Come on, Peter," Coughlin said. "You didn't come on the job last week. You know what they can do to somebody—civil service be damned—when they want to get rid of him. If you can put up with going back in uniform and Night Command, he'll think of something else."

Peter didn't reply.

"It would probably help some if you could catch whoever hacked up the Nelson boy and shot his boyfriend," Coughlin said.

They were in the cemetery now, winding slowly down access roads. He could see Dutch Moffitt's grave site. Highway Patrolmen were already lined up on both sides of the path down which they would carry Dutch's casket.

Jesus, Peter thought. *Maybe that was my mistake. Maybe I should have just stayed in Highway, and rode around on a motorcycle, and been happy to make Lieutenant at forty-five. That way there wouldn't have been any of this goddamned politics.*

But then he realized he was wrong.

There's always politics. In Highway, it's who gets a new motorcycle and who doesn't. Who gets to do interesting things, or who rides up and down Interstate 95 in the rain, ticketing speeders. Same crap. Just a different level.

"Thank you, Chief," Peter said. "I appreciate the vote of confidence."

"I owe your father one," Chief Inspector Dennis V. Coughlin said, matter-of-factly. "He saved my ass, one time."

"Hello?"

Peter's heart jumped at the sound of her voice.

"Hi," he said.

"I thought it might be you," she said.

"You don't seem thrilled to hear my voice," Peter said.

"I don't get very many calls at midnight," she said, ignoring his reply.

"It took me that long to get up my courage to call," he said.

"Where are you, home? Or out on the streets, protecting the public?"

"I'm in Atlantic City," he said.

"What are you doing there?"

"Working on the Nelson job," he said.

"At two o'clock this afternoon, I had a call from WCTS-TV, Channel Four, Chicago," Louise said. "They want me to co-anchor their evening news show."

"Oh?"

"They want me so bad that they will give me twenty thousand a year more than I'm making now, and they will buy out my contract here," Louise said. "That may be because I am very good, and have the proper experience, and it may be because my father owns WCTS-TV."

"What are you going to do?"

"I'd like to talk to you about that," she said. "Preferably in a public place. I don't want to be prone to argue."

He didn't reply.

"That was a joke," she said. "A clever double entendre on the word 'prone.' "

"I've heard it before," Peter said.

"But if you promise to just talk, you could come here. How long will it take you to drive from Atlantic City?"

"I can't come," Peter said.

"Why not?" she asked.

"I just can't, Louise."

"Your girlfriend down there with you? Taking the sea air? I saw her kiss you this morning."

"No," he said. "I told you I'm working."

"At midnight?"

"I can't come back to Philadelphia right now," he said.

"Somebody told your girlfriend about me? She's looking for you with a meat cleaver?" She heard what she said. "That was really first-class lousy taste, wasn't it? I'm upset, Peter."

"Why?"

"My father is a very persuasive man," she said. "And then he topped his hour and a half of damned-near-irrefutable arguments why you and I could never build anything permanent with that lovely WCTS-TV carrot. And seeing good ol' whatsername kiss you didn't help much, either. I think it would be a very good idea if you came here, as soon as you could, and offered some very convincing counter arguments."

"Would you be happy with the carrot? Knowing it was a carrot?"

"I think the news director at WCTS-TV will be very pleasantly surprised to find out how good I am. Since I have been shoved down his throat, he expects some simpering moron. And I'm not, Peter. I'm good. And Chicago is one step from New York, and the networks."

"Is that what you want? New York and the networks?"

"I don't know right now what I want, except that I want to talk to you," she said.

"I can't come tonight, Louise," Peter said.

"Why not? I can't seem to get an answer to that question."

"I'm in trouble with the department," Peter said.

"What kind of trouble?"

"Political trouble."

"Any chance they'll fire you, I hope, I hope?"

"Thanks a lot," he said.

"Sorry, I forgot how important being a policeman is to you," she said, sarcastically. There was a long pause.

"We're fighting, and saying things we won't be able to take back," she said. "That's not what I wanted."

"I love you," Peter said.

"One of the interesting thoughts my father offered was that people tend to confuse love with lust. Lust comes quickly and eventually burns itself out. Love has to be built, slowly."

"Okay," Peter said. "I lust you, and I'm willing to work on the other thing."

She laughed, but stopped abruptly.

"I don't know why I'm laughing," she said. "I'm not sure whether I should cry or break things, but I know I shouldn't be laughing. I want you to come here, Peter. I want to look at you when we're talking."

"I can't come," he said. "I'm sorry."

"When can you come?"

"I don't know," he said. "Three, four days, maybe."

"Why not now?" Louise demanded plaintively.

"Because I'm liable to lose my job if I come back right now."

There was a long pause. When Louise finally spoke, her voice was calm.

"You know what you just said, of course? That your goddamned job is more important in your life than me."

"Don't be silly, Louise," Peter said.

"No, I won't," she said. "Not anymore."

The phone went dead in his ear.

When he dialed again, he got her answering device. He tried it three more times and then gave up.

When he tried to call her at WCBL-TV the next day, she was either not in, or could not be called to the telephone, and would he care to leave a message?

● ● ●

Staff Inspector Peter Wohl paid lip service to the notion that he was in Atlantic City working on the Nelson homicide job. He went to the hospital where the autopsy on Errol F. Watson, also known as Pierre St. Maury, was performed, and looked at the corpse, and read the coroner's report. Errol F. Watson had died of destruction of brain tissue caused by three projectiles, believed to be .32 caliber, of the type commonly associated with caliber .32 Colt semiautomatic pistols.

That didn't mean he had been shot with a Colt. There were a hundred kinds of pistols that fired the .32 ACP cartridge. No fired cartridge cases had been found, despite what Wohl believed had been a very thorough search of the area where the body had been found. They had found blood and bone and brain tissue.

Very probably, whoever had shot Errol F. Watson also known as Pierre St. Maury had marched him away from the Jaguar, and then shot him in the back of the head. And then twice more, at closer range. God only knew what had happened to the ejected cartridge cases. If they had been ejected. There were some revolvers (which do not eject fired cases), chambered for .32 ACP. Whatever the pistol was, it was almost certainly already sinking into the sandy ocean floor off Atlantic City, or into the muck of a New Jersey swamp, and the chances of recovering it were practically nil.

He also spent most of a day at the state trooper garage, watching, with professional admiration, the lab technicians working on the Jaguar. They knew their business, and they lifted fingerprints and took soil samples and did all the clever things citizens have grown to expect by watching cop stories on television.

Lieutenant Bob McGrory, who had taken him to the garage, picked him up after work there and then insisted he come home with him for supper. He had been at first reluctant and uncomfortable, but McGrory's wife, Mary-Ellen, made him feel welcome, and McGrory produced a bottle of really good scotch, and they sat around killing that, and telling Dutch Moffitt stories, and Peter's mouth finally loosened, and he told McGrory why he really had been sent to Atlantic City.

He left then, aware that he was a little drunk, and not wanting to confide in Bob McGrory the painful details of his romance with Miss Louise Dutton.

On his arrival in Atlantic City, in a fey mood, he had taken a room in the Chalfonte-Haddon Hall, a thousand-room landmark on the boardwalk, rather than in a smaller hotel or a motel. He had told himself that he would endure his time in purgatory at least in luxury.

It was, he decided, *faded grandeur* rather than *luxury*. But it did have a bar, and he stopped there for a nightcap before he went to his room. He had just had another one-way conversation with Louise Dutton's answering machine, the machine doing all the talking, when there was a knock at his door.

"Hi," she said. "I saw you downstairs in the bar, and thought you might like a little company."

He laughed.

"What's so funny?"

"I'm a cop," he said.

"Oh, *shit!*"

He watched her flee down the corridor, and then, smiling, closed the door and walked across the room to his bed.

The phone rang.

Please, God, let that be Louise! Virtue is supposed to be its own reward.

"Did I wake you up?" Lieutenant Bob McGrory asked.

"No problem, I had to answer the phone anyway," Wohl said, pleased with his wit.

"I just had a call from a friend of mine on the Atlantic City vice squad," McGrory said. "Two gentlemen were in an establishment called the Black Banana earlier this evening. They paid for their drinks with a Visa credit card issued to Jerome Nelson. The manager called it in. I understand he needs a friend—several friends—in the police department right now."

"The Black Banana?" Wohl asked. "If it's what it sounds like, we've got one of those in Philly."

"Maybe it's a franchise," McGrory said, chuckling.

"They still there?"

"No. The cops are checking the hotels and motels. They have what may be a name from the manager of the Black Banana, and they're also checking to see if anyone is registered as Jerome Nelson. They have a stakeout at the Banana, too."

"Interesting," Peter said.

"I told my friend I'd call him back and tell him if you wanted to be waked up if they find them."

"Oh, yes," Peter Wohl said. "Thank you, Bob."

On his fifth day in Atlantic City, when Peter Wohl walked into the state trooper barracks, Lieutenant Robert McGrory told him that he had just that moment hung up from talking with Chief Inspector Dennis V. Coughlin.

" 'Almost all is forgiven, come home' is the message, Peter," Lieutenant McGrory said.

"Thank you," Peter said. "Thanks for everything."

"Anytime. You going right back?"

"Yeah," Peter said. "My girlfriend's probably finally given up on me."

"The one at the church? Very nice."

"Her, too," Peter said.

There was a Mayflower moving van parked on the cobblestone street before Six Stockton Place.

It is altogether fitting and proper, Peter Wohl thought, *that I should arrive here at the exact moment they are carrying out Louise's bed.*

But he got out of the LTD anyway, and walked into the building and rode up in the elevator. The door to Louise's apartment was open, and he walked in.

There were two men standing with a packing list.

"Where are you taking this stuff?" Peter asked.

"What's it to you?"

"I'm a police officer," Peter said, and took out his ID.

The man handed him a clipboard with forms on it. The household furnishings listed below were to be shipped to 2710 Lake Shore Drive, Chicago, Illinois, Apartment 1705.

"Thank you," Peter said.

"Something wrong?"

"Nothing at all," Peter said, and left the apartment and got in the LTD and drove to the Roundhouse.

He parked the car and went in and headed for the elevators, then turned and went to the receptionist's desk.

"Let me have that phone, will you, please?" Peter asked.

He knew the number of WCBL-TV by memory now.

They told him they were sorry, Miss Louise Dutton was no longer connected with WCBL-TV.

He pushed the phone back to the officer on duty and walked toward the elevators.

When the door opened, Commissioner Thaddeu Czernich and Sergeant Jankowitz got out. Jankowitz's eyes widened when he saw Wohl.

"Good afternoon, Commissioner," Peter said.

"Got a minute, Peter?" Czernich said, and took Wohl's arm and led him to one side.

"I think I owe you an apology," Czernich said.

"Sir?"

"I should have known you weren't the one with diarrhea of the mouth," Czernich said.

"No apology is necessary, Commissioner," Peter said.

Czernich met his eyes for a moment, and nodded.

"Well, I suppose you're ready to go back to your regular duties, aren't you, Peter?"

"Yes, sir."

"Give my regards to your dad, when you see him," Czernich said. He smiled at Peter, patted his shoulder, and walked away.

Peter got on the elevator and rode up to Chief Inspector Dennis V. Coughlin's office.

"Well, good afternoon, Inspector," Sergeant Tom Lenihan said, smiling broadly at him. "How nice to see you. I'll tell the chief you're here."

Dennis V. Coughlin greeted him by saying, "I was hoping you would walk in here about now. You can buy me lunch. You owe me one, I figure."

"Yes, sir. No argument about that."

They went, with Tom Lenihan, to Bookbinder's Restaurant. Coughlin ate a dozen cherrystone clams and drank a bottle of beer before he got into the meat of what he wanted to say.

"Commissioner Czernich happened to run into Mickey O'Hara," Coughlin said. "And the subject somehow turned to the story Mickey wrote quoting an unnamed senior police officer to the effect that we were looking for a Negro homosexual in connection with the Nelson murder."

"You set that up, didn't you, Chief?" Peter said.

"Mickey wouldn't tell him who the unnamed police officer was, but he did tell him, swearing by all that's holy, that it wasn't you."

"And the commissioner believed him?"

"I think so. I'd stay out of his way for a while, if I were you."

"I ran into him getting on the elevator in the Roundhouse," Peter said.

"And?"

"He apologized, I said none was necessary, and then he said he thought I would be happy to be getting back to my regular duties, and that I should give his regards to my dad."

"Okay," Coughlin said. "Even better than I would have hoped."

"I'm off the hook, then?"

"You weren't listening. I said that if I were you, I'd stay out of his sight for a while."

"Yes, sir."

"Since it wasn't you, who had the big mouth? That wasn't hard to figure out. DelRaye. So DelRaye has been transferred from Homicide to the Twenty-Second District—in uniform—and he can kiss away, for good, his chances, not that there were many, to make captain. And then, I understand, Hizzoner the Mayor called Mr. Nelson, and told him what had happened, that he had found out who had the big mouth, and taken care of him, and that, proving our dedication to finding the murderers of his son, we sent you to Atlantic City where you did in fact assist the local police in apprehending the men we are sure are the murderers of his son, and couldn't we be friends again? Whereupon, Mr. Nelson let the mayor have it. I have it on reliable information that they said some very unpleasant things to each other."

"Oh, Christ!"

"I don't know what that will do to the mayor in the election, but right now he thinks that Nelson is crazy. I mean, really. He thinks Nelson is out of his mind, which gets you off the hook with him. I mean, it's you and him against the crazy man at the *Ledger.*"

Wohl's eyebrows rose thoughtfully, but he didn't say anything.

Coughlin looked around for the waitress, found her, and ordered another beer and broiled swordfish.

"Same for me, please," Wohl said.

"I think I'll have some steamers," Lenihan said. "I'm trying to lose a little weight."

"That little bowl of melted butter will sure help, Tom," Coughlin said, and then turned to Peter. "Your friend Miss Dutton has left town."

"I know."

"That going to bother you, Peter?" Coughlin asked.

"Yeah," Peter said. "Yeah, it will. How did you know about that?"

Coughlin chuckled, but didn't answer.

"You'll get over it," Coughlin said. "It happens to everybody, and everybody gets over it, sooner or later."

"How late is later?" Peter asked.

"Find some nice girl, a nurse, for example, and take her out. You'd be surprised how quickly some things pass when there's a nice girl around."

Staff Inspector Peter Wohl didn't reply. But he picked up his beer glass and raised it to Chief Inspector Dennis V. Coughlin. He smiled, and then took a deep sip.

SPECIAL
OPERATIONS

FOR SERGEANT ZEBULON V. CASEY

INTERNAL AFFAIRS DIVISION

RETIRED

POLICE DEPARTMENT, THE CITY OF PHILADELPHIA.

HE KNOWS WHY.

1 Mary Elizabeth Flannery first came to the attention of the Police Department of the City of Philadelphia at 9:21 P.M., June 29, 1973, when an unidentified civilian called the Police Emergency number and reported that as she and her husband had been driving through Fairmount Park, going down Bell's Mill Road toward Chestnut Hill, they had seen a naked woman, just walking around, on the Chestnut Hill side of the bridge over Wissahickon Creek.

The call was taken in the Police Radio Room, which is on the second floor of the Police Building in downtown Philadelphia. The operator who took the call was a civilian, a temporary employee, a twenty-two-year-old, 227-pound, six-foot-three-inch black man named Foster H. Lewis, Jr.

Foster H. Lewis, Sr., was a sergeant in the Eighteenth District. That hadn't hurt any when Foster H. Lewis, Jr., had appeared three years before in the City Administration Building across from City Hall to apply for a part-time job to help him with his tuition at Temple University, where he was then a premedical sophomore.

Foster H. Lewis, Jr., who was perhaps predictably known as "Tiny," had been at first more than a little awed by the Radio Room, with its rows of operators sitting before control consoles, and made more than a little uncomfortable by the steady stream of calls for help, often from people on the edge of hysteria.

Alone of America's major city police forces, Philadelphia police respond to any call for help, not just to reports of crime. It is deeply embedded in the subconscious minds of Philadelphia's 2.1 million citizens (there are more than five million people in the Philadelphia metropolitan area) that what you do when Uncle Charley breaks a leg or the kid falls off his bike and is bleeding pretty bad at the mouth or when you see a naked woman just walking around in Fairmount Park is "call the cops."

Tiny Lewis had worked in the Radio Room two, three nights a week, and weekends, and full time during the summers for three years now, and he was no longer awed by either the Radio Room or his responsibilities in dealing with a citizen who was calling for help.

For one thing, he was reasonably sure that this citizen's call was for real, and that the citizen herself was neither hysterical nor drunk, nor both.

"May I have your name, please, ma'am?" Tiny Lewis asked, politely.

"Never mind about that," the caller snapped. "Just help that poor woman."

"Ma'am, I have to have your name," Tiny Lewis said, reasonably. Sometimes that worked, and sometimes it didn't. It didn't now. The phone went dead.

"Joe!" Tiny Lewis called, just loud enough to catch the attention of the Police Dispatcher, a sworn police officer named Joe Bullock.

Joe Bullock had had sixteen years on the job when he pulled a drunk to the curb on the Baltimore Pike in West Philadelphia. He had him standing outside his car when another drunk had come along and rear-ended the stopped car. Neither civilian had been seriously injured, but Joe Bullock had spent seven months in University Hospital. The Department had wanted to put him out on a Thirty-Two, a Civil Service Disability Pension for Injuries Received in the Line of Duty, but Bullock had appealed to the Police Commissioner.

The Police Commissioner, then the Honorable Jerry Carlucci, had found time to see Officer Bullock, even though his time was pretty much taken up with his campaign to get himself elected mayor. Commissioner Carlucci only vaguely remembered Officer Bullock, when Bullock politely reminded him that he used to see him when the Commissioner had been a Highway Sergeant, but he shook his hand warmly, and assured him that as long as he was either Police Commissioner or mayor, the expletive-deleted paper pushers on the Civil Service Commission were not going to push out on a Thirty-Two any good cop who wanted to stay on the job and had a contribution to make.

Officer Bullock was assigned to the Radio Division as a Police Dispatcher.

"What have you got, Tiny?" Officer Bullock inquired of Tiny Lewis.

"A naked woman in the park at Bell's Mill and Wissahickon Creek, around the Forbidden Drive," Tiny said. "I think there's something to it."

"It could be some girl changed her mind at the last minute," Joe Bullock said.

Forbidden Drive, despite the ominous name, was an unpaved road running along Wissahickon Creek, used in the daylight hours by respectable citizens for horseback riding, hiking, and at night by young couples seeking a place to park a car in reasonable privacy.

"I don't think so," Tiny said, repeating, "I think there's something to this."

Joe Bullock nodded. He knew that Tiny Lewis had a feel for his job, and very rarely got excited. He knew too that the location was in Chestnut Hill. It was said that ninety-five percent of Philadelphia was owned by people who lived in Chestnut Hill, very often in very large houses on very large pieces of property; the sort of people who were accustomed to the very best of police protection and who could get through to the mayor immediately if they didn't think they were getting it.

Bullock went to his console, and checked the display for the Fourteenth Police District, which was charged with maintaining the peace in the area of Northwest Philadelphia including Chestnut Hill. He was not surprised to find that an indicator with "1423" on it was lit up. The "14" made reference to the district; "23" was the Radio Patrol Car (RPC) assigned to cover Chestnut Hill. He would have been surprised if 1423 was not lit up, signifying that it was on a job, and not available. Chestnut Hill was not a high-crime area, or even an area with a traffic problem.

"Fourteen Twenty-Three," Joe Bullock said into the microphone.

There was an immediate response: "Fourteen Twenty-Three."

"Fourteen Twenty-Three," Joe Bullock said to his microphone, "report of a naked female on Forbidden Drive, in the vicinity of Bell's Mill Road and the bridge. Civilian by phone."

"Fourteen Twenty-Three, okay," Police Officer William Dohner, who was cruising his district on Germantown Avenue, near Springfield Street, said into his microphone. He then put the microphone down, flipped on the siren and the flashing lights, and turned his 1972 Ford around and headed for Forbidden Drive.

As this was going on, Tiny Lewis was writing the pertinent information on a three-by-eight-card. At this stage, the incident was officially an "Investigation, Person." He then put the card between electrical contacts on a shelf above his console. Doing so interrupted the current lighting the small bulb behind the "1423" block on the display console. The block went dark, signifying that Fourteen Twenty-Three had a job.

Joe Bullock's Police Radio call vis-à-vis the naked woman in Fairmount Park was received as well over the radios installed in other police vehicles. Almost immediately, a 1971 Ford van, EPW 1405, one of the two-man Emergency Patrol Wagons assigned to the Fourteenth District to transport the injured, prisoners, and otherwise assist in law enforcement, turned on its flashing lights and siren and headed for Forbidden Drive. So did Highway Nineteen, which happened to be in the area. So did D-209, an unmarked car assigned to the Northwest Detective District. And others.

It had been a relatively quiet night, and a naked female on Forbidden Drive certainly required all the assistance an otherwise unoccupied police officer could render.

Joe Bullock's call was also received over the police-bands short-wave radio installed in a battered, four-year-old Chevrolet *Impala* coupe registered to one Michael J. O'Hara of the 2100 block of South Shields Street in West Philadelphia.

Mr. O'Hara had spent Sunday evening having dinner with his widowed mother, who resided in the Cobbs Creek Nursing Center, in the Mr. and Mrs. J. K. McNair Memorial Dining Facility. Mickey was a dutiful son and loved his mother, and made a valiant effort to have dinner with her twice a week. It was always a depressing experience. Mrs. O'Hara's mind was failing, and she talked a good deal about people who were long dead, or whom he had never known. And about fellow residents in the Cobbs Creek Nursing Center, who, if she was to be believed, carried on sinful sexual relations that would have worn out twenty-year-olds when they were not engaged in stealing things from Mrs. O'Hara. The food was also lousy; it reminded Mickey of what they used to feed him in basic training in the army.

After pushing his mother's wheelchair down the polished, slippery corridors of the Cobbs Creek Nursing Center to her room, Mickey O'Hara usually went directly to Brannigan's Bar & Grill, two blocks away at Seventieth and Kingessing, where he had a couple of quick belts of John Jamison's with a beer chaser.

Tonight, however, he had gone directly home, not because he didn't need a drink— quite the contrary—but because there was a recent development in his life that left him feeling more uneasy than he could ever remember having felt before. And Mickey knew himself well enough to know that the one thing he should not do in the circumstances was tie one on.

Home was the house in which he had grown up, the fourth row house on the right from the end of the 2100 block of South Shields Street. He had been living here alone now for two and a half years, since Father Delahanty of the Good Shepherd Roman Catholic Church had managed to convince Mrs. O'Hara that moving "temporarily" to the Cobbs Creek Nursing Center was the best thing for her to do until she got her health back.

She was never going to leave Cobbs Creek, and everybody but Mrs. O'Hara knew that, but she kept talking about when she'd be going home, and Mickey didn't feel it would be right to go and see her and lie about selling the goddamned house and taking an apartment somewhere.

He went into the house and put the photo album back on the shelf where it had been kept since he was in short pants. He had carried the damned thing back and forth to Cobbs Creek two dozen times. She would ask him to bring it, and he would take it to her, and a week later, she would tell him to take it home and put it on the shelf; Cobbs Creek was full of thieves who were always stealing anything that wasn't chained down, and she didn't want to lose it.

Then he went into the kitchen and decided that one lousy glass of beer wasn't going to get him in trouble, and filled a Pabst Blue Ribbon glass from a quart bottle of Ortlieb's, which was a dime less a quart than Pabst, and so far as Mickey was concerned, a better beer to boot. He went into the living room, turned the TV on, and watched a rerun of *I Love Lucy* until it was time to go downtown.

Bull Bolinski, who was probably his oldest friend, said his plane would arrive at half past eight, and that Mickey should give him an hour or so to get to his hotel, and make a couple of phone calls. Mickey had offered to meet Bull at the airport, but Bull said there was no sense doing that, he would catch a cab.

When it was time to go meet the Bull, Mickey turned the TV off, rinsed out the Pabst Blue Ribbon glass in the sink, then went out and got in the car. He turned on the police-band radio without thinking about it. The *"naked lady in Fairmount Park"* call from Police Radio came before he had pulled away from the curb.

He had two reactions to the call: First, that what he had heard was all there was to it, that some broad—drunk, stoned, or crazy—was running around Fairmount Park in her birthday suit. If she was a good-looking broad, there might be a funny piece in it for him, providing she was drunk or stoned or maybe mad at her husband or her boyfriend. Every cop in Northwest Philly would go in on a "naked lady" call; it would look like a meeting of the FOP, the Fraternal Order of Police.

But not if she was a looney. Mickey had his principles, among them that looney people aren't funny. Unless, of course, they thought they were the King of Pennsylvania or something. Mickey never wrote about loonies who were pitiful.

The second thought he had was more of a hunch than anything else. It *could* have something to do with a real looney, a dangerous one, a white male scumbag who had been running around lately raping women. Not just any women, but nice, young, middle-class white women, and not just raping them, either, but making them do all kinds of dirty things, weird things. Or doing the same to them. Jack Fisher, one of the Northwest detectives, had told Mickey that the looney had tied one girl down on her bed, taken off his own clothes, and then pissed all over her.

Then Mickey had a third thought: Whatever was going on was not, at the moment, of professional interest to Michael J. O'Hara. There would probably be a story in the *Philadelphia Bulletin,* either a two-graph piece buried with the girdle ads in section C, or maybe even a bylined piece on the front page, but it would not be written by Michael J. O'Hara.

Michael J. O'Hara was *withholding his professional services* from the *Bulletin,* pending resolution of contractual differences between the parties. Bull Bolinski had told him, *"No, you're not on strike. Bus drivers strike, steel workers strike. You're a fucking professional. Get that through your thick head."*

Mickey O'Hara had been *withholding his professional services* for three weeks now. He had never been out of work that long in his life, and he was getting more than a little worried. If the *Bulletin* didn't give in, he thought it entirely possible that he was through. Not only with the *Bulletin*, but with the other newspapers in Philadelphia, too. The bastards in management all knew each other, they all had lunch at the Union League together, and there was no question in Mickey's mind that if the *Bulletin* management decided to tell him or the Bull to go fuck himself, they wouldn't stop there, they would spread the word around that Mickey O'Hara, always a troublemaker, had really gone off the deep end this time.

And it was already past the point where he could tuck his tail between his legs and just show up in the City Room and go back to work. The only thing he could do was put his faith in the Bull. And sweat blood.

Mickey reached over and turned off the police-bands shortwave radio, then headed downtown, via the Roosevelt Boulevard Extension to North Broad Street, then down Broad toward City Hall.

Bill Dohner, a wiry, graying, forty-two-year-old cop who had been on the job for exactly half his life, turned off his lights and siren when he was four blocks away from Forbidden Drive, although he didn't slow down. Sometimes, flashing lights and a howling siren were the wrong way to handle a job.

He reached over on the front seat and found his flashlight, and had it in his hand as he braked sharply at the entrance to Forbidden Drive. The unpaved road looked deserted to him, so he continued down Bell's Mill Road and crossed the bridge over Wissahickon Creek. He didn't see anything there, either, so he turned around, quickly, but without squealing his tires, and returned to Forbidden Drive and turned right into it.

His headlights illuminated the road for a hundred yards or so, and there was nothing on it. Dohner drove very slowly down it, looking from side to side, down into Wissahickon Creek on his right, and into the woods on his left.

And then Dohner saw Mary Elizabeth Flannery. She was on her feet, just at the end of the area illuminated by his headlights, on the edge of the road. She had her head down and her hands behind her, as if they were tied, and she was naked.

Dohner accelerated quickly, reaching for his microphone.

"Fourteen Twenty-Three. I got a naked woman on Forbidden Drive. Can you send me backup?"

He braked sharply when he reached Mary Elizabeth Flannery, then reached onto the passenger-side floorboard, coming up with a folded blanket. Then he jumped out of the car.

Dohner saw the blank look in Mary Elizabeth Flannery's eyes when she saw him, and saw that his guess had been right; her hands were tied behind her.

"It's going to be all right, miss," Bill Dohner said, gently, as he draped the blanket around her shoulders. "Can you tell me what happened?"

At that moment, every radio in every police car in the city of Philadelphia went *beep beep beep,* and then they heard Joe Bullock's voice. "Assist Officer, Forbidden Drive at Bell's Mill Road. Police by radio. Assist Officer. Forbidden Drive at Bell's Mill Road. Police by radio."

Flashing lights and sirens on all the cars that had previously been headed toward Bell's Mill Road went on, and feet pressed more heavily on accelerator pedals: flashing lights and sirens went on in cars driven by Bill Dohner's Sergeant (14A); Bill Dohner's Lieutenant (14DC); two of Dohner's peers, patrolling elsewhere in the Fourteenth District (1421 and 1415); on Highway Twenty-Six, D-Dan 209, and others.

Bill Dohner took a well-worn but very sharp penknife from his pocket and cut the white lamp cord binding Mary Elizabeth Flannery's hands behind her. He did not attempt to untie the lamp cord. Sometimes a knot could be used as evidence; the critters who did things like this sometimes used unusual knots. He dropped the cord in his trousers pocket, and gently led Mary Elizabeth Flannery to his car.

"Can you tell me what he looked like?" Bill Dohner asked. "The man who did this to you?"

"He came in the apartment, and I didn't hear him, and he had a knife."

"Was he a white man?" Dohner opened the rear door of the car.

"I don't know . . . Yes, he was white. He had a mask."

"What kind of a mask?"

"A kid's mask, like the Lone Ranger."

"And was he a big man, a little man, or what?" Dohner felt Mary Elizabeth Flannery's back stiffen under his hand. "What's the matter?" he asked, very gently.

"I don't want to get in the back," she said.

"Well, then, I'll put you in the front," he said. "Miss, what did this man do to you?"

"Oh, Jesus, Mary and Joseph," Mary Elizabeth Flannery said, sucking in her breath, and then sobbing.

"Did he do anything to you?"

"Oh, Jesus!" she wailed.

"I have to ask, miss, what did he do to you?"

"He made me—he *urinated* on me!"

"Is that all?" Dohner asked softly.

"Oh, Jesus," Mary Elizabeth Flannery wailed. "He made me . . . he put his thing in my mouth. He had a knife—"

"What kind of a knife?"

"A *knife*," she said. "A butcher knife."

"What's your name, miss? Can you tell me that, please?"

He installed her in the front seat of the car, then ran around and got in beside her. She did not look at him as he did.

"What's your name, miss?" Dohner asked again.

"Flannery," she said. "Mary Flannery."

"If we're going to catch this man, you're going to have to tell me what he looks like," Bill Dohner said. "What kind of clothes was he wearing? Can you tell me that?"

"He was *naked.*"

"He brought you here from your apartment, right?" Dohner asked, and she nodded.

"How did he bring you here?"

"In a van,"

"Was he naked then?"

"Oh, Jesus!"

"Do you remember what kind of a van? Was it dark or light?"

She shook her head from side to side.

"Was it new or old?"

She kept shaking her head.

"Was it like a station wagon, with windows, or was it closed in the back?"

"Closed."

"And was he a small man?" There was no response. "A large man? Did you see the color of his hair? Did he have a beard, or scars or anything like that?"

"He was big," Mary Elizabeth Flannery said. "And he was *hairy.*"

"You mean he had long hair, or there was a lot of hair on his body?"

"On his body," she said. "What's going to happen to me?"

"We're going to take care of you," Dohner said. "Everything's going to be all right now. But I need you to tell me what this man looked like, what he was wearing, so we can lock him up. Can you tell what he wore when he brought you over here?"

"Overalls," she said. *"Coveralls.* You know?"

"Do you remember what color they were?"

"Black," she said. "They were black. I saw him put them on. . . ."

"And what color was the van?"

"I didn't see. Maybe gray."

"And when he left you here, which way did he go? Did he go back out to Bell's Mill Road, or the other way?"

"Bell's Mill Road."

"And which way did he turn when he got there?"

"Right," she said, with certainty.

Dohner reached for the microphone.

"Fourteen Twenty-Three," he said.

"Fourteen Twenty-Three," Police Radio replied.

"Fourteen Twenty-Three," Dohner said. "Resume the Assist."

"Resume the Assist" was pure police cant, verbal shorthand for "Those police officers who are rushing to this location with their sirens screaming and their warning lights flashing to assist me in dealing with the naked lady may now resume their normal duties. I have things in hand here, am in no danger, and expect my supervisor, a wagon, and probably a District detective to appear here momentarily."

As police cars slowed, and sirens and flashing lights died all over the Northwest, Dohner went on: "We have a sexual assault, kidnapping, assault with a deadly weapon. Be on the lookout for a white male in a gray van, make unknown. He's wearing black coveralls and may be in possession of a black mask and a butcher knife. Last seen heading east on Bell's Mill Road toward Germantown."

As he put the microphone down, a police car turned onto Forbidden Drive, lights flashing, siren screaming. It skidded to a stop beside Bill Dohner's car, and two Highway Patrolmen jumped out of it.

Joe Bullock's voice came over the radio: "Flash information on a kidnapping, assault with a deadly weapon and rape on Forbidden Drive. Be on the lookout for a white male in black coveralls driving a gray van. Suspect fled east on Bell's Mill Road toward Germantown. May be in possession of a large knife. May have a black mask."

"Mary," Bill Dohner said, kindly. "I'm going to speak to these officers for a moment and tell them what's happened, and then I'm going to take you to the hospital."

As Dohner opened the door, two more police cars, one of them another Fourteenth District RPC and the other an unmarked Northwest Detectives car, came onto Forbidden Drive, one from Bell's Mill Road, and the other from Northwestern Avenue, which is the boundary between Philadelphia and Montgomery counties.

When Bill Dohner got back into the car beside Mary Elizabeth Flannery, she was shaking under the blanket, despite the heat.

He picked up the microphone: "Fourteen Twenty-Three, I'm en route with the victim to Chestnut Hill Hospital."

As he started to drive off, Bill Dohner looked at Mary Elizabeth Flannery again and said, "Shit," under his breath. She was probably going into shock. Shock can be fatal.

"You all right, Mary?"

"Why did he do that to me?" Mary Elizabeth Flannery asked, wonderingly, plaintively.

2   Mickey O'Hara drove the battered Chevrolet around City Hall, then down South Broad Street, past the dignified Union League Club. When he came to the equally dignified Bellevue-Stratford Hotel, Mickey pulled to the curb at the corner, directly beside a sign reading NO PARKING AT ANY TIME TOW AWAY ZONE.

He slid across the seat and got out the passenger-side door. Then he walked the fifty feet or so to the revolving door of the Bellevue-Stratford and went inside.

He walked across the lobby to the marble reception desk. There was a line, two very well dressed middle-aged men Mickey pegged to be salesmen, and a middle-aged, white-haired couple Mickey decided were a wife and a husband who, if he had had a choice, would have left her home.

All the salesmen did was ask the clerk for their messages. The wife had apparently badgered her husband into complaining about their room, which didn't offer what she considered a satisfactory view, and then when he started complaining, took over from him. She obviously, and correctly, considered herself to be a first-class bitcher.

The desk clerk apparently had the patience of a saint, Mickey thought; and then—by now having gotten a good look at her—he decided she looked like one, too. An angel, if not a saint. Tall, nicely constructed, with rich brown hair, a healthy complexion, and very nice eyes. And she was wearing, Mickey noticed, no rings, either engagement or wedding, on the third finger on her left hand.

She gave the big-league bitcher and her consort another room, apologizing for any inconvenience the original room assignment might have caused. Mickey thought the big-league bitcher was a little disappointed, like a bantamweight who sent his opponent to the canvas for the count with a lucky punch in the first round. All keyed up, and nobody around to fight with.

"Good evening, sir," the desk clerk said. "How may I help you?"

Her voice was low and soft, her smile dazzling; and her hazel eyes were fascinating.

"What room is Bull Bolinski in?" Mickey asked.

"Mr. Bolinski isn't here, sir," she replied immediately.

"He isn't?"

"Are you Mr. O'Hara, sir? Mr. Michael J. O'Hara?"

"Guilty."

She smiled. Warmly, Mickey thought. Genuinely amused.

"I thought I recognized you from your pictures," she said. "I'm one of your . . . what . . . avid readers . . . Mr. O'Hara."

"Oh, yeah?"

She nodded confirmation. "Mr. Bolinski called, Mr. O'Hara," she said. "Just a few moments ago. He's been delayed."

"Oh?"

"He said you would be here, and he asked me to tell you that he will be getting into Philadelphia very late, and that he hopes you'll be free to have breakfast with him, somewhere around ten o'clock."

"Oh."

"Is there anything I can do for you, Mr. O'Hara?"

"No. No, thanks."

She smiled at him again, with her mouth and her eyes.

By the time he got to the revolving door, Mickey realized that opportunity had knocked, and he had as usual blown it again.

Well, what the hell was I supposed to say, "Hey, honey, what time do you get off? Let's you and me go hoist a couple"?

Mickey got back in the Chevy and drove home, nobly resisting the temptation to stop in at six different taverns en route for just one John Jamison's. He went into the kitchen, finished the quart bottle of Ortleib's, and then two more bottles as he considered what he would do if he couldn't be a police reporter anymore. And, now that the opportunity was gone, thinking of all the clever, charming and witty things he should have said to the desk clerk with the soft and intimate voice and intelligent, hazel eyes.

George Amay, the Northwest Detectives Division detective, who, using the designator D-Dan 209, had gone in on the naked woman call, stayed at the crime scene just long enough to get a rough idea of what was going down. Then he got back in his car and drove to an outside pay phone in a tavern parking lot on Northwestern Avenue and called it in to the Northwest Detectives desk man, one Mortimer Shapiro.

Detective Shapiro's place of duty was a desk just inside the Northwest Detectives squad room, on the second floor of the Thirty-fifth Police District Building at North Broad and Champlost streets.

"Northwest Detectives, Shapiro," Mort said, answering the telephone.

"George Amay, Mort," Amay said. "I went in on a Thirty-fifth District call for a naked lady on Forbidden Drive. It's at least Criminal Attempt Rape, Kid napping, et cetera et cetera."

"Where are you?"

"In a phone booth on Northwestern. The victim's been taken to Chestnut Hill Hospital. The Thirty-fifth Lieutenant and Sergeant are at the scene. And Highway. And a lot of other people."

"Go back to the scene, and see if you can keep Highway from destroying all the evidence," Shapiro said. "I'll send somebody over."

Detective Shapiro then consulted the Wheel, which was actually a sheet of paper on which he had written the last names of all the detectives present for duty that night in the Northwest Detectives Division.

Assignment of detectives to conduct investigations, called jobs, was on a rotational basis. As jobs came in, they were assigned to the names next on the list. Once assigned a job, a detective would not be assigned another one until all the other detectives on the wheel had been assigned a job, and his name came up again.

The next name on the wheel was that of a detective Mort Shapiro privately thought of as Harry the Farter. Harry, aside from his astonishing flatulence, was a nice enough guy, but he was not too bright.

What Amay had just called in was not the sort of job that should be assigned to detectives like Harry the Farter, if there was to be any real hope to catch the doer. The name below Harry the Farter's on the Wheel was that of Richard B. "Dick" Hemmings, who was, in Mort Shapiro's judgment, a damned good cop.

Shapiro opened the shallow drawer in the center of his desk, and took from it a report of a recovered stolen motor vehicle, which had come in several hours before, and which Detective Shapiro had "forgotten" to assign to a detective.

When a stolen motor vehicle is recovered, or in this case, found deserted, a detective is assigned to go to the scene of the recovery to look for evidence that will assist in the prosecution of the thief, presuming he or she is ultimately apprehended. Since very few auto thefts are ever solved, investigation of a recovered stolen motor vehicle is one of those time-consuming futile exercises that drain limited manpower resources. It was, in other words, just the sort of job for Harry the Farter.

"Harry!" Mort Shapiro called, and Harry the Farter, a rather stout young man in his early thirties, his shirt showing dark patches of sweat, walked across the squad room to his desk.

"Jesus," Harry the Farter said when he saw his job. "Another one?"

Shapiro smiled sympathetically.

"Shit!" Harry the Farter said, broke wind, and walked back across the squad room to his desk. When, in Shapiro's judgment, Harry the Farter was sufficiently distracted, Shapiro got up and walked to the desk occupied by Detective Hemmings, who was typing out a report on an ancient manual typewriter. He laid a hand on his shoulder and motioned with his head for Hemmings to join him at the coffee machine.

"Amay just called in," Shapiro said after Hemmings had followed him to the small alcove holding the coffee machine. "We've got another rape, it looks like, on Forbidden Drive by the Bell's Mill bridge over the Wissahickon."

Hemmings, a trim man of thirty-five, just starting to bald, pursed his lips and raised his eyebrows.

"Amay said that he could use some help protecting the crime scene," Shapiro said. "I just gave Harry a recovered stolen vehicle."

Hemmings nodded his understanding, then walked across the room to a row of file cabinets near Shapiro's desk. He pulled one drawer open, reached inside, and came out with his revolver and ankle holster. He knelt and strapped the holster to his right ankle. Then he went to Shapiro's desk, opened the center drawer, and took out a key to one of the Northwest Detectives unmarked cars, then left the squad room.

Shapiro, first noting with annoyance but not surprise that Harry the Farter was still fucking around with things on his desk and had not yet left, entered the Lieutenant's office, now occupied by the tour commander, Lieutenant Teddy Spanner.

"Amay called in an attempted criminal rape, kidnapping, et cetera," Shapiro said. "It looks as if our scumbag is at it again. I gave it to Hemmings."

"Where?" Spanner asked.

"Forbidden Drive, by the bridge over the Wissahickon."

"Who's next up on the Wheel?" Spanner said.

"Edgar and Amay," Shapiro said.

"What's Harry Peel doing?" Lieutenant Spanner asked.

"I just sent him on a recovered stolen vehicle," Shapiro said.

Spanner met Shapiro's eyes for a moment.

"Well, send Edgar if he's next up on the Wheel, over to help, and tell him to tell Amay to stay with it. Or, I will. I better go over there myself."

"Yes, sir," Mort Shapiro said, and walked back across the squad room to his desk, where he sat down and waited for the next job to come in.

Officer Bill Dohner used neither his siren nor his flashing lights on the trip to the Chestnut Hill Hospital Emergency Room. For one thing, it wasn't far, and there wasn't much traffic. More importantly, he thought that the girl was upset enough as it was without adding the scream of a siren and flashing lights to her trauma.

"You just stay where you are, miss," Dohner said. "I'll get somebody to help us."

He got out of the car and walked quickly through the doors to the Emergency Room.

There was a middle-aged, comfortable-looking nurse standing by the nurse's station.

"I've got an assaulted woman outside," he said. "All she has on is a blanket."

The nurse didn't even respond to him, but she immediately put down the clipboard she had been holding in her hands and walked quickly to a curtained cubicle, pushing the curtains aside and then pulling out a gurney. She started pushing it toward the doors. By the time she got there, she had a licensed practical nurse, an enormous red-haired woman, and a slight, almost delicate black man in a white physician's jacket at her heels.

"Any injuries that you saw?" the doctor asked Dohner, who shook his head. "No."

The LPN, moving with surprising speed for her bulk, was at the RPC before anyone else. She pulled the door open.

"Can you get out of there without any help, honey?" she asked.

Mary Elizabeth Flannery looked at her as if the woman had been speaking Turkish.

The LPN leaned into the car and half pulled Mary Elizabeth Flannery from it, and then gently put her on the gurney. She spread a white sheet over her, and then, with a little difficulty, pulled Dohner's blanket from under the sheet.

"You're going to be all right, now, dear," the LPN said.

Dohner took the blanket. The doctor leaned over Mary Elizabeth Flannery as the LPN started pushing the gurney into the Emergency Room. Dohner folded the blanket and put it on the front passenger-side floorboard. Then he picked up the microphone.

"Fourteen Twenty-Three. I'm at Chestnut Hill Hospital with the victim."

"Fourteen Twenty-Three, a detective will meet you there."

"Fourteen Twenty-Three, okay," Dohner said, and then walked into the Emergency Room.

None of the people who had taken Mary Elizabeth Flannery from his car were in sight, but he heard sounds and detected movement inside the white-curtained cubicle from which the nurse had taken the gurney. Dohner sat down in a chrome and plastic chair to wait for the detective, or for the hospital people to finish with the victim.

The LPN came out first, rummaged quickly through a medical equipment cabinet, muttered under her breath when she couldn't find what she was looking for, then went back into the cubicle. The nurse then came out, went to the same cabinet, swore, and then reached for a telephone.

Then she spotted a ward boy.

"Go to supply and get a Johnson Rape Kit," she ordered. "Get a half dozen of them, if you can."

She looked over at Dohner.

"She hasn't been injured," she said. "Cut, or anything like that."

"I'd like to get her name and address," Dohner said.

"That'll have to wait," the nurse said.

A minute or two later, the ward boy came running down the waxed corridor with an armful of small packages. He went to the curtained cubicle, handed one of the packages to someone inside, then put the rest in the medical equipment cabinet.

Officer Dohner knew what the Johnson Rape Kit contained, and how it was used, and he felt a wave of mixed rage and compassion for Mary Elizabeth Flannery, who seemed to him to be a nice young woman, and was about to undergo an experience that would be almost as shocking and distasteful for her as what the scumbag had already done to her.

The Johnson Rape Kit contained a number of sterile vials and swabs. Blood would be drawn from Mary Elizabeth Flannery into several of the vials. Tests for venereal disease and pregnancy would be made. The swabs would be used to take cultures from her throat, vagina, and anus, to determine the presence of semen and alien saliva, urine or blood.

It would be uncomfortable for her, and humiliating, but it was necessary to successfully prosecute the sonofabitch who did this to her, presuming they could catch him.

The "chain of evidence" would be carefully maintained. The assistant district attorney who prosecuted the case, presuming again that the police could catch the rapist, would have to be prepared to prove in court that the results of the probing of Mary Elizabeth Flannery's bodily orifices had been in police custody from the moment the doctor handed them to Dohner (or a detective, if one had shown up by the time the doctor was finished with his tests) until he offered them as evidence in a courtroom.

Detective Dick Hemmings arrived at the Chestnut Hill Hospital Emergency Room twenty minutes after Officer Bill Dohner had taken her there. He found Dohner sitting in a chair, filling out a Form 75-48, which is the initial Report of Investigation. It is a short form, providing only the bare bones of what has happened.

Dohner nodded at Hemmings, who sat down beside him and waited until he had finished. Dohner handed the 75-48 to him. In a neat hand, he had written: *"Compl. states a W/M broke into her apt, forced her to perform Involuntary Deviate Sex. Intercourse, urinated on her, tied her up, forced her into a van, & left her off at Bell's Mill Road & Forbidden Dr."*

"Jesus," Hemmings said. "Where is she?"

"In there with the doctor," Dohner said, nodding toward the white-curtained cubicle.

"Hurt?"

"No."

Dohner reached in his pocket and took out the cord he had cut from Mary Elizabeth Flannery's wrists. "This is what he tied her up with."

Hemmings saw that Bill Dohner had not untied the knot in the cord.

"Good job," he said. "Make sure the knot doesn't come untied. Give me a couple of minutes here to find out what we have, and then take the cord to Northwest and put it on a Property Receipt."

Dohner nodded. He held up a clear plastic bag, and dropped the cord in it.

"I got this from one of the nurses," he said.

A Property Receipt—Philadelphia Police Department Form 75-3—is used to maintain the *"chain of evidence."* As with the biologic samples to be taken from Mary Elizabeth Flannery's body, it would be necessary, presuming the case got to court, for the assistant district attorney to prove that the cord allegedly used to tie the victim's hands had never left police custody from the time Dohner had cut it from her wrists; that the chain of evidence had not been broken.

Property Receipts are numbered sequentially. They are usually kept in the desk of the Operations Room Supervisor in each district. They must be signed for by the officer asking for one, and strict department policy insists that the information on the form must either be typewritten or *printed* in ink. Consequently, evidence is almost always held until the officer using a Property Receipt can find a typewriter.

"Anything happen at the scene?" Dohner asked.

"The Mobile Crime Lab got there when I was there," Hemmings said. "Nobody that looks like the doer has shown up. How long did he have her there?"

"I didn't get hardly anything out of her," Dohner said. "Just her name, and what this guy did to her. She's pretty shook up."

Hemmings finished filling out the form, acknowledging receipt of one length of knotted cord used to tie up Mary Elizabeth Flannery, signed it, and handed the original to Dohner, who handed him the cord.

"You might as well go, Bill," Hemmings said. "I'll take it from here."

"I hope you catch him," Dohner said, standing up and giving his hand to Hemmings.

Then he went outside and got in his car and started the engine and called Police Radio and reported that Fourteen Twenty-Three was back in service.

Mary Elizabeth Flannery looked with frightened eyes at the stranger who had entered the curtained cubicle.

"Miss Flannery, my name is Dick Hemmings, and I'm a detective. How are you doing?"

She did not reply.

"Is there anyone you would like me to call? Your parents, maybe? A friend?"

"No!" Mary Elizabeth Flannery said, as if the idea horrified her.

"I know what you've been going through," Hemmings said.

"No, you don't!"

"But the sooner we can learn something about the man who did this to you, the better," Hemming went on, gently. "Would it be all right if I asked you a couple of questions?"

She eyed him suspiciously, but didn't reply.

"I need your address, first of all," he said.

"210 Henry Avenue," she said. "Apartment C. They call it the Fernwood."

"That's one of those garden apartments, isn't it?" Hemmings asked, as a mental image of that area of Roxborough came to his mind.

"Yes," she said.

"How do you think this man got into your apartment?" Hemmings asked.

"How do I know?" she snapped.

"Is there a fire escape? Were there open windows?"

"There's a back," she said. "Little patios."

"You live on the ground floor?"

"Yes."

"Did you hear any noises, a window breaking, a door being forced, by any chance?"

"The windows were open," she said. "It's been hot."

She thinks I'm stupid, but at least she's talking.

"When were you first aware that this man was in your apartment?"

"When I saw him," Mary Elizabeth Flannery snapped.

"Where were you, what were you doing, when you first saw him?"

"I was in my living room, watching television."

"And where was he, when you first saw him?"

"Just standing there, in the door to my bedroom." She grimaced.

"Can you describe him?"

"No."

"Not at all?"

"He was wearing black overalls, coveralls, whatever they call them, and a mask. That's all I could see."

"What kind of a mask?"

"A mask, over his eyes."

"I mean, what color was the mask? Did you notice?"

"It was a Lone Ranger mask," she said. "The kind with a flap over the mouth."

"Black?"

"Yes, black," she said.

The Lone Ranger, Hemmings thought, *wore a mask that covered his eyes only, not with a flap over his mouth.*

"Did he have anything with him?"

"He had a knife," she said, impatiently, as if she expected Hemmings to know all these details.

"What kind of knife?"

"A butcher knife."

"Was it your knife?"

"No, it wasn't my knife."

"Do you remember if the windows in your bedroom were open?" Hemmings asked.

"I told you they were; it was hot."

"How big was the knife?" Hemmings asked, extending his index fingers as he spoke, and then moving his hands apart.

"That big," Mary Elizabeth Flannery said, when she thought his hands were as far apart as the knife had been large.

"And it was a butcher knife, right?"

"I told you that."

"I mean, it couldn't have been a hunting knife, or a bayonet, or some other kind of a knife?"

"I know a butcher knife when I see one."

"Miss Flannery, I'm on your side."

"Why do you let people like that run the streets, then?" she challenged.

"We try not to," Hemmings said, sincerely. "We try to catch them, and then to see that they're put behind bars. But we need help to catch them."

There was no response to this.

"What happened then, Miss Flannery?" Hemmings asked, gently.

"I told the cop what that filthy bastard did to me."

"But I have to know, and in some detail, I'm afraid." Hemmings said.

"He threatened me with his knife, and made me . . . oh, Jesus!"

"Can you tell me exactly what he said?"

She snorted. "You want to know exactly what he said? I'll tell you exactly what he said, he said *'Very nice,'* that's what he said."

"What kind of a voice did he have?"

"What do you mean, what kind of a voice?"

"Was it deep, or high pitched? Did he have any kind of an accent?"

"He had a regular voice," she said. "No accent."

"And then what happened?"

"Then . . . he came over to me, and cut my clothes."

"You were sitting where? In an armchair? On a couch?"

"I was laying down on my couch."

"What part of your clothes did he cut? What were you wearing?"

She flushed and turned her face away from him.

"Jesus!" she said.

"Miss Flannery," Hemmings said. "Sometimes, when it's hot like this, and my air conditioner's not working, and there's nobody around to see me, when I watch television, I do it in my underwear. Was that what happened with you?"

She nodded her head, but still kept her head turned away from him.

"Bra and pants, is that what you were wearing, because it was so damned hot?"

"Just my panties," she said, faintly, after a moment, and then she flared. "You're trying to make it sound like it was my fault."

"No, I'm not, Miss Flannery," Hemmings said, with all the sincerity he could muster.

He probably would have broken in if you had been wearing an ankle-length fur coat, but looking through the window and seeing you wearing nothing but your underpants didn't discourage him any, either, Hemmings thought. And was immediately ashamed of himself.

"You say he cut your clothing? You mean your underclothes?"

"He came over to me and put the knife down the front of my panties and jerked it," she said.

"Did he say anything? Or did you?"

"I tried to scream when I first saw him, and couldn't," she said. "And then when he was using the knife, I was too scared to scream."

"Did he say anything?"

"He said, 'Let's see the rest,' " she said, very faintly.

"What was he doing with the knife at this time?" Hemmings asked, gently.

"Oh, my God! Is this *necessary?*"

"Yes, ma'am, I'm afraid it is."

"He was pushing me in the breast with it, with the point."

She turned her face to look at him, then as quickly averted it.

"Then he said, 'Take your panties off,' and I did," she said, quickly, softly. "And then he took me into my bedroom and made me get on the bed, and then he tied me to the bed—"

"What did he use to tie you to the bed?"

"My panty hose," she said. "He went in my dresser and got panty hose and tied me up."

"Up?" Hemmings interrupted. "Or to the bed?"

"To the bed," she said. "I've got a brass bed, and he tied me to the headboard and footboard."

"On your back? Or on your stomach?"

"On my back," she said.

"And then what?"

"Then he started talking dirty," she said.

"Do you remember what he said?"

"What do you think?" she flared.

"Can you tell me exactly what he said?" Hemmings asked.

"Jesus!" she said. "He used words like 'teats' and . . . and 'pussy' and words like that."

"Anything else?"

"Isn't that enough? Or do you mean what he did to me?"

"Anything and everything you can tell me, Miss Flannery . . ."

"Then he started taking off his overalls—"

"Let's get that fact straight," Hemmings said. "*Overalls* are what farmers wear, if you follow me. They have straps over the shoulders, and a sort of flap in front. *Coveralls* are what mechanics sometimes wear. They cover everything; they have sleeves. Which was he wearing?"

"Coveralls," she said. "Black coveralls."

"Black, or maybe dark blue?"

"*Black,*" she said firmly.

"Sometimes people who wear coveralls get them at work," Hemmings said. "And they have embroidery on them, or little patches. 'Joe's Garage,' or something like that. Or a name embroidered. Did you notice anything like that?"

"No," she said, surely.

"When he took off his coveralls, did you notice what kind of underclothes he was wearing?"

"When I saw what he was doing, I closed my eyes."

"And?"

"And said Hail Marys," she said.

"And then what happened?"

"He wasn't wearing a T-shirt," she said, "an undershirt. I saw that much. He was bare-chested. He was hairy. He had a lot of hair."

"And then what happened."

"I felt him getting on the bed, and when I opened my eyes, he was on top of me."

"Lying on top of you?"

"No! Kneeling, squatting, over me. Over my head. And he had all his clothes off."

"And then what did he do?"

"He told me to suck it," she said, bitterly.

"He meant his penis?"

"What do you think?"

"Was he erect? Did he have an erection?"

"No," she said. "No. He said, 'Suck it and make it hard.' "

"And he put his penis in your mouth?"

"He had his goddamned knife on my throat!"

"And forced his penis into your mouth?"

"Yes, God damn you, yes!"

"And did he ejaculate?"

"What? Oh. No. No, thank God, he didn't."

"What did he do?"

"After a while he took it out, and sat back on his heels and . . . played with himself."

"Did he ejaculate then?"

"All over me," she said, almost moaning, "my face, my mouth, my chest . . ."

"You said he was hairy," Hemmings asked. "Did you notice anything else? Were there any scars on his body? Any marks? Any tattoos? Anything like that?"

"I was trying not to look at him."

"You had your eyes closed all this time?"

"He pushed me with the knife and made me open them," she said. "He said he wanted me to watch."

"And after he had masturbated, what did he do?"

"He sat there, on my legs, for a while, and then he got off and put his overalls, coveralls, back on."

"Did he go to the bathroom, anything like that?"

"He went to the bathroom on me," she said, in mingled horror and fury. "He got off me, off the bed, and then stood by the side of it and . . . pissed all over me."

"He stood by the side of the bed and urinated on you. Before or after he put his coveralls back on?"

"Before," she said.

"And you didn't see any markings of any kind on his body?"

"I told you already, no."

"And then what happened?"

"He cut me loose and made me roll over, and then he tied me up again," she said.

"When Officer Dohner found you, Miss Flannery, your hands were tied with lamp cord. Do you remember where he got that?"

"No," she said.

"He cut the panty hose with which you were tied, is that right? He didn't untie you?"

"He tried," she said. "And then when he couldn't, he got mad. And then he got even madder when he couldn't find any more panty hose. He pulled the dresser drawer all the way out and threw it on the floor."

"And after he had tied your hands behind you, what did he do?"

"He said we were going for a little ride, he wanted everybody to—"

"To what?"

"To have a look at me."

"Are those, more or less, his exact words?"

"He said he wanted everybody to see . . . my private parts, and to see his come all over me."

"Then what?"

"He found my raincoat . . ."

"Where was that?"

"In the hall closet," she said. "And he told me to get up, and he put my raincoat over my shoulders. And he said that if I tried to run away, he'd . . . he'd stick the knife up . . . in me . . . he'd stick the knife between my legs."

"And then?"

"He took me out the back and put me in the back of his van."

"Tell me about the van," Hemmings said. "Where was it?"

"In the parking lot behind my apartment."

Hemmings tried and failed to recall a mental image of the garden apartment complex parking lot.

"What kind of a van was it?"

"A *van,*" she said, impatiently.

"Where did he put you in the van?"

"In the back."

"Was there a door on the side, a sliding door, maybe? Or did you get in the front?"

"There was a sliding door. He opened it, and told me to get in and lay down on my face."

"Did you see anything in the back of the van? I mean, was it plain in there, or did he have it fixed up with chairs and upholstery? Was there a carpet, maybe?"

"No. The floor was metal. And there was nothing in there. Just a *van.*"

"Did it look to you like a new van, or one that has been around awhile? Was it scratched up, maybe? Was there a peculiar smell? Anything like that?"

"It was dark, and I had my face on the floor, and I couldn't see anything," she said.

"And then what happened?"

"He got in front and started it up, and I guess he just drove me to where he pushed me out and the cop found me."

"Did anything happen while you were in the van? Did you hear something, maybe, that stuck in your mind. Can you think of anything at all?"

"I thought he was going to kill me," she said. "I was praying."

"Tell me about what happened when you got to Forbidden Drive," Hemmings said.

"I knew we'd left the street," she said. "A regular street, I mean. It sounded different under the wheels."

That response disappointed Dick Hemmings a little; if she had picked up on that, she more than likely would have picked up on anything else odd that had happened. Therefore, nothing interesting had happened.

"And?"

"And then he stopped, and I heard him opening the door, and then he told me to get out. He said that I should walk away from him, and if I turned around to look, he would kill me."

"And he was still wearing his mask?"

"Yeah."

"And then?"

"He took my raincoat off, and pushed me, and I started walking," she said. "And then I heard him driving off."

"Did you know where you were?"

"I thought the park," she said. "We hadn't come that far. But where in the park, I didn't have any idea."

"Did anyone come by before Officer Dohner got there?"

"No," she said. "I saw lights, headlights, and started walking toward where they were going past."

"I'll certainly be talking to you again, Miss Flannery," Hemmings said. "But this is enough to get us started. Thank you for being so frank with me."

"I hope he runs away when you catch him, so you can shoot the sonofabitch!" she said.

"Maybe we'll get lucky," Hemmings said.

I shouldn't have said that.

"What happens to me now?" Mary Elizabeth Flannery said.

"Well, I guess that's up to the doctor," Hemmings said. "He'll probably want you to spend the night here."

"I don't want to spend the night here," she said, angrily. "I want to go home."

"Well, that's probably your decision. . . ."

"How am I going to get home? I don't have any clothing, my purse . . ."

"If you'd like me to, Miss Flannery," Hemmings said. "I'll be going to your apartment. I could bring you some clothing, and if you can work it out with the doctor, I'd be happy to drive you home. But if you want my advice, I'd stay here, or at least spend the night with your family, or a friend—"

" 'Hello, Daddy, guess what happened to me?' "

"I'm sure your father would understand," Hemmings said.

She snorted.

"What my father would say would be, 'I told you if you insisted on getting an apartment by yourself, something like this would happen.' "

"Well, what about a friend?"

"I don't want to have to answer any more questions from anybody," she said.

"Well, I'll go get you some clothing," Hemmings said. "And bring it here. You think about it."

 As Mickey O'Hara had walked across the fine carpets laid over the marble floor of the lobby of the Bellevue-Stratford Hotel, and then onto South Broad Street, 6.3 miles to the north, where Old York Road cuts into Broad Street at an angle, about a mile south of the city line, the line of traffic headed toward downtown Philadelphia from the north suddenly slowed, taking the driver of a 1971 Buick Super sedan by surprise.

He braked sharply and the nose of the Buick dipped, and there was a squeal from the brakes. The driver of the Mercury in front of him looked back first with alarm, and then with annoyance.

I'm probably a little gassed, the driver of the Buick thought. *I'll have to watch myself.*

His name was David James Pekach, and he was thirty-two years old. He was five feet nine inches tall, and weighed 143 pounds. He was smooth shaven, but he wore his hair long, parted in the middle, and gathered together in the back in a pigtail held in place by a rubber band. He was wearing a white shirt and a necktie. The shirt was mussed and sweat stained. The jacket of his seersucker suit was on the seat beside him.

The Buick Super was not quite three years old, but the odometer had already turned over at 100,000 miles. The shocks were shot, and so were the brakes. The foam rubber cushion under David James Pekach's rear end had long ago lost its resilience, and the front-end suspension was shot, and the right-rear passenger door had to be kicked to get it open. But the air conditioner still worked, and Pekach had been running it full blast against the ninety-eight-percent humidity and ninety-three-degree temperature of the late June night.

David James Pekach was on his way home from upper Bucks County. His cousin Stanley had been married at eleven o'clock that morning at Saint Stanislaus's Roman Catholic Church in Bethlehem, and there had been a reception following at the bride's home near Riegelsville, on the Delaware River, at the absolute upper end of Bucks County.

The booze had really flowed, and he had had more than he could handle. He was a little guy, at least compared to his brothers and cousins, and he couldn't handle very much, anyway.

There had been the usual cracks about his size, and of course the pigtail, at the reception (*"You know what Davie is? With that pigtail? One Hung Low. The world's only Polack Chink."*) and every time he'd looked at the priest, he'd found the priest looking at him, then suddenly turning on an uneasy smile. He wasn't their priest, he was the bride's family's priest, and what he was obviously thinking was, *"What's a bum like that doing in the Pekach family?"*

He saw the reason for the sudden slowdown, flashing blue lights on two Philadelphia police cars at the corner. A wreck. *Probably a bad one,* he thought, with two cars at the scene.

He hadn't been paying much attention to where he was. He looked around to see where he was.

When he got to the cop directing traffic, the cop signaled him to stop. Dave Pekach rolled down the window.

"You almost rear-ended the Mercury," the cop accused. From the way the cop looked at him, Dave Pekach knew that he didn't like men who wore long blond hair in a pigtail any more than the priest had.

"I know," Dave Pekach said, politely. "I wasn't paying attention."

"You been drinking?" It was an accusation, not a question.

"I just came from a wedding," Pekach admitted. "But I'm all right."

The cop flashed his light around the inside of the Buick, to see what he could see, then let Pekach sweat twenty seconds, then waved him on.

Pekach drove fifty feet, swore, and then braked hard again. The brakes squealed again, and there was a loud, dull groan from the front end as he bounced over a curb and stopped.

He opened the door and got out and started walking toward two men standing by the hood of a five-year-old Ford sedan.

"Hey, buddy!" the cop who had stopped him called. "What do you think you're doing?"

Pekach ignored him.

The cop, trotting over, reached the old Ford just as Pekach did, just in time to hear one of the men greet Pekach: "Hey, Captain," one of the men said. He was a heavy, redheaded Irishman in a T-shirt and blue jeans. "Don't you look spiffy!"

The cop was embarrassed. He had sensed there was something not quite right with the car, or the man driving it. There were some subtle things. The relatively new automobile had obviously not been washed, much less polished, in some time. It looked as if it had been used hard. The driver's-side vent window had a thumb-sized piece of glass missing, and was badly cracked. The tires had black walls, and on closer examination were larger than the tires that had come with the car.

But until right now, the cop had been looking for something *wrong,* something that would have given him reasonable cause to see what the clown in the pigtail might have under the seat or in the glove compartment or in the trunk. Now he looked at the car again, and saw that he had missed the real giveaway: On the shelf between the top of the backseat and the window was a thin eight-inch-tall shortwave radio antenna.

The battered Buick was a police car, and the funny-looking little guy with the hippy pigtail was a police officer. More than a cop. One of the narcotics guys had called him "Captain."

And then the cop put it all together. The little guy with the pigtail was Captain David Pekach, of the Narcotics Division of the Philadelphia Police Department. He remembered now, too, that Pekach had just made captain. Now that he was a captain, the cop thought, Pekach was probably going to have to get rid of the pigtail. Captains don't work undercover; neither do lieutenants, and only rarely a sergeant. The cop remembered a story that had gone around the bar of the Fraternal Order of Police. A Narcotics Lieutenant (obviously, now Pekach) had been jumped on by the Commissioner himself for the pigtail. Pekach had stood up to him. If he was supposed to supervise his undercover men working the streets, the only way he could do that was, from time to time, to go on the streets with them. And a very good way to blow the cover of plainclothes cops working Narcotics dressed like addicts was to have them seen talking to some guy in a business suit and a neat, show-your-ears haircut. No questions were likely to be asked about a guy in a dirty sweatshirt and a pigtail. The story going around the FOP bar was that Commissioner Czernich had backed off.

"What's going on?" Captain Pekach asked the red-haired Narc, whose name was Coogan.

"We were cutting the grass in Wissahickon Park," the other Narcotics officer said. He was a Latin American, wearing a sleeveless denim jacket, his naked chest and stomach sweaty under it. He was a small man, smaller than Captain Pekach. At five feet seven even, he had just made the height requirement for police officers.

"Cutting the grass" was a witticism. Parks have grass. *Cannabis sativa,* commonly known as marijuana, is known on the street as "grass." But arresting vendors of small quantities of grass is not a high-priority function of plainclothes officers of the Narcotics Division. The Narcotics officers knew that, and they knew that Captain David Pekach knew it.

"And?" Pekach asked.

"It was a slow night, Captain," Alexandro Gres-Narino said, uncomfortably.

"Except for the naked lady," Tom Coogan said.

"What naked lady?" Pekach asked.

"Some dame was running around without any clothes in the park by the Wissahickon Bridge," Tom Coogan said. "Every car north of Market Street went in on it."

"Tell me about this," Pekach said, impatiently, gesturing vaguely around him.

"So there was a buy, and they run," Coogan said. "And we chased them. And they run off the road here."

"High-speed pursuit, no doubt?" Pekach asked, dryly.

"Not by us, Captain," Coogan said, firmly and righteously. "We got on the radio and gave a description of the car, and a Thirty-fifth District car spotted it, and they chased them. We only come over here after they wrecked the car."

"So what have you got?" Pekach asked, a tired, disgusted tone in his voice.

Without waiting for a reply, he walked over to one of the Thirty-fifth District patrol cars, and looked through the partially opened rear seat window. There were four white kids crowded in the back, two boys and two girls, all four of them looking scared.

"Anybody hurt?" Pekach asked.

Four heads shook no, but nobody said anything.

"Whose car?" Pekach asked.

There was no reply immediately, but finally one of the boys, mustering what bravado he could, said, "Mine."

"Yours? Or your father's?" Pekach asked.

"My father's," the boy said.

"He's going to love you for this," Pekach said, and walked back to the Narcotics Division officers.

"Well, what have you got on them?" he asked Officer Coogan.

"About an ounce and a half," Coogan replied, uncomfortably.

"An *ounce* and a *half!*" Pekach said in sarcastic wonderment.

"Failure to heed a flashing light, speeding, reckless driving," Coogan went on, visibly a little uncomfortable.

"You like traffic work, do you, Coogan? Keeping the streets free of reckless drivers? Maybe rolling on a naked lady?"

Officer Coogan did not reply.

There was the growl of a siren, and Pekach looked over his shoulder and saw a Thirty-fifth District wagon pulling up. The two policemen in it got out, spoke to one of the patrol car cops, and then one of them went to the van and opened the rear door while the other went to the patrol car with the patrol car cop. The patrol car cop opened the door and motioned the kids out.

"Wait a minute," Pekach called. He walked over to them.

One of the girls, an attractive little thing with long brown hair parted in the middle and large dark eyes, looked as if she was about to cry.

"You got any money?" Pekach asked.

"Who are you?" the van cop asked.

"I'm Captain Pekach," he said. "Narcotics."

The girl shook her head.

Pekach pointed at one of the boys, the one who had told him it was his father's car. "You got any money, Casanova?"

There was a just perceptible pause before the boy replied, "I got some money."

"You got twenty bucks?" Pekach asked.

The boy dug his wallet out of his hip pocket.

"Give it to her," Pekach ordered. Then he turned to the patrol car cop. "You have the names and addresses?"

"Yes, sir."

"Put the girls in a cab," Pekach said.

He turned to the girl with the large dark eyes.

"Your boyfriends are going to jail," he said. "First, they're going to the District, and then they'll be taken downtown to Central lockup. When they get out, ask them what it was like."

Pekach found Officers Alexandro Gres-Narino and Thomas L. Coogan.

"If you can fit me into your busy schedule, I would like a moment of your time at half past three tomorrow in my office," he said.

"Yes, sir," they said, almost in unison.

Pekach took one more look at the girl with the large dark eyes. There were tears running down her cheeks.

"Thank you," she said, barely audibly.

Captain Dave Pekach then walked to the worn-out Buick, coaxed the engine to life, and drove home.

At five minutes after nine the next morning, Mickey O'Hara again pulled his battered Chevrolet Impala to the curb in front of the Bellevue-Stratford Hotel by the NO PARKING AT ANY TIME TOW AWAY ZONE sign. He was not worried about a ticket. There was about as much chance a police officer would cite him for illegal parking, much less summon a police tow truck to haul Mickey O'Hara's car away, as there was for a white hat to slap a ticket on His Honor, Mayor Jerry Carlucci's mayoral Cadillac limousine.

There were perhaps a couple of dozen police officers among the eight thousand or so cops on the force who would not recognize the battered, antennae-festooned Chevrolet as belonging to Mr. Mickey O'Hara, of the editorial staff of the *Philadelphia Bulletin*. The others, from Commissioner Thaddeu Czernich to the most recent graduates of the police academy, if they saw Mickey O'Hara climb out of his illegally parked vehicle, would wave cheerfully at him, or, if they were close enough, offer their hands, and more than likely say, "Hey, Mickey, how's it going? What's going on?"

It was generally conceded that Mickey O'Hara knew more of what was going on at any given moment, in the area of interesting crime, than the entire staff of the Police Radio Room on the second floor of the Roundhouse. Equally important, Mickey O'Hara was nearly universally regarded as a good guy, a friend of the cops, someone who understood their problems, someone who would put it in the paper the way it had really gone down. Mickey O'Hara, in other words, was accustomed to ignoring NO PARKING signs.

But today, when he got out of his car, Mickey looked at the sign, and read it, and for a moment actually considered getting back in, and taking the car someplace to park it legally. The cold truth was that right now he was not a police reporter. The Bull could call it *"withholding professional services"* all day and all night, but the truth of the matter was that Mickey O'Hara was out of work. If you didn't have a job, and nobody was going to hand you a paycheck, you were, *ergo sum,* out of work.

Mickey decided against moving the car someplace legal. That would have been tantamount to an admission of defeat. He didn't *know* that the *Bulletin* was going to tell him, more accurately tell his agent, to "go fuck yourselves, we don't need him." That struck Mickey as the most likely probability in the circumstances, but he didn't *know* that for *sure.*

He had hoped to have the issue resolved, one way or the other, last night. But the Bull's plane had been late, so that hadn't happened. It had been pretty goddamned depressing, and he had woken up, with a minor hangover, rather proud of himself for not, after he'd drained the last bottle of Ortleib's, having gone out and really tied one on.

Mickey straightened his shoulders and marched resolutely toward the revolving door giving access to the lobby of the Bellevue-Stratford. There was nothing to really worry about, he told himself. For one thing, he was the undisputed king of his trade in Philadelphia. There were four daily newspapers in the City of Brotherly Love, and at least a dozen people, including, lately, a couple of females, who covered crime. The best crime coverage was in the *Bulletin,* and the best reporter on the *Bulletin* was Michael J. O'Hara, even if most of the other reporters, including both women, had master's degrees in journalism from places like Columbia and Missouri.

Mickey himself had no college degree. For that matter, he didn't even have a high school diploma. He had begun his career, as a copy boy, in the days when reporters typed their stories on battered typewriters, and then held it over their head, bellowing "copy" until a copy boy came to carry it to the city desk.

Mickey had been expelled from West Catholic High School in midterm of his junior year. The offenses alleged involved intoxicants, tobacco, and so far as Monsignor John F. Dooley, the principal, was concerned, incontrovertible proof that Michael J. O'Hara had been running numbers to the janitorial staff and student body on behalf of one Francisco Guttermo, who, it was correctly alleged, operated one of the most successful numbers routes in Southwest Philly.

It had been Monsignor Dooley's intention to teach Mickey something about the wages of sin by banishing him in shame from the company of his classmates for, say, three weeks, and then permitting him to return, chastened, to the halls of academe.

The day after he was expelled, Mickey spotted a sign, crudely lettered, thumbtacked to the door of the *Philadelphia Daily News,* which in those days occupied a run-down building on Arch Street, way up by the Schuylkill River. The sign read, simply, COPY BOY WANTED.

Mickey had no idea what a copy boy was expected to do, but in the belief that it couldn't be any worse than his other options, becoming a stock boy in an Acme Supermarket, or an office boy somewhere, he went inside and upstairs to the second floor and applied for the position.

James T. "Spike" Dolan, the City Editor of the *Daily News,* saw in young Mickey O'Hara a kindred soul and hired him. Within hours Mickey realized that he had found his niche in life. He never went back to West Catholic High School, although many years later, in a reversal of roles in which he found himself the interviewee for a reporter for *Philadelphia Magazine,* he gave West Catholic High, specifically the nearly three years of Latin he had been force-fed there, credit for his skill with words. The interview came after Mickey had been awarded the Pulitzer Prize for investigative reporting. The series of stories had dealt with chicanery involving the bail bond system then in effect.

He told himself too that not only was he the best police reporter in town, but that his agent was one of the best agents there was, period. He didn't do too well with this, because there were a couple of things wrong with it, and he knew it. For one thing, newspaper reporters don't have agents. Movie stars have agents, and television personalities have agents, and sports figures have agents, but not newspaper police beat reporters.

Police reporters don't have contracts for their professional services. Police reporters are employed at the pleasure of the city editor, and subject to getting canned whenever it pleases the city editor, or whenever they displease the city editor. Mickey, who had been fired at least once from every newspaper in Philadelphia, plus the *Baltimore Sun* and the *Washington Post* during his journalistic career, knew that from experience. And police reporters don't make the kind of money his agent had assured him he would get him, or kiss his ass at Broad and Market at high noon.

What had happened was that Casimir "the Bull" Bolinski had come to town a month before, and Mickey had gone to see him at the Warwick. Mickey and the Bull went way back, all the way to the third grade at Saint Stephen's Parochial School, at Tenth and Butler streets where Roosevelt Boulevard turns into the Northeast Extension. So far back that he still called the Bull "Casimir" and the Bull called him "Michael."

Sister Mary Magdalene, principal of Saint Stephen's, had had this thing about nicknames. Your name was what they had given you when you were baptized, and since baptism was a sacrament, sacred before God, you used that name, not one you had made up yourself. Sister Mary Magdalene had enforced her theologic views among her charges with her eighteen-inch, steel-reinforced ruler, which she had carried around with her, and used either like a cattle prod, jabbing it in young sinners' ribs, or like a riding crop, cracked smartly across young bottoms.

Casimir Bolinski had gone on to graduate from West Catholic High School, largely because when Monsignor Dooley had caught Michael J. O'Hara with a pocketful of Frankie the Gut Guttermo's numbers slips, Mickey had refused to name his accomplice in that illegal and immoral enterprise.

Casimir Bolinski had gone on to Notre Dame, where he was an All-American tackle, and then on to a sixteen-year career with the Green Bay Packers. His professional football career ended only when the chief of orthopedic surgical services at the University of Illinois Medical College informed Mrs. Bolinski that unless she could dissuade her husband from returning to the gridiron she should start looking for a wheelchair in which she could roll him around for the rest of his life.

It was then, shortly after Bull Bolinski's tearful farewell-to-professional-football news conference, that his secret, carefully kept from his teammates, coaches and the management of the Green Bay Packers, came out. Bull Bolinski was also Casimir J. Bolinski, D. Juris (cum laude), the University of Southern California, admitted to the

California, Pennsylvania, Wisconsin, Illinois, and New York bars, and admitted to practice before the Supreme Court of the United States of America.

He had not, as was popularly believed, spent his off seasons on the West Coast drinking beer on the beach and making babies with Mrs. Bolinski. And neither was Mrs. Antoinette Bolinski quite what most people on the Packers thought her to be, that is just a pretty, good li'l old broad with a spectacular set of knockers who kept the Bull on a pretty short leash.

Mrs. Bolinski had been a schoolteacher when she met her husband. She had been somewhat reluctantly escorting a group of sixth-graders on a field trip to watch the Packers in spring training. She held the view at the time that professional football was sort of a reincarnation of the Roman games, a blood sport with few if any redeeming societal benefits.

The first time she saw Casimir, he had tackled a fellow player with such skill and enthusiasm that there were three people kneeling over the ball carrier, trying to restore him to consciousness and feeling for broken bones. Casimir, who had taken off his helmet, was standing there, chewing what she later learned was Old Mule rough cut mentholated chewing tobacco, watching.

Antoinette had never before in her entire (twenty-three-year) life seen such tender compassion in a man's eyes, or experienced an emotional reaction such as that she felt when Casimir glanced over at her, spat, smiled shyly, winked, and said, "Hiya, honey!"

By the time, two months later, Mr. and Mrs. Casimir Bolinski returned from their three-day honeymoon in the Conrad Hilton Hotel in Chicago, she had him off Old Mule rough cut mentholated chewing tobacco and onto mint Life Savers, and already thinking about his—now their—future, which, pre-Antoinette, had been a vague notion that when he couldn't play anymore, he would get a job as a coach or maybe get a bar and grill or something.

Two days after the management of the Green Bay Packers had stood before the lights of the television cameras of all three networks and given Bull Bolinski a solid gold Rolex diver's watch, a set of golf clubs, a Buick convertible and announced that the number he had worn so proudly on his jersey for sixteen years would be retired, they received a letter on the engraved crisp bond stationery of Heidenheimer & Bolinski, Counselors At Law, advising them that the firm now represented Messrs. J. Stanley Wozniski; Franklin D. R. Marshall; and Ezra J. Houghton, and would do so in the upcoming renegotiation of the contracts for their professional services, and to please communicate in the future directly with Mr. Bolinski in any and all matters thereto pertaining.

This was shortly followed by that legendary television interview with linebacker F. D. R. Marshall and quarterback E. J. Houghton, during which Mr. Marshall had said, "If the *bleep*ing Packers don't want to deal with the Bull, so far's I'm concerned, they can shove that *bleep*ing football up their *bleep*," only to be chastised by Mr. Houghton, who said, "Shut up, FDR, you can't talk dirty like that on the *bleep*ing TV."

So Mickey O'Hara was aware from the very beginning that the Bull had not only succeeded in getting a fair deal for his former teammates from the Packers, but had also, within a matter of a couple of years, become the most successful sports agent in the business, and grown rich in the process.

But it wasn't until the Bull had come to town and Mickey had picked him up at the Warwick and they had driven into South Philadelphia for some real homemade Italian sausage and some really good lasagna that he even dreamed that it could have anything to do, however remotely, with him.

"Turn the fucking air conditioner on, Michael, why don't you?" the Bull said to Mickey when they were no more than fifty yards from the Warwick.

"It's broke," Mickey had replied.

"What are you riding around in this piece of shit for anyway?" The Bull then looked around the car and warmed to the subject. "Jesus, this is really a goddamned junker, Michael."

"Fuck you, Casimir. It's reliable. And it's paid for."

"You always were a cheapskate," the Bull said. "Life ain't no rehearsal, Michael. Go buy yourself some decent wheels. You can afford it, for Christ's sake. You ain't even married."

"Huh!" Mickey snorted. "That's what you think."

"What *do* they pay you, Michael?"

Mickey told him and the Bull laughed and said "Bullshit," and Mickey said, "That's it. No crap, Casimir."

"I'll be goddamned, you mean it," the Bull had said, genuinely surprised. Then he grew angry: "Why those cheap sonsofbitches!"

Three days later, the publisher of the *Bulletin* had received a letter on Heidenheimer and Bolinski stationery stating that since preliminary negotiations had failed to reach agreement on a satisfactory interim compensation schedule for Mr. Michael J. O'Hara's professional services, to be in effect while a final contract could be agreed upon between the parties, Mr. O'Hara was forced, effective immediately, to withhold his professional services.

When Mickey heard that what the Bull meant by "interim compensation schedule" was $750 a week, plus all reasonable and necessary expenses, he began to suspect that, despite the Bull's reputation in dealing with professional sports management, he didn't know his ass from second base *vis-à-vis* the newspaper business. Mickey had been getting $312.50 a week, plus a dime a mile for the use of his car.

"Trust me, Michael," the Bull had said. "I know what I'm doing."

That was damned near a month ago, and there hadn't been a peep from the *Bulletin* in all that time.

The good-looking dame, from last night, her hair now done up in sort of a bun, was behind the marble Reception desk in the lobby of the Bellevue-Stratford.

What the hell is that all about? How many hours do these bastards make her work, for Christ's sake?

This time there was no line, and she saw Mickey walking across the lobby, and Mickey smiled at her, and she smiled back.

"Good morning, Mr. O'Hara," she said.

"Mickey, please."

"Mr. and Mrs. Bolinski are in the house, Mr. O'Hara. If you'll just pick up a house phone, the operator will connect you."

"If I wanted to talk to him on the telephone," Mickey replied, "I could have done that from home. I want to see him."

"You'll have to be announced," the good-looking dame said, her delicate lips curling in a reluctant smile.

"You got your hair in a bun," Mickey said.

"I've been here all night," she said.

"How come?"

"My relief just never showed up," she said.

"Jesus! She didn't phone or anything?"

"Not a word," she said.

"You didn't get any sleep at all?"

She shook her head.

"You sure don't look like it," Mickey blurted.

Her face flushed, and she smiled shyly.

Then she picked up a telephone. She spoke the Bull's room number so softly he couldn't hear it.

The phone rang a long time before the Bull's wife answered it.

"Good morning, Mrs. Bolinski," she said. "This is Miss Travis at the front desk. I hope I haven't disturbed you. Mr. O'Hara is here."

Travis, huh? It figures she would have a nice name like that.

"May I send him up?" Miss Travis said, glancing at Mickey. Then she said, "Thank you, madam," and hung up. "Mr. Bolinski is in the Theodore Roosevelt Suite, Mr. O'Hara. That's on ten. Turn to your right when you exit the elevator."

"Thanks."

"My pleasure."

Mickey turned and started to walk to the bank of elevators. Then he turned again.

"You get yourself some sleep," he commanded.

The remark startled her for long enough to give Mickey the opportunity to conclude that whenever it came to saying exactly the right thing to a woman he really liked, he ranked right along with Jackie Gleason playing the bus driver on TV. Or maybe the Marquis de Sade.

But she smiled. "Thank you. I'll try," she said. "I should be relieved any minute now."

Mickey nodded at her, and walked to the elevator. When he got inside and turned around and looked at her, she was looking at him. She waved as the elevator door closed.

It doesn't mean a fucking thing. She was smiling at the old blue-haired broad last night, too.

Mickey had no trouble finding the Theodore Roosevelt Suite, and when he did the door was open, and he could hear Antoinette's voice. He rapped on the door, and pushed it open.

Antoinette was sitting on one of the two couches in front of a fireplace, in a fancy bathrobe, her legs tucked under her, talking on the telephone. She waved him inside, covered the mouthpiece with her hand, and said, "Come in, Michael. Casimir's in the shower."

Then she resumed her conversation. Mickey picked up that she was talking to her mother and at least one of the kids.

Casimir Bolinski entered the room. He was wearing a towel around his waist. It was an average-size towel around an enormous waist, which did little to preserve Mr. Bolinski's modesty.

"I can't find my teeth, sweetie," he mumbled.

Mrs. Bolinski covered the mouthpiece again.

"They're in that blue jar I bought you in Vegas," Mrs. Bolinski said.

"Be with you in a jiff, Michael," the Bull mumbled, adding, "You're early."

He walked out of the sitting room. Mickey saw that his back, and the backs of his legs, especially behind the knees, were laced with surgical scars.

"Kiss, kiss," Antoinette said to the telephone and hung up. "We left the kids with my mother." she said. "Casimir and I have to really work at getting a little time alone together. So I came with him."

"Good for you," Mickey said.

"I didn't know we were coming here," Antoinette said, "until we got to the airport."

Mickey wondered if he was getting some kind of complaint, so he just smiled, instead of saying anything.

"How's your mother, Michael?" Antoinette asked.

"I had dinner with her yesterday."

"That's nice," Antoinette said. Then she picked up the telephone again, dialed a number, identified herself as Mrs. Casimir Bolinski, and said they could serve breakfast now.

The Bull returned to the room, now wearing a shirt and trousers, in the act of hooking his suspender strap over his shoulder.

"I told them to come at ten," he announced, now, with his teeth in, speaking clearly. "We'll have time to eat breakfast. How's your mother?"

"I had dinner with her yesterday. Who's coming at ten?"

"She still think the other people are robbing her blind?"

"Yeah, when they're not . . . making whoopee," Mickey said. "Who's coming at ten?"

"Who do you think?" the Bull said. "I told them we were sick of fucking around with them."

"Clean up your language," Antoinette said, "there's a lady present."

"Sorry, sweetie," the Bull said, sounding genuinely contrite. "Ain't there any coffee?"

"On that roll-around cart in the bedroom," Antoinette said.

The Bull went back into the bedroom and came out pushing a cart holding a coffee service. He poured a cupful and handed it to Mickey, then poured one for himself.

"What am I, the family orphan?" Antoinette asked.

"I thought you had yours," the Bull said.

"I did, but you should have asked."

"You want a cup of coffee, or not?"

"No, thank you, I've got to get dressed," Antoinette said, snippily, and left the sitting room.

"She's a little pissed," the Bull said. "She didn't know I was coming here. She thought I was going to Palm Beach."

"Palm Beach?"

"Lenny Moskowitz is marrying Martha Bethune," the Bull explained. "We got to get the premarital agreement finalized."

Mickey knew Lenny Moskowitz. Or knew of him. He had damned near been the Most Valuable Player in the American League.

"Who's Martha Whateveryousaid?"

"Long-legged blonde with a gorgeous set of knockers," the Bull explained. "She's damned near as tall as Lenny. Her family makes hubcaps."

"Makes what?"

"Hubcaps. For cars? They have a pisspot full of dough, and they're afraid Lenny's marrying her for her dough. Jesus, I got him five big ones for three years. He don't need any of her goddamned dough."

Mickey smiled uneasily, as he thought again of the enormous difference between negotiating a contract for the professional services of someone who was damned near the Most Valuable Player in the American League and a police reporter for the *Philadelphia Bulletin.*

A few minutes later, two waiters rolled into the suite with a cart and a folding table and set up breakfast.

"I told you, I think," the Bull said, as he shoveled food onto his plate, "that you can't get either Taylor ham or scrapple on the West Coast?" Scrapple, a mush made with pork by-products, which was probably introduced into Eastern Pennsylvania by the Pennsylvania Dutch (actually Hessians), was sometimes referred to as "poor people's bacon."

"Yeah, you told me," Mickey said. "How do you think we stand, Casimir?"

"What do you mean, stand? Oh, you mean with those bastards from the *Bulletin?*"

"Yeah," Mickey said, as Antoinette came back into the room, and Casimir stood up and politely held her chair for her.

"Thank you, darling," Antoinette said. "Has Casimir told you, Michael, that they don't have either Taylor ham or scrapple on the West Coast?"

"I could mail you some, if you like," Mickey said.

"It would probably go bad before the goddamned post office got it there," the Bull said, "but it's a thought, Michael."

"I never heard of either before I met Casimir," Antoinette said, "but now I'm just about as crazy about it as he is."

"Casimir was just about to tell me how he thinks we stand with the *Bulletin,*" Mickey said.

"Maybe you could send it Special Delivery or something," the Bull said. "If we wasn't going from here to Florida, I'd put a couple of rolls of Taylor ham and a couple of pounds of scrapple in the suitcase. But it would probably go bad before we got home."

"Of course it would," Antoinette said. "And it would get warm and greasy and get all over our clothes."

"So how do you think we stand with the *Bulletin?*" Mickey asked, somewhat plaintively.

"You sound as if you don't have an awful lot of faith in Casimir, Michael," Antoinette said.

"Don't be silly," Mickey said.

"It would probably take two days to get to the Coast Air-Mail Special Delivery," the Bull said. "What the hell, it's worth a shot."

He reached into his trousers pocket, took out a stack of bills held together with a gold clip in the shape of a dollar sign, peeled off a fifty-dollar bill, and handed it to Mickey.

"Two of the big rolls of Taylor ham," the Bull ordered thoughtfully, "and what—five pounds?—of scrapple. I wonder if you can freeze it."

"Probably not," Antoinette said. "If they could freeze it, they would probably have it in the freezer department in the supermarket."

"What the hell, we'll give it a shot anyway. You never get anywhere unless you take a chance, ain't that right, Michael?"

"Right."

4 The Philadelphia firm of Mawson, Payne, Stockton, McAdoo & Lester maintained their law offices in the Philadelphia Savings Fund Society Building at Twelfth and Market streets, east of Broad Street, which was convenient to both the federal courthouse and the financial district. The firm occupied all of the eleventh floor, and part of the tenth.

The offices of the two founding partners, Brewster Cortland Payne II and Colonel J. Dunlop Mawson, together with the Executive Conference Room and the office of Mrs. Irene Craig, whose title was Executive Secretary, and whose services they had shared since founding their partnership, occupied the entire eastern wall of the eleventh floor, Colonel Mawson in the corner office to the right and Mr. Payne to the left, with Mrs. Craig between them.

Although this was known only to Colonel Mawson and Mr. Payne, and of course to Mrs. Craig herself, her annual remuneration was greater than that received by any of the twenty-one junior partners of the firm. She received, in addition to a generous salary, the dividends on stock she held in the concern.

Although her desk was replete with the very latest office equipment appropriate to an experienced legal secretary, it had been a very long time since she had actually taken a letter, or a brief, or typed one. She had three assistants, two women and a man, who handled dictation and typing and similar chores.

Irene Craig's function, as both she and Colonel Mawson and Mr. Payne saw it, was to control the expenditure of their time. It was, after all, the only thing they really had to sell, and it was a finite resource. One of the very few things on which Colonel Mawson and Mr. Payne were in complete agreement was that Mrs. Craig performed her function superbly.

Brewster C. Payne, therefore, was not annoyed when he saw Mrs. Craig enter his office. She knew what he was doing, reviewing a lengthy brief about to be submitted in a rather complicated maritime disaster, and that he did not want to be disturbed unless it was a matter of some import that just wouldn't wait. She was here, *ergo sum*, something of bona fide importance demanded his attention.

Brewster Cortland Payne II was a tall, dignified, slim man in his early fifties. He had sharp features and closely cropped gray hair. He was sitting in a high-backed chair, upholstered in blue leather, tilted far back in it, his crossed feet resting on the windowsill of the plate-glass window that offered a view of the Benjamin Franklin Bridge and Camden, New Jersey. The jacket of his crisp cord suit was hung over one of the two blue leather upholstered Charles Eames chairs facing his desk. The button-down collar of his shirt was open, and his regimentally striped necktie pulled down.

His shirt cuffs were rolled up. He had not been expecting anyone, client or staff, to come into his office.

"The building is gloriously aflame, I gather," he said, smiling at Irene Craig, "and you are holding the door of the very last elevator?"

"You're not supposed to do that," she said. "When there's a fire, you're supposed to walk down the stairs."

"I stand chastised," he said.

"I hate to do this to you," she said.

"But?"

"Martha Peebles is outside."

Brewster C. Payne II's raised eyebrows made it plain that he had no idea who Martha Peebles was.

"Tamaqua Mining," Irene Craig said.

"Oh," Brewster C. Payne said. "She came to us with Mr. Foster?"

"Right."

One of the factors that had caused the Executive Committee of Mawson, Payne, Stockton, McAdoo & Lester to offer James Whitelaw Foster, Esq., a junior partnership with an implied offer somewhere not too far down the pike of a full partnership was that he would bring with him to the firm the legal business of Tamaqua Mining Company, Inc. It was a closely held corporation with extensive land and mineral holdings in northeast Pennsylvania near, as the name implied, Tamaqua, in the heart of the anthracite region.

"And I gather Mr. Foster is not available?" Payne asked.

"He's in Washington," Irene said. "She's pretty upset. She's been robbed."

"Robbed?"

"Robbed. I think you better see her."

"Where's the colonel?" Payne asked.

"If he was here, I wouldn't be in here," she said. Payne couldn't tell if she was annoyed with him, or tolerating him. "He's with Bull Bolinski."

"With whom?"

"World-famous tennis player," Irene Craig said.

"I don't place him, either," Payne said, after a moment.

"Oh, God," she said, in smiling exasperation. *"Bull Bolinski.* He was a tackle for the Green Bay Packers. You really never heard the name, did you?"

"No, I'm afraid I haven't," Payne said. "And now you have me wholly confused, Irene."

"The colonel's at the Bellevue-Stratford, with the Bull, who is now a lawyer and representing a reporter, who's negotiating a contract with the *Bulletin."*

"Why is he doing that?" Payne asked, surprised, and thinking aloud. The legal affairs of the *Philadelphia Bulletin* were handled by Kenneth L. McAdoo.

"Because he wanted to meet the Bull," Irene Craig said.

"I think I may be beginning to understand," Payne said. "You think I should talk to Mrs. . . . Whatsername?"

"Peebles," Irene Craig replied. *"Miss* Martha Peebles."

"All right," Payne said. "Give me a minute, and then show her in."

"I think you should," Irene Craig said, and walked out of the office.

"Damn," Brewster C. Payne said. He slipped the thick brief he had in his lap and the notes he had made on the desk into the lower right-hand drawer of his desk. Then he stood up, rolled down and buttoned his cuffs, buttoned his collar, pulled up his tie, and put his suit jacket on.

Then he walked to the double doors to his office and pulled the right one open.

A woman, a young one (he guessed thirty, maybe thirty-two or -three), looked at him. She was simply but well dressed. Her light brown hair was cut fashionably short, and she wore short white gloves. She was almost, but not quite, good-looking.

Without thinking consciously about it, Brewster C. Payne categorized her as a lady. What he thought, consciously, was that she, with her brother, held essentially all of the stock in Tamaqua Mining, and that that stock was worth somewhere between twenty and twenty-five million dollars.

No wonder Irene made me see her.

"Miss Peebles, I'm Brewster Payne. I'm terribly sorry to have kept you waiting. Would you please come in?"

Martha Peebles smiled and stood up and walked past him into his office. Payne smelled her perfume. He didn't know the name of it, but it was, he thought, the same kind his wife used.

"May I offer you a cup of coffee? Or perhaps tea?" Payne asked.

"That would be very nice," Martha Peebles said. "Coffee, please."

Payne looked at Irene Craig and saw that she had heard. He pushed the door closed, and ushered Martha Peebles onto a couch against the wall, and settled himself into a matching armchair. A long teakwood coffee table with drawers separated them.

"I'm very sorry that Mr. Foster is not here," Payne said. "He was called to Washington."

"It was very good of you to see me," Martha Peebles said. "I'm grateful to you."

"It's my pleasure, Miss Peebles. Now, how may I be of assistance?"

"Well," she said, "I have been robbed . . . and there's more."

"Miss Peebles, before we go any further, how would you feel about my turning on a recording machine? It's sometimes very helpful . . ."

"A recording machine?" she asked.

"A recording is often very helpful," Payne said.

She looked at him strangely, then said, "If you think it would be helpful, of course."

Payne tapped the switch of the tape recorder, under the coffee table, with the toe of his shoe.

"You say you were robbed?"

"I thought you said you were going to record this," Martha Peebles said, almost a challenge.

"I am," he said. "I just turned it on. The switch is under the table. The microphone is in that little box on the table."

"Oh, really?" she said, looking first at the box and then under the coffee table. "How clever!"

"You were saying you were robbed?"

"You could have turned it on without asking, couldn't you?" Martha Peebles said. "I would never have known."

"That would have been unethical," he said. "I would never do something like that."

"But you could have, couldn't you?"

"Yes, I suppose I could have," he said, realizing she had made him uncomfortable. "But you were telling me you were robbed. What happened?"

There was a brief tap at the door, and Edward F. Joiner, a slight, soft-spoken man in his middle twenties who was Irene Craig's secretary, came in, carrying a silver coffee set. He smiled at Martha Peebles, and she returned it shyly, as he set the service on the table.

"I'll pour, Ed," Payne said. "Thank you."

Martha Peebles took her coffee black, and did not care for a doughnut or other pastry.

"You were saying you were robbed?" Payne said.

"At home," she said. "In Chestnut Hill."

"How exactly did it happen? A burglar?"

"No, I'm quite sure it's not a burglar," she said. "I even think I know who did it."

"Why don't you start at the very beginning?" Payne said.

Martha Peebles told Brewster Payne that two weeks before, two weeks plus a day, her brother Stephen had brought home a young man he had met.

"A tall, rather good-looking young man," she said. "His name was Walton Williams. Stephen said that he was studying theater at the University of Pennsylvania."

"And is your brother interested in the theater?" Payne asked, carefully.

"I think rather more in young actors than in the theater, per se," Martha Peebles said, matter-of-factly, with neither disapproval nor embarrassment in her voice.

"I see," Payne said.

"Well, they stayed downstairs, in the recreation room, and I went to my room. And then, a little after midnight, I heard them saying goodnight on the portico, which is directly under my windows."

"And you think there's a chance this Williams chap is involved in the robbery?"

"There's no question about it," she said.

"How can you be sure?"

"I saw him," she said.

"I'm afraid I've become lost somewhere along the way," Payne said.

"Well, the next night, about half past eight, I was having a bath when the doorbell rang. I ignored it—"

"Was there anyone else in the house? Your brother? Help?"

"We keep a couple," she said. "But they leave about seven. And Stephen wasn't there. He had gone to Paris that morning."

"So you were alone in the house?"

"Yes, and since I wasn't expecting anyone, I just ignored the bell."

"I see. And then what happened?"

"I heard noises in my bedroom. The door opening, then the sound of drawers opening. So I got out of the tub, put a robe on, and opened the door a crack. And there was Walton Williams, at my dresser, going through my things."

"What did you do then?" Payne asked. *This is a very stupid young woman,* he thought. *She could have gotten herself in serious difficulty, killed, even, just walking in on a situation like that.*

And then he changed *"stupid"* in his mind to *"naive"* and *"inexperienced and overprotected."*

"I asked him just what he thought he was doing," Martha Peebles said, "and he just looked at me for a moment, obviously surprised to find someone home, and then he ran out of the room and down the stairs and out of the house."

"And you believe he stole something?" Payne asked.

"I *know* he stole things," she said. "I know *exactly* what he stole from me. All my valuable pins and pendants, and all of Mother's jewelry that was in the house."

"And where was your mother when this was going on?" Payne asked.

This earned him a cold and dirty, almost outraged, look.

"Mother passed on in February," she said. "I would have thought you would know that."

"I beg your pardon," Payne said. "I did not."

"Most of her good things were in the bank, of course, but there were some very nice pieces at home. There was a jade necklace, jade set in gold, that she bought in Djakarta, and this Williams person got that. I know she paid ten thousand dollars for that; I had to cable her the money."

"You called the police, of course?" Payne asked.

"Yes, and they came right away, and I gave them a description of Stephen's friend, and an incomplete list, later completed, of everything that was missing. Mr. Foster took care of that for me."

"Well, I'm glad the firm was able to be of some help," Payne said. "Would you take offense if I offered a bit of advice?"

"I came here seeking advice," Martha Peebles said.

"I don't think anything like this will ever happen to you again in your lifetime," Payne said. "But if it should, I really think you would be much better off not to challenge an intruder. Just hide yourself as well as you can, let him take what he wants, and leave. And then you call the police."

"It's already happened again," she said, impatiently.

"I beg your pardon?"

"Last Sunday, Sunday a week ago, not yesterday. I had gone out to the Rose Tree Hunt for the buffet—"

"I was there," Payne interrupted, "my wife and I. And my oldest son."

"—and when I returned home," Martha Peebles went on, oblivious to the interruption, "and stepped inside the door from the driveway, I heard sounds, footsteps, in the library. And then he must have heard me . . . I'm convinced it was Stephen's young man, but I didn't actually see him, for he ran out the front door."

"You didn't confront him again?"

"No, I called the police from the telephone in the butler's pantry."

"And they came?"

"Right away," she said. "And they searched the house, and they found where he had broken a pane of glass in the greenhouse to gain entrance, and I found out what was stolen this time. A Leica camera, Stephen's—I don't know why he didn't take it to France, but he didn't, I had seen it that very morning—and some accessory lenses for it, and Daddy's binoculars . . . and some other things."

"Miss Peebles," Payne said. "The unpleasant fact is that you will probably never be able to recover the things that were stolen. But if Mr. Foster has been looking after your interests, I'm confident that your insurance will cover your loss."

"I'm not concerned about a *camera,* Mr. Payne," she said. "I'm concerned for my safety."

"I really don't think whoever has done this will return a third time, Miss Peebles," Payne said. "But a few precautions—"

"He was back again last night," she interrupted him. "That's why I'm here now."

"I didn't know," Payne said.

"This time he broke in the side door," she said. "And cut himself when he was reaching through the pane he broke out; there was blood on the floor. This time he stole a bronze, a rather good Egyptian bronze Daddy had bought in Cairo as a young man. Small piece, about eight inches tall. And some other, personal items."

"Such as?"

Her face flushed.

"He went through my dresser," she said, softly, embarrassed, "and stole a half dozen items of underclothing."

"I see," Payne said.

"Specifically," she said, apparently having overcome her discomfiture, "he made off with all my black undies, brassieres, and panties."

"Just the black?" Payne asked, furious with himself for wanting to smile. What this young woman was telling him was not only of great importance to her, but very likely was symptomatic of a very dangerous situation. While a perverse corner of his brain was amused by the notion of an "actor," almost certainly a young gentleman of exquisite grace, making off with this proper young woman's black underwear, it wasn't funny at all.

"Just the black," she said.

"Well, the first thing I think you might consider is the installation of a security system—"

"We've had Acme Security since Daddy built the house," she said. "Until now, I thought it provided a measure of security. Their damned alarm system doesn't seem to work at all."

"May I suggest that you ask them to come and check it out?" Payne said.

"I've already done that," she said. "They say there's absolutely nothing wrong with it. What *I* think is that people like Stephen's young man know about things like that, and know how to turn them off, render them useless, and Acme just doesn't want to admit that's possible."

She's probably right.

"Another possibility, for the immediate future," Payne said, "until the police can run this Williams chap to ground, is to move, temporarily, into a hotel."

"I have no intention of having someone like that drive me from my home," Martha Peebles said, firmly. "What I had hoped to hear from Mr. Foster, Mr. Payne, is that he has some influence with the police, and could prevail upon them to provide me with more protection than they so far have."

"I frankly don't know what influence Mr. Foster has with the police, Miss Peebles—"

"Well, that's certainly a disappointment," she interrupted him.

"But as I was about to say, Colonel Mawson, a senior partner of the firm, is a close personal friend of Police Commissioner Czernich."

"Well, then, may I see him, please?"

"That won't be necessary, Miss Peebles. As soon as he walks through the door, I'll bring this to his attention."

"Where is he now?"

"Actually," Payne said, "he's at the Bellevue-Stratford. With a chap called Bull Bolinski."

"The Packers' Bull Bolinski?" Miss Peebles asked, brightening visibly.

"Yes, the Packers' Bull Bolinski."

"Oh, I almost cried when he announced his retirement," Martha Peebles said.

"He's now an attorney, you know."

"I hadn't heard that," she said. "And I'd forgotten this has all been recorded, hasn't it?"

"Yes, it has. And I'll have it transcribed immediately."

Martha Peebles stood up and offered Brewster C. Payne II her hand.

"I can't tell you how much better I feel, Mr. Payne, after having spoken to you. And thank you for seeing me without an appointment."

"That was my pleasure," Payne said. "Anytime you want to see me, Miss Peebles, my door is always open. But I wish you would consider checking into a hotel for a few days. . . ."

"I told you, I will not be run off by people like that," she said, firmly. "Good morning, Mr. Payne."

He walked with her to the door, then to the elevator, and saw her on it.

When he walked back into his office, Irene Craig followed him.

"What the devil is wrong with the cops?" she asked. "She gave them a description of this creep, even if that was a phony name."

"Why do I suspect that you were, as a figure of speech, out there all the time with your ear to my keyhole?" he asked.

"You knew I would be monitoring that," she said. "I also had Ed take it down on the Stenotype machine. I should have a transcript before the colonel gets back."

"Good girl!" he said.

"There are some women in my position who would take high umbrage at a sexist remark like that," she said. "But I'll swap compliments. You handled her beautifully."

"Now may I go back to work, boss?" Payne said.

"Oh, I think the colonel can handle this from here," she said, and walked out of his office.

Brewster Cortland Payne II returned to his brief.

 The eight men gathered in the conference room of the suite of third-floor offices in the Roundhouse assigned to the Police Commissioner of the City of Philadelphia chatted softly among themselves, talking about anything but business, waiting for the Commissioner to more or less formally open the meeting.

He did not do so until Deputy Commissioner for Administration Harold J. Wilson, a tall, thin, dignified man, entered the room, mumbled something about having been hung up in traffic, and sat down.

Police Commissioner Thaddeu Czernich then matter-of-factly thumped the table with his knuckles, and waited for the murmur of conversation to peter out.

"The mayor," Commissioner Czernich said, evenly, even dryly, "does not want Mike Sabara to get Highway Patrol."

Thaddeu Czernich was fifty-seven years old, a tall, heavyset man with a thick head of silver hair. His smoothly shaven cheeks had a ruddy glow. He was just starting to jowl. He was wearing a stiffly starched shirt and a regimentally striped necktie with a dark blue, pin-striped, vested suit. He was a handsome, healthy, imposing man.

"He say why?" Chief Inspector of Detectives Matt Lowenstein asked.

"He said, 'In uniform, Mike Sabara looks like a guard in a concentration camp,' " Czernich quoted.

Chief Inspector Lowenstein, a stocky, barrel-chested man of fifty-five, examined the half-inch ash on his six-inch-long light green *Villa de Cuba "Monarch"* for a moment, then chuckled.

"He does," Lowenstein said, "if you think about it, he does."

"That's hardly justification for not giving Sabara the Highway Patrol," Deputy Commissioner Wilson said, somewhat prissily.

"You tell the dago that, Harry," Lowenstein replied.

Deputy Commissioner Wilson glowered at Lowenstein, but didn't reply. He had long ago learned that the best thing for him to say when he was angry was nothing.

And he realized that he was annoyed, on the edge of anger, now. He was annoyed that he had gotten hung up in traffic and had arrived at the meeting late. He prided himself on being punctual, and when, as he expected to do, he became Police Commissioner himself, he intended to instill in the entire department a more acute awareness of the importance of time, which he believed was essential to efficiency and discipline, than it had now.

He was annoyed that when he had walked into the meeting, the only seat remaining at the long conference table in the Commissioner's Conference Room was beside Chief Inspector Lowenstein, which meant that he would have to inhale the noxious fumes from Lowenstein's cigar for however long the meeting lasted.

He was annoyed at Chief Inspector Lowenstein's reference to the mayor of the city of Philadelphia, the Honorable Jerry Carlucci, as "the dago," and even more annoyed with Commissioner Czernich for not correcting him for doing so, and sharply, on the spot.

So far as Deputy Commissioner Wilson was concerned, it was totally irrelevant that Mayor Carlucci and Chief Lowenstein were lifelong friends, going back to their service as young patrolmen in the Highway Patrol; or that the mayor very often greeted Chief Lowenstein in similarly distasteful terms. ("How's it going, Jew boy?") The mayor was the mayor, and senior officials subordinate to him were obliged to pay him the respect appropriate to his position.

Deputy Commissioner Wilson was also annoyed with the mayor. There was a chain-of-command structure in place, a standing operating procedure. When it became necessary to appoint a senior police officer to fill a specific position, the Deputy Commissioner for Administration, after considering the recommendations made to him by appropriate personnel, and after personally reviewing the records of the individuals involved, was charged with furnishing the commissioner the names, numerically ranked, of the three best-qualified officers for the position in question. Then, in consultation with the Deputy Commissioner for Administration, the Commissioner would make his choice.

Deputy Commissioner for Administration Wilson had not yet completed his review of the records of those eligible, and recommended for, appointment as Commanding Officer, Highway Patrol. Even granting that the mayor, as chief executive officer of the City of Philadelphia, might have the right to enter the process, voicing his opinion, doing so interfered with both the smooth administration of Police Department personnel policy, and was certain to affect morale adversely.

It had to do with Mayor Carlucci's mind-set, Deputy Commissioner Wilson believed. It was not that the mayor thought of himself as a retired policeman. Mayor Carlucci thought of himself as a cop who happened to be mayor. And even worse than that, Mayor Carlucci, who had once been Captain Carlucci, Commanding Officer, Highway Patrol, thought of himself as a Highway Patrolman who also happened to be mayor.

The mayoral Cadillac limousine, in previous administrations chauffeured by a plainclothes police officer, was now driven by a uniformed Highway Patrol sergeant. It was equipped with shortwave radios tuned to the Highway Patrol and Detective bands, and the mayoral limousine was famous, or perhaps infamous, for rolling on calls the mayor found interesting.

Police Radio would, in Deputy Commissioner Wilson's judgment, far too often announce that there was a *robbery in progress,* or *officer needs assistance,* or *man with a gun, shots fired,* only to have the second or third reply—sometimes the first—be "M-Mary One in on the shots fired," from the mayoral Cadillac limousine, by then already racing down Lancaster Avenue or South Broad Street or the Schuylkill Expressway with the siren whooping and red lights flashing.

Deputy Commissioner Wilson was not really sure in his own mind why the mayor behaved this way, whether it was because, as the mayor himself had said, he was unable to dilute his policeman's blood to the point where he could *not* respond to an *officer needs assistance* call, or whether it was calculated, on purpose. The mayor very often got his picture in the newspapers, and his image on the television, at one crime scene or another, often standing with his hands on his hips, pushing back his suit jacket so that the butt of his Smith & Wesson Chief's Special .38-caliber snub-nose revolver could be seen.

Commissioner Wilson was very much aware that one did not become mayor of the nation's fourth-largest city if one was either stupid, childish, or unaware of the importance of public relations and publicity. There were a lot of voters who liked the idea of having their mayor rush to the scene of a crime wearing a gun.

"I think it probably has to do with the *Ledger* editorial last Sunday," Commissioner Czernich said now.

This produced a chorus of grunts, and several mildly profane expressions. Following a Highway Patrol shooting, in which two North Philadelphia youths, interrupted while they were holding up a convenience store, were killed, one of them having six wounds in his body, the *Ledger* published an indignant editorial, under the headline, "POLICE FORCE? OR A JACKBOOTED GESTAPO?"

It was not the first time the *Ledger* had referred to the highly polished motorcyclist's black leather boots worn by police officers assigned to Highway Patrol as Gestapo Jackboots.

"Has he got someone in mind?" Chief Inspector Dennis V. Coughlin asked.

Coughlin looked not unlike Commissioner Czernich. He was tall, and large boned, and had all his teeth and all his curly hair, now silver. He was one of eleven Chief Inspectors of the Police Department of the City of Philadelphia. But it could be argued that he was first among equals. Under his command, among others, were the Narcotics Unit, the Vice Unit, the Internal Affairs Division, the Staff Investigation Unit, and the Organized Crime Intelligence Unit.

The other ten Chief Inspectors reported to either the Deputy Commissioner (Operations) or the Deputy Commissioner (Administration), who reported to the Commissioner. Denny Coughlin reported directly to the Commissioner, and, not unreasonably, believed that what happened anywhere in the Police Department was his business.

"The mayor has several things in mind," Commissioner Czernich said, carefully, "thoughts which he has been kind enough to share with me."

"Uh-oh," Lowenstein said.

"He thinks that David Pekach would make a fine commander of Highway," Commissioner Czernich said.

Chief Lowenstein considered that for a moment, then said, chuckling, "But he'd have to cut off his pigtail. Do you think David would be willing to do that?"

There were chuckles from everyone around the conference table except for Deputy Commissioner for Administration Wilson. Newly promoted Captain Pekach wasn't even on the preliminary list of fourteen captains Commissioner Wilson had drawn up to fill the vacancy of Commanding Officer, Highway Patrol, created when Captain Richard C. Moffitt had been shot to death trying to stop an armed robbery.

"Mike Sabara was next in line for Highway," Chief Inspector Coughlin said. "And he's qualified. I guess the mayor's thought about that?"

"The mayor thinks Mike would fit in neatly as Deputy Commander of Special Operations Division," Commissioner Czernich said, "especially if I went along with his suggestion to take Highway away from Traffic and put it under Special Operations. Then it would be sort of a promotion for Sabara, the mayor says."

"I thought that Special Operation Division idea was dead," Deputy Commissioner for Operations Francis J. Cohan said. It was the first time he'd spoken. "I didn't like it, said so, and now I'm going to get it anyway?"

"Denny's going to get it," Commissioner Czernich said, nodding his head toward Chief Inspector Coughlin.

"My God!" Cohan said. "If Highway isn't Operations, what is?"

"Everything you have now, except Highway," Commissioner Czernich said. "Highway is now under *Special* Operations."

"Highway and what else?" Cohan asked.

"Highway and ACT," Czernich said.

"The ACT grant came through?" Deputy Commissioner Wilson asked, both surprised and annoyed.

ACT was the acronym for Anti-Crime Teams, a federally funded program administered by the Justice Department. It was a test, more or less, to see what effect saturating a high-crime area with extra police, the latest technology, and special assistance from the district attorney in the form of having assistant district attorneys with nothing to do but push ACT-arrested criminals through the criminal justice system would have, short and long term, on crime statistics.

"When did all this happen?" Cohan asked.

"The mayor told me he had a call from the senator Friday afternoon about the

ACT grant," Czernich said. "I suppose it'll be in the papers today, or maybe on the TV tonight. The mayor says we'll start getting money, some of it right away."

"I meant about this Special Operations," Cohan said.

"Wait a minute," Czernich said. "I'm glad this came up." He shifted in his chair to look at Deputy Commissioner for Administration Wilson. "Harry, I don't want to be told that, in setting up Special Operations, something can't be done because there's no money. You authorize whatever is necessary, using contingency funds, until the federal money comes in. Then reimburse the contingency fund. Understand?"

"Yes, sir," Deputy Commissioner Wilson said.

Czernich turned back to Deputy Commissioner Cohan.

"To answer your question, it happened yesterday. I don't know how long he's been thinking about it, but it happened about half past ten yesterday morning. When he came home from mass, he called me up and said if I didn't have anything important going on, I should come by and he'd give me a cup of coffee."

"Was that before or after he read the *Ledger?*" Lowenstein asked.

"He asked me if I'd seen it the moment I walked in the door," Czernich said.

"And when is all this *going* to happen?" Cohan asked.

"It's happening right now, Frank," Czernich said. "It's effective today."

"Am I going to get to pick a commander for this Special Operations Division?" Coughlin asked.

"Anybody you want, Denny," Commissioner Czernich said, "just so long as his name is Peter Wohl."

"Jesus," Coughlin exploded, "why doesn't he just move in here if he's going to make every goddamned decision?" He paused, then added, "Not that I have anything against Peter Wohl. But . . . Jesus!"

"He doesn't have to move in here, Denny," Commissioner Czernich said. "Not as long as he has my phone number."

"Did Mayor Carlucci give you his reasons for all this?" Deputy Commissioner Wilson asked. "Or for any of it?"

"No, but what he did do when he explained everything—there's a little more I haven't gotten to yet—was to ask me if I had any objections, if there was something wrong with it that he'd missed."

"And you couldn't think of anything?" Cohan asked, softly.

"He wants a Special Operations Division," Czernich said. "He knows you don't want it. So he gave it to Denny Coughlin. He wants Peter Wohl to run it. What was I supposed to say, 'Peter isn't qualified'? He thinks Mike Sabara is bad for Highway's image. What was I supposed to say, for Christ's sake, that 'beauty is only skin deep'?"

Cohan shrugged. "You said there's more," he said.

"Just as soon as Peter Wohl has a little time to get his feet wet," Czernich said, "Denny will ask him to recommend, from among Highway Patrol sergeants, someone to take over as the mayor's driver. Sergeant Lucci, who is driving the mayor now, made it onto the lieutenants' list. As soon as Peter can find a replacement for him, *Lieutenant* Lucci will return to ordinary supervisory duties commensurate with his rank, in Highway."

"You don't happen to think," Chief Lowenstein said, dryly sarcastic, "that Lieutenant Lucci might have in mind getting some of this ACT money for Highway, do you?

Or that he might just happen to bump into the dago every once in a while, say once a week, and just happen to mention in idle conversation that Highway didn't get as much of it as he thinks they should? Nothing like that could be happening, could it, Tad?"

"I don't know," Czernich said, coldly. "But if he did, that would be Peter Wohl's problem, wouldn't you say? Wohl's and Denny's?"

"What's he really got in mind, long term, for this Special Operations?" Chief Coughlin asked.

"Long term, I haven't any idea," said Czernich. "Short-term, yeah, I know what he's got in mind."

There was a pause, and when it didn't end, Denny Coughlin said, "You going to tell us?"

"What he said, Denny, was that he thought it would be nice if he could hold a press conference in a couple of weeks, where he could announce that an Anti-Crime Team of the new Special Operations Division, which was a little suggestion of his to the Police Department, had just announced the arrest of the sexual pervert who had been raping and terrorizing the decent women of Northwest Philadelphia."

"That scumbag is none of the Anti-Crime Team, or Special Operations, or Highway's business," Chief Inspector Lowenstein said, coldly angry. "Rape is the Detective Bureau's business. It always has been."

"It still is, Matt," Czernich said, evenly, "except for what's going on in Northwest Philadelphia. That's now in Peter Wohl's lap because Jerry Carlucci says it is."

"He was at it again last night," Deputy Commissioner Cohan said. "He broke into the apartment of a woman named Mary Elizabeth Flannery, on Henry Avenue in Roxborough, tied her to her bed, cut her clothes off with a hunting knife, took off his clothes, committed an incomplete act of oral sodomy on her, and when that didn't get his rocks off, he pissed all over her. Then he tied her hands behind her back, loaded her in a van, and dumped her naked on Forbidden Drive in Fairmount Park."

"What do you mean, dumped her naked in the park?" Lowenstein asked.

"Just that, Matt. He carried her over there in a van, then pushed her out. Hands tied behind her back. Not a stitch on her."

"You catch somebody like that," Lowenstein said, "what you should do is cut the bastard's balls off and leave him to bleed to death."

"Let's just hope that Peter Wohl can catch him," Czernich said.

At five minutes after ten, Colonel J. Dunlop Mawson, of Mawson, Payne, Stockton, McAdoo & Lester, legal counsel to the *Philadelphia Bulletin,* presented himself at the door of the Theodore Roosevelt Suite.

"Mr. Bolinski," Colonel Mawson said, as he enthusiastically pumped the Bull's hand, "I'm one of your greatest fans."

"And I of yours, Colonel," the Bull said. Before the sentence was completely out of the Bull's mouth, Mickey O'Hara realized that the Bull no longer sounded like your typical Polack Catholic product of West Philly. "I can only hope that the presence of the dean of the Philadelphia Criminal Bar does not carry with it any suggestion that larceny is at hand."

Colonel J. Dunlop Mawson beamed.

"Bull," he said, "—may I call you Bull?"

"Certainly," the Bull said. "I do hope we're going to be friends."

"Bull, the truth of the matter is that I pulled a little rank. I'm a senior partner in the firm, and I took advantage of that so that I would have a chance to meet you."

"I'm flattered," the Bull said, "and honored to meet you, Colonel."

"The honor is mine," Mawson said, "to meet the man who is arguably the best tackle football has ever known."

"This is my wife, Colonel," the Bull said, "and I believe you know Mr. O'Hara?"

"A privilege to meet you, ma'am," Mawson said.

"May we offer you some coffee, Colonel? Or perhaps something else?" Antoinette said.

"Coffee seems like a splendid idea," Colonel Mawson said. He nodded at Mickey, but said nothing and did not offer his hand.

This was followed by a ten-minute tour, conducted by Colonel J. Dunlop Mawson, down Football Memory Lane. Then came a detour, via Bull's mentioning that he represented Lenny Moskowitz, lasting another ten minutes, in which the intricacies of premarital agreements were discussed in terms Mickey couldn't understand at all.

Finally, the Bull said, "Colonel, I really hate to break this off, but Antoinette and I are on a tight schedule."

"Of course," Colonel J. Dunlop Mawson said, "forgive me."

He reached into his alligator attachè case and came up with a manila folder, which he passed to the Bull.

"I think you'll find that brings us to a state of agreement," he said.

The Bull read the document very carefully, while Colonel J. Dunlop Mawson hung on every word of Mrs. Bolinski's tour guide of the better restaurants in the Miami/Palm Beach area.

"With one or two minor caveats," the Bull said, "this appears to be what I discussed with—what was his name?"

"Lemuelson," Colonel Mawson said, "Steve Lemuelson. What seems to trouble you, Bull?"

"I'd like to add a phrase here," the Bull said.

Colonel Mawson scurried to Bull's armchair and looked over his shoulder, then read aloud what the Bull had written in: ". . . it being understood between the parties that the annual increase will ordinarily be approximately ten percentum of both compensation and reimbursement of expenses, unless the annual rate of inflation has exceeded four percentum, in which case the annual increase in compensation will ordinarily be ten percentum plus seventy percentum of the rate of inflation, according to the latest then published figures by the U.S. Department of Commerce."

Colonel Mawson grunted.

"You see the problem, of course, Counselor," the Bull said.

"I think we can live with that, Bull," Colonel Mawson said.

Mickey didn't know what the fuck they were talking about.

"And then here in fourteen (c) six," the Bull said, "I think a little specificity would be in order. You can see what I've penciled in."

And again Colonel Mawson read the modified clause aloud, "A Buick Super, Mercury Monterey, or equivalent automobile, including special radio apparatus, satisfactory to Mr. O'Hara, including installation, maintenance, and all related expenses thereto pertaining."

Colonel Mawson paused thoughtfully for a moment, then said, "Oh, I see. Well, that certainly seems reasonable enough."

"Good," the Bull said, "and last, I have added a final paragraph, thirty-six." He flipped through the document and then pointed it out to Mawson, This time he read it aloud: "The terms of this agreement shall be effective as of from 1 June 1973."

"But, Bull," the colonel protested, "he hasn't been working all that time."

"He would have been working, if you had then agreed to the terms agreed to here," the Bull said.

The colonel hesitated, then said, "Oh, hell, what the hell, Bull, why not?"

"I don't think Mr. O'Hara is being unreasonable," the Bull said.

"I'm sorry it got as far as withholding services," Colonel Mawson said.

"What I suggest we do now is have Mr. O'Hara sign, and initial all the modified sections," the Bull said. "And then when I get back to the office I'll have my girl run off a half dozen copies on the Xerox and pop them in the mail to you."

When Mickey O'Hara scrawled his initials in the margin beside *Section 11-Compensation,* he saw that a line had been drawn through what had originally been typed, SEVEN HUNDRED AND FIFTY DOLLARS AND NO CENTS ($750.00), and that his corrected weekly compensation was to be ONE THOUSAND DOLLARS AND NO CENTS ($1,000.00), *said sum to be paid weekly by check payable to Heidenheimer & Bolinski, P.C., who herewith assume responsibility for the payment of all applicable federal, state, and local income taxes and Social Security contributions.*

When he came down from the Theodore Roosevelt suite, there were two people behind the front desk of the Bellevue-Stratford, neither of them Miss Travis. He was torn between disappointment and relief that somebody had finally shown up to take her place.

He wondered how she would react if he just happened to come by the Bellevue-Stratford and say hello, and maybe ask her if she wanted to go get something to eat, or go to a movie, or something.

Then he realized that was foolish. She had given him the same smile she had given the blue-haired broad who had bitched about her room. Maybe the smile was a little more genuine, but even so that would be because he was at the Bellevue-Stratford to see the Bull, who was staying in one of the more expensive suites.

But maybe not. She had said she was a—what did she say?—*an avid reader.*

And then Mickey O'Hara pushed through the revolving door and onto South Broad Street, and there she was, coming up the street headed toward City Hall, carrying a paper sack in each arm. He saw paper towels in one of them.

"Hi!" she said.

"I thought you was going to bed."

"I'm on my way," she said.

"Can I take you?"

There you go, O'Hara, both fucking feet in your mouth!

"I didn't mean that the way it sounded," Mickey said. "I mean, I got my car . . ."

"I'm probably going nowhere near where you are," she said, after a just perceptible pause.

"Where?"

"Roxborough."

"Practically on my way," he said.

"Really?"

"Really."

It would be on my way if you were going to Mexico City.

"Where's your car?" she asked.

He pointed to it.

"You're sure you're really going that way?" she asked.

"Positive."

Miss Travers didn't seem to think anything was wrong with his car, but Mickey managed to drop into their conversation that he was about to get a new one, that he was thinking of either a Mercury or Buick.

More important, she told him her first name was Mary, and that she would love to have dinner with him, but it would probably be hard to arrange it, because she was stuck on the seven-to-three-in-the-morning shift—it was determined by seniority—and that made any kind of a normal social life nearly impossible.

"I know," Mickey said. "The *Bulletin* goes to bed at half-past two."

"You mean that's when you quit for the day?"

He nodded and she smiled at him, and he thought, *We already have something in common.*

Forty minutes later, when he steered the battered Chevrolet Impala off North Broad Street and into the parking lot behind the Thirty-fifth District Station, where he stopped in a space marked INSPECTOR PARKING ONLY, Mickey still wasn't sure he really believed what had happened.

I've got a date with Mary Travis. Tonight. Tomorrow morning. At five minutes after three, at the front door of the Bellevue-Stratford.

And that wasn't all that had happened.

I'm making as much dough as the fucking Police Commissioner, for Christ's sake!

He sat there for a moment, then lit a cigarette. Then he got out of the car, entered the building through a door marked POLICE USE ONLY and went inside. He waved at the uniformed cops in the ground-floor squad room, then climbed the stairs to the second floor, which housed the Northwest Detectives Division.

On the landing at the top of the stairs were several vending machines, a garbage can, and two battered chairs. A concrete block wall with a wide open window counter and a door separated the landing from the squad room of Northwest Detectives. A sign beneath the window counter read POLICE PERSONNEL ONLY BEYOND THIS POINT, and just inside the door the desk man, a detective, sat at a battered desk.

Mickey walked through the door, waved at the desk man, and exchanged casual greetings, a nod of the head, or a smile, with the half dozen detectives working at their own battered desks, then took a quick, practiced glance at the large, yellow legal pad on the desk man's desk. On it, the desk man would have written the names of any citizens brought into the squad room for "interviews" on the shift. It was an informal record, intended primarily to remind the desk man who had hauled in who, and was responsible for the critter. If a citizen got as far as the detective squad room, the odds were the "interview" would be followed by an arrest.

Mickey found nothing that looked particularly interesting, so he walked across the squad room to a small alcove at the rear, which held a coffee machine. He helped himself to a cup, black, then tucked a dollar bill in the coffee kitty can.

When he came out of the alcove, he looked into the window of the small office used by the Lieutenants of Northwest Detectives. Lieutenant Teddy Spanner, who had the watch, and Lieutenant Louis Natali of Homicide were inside. That was unusual; you rarely saw a Homicide Lieutenant in one of the Detective District Squad Rooms, unless something important was going down.

Lou Natali, a slight, olive-skinned man who was losing his hair, was leaning on the glass wall. Behind the desk, Spanner, a very large fair-skinned man in his shirtsleeves, waved at Mickey, calling him inside.

"How goes it, Mickey?" Spanner said, as Mickey leaned over the desk to shake his hand.

"Can't complain," Mickey said, and turned to Lou Natali. "What do you say, Lou?"

"Haven't seen you around lately, Mick," Natali said. "You been sick or something?"

"I took a couple of weeks off," Mickey said.

"You go down to the shore?" Spanner asked.

"The shore?" Mickey asked.

"You told me, Mick, the last time I saw you, that what you needed was to go lay on the beach."

"I just hung around the house and watched the wallpaper peel," Mickey said.

"So what's new, Mick?" Natali asked, chuckling.

What's new? I'm now making a thousand bucks a week, less a hundred for the Bull, plus a Buick Super, Mercury Monterey, or equivalent automobile. And I just met a really interesting girl. That's what's new.

"Nothing much," Mickey said. "You tell me."

Both police officers shrugged their shoulders.

Mickey was disappointed. He had had a gut feeling when he saw Lou Natali that something was up. Mickey knew both of them well enough not to press the question. Probably nothing was. If there was, either Spanner or Natali would have told him, maybe prefacing it with *"Off the record, Mick"* but they would have told him.

"Tell me about the naked lady in Fairmount Park," Mickey said. "I heard the call last night."

"Every car in the District, plus half the Highway Patrol, went in on that, Mick," Spanner said. "But aside from that, it's not very funny. Lou and I were just talking about it."

"Tell me," Mickey said.

"Off the record?"

Goddamn, I knew there was something!

"Sure."

"You heard, I suppose, about the guy who's been raping women in Manayunk and Roxborough?"

Mickey nodded.

"From what I understand, he's the same guy who dumped the woman in Fairmount Park."

"Raped her first, you mean?"

"Not quite," Spanner said. "This is a real sick guy. Getting sicker, too."

"I don't know what you mean," Mickey said.

"He's not even screwing them anymore," Spanner said. "What he's doing now is getting his rocks off humiliating them. Pissing on them, and worse."

"Jesus!" Mickey said. "Worse?"

"What he did last night was put a knife to her throat and make her take it in the mouth. Then when he couldn't get his rocks off, he pissed all over her. Then he tied her hands behind her back and dumped her out on Forbidden Drive."

"Nice fella," Mickey said.

"Sure as Christ made little apples," Natali said, "unless they bag this scumbag, he's going to kill somebody. Cut 'em up, probably. I'm afraid he's going to start going after young girls."

"Jesus," Mickey said. He felt a little sick to his stomach when he thought of some slimeball doing something like that to a nice girl like Mary Travis. "You got anything going?"

"Not much. No good description. All we know is that he's a white guy with a van. And likes to wear a mask," Spanner said.

"You didn't get that here, Mickey," Natali said, "What I'm worried about is that I don't want to give the sonofabitch any ideas."

Mickey made a gesture signifying that he wouldn't violate the confidence.

"Who's got this job?" Mickey asked.

"Dick Hemmings," Spanner said. Mickey knew Dick Hemmings to be a brighter than usual Northwest Detective, which was saying something because, with a couple of exceptions, Northwest Division had some really good detectives.

"Who was the cop who answered the call?" Mickey asked.

"Bill Dohner," Spanner said. "I don't know where you can find him until he comes in tonight, but Dick Hemmings is in court. I got the feeling he'll be in there all day."

"Well, then I guess I'd better get down there," Mickey said. "And start earning my living."

He returned to the coffee machine alcove and washed out his cup, then put it in the rack. Then he picked up a telephone on one of the unoccupied desks in the detective squad room and dialed a number from memory.

"City desk," a male voice came on the line.

"This is O'Hara," he said.

"Mr. Michael J. O'Hara?" Gerald F. Kennedy, the city editor of the *Bulletin*, replied in mock awe. "Might one dare to hope, Mr. O'Hara, that there is a small germ of truth in the rumor going around that you are no longer withholding your professional services?"

"Fuck you, Kennedy."

"Then to what do I owe the honor of this telephone call, Mr. O'Hara?"

"Who's been covering the Northwest Philly rapes?"

"Why do you want to know, Mickey?"

"I think I'm onto something."

"Are you?" Gerry Kennedy asked.

"Yeah, I am," Mickey said.

"Odd, but I don't seem to recall assigning this story to you."

"Are we going to play games? In which case, Kennedy, go fuck yourself. I get paid whether or not I work."

"I assigned the story to Cheryl Davies," Kennedy said. "She's not going to like it if I take it away from her and give it to you."

"Fuck her."

"I would love to," Gerry Kennedy said. "But I don't think it's likely. What do you want with her, Mickey?"

"Not a goddamned thing," Mickey said. "What I'm going to do, Kennedy, is cover this myself. And you decide whose stuff you want to run."

"How about working together with her, Mick?" Gerry Kennedy asked. "I mean, she's been on it for three weeks—"

He broke off in midsentence when he realized that Mickey O'Hara had hung up.

6 "Good afternoon, sir," Jesus Martinez, who was of Puerto Rican ancestry, and who was five feet eight inches tall and weighed just over 140 pounds, said to the man who had reached into the rear seat of a 1972 Buick sedan in the parking lot of the Penrose Plaza Mall at Lindbergh Avenue and Island Road in West Philadelphia, and taken out two shopping bags, one of them emblazoned *John Wanamaker & Sons*.

"What the fuck?" the man replied. His name was Clarence Sims, and he was six feet three and weighed 180 pounds.

"Been doing a little shopping, have you, sir?"

"Get out of my face, motherfucker," Clarence Sims replied.

"I'm a police officer," Jesus Martinez said, pulling up his T-shirt, which he wore outside his blue jeans, so that his badge, through which his belt was laced, came into sight. "May I see your driver's license and vehicle registration, please?"

Clarence Sims considered, briefly, the difference in size between them, and his options, and then threw the *John Wanamaker & Sons* shopping bag at Jesus Martinez and started running.

He got as far as the Buick's bumper when he stumbled over something. The next thing Clarence Sims knew he was flat on the ground, with an enormous honky sitting on him, and painfully twisting his arms behind him. He felt a steel handcuff snap shut around one wrist, and then around the other.

And the little spick was in his face, the spick and a gun, shoved hard against his nostrils.

"Don't you *ever* call me motherfucker, you motherfucker!" Officer Jesus Martinez said, furiously. "I ought to blow your fucking brains out, cocksucker!"

"Hay-zus," the enormous honky said, "cool it!"

"I don't like that shit!" Officer Martinez replied, still angry. But the revolver barrel withdrew from Clarence Sims's nostril.

Clarence Sims felt hands running over his body. From one hip pocket a switchblade was removed, from the other his wallet. His side pockets were emptied, spilling a collection of coins and chewing gum wrappers onto the macadam of the parking lot. His groin was probed dispassionately, and then he felt the hands moving down his legs. From his right sock, fingers removed a joint of marijuana, a small plasticine bag of marijuana—known on the street as a "nickel bag," because they sold for five dollars—and a book of matches.

"Oh, my God!" a female voice said, in shock.

"It's all right, ma'am," Clarence heard the spick say, "we're police officers. Is this your car, ma'am?"

"Yes, it is," the female voice said, and then she spotted the shopping bags, and the tone of indignation came into her voice. "Those are my things!"

"Somehow, I didn't think they were his," Martinez said.

Clarence felt the weight of the man kneeling on his back go away.

"Your name Clarence Sims?" Martinez asked.

"Go fuck yourself!"

Clarence Sims's face, which he had raised off the macadam of the parking lot, suddenly encountered it again, as if something—a foot, say—had pushed the back of his head.

"You're under arrest, Clarence," the honky said.

"What happened here?" the female voice asked.

"I saw him taking those bags out of the backseat," Martinez said. "Ma'am, can you tell me how much the stuff in them is worth?"

The victim thought about that a moment. "Two hundred dollars," she said, finally. "Maybe a little more."

"It would help if you could tell us if it's *for sure* worth more than two hundred dollars," Martinez pursued.

The victim considered that for a moment, then said, "Now that I've had a chance to think, it's all worth closer to three hundred dollars than two."

"Bingo," Charley McFadden said. "M-1."

The victim looked at him strangely.

The crime of which Clarence Sims now stood accused, *theft from auto,* was a misdemeanor. There were three subcategories: M-3, where the stolen property is worth less than fifty dollars; M-2, where the property is worth between fifty and two hundred dollars; and M-1, where the property is worth more than two hundred dollars.

Like most police officers, Charley McFadden was pleased that the critter he had arrested was not as unimportant as he might have been. An M-1 thief was a better arrest than an M-3.

A faint but growing glimmer of hope that he might be able to extricate himself from his current predicament came into Clarence Sims's mind: The fucking pigs had not read him his goddamned rights. Like most people in his line of work, Clarence Sims was well aware of what had come to be known as the *Miranda* Decision. If the fucking pigs didn't read you the whole goddamned thing, starting with *"You have the right to remain silent"* and going through the business about them getting you a lawyer if you couldn't afford one, and could prove it, then you told the judge and the judge let you walk.

Clarence Sims erred. Under the law it is necessary to advise a suspect of his rights under *Miranda* only when the suspect is to be questioned concerning a crime. Since it was not the intention of the arresting officers to ask him any questions at all about the crime, it was not necessary for them to inform Mr. Sims of his rights under *Miranda.*

The man Clarence Sims thought of as the big honky, who was a twenty-two-year-old police officer named Charles McFadden, opened the door of a battered old Volkswagen, and picked up a small portable radio.

The battered old Volkswagen was his personal automobile. He had been authorized to use it on duty. Authorized, but not required. Since he had chosen to use it, he had been issued sort of a Police Department credit card, which authorized him to gas up at any Police Department gas pump—there is one at every District Headquarters—up to a limit of 100 gallons per month, no questions asked. If he had not elected to use his personal vehicle on duty, he could have performed that duty on foot.

"Twelfth District BD," Charley McFadden said into the radio. (Burglary Detail.)

"Twelfth District BD," Police Radio promptly responded.

"Twelfth District BD," Charley McFadden said. "I need a wagon for a prisoner. We're in the parking lot of the Penrose Plaza at Island Road and Lindbergh."

Police Radio did not respond to Officer McFadden directly, but instead, after checking the board to see what was available, called the Emergency Patrol Wagon directly:

"Twelve Oh One."

"Twelve Oh One," the wagon replied.

"Meet the burglary detail at the parking lot of Penrose Plaza, Island at Lindbergh, with a prisoner."

"Twelve Oh One, okay," EPW 1201 replied.

Charley McFadden put the portable radio back on the seat of his Volkswagen.

When the two police officers assigned to 1201, the Twelfth District wagon responding to the call to transport a prisoner, arrived at the scene, they found that the arresting officers were having more trouble with the victim than with the prisoner.

The prisoner was on his feet, his hands cuffed behind him, leaning on the victim's car and apparently resigned to his fate. Even, to judge by the look on his face, a little smug about it.

The victim, having been informed that her two packages had become evidence, and could not be returned to her until released by proper authority, was engaged in a heated conversation with Officer McFadden, telling him that she had to have the shopping bags, at least the one from *John Wanamaker & Sons* which contained a formal dress shirt for her husband, a shirt he absolutely had to have for a dinner party that night.

"Ma'am, if you'll just go to the West Detectives, at Fifty-fifth and Pine, and sign the Property Receipt, they'll give you your stuff right back."

"What I don't understand is why I can't sign whatever it is I have to sign right here," she said.

"I don't have the form, lady; you have to do it at West Detectives," Charley McFadden said. "That's the rules."

That was not the truth, the whole truth, and nothing but the truth. But it had been Officer McFadden's experience that if he gave the victim back her property here and now, that would be the last he, or more importantly, the criminal justice system, would ever see of her. It had been his experience that the ordinary citizen's interest in law enforcement ended when they had to make their own contribution, like showing up in court and swearing under oath that the stuff the critter had stolen belonged to her.

The chances of her showing up in court, and thus perhaps aiding in sending Mr. Sims off to jail, would be aided if she got the idea, by signing a Property Receipt, that she was already involved and *had* to show up in court.

"And what if I refuse to press charges?" the victim said, finally, in desperate exasperation.

"Lady, I'm pressing charges," Charley McFadden said, equally exasperated. "Or Hay-zus is. The *city* is. We *caught* him stealing that stuff from your car."

"Well, we'll see about that, young man," the victim said. "We'll just see about that. My brother-in-law just happens to be a very prominent attorney."

"Yes, ma'am," Charley McFadden said. He turned to the two wagon cops. "You can take him," he said.

"And I'm going to get on the telephone right now and tell him about this," the victim said. "This is simply outrageous."

"Yes, ma'am," Charley McFadden said.

Clarence Sims was led to the wagon, helped inside, and driven to the West Detectives District at Fifty-fifth and Pine streets, where his glowing ember of hope that he was going to walk was extinguished by a detective who began their discussion by explaining his rights under *Miranda*.

Lieutenant Ed Michleson, the Day Watch commander at the Twelfth District, was not at all surprised to get the telephone call from Sergeant Willoughby of Chief Inspector Coughlin's office informing him that he was about to lose the services of Officers Jesus Martinez and Charles McFadden.

When they had been assigned to the Twelfth District, it had been with the understanding that it was only temporary, that they would be reassigned. The District Commander had told him that he had gotten it from Chief Coughlin himself that their assignment was only until he could find a good job for them.

They had been previously working plainclothes in Narcotics, a good, but not unusual assignment for young cops who showed promise and whose faces were not yet known on the street, and who, if they let their hair grow and dressed like bums, could sort of melt into the drug culture.

When their faces became known, which was inevitable, the next step was usually back into uniform. But McFadden and Martinez had, on their own, staked out the Bridge & Pratt Streets terminal of the subway, and there found the junkie who had shot Captain Dutch Moffitt, of Highway Patrol, to death. McFadden had chased Gerald Vincent Gallagher down the tracks where Gallagher had fallen against the third rail and then gotten himself run over by a subway train.

In the movies, or in a cop-and-robbers program on TV, with the mayor and assorted big shots beaming in the background, the Commissioner would have handed them detectives' badges, and congratulations for a job well done. But this was real life, and promotions to detective in the Philadelphia Police Department came only after you had taken, and passed, the civil service examination. Martinez had taken the exam and flunked it, and McFadden hadn't been a cop long enough to be eligible to even take it.

But it was good police work, and Chief Inspector Coughlin, who was a good guy, didn't want to put them back into uniform—which young cops working plainclothes considered a demotion—even though with their pictures on the front page of every newspaper in Philadelphia, and on TV, their effectiveness as undercover Narcs was destroyed.

So he'd loaned them to Twelfth District, which was understrength, and had a problem with thieves working shopping mall parking lots, until he could find someplace to assign them permanently. And now he had.

Lieutenant Michleson got up and walked into the Operations Room and asked the corporal where Mutt and Jeff were. They looked like Mutt and Jeff. McFadden was a great big kid, large boned, tall and heavy. Martinez was a little Latin type, wiry and just over Department minimums for height and weight.

"They're on their way in," the corporal said. "They just arrested a guy robbing a car in the parking lot at Penrose Plaza. That makes five they caught since they been here."

"When they finish up the paperwork, send them into me," Michleson said. "We're going to lose them."

"Where they going?"

"Highway."

"Highway?" the corporal replied, surprised, then laughed. "Those two?"

"That's not kind, Charley," Michleson said, smiling at the mental image of Mutt and Jeff all decked out in Highway Patrol regalia.

"I don't think Hay-zus is big enough to straddle a Harley," the corporal said.

"Maybe somebody figures they paid their dues," Lieutenant Michleson said. "Highway didn't catch the critter who shot Captain Moffitt. They did."

"When are they going?"

"They're to report in the morning."

Staff Inspector Peter Wohl, at thirty-five the youngest of the eighteen Staff Inspectors of the Police Department of the City of Philadelphia, who was lying on his back, looked up from what he was doing and found himself staring up a woman's shorts at her underpants. The underpants were red, and more or less transparent, and worn under a pair of white shorts.

He pushed himself, on his mechanic's crawler, the rest of the way out from under the Jaguar XK-120, and sat up. There was grease on his face, and on his bare, smoothly muscled chest, but there was still something about him that suggested more the accountant, or the lawyer, than a mechanic. Or a police officer.

"Hi," the wearer of the red underpants and white shorts said.

"Hi," Peter Wohl said, noticing now that she was also wearing a man's white shirt, the bottom rolled up and tied in a knot under her bosom, which served to bare her belly and put her not at all unattractive navel on display.

"I saw you working out the window," the woman said, "and I figured you could use this." She extended a bottle of Budweiser to him.

Peter Wohl noticed now that the hand holding the bottle had both an engagement and a wedding ring on the appropriate finger.

He took the beer.

"Thank you," he said, and took a pull at the neck.

"Naomi," the woman said. "Naomi Schneider."

"Peter Wohl," he said.

Naomi Schneider, it registered on Peter Wohl's policeman's mind, was a white female, approximately five feet six inches tall, approximately 130 pounds, approximately twenty-five years of age, with no significant distinguishing marks or scars.

"We're in Two-B," Naomi Schneider volunteered. "My husband and I, I mean. We moved in last week."

"I saw the moving van," Peter said.

Two-B was the apartment occupying the rear half of the second floor of what Peter thought of as the House. There were six apartments in the House, a World War I–era mansion on the 8800 Block of Norwood Road in Chestnut Hill, which had been converted into what the owner, a corporation, called "luxury apartments." The apartments in the rear of the building looked out on the four-car garage, and what had been the chauffeur's quarters above it. Peter Wohl lived in the ex-chauffeur's quarters, and to the often undisguised annoyance of the tenants of the House occupied two of the four garages.

It was possible, he thought, that Mr. Schneider had suggested to his wife that maybe if they made friends with the guy in the garage apartment with the Jaguar and *two* garages they could talk him out of one of them. There had been, he had noticed lately, a Porsche convertible coupe parked either on the street, or behind the house. They could probably make the argument that as fellow fine sports car *aficionados* he would appreciate that it was nearly criminal to have to leave a Porsche outside exposed to the elements.

But he dismissed that possible scenario as being less likely than the possibility that Mr. Schneider knew nothing of his wife's gesture of friendliness, and that Naomi had something in mind that had nothing to do with their Porsche.

"My husband travels," Naomi offered. "He's in floor coverings. He goes as far west as Pittsburgh."

Bingo!

"Oh, really?"

He now noticed that Naomi Schneider's eyes were very dark. Dark-eyed women do not have blond hair. Naomi's hair was, therefore, dyed blond. It was well done, no dark roots or anything, but obviously her hair was naturally black, or nearly so. Peter had a theory about that. Women with dark hair who peroxided it should not go out in the bright sunlight. Dyed blond hair might work inside, especially at night, but in the sunlight, it looked . . . dyed.

"He's generally gone two or three nights a week," Naomi offered. "What do you do?"

Peter elected to misunderstand her. "I just had the seats out," he said. "I took them to a place downtown and had the foam rubber replaced, and now I'm putting them back in."

Naomi stepped to the car and ran her fingers over the softly glowing red leather.

"Nice," she said. "But I meant, what do you do?"

"I work for the city," Peter said. "I see a Porsche around. That yours?"

"Yeah," Naomi said. "Mel, my husband, sometimes drives it on business, but there's not much room in it for samples, so usually he takes the station wagon, and leaves me the Porsche."

"I don't suppose," Peter agreed amiably, "that there *is* much room in a Porsche for floor-covering samples."

"This is *nice,*" Naomi said, now stroking the Jaguar's glistening fender with the balls of her fingers. "New, huh?"

Peter Wohl laughed. "It's older than you are."

She looked at him in confusion. "It looks new," she said.

"Thank you, ma'am," Peter said. "But that left Coventry in February 1950."

"Left where?"

"Coventry. England. Where they make them."

"But it looks new."

"Thank you again."

"I'll be damned," Naomi said. She looked down at Peter and smiled. "You hear what happened last night?"

"No."

"About the woman who was raped? Practically right around the corner?"

"No," Peter Wohl replied truthfully. He had spent the previous day, and the day before that, the whole damned weekend, in Harrisburg, the state capital, in a hot and dusty records depository.

"He forced her into his van, did—you know—to her, and then threw her out of the van in Fairmount Park. It was on the radio, KYW."

"I hadn't heard."

"With Mel gone so much, it scares me."

"Did they say, on the radio, if it was the same man they think has done it before?" Peter asked.

"They said they *think* it is," Naomi said.

Interesting, Peter Wohl thought, *if it is the same guy, it's the first time he's done that.*

"Naked," Naomi said.

"Excuse me?"

"He threw her out of the van naked. Without any clothes."

Well, that would tie in with the humiliation that seems to be part of this weirdo's modus operandi.

There was the sound of tires moving across the cobblestones in front of the garages, and Peter's ears picked up the slightly different pitch of an engine with its idle speed set high; the sound of an engine in a police car.

He hoisted himself off the mechanic's crawler. A Highway Patrol car pulled to a stop. The door opened, and a sergeant in the special Highway Patrol uniform (crushed crown cap, Sam Browne belt, and motorcyclist's breeches and puttees) got out. Wohl recognized him. His name was Sergeant Alexander W. Dannelly. Wohl remembered the name because the last time he had seen him was the day Captain Dutch Moffitt had been shot to death at the Waikiki Diner, over on Roosevelt Boulevard. Sergeant Dannelly had been the first to respond to the call, "Officer needs assistance; shots fired; officer wounded."

And Dannelly recognized him, too. He smiled, and started to wave, and then caught the look in Wohl's eyes and the barely perceptible shake of his head, and stopped.

"Can I help you, Officer?" Wohl asked.

"I'm looking for a man named Wohl," Sergeant Dannelly said.

"I'm Wohl."

"May I speak to you a moment, sir?"

"Sure," Wohl said. "Excuse me a minute, Naomi."

She smiled uneasily.

Wohl walked to the far side of the Highway Patrol car.

"What's up, Dannelly?" he asked.

"You're not answering your phone, Inspector."

"I've got the day off," Wohl said. "Who's looking for me?"

"Lieutenant Sabara," Dannelly said. "He said to send a car by here to see if you were home; that maybe your phone wasn't working."

"The phone's upstairs," Wohl said. "If it's been ringing, I didn't hear it."

"Okay with you, sir, if I get on the radio and tell him you're home?"

"Sure." Wohl wondered what Sabara wanted with him that was so important he had sent a car to see if his phone was working. "Tell him to give me fifteen minutes to take a bath, and then I'll wait for his call."

"You want to wait while I do it?"

"No," Wohl said, smiling. "You get out of here and then you call him."

"I understand, sir," Dannelly said, nodding just perceptibly toward Naomi.

"No, you don't," Wohl said, laughing. "The only thing I'm trying to hide, Sergeant, is that I'm a cop."

"Whatever you say, Inspector," Dannelly said, unabashed, winking at Wohl.

Wohl waited until Sergeant Dannelly had gotten back in the car and driven off, then walked back to Naomi Schneider. Her curiosity, he saw, was about to bubble over.

"I saw an accident," Peter lied easily. "I have to go to the police station and make a report."

Sometimes, now for example, Peter Wohl often wondered if going to such lengths to conceal from his neighbors that he was a cop was worth all the trouble it took. It had nothing to do with anything official, and he certainly wasn't ashamed of being a damned good cop, the youngest Staff Inspector in the department; but sometimes, with civilians, especially civilians like his neighbors—bright, young, well-educated, well-paid civilians—it could be awkward.

Before he had, just after his promotion to Staff Inspector, moved into the garage apartment, he had lived in a garden apartment on Montgomery Avenue in the area of West Philadelphia known as Wynnfield. His neighbors there had been much the same kind of people, and he had learned that their usual response to having a cop for a neighbor was one of two things, and sometimes both. What was a lowlife, like a cop, doing in among his social betters? And what good is it having a cop for a neighbor, if he can't be counted on to fix a lousy speeding ticket?

He had decided, when he moved into the garage apartment, not to let his neighbors know what he did for a living. He almost never wore a uniform, and with his promotion to Staff Inspector had come the perk of an official car that didn't look like a police car. Not only was it unmarked, but it was new (the current car was a two-tone Ford LTD) and had whitewall tires and no telltale marks; the police shortwave radio was concealed in the glove compartment and used what looked like an ordinary radio antenna.

When his neighbors in the garage apartment asked him what he did, he told them he worked for the city. He didn't actually come out and deny that he was a cop, but he managed to convey the impression that he was a middle-level civil servant, who worked in City Hall.

He didn't get chummy with his neighbors, for several reasons, among them that, like most policemen, he was most comfortable with other policemen, and also because there was no question in his mind that when he was invited to come by for a couple of beers, at least marijuana, and probably something even more illegal, would be on the menu as well.

If he didn't see it, he would not have to bust his neighbors.

"Oh," Naomi Schneider said, when he told her about the accident he had seen and would have to go to the station to make a report about.

"Actually," Peter said, "I'm a suspect in a bank robbery."

Naomi laughed delightedly, which made her bosom jiggle.

"Well, it was nice to meet you, Naomi," Peter said. "And I thank you for the beer—"

"My pleasure," Naomi interrupted. "You looked so *hot!*"

"And I look forward to meeting Mr. Schneider."

"Mel," she clarified. "But he won't be home until Thursday. He went to Pittsburgh, this time."

"But now I have to take a shower and go down to the police station."

"Sure, I understand," Naomi said. "How come you're home all the time in the day-time, if you don't mind my asking?"

"I have to work a lot at night," he explained. "So instead of paying me overtime, they give me what they call compensatory time."

"Oh," Naomi said.

He handed her the empty Budweiser bottle, smiled, and went up the stairs at the end of the building to his apartment.

The red light on his telephone answering machine in the bedroom was flashing. That was probably Sabara, he decided. But even if it wasn't, if it was either business, or more likely his mother, who was not yet convinced that he was really eating prop-erly living by himself that way, it would have to wait until he had his shower.

He showered and shaved in the shower, a trick he had learned in the army, and started to dress. After he pulled on a pair of DAK slacks, he stopped. He knew Mike Sabara—now the Acting Commander of Highway Patrol, until they made it official—but they were not close friends. That made it likely that what Sabara wanted was of-ficial; that he would have to meet him somewhere, and he could not do that in lemon-colored DAKs and a polo shirt.

Barefoot, wearing only the DAKs, he pushed the PLAY button on the answering machine. The tape rewound, and then began to play. He had had a number of calls while he was outside putting the seats back in the XK-120. But most of the callers had either hung up when they heard the recorded message, or cussed and then hung up. Finally, he heard Mike Sabara's voice:

"Inspector, this is Mike Sabara. I'd like to talk to you. Would you call Radio and have them give me a number where you can be reached? Thank you."

This was followed by his mother's voice ("I don't know why I call, you're never home") and three more beeps and clicks indicating his callers' unwillingness to speak to a damned machine.

He looked at his watch and decided he didn't want to hang around until Sabara called him. He dialed the number of Police Radio from memory.

"This is Isaac Seventeen," he said. "Would you get word to Highway One that I'm at 928-5923 waiting for his call? No. Five nine *two* three. Thank you."

He decided another beer was in order, and went to the refrigerator in the kitchen and got one. Then he went back into the living room and sat down on his long, low, white leather couch and put his feet on the plate-glass coffee table before it to wait for Sabara's call.

Peter Wohl had once had a girlfriend, now married to a lawyer and living in Swarthmore, who had been an interior decorator, and who had donated her professional services to the furnishing of the apartment when it had seemed likely they would be married. From time to time he recalled what the couch, two matching chairs, and the plate-glass coffee table had cost him, even with Dorothea's professional discount. Every time he did, he winced.

His door chimes went off. They were another vestige of Dorothea. She said they were darling. They played the first few bars of *"Be It Ever So Humble, There's No Place Like Home."* They were "custom," and not only had cost accordingly, but were larger than common, ordinary door chimes, so that when, post-Dorothea, he had tried to replace them, he couldn't, without repainting the whole damned wall by the door.

It was Naomi Schneider. He was annoyed but not surprised.

"Hi," she said. "All cleaned up?"

"I hope so," he said. "What can I do for you?"

"Mel, my husband, asked me to ask you something," she said.

The phone began to ring.

"Excuse me," he said, and went toward it. When he realized that she had invited herself in, he walked past the phone on the end table and went into his bedroom and picked up the bedside phone.

"Hello?"

"Tom Lenihan, Inspector," his caller said.

Sergeant Tom Lenihan worked for Peter's boss, Chief Inspector Dennis V. Coughlin. He was sort of a combination driver and executive assistant. Peter Wohl thought of him as a nice guy, and a good cop.

"What's up, Tom?"

"The Chief says he knows you worked all weekend, and it's your day off, and he's sorry, but something has come up, and he wants to see you this afternoon. I've got you scheduled for three-thirty. Is that okay?"

"What would you say if I said no?"

"I think I'd let you talk to the Chief." Lenihan chuckled.

"I'll be there."

"I thought maybe you could fit the Chief into your busy schedule," Lenihan said. "You being such a nice guy, and all."

"Go to hell, Tom," Wohl said, laughing, and hung up. He wondered for a moment if the Chief wanting to see him was somehow connected with Lieutenant Mike Sabara wanting to talk to him.

Then he became aware that Naomi Schneider was standing in the bedroom door, leaning on the jamb, and looking at the bed. On the bed were his handkerchief, his wallet, his keys, the leather folder that held his badge and photo-identification card, and his shoulder holster, which held a Smith & Wesson "Chief's Special" five-shot .38 Special revolver, all waiting to be put into, or between layers of, whatever clothing he decided to wear.

"What are you, a cop or something?" Naomi asked.

"A cop."

"A detective, maybe?" Naomi asked, visibly thrilled.

"Something like that."

Christ, now it will be all over the House by tomorrow morning!

"What does that mean?" Naomi asked. "Something like that?"

"I'm a Staff Inspector," he said. "And, Naomi, I sort of like for people not to know that I am."

"What's a Staff Inspector?"

"Sort of like a detective."

"And that's sort of a secret."

The phone rang again, and he picked it up.

"Peter Wohl," he said.

"Inspector, this is Mike Sabara."

Wohl covered the mouthpiece with his hand.

"Excuse me, please, Naomi?"

"Oh, sure," she said, and put her index finger in front of her lips in a gesture signifying she understood the necessity for secrecy.

When she turned around, he saw that her red underpants had apparently gathered in the décolletage of her buttocks; her cheeks peeked out naked from beneath the white shorts.

"What's up, Mike?" Wohl asked.

"I'd like to talk to you, if you can spare me fifteen minutes."

"Anytime. Where are you?"

"Harbison and Levick," Sabara said. "Could I come over there?"

The headquarters of the Second and Fifteenth districts, and the Northeast Detectives, at Harbison and Levick streets, was in a squat, ugly, two-story building whose brown-and-tan brick had become covered with a dark film from the exhausts of the heavy traffic passing by over the years.

"Mike, I've got to go downtown," Wohl said, after deciding he really would rather not go to Harbison and Levick. "What about meeting me in DaVinci's Restaurant? At Twenty-first and Walnut? In about fifteen minutes?"

"I'll be there," Lieutenant Sabara said. "Thank you."

"Be with you in a minute, Naomi," Wohl called, and closed the door. He dressed in a white button-down shirt, a regimentally striped necktie, and the trousers to a blue cord suit. He slipped his arms through the shoulder holster straps, shrugged into the suit jacket, and then put the wallet and the rest of the impedimenta in various pockets. He checked his appearance in a mirror on the back of the door, then went into the living room, where he caught Naomi having a pull at the neck of his beer bottle.

"Very nice!" Naomi said.

"Naomi, I don't want to sound rude, but I have to go."

"I understand."

"What was it Mr. Schneider wanted you to ask me?" he asked.

"He said I should see if I could find out if you would consider subletting one of your garages."

"I'm sorry, I can't do that. I need one for the Jaguar, and my other car belongs to the city, and that has to be kept in a garage."

"Why?" It was not a challenge, but simple curiosity.

"Well, there's a couple of very expensive radios in it that the city doesn't want to have boosted."

"Boosted? You mean stolen?"

"Right."

"That makes sense," she said. "I'll tell Mel."

She got off the couch, displaying a large and not at all unattractive area of inner thigh in the process.

"Well," she said. "I'll let you go."

He followed her to the door, aware that as a gentleman he should not be paying as much attention as he was to her naked *gluteus maximus,* which was peeking out the hem of her shorts.

"Naomi," he said, as he pulled the door open for her, "when you talk to your husband about me, would you tell him that I would consider it a favor if he didn't spread it around that I'm a cop?"

"I won't even tell him."

"Well, you don't have to go that far."

"There's a lot of things I don't tell Mel," Naomi said, softly.

And then her fingers brushed his crotch. Peter pulled away, in a reflex action, and had just decided it was an accidental contact, when that theory was disproved. Naomi's fingers followed his retreating groin, found what she was looking for, and gave it a gentle squeeze.

"See you around, Peter," she said, looking into his eyes. Then she let go of him, laughed, and went quickly down the stairs.

 Peter Wohl glanced at the fuel gauge of the Ford LTD as he turned the ignition key off in the parking lot on Walnut Street near the DaVinci Restaurant. The needle was below E; he was running on the fumes. Since he had driven only from his apartment here, that meant that it had been below E when he had arrived home; and *that* meant he had come damned close to running out of gas on the Pennsylvania Turnpike, or on the Schuylkill Expressway, which would have been a disaster. It would have given him the option of radioing for a police wrecker to bring him gas, which would have been embarrassing, or getting drowned in the torrential rain trying to walk to a gas station. Drowned and/or run over.

Periodically in his life, Wohl believed, he seemed to find himself walking along the edge of a steep cliff, a *crumbling* cliff, with disaster a half-step away. He was obviously in that condition now. The gas gauge seemed to prove that; and so did Naomi of the traveling husband and groping fingers. And, he decided, he probably wasn't going to like at all what Mike Sabara had on his mind.

He got out of the car, and locked it, aware that when he got back in it, the inside temperature would be sizzling; that he would sweat, and his now natty and freshly pressed suit would be mussed when he went to see Chief Coughlin. And he had a gut feeling that was going to be some sort of a disaster, too. It wasn't very likely that Coughlin was going to call him in on a day off to tell him what a splendid job he had been doing and why didn't he take some time off as a reward.

A quick glance around the parking lot told him that Sabara wasn't here yet. He would have spotted a marked Highway Patrol car immediately, and even if Sabara was in an unmarked car, he would have spotted the radio antenna and black-walled tires.

And, he thought, as he walked into the DaVinci, if what Coughlin was after was to hear how his current investigation was going, the reason he had been in Harrisburg, he wasn't going to come across as Sherlock Holmes, either. The only thing two days of rooting around in the Pennsylvania Department of Records had produced was a couple of leads that were weak at best and very probably would turn out to be worthless.

The DaVinci restaurant, named after the artist/inventor, not the proprietor, served very good food despite what Peter thought of as restaurant theatrics. As a general rule of thumb, he had found that restaurants that went out of their way to convert their space into something exotic generally served mediocre to terrible food. The DaVinci had gone a little overboard, he thought, trying to turn their space into rustic Italian. There were red checkered tableclothes; a lot of phony trellises; plastic grapes; and empty Chianti bottles with candles stuck in their necks. But the food was good, and the people who ran the place were very nice.

He asked for and got a table on the lower level, which gave him a view of both the upper level and the bar just inside the door. The waitress was a tall, pretty young brunette who looked as though she should be on a college campus. Then he remembered hearing that the waitresses in DaVinci's were aspiring actresses, hoping to meet theatrical people who came to Philly, and were supposed to patronize DaVinci's.

Her smile vanished when he ordered just coffee.

Or can she tell I'm not a movie producer?

When she delivered his coffee, he handed her a dollar and told her to keep the change. That didn't seem to change her attitude at all.

Mike Sabara came into the room a few minutes later, immediately after Peter had scalded his mouth on the lip of the coffee cup, which had apparently been delivered to his table fresh from the fires of hell.

Mike was in uniform, the crushed-crown cap and motorcyclist's breeches and puttees peculiar to Highway Patrol, worn with a Sam Browne belt festooned with a long line of cartridges and black leather accoutrements for the tools of a policeman's trade, flashlight, handcuffs, and so on. Mike was wearing an open-collared white shirt, with a captain's insignia, two parallel silver bars, on each collar point.

The Highway Patrol and its special uniform went back a long time, way before the Second World War. It had been organized as a traffic law enforcement force, as the name implied, and in the old days, it had been mounted almost entirely on motorcycles, hence the breeches and puttees and soft-crowned cap.

There were still a few motorcycles in Highway—from somewhere Wohl picked out the number twenty-four—but they were rarely used for anything but ceremonial purposes, or maybe crowd control at Mummers Parades. The Highway Patrol still patrolled the highways—the Schuylkill Expressway and Interstate 95—but the Patrol had evolved over the years, especially during the reign of Captain Jerry Carlucci, and even more during the reign of Mayor Carlucci, into sort of a special force that was dispatched to clean up high-crime areas.

Highway Patrol cars carried two officers, while all other Philadelphia police cars carried only one. Unless they had specific orders sending them somewhere else, Highway Patrol cars could patrol wherever, within reason, they liked, without regard to District boundaries. They regarded themselves, and were regarded by other policemen, as an elite force, and there was always a long waiting list of officers who had applied for transfer to Highway Patrol.

Anyone with serious ambitions to rise in the police hierarchy knew the path led through Highway Patrol. Wohl himself had been a Highway Patrol Corporal, and had liked the duty, although he had been wise enough to keep to himself his profound relief that his service in Highway had been after the motorcycles had been all but retired and he had rarely been required to get on one. Going through the "wheel training course," which he had considered necessary to avoid being thought of as less than wholly masculine, had convinced him that anybody who rode a motorcycle willingly, much less joyfully, had some screws in urgent need of tightening.

Wohl had several thoughts as he saw Mike Sabara walking across the room to him, wearing what for Sabara was a warm smile. He thought that Mike was not only an ugly sonofabitch but that he was menacing. Sabara's swarthy face was marked with the scars of what could have been smallpox, but more probably were the remnants of adolescent acne. He wore an immaculately trimmed pencil-line mustache. If it was designed to take attention from his disfigured skin, Wohl thought, it had exactly the opposite effect.

He was a short, stocky, barrel-chested man, with an aggressive walk. He was also hairy. Thick black hair showed at the open collar of his shirt and covered his exposed arms.

All of these outward things, Wohl knew, were misleading. Mike Sabara was an extraordinarily gentle man, father of a large brood of well-cared-for kids. He was a Lebanese, and active—he actually taught Sunday School—in some kind of Orthodox Church. Wohl had seen him crying at Dutch Moffitt's funeral, the tears running unashamedly down his cheeks as he carried Dutch to his grave.

Sabara put out his large hand as he slipped into the seat across from Wohl. His grip was firm, but not a demonstration of all the strength his hand possessed.

"I appreciate you meeting me like this, Inspector," Sabara said.

"I know why you're calling me 'Inspector,' Mike," Wohl said, smiling, "so I'll have to reply, 'My pleasure, *Captain* Sabara.' Congratulations, Mike, it's well deserved, and how come I wasn't invited to your promotion party?"

Wohl immediately sensed that what he had intended as humor had fallen flat. Sabara gave him a confused, even wary, look.

"The Commissioner called me at home last night," Sabara said. "He said to come to work today wearing captain's bars."

Which you just happened to have lying around, Wohl thought, and was immediately ashamed of the unkind thought. He himself had bought a set of lieutenant's bars the day the examination scores had come out, even though he had known it would be long months before the promotion actually came through.

"So it's official, then?" Wohl said. "Well, congratulations. I can't think of anybody better qualified."

Wohl saw that, too, produced a reaction in Sabara different from what he expected. More confusion, more wariness.

The waitress reappeared.

"Get you something?"

"Iced tea, please," Captain Sabara said. The waitress looked at him strangely. Sabara, Wohl thought, was not the iced tea type.

"Can I get right to it, Inspector?" Sabara asked, when the waitress had left.

"Sure."

"If it's at all possible," Sabara said, "I'd like Highway Patrol."

Sabara had, Wohl sensed, rehearsed that simple statement.

"I'm not sure what you mean, Mike."

"I mean, I'd really like to take over Highway," Sabara said, and there was more uncertainty in his eyes. "I mean, Christ, no one knows it better than I do. And I know I could do a good job."

What the hell is he driving at?

"You want me to put in a good word for you? Is that it, Mike? Sure. You tell me to who, and I'll do it."

There was a pause before Sabara replied.

"You don't know, do you?" he said, finally.

"Know what?"

"About Highway and Special Operations."

"No," Wohl said, and searched his memory. "The last I heard about Special Operations was that it was an idea whose time had not yet come."

"It's time has come," Sabara said, "and Highway's going under it."

"And who's getting Special Operations?"

"You are," Sabara said.

Jesus H. Christ!

"Where did you get that?" Wohl asked.

Sabara looked uncomfortable.

"I heard," he said.

"I'd check out that source pretty carefully, Mike," Wohl said. "This is the first I've heard anything like that."

"You're getting Special Operations and David Pekach is getting Highway," Sabara said. "I thought Pekach was your idea, and maybe I could talk you out of it."

"Did your source say what's in mind for you?" Wohl asked.

"Your deputy."

"Where the hell did you get this?"

"I can't tell you," Sabara said. "But I believe it."

And now I'm beginning to. Sabara has heard something he believes. Jesus, is this why Chief Coughlin sent for me?

Why me?

"I'm beginning to," Wohl said. "Chief Coughlin wants to see me at half past three. Maybe this is why."

"Now I'm on the spot," Sabara said. "I'd appreciate it if you didn't—"

"Tell him we talked? No, of course not, Mike. And I really hope you're wrong."

From the look in Sabara's eyes, Wohl could tell he didn't think there was much chance he was wrong. That meant his source was as good as he said it was. And that meant it had come from way up high in the police department hierarchy, a Chief Inspector, or more likely one of the Deputy Commissioners.

Someone important, who didn't like the idea of Special Operations, of Peter Wohl being given command of Special Operations, of David Pekach being given command of Highway over Mike Sabara. Or all of the above.

"Peter," Mike Sabara said. It was the first time he had used Wohl's Christian name. "You understand . . . there's nothing personal in this? You're a hell of a good cop. I'd be happy to work for you anywhere. But—"

"You think you're the man to run Highway?" Wohl interrupted him. "Hell, Mike, so do I. And I don't think I'm the man to run Special Operations. I don't even know what the hell it's supposed to do."

There was something about Police Recruit Matthew M. Payne that Sergeant Richard B. Stennis, Firearms Instructor and Assistant Range Officer of the Police Academy of the City of Philadelphia, did not like, although he could not precisely pin it down.

He knew when it had begun, virtually the first time he had ever laid eyes on Payne. Dick Stennis, whose philosophy *vis-à-vis* firearms, police or anyone else's, was *"You never need a gun until you need one badly,"* took his responsibility to teach rookies about firearms very seriously.

Sergeant Stennis—a stocky, but not fat, balding man of forty—was aware that statistically the odds were about twenty to one that his current class of rookies would go through their entire careers without once having drawn and fired their service weapon in the line of duty. He suspected that, the way things were going, the odds might change a little, maybe down to ten to one that these kids would never have to use their service revolvers; but the flip side of even those percentages was that one in ten of them *would* have to use a gun in a situation where his life, or the life of another police officer, or a civilian, would depend on how well he could use it.

Some of Dick Stennis's attitude toward firearms came, and he was aware of this, from the United States Marine Corps. Like many police officers, Stennis had come to the department after a tour in the military. He had enlisted in the Corps at eighteen, a week after graduating from Frankford High School in June of 1950. He had arrived in Korea just in time to miss the Inchon Invasion, but in plenty of time to make the Bug Out from the Yalu and the withdrawal from Hamhung on Christmas Eve of the same year.

He was back from Korea in less than a year, wearing corporal's chevrons and a Silver Star and two Purple Hearts, the reason for the second of which had kept him in the Philadelphia Navy Hospital for four months. When he was restored to duty, the Corps sent him back to Paris Island, and made him a firearms instructor, which was something, but not entirely, like being a drill instructor.

When his three-year enlistment was over and he went back to Philadelphia, he joined the Police Department. Two years after that, about the time he was assigned to the Police Academy, he had gotten married and joined the Marine Corps Reserve because he needed the money.

One weekend a month and two weeks each summer Sergeant Stennis of the Police Department became Master Gunnery Sergeant Stennis of the United States Marine Corps Reserve. He had been called up for the Vietnam War, fully expecting to be sent to Southeast Asia, but the Corps, reasoning that a Philadelphia cop called up from the Reserve was just the guy to fill the billet of Noncommissioned Officer in Charge of the Armed Forces Military Police Detachment in Philadelphia, had sent him back to Philly two weeks after he reported in at Camp LeJeune.

Practically, it had been a good deal. He had done his two years of active duty living at home. The Marine Corps had paid him an allowance in lieu of rations, and an allowance, in lieu of housing, that was greater than the mortgage payment on his house on Leonard Street in Mayfair. And he had been building double-time. His seniority with the Police Department had continued to build while he was "off" in the Corps, and he had added two years of active duty time to his Marine Corps longevity. When he turned sixty, there would be a pension check from the Corps to go with his police pension and, when he turned sixty-five, his Social Security.

When he went on inactive duty again, the Corps gave him a Reserve billet with the Navy Yard, as an investigator on the staff of the Provost Marshal. He generally managed to pick up two or three days of "active duty" a month, sometimes more, in addition to the one weekend, which meant that much more in his Reserve paycheck every three months. It also meant that his Corps pension, when he got to it, would be that much larger.

It was a pretty good deal, he had reminded himself, when he had failed the Police Department's Lieutenant's examination for the second time. If he had passed it, there was no telling where the Department would have assigned him, but it would have meant leaving the Academy, which he liked, and almost certainly would have kept him from picking up an extra two or three days Master Gunnery Sergeant's pay and allowances every month. The Academy had an eight-to-five, Monday-through-Friday work schedule. As a new Lieutenant, he could have expected to work nights and weekends.

And he liked what he was doing, and thought it was important. Sometimes, Dick Stennis thought, very privately, that if his supervision of the firearms instruction at the Police Academy kept *just one* cop, or *just one* civilian, alive, it was worth being thought of by one class of rookies after another as "that bald-headed prick."

The first time Police Recruit Matthew M. Payne had come to the attention of Sergeant Richard Stennis was during the lecture Sergeant Stennis customarily delivered to the class as the first step in the firearms phase of their training. Sergeant Stennis believed, not unreasonably, that over the years he had been able to hone and polish his introductory lecture to the point where it was both meaningful and interesting.

Police Recruit Matthew M. Payne apparently was not so affected. The first time Stennis saw Payne, who was sitting toward the rear of the classroom, he was yawning. He was *really* yawning, holding a balled fist to his widely gaping mouth.

Sergeant Stennis had stopped in midsentence, and pointed a finger at him.

"You!" he said sharply, to get his attention. "What's your name?"

Payne had looked uncomfortable. "Payne, sir."

"Perhaps it would be easier for you to stay awake if you stood up."

Payne had jumped to his feet and assumed what is known in the military as the position of "parade rest," that is, he stood stiffly, with his feet slightly apart, and his hands folded neatly in the small of his back, staring straight ahead.

That little fucker is making fun of me, Stennis decided, and then modified that slightly. Payne was not a *little* fucker. He was probably six feet one, Stennis judged, maybe a little over that. And he was well set up, a muscular, good-looking young man.

Well, fuck you, sonny. I've been dealing with wiseasses like you all my life. You want to stand there at parade rest, fine. You'll stand there until this class is over.

And Police Recruit Matthew M. Payne had done just that, for the remaining forty, forty-five minutes of the class, which served to give Sergeant Stennis some food for thought. That was the sort of thing a serviceman would do. Perhaps he had jumped the kid a little too hard.

When he checked Payne's records, however, he found no indication that Payne had ever worn any uniform but the one he was wearing now; he was not an ex-serviceman. His records indicated further that Matthew M. Payne had just graduated from the University of Pennsylvania, Bachelor of Arts, cum laude.

That was unusual. Very few college graduates took the Civil Service exam for the Police Department. The starting pay for a rookie policeman was low (in Dick Stennis's opinion, a disgrace) and a college degree was worth more money almost anyplace else.

Making an effort not to make a big deal of it, he asked other instructors what they thought of Payne. The responses had been either a shrug, meaning that they hadn't formed an opinion of him one way or another, or that he was just one more recruit, except for a few instructors who replied that he seemed smart. Not smartass, but smart. Bright. Payne had apparently given no one else any trouble; if he had, Stennis would have heard.

The first day of actual firing on the Police Academy Pistol Range was, Stennis had learned, most often one of shock, even humiliation for rookies. Very few recruits, excepting, of course, ex-servicemen, had much experience with any kind of firearm, and even less with handguns.

What they knew of pistols most often came from what they had seen in the movies and on TV, where Hollywood cops, firing snub-nosed revolvers, routinely shot bad guys between the eyes at fifty yards.

The targets on the Academy Pistol Range were life-sized silhouettes, with concentric "kill rings" numbered (K5, K4, and so on) for scoring. Ideally, all bullets would land in a K5 kill ring. The targets were set up for the recruit's first firing at fifteen yards. The weapon used was the standard service revolver, the Smith & Wesson Model 10 "Military & Police." It was a six-shot, .38 Special caliber, fixed-sight weapon, which could be fired in either single action (the hammer was cocked, using the thumb, before the trigger was pulled) or double action (simply pulling the trigger would cock the hammer and then release it).

For their first live firing exercise, the recruits were instructed in the double-hand hold, and told to fire the weapon single action, that is by cocking the hammer before lining up the sights and pulling the trigger.

It seemed so easy when the recruits first took their positions. *Anyone* should be able to hit a man-sized target at that short range. You could practically reach out and touch the damned target. The result of this was that many, even most recruits, decided it would be safe to show off a little, and perhaps even earn a smile from Sergeant Stennis, by shooting the target in the head, a K5 kill ring.

The result of this, many times, was that there were no holes at all in the target, much less in the head, after the recruit had fired his first six rounds. Shooting a pistol is infinitely more difficult than it is made to appear in the movies.

Sergeant Stennis didn't mind that the first six rounds were normally a disaster for their firers. It humbled them; and humbled, they were that much easier to teach.

When Recruit Matthew M. Payne stepped to the firing line, Sergeant Stennis waited until he was in position, and then moved so that he was standing behind him. Payne did not look particularly uncomfortable when, on command, he looked at the revolver. He fed six cartridges into the cylinder without dropping any of them, which sometimes happened, and he closed the cylinder slowly and carefully.

Some recruits, even though cautioned not to do so, followed the practice of Hollywood cops by snapping the pistol sharply to the right, so that the cylinder slammed home by inertia. This practice, Stennis knew, soon threw the cylinder out of line with the barrel, and the pistol then required the services of a gunsmith.

Sergeant Stennis would not have been surprised if Recruit Payne had flipped the cylinder shut. Even when he didn't, he sensed that Payne was going to do something wiseass, like fire his six rounds at the silhouette's head, rather than at the torso of the target.

And when the command to fire was given, Payne did just that.

And hit the silhouette in the head, just above where the right eye would be.

Beginner's luck, Stennis decided.

Payne's second shot hit the silhouette in the upper center of the head, where the forehead would be.

I'll be damned!

Payne's third shot hit the target head where the nose would be; and so did the fourth. The fifth went a little wide, hitting the tip of the silhouette head, but still inside the K5 ring, which Payne made up for by hitting the silhouette head where the left eye would be with his sixth shot.

I really will be damned. That wasn't at all bad.

When the recruits went forward to examine their targets, and to put gummed pasters on the bullet holes, Sergeant Stennis followed Payne.

"Not bad at all," he said to Payne, startling him. "Where did you learn to shoot a pistol?"

"At Quantico," Payne replied. "The Marine base."

"I know what it is," Stennis said. "How come your records don't say anything about you being in the Corps?"

"I was never in the Corps," Payne replied. "I was in the Platoon Leader Program. I went there two summers."

"What happened?" Stennis asked. Payne understood, he saw, what he was really asking: *If you were in the Platoon Leader Program, how come you're here, and not a second lieutenant in the Corps?*

"I busted the commissioning physical," Payne said.

"You tell them that when you joined the Department?" Stennis demanded, sharply.

"Yes, sir."

They locked eyes for a moment, long enough for Stennis to decide that Payne was telling the truth.

Is that why he came in? Stennis wondered. *Because he flunked the Marine Corps physical, and wants to prove he's a man, anyway? Well, what the hell is wrong with that?*

"Well, that was pretty good shooting," Stennis said.

"I could do better if the pistol had better sights," Payne said, adding, "and this could use a trigger job, too."

Stennis's anger returned.

"Well, Payne," he replied sarcastically, "I'm afraid you'll just have to learn to cope with what the Department thinks they should give you."

He turned and walked back to the firing line.

Almost immediately, he felt like a hypocrite. Wiseass or not, the kid was right. You couldn't get a very good sight picture with the standard service revolver. The front sight was simply a piece of rounded metal, part of the barrel. The rear sight was simply an indentation in the frame. Stennis's own revolver was equipped with adjustable sights—a sharply defined front sight, and a rear sight that was adjustable for both height and windage, with a sharply defined aperture. That, coupled with a carefully honed action, a "trigger job," which permitted a smooth "let off," resulted in a pistol capable of significantly greater accuracy than an off-the-shelf revolver.

And Stennis was suddenly very much aware that his personal pistol was not regulation, and that he got away with carrying it solely because no one in the Department was liable to carefully scrutinize the pistol carried by the Police Academy's Firearms Instructor.

When he reached the firing line, he was not especially surprised to see Chief Inspector Heinrich "Heine" Matdorf, Chief of the Training Bureaus, and thus sort of the headmaster of the Police Academy, standing at the end of the line, to the right, where a concrete pathway led to the main Police Academy Building.

Heine Matdorf, a large, portly, red-faced man who was nearly bald, believed in keeping an eye on what was going on. Stennis liked him, even if they could not be called friends. When Matdorf had come to the Training Bureau two years before, he had made everyone nervous by his unannounced visits to classrooms and training sites. He was taciturn, and his blue eyes seemed cold.

But they had quickly learned that he was not hypercritical, as prone to offer a word of approval as a word of criticism. The new broom had swept only those areas in need of it.

As was his custom, Stennis acknowledged the presence of Chief Matdorf with a nod, expecting a nod in return. But Matdorf surprised him by walking over to him.

"Chief," Stennis greeted him.

"That kid you were talking to, Payne?"

"Yes, sir."

"I want a word with him," Matdorf said. "Stick around."

"He put six shots into the head, first time up," Stennis offered.

Matdorf grunted again, but didn't otherwise respond.

Matthew Payne finished pasting his target and walked back to the firing line. Stennis saw in his eyes that he was curious, but not uneasy, to see Chief Matdorf standing there beside him.

"You know who I am?" Matdorf asked as Payne walked up.

"Yes, sir."

"We met at Captain Moffitt's wake," Chief Matdorf said. "Chief Coughlin introduced us."

"Yes, sir, I remember."

What the hell was this kid doing at Dutch Moffitt's wake? And Chief Coughlin introduced him to Matdorf?

"I just had a call from Chief Coughlin about you," Matdorf said.

"Yes, sir?"

"Turn in your gear," Matdorf said. "Clean out your locker. If anybody asks what you're doing, tell them 'just what I'm told.' At eight-thirty tomorrow morning, report to Captain Sabara at Highway Patrol. You know where that is? Bustleton and Bowler?"

"I don't understand."

"I'm sure Captain Sabara will explain everything to you tomorrow morning," Matdorf said. "If I didn't make this clear, you won't be coming back here."

"And I'm to ... clean out my locker right now?"

"That's right," Matdorf said. "And don't tell anybody where you're going."

"Yes, sir," Payne said. Stennis saw that he didn't like what he had been told, but was smart enough to sense that asking Chief Matdorf would be futile.

"So get on with it," Matdorf said.

"Yes, sir," Payne said. Then he picked up his earmuffs and other shooting equipment from the firing position and walked off the line.

"You don't say anything to anybody about him going to Highway, either, Dick," Matdorf said.

"No, sir," Stennis said.

"Curiosity about to eat you up?" Matdorf asked, flashing a rare, shy smile.

"Yes, sir."

"The reason he was at Dutch Moffitt's funeral was that Dutch was his uncle."

"I didn't know that."

"His father was a cop, too. Sergeant John X. Moffitt," Matdorf went on. "He got himself killed answering a silent burglar alarm in a gas station in West Philadelphia."

"I didn't know that, either. What are they going to do with him in Highway?" Stennis asked, and then, without giving Matdorf a chance to reply, went on, "How come his name is Payne?"

"His mother remarried; the new husband adopted him," Matdorf said. "And I don't know what they're going to do with him in Highway. This was one of those times when I didn't think I should ask too many questions."

"Coughlin set it up?" Stennis asked.

Matdorf nodded. "Chief Coughlin and the boy's father went through the Academy together. They were pretty tight. I know, because I was in the same class."

His face expressionless, Matdorf met Stennis's eyes for a long moment. Then he turned and walked off the firing line.

8 When Peter Wohl drove into the parking lot behind the Police Administration Building at Eighth and Arch, he pulled up to the gasoline pump and filled the Ford's gas tank.

It took 19.7 gallons. He had heard somewhere that the Ford held 22 gallons. That meant that despite the gas gauge needle pointing below E, he really had been in no danger of running out of gas.

There was a moral to be drawn from that, he thought, as he drove around the parking lot, looking for a place to park. *For yea, though I walk along the edge of the crumbling cliff, I seem to have an unnatural good luck that keeps me from falling off.*

He pulled the Ford into one of the parking slots reserved for official visitors and got out, leaving the windows open a crack to let the heat out. There was, he rationalized, not much of a chance that even the most dedicated radio thief would attempt to practice his profession in the Roundhouse parking lot.

The Police Administration Building was universally known as the Roundhouse. It was not really round, but curved. The building and its interior walls, including even those of the elevators, were curved. It was, he thought, called the Roundhouse because that came easier to the tongue than "Curved House."

He entered the building by the rear door. Inside, to the right, was a door leading to the Arraignment Room. The Roundhouse, in addition to housing the administrative offices of the Police Department on the upper floors, was also a jail. Prisoners were transported from the districts around the city to a basement facility where they were fingerprinted, photographed, and put in holding cells until it was their turn to face the magistrate, who would hear the complaint against them, and either turn them loose or decide what their bail, if any, should be.

There was sort of a small grandstand in which the family and friends of the accused could watch through a plate-glass wall as the accused was brought before the magistrate.

To the left was the door leading to the lobby of the Roundhouse. It was kept closed and locked. A solenoid operated by a Police Officer, usually a Corporal, sitting behind a thick, shatterproof window directly opposite the door, controlled the lock.

Most senior officers of the Police Department of the City of Philadelphia, that is to say from Deputy Commissioners on down through the Captains, were known by sight to the cop controlling the door. Peter Wohl, as a Staff Inspector, was rather high in the police hierarchy. He was one of seventeen Staff Inspectors, a rank immediately superior to Captains, and immediately subordinate to Inspectors. On the rare occasions when Staff Inspector Wohl wore his uniform, it carried a gold oak leaf, identical to that of majors in the armed forces. Inspectors wore silver oak leaves, and Chief Inspectors a colonel's eagle.

Senior officers were accustomed, when entering the Roundhouse, to having the solenoid to the locked door to the lobby buzzing when they reached it. When Peter Wohl reached it, it remained firmly locked. He looked over his shoulder at the cop, a middle-aged Corporal behind the shatterproof glass. The Corporal was looking at him, wearing an official, as opposed to genuine, smile, and gesturing Wohl over to him with his index finger.

Peter Wohl had been keeping count. This made it thirteen-six. Of the nineteen times he had tried to get through the door without showing his identification to the cop behind the shatterproof glass window, he had failed thirteen times; only six times had he been recognized and passed.

He walked to the window.

"Help you, sir?" the Corporal asked.

"I'm Inspector Wohl," Peter said. The corporal looked surprised and then uncomfortable as Wohl extended the leather folder holding his badge (a round silver affair embossed with a representation of City Hall and the letters STAFF INSPECTOR) and identification for him to see.

"Sorry, Inspector," the Corporal said.

"You're doing your job," Peter said, and smiled at him.

He went back to the door, and through it, and walked across the lobby to the elevators. Then he stopped and walked to a glass case mounted on the wall. It held the photographs and badges of Police Officers killed in the line of duty. There was a new one, of an officer in the uniform of a captain of Highway Patrol. Richard C. Moffitt.

Captain Dutch Moffitt and Peter Wohl had been friends as long as Wohl could remember. Not close friends—Dutch had been too flamboyant for that—but friends. They had known they could count on each other if there was a need; they exchanged favors. Wohl thought that the last favor he had done Dutch was to convince Jeannie, the Widow Moffitt, that Dutch had business with the blonde Dutch had been with in the Waikiki Diner on Roosevelt Boulevard when he had been fatally wounded by a junkie holding the place up.

Wohl turned and entered the elevator and pushed the button for the third floor, the right wing of which was more or less the Executive Suite of the Roundhouse. It housed the offices of the Commissioner, the Deputy Commissioners, and some of the more important Chief Inspectors, including that of Chief Inspector Dennis V. Coughlin.

The corridor to that portion of the building was guarded by a natty man in his early thirties, either a plainclothesman or a detective, sitting at a desk. He knew Wohl.

"Hello, Inspector, how are you?"

"About to melt," Wohl said, smiling at him. "I heard some of the cops in Florida can wear shorts. You think I could talk Chief Coughlin into permitting that?"

"I don't have the legs for that," the cop said, as Wohl went down the corridor.

Chief Inspector Dennis V. Coughlin shared an outer office with Police Commissioner Thaddeu Czernich, separated from it by the Commissioner's Conference Room.

Sergeant Tom Lenihan sat at a desk to the left. A pleasant-faced, very large man, his hair was just starting to thin. He was in his shirtsleeves; a snub-nosed revolver could be seen on his hip.

"Well, I'm glad you could fit the Chief into your busy schedule," Lenihan said, with a smile. "I know he'll be pleased."

"How do you think you're going to like the last-out shift in the Seventeenth District, Sergeant?" Wohl said.

Lenihan chuckled. "Go on in. He's expecting you."

Wohl pushed open the door to Chief Inspector Coughlin's office. Coughlin's desk, set catty-cornered, faced the anteroom. Coughlin was also in his shirtsleeves, and he was talking on the telephone. He smiled and motioned Wohl into one of the two chairs facing his desk.

"Hold it a minute," he said into the telephone. He tucked it under his chin and searched through the HOLD basket on his desk. He came out with four sheets of teletype paper and handed them to Wohl. He smiled—rather smugly, Peter thought—at him, and then he resumed his telephone conversation.

The teletype messages had been passed over the Police Communications Network. There was a teletype machine in each of the twenty-two districts (in New York City, and many other cities, the term used for district police stations was "precinct"); in each Detective Division; and elsewhere.

Wohl read the first message.

> GENERAL: 0650 06/30/73 FROM COMMISSIONER
> PAGE 1 OF 1
> CITY OF PHILADELPHIA
> POLICE DEPARTMENT

> ANNOUNCEMENT WILL BE MADE AT ALL ROLL CALLS OF THE
> FOLLOWING COMMAND ASSIGNMENT: EFFECTIVE IMMEDIATELY
> CAPTAIN DAVID S. PEKACH IS REASSIGNED FROM NARCOTICS
> BUREAU TO HIGHWAY PATROL AS COMMANDING OFFICER.

Well, there goes whatever small chance I had to plead Mike Sabara's case. Now that it's official, it's too late to do anything about it.

He read the second message.

> GENERAL: 0651 06/30/73 FROM COMMISSIONER
> PAGE 1 OF 1
> CITY OF PHILADELPHIA
> POLICE DEPARTMENT

> THE FOLLOWING COMMAND REORGANIZATION WILL BE
> ANNOUNCED AT ALL ROLL CALLS: EFFECTIVE IMMEDIATELY A
> SPECIAL OPERATIONS DIVISION IS FORMED WITH HEADQUATERS
> IN THE 7TH POLICE DISTRICT/HIGHWAY PATROL BUILDING.
> COMMANDING OFFICER SPECIAL OPERATIONS DIVISION WILL BE
> IMMEDIATELY SUBORDINATE TO THE COMMISSIONER, REPORTING
> THROUGH CHIEF INSPECTOR COUGHLIN. THE SPECIAL OPERATIONS
> DIVISION WILL CONSIST OF THE HIGHWAY PATROL, THE ANTI-
> CRIME TEAM (ACT) UNIT, AND SUCH OTHER UNITS AS MAY BE
> LATER ASSIGNED. THE SPECIAL OPERATIONS DIVISION HAS
> CITYWIDE JURISDICTION. SPECIAL OPERATIONS DIVISION MOTOR
> VEHICLES (EXCEPT HIGHWAY PATROL) ARE ASSIGNED RADIO CALL
> SIGNS S-100 THROUGH S-200, AND WILL USE THE PHONETIC
> PRONUNCIATION "SAM."

The radio designator "Sam" was already in use, Wohl knew. Stakeout and the Bomb Squad used it. It was "Sam" rather than the military "Sugar" because the first time a Bomb Squad cop had gone on the air and identified himself as "S-Sugar Thirteen" the hoots of derision from his brother officers had been heard as far away as Atlantic City.

Special Operations had been given, he reasoned, the "Sam" designator because Special Operations, also "S," was going to be larger than "S" for Stakeout. So what were they going to use for Stakeout and the Bomb Squad? It would not work to have both using the same designator.

But that was a problem that could wait.

He read the third and fourth teletype messages.

GENERAL: 0652 06/30/73 FROM COMMISSIONER
PAGE 1 OF 1
CITY OF PHILADELPHIA
POLICE DEPARTMENT
ANNOUNCEMENT WILL BE MADE AT ALL ROLL CALLS OF THE
FOLLOWING COMMAND ASSIGNMENT: EFFECTIVE IMMEDIATELY
STAFF INSPECTOR PETER F. WOHL IS REASSIGNED FROM INTERNAL
AFFAIRS DIVISION TO SPECIAL OPERATIONS DIVISION AS
COMMANDING OFFICER.

GENERAL: 0653 06/30/73 FROM COMMISSIONER
PAGE 1 OF 1
CITY OF PHILADELPHIA
POLICE DEPARTMENT

ANNOUNCEMENT WILL BE MADE AT ALL ROLL CALLS OF THE
FOLLOWING COMMAND ASSIGNMENT: EFFECTIVE IMMEDIATELY
CAPTAIN MICHAEL J. SABARA IS REASSIGNED FROM (ACTING)
COMMAND OFFICER HIGHWAY PATROL TO SPECIAL OPERATIONS
DIVISION AS DEPUTY COMMANDER.

"I'll be in touch," Chief Coughlin said to the telephone, and hung up. He turned to Wohl, smiling.

"You don't seem very surprised, Peter," Coughlin said.

"I heard."

"You did?" Coughlin said, surprised. "From who?"

"I forget."

"Yeah, you forget," Coughlin said, sarcastically. "I don't know why I'm surprised."

"I don't suppose I can get out of this?" Wohl asked.

"You're going to be somebody in the Department, Peter," Coughlin said. "It wouldn't be much of a surprise if you got to be Commissioner."

"That's very flattering, Chief," Wohl said. "But that's not what I asked."

"Don't thank me," Coughlin said. "I didn't say that. The mayor did, to the Commissioner. When the mayor told him he thought you should command Special Operations."

Wohl shook his head.

"That answer your question, Inspector?" Chief Coughlin asked.

"Chief, I don't even know what the hell Special Operations is," Wohl said, "much less what it's supposed to do."

"You saw the teletype. Highway and ACT. You were Highway, and you've got Mike Sabara to help you with Highway."

"I don't suppose anybody asked Mike if he'd like to have Highway?" Wohl asked.

"The mayor says Mike looks like a concentration camp guard," Coughlin said. "Dave Pekach, I guess, looks more like what the mayor thinks the commanding officer of Highway Patrol should look like."

"This is a reaction to that *'Gestapo in Jackboots'* editorial? Is that what this is all about?"

"That, too, sure."

"The *Ledger* is going after Carlucci no matter what he does," Wohl said.

"His Honor the Mayor," Coughlin corrected him.

"And after me, too," Wohl said. "Arthur J. Nelson blames me for letting it out that his son was . . . involved with other men."

Arthur J. Nelson was Chairman of the Board and Chief Executive Officer of Daye-Nelson Publishing, Inc., which owned the *Ledger* and twelve other newspapers across the country.

" 'Negro homosexuals,' " Coughlin said.

It had been a sordid job. Jerome Nelson, the only son of Arthur J. Nelson, had been murdered, literally butchered, in his luxurious apartment in a renovated Revolutionary War–era building on Society Hill. The prime suspect in the case was his live-in boyfriend, a known homosexual, a man who called himself "Pierre St. Maury." A fingerprint search had identified Maury as a twenty-five-year-old black man, born Errol F. Watson, with a long record of arrests for minor vice offenses and petty thievery. Watson had himself been murdered, shot in the back of the head with a .32 automatic, by two other black men known to be homosexuals.

Wohl believed he knew what had happened: It had started as a robbery. The almost certain doers, and thus the almost certain murderers, were Watson's two friends. They were currently in the Ocean County, New Jersey jail, held without bail on a first-degree murder charge. Watson's body had been found buried in a shallow grave not far from Atlantic City, near where Jerome Nelson's stolen Jaguar had been abandoned. When the two had been arrested, they had been found in possession of Jerome Nelson's credit card, wristwatch, and ring. Other property stolen from Jerome Nelson's apartment had been located and tied to them, and their fingerprints had been all over the Jaguar.

The way Wohl put it together in his mind, the two critters being held in New Jersey had gotten the keys to the Nelson apartment from Watson, probably in exchange for a promise to split the burglary proceeds with him. Surprised to find Jerome Nelson at home, they had killed him. And then they had killed Watson to make sure that when the police found him, he couldn't implicate them.

But the two critters had availed themselves of their right under the *Miranda* Decision to have legal counsel. And their lawyer had pointed out to them that while they were probably going to be convicted of the murder of Watson, if they professed innocence of the Nelson robbery and murder, the Pennsylvania authorities didn't have either witnesses or much circumstantial evidence to try them with.

It was a statement of fact that sentences handed down to critters of whatever color for having murdered another critter tended to be less severe than those handed down to black men for having murdered a rich and socially prominent white man. And if the two critters in the Ocean County jail hadn't known this before the State of New Jersey provided them with free legal counsel, they knew it now.

Their story now was that they had met Watson riding around in a Jaguar, and bought certain merchandise he had for sale from him. They had last seen him safe and sound near the boardwalk in Atlantic City. They had no idea who had killed him, and they had absolutely no knowledge whatever of a man named Jerome Nelson, except that his had been the name on the credit card they bought from Errol Watson/Pierre St. Maury.

Ordinarily, it wouldn't have mattered. It would have been just one more sordid job in a long, long list of sordid jobs. The critters would have gone away, even if the New Jersey prosecutor had plea-bargained Watson's murder down to second-degree murder or even first-degree manslaughter. They would have gotten twenty-to-life, and the whole job would have been forgotten in a month.

But Jerome Nelson was not just one more victim. His father was Arthur J. Nelson, who owned the *Ledger,* and who had naturally assumed that when Mayor Jerry Carlucci and Police Commissioner Thaddeu Czernich had called on him immediately after the tragedy to assure him that the full resources of the Philadelphia Police Department would be brought to bear to bring whoever was responsible for this heinous crime against his son to justice, that the Police Department would naturally do what it could to spare the feelings of the victim's family. That, in other words, the sexual proclivities of the prime suspect, or his racial categorization, or that he had been sharing Jerome's apartment, would not come out.

Mayor Carlucci had seemed to be offering what Arthur J. Nelson had, as the publisher of a major newspaper, come to expect as his due: a little special treatment. Commissioner Czernich had even told Nelson that he had assigned one of the brightest police officers in the Department, Staff Inspector Peter Wohl, to oversee the detectives in the Homicide Division as they conducted their investigation, and to make sure that everything that could possibly be done was being done.

That hadn't happened.

Mr. Michael J. O'Hara, of the *Bulletin,* had fed several drinks to, and stroked the already outsized ego of, a Homicide Division Lieutenant named DelRaye, which had caused Lieutenant DelRaye to say something he probably would not have said had he been entirely sober. That resulted in a front-page, bylined story in the *Bulletin* announcing that "according to a senior police official involved in the investigation" the police were seeking Jerome Nelson's live-in lover, who happened to be a black homosexual, or words to that effect.

Once Mickey O'Hara's story had broken the dam, the other two major newspapers in Philadelphia, plus all the radio and television stations, had considered it their sacred journalistic duty to bring all the facts before the public.

Mrs. Arthur J. Nelson, who had always manifested some symptoms of nervous disorder, had had to be sent back to the Institute of Living, in Hartford, Connecticut, said to be the most expensive psychiatric hospital in the country, after it had come out, in all the media except the *Ledger,* that her only child had been cohabiting with a Negro homosexual.

Mr. Arthur J. Nelson had felt betrayed, not only by his fellow practitioners of journalism, but by the mayor and especially by the police. If that goddamned cop hadn't had diarrhea of the mouth, Jerome could have gone to his grave with some dignity, and his wife wouldn't be up in Hartford again.

Peter Wohl had been originally suspected by both Arthur J. Nelson and the mayor as the cop with the big mouth, but Commissioner Czernich had believed Wohl's denial, and found out himself, from Mickey O'Hara, that the loudmouth had been Lieutenant DelRaye.

When Mayor Carlucci had called Mr. Nelson to tell him that, and also that Lieutenant DelRaye had been relieved of his Homicide Division assignment and banished in disgrace—and in uniform—to a remote district; and also to tell him that Peter Wohl had been in on the arrest of the two suspects in Atlantic City, what had been intended as an offering of the olive branch had turned nasty. Both men had tempers, and things were said that could not be withdrawn.

And it had quickly become evident how Arthur J. Nelson intended to wage the war. Two days later, a young plainclothes Narcotics Division cop had caught up with Gerald Vincent Gallagher, the drug addict who had been involved in the shooting death of Captain Dutch Moffitt. It had been a front-page story in all the newspapers in Philadelphia, the stories generally reflecting support for the police, and relief that a drug-addict cop-killer had been run to ground. The *Ledger* had buried the story, although factually reported, far inside the paper. The *Ledger* editorial, headlined *"Vigilante Justice?"* implied that Gerald Vincent Gallagher, who had fallen to his death under the wheels of a subway train as he tried to escape the Narcotics cop, had instead been pushed in front of the train.

The most recent barrage had been the *"Jackbooted Gestapo"* editorial. Arthur J. Nelson wanted revenge, and apparently reasoned that since Mayor Carlucci had risen to political prominence through the ranks of the Police Department, a shot that wounded the cops also wounded Carlucci.

"What is he doing," Wohl asked, "putting me between him and the *Ledger?"*

"Peter, I think what you see is what you get," Coughlin said.

"What I see is me," Wohl said, "who hasn't worn a uniform or worked anywhere but headquarters in ten years being put in charge of Highway, and of something called ACT that I don't know a damned thing about. I don't even know what it's supposed to do."

"The mayor told the Commissioner he has every confidence that, within a short period of time—I think that means a couple of weeks—he will be able to call a press conference and announce that his Special Operations Division has arrested the sexual deviate who has been raping the decent women of Northwest Philadelphia."

"Rape is under the Detectives' Bureau," Wohl protested.

"So it is," Coughlin said. "Except that the Northwest Philly rapist is yours."

"So it *is* public relations."

"What it is, Peter, is what the mayor wants," Coughlin said.

"Matt Lowenstein will blow a blood vessel when he hears I'm working his territory."

"The Commissioner already told him," Coughlin said. "Give up, Peter. You can't fight this."

"Who's in ACT? What kind of resources am I going to find there?"

"I've sent you three people," Coughlin said, "to get you started. Officers Martinez and McFadden. They've been ordered to report to you at eight tomorrow morning."

Officer Charley McFadden was the plainclothes Narc the *Ledger* had as much as accused of pushing Gerald Vincent Gallagher in front of the subway train; Officer Jesus Martinez had been his partner.

Wohl considered that for a moment, then said, "You said three?"

"And Officer Matthew Payne," Coughlin said. "Dutch's nephew. You met him."

After a moment, Wohl said, "Why Payne? Is he through the Academy?"

"I had a hunch, Peter," Coughlin said, "that Matt Payne will be of more value to you, and thus to the Department, than he would be if we had sent him to one of the districts."

"I'm surprised he stuck it out at the Academy," Wohl said.

"I wasn't," Coughlin said, flatly.

"What are you talking about? Using him undercover?" Wohl asked.

"Maybe," Coughlin said. "We don't get many rookies like him. Something will come up."

"The only orders I really have are to do something about this rapist?" Wohl asked.

"Your orders are to get the Special Operations Division up and running. That means trying to keep Highway from giving the *Ledger* an excuse to call them the Gestapo. And it means getting ACT up and running. There's a Sergeant, a smart young guy named Eddy Frizell, in Staff Services, who's been handling all the paperwork for ACT. The Federal Grant applications, what kind of money, where it's supposed to be used, that sort of thing. I called down there just before you came in and told him to move himself and his files out to Highway. He'll probably be there before you get there. Czernich told Whelan to give you whatever you think you need in terms of equipment and money, from the contingency fund, to be reimbursed when the Federal Grant comes in. Frizell should be able to tell you what you need."

"The mayor expects me to catch the rapist," Wohl said, and paused.

"That's your first priority."

"Who am I supposed to use to do that? Those kids from Narcotics?" He saw a flash of annoyance, even anger, on Coughlin's face. "Sorry, Chief," he added quickly. "I didn't mean for that to sound the way it came out."

"The initial manning for ACT is forty cops, plus four each Corporals, Sergeants, and Lieutenants; a Captain, four Detectives, and of course, you," Coughlin said. "I already sent a teletype asking for volunteers to transfer in. You can pick whoever you want."

"And if nobody volunteers? Or if all the volunteers are guys one step ahead of being assigned to rubber gun squad or being sent to the farm in their districts?"

Coughlin chuckled. "Being sent to the farm" was the euphemism for alcoholic officers being sent off to dry out; the rubber gun squad was for officers whose peers did not think they could be safely entrusted with a real one.

"Then you can pick, within reason, anybody you want," Coughlin said. "Making this thing work is important to the mayor; therefore to Czernich and me. You're not going to give me trouble about this, Peter, are you?"

"No, of course not, Chief," Wohl said. "It just came out of the blue, and it's taking some getting used to."

Chief Coughlin stood up and put out his hand.

"You can handle this, Peter," Coughlin said. "Congratulations and good luck."

He had, Peter Wohl realized as he put out his hand to take Coughlin's, not only been dismissed but given all the direction he was going to get.

"Thank you, Chief," he said.

Wohl went to the parking lot, opened the door of his car, and rolled down the windows, standing outside a moment until some of the heat could escape. Then he got in and started the engine, and turned on the air conditioner. He cranked up the window and shifted into reverse.

Then he changed his mind. He reached over to the glove compartment and took out the microphone.

"Radio, S-Sam One Oh One," he said.

"S-Sam One Oh One, Radio," Police Radio replied. They didn't seem at all surprised to hear the new call sign, Wohl thought.

"Have you got a location on Highway One?" Wohl asked.

The reply was almost immediate: "Out of service at Highway."

"What about N-Two?" Wohl asked, guessing that Dave Pekach, who was, now that he had been promoted, the second-ranking man in Narcotics, would be using that call sign.

"Also out of service at Highway, S-Sam One Oh One," Police Radio replied.

"If either of them come back on the air, ask them to meet me at Highway. Thank you, Radio," Wohl said, and put the microphone back in the glove compartment. Then he backed out of the parking space and headed for Highway Patrol headquarters.

Elizabeth Joan Woodham did not like to be called "Woody" as most of her friends did. She thought of herself as too tall, and skinny, and somewhat awkward, and thus "wooden."

She was, in fact, five feet ten and one-half inches tall. She weighed 135 pounds, which her doctor had told her was just about right for her. She thought she had the choice between weighing 135, which she was convinced made her look skinny, and putting on weight, which would, she thought, make her a large woman.

She thought she had a better chance of attracting the right kind of man as a skinny woman. Large women, she believed, sort of intimidated men. Elizabeth J. Woodham, who was thirty-three, had not completely given up the hope that she would finally meet some decent man with whom she could develop a relationship. But she had read a story in *Time* that gave statistics suggesting that the odds were against her. Apparently someone had taken the time to develop statistics showing that, starting at age thirty, a woman's chances of ever marrying began to sharply decline. By age thirty-five, a woman's chances were remote indeed, and by forty practically neglible.

She had come to accept lately that what she wanted, really, was a child, rather than a man. She wondered if she really wanted to share her life with a man. Sometimes, in her apartment, she conjured up a man living there with her, making demands on her time, on her body, confiscating her space.

The man was a composite of the three lovers she had had in her life, and she sometimes conjured him up in two ways. One was a man who had all the attractive attributes of her three lovers, including the physical aspects, rolled into one. The other man had all the unpleasant attributes of her lovers, which had ultimately caused her to break off the relationships.

The conjured-up good man was most often the lover she had had for two and a half years, a kind, gentle man with whom the physical aspects of the relationship had been really very nice, but who had had one major flaw: he was married, and she had gradually come to understand that he was never going to leave his wife and children; and that in fact his wife was not the unfeeling and greedy bitch he had painted, but rather someone like herself, who must have known he was playing around when he came home regularly so late, and suffered through it in the belief that it was her wifely duty; or because of the children; or because she believed practically any man was better than no man at all.

Elizabeth had decided, at the time she broke off the relationship, that it was better to have no man at all than one who was sleeping around.

Elizabeth Woodham, during the winters, taught the sixth grade at the Olney Elementary School at Taber Road and Water Street. This summer, more for something to do than for the money, she had taken a job as a storyteller with the Philadelphia Public Library system, the idea being that the way to get the kids to read was to convince them that something interesting was between the covers of a book; and the way to do that was by gathering them together and telling them stories.

If it also served to keep them off the streets at night, so much the better. Mayor Carlucci had gotten a Federal Grant for the program, and Elizabeth Woodham, the Project Administrator had told her when she applied for the job, was just the sort of person she had hoped to attract.

The hours were from three to nine, with an hour off for dinner. Elizabeth usually got to the playground at two, to set things up and attract a crowd for the three-thirty story hour for the smaller children. The story "hour" almost always ran more than an hour, usually two. She kept it up until she sensed her charges were growing restless. And she took a sort of professional pride in keeping their attention up as long as she could, scrupulously stopping when they showed the first signs of boredom, but taking pride in keeping it longer than you were supposed to be able to keep it.

The playground was on East Godfrey Avenue in Olney. West Godfrey Avenue becomes East Godfrey when it crosses Front Street. It is close to the city line, Cheltenham Avenue. East Godfrey is a dead-end street. A playground runs for two blocks off it to the south, down to where Champlost Avenue turns north and becomes Crescentville Avenue, which forms the western boundary of Tacony Creek Park.

The evening story hour was at seven-thirty, and was thus supposed to be over at eight-thirty, to give Elizabeth time to close things up before the park was locked for the night at nine.

But she'd managed to prolong the expected attention span and it was close to nine before she had told the kids the story of *The Hound of the Baskervilles,* and sown, she hoped, the idea that there were more stories by A. Conan Doyle about Sherlock Holmes and Dr. Watson available in the public library.

It was thus a few minutes after nine when she left the park and walked down East Godfrey Avenue toward where she had parked her car, a two-year-old Plymouth coupe.

"If you scream, I'll cut off your boobies right here," the man with the black mask covering his face said as he pulled Elizabeth J. Woodham through the side door of a van.

Barbara Crowley, a tall, lithe woman of twenty-six, entered Bookbinder's Restaurant at Second and Walnut streets and looked around the main dining room until she spotted Peter Wohl, who was sitting at a table with an older couple. Then she walked quickly across the room to the table.

Peter Wohl saw her coming and got up.

"Sorry I'm late," Barbara Crowley said.

"We understand, dear," the older woman said, extending her cheek to be kissed. She was a thin, tall woman with silver gray hair simply cut, wearing a flower-print dress. She was Mrs. Olga Wohl, Peter Wohl's mother. It was her birthday. The older man, larger and heavier than Peter, with a florid face, was his father, Chief Inspector (Retired) August Wohl.

"How are you, Barbara?" Chief Wohl said, getting half out of his chair to smile at her and offer his hand.

"Bushed," Barbara Crowley said. As she sat down, she put her purse in her lap, opened it, and removed a small tissue-wrapped package. She handed it to Olga Wohl. "Happy birthday!"

"Oh, you shouldn't have!" Olga Wohl said, beaming, as she tore off the tissue. Underneath was a small box bearing the *Bailey, Banks & Biddle, Jewelers, Philadelphia* logotype. Olga Wohl opened it and took out a silver compact.

"Oh, this is too much," Olga Wohl said, repeating, "You shouldn't have, dear."

"If you mean that, Mother," Peter said, "she can probably get her money back."

His father chuckled; his mother gave him a withering look.

"It's just beautiful," she said, and leaned across to Barbara Crowley and kissed her cheek. "Thank you very much."

"She doesn't look seventy, does she?" Peter asked, innocently.

"I'm fifty-seven," Olga Wohl said, "still young enough to slap a fresh mouth if I have to."

August Wohl laughed.

"Watch it, Peter," he said.

"So how was your day?" Barbara asked, looking at Peter.

"You mean aside from getting my picture in the papers?" Peter asked.

"What?" Barbara asked, confused.

A waiter appeared, carrying a wine cooler on a three-legged stand.

"Peter was promoted," Olga Wohl said. "You didn't see the paper?"

"I don't think 'promoted,' " Peter said. " 'Reassigned.' "

The waiter, with what Peter thought was an excessive amount of theatrics, unwrapped the towel around the bottle, showed Peter the label, uncorked the bottle, and poured a little in a glass for his approval.

"I didn't see the paper," Barbara said.

"Mother just happens to have one with her," Peter said, and then, after sipping the wine, said to the waiter, "That's fine, thank you."

The waiter poured wine in everyone's glass and then rewrapped the bottle in its towel as Olga Wohl took a folded newspaper from her purse, a large leather affair beside her chair, and handed it to Barbara Crowley. The story was on the front page, on the lower right-hand side, beside an old photograph of Peter Wohl. The caption line below the photograph said, simply, "P. Wohl."

POLICE ORGANIZATION
RESHUFFLED

By Cheryl Davies
Bulletin Staff Writer

Police Commissioner Thaddeu Czernich today announced the formation of a new division, to be called Special Operations, within the Philadelphia Police Department. Although Czernich denied the reshuffling has anything to do with recent press criticism of some police operations, knowledgeable observers believe this to be the case.

Highway Patrol, the elite police unit sometimes known as "Carlucci's Commandos," which has been the subject of much recent criticism, has been placed under the new Special Operations Division, which will be commanded by Inspector Peter Wohl. Captain Michael J. Sabara, who had been in temporary command of the Highway Patrol since Captain Richard C. Moffitt was shot and killed, was named as Wohl's deputy. Captain David S. Pekach, who had been assigned to the Narcotics Bureau, was named to command the Highway Patrol.

Inspector Wohl, who was previously assigned to the Special Investigations Division, and Pekach are little known outside the police department, but are regarded by insiders as "straight arrows," officers who go by the book, lending further credence to the theory that the reorganization is intended to tame the Highway Patrol, and lessen press criticism of its alleged excesses. One Philadelphia newspaper recently editorialized that the Highway Patrol was acting like the Gestapo.

The new Special Operations Division will also have under its wing a special, federally funded, yet-to-be-formed unit called Anti-Crime Teams (ACT). According to Commissioner Czernich, specially trained and equipped ACT teams will be sent to high-crime areas in Philadelphia as needed to augment existing Police resources.

"That's very nice," Barbara said. Peter Wohl snorted derisively. "Congratulations, Peter." Peter snorted again. "Am I missing something?" Barbara asked, confused. "What's wrong with it?"

"I'm a Staff Inspector, for one thing," Peter said. "Not an Inspector."

"Well, so what? That's a simple mistake. She didn't know any better."

"For another, there's a pretty clear implication in there that Highway has been doing something wrong, and they haven't, and that Mike Sabara, who is a really good cop, didn't get Highway because he's involved with what's wrong with it."

"Why didn't he get it?"

"Because the mayor thinks he looks like a concentration camp guard," Peter said.

"Really?" Barbara said.

"Really," Peter said. "And I wasn't sent over there to 'tame' Highway, either."

"But Carlucci will be very pleased if you can keep the newspapers from calling it the Gestapo," Chief Inspector August Wohl said.

"Only one newspaper's doing that, Dad," Peter replied, "and you know why."

"*I* don't," Barbara said.

"Arthur J. Nelson, who owns the *Ledger,* has got it in for the police," Peter said, "because it got out that his son, the one who was murdered—Jerome?—was a homosexual."

"Oh," Barbara said. "How did it get out?"

"A cop who should have known better told Mickey O'Hara," Peter said. "Not that it wouldn't have come out inevitably, but he blames the Police."

Barbara considered that a moment, and then decided to change the subject: "Well, what are you going to do over there, anyway?" she asked.

"He's the commanding officer," Olga Wohl said, a touch of pride in her voice.

"You asked me how my day was," Peter said, dryly.

"Yes, I did."

"Well, I went over to my new *command,*" he said, wryly, "about four-thirty. Special Operations will operate out of what until this morning was Highway Patrol headquarters, at Bustleton and Bowler. Three people were waiting for me. Captain Mike Sabara, his chin on his knees, because until this morning, he thought he was going to get Highway; Captain Dave Pekach, who had his chin on his knees because he's got the idea that somebody doesn't like him; *because* they gave *him* Highway—in other words he thinks he's being thrown to the wolves; and a sergeant named Ed Frizell, from Staff Planning, whose chin is on his knees because when he dreamed up this ACT thing it never entered his mind that he would be involved in it—banished, so to speak, in disgrace from his office in the Roundhouse to the boondocks, forced to wear a uniform and consort with ordinary cops, and possibly even have to go out and arrest people."

Chief Wohl chuckled.

"And then I went to the Highway roll call," Peter went on. *"That* was fun."

"I don't understand, dear," his mother said.

"Well, I was practicing good leadership techniques," Peter said. "I thought I was being clever as hell. I got there, and made my little speech. I was proud to be back in Highway, as I was sure Captain Pekach was. I said that I had always thought of Highway as the most efficient unit in the Department, and felt sure it would stay that way. I even included the standard lines that my door was always open, and that I looked forward to working with them."

"What's wrong with that?" Barbara asked.

"Well, I didn't know that they thought I was the SOB who took Highway away from Mike Sabara, who everybody likes, and gave it to Pekach, who nobody in Highway likes."

"Why don't they like Pekach?" Chief Wohl asked. "I thought he was a pretty good cop. And from what I hear, he did a good job in Narcotics. And he came out of Highway."

"He did a great job in Narcotics," Peter said. "But what I didn't know—and it was my fault I didn't—was that the *one* time a Highway cop got arrested for drugs, Dave Pekach was the one who arrested him."

"The Sergeant? About a year ago?" Chief Wohl asked, and Peter nodded.

"I knew about that," Chief Wohl said, "but I didn't know Pekach was involved."

"And I hadn't seen Miss Cheryl Davies's clever little newspaper article, and they had," Peter went on, "so my attempt at practicing the best principles of command left the indelible impression on my new command that I am a fool or a liar, or both."

"Oh, Peter," his mother said. "You don't know that!"

"I know cops, Mother," Peter said. "I know what those guys were thinking."

"If they think that now, they'll come to know better," Barbara said, loyally.

"Would you care to order now?" the waiter asked.

"Yes, please," Peter said. "I'm going to have something hearty. That's traditional for condemned men."

Chief Wohl chuckled again. Barbara leaned across the table and put her hand on Peter's. Mrs. Wohl smiled at them.

They were on dessert when the manager called Peter to the telephone.

"Inspector Wohl," Peter said.

"Lieutenant Jackson, sir," the caller said. "You said you wanted to be notified when anything came up."

Wohl now placed the name and face. His caller was the Highway Tour Commander on duty.

"What's up, Jackson?"

"We got a pretty bad wreck, I'm afraid. Highway Sixteen was going in on a call and hit a civilian broadside. At Second and Olney."

"Anybody hurt?"

"Both of our guys were injured," Jackson said, reluctance in his voice. "One of the passengers in the civilian car is dead; two others are pretty badly injured."

"My God!"

"It was a little boy that got killed, Inspector," Jackson said.

"Jesus H. Christ!" Wohl said. "Has Captain Pekach been notified?"

"Yes, sir."

"You say they were answering a call?"

"Yes, sir," Jackson said. "They went in on a call to the Thirty-fifth District. Somebody saw a woman being forced into a van by a guy with a knife at Front and Godfrey, one of the apartment buildings. In the parking lot."

"Where are you?"

"At the scene, sir."

"What scene, the wreck or the kidnapping?"

"The wreck, sir. I sent Sergeant Paster to the kidnapping."

"Get on the radio, and tell Captain Pekach I said for him to handle the wreck, and then tell Sergeant—"

"Paster, sir," Lieutenant Jackson furnished.

"Tell Sergeant Paster to meet me at the scene of the kidnapping," Wohl said.

"Yes, sir."

Wohl hung up without saying anything else.

He found the manager and arranged to settle the bill before returning to the table.

"A Highway car hit a civilian," he said, looking at his father. "A little boy is dead."

"Oh, God!" his father said.

"They were going in on a Thirty-fifth District call," Peter said. "Someone reported a woman being forced into a van at knifepoint. I've got to go."

His father nodded his understanding.

Peter looked at Barbara. "Sorry," he said. "And I don't know how long this will take."

"I understand," she said. "No problem, I've got my car."

"And I'm sorry to have to walk out on your party, Mother."

"Don't be silly, dear," she said. "At least you got to eat your dinner."

"I'll call you," he said, and walked quickly out of the restaurant.

You are a prick, Peter Wohl, he thought, as he walked through the parking lot. *A little boy has been killed and a woman has been kidnapped, and your reaction to all this is that you are at least spared the problem of how to handle Barbara.*

Until Dutch Moffitt had gotten himself killed, everybody concerned had been under the impression that he and Barbara had an *understanding,* which was a half-step away from a formal engagement to be married. But the witness to the shooting of Captain Moffitt had been a female, specifically a stunning, long-legged, long-haired, twenty-five-year-old blonde named Louise Dutton, who was co-anchor of WCBL-TV's "Nine's News."

Less than twenty-four hours after he had met Louise Dutton in the line of duty, they had been making the beast with two backs in his apartment, and Peter had been convinced that he had finally embarked on the Great Romance of his life. And for a little while, the Grand Passion had seemed reciprocal, but then there had been, on Louise's part, a little sober consideration of the situation.

She had asked herself a simple question: "Can a talented, ambitious young television anchor whose father just happens to own a half dozen television stations around the country find lasting happiness in the arms of an underpaid cop in Philadelphia?"

The answer was no. Louise Dutton was now working for a television station in Chicago, one that not coincidentally happened to be owned by her father—who, Peter understood, while he liked Peter *personally,* did not see him as the father of his grandchildren.

There was no question in Peter's mind that Barbara knew about Louise, and not only because he had covered Dutch's ass one last time by telling the Widow Moffitt that Dutch could not have been fooling around with Louise Dutton because she was his, Peter's, squeeze. That he was "involved" with Louise Dutton had been pretty common knowledge around the Department; even Chief Coughlin knew about it. Barbara had two uncles and two brothers in the Department. Peter had known them all his life, and there is no human being more self-righteous than a brother who hears that some sonofabitch is running around on his baby sister. Barbara knew, all right.

But Barbara had decided to forgive him. Her presence at his mother's birthday dinner proved that. He had called her twice, post-Louise, and both times she hadn't "been able" to have dinner or go to a movie with him. He would not have been surprised if she hadn't "been able" to have dinner with him and his parents, but she'd accepted that invitation. And there wasn't much of a mystery about how she planned to handle the problem: she was going to pretend it didn't exist, and never had.

And when her knee found his under the table, he had understood that after they had said good night to his parents, they would go either to his apartment or hers, and get in bed, and things would be back to normal.

The problem was that Peter wasn't sure he wanted to pick things up where they had been, pre-Louise. He told himself that he had either been a fool, or been made a fool of, or both; that Barbara Crowley was not only a fine woman, but just what he needed; that he should be grateful for her tolerance and understanding; that if he had any brains, he would be grateful for the opportunity she was offering; and that he should manifest his gratitude by taking a solemn, if private, vow never to stray again from the boundaries of premarital fidelity.

But when he had looked at Barbara, he had thought of Louise, and that had destroyed 90 percent of his urge to take Barbara to bed.

He got in his car, started the engine, and then thought of Mike Sabara.

"Jesus!" he said.

He reached into the glove compartment and took out the microphone.

"Radio, S-Sam One Oh One," he said. "Have you got a location on S-Sam One Oh Two?"

After a longer than usual pause, Police Radio replied that S-Sam One Oh Two was not in service.

Peter thought that over a moment. If he and Pekach had been informed of the crash, Sabara certainly had. And Sabara was probably still using his old radio call, Highway Two, for the number two man in Highway.

"Radio, how about Highway Two?"

"Highway Two is at Second and Olney Avenue."

"Radio, please contact Highway Two and have him meet S-Sam One Oh One at Front and Godfrey Avenue. Let me know if you get through to him."

"Yes, sir. Stand by, please."

I'm going to have to get another band in here, Peter thought, as he backed out of the parking space. *Bands. I'm going to have to get Highway and Detective, too.*

Every Police vehicle was equipped with a shortwave radio that permitted communication on two bands: the J-Band and one other, depending on what kind of car it was. Cars assigned to the Detective Bureau, for example, could communicate on the J-Band and on H-Band, the Detective Band. Cars assigned to a District could communicate on the J-Band and on a frequency assigned to that District. Peter's car had the J-Band and the Command Band, limited to the Commissioner, the Chief Inspector, the Inspectors, and the Staff Inspectors.

He was six blocks away from Bookbinder's Restaurant when Radio called him.

"S-Sam One Oh One, Radio."

"Go ahead."

"Highway Two wants to know if you are aware of the traffic accident at Second and Olney Avenue."

"Tell Highway Two I know about it, and ask him to meet me at Front and Godfrey."

"Yes, sir," Radio replied.

Peter put the microphone back in the glove compartment and slammed it shut.

Now Sabara, who had very naturally rushed to a scene of trouble involving "his" Highway Patrol, was going to be pissed.

It can't be helped, Peter thought. *Mike's going to have to get it through his head that Highway is now Pekach's.*

When Matthew Payne walked into the kitchen of the house on Providence Road in Wallingford, he was surprised to find his father standing at the stove, watching a slim stream of coffee gradually filling a glass pot under a Krups coffee machine.

"Good morning," his father said. He was wearing a light cotton bathrobe, too short for him, and a pair of leather bedroom slippers. "I heard you in the shower and thought you could probably use some coffee."

"Can I!" Matt replied. He was dressed in a button-down-collar shirt and gray slacks. His necktie was tied, but the collar button was open, and the knot an inch below it. He had a seersucker jacket in his hand. When he laid it on the kitchen table—of substantial, broad-planked pine, recently refinished after nearly a century of service—there was a heavy thump.

"What have you got in there?" Brewster C. Payne asked, surprised.

"My gun," Matt said, raising the jacket to show a Smith & Wesson Military & Police Model .38 Special revolver in a shoulder holster. "What every well-dressed young man is wearing these days."

Brewster Payne chuckled.

"You're not wearing your new blue suit, I notice," he said.

"He said, curiosity oozing from every pore," Matt said, gently mockingly.

"Well, we haven't had the pleasure of your company recently," his father said, unabashed.

"I communed with John Barleycorn last night," Matt said, "at Rose Tree. I decided it was wiser by far to spend the night here than try to make it to the apartment. Particularly since the bug is one-eyed."

"Anything special, or just kicking up your heels?" Brewster Payne asked.

"I don't know, Dad," Matt said, as he took two ceramic mugs from a cabinet and set them on the counter beside the coffee machine. "All I know is that I had more to drink than I should have had."

"You want something to eat?" Brewster Payne asked, and when he saw the look on Matt's face, added, "If you've been at the grape, you should put something in your stomach. Did you have dinner?"

"I don't think so," Matt replied. "The last thing I remember clearly is peanuts at the bar."

His father went to the refrigerator, a multidoored stainless steel device filling one end of the room. He opened one door after another until he found what he was looking for.

"How about a Taylor ham sandwich? Maybe with an egg?"

"I'll make it," Matt said. "No *egg.*"

Brewster Payne chuckled again, and said, "You were telling me what you were celebrating. . . ."

"No, I wasn't," Matt said. "You're a pretty good interrogator. You ever consider practicing law? Or maybe becoming a cop?"

"Touché," Brewster Payne said.

"I was on the pistol range yesterday," Matt said, "when Chief Matdorf, who runs the Police Academy, came out and told me to clean out my locker and report tomorrow morning, this morning, that is, at eight o'clock, to the commanding officer of Highway Patrol." He paused and then added, "In plainclothes."

"What's that all about?" Brewster Payne said.

"John Barleycorn didn't say," Matt said. "Although I had a long, long chat with him."

"You think Dennis Coughlin is involved?"

"Uncle Denny's involved in everything," Matt said as he put butter in a frying pan. "You want one of these?"

"Please," Brewster Payne said. "Were you having any trouble in the academy?"

"No, not so far as I know."

"Highway Patrol is supposed to be the elite unit within the Department," Brewster Payne said. "You think you're getting special treatment, is that it?"

"Special, yeah, but I don't know what kind of special," Matt said. "To get into Highway, you usually need three years in the Department, and then there's a long waiting list. It's all volunteer, and I didn't volunteer. And then, why in plainclothes?"

"Possibly it has something to do with ACT," Brewster Payne said.

"With what?"

"ACT," Brewster Payne said. "It means Anti-Crime Team, or something like that. It was in the paper yesterday. A new unit. You didn't see it?"

"No, I didn't," Matt said. "Is the paper still around here?"

"It's probably in the garbage," Brewster Payne said.

Matt left the stove and went outside. His father shook his head and took over frying the Taylor ham.

"It's a little soggy," Matt called a moment later, "but I can read it."

He reappeared in the kitchen with a grease-stained sheet of newspaper. When he laid it on the table, his father picked it up and read the story again.

"May I redispose of this?" he asked, when he had finished, holding the newspaper distastefully between his fingers.

"Sorry," Matt said. "That offers a lot of food for thought," he added. "This ACT, whatever it is, makes more sense than putting me in Highway. But it still smacks of special treatment."

"I think you're going to have to get used to that."

"What do you mean?"

"How many of your peers in the Academy had gone to college?" Brewster Payne asked.

"Not very many," Matt said.

"And even fewer had gone on to graduate?"

"So?"

"Would it be reasonable to assume that you were the only member of your class with a degree? A cum laude degree?"

"You think that's it, that I have a degree?"

"That's part of it, I would guess," Brewster Payne said. "And then there's Dennis Coughlin."

"I think that has more to do with this than my degree," Matt said.

"Dennis Coughlin was your father's best friend," Brewster C. Payne said. "And he never had a son; I'm sure he looks at you in that connection, the son he never had."

"I never thought about that," Matt said. "I wonder why he never got married?"

"I thought you knew," Brewster Payne said, after a moment. "He was in love with your mother."

"And she picked you over him?" Matt said, genuinely surprised. "I never heard that before."

"He never told her; I don't think she ever suspected. Not then, anyway. But I knew. I knew the first time I ever met him."

"Jesus!" Matt said.

"Would you like to hear my theory—theories—about this mysterious assignment of yours?"

"Sure."

"I think Dennis Coughlin is about as happy about you being a policeman as I am; that is to say he doesn't like it one little bit. He's concerned for your welfare. He doesn't want to have to get on the telephone and tell your mother that you've been hurt, or worse. Theory One is that you are really going to go to Highway. Dennis hopes that you will hate it; realize the error of your decision, and resign. Theory Two, which will stand by itself, or may be a continuation of Theory One, is that if you persist in being a policeman, the best place for you to learn the profession is from its most skilled practitioners, the Highway Patrol generally, and under Inspector Wohl. I found it interesting that Wohl was given command of this new Special Operations Division. Even I know that he's one of the brightest people in the Police Department, a real comer."

"I met him the night of Uncle Dutch's wake," Matt said. "In a bar. When I told him that I was thinking of joining the department, he told me I would think better of it in the morning; that it was the booze talking."

"Theory Three," Brewster Payne said, "or perhaps Two (a), is that Dennis has sent you to Wohl, with at least an indication on his part that he would be pleased if Wohl could ease you out of the Police Department with your ego intact."

Matt considered that a moment, then exhaled audibly. "Well, I won't know, will I, until I get there?"

"No, I suppose not."

Matt wolfed down his Taylor ham on toast, then started to put on his shoulder holster.

"They issue you that holster?" Brewster Payne asked.

"No, I bought it a week or so ago," Matt said. "When I wear a belt holster under a jacket, it stands out like a sore thumb."

"What about getting a smaller gun?"

"You can't do that until you pass some sort of examination, qualify with it," Matt said. "I wasn't that far along in the Academy when I was—I suppose the word is 'graduated.' "

"There's something menacing about it," Brewster Payne said.

"It's also heavy," Matt said. "I'm told that eventually you get used to it, and feel naked if you don't have it." He shrugged into the seersucker jacket. "Now," he said, smiling. "No longer menacing."

"Unseen, but still menacing," his father responded, then changed the subject. "You said you were having headlight trouble with the bug?"

The bug, a Volkswagen, then a year old, had been Matt Payne's sixteenth-birthday present, an award for making the Headmaster's List at Episcopal Academy.

"I don't know what the hell is the matter with it; there's a short somewhere. More likely a break. Whenever I start out to fix it, it works fine. It only gives me trouble at night."

"There is, I seem to recall, another car in the garage," Brewster Payne said. "On which, presumably, both headlights function as they should."

The other car was a silver, leather-upholstered Porsche 911T, brand new, presented to Matthew Payne on the occasion of his graduation, cum laude, from the University of Pennsylvania.

"Very tactfully phrased," Matt said. "Said the ungrateful giftee."

He had not driven the Porsche to Philadelphia, or hardly at all, since he had joined the police department.

His father read his mind: "You're afraid, Matt, that it will ... set you apart?"

"Oddly enough, I was thinking about the Porsche just now," Matt said. "Hung for a sheep as a lion, so to speak."

"I think you have that wrong; it's sheep and lamb, not lion," Brewster Payne replied, "but I take your point."

"I am being—what was it you said?—being 'set apart' as it is," Matt said. "Why not?"

"I really do understand, Matt."

"If I am sexually assaulted by one or more sex-crazed females driven into a frenzy when they see me in that car. . . ."

"What?" his father, asked, chuckling.

"I'll tell you how it was," Matt said, and smiled, and went out of the kitchen, pausing for a moment to throw an affectionate arm around Brewster C. Payne.

Payne, sipping his coffee, went to the kitchen window and watched as Matt opened one of the four garage doors, then emerged a moment later behind the wheel of the Porsche.

He should not be a policemen, he thought. *He should be in law school. Or doing almost anything else.*

Matt Payne tooted "Shave and a Haircut, Two Bits" on the Porsche's horn, and then headed down the driveway.

10 Officers Jesus Martinez and Charles McFadden arrived together, in Officer McFadden's Volkswagen, at Highway Patrol headquarters at quarter to eight, determined to be on time and otherwise to make a good first impression. They were both wearing business suits and ties, McFadden a faintly plaided single-breasted brown suit, and Martinez a sharply tailored double-breasted blue pinstripe.

He looked, McFadden accused him, not far off the mark, like a successful numbers operator on his way to a wedding.

The available parking spaces around the relatively new building were all full. There were a row of Highway motorcycles parked, neatly, as if in a military organization, at an angle with their rear wheels close to the building; and a row of Highway radio cars, some blue-and-whites identifiable by the lettering on their fenders, and some, unmarked, by their extra radio antennae and black-walled high-speed tires.

There were also the blue-and-whites assigned to the Seventh District, the Seventh District's unmarked cars, and several new-model cars, which could have belonged to any of the department's senior officers.

And there was a battered Chevrolet, festooned with radio antennae, parked in a spot identified by a sign as being reserved for Inspectors.

"That's Mickey O'Hara's car," Charley McFadden said. "I wonder what he's doing here?"

"There was a woman kidnapped last night," Hay-zus said. "It was on the radio."

"Kidnapped?" McFadden asked.

"Couple of people saw some nut forcing her into a van, with a knife," Hay-zus said.

They had driven through the parking area without having found a spot to park. McFadden drove halfway down the block, made a U-turn, and found a parking spot at the curb.

"That's *abducting,*" McFadden said.

"What?"

"What you said was kidnapping was abducting," McFadden said. "Kidnapping is when there's ransom."

"Screw you," Hay-zus said, in a friendly manner, and then, "Hey, look at them wheels!"

A silver Porsche was coming out of the parking lot, apparently after having made the same fruitless search for a place to park they had.

"I'd hate to have to pay insurance on a car like that," McFadden said.

"You got enough money to buy a car like that, you don't have to worry about how much insurance costs," Hay-zus said.

Both of them followed the car as it drove down Bowler Street past them.

"I know that guy," Charley McFadden said. "I seen him someplace."

"Really? Where?"

"I don't know, but I know that face."

Jesus Martinez looked at his watch, a gold-cased Hamilton with a gold bracelet and diamond chips on the face instead of numbers, and on which he owed eighteen (of twenty-four) payments at Zale's Credit Jewelers.

"Let's go in," he said. "It's ten of."

McFadden, not without effort, worked himself out from under the Volkswagen's steering wheel, then broke into a slow shuffle to catch up with Martinez.

They went into the building through a door off the parking lot, through which they could see Highway Patrolmen entering.

They looked for and found the to-be-expected window counter opening on the squad room. A Corporal was leaning on the counter, filling out a form. They waited until he was through, and looked at them curiously.

"We were told to report to the Commanding Officer of Highway at eight," Hay-zus said.

"You're a police officer?" the Corporal asked, doubtfully.

"Yeah, we're cops," Charley McFadden said.

"I know you," the Corporal said. "You're the guy who ran down the shit who was the doer in Captain Moffitt's shooting."

McFadden almost blushed.

"*We* were," he said, nodding at Martinez. "This is my partner, Hay-zus Martinez."

"What do you want to see the Captain about? The reason I ask is that he's busy as hell right now; I don't know when he'll be free."

"Beats me," McFadden said. "We was told to report to him at eight."

"Well, have a seat. When he's free, I'll tell him you're here. There's a coffee machine and a garbage machine around the corner." He pointed.

"Thanks," Charley said, and walked around the corner to the machines, not asking Hay-zus if he wanted anything. Hay-zus was a food freak; he didn't eat anything that had preservatives in it, or drink anything with chemical stimulants in it, like coffee, which had caffeine, or Coke, which had sugar and God only knows what other poison for the body.

When Charley returned, a minute or two later, holding a Mounds bar in one hand and a can of Coke in the other, Hay-zus nodded his head toward the counter. The guy they had seen in the Porsche, the one Charley said he knew from someplace, was talking to the Corporal. As Charley watched, he turned and headed for where Hay-zus was sitting on one of the row of battered folding metal chairs.

Charley walked over and sat down, and then leaned over Hay-zus.

"Don't I know you from somewheres?"

"Is your name McFadden?" Matt Payne asked.

"Yeah."

"I was at your house the night you got Gerald Vincent Gallagher."

"You were?" Charley asked. "I don't remember that."

"I was there with Chief Coughlin," Matt said. "And Sergeant Lenihan."

"Oh, yeah, I remember now," Charley said, although he did not. "How are you?"

"Fine," Matt said. "Yourself?"

There was a sort of stir as someone else came through the door from the parking lot. Matt recognized Peter Wohl; he wondered if Wohl would recognize him.

Wohl recognized all three of the young men on the folding metal chairs. He gave them a nod, and kept walking toward his office.

God damn it, you're a commanding officer now. Act like one.

He turned and walked to the three of them, his hand extended first to Martinez.

"How are you, Martinez?" he said, and turned before Martinez, who wasn't quite sure of Wohl's identity, could reply. "And McFadden. How's it going? And you're Payne, right?"

"Yes, sir."

"I'll be with you as soon as I'm free," Wohl said. "The way things are going, that may be a while."

"Yes, sir," McFadden and Martinez said, having found their voices.

Wohl then walked across the room and through the door to his outer office. Three people were in it: a Highway Sergeant, who had been Dutch Moffitt's Sergeant, then Mike Sabara's, and was *not* Dave Pekach's; Sergeant Eddy Frizell, in uniform, and looking a little sloppy compared to the Highway Sergeant; and Michael J. O'Hara, of the *Bulletin*.

The Highway Sergeant got to his feet when he saw Wohl, and after a moment, Frizell followed suit.

"Good morning, Inspector," the Highway Sergeant said.

"Good morning," Wohl said. "What do you say, Mickey? You waiting to see somebody?"

"You," O'Hara said.

"Well, then, come on in," Wohl said. "You can watch me drink a cup of coffee." He turned to look at the Highway Sergeant. "There *is* coffee?"

"Yes, sir," the Sergeant said. "Sir, Chief Coughlin wants you to phone as soon as you get in."

"Get me and Mickey a cup of coffee, and then get the Chief on the line," Wohl ordered.

Captains Sabara and Pekach were in what until yesterday had been the office of the Commanding Officer of Highway Patrol, and what was now, until maybe other accommodations could be found, the office of the Commanding Officer of Special Operations Division. Sabara, who was wearing black trousers and plain shoes, and not the motorcyclist's boots of Highway, was sitting in an armchair. Pekach, who was wearing Highway boots, and a Sam Browne belt, was sitting across from him on a matching couch.

They both started to get up when they saw Wohl. He waved them back into their seats.

"Good morning," Wohl said.

"Good morning, Inspector," they both said. Wohl wondered if that was, at least on Mike Sabara's part, intended to show him that he was pissed, or whether it was in deference to the presence of Mickey O'Hara.

"Chief Coughlin wants you to call him as soon as you get in," Sabara said.

"The sergeant told me," Wohl said. "Well, anything new?"

"No van and no woman," Sabara said.

"Damn!" Peter said.

"I called the hospital just a moment ago," Pekach said. "We have two still on the critical list, one of ours and the wife. The other two, the husband and our guy, are 'stabilized' and apparently out of the woods."

The Highway Sergeant came in and handed first Wohl and then Mickey O'Hara a china mug of coffee.

"Nothing on the woman? Or the van? *Nothing?*" Wohl asked.

"All we have for a description is a dark van, either a Ford or a Chevy," Sabara said. "That's not much."

One of the two telephones on Wohl's desk buzzed. He looked at it to see which button was illuminated, punched it, and picked up the handset.

"Inspector Wohl," he said.

"Dennis Coughlin, Peter," Chief Coughlin said.

"Good morning, sir."

"You got anything?"

"Nothing on the van or the woman," Peter said. "Pekach just talked to the hospital. We have one civilian, the wife, and one police officer on the critical list. The husband and the other cop are apparently out of danger."

"Have you seen the paper? The *Ledger,* especially?"

"No, sir."

"You should have a look at it. You'll probably find it interesting," Coughlin said. "Keep me up to date, up to the moment, Peter."

"Yes, sir," Peter said.

He heard Coughlin hang the phone up.

"Has anybody seen the *Ledger?*" Peter asked.

Pekach picked up a folded newspaper from beside him on the couch, walked across the room to Wohl's desk and laid it out for him.

There was a three-column headline, halfway down the front page, above a photograph of the wrecked cars.

SPEEDING HIGHWAY PATROL CAR KILLS FOUR-YEAR-OLD

Below the photograph was a lengthy caption:

This Philadelphia Highway Patrol car, racing to the scene of a reported abduction, ran a red light on Second Street at Olney Ave. and smashed into the side of a 1970 Chevrolet sedan at 8:45 last night, killing Stephen P. McAvoy, Jr., aged four, of the 700 block of Garland Street, instantly. His father and mother, Stephen P., 29, and Mary Elizabeth McAvoy, 24, were taken to Albert Einstein Northern Division Hospital, where both are reported in critical condition. Both policemen in the police car were seriously injured.

The tragedy occurred the day after Peter Wohl, a Police Department Staff Inspector, was given command of the Highway Patrol, in a move widely believed to be an attempt by Commissioner Thaddeu Czernich to tame the Highway Patrol, which has been widely criticized in recent months.

(More photos and the full story on page 10A. The tragedy is also the subject of today's editorial.)

Peter shook his head and looked around the office.

"We didn't run the stoplight," David Pekach said. "The guy in the Ford ran it." Peter met his eyes.

"Hawkins told me the light had just turned green as he approached Olney Avenue," Pekach said. "I believe him. He was too shook up to lie."

"He was driving?" Peter asked.

"Nobody's going to believe that," Mickey O'Hara said. "You guys better find a witness."

"I hope we're working on that," Wohl said.

"I've got guys ringing doorbells," Pekach said.

"How's the *Bulletin* handling this story, Mickey?" Wohl asked.

"It wasn't quite as bad as that," Mickey O'Hara said. "Cheryl Davies wrote the piece. But I'm here for a statement."

"We deeply regret the tragedy," Wohl said. "The incident is under investigation."

O'Hara shrugged. "Why did I suspect you would say something like that?" he said.

"It's the truth," Wohl said. "It's all I have to give you."

"What about the abducted female? The Northwest Philly rapist? On or *off* the record," O'Hara said.

Wohl's phone buzzed again, and he picked it up.

"Inspector Wohl," he said.

"Thaddeu Czernich, Peter. How are you?"

"Good morning, Commissioner," Peter said.

Both Pekach and Sabara got up, as if to leave.

Probably, Peter thought, *because they figure if they leave, Mickey O'Hara will take the hint and leave with them.*

He waved them back into their seats.

"Fine, sir. How about yourself?"

"It looks as if we sent you over at just the right time," Czernich said. "You've seen the papers?"

"Yes, sir. I just finished reading the *Bulletin.*"

"A terrible thing to have happened," Czernich said, "in more ways than one."

"Yes, sir, it is."

"Anything on the missing woman?"

"No, sir."

"Well, I have full confidence in your ability to handle whatever comes up; otherwise we wouldn't have sent you over there. But let me know if there's anything at all that I can do."

"Thank you, sir."

"The reason I'm calling, Peter—"

"Yes, sir?"

"Colonel J. Dunlop Mawson called me yesterday afternoon. You know who I mean?"

"Yes, sir."

"Under the circumstances, if you take my meaning, we can use all the friends we can get."

"Yes, sir."

"He has a client, a woman named Martha Peebles. Chestnut Hill. Very wealthy woman. Has been burglarized. Is *being* burglarized. She is not happy with the level of police service she's getting from the Fourteenth District and/or Northwest Detectives. She complained to Colonel Mawson, and he called me. Got the picture?"

"I'm not sure," Peter said.

"I think it would be a very good idea, Peter," Commissioner Czernich said, "if police officers from the Special Operations Division visited Miss Peebles and managed to convince her that the Police Department—strike that, *Special Operations*—is taking an avid interest in her problems, and is doing all that can be done to resolve them."

"Commissioner, right now, Special Operations is me and Mike Sabara and Sergeant Whatsisname—Frizell."

"I don't care how you do this, Peter," Czernich said, coldly. "Just do me a favor and do it."

"Yes, sir."

"I seem to recall that Denny Coughlin got me to authorize the immediate transfer to you of forty volunteers. For openers."

"Yes, sir."

"Well then, you ought to have some manpower shortly," Czernich said.

"Yes, sir."

"Keep me informed about the abducted woman, Peter," Czernich said. "I have an unpleasant gut feeling about that."

"Yes, sir, of course."

"Tell your Dad I said hello when you see him," Czernich said, and hung up.

Peter put the handset back in its cradle and turned to Mickey O'Hara.

"What can I do for you, Mickey?"

"Don't let the doorknob hit me in the ass?" O'Hara said.

"No. What I said was 'What can I do for you, Mickey?' " When I throw you out, I won't be subtle. Is there something special, or do you just want to hang around?"

"I'm interested in the abducted woman," O'Hara said. "I figure when something breaks, this will be the place. So I'll just hang around, if that's okay with you."

"Fine with me," Wohl said. He turned to Mike Sabara. "Mike, get on the phone to the Captain of Northwest Detectives, and the Fourteenth District Commander. Tell them that Commissioner Czernich just ordered me to stroke a woman named Peebles, and that before I send a couple of our people out to see her, I'm going to send them by to look at the paperwork. She's—what the commissioner said was—*being* burglarized, and she's unhappy with the service she's been getting, and she has friends in high places."

"Who are you going to send over?"

"Officers Martinez and McFadden," Wohl said.

"Who are they?" Sabara asked, confused.

"Two of the three kids sitting on the folding chairs in the foyer," Wohl said. "I'm doing what I can with what I've got. Then, the next item on the priority list: We need people. I would like to have time to screen them carefully, but we don't have any time. A teletype went out yesterday, asking for volunteers. I don't know if there have been any responses yet, but find out. If there have not been any, or even, come to think of it, if there have—"

"McFadden and Martinez used to work undercover for me in Narcotics," Pekach said to Sabara. "They're the two that found Gerald Vincent Gallagher. They're here?"

"Chief Coughlin sent them over," Wohl said. "To Special Operations, David, not Highway."

"They're good cops. Not much experience in Chestnut Hill . . ." Pekach said.

"Like I said, I'm doing what I can with what I have," Wohl said. "As I was saying, Mike, get us some people. If you, or Dave, can think of anybody you can talk into volunteering, do it. Then call around, see if there have been volunteers. Check them out. Have them sent here today. Go to the Districts if that's necessary. The only thing: tell them that if they don't work out, they go back where they came from."

"You want to talk to them?" Sabara asked. "Before we have them sent over here?"

"After you've picked them, I want to talk to them, sure," Wohl said. "But you know what we need, Mike."

Peter picked up his telephone and pushed one of the buttons. "Sergeant, would you ask Sergeant Frizell to come in here? And send in the three plainclothes officers waiting in the foyer?" There was a pause, then: "Yeah, all at once."

"Now, I'll be polite," Mickey O'Hara said. "Am I in the way?"

"Not at all," Peter said. "I'll let you know when you are, Mickey."

Sergeant Frizell, trailed by Officers McFadden, Martinez, and Payne, came into the office.

"What do we know about cars?" Wohl asked.

"For the time being," Frizell replied, "we have authority to draw cars, unmarked, from the lot at the Academy on the ratio of one car per three officers assigned."

"And then they'll have to be run by Radio, right, to get the proper radios?"

"Right."

"I want all our cars to have J-Band, Detective, Highway, and ours, whenever we get our own," Peter said.

"I'm not sure that's in the plan, Inspector," Frizell said.

"I don't give a damn about the plan," Peter said. "You call Radio and tell them to be prepared to start installing the radios. And call whoever has the car pool, and tell them we're going to start to draw cars today. Tell them we have fifty-eight officers assigned; in other words that we want twenty cars."

"But we don't have fifty-eight officers assigned. We don't have any."

"We have three at this moment," Wohl said. "And Captain Sabara is working hard on the others."

"Yes, sir," Sergeant Frizell said. "But, Inspector, I really don't think there will be fifteen unmarked cars available at the Academy."

"Then take blue-and-whites," Wohl said. "We can swap them for unmarked Highway cars, if we have to."

"Inspector," Frizell said, nervously, "I don't think you have the authority to do that."

"Do that right now, please, Sergeant," Wohl said, evenly, but aware that he was furious and on the edge of losing his temper.

The last goddamned thing I need here is this Roundhouse paper pusher telling me I don't have the authority to do something.

Frizell, sensing Wohl's disapproval, and visibly uncomfortable, left the room.

Wohl looked at the three young policemen.

"You fellows know each other, I guess?"

"Yes, sir," they chorused.

"Okay, this is what I want you to do." He threw car keys at Matt Payne, who was surprised by the gesture, but managed to snag them. "Take my car, and drive McFadden and Martinez to the motor pool at the Police Academy. There, you two guys pick up two unmarked cars. Take one of them to the radio shop and leave it. You take my car to the radio shop, Payne, and stay with it until they put another radio in it. Then bring it back here. Then you take Captain Sabara's car and have them install the extra radios in it. Then you bring that back. Clear?"

"Yes, sir," Matt Payne said.

"You two bring the other car here. I've got a job I want you to do when you get here, and when you finish that, then you'll start shuttling cars between the motor pool and the radio garage and here. You understand what I want?"

"Yes, sir."

Getting cars, and radios for them, and handing out assignments to newly arrived replacements, is a Sergeant's job, Wohl thought, *except when the man in charge doesn't really know what he's doing, in which case he is permitted to run in circles, wave and shout, making believe he does. That is known as a prerogative of command.*

Lieutenant Teddy Spanner of Northwest Detectives stood up when Peter Wohl walked into his office, and put out his hand.

"How are you, Inspector?" he said. "I guess congratulations are in order."

"I wonder," Wohl said, "but thanks anyway."

"What can Northwest Detectives do for Special Operations?"

"I want a look at the files on the burglary—is it burglaries?—job on a woman named Peebles, in Chestnut Hill," Wohl said.

"Got them right here," Spanner said. "Captain Sabara said somebody was coming over. He didn't say it would be you."

"The lady," Wohl said, "the Commissioner told me, has friends in high places."

Spanner chuckled. "Not much there; it's just one more burglary."

"Did Mike say we were also interested in the Flannery sexual assault and abduction?"

"There it is," Spanner said, pointing to another manila folder.

Wohl sat down in the chair beside Spanner's desk and read the file on the Peebles burglary.

"Can I borrow this for a couple of hours?" Wohl asked. "I'll get it back to you today."

Spanner gave a deprecatory wave, meaning *Sure, no problem,* and Wohl reached for the Flannery file and read that through.

"Same thing," he said. "I'd like to take this for a couple of hours."

"Sure, again."

"What do you think about this?" Wohl said.

"I think we're dealing with a real sicko," Spanner said. "And I'll lay odds the doer is the same guy who put the woman in the van. Anything on that?"

"Not a damned thing," Wohl said. "Push me the phone, will you?"

He dialed a number from memory.

"This is Inspector Wohl," he said. "Would you have the Highway car nearest Northwest Detectives meet me there, please?"

He hung up and pushed the telephone back across the desk.

"I need a ride," he explained.

"Something wrong with your car? Hell, I'd have given you a ride, Inspector. You want to call and cancel that?"

"Thanks but no thanks," Wohl said.

"Well, then"—Spanner smiled—"how about a cup of coffee?"

"Thank you," Wohl said.

A Highway Patrol officer came marching through the Northwest Detectives squad room before Wohl had finished his coffee. Wohl left the unfinished coffee and followed him downstairs to the car.

"I need a ride to the Roundhouse," Wohl said, as he got in the front beside the driver. "You can drop me there."

"Yes, sir," the driver said.

They pulled out of the District parking lot and headed downtown on North Broad Street. Wohl noticed, as he looked around at the growing deterioration of the area, that the driver was scrupulously obeying the speed limit.

"If you were God," Wohl said to the driver, "or me, and you could do anything you wanted to, to catch the guy who's been assaulting the women in Northwest Philly—and I think we're talking about the same doer who forced the woman into the van last night—what would you do?"

The driver looked at him in surprise, and took his time before answering, somewhat uneasily. "Sir, I really don't know."

Wohl turned in his seat and looked at the Highway Patrol officer in the backseat. "What about you?"

The man in the backseat raised both hands in a gesture of helplessness.

"The way I hear, we're doing everything we know how."

"You think he's going to turn the woman loose?" Wohl asked.

"I dunno," the driver replied. "This is the first time he's . . . kept . . . one."

"If you think of something, anything," Wohl said, "don't keep it to yourself. Tell Captain Pekach, or Captain Sabara, or me."

"Yes, sir," the driver said.

"Something wrong with this unit?" Wohl asked.

"Sir?"

"Won't it go faster than thirty-five?"

The driver looked at him in confusion.

"Officer Hawkins says it was the civilian who ran the stoplight last night," Wohl said. "I believe him. We're looking for witnesses to confirm Hawkins's story."

The driver didn't react for a moment. Then he pushed harder on the accelerator and began to move swiftly through the North Broad Street traffic.

With a little luck, Wohl thought, *these guys will have a couple of beers with their pals when their tour is over, and with a little more luck, it will have spread through Highway by tomorrow morning that maybe Inspector Wohl ain't the complete prick people say he is; that he asked for advice; said he believed Hawkins; and even told the guy driving him to the Roundhouse to step on it.*

11 As they drove down Delaware Avenue Officer Charley McFadden pushed himself off the backseat of Staff Inspector Peter Wohl's car and rested his elbows on the backrest of the front seat.

"I never been in an Inspector's car before," he said, happily. "Nice."

"It certainly doesn't look like a police car, does it?" Matt Payne, who was driving, said.

McFadden looked at him curiously.

"It's not supposed to," Jesus Martinez said, and then put into words what was in his mind. "Where'd you come from, if you don't mind my asking?"

"The Academy," Matt said.

"You was teaching at the Academy?"

"I was going through the Academy," Matt said. "I was on the range yesterday when Chief Matdorf came out and told me to report to Highway in plainclothes this morning."

"I'll be goddamned," Charley McFadden said, and then added, "we was in Narcotics. Hay-zus and me. We were partners, working undercover."

"For the last week, we were over in the Twelfth District, catching guys robbing stuff from parked cars," Jesus said. "I wonder what the hell this is all about?"

Both Matt Payne and Charley McFadden shrugged their shoulders.

"We're gonna find out, I guess."

"Where we're going is to that area behind the fence on the way to the Academy, right?" Matt asked.

"Yeah," Martinez said.

"I sure like your wheels," Charley said. "Porsche, huh?"

"Nine Eleven T," Matt said.

"What did something like that set you back?" Charley asked.

"Christ, Charley!" Martinez said. "You don't go around asking people how much things cost."

"I was just curious, Hay-zus, is all," Charley said. "No offense."

"I don't know what it cost," Matt said. "It was a present. When I graduated from college."

"*Nice* present!" Charley said.

"I thought so," Matt said. "What do you call him? Hay-zus?"

"That's his name," Charley said. "It's spick for Jesus."

"*Spanish,* you fucking Mick," Jesus Martinez said.

"I didn't get your name," Charley said, ignoring him.

"Matt Payne," Matt said.

Charley put his hand down over Matt's shoulder.

"Nice to meet you," Charley said as Matt shook it.

"Me, too," Jesus said, offering his hand.

They were able to draw two cars—both new Plymouths, one blue, and the other a dark maroon—from the Police Motor Pool without trouble, but when they got to the Police Radio Shop in the 800 block of South Delaware Avenue, things did not go at all smoothly.

It even began badly. The man in coveralls in the garage examined all three cars carefully as they drove in, and then returned his attention to what he was doing, which was reading *Popular Electronics.*

He did not look up as, one after the other, Matt, Jesus, and Charley walked up to stand in front of his desk.

"Excuse me." Matt spoke first. "I have Inspector Wohl's car."

"Good for you," the man said without looking up.

"You're supposed to install some communications equipment in it," Matt said.

"I ain't seen nothing on it," the man said. "You got the paperwork?"

"No," Matt said. "I'm afraid I wasn't given any."

"Well, then," the man said, returning to *Popular Electronics.*

"My instructions are to wait while the work is done," Matt said.

"And my instructions are no paperwork, no work," the man said. "And we don't do work while people wait. Who the hell do you guys think you are, any-way?"

"We're from Special Operations," Matt said.

"La dee da," the man said.

"Well, I'm sorry you fell out of bed on the wrong side," Matt said, "but that doesn't help me with my problem. Where can I find your supervisor?"

"I'm in charge here," the man flared.

"Good, then you pick up the telephone and call Inspector Wohl and tell him what you told me."

"What are you, some kind of a wiseass?"

Matt didn't reply.

"You can leave the car here, and when the paperwork catches up with it, we'll see what we can do," the man said.

"May I use your telephone, please?" Matt asked.

"What for?"

"So I can call Inspector Wohl, and tell him that not only are you refusing to do the work, but refusing, as well, to telephone him to say so."

The man gave him a dirty look, then reached for the telephone. He dialed a number.

"Sergeant, I got a hotshot here, says he's from Special Operations, without a sheet of paperwork, and demanding we do something—I don't know what—to three unmarked cars."

There was a reply, unintelligible, and then the man handed Matt the telephone.

"This is Sergeant Francis," the voice said. "What can I do for you?"

"My name is Payne. I'm assigned to Special Operations, and there has apparently been a breakdown in communications somewhere," Matt said. "I'm here with three unmarked cars, one of them Inspector Wohl's. Somebody was to have telephoned down here to arrange all this."

"I don't know anything about it," Sergeant Francis said. "Why don't you go back where you came from and ask somebody?"

"No, Sergeant," Matt said. "What I would like to do is speak to your commanding officer. Can you give me his number, please?"

"I'll do better than that," Sergeant Francis said. And then, faintly, Matt heard, "Lieutenant, you want to take this?"

"Lieutenant Warner."

"Sir, this is Officer Payne, of Special Operations. I'm at the radio shop. I was told to bring Inspector Wohl's car here to have—"

"Christ, you're there already?"

"Yes, sir. With Inspector Wohl's car, and two others."

"I thought when your Sergeant called, he was talking about tomorrow, at the earliest."

"We're here now, sir. Inspector Wohl sent us."

"So you said. Is there a man named Ernie around there, somewhere?"

Matt looked at the man at the desk.

"Is there somebody named Ernie here?" he asked.

"I'm Ernie."

"Yes, sir, there is," Matt said.

"Let me speak to him," Lieutenant Warner said.

Matt handed him the telephone.

Ernie, to judge by the look on his face, did not like what he was being told.

"Yes, sir, I'll get right on it," Ernie said, finally, and hung up. He looked at Matt. "Four bands in every car? What the fuck is this Special Operations, anyway?"

"We're sort of a super Highway Patrol," Matt said, with a straight face.

"Well, what do you think of him?" Charley McFadden asked as Jesus Martinez turned the unmarked Plymouth onto Harbison Avenue and headed north, toward Highway Patrol headquarters.

"I think he's a rich wiseass," Jesus said.

"Meaning you don't like him? I sort of like him."

"Meaning he's a rich wiseass," Jesus said. "Either that or he's a gink."

"Well, he got that shit-for-brains working on the radios, didn't he? I thought he handled that pretty well."

Jesus grunted. "That's what makes me think he may be a gink. He didn't act like a rookie in there. He as much as told that sergeant on the phone to go fuck himself. Rookies don't do that."

"Why would Internal Affairs send a gink in? Christ, they just formed Special Operations today. Internal Affairs sends somebody in undercover when they hear something is dirty. There hasn't been time for anything dirty to happen."

"He could be watching Highway."

"I think you're full of shit," Charley said, after a moment's reflection. "Whatever he is, he's no gink."

"So, you tell me: what is a rich guy who went to college doing in the Police Department?"

"Maybe he wants to be a cop," Charley said.

"Why? Ask yourself that, Charley."

"I dunno," Charley replied. "Why do you want to be a cop?"

"Because, so far as I'm concerned, it's a good job where I can make something of myself. But I didn't go to college, and nobody gave me a Porsche."

"Well, fuck it. I sort of like him. I liked the way he told that shit-for-brains where to head in."

When they got to Highway, the corporal told them that Captain Sabara wanted to see them. There were a lot of people in the outer office, and they both figured they were in for a long wait. Jesus settled himself in as comfortably as he could, and Charley went looking for the Coke and garbage machines.

He had just returned with a ham and cheese on rye and a pint of chocolate drink when the door to the Commanding Officer's office opened, and a middle-aged cop with a white-topped Traffic Bureau cap in his hand came out.

"Is there somebody named McFadden out here?"

Charley couldn't reply, for his mouth was full of ham and cheese, but he waved his hand, with the rest of the sandwich in it, over his head, and caught the traffic cop's attention.

"Captain Sabara wants to see you," the traffic cop said. "You and Gonzales, I think he said."

"Martinez?" Jesus asked, bitterly.

"Yeah, I think so."

Charley laid the sandwich on the chair next to Jesus, and, chewing furiously, followed him into the office.

"You wanted to see us, sir?" Jesus asked, politely.

"Yeah," Sabara said. "You got the cars all right?"

"Yes, sir, we left the blue-and-white at Radio," Jesus said.

"This is bullshit," Sabara said. "But from time to time, like when the Commissioner says to, we do bullshit. There have been a couple of minor burglaries in Chestnut Hill. A lady named Peebles. She's rich, and she has friends. And she doesn't think that she's been getting the service she deserves from the Police Department. She talked to one of her friends and he talked to the Commissioner, and the Commissioner called Inspector Wohl. Getting the picture?"

"Yes, sir," Jesus said.

Charley McFadden made one final, valiant swallow of the ham and cheese and chimed in, a moment later, "Yes, sir."

"Here's the file. Inspector Wohl borrowed it from Northwest Detectives. Read it. Then go see the lady. Charm her. Make her believe that we, and by we I mean Special Operations especially, but the whole Department, too, are sympathetic, and are going to do everything we can to catch the burglar, and protect her and her property. Getting all this?"

"Yes, sir," they chorused.

"On the way back, return the file to Northwest Detectives," Sabara said, "and be prepared to tell me, and Inspector Wohl, what you said to her, and how she reacted."

"Yes, sir."

"Okay, go do it," Sabara said, and they said "yes, sir" again and turned to leave. Jesus was halfway through the door when Sabara called out, "Hey!"

They stopped and turned to look at him.

"I know what a good job you guys did getting the doer in the Captain Moffitt shooting," Sabara said. "And Captain Pekach told me you did a good job for him in Narcotics before that. But you got to understand that Chestnut Hill isn't the street, and you have to treat people like this Miss Peebles gentle. It's bullshit, but it's important bullshit. So be real concerned and polite, okay?"

"Yes, sir," they chorused.

Peter Wohl had to show the officer on duty his identification before he was permitted to go through the locked door into the lobby of the Roundhouse. That made the score fourteen-six.

He got on the elevator and went to the Homicide Bureau on the second floor. When he pushed open the door to the main room, he saw that Captain Henry C. Quaire was in his small, glass-walled office.

The door was closed, and Quaire, a stocky muscular man in his early forties, was on the telephone, but when he saw Wohl he gestured for him to come in.

"I'll be in touch," he said after a moment, and then hung up the telephone. Then he half got out of his chair and offered his hand.

"Congratulations on your new command," Quaire said.

"Thank you, Henry," Wohl said.

"I don't know what the hell it is," Quaire said, "but it sounds impressive."

"That sums it up very neatly." Wohl said. "I'm already in trouble, and I just got there."

"I heard about the little boy," Quaire said. "That's a bitch."

"The civilian ran the red light, not our guy," Peter said.

"I hope you can prove that," Quaire said.

"That's what Mickey O'Hara said," Wohl said. "I've got people looking for witnesses. I really hope they can turn some up. But that's not why I'm here, Henry."

"Why do I think I'm not going to like what's coming next?" Quaire asked, dryly.

"Because you won't," Wohl said. "I want two of your people, Henry."

"Which two?"

"Washington and Harris," Wohl said.

"Can I say no, politely or otherwise?"

"I don't think so," Wohl said. "Chief Coughlin said I can have anybody I want. I'm going to hold him to it."

"Can I ask why, then?" Quaire said, after a moment.

Wohl laid the file he had borrowed from Lieutenant Teddy Spanner of Northwest Detectives on Captain Quaire's desk.

"That's what Northwest Detectives has on the Northwest Philly rapist," he said.

"They found the woman he forced into the van?"

"No. Not yet."

"I'll say the obvious, Inspector," Quaire said, tapping the folder with his fingertips but not opening it. "Rape, sexual assault, is none of Homicide's business. What are you showing this to me for?"

"The Northwest Philadelphia rapist is now my business, Henry," Wohl said.

"Okay. But still, why are you showing this to me?"

"I don't think we're going to find that woman alive," Wohl said.

"Then it will be my business," Quaire said. "But not until."

"No. It will still be my business," Wohl said.

Quaire's eyebrows rose.

"Not that it's any of my business, but how did that sit with Chief Lowenstein when he heard that? Or has he?"

Chief Inspector Matt Lowenstein, under whom Homicide operated, was notoriously unsympathetic to what he considered invasions of his territory.

"I devoutly hope he knows it wasn't my idea," Wohl said. "But he's been told."

"What are you asking for, Inspector?" Quaire asked. "That if this abduction turns into homicide, that I assign Washington and Harris? Frankly, I don't like being told how to run my shop."

"No, I want them transferred to Special Operations, now," Peter said.

Quaire considered that for a moment.

"I was about to say no," he said, finally, "but you've already told me I can't, haven't you?"

"Why don't you call Lowenstein?" Wohl said.

"I believe you, Peter, for Christ's sake," Quaire said.

"Thank you," Wohl said. "But maybe Lowenstein would like to think he's not the only one pissed off about this."

Quaire looked at him a moment, and then grunted.

He dialed a number from memory and told Chief Inspector Lowenstein that Staff Inspector Wohl was in his office, saying he wanted Detectives Washington and Harris transferred to Special Operations.

The reply was brief, and then Captain Quaire put the handset back in its cradle without saying good-bye.

"That was quick," Peter said with a smile. "What did he say?"

"You don't want to know," Quaire said.

"Yeah, I do."

"Okay," Quaire said, with a strange smile. " 'Give the little bastard whatever he wants, and tell him I said I hope he hangs himself.' End quote."

"That's all? He must be in a very good mood today," Wohl said, smiling. *But it's not funny. Lowenstein is, understandably, angry, and if he thinks I'm abusing the au-*

thority Czernich and Coughlin gave me, I'll pay for it. Maybe tomorrow, maybe next year, but sometime.

"So when would you like Detectives Washington and Harris?" Quaire asked.

"Now."

"You mean today?" Quaire asked, incredulously.

"Yeah, and if they could keep their cars for a couple of days, until I can get cars for them, I'd appreciate it."

Quaire thought that over for a moment.

"Inspector, I'm short of cars. If you *tell* me to let them keep their cars, I will, but—"

"Okay. I'll work something out with the cars," Wohl said. "But I want them today."

"They're working the streets," Quaire said. "I'll get word to them to come in here. And then I'll send them out to you. Where are you, in Highway?"

"Yeah. Henry, there is a chance we can do something before that woman is . . . before the abduction turns into a homicide. That's why I need them now."

"What you're saying is that you don't like the way Northwest Detectives are handling the job," Quaire said.

Now it was Wohl's turn to consider his reply.

"I hadn't thought about it quite that way, Henry. But yeah, I guess I am. The Northwest Philly rapist is out there somewhere; Northwest Detectives doesn't seem to have been able to catch him. Look at the file—nothing."

Quaire pushed the file across the desk to Wohl.

"I don't want to look at that file, Inspector," he said. "It's none of my business."

Wohl bit off the angry reply that popped into his mind before it reached his mouth. He picked up the file and stood up.

"Thank you, Captain," he said.

"Yes, sir," Captain Quaire said.

In the elevator on the way down to the lobby, Peter's stomach growled, and then there was actually pain.

I didn't have any breakfast, that's what it is.

And then he realized that his having skipped breakfast because he didn't want to be late his first morning on his new command had nothing to do with it.

He thought of a sandwich shop not far from The Roundhouse where he could get an egg sandwich or something and a half pint of milk. But when he walked out of the rear door of the Roundhouse, he saw a Highway Patrol car coming out of the Central Lockup ramp.

He trotted over to it, tapped on the closed window, and told the surprised driver to take him to Highway.

As Peter got out of the Highway car, out of the corner of his eye he saw another unmarked car, Sabara's, pull into the parking lot. The driver was Matt Payne. He looked around the parking lot and saw that his car, now wearing another short-wave antenna, was in the parking spot marked INSPECTOR.

He waited until Payne found a spot to park Sabara's car and then walked to the building.

"Payne!"

Payne looked around and saw him, and walked over.

"Yes, sir?"

"You got radios in the cars?"

"Yes, sir."

"That was quick," Wohl thought aloud.

"Well, there really wasn't much to it," Payne said. "Just screw the mounting to the transmission tunnel, install the antenna, and make a couple of connections."

"Come on in the office," Wohl said, "I want to talk to you."

"Yes, sir," Payne said.

Wohl had a quick mental picture of himself having a short chat in his office, to feel the boy out, to get a better picture of him to see what he could do with him.

As soon as he got in the building, he saw that would be impossible. All the folding chairs were occupied. Some of the occupants were in uniform, and he didn't have to be Sherlock Holmes to decide that the ones in plainclothes were policemen, too.

Sabara had gotten right to work, he decided. These people appeared to be looking for a job.

Sergeant Frizell immediately confirmed this: "Captain Sabara is interviewing applicants in there, sir," he said.

"Wait here a minute, Payne," Wohl said.

"Inspector," Payne said, as Wohl put his hand on the office doorknob, and Wohl looked at him. "Captain Sabara's keys, sir," Payne said, handing them to him.

"Thank you," Wohl said. He took the keys and went inside.

Sabara was behind the desk, with a personnel folder spread out before him. A uniformed cop sat nervously on the edge of a straight-backed chair facing the desk. Sabara started to get up, and Wohl waved him back.

There was something about the uniformed cop Wohl instinctively disliked. He had a weak face, Wohl decided. He wondered how he knew. Or if he knew.

"This is Inspector Wohl," Sabara said, and the cop jumped to his feet and put out his hand.

"How do you do, sir?" the cop said.

Confident that the cop couldn't see him, Sabara made a wry face, and then shook his head, confirming Wohl's own snap judgment that this cop was something less than they desired.

Why am I surprised? When there is a call for volunteers, ninety percent of the applicants are sure to be people unhappy with their present assignment, and, as a general rule of thumb people are unhappy with their jobs because they are either lazy or can't cut the mustard.

"Here's your keys, Mike," Wohl said.

"So quick?" Sabara asked.

Before Wohl could reply, one of the phones rang and Sabara picked it up.

"Yes?" he said, and listened briefly, and then covered the receiver with his hand. "Detective Washington for you, sir."

Wohl took the telephone.

"Hello, Jason," he said.

"Sir, I'm ordered to report to you," Washington said, his tone of voice making it quite clear what he thought of his orders.

"Where are you, Jason?" Wohl asked.

"At the Roundhouse, sir."

"You need a ride?"

"Sir, I called to ask if you wanted me to drive my car out there."

"Wait around the rear entrance, Jason," Wohl said. "I'll have someone pick you up in the next few minutes."

"Yes, sir," Washington said.

"Is Tony Harris there, too?"

"No, sir," Washington said, and then blurted, "Him, too?"

"I'm trying to get the best people I can, Jason," Wohl said.

"Yes, sir," Washington said, dryly, making it quite clear that he was not in a mood to be charmed.

"I'll have someone pick you up in a couple of minutes, Jason," Wohl said, and hung up.

He looked at Mike Sabara. "Detectives Washington and Harris will be joining us, Captain," he said. "That was Washington. I'm going to have someone pick him up and bring him here."

"You want me to take care of that, Inspector?" Sabara asked.

"I can do it," Wohl said, and smiled at the cop. "Nice to have met you," he said. *I hope he doesn't take that guy.*

Matt Payne was leaning on the concrete-block wall of the outside room when Wohl returned to it. When Payne saw him, he pushed himself off the wall.

"Payne, take my car again—" Wohl began and then stopped.

"Yes, sir?"

"How long did it take you to get a car out of the motor pool?"

"Just a couple of minutes," Payne said. "They have a form; you have to inspect the car for damage and then sign for it."

"Okay, let's go get another one," Wohl said, making up his mind.

As they walked to the car, Payne asked, "Would you like me to drive, sir?"

Wohl considered the question.

I liked my first ride downtown; it gave me a chance to look around. All I usually see is the stoplight of the car ahead of me.

"Please," he said, and handed Payne the keys.

Three blocks away, Payne looked over at Wohl and said, "I don't know the ground rules, sir. Am I expected to keep the speed limit?"

"Christ," Wohl replied, annoyed, and then looked at Payne. *It was an honest question, he decided, and deserves an honest answer.*

"If you mean, can you drive like the hammers of hell, no. But on the other hand . . . use your judgment, Payne." And then he added, "That's all police work really is, Payne, the exercise of good judgment."

"Yes, sir," Payne said.

Well, didn't you sound like Socrates, Jr., Peter Wohl?

But then he plunged on: "It's not like you might think it is. Brilliant detective work and flashing lights. Right now every cop in Philadelphia, and in the area, is looking for a woman that some lunatic with sexual problems forced into the back of his van at the point of a knife. Since we don't have a good description of the van, or the tag number—and, even if we had the manpower, and we don't—we can't stop every van and look inside. That's unlawful search. So we're just waiting for something to happen. I don't like to consider what I think will happen."

"My sister says rapists are more interested in dominating their victims, rather than in sexual gratification," Payne said.

"Your sister, no doubt," Wohl said, sarcastically, "is an expert on rape and rapists?"

"She's a psychiatrist," Payne said. "I don't know how much of an expert she is. As opposed to how much of an expert she thinks she is."

Wohl chuckled. "Well, maybe I should talk to her. I need all the help I can get."

"She'd love that," Payne said. "She would thereafter be insufferably smug, having been consulted by the cops, but if you mean it, I could easily set it up."

"Let's put it on the back burner," Wohl said. "What we're going to do now . . . Chief Coughlin gave me the authority to pick anybody I want for Special Operations. I just stole two of the best detectives from Homicide, which has grievously annoyed the head of Homicide, Chief Lowenstein, and at least one of the two detectives. I haven't talked to the other one yet. Anyway, after we pick up the car, we're going to go to the Roundhouse and pick up a detective named Jason Washington, Jr. I think he's the best detective in Homicide. The car we're going to pick up is for him. I want him to interview all the previous victims. He's damned good at that. Maybe he can get something out of them the other guys missed. Maybe we can find the rapist that way. And maybe Jason Washington would like to talk to your sister."

Payne didn't reply.

Thirty-five minutes later, Matt Payne, at the wheel of a light green Ford LTD, followed Peter Wohl's light tan LTD into the parking area behind the Roundhouse. Wohl pulled to the curb by the rear entrance and got out.

"Stay in the car," he said. "I'll be right out."

He went inside the building, waited in line behind the civilian who was talking to the Corporal behind the shatterproof glass, and then showed his identification.

"Oh, hell, Inspector," the Corporal said, "I know you."

"Thank you," Peter said.

That makes it fourteen-seven, Peter thought.

When the solenoid buzzed, he pushed the door open and entered the lobby.

Two men sitting on chairs stood up. One of them was very large, heavy, and dressed very well, looking more like a successful businessman than a cop.

Or a colored undertaker, Peter thought, wondering if that made him racist; and then decided it didn't. Jason Washington was more than colored, he was jet black; and in his expensive, well-tailored suit, he looked like an undertaker.

The other man was white, slight, and looked tired and worn. His clothes were mussed and looked as if they had come, a long time ago, from the bargain basement at Sears. His name was Anthony C. "Tony" Harris, and he was, in Wohl's judgment, the second-sharpest detective in Homicide.

Neither smiled when Wohl walked over to them.

"Sorry to keep you waiting," Wohl said. "I stopped by to get you a car."

"Inspector," Tony Harris said, "before this goes too far, can we talk about it?"

"Have either of you had lunch?" Peter asked.

Both shook their heads no.

"Neither have I," Peter said. "So, yes, Tony, we can talk about it, over lunch. I'll even buy."

"I'd appreciate that, Inspector," Tony Harris said.

"Where would you like to eat? The Melrose Diner okay?"

There was no response from either of them.

"Jason, I'm not sure the kid driving your car knows where the Melrose is," Wohl said. "You want to ride with him and show him? I'll take Tony with me."

"Where's the car?" Jason Washington asked. It was the first time he had opened his mouth.

"Behind mine," Wohl said, "at the curb."

Washington marched out of the lobby.

He's really pissed, Peter thought, and wondered again if he was doing the right thing. And then he felt a wave of anger. *Fuck him! He's a cop. Cops do what they're told. Nobody asked me if I wanted this goddamned job, either!*

"Tony," Wohl said, "aside from telling you that you can make as much overtime in Special Operations as you've been making in Homicide, what we're going to talk about at lunch is how I want you to do this job, not whether or not you like it."

Tony Harris met his eyes, looked as if he was going to reply, but didn't; then he walked toward the door from the lobby.

 Officer Matt Payne had more than a little difficulty complying with Staff Inspector Peter Wohl's order to "Call the office, Payne; tell them where we are. And you better ask if anything's new about the abduction."

It was, he thought, as he fished the thick Philadelphia telephone book from under the pay phone in the foyer of the Melrose Diner, the first time he had ever called the Police Department.

And the phone book was not much help.

The major listing under POLICE was the POLICE ATHLETIC LEAGUE. A dozen addresses and numbers were furnished, none of which had anything to do with what he wanted.

Under POLICE DEPARTMENT were listings to

STOP A CRIME   911
OR SAVE A LIFE 911

neither of which was what he was looking for.

A little farther down the listing was

FOR OTHER POLICE HELP 231-3131
ADMIN OFCS 7&RACE   686-1776
POLICE ACADEMY   686-1776

Matt tried the OTHER POLICE HELP number first.

"Police Emergency," a male voice responded on the fifth ring. "May I help you?"

"Sorry," Matt said, "wrong number," and hung up. He chuckled and said, "Shit," and put his finger back on the listing. By ADMIN OFCS 7&RACE they obviously meant the Roundhouse. But the number listed was the same as the one listed for the POLICE ACADEMY, which was to hell and gone the other side of town.

He put another dime in the slot and dialed 686-1776.

"City of Philadelphia," a bored female replied on the ninth ring.

"May I speak to the Special Operations Division of the Police Department, please."

"What?"

"Special Operations, please, in the Police Department."

"One moment, please," the woman replied, and Matt exhaled in relief.

But there was no ringing sound, and after a long pause, the woman came back on the line. "I have no such listing, sir," she said, and the line went dead.

He fumbled through his change for another dime and couldn't find one. But he had a quarter and dropped it in the slot and dialed 686-1776 again.

"City of Philadelphia," another bored female answered on the eleventh ring.

"Highway Patrol Headquarters, please," Matt said.

"Is this an emergency, sir?"

"No, it's not."

"One moment, please."

Now the phone returned a busy signal.

"That number is busy," the operator said. "Would you care to hold?"

"Please."

"What?"

"I'll hold."

"Thank you, sir," she said, and the line went dead.

He dropped his last quarter in the slot, dialed 686-1776 again, and asked a third woman with a bored voice for Highway Patrol.

"Special Operations, Sergeant Frizell."

"This is Officer Payne, Sergeant," Matt said. That was, he thought, the first time he had ever referred to himself as "Officer Payne." It had, he thought, a rather nice ring to it.

"You a volunteer, Payne?"

"Excuse me?"

"I said, are you a volunteer?"

"No, I'm not," Matt said.

"Well, what can I do for you?"

"Inspector Wohl told me to check in," Matt said. "We're at the Melrose Diner."

"Oh, you're his driver. Sorry, I didn't catch the name."

"The number here is 670-5656," Matt said.

"Got it. He say when he's coming in?"

"No. But he said to ask if anything has happened with the abducted woman."

"Not a peep."

"Thank you," Matt said. "Good-bye."

"What?"

"I said good-bye."

"Yeah," Sergeant Frizell said, and the line went dead.

When he went into the dining room of the Melrose Diner, he looked around until he spotted them. They were in a corner banquette, and a waitress was delivering drinks.

"Anything?" Inspector Wohl asked him.

"No, sir."

"Damn," Wohl said. "What are you drinking?"

Drinking on duty, Matt saw, was not the absolute no-no he had been led to believe, from watching *Dragnet* and the other cop shows on television. Both Wohl and Washington had small glasses dark with whiskey in front of them, obviously something-on-the-rocks, and Harris had a taller glass of clear liquid with a slice of lime on the rim, probably a vodka tonic.

"Have you any ale?" Matt asked the waitress.

She recited a litany of the available beers and ales and Matt picked one.

"You going to eat, too?" the waitress asked. "I already got their orders."

Matt took a menu, glanced at it quickly, and ordered a shrimp salad.

From the look—mixed curiosity and mild contempt—he got from Detective Washington, Matt surmised that both the ale and the shrimp salad had been the wrong things to order.

When the waitress left, Peter Wohl picked up his glass, and with mock solemnity said, "I would like to take this happy occasion to welcome you aboard, men."

"Shit," Jason Washington said, unsmiling.

"Jason, I need you," Wohl said, seriously.

"Oh, I know why you did it," Washington said. "But that doesn't mean I agree that it was necessary, or that I have to like it."

Wohl looked as if he had started to say something and then changed his mind.

"I told Tony in the Roundhouse lobby, Jason, that if it's overtime you're worried about, you can have as much as you want."

"I should have drowned you when you were a sergeant in Homicide," Washington said, matter-of-factly. "Inspector, you know what Homicide is."

"Yeah, and I know you two guys are the best detectives in Homicide. *Were* the best two."

"When he's through shoveling the horseshit, Tony," Washington said, "hand the shovel to me. It's already up to my waist, and I don't want to suffocate."

Harris grunted.

"What you're doing, Inspector, is covering your ass, and using Tony and me to do it."

"Guilty, okay?" Wohl said. "Now can we get at it?"

"Now that the air, so to speak, is clear between us," Washington said, "why not?"

"Special Operations has the Northwest Philadelphia rapist job," Wohl said. "That came from the Commissioner, and I think he was following orders."

Jason Washington's eyebrows rose.

"This is the file," Wohl said. "I borrowed it from Northwest Detectives."

They were interrupted by the waitress, who set a bottle of ale and a glass in front of Matt, and then a shrimp cocktail in front of each of the others.

"I want it handled like a homicide," Wohl said.

"It's not a homicide," Washington said. "Yet. Or is it?"

"Not yet," Wohl said.

Tony Harris, who had been sitting slumped back in his chair, now leaned forward and pulled the manila folder from under Wohl's hand. He laid it beside his plate, then picked up his seafood fork. He stabbed a shrimp, dipped it in the cocktail sauce, put it in his mouth, and started to read the file.

"Who had the job at Northwest Detectives?" Jason Washington asked.

"As they came up on the wheel," Wohl said. "But, starting with the Flannery job—"

"That's the one that's missing?" Washington interrupted.

"The one before that. The one he turned loose naked with her hands tied behind her in Fairmount Park."

Washington nodded his understanding, put a shrimp in his mouth, and waited for Wohl to continue.

"Dick Hemmings got the Flannery job on the Wheel," Wohl said. "Then Teddy Spanner gave him the whole job. When it became pretty certain what it was, one doer."

"Dick Hemmings is a good cop," Washington said. "What do you think we can do he hasn't already done?"

Then he raised his whiskey glass, which Matt saw was now empty, over his head. When he had caught the waitress's eye, he raised his other hand and made a circular motion, ordering another round.

Matt took another sip of his ale. He was doing his best to follow the conversation, which he found fascinating. He wondered what "the wheel" they were talking about was, but decided it would not to be wise to ask. Washington had already made it plain he held him in contempt; a further proof of ignorance would only make things worse.

"The one thing we need is a—two things. We need first a good description of the doer. Since we don't have a description, we need a profile. I've been thinking of talking to a psychiatrist—"

"Save your time," Tony Harris said. "I can tell you what a shrink will tell you. We're dealing with a sicko here. He gets his rocks off humiliating women. He hates his mother. Maybe he was screwing his mother, or she kept bringing guys home and taking them to bed. Something. Anyway, he hates her, and is getting back at her by hitting on these women. No hookers, you notice. Nice little middle-class women. That's what you'd get from a shrink."

He closed the file and handed it across the table to Washington.

"Jason's very good with people," Wohl said. "I thought it would be a good idea if he reinterviewed all the victims."

If Jason Washington heard Wohl, there was no sign. He was very carefully reading the file.

"I'll lay you ten to one that when we finally catch this scumbag," Tony Harris said, "it will come out that he's been going to one of your shrinks, Inspector, and that one of *those* scumbags has been reading the papers and knows fucking well his seventy-five-dollar-an-hour patient is the guy who's been doing this. But he won't call us. Physician-patient confidentiality is fucking sacred. Particularly when the patient is coughing up seventy-five bucks an hour two, three times a week."

"I don't know how far Hemmings, or anybody, has checked out sexual offenders," Wohl said.

"I'll start there," Harris said. "These fuckers don't just start out big. Somewhere there's a record on him. Even if it's for something like soliciting for prostitution."

He said this as the waitress delivered the fresh round of drinks. She gave him a very strange look.

"I'm going to be in court most of this week and next," Washington said, without looking up from the file any longer than it took to locate the fresh drink.

"I figured that would probably be the case," Wohl said. "So why don't you work the four-to-midnight shift? It is my professional judgment that the people you will be interviewing will be more readily available in the evening hours."

Washington snorted, but there was a hint of a smile at his eyes and on his lips. He knew the reason Wohl had assigned him to the four-to-twelve shift had nothing to do with more readily available witnesses. It would make all the time he spent in court during the day overtime.

"I'm going to be in court a lot, too," Tony Harris said. "That apply to me, too?"

"Since it is also my professional judgment that you can do whatever you plan to do during the evening hours better than during the day, sure," Wohl said.

Peter Wohl had been in Homicide and knew that, because of the overtime pay, Homicide detectives were the best-paid officers in the Police Department. There was no question in his mind that Washington and Harris were taking home as much money as a Chief Inspector. That was the major, but not the only, reason they were unhappy with their transfer to Special Operations; they thought it was going to cut their pay.

It posed, he realized, what Sergeant Frizell would term a "personnel motivation problem" for him: if they didn't want to work for him, they didn't have to. About the only weapon he had as a supervisor short of official disciplinary action—and both Washington and Harris were too smart to make themselves vulnerable to something like that—was to send his men back where they had come from. Which would not make either Washington or Harris at all unhappy.

He had a somewhat immodest thought: *If they didn't like me, to the point where they are willing to give me and Special Operations a chance, they would already have come up with twenty reasons to get themselves fired.*

"Is the Flannery woman still in the hospital?" Washington asked.

"I don't know," Wohl said.

"She saw more of this guy than any of the others," Washington said, closing the file. "Can I have this?"

"No," Wohl said. "But I'll get you both a copy. Payne, when we get back to the office, Xerox this in four copies."

"Yes, sir."

"Ah," Washington said, looking around the room. "Here comes my lunch!"

The waitress delivered two New York strip steaks, a filet mignon (to Washington) and a shrimp salad.

If I had ordered a steak, Matt thought, *they would have ordered bacon, lettuce, and tomato sandwiches.*

Nobody spoke another word until Washington laid his knife and fork on the plate, and delicately dabbed at his mouth with his napkin.

"We work for you, right?" he asked. "I don't have to check with Sabara every time I sharpen a pencil?"

"Mike is the Deputy Commander," Wohl said.

"We work for you, right?" Washington repeated.

"Mike is the Deputy Commander," Wohl repeated, "but I will tell him that the only job you two have is the Northwest Philly rapist. What have you got against Sabara?"

"He's a worrier," Washington said. "Worriers make me nervous."

Wohl chuckled.

Washington looked at Matt Payne. "You open to a little advice, son?"

"Yes, sir," Payne said.

" 'Yes, sir,' " Harris quoted mockingly.

"That's a very nice jacket," Washington said, giving Harris a dirty look, and then turning his face to Matt. "Tripler?"

"Yes," Matt said, surprised. "As a matter of fact it is."

"If you're going to wear a shoulder holster, you have to have them make allowance for it," Washington said. "Cut it a little fuller under the left arm. What you look like now, with the material stretched that way, is a man carrying a pistol in a shoulder holster."

Matt, smiling uneasily, looked at Inspector Wohl, whom he found grinning at him.

"Listen to him, Payne," Wohl said. "He's the recognized sartorial authority in the police department."

"The whole idea of plainclothes is to look like anything but a cop," Washington said. "What you really should do, in the summer, is get a snub-nose and carry it in an ankle holster. Very few people look at your ankles to see if you're carrying a gun, and even if they do, unless you wear peg-leg trousers like Harris here, they're pretty much out of sight on your ankles."

Wohl laughed.

Washington stood up and put out his hand to Wohl.

"Thank you for the lunch," he said. "I'll check in if I come up with anything."

"My pleasure," Wohl said. "Jason, what you have for radios in the car is J-Band and I don't know what else. It's arranged with Radio to give you Detectives and Highway, too. I mean, if you take the car there, they're set up to do the work right away. Tony, you paying attention?"

"When do I get a car?" Harris asked.

"As soon as Jason drives you over to get one."

Harris grunted.

"Sabara's not going to worry if I take the car home with me at night, is he?" Washington asked.

"No, he's not," Wohl said. "You stop worrying. You're going to be the star of our little operation."

"Here comes the horse manure again," Washington said, and walked out of the room.

"Nice to meet you, Payne," Harris said, offering him his hand. "See you around."

When they had left the restaurant, Wohl held up his coffee cup to catch the waitress's attention, and when she had refilled his cup from a stainless steel pot, he turned to Matt.

"Now we get to you, Officer Payne," he said.

"Sir?"

"It is generally accepted as a fact of life in the Police Department that before you do anything else with a rookie, you give him a couple of years in a District. In the case of someone your size, you assign him to a wagon. You know what a wagon is?"

"Yes, sir, a paddy wagon."

"Be careful where you say that," Wohl said. "To some of our brother officers of Irish extraction, paddy wagon is a pejorative term, dating back to the days when Irishmen were known as 'Paddys' and were hauled off to jail in a horse-drawn vehicle known as the 'Paddy Wagon.' "

"Sir, I'm half-Irish."

"Half doesn't count. It's not like being a little pregnant. My mother's Catholic. But neither you nor I are products of the parochial school system, or alumni of Roman or Father Judge or North Catholic High. Neither are we Roman Catholics. Half-Irish or ex–Roman Catholic doesn't count."

"Yes, sir," Matt said, smiling. "I'll say 'wagon.' "

"As I was saying, broad-backed young rookies like yourself generally begin their careers in a District with a couple of years in a wagon. That gives them practical experience, and the only way to really learn this job is on the job. After a couple of years in a wagon, rookies move on, either, usually, to an RPC, or somewhere else. There are exceptions to this, of course. Both Charley McFadden and Jesus Martinez went right from the Academy to Narcotics, as plainclothes, undercover. The reasoning there was that their faces weren't known to people in the drug trade, and that, presuming they dressed the part, they could pass for pushers or addicts. But that sort of thing is the exception, not the rule."

"Yes, sir."

"Speaking of our Irish-American friends, when was the last time you saw Chief Coughlin?"

"I had dinner with him one night last week," Matt said.

"Would you be surprised to learn that Chief Coughlin sent you to Special Operations?"

"Chief Matdorf told me that he had arranged for me to be sent to Highway," Matt said, hesitated, and then went on, "but Chief Coughlin didn't say anything to me about it."

"He told me he was sending you over," Wohl said, "but he didn't tell me what he expected me to do with you. What would you like to do?"

The question surprised Matt; he raised both his hands in a gesture of helplessness.

"I don't think he had in mind putting you on a motorcycle," Wohl said. "And since, for the moment at least, I'm not even thinking of any kind of undercover operations, I really don't know what the hell to do with you. Can you type?"

"Yes, sir."

"Well?"

"Yes, sir. I think so."

"Well, I don't think Chief Coughlin wants me to turn you into a clerk, either," Wohl said, "but we're going to start generating a lot of paperwork to get Special Operations up to speed. More than Sergeant Frizell can handle. More than he can handle while he does things for me, too, anyway. The thought that occurs to me is that you could work for me, as sort of a gofer, until I can sort this out. How does that sound?"

"That sounds fine, sir."

"And, for the time being, anyway, I think in plainclothes," Wohl said.

He looked around, caught the waitress's eye, and gestured for the check.

He turned back to Matt. "Jason Washington was right," he said. "You should get yourself a snub-nose and an ankle holster. You'll have to buy it yourself, but Colosimo's Gun Store offers an alleged police discount. Know where it is?"

"No, sir."

"The nine-hundred block on Spring Garden," Wohl said.

"Sir, I thought you had to qualify with a snub-nose," Matt said.

"How did you do on the pistol range in the Academy?" Wohl asked.

"All right, I think," Matt said. "Better than all right. I made Expert with the .45 at Quantico."

"That's right," Wohl said. "You told me that the night I first met you, the night of Dutch's wake. You were planning to be a Marine, weren't you? And then you busted the physical."

"Yes, sir."

"Is that why you came on the cops? To prove you're a man, anyway?"

"That's what my sister says," Matt said. "She says I was psychologically castrated when I flunked the physical, and that what I'm doing is proving my manhood."

"Your sister the psychiatrist?"

"Yes, sir."

"Did you get the feeling that Tony Harris is not too impressed with psychiatrists?" Wohl asked.

"Yes, sir, that came through pretty clearly."

"Or did you come on the job because of what happened to Dutch? And/or your father?" Wohl asked, picking that up again.

"That's probably got something to do with it," Matt said. "It probably was impulsive. But from what I've seen so far—"

"What?"

"It's going to be fascinating," Matt said.

"You haven't seen enough of it to be able to make that kind of judgment," Wohl said. "All you've seen is the Academy."

"And Washington and Harris," Matt argued gently.

"You're a long way, Matt, from getting close to guys like those two. The folklore is that being a detective is the best job in the Department; and that being a Homicide detective is the best of detective jobs. Washington and Harris, in my judgment, are the best two Homicide detectives, period. But that does trigger a thought: it would be a good idea for you to hang around with somebody, some people, who know what they're doing. I'm talking about McFadden and Martinez. I'll tell them to show you the ropes. That'll mean a lot of night work, overtime. How do you feel about overtime?"

"I really don't have anything better to do," Matt said, honestly. "Sure, I'd like that."

"The eyes of the average police officer would light up when a supervisor mentioned a lot of overtime," Wohl said.

"Sir?" Matt asked, confused.

The waitress appeared with the check on a small plastic tray. Matt had to wait until Wohl had carefully added up the bill and handed her his American Express card before he got an explanation.

"Overtime means extra pay," Wohl said. "Washington and Harris take home as much money as I do. More, probably. Supervisors get, at least, compensatory time, not pay for overtime. To most cops, overtime pay is very important."

"I wondered why you kept mentioning to them they could have all the overtime they wanted," Matt said.

"My point is that you weren't thinking about the money, were you? Money isn't much of a consideration for you, is it? You remember, you told me about that the night we met."

"I don't think that will keep me from doing my job," Matt said.

"I don't think it will, either," Wohl said. "But I think you should keep it in mind."

"Yes, sir."

"About the snub-nose," Wohl said, as he signed the American Express bill, "I don't think anyone will challenge you, but if that happens, the paperwork will come through me, and I'll handle it. But don't buy a Smith & Wesson Undercover, or a Colt with a hammer shroud."

"Sir?"

"An Undercover comes with a built-in shroud over the hammer; it's intended to keep you from snagging the gun on your clothing, if you should ever need to get at it in a hurry. And they sell shrouds for Colts. The problem is you can't carry a gun with a shroud in an ankle holster; there's no place for the strap on the holster to catch."

"I understand, sir."

"The odds that you will ever have to use your revolver, which I hope they told you at the Academy, are about a thousand to one. But as the Boy Scouts say, *"Be Prepared!"*

He smiled at Matt and got up and walked out of the restaurant with Matt at his heels.

When Peter Wohl walked into what had been Mike Sabara's office as Acting Commanding Officer of Highway Patrol, and was now his, it was empty; all of Mike's photographs and plaques were gone from the walls, and so were the pistol shooting and bowling trophies Sabara had had on display on top of filing cabinets and other flat surfaces. Wohl walked to the desk, pulled drawers open, and saw that they too had been emptied.

He walked to the door.

"What happened to Captain Sabara?" he asked Sergeant Frizell.

"He and Captain Pekach moved in there," Frizell said, pointing to a door.

Wohl walked to it and pulled it open. He had been unaware of the room's existence until that moment, and now that he saw it, he realized that it was really too small for two captains, and felt a moment's uneasiness at having the relatively large office to himself. He hadn't had an office when he had been just one more Staff Inspector. He had shared a large room with all of his peers, and he had not had a Sergeant to handle his paperwork.

I guess it goes with the territory, he decided, *but I don't like it.*

"We're going to have to do better than that," he said, to Sergeant Frizell. "In your planning, did the subject of space come up?"

"Space is tight, Inspector."

"That's not what I asked."

"There's an elementary school building at Frankford and Castor," Frizell said.

"Not being used. The Department's been talking to the Board of Education about that."

"And?"

"It's a *school building,*" Frizell said. "There's no detention cells, nothing but a bunch of classrooms. Not even much space for parking."

"And there's no room in this building to move in fifty, maybe a hundred, maybe two hundred cops," Wohl said. "Find out what's being said, and to whom, about us getting it, will you?"

"Yes, sir," Frizell said. "There was some discussion about giving Special Operations, if it grows as large as it might with the ACT Grants, Memorial Hall."

"At Forty-fourth and Parkside in Fairmount Park?"

"Yes, sir."

"That would be nice. Keep your ears open and keep me advised," Wohl said.

Frizell nodded. "Inspector, what do you want me to do about these?" He held up the Northwest Philadelphia rape files.

"I told Payne to Xerox them in four copies."

"Our Xerox is down."

"What about the machine in the District?"

"Well, they're not too happy with us using theirs," Frizell said. "They'll do it, but they make us wait."

I will be damned if I will go find the District Captain and discuss Xerox priorities with him.

"Sergeant," Wohl said, his annoyance showing in his voice, "high on your list of priorities is getting us a new Xerox machine. Call Deputy Commissioner Whelan's office and tell them I said we need one desperately."

"Yes, sir," Frizell said. "And in the meantime, sir, what do I do with this?"

"Payne," Wohl ordered. "Go get that Xeroxed someplace. You're a bright young man, you'll find a machine somewhere."

"Yes, sir," Matt said.

"There's one more thing, Inspector," Sergeant Frizell said, and handed him a teletype message.

GENERAL: 0698 06/30/73 FROM COMMISSIONER
PAGE 1 OF 1
CITY OF PHILADELPHIA
POLICE DEPARTMENT

THE FOLLOWING WILL BE ANNOUNCED AT ALL ROLL CALLS:
EFFECTIVE IMMEDIATELY SPECIAL OPERATIONS DIVISION MOTOR
VEHICLES (EXCEPT HIGHWAY PATROL) ARE ASSIGNED RADIO CALL
SIGNS W-1 THROUGH W-200, AND WILL USE THE PHONETIC
PRONUNCIATION "WILLIAM."

Jesus! I just got here, and they're already changing things.
"William"? That's awkward. Why not "Whiskey"?
Obviously, "Whiskey" wouldn't work.
And "Wine" and "Women" wouldn't work, either. But "William"?

In two or three days, if not already, that will be "Willy" and I will get an interdepartmental memorandum crisply ordering me to have my men follow official Department Radio procedures.

"Did you get the word out?" Wohl asked Frizell.

"Yes, sir."

Wohl, without thinking about it, handed the teletype to Matt Payne. Then he saw Charley McFadden and Jesus Martinez coming into the outer office.

"Wait a minute, Payne," he said, as he walked into the outer office.

"Good afternoon, sir," Martinez said.

"I hope you're here to report that you have seen Miss Peebles, and that she now loves the Police Department and all we're doing for her," Wohl asked.

"I don't know if she loves us or not," McFadden said, smiling. "But she made us a cup of coffee."

"What's going on over there?" Wohl said, gesturing for the two of them to go into his office, and then adding, "You, too, Matt. I want you in on this."

Wohl sat in the upholstered chair and indicated that Martinez, McFadden, and Payne should sit on the couch.

"Okay, what happened? What's going on with Miss Peebles?"

"She's all right," McFadden said. "A little strange. Rich. Scared, too."

"Explain all that to me," Wohl said. "Did Captain Sabara explain that she has friends in high places?"

"Yes, sir," Martinez said. "Well . . . do you want to hear what I think, Inspector?"

"That would be nice," Wohl said, dryly.

"She's a nice lady, with a fag for a brother," Martinez said. "I don't even know if she knows the brother is a fag, she's that dumb. I mean, nice but *dumb*, you follow me?"

"I'm sure that you're going to tell me what her brother's sexual proclivities have to do with the burglary. Burglaries."

"She knows all right," McFadden said.

"Anyway, the brother brought a guy home. An actor."

"Going under the name Walton Williams," McFadden said. "Nothing in criminal records under that name."

"That was in the report I told you to read," Wohl said.

"Anyway, the way we see it," Martinez went on, "the fag took one look around the place, saw all the expensive crap—what do you call it, 'bric-a-brac'?"

"If it's worth more than fifty dollars, we usually say, *'objets d'art,' "* Wohl said.

"Expensive *knickknacks,"* McFadden offered.

"—and figured he was in a toy store. Especially after the brother went to France. So he's been ripping her off."

"How would you handle this crime wave?"

"Find the fag," McFadden said.

"Cherchez la pouf," Wohl said.

Matt Payne laughed.

"Excuse me?" Martinez said.

"Go on," Wohl said. "How would you do that?"

"Give us a couple of days," McFadden said. "We'll find him."

"You think you know where to look?"

"There's a couple of fairies around who owe me some favors," Martinez said.

"Just off the top of my head, do you think there is any chance this Mr. Williams could be the doer in the rapes?"

"I called Detective Hemmings at Northwest Detectives," McFadden said. "The best description of *that* doer is that he's hairy. Black hairy. The description we got from Miss Peebles is that the brother's boyfriend is blond."

"And 'delicate,' " Martinez said.

Well, they're thinking, Wohl thought.

"What about his stealing her underwear?"

"That's a puzzler," Martinez said. "When I catch him, I'll ask him."

"We could stake out the house, Inspector," McFadden said. "Until he comes back. I'm sure he'll be back. But I think the easiest and cheapest way to catch him is for you to let us go look for him."

"What did you say 'cheapest'?" Wohl asked.

"I got the feeling that when we catch this guy, Miss Peebles isn't going to want to go testify against him," McFadden said. "Because of the brother. What he is would get out. And the brother may not want the guy locked up."

"I see."

"But if we can find him, maybe we can talk to him," Martinez said. "Maybe we can even get some of the stuff back. But I think we can discourage him from going back there again."

"You're not suggesting anything that would violate Mr. Williams's civil rights, are you, Martinez?"

"No, sir," Martinez said, straight-faced. "As a minority member myself, I am very sensitive about civil rights."

"I'm glad to hear that," Wohl said. "I would be very annoyed if I learned any of my men were slapping some suspect around. You understand that?"

"Yes, sir."

"You, too, McFadden?"

"Yes, sir."

"Okay, go look for him," Wohl said.

"Yes, sir," they said in unison, pleased.

"Sir, the best time to deal with people like that is at night, say from nine o'clock on, until the wee hours," McFadden said.

"You're talking about overtime?" Wohl asked, looking at Matt Payne as he spoke.

"Yes, sir," McFadden said.

"Put in as much overtime as you think is necessary," Wohl said. "I want you to take Officer Payne along with you, to give him a chance to see how you work."

"Yes, sir," McFadden said, immediately.

"Inspector, that might be a little awkward," Martinez said.

"That wasn't a suggestion," Wohl said.

"Yes, sir," Martinez said.

"Can we keep the car we've been driving, sir?" McFadden asked.

"If you mean, do you have to turn it in when you go off duty, the answer is no, not for the time being. I don't care which one of you keeps it overnight, but I don't want to hear that somebody stole the radios, or the tires, or ran a key down the side to show his affection for the police."

"I'll take good care of it, sir," Martinez said.

"For right now, for the rest of the afternoon, I want you to keep drawing cars and taking them for radios and bringing them here. Take Payne with you. He's doing an errand for me, and he'll need a car to do it."

"Yes, sir," McFadden said.

"That's all," Wohl said. He looked at Payne. "Get that Xeroxed, and then come back here."

"Yes, sir," Payne said.

"I have every confidence that in the morning, Mr. Williams will be in the hands of the law, and that I can call the Commissioner and tell him that not only has justice been done, but that Miss Peebles is more than satisfied with her police support."

Martinez and McFadden flashed smiles that were not entirely confident, and got up. As Payne started to follow them out of the office Wohl said, softly, "Keep your eyes open and your mouth shut tonight, Matt."

13 Matt Payne turned off Seventh Street into the parking lot behind the Round-house at the wheel of an almost new Plymouth Fury. Forty-five minutes before, he had picked it up at the Radio garage, and it was equipped with the full complement of radios prescribed for Special Operations by Staff Inspector Peter Wohl.

He knew the radio worked, because he had tried it.

"W-William Two Oh Nine," he had called on the Highway Band. "Out of service at Colosimo's Gun Store in the nine-hundred block of Spring Garden."

And Radio had called back, "W-William Two Oh Nine, is that the nine-hundred block on Spring Garden?"

The Radio Dispatcher was Mrs. Catherine Wosniski, a plump, gray-haired lady of sixty-two who had been, it was said, a dispatcher since Police Dispatch had been a couple of guys blowing whistles from atop City Hall, long before Marconi had even thought of radio.

Mrs. Wosniski had been around long enough to know, for example, that:

Special units—and Special Operations was certainly a Special Unit—did not have to report themselves out of service as did the RPCs in the Districts. The whole idea of reporting out of (or back in) service was to keep the dispatchers aware of what cars were or were not available to be sent somewhere by the dispatchers. Dispatchers did not dispatch special unit vehicles.

Catherine Wosniski also knew about Colosimo's Gun Store. It was where three out of four cops in Philadelphia, maybe more, bought their guns. And she also knew that many of them stopped by Colosimo's to shop on a personal basis when they had been officially sent to the Roundhouse; that they shopped there, so to speak, on company time, almost invariably "forgetting" to call Police Radio to report themselves out of service.

So what she had here was a car that was not required to report itself out of service doing just that, and at a location where cars rarely reported themselves out of service, because supervisors, who also had radios, frowned on officers shopping on company time.

Although Mrs. Catherine Wosniski was a devout and lifelong member of the Roman Catholic Church, she was also conversant with certain phrases used by those of the Hebraic persuasion: What she thought was, *there's something not kosher here.*

"W-William Two Oh Nine," she radioed back. "Do you want numbers on this assignment?"

What she was asking was whether the officer calling wanted the District Control Number for whatever incident was occurring at Colosimo's Gun Store that he had elected to handle. A District Control Number is required for every incident of police involvement.

Officer Matthew Payne had no idea at all what she was talking about.

"W-William Two Oh Nine. No, thank you, ma'am, I don't need any numbers."

It had been at least two years since anyone had said thank you to Catherine Wosniski over the Police Radio; she could never remember anyone who had ever called her 'ma'am' over the air.

"W-William Two Oh Nine," she radioed, a touch of concern in her voice, "is everything all right at that location?"

"W-William Two Oh Nine," Officer Payne replied, "everything's fine here. I'm just going inside to buy a gun."

There was a pause before Mrs. Wosniski replied. Then, very slowly, she radioed, "Ooooooo-kaaaaaay, W-Two Oh Nine."

Everyone on this band thus knew that Mrs. Wosniski knew that she was dealing with an incredible dummy who hadn't the foggiest idea how to cover his tracks when he was taking care of personal business.

Blissfully unaware of the meaning of his exchange with Police Radio, and actually complimenting himself on the professional way he had handled the situation, Matt Payne got out of the car and went into Colosimo's Gun Store.

Thirty minutes after that, after equipping himself with a Smith & Wesson Model 37 Chief's Special Airweight J-Frame .38 Special caliber revolver and an ankle holster for it, he had called Radio again and reported W-William Two Oh Nine back in service.

Getting the pistol had been far more complicated than he had imagined. He had—naively, he now understood—assumed that since he was now a sworn Police Officer, and equipped with a badge and a photo identification card to prove it, buying a revolver would be no more difficult than buying a pair of shoes.

But that hadn't been the case. First there had been a long federal government form to fill out, on which he had to swear on penalty of perjury, the punishments for which were spelled out to be a $10,000 fine and ten years imprisonment, that he was not a felon, a drunk, or a drug addict; and that neither was he under psychiatric care or under any kind of an indictment. And when that was complete, the salesman took his photo identification to a telephone and called the Police Department to verify that there was indeed a Police Officer named Matthew Payne on their rolls.

But finally the pistol was his. He carried it out to the car and, with more trouble than he thought it would be, managed to fasten the ankle holster to his right ankle. Then, sitting in the car, he had gone through some actually painful contortions to take off his jacket and his shoulder holster.

He took the revolver from the holster, opened the cylinder, and dumped the six shiny, somehow menacing, cartridges into his hand. He loaded five of them, all it held, into the Undercover revolver's cylinder and put it back into the ankle holster. He slipped the leftover cartridge into his trousers pocket.

When he tried to put the service revolver and the shoulder holster in the glove compartment, it was full of shortwave radio chassis. He finally managed to shove it all under the passenger-side seat.

The ankle holster, as he drove to the Roundhouse, had felt both strange and precariously mounted, raising the very real possibility that he didn't have it on right.

As he looked for a parking place, other doubts rose in his mind. He had never been inside the Roundhouse; the closest he'd come was waiting outside while Inspector Wohl had gone inside to get Detectives Washington and Harris.

He had no idea where to go inside to gain access to a Xerox machine. And there was, he thought, a very good possibility that as he walked down a corridor somewhere, the ankle holster would come loose and his new pistol would go sliding down the corridor before the eyes of fifty Police Officers, most of them Sergeants or better.

He found a parking place, pulled the Fury into it, and almost immediately backed out and left the Roundhouse parking lot. He knew where there was a Xerox machine, and where to park the car to get to it. He picked up the microphone.

"W-William Two Oh Nine," he reported, "out of service at Twelfth and Market."

"Why hello, Matt," Mrs. Irene Craig, executive secretary to the senior partners of Mawson, Payne, Stockton, McAdoo & Lester, said. "How are you?"

"Just fine, Mrs. Craig," Matt said. "And yourself?"

His confidence in the ankle holster had been restored. He had walked, at first very carefully, and then with growing confidence through the parking building to the elevator, and it had not fallen off.

"What can I do for you?"

"I need to use the Xerox machine," he said.

"Sure," she said. "It's in there. Do you know how to use it?"

"I think so," he said.

"Come on," she said. "I'll show you."

When the fifth sheet was coming out of the Xerox machine, she turned to him. "What in the world is this?"

"It's the investigation reports of the Northwest Philadelphia rapes," Matt said.

"What are you doing with them?" she asked. "Or can't I ask?"

"I'm working on them," Matt said, and then the lie became uncomfortable. "My boss told me to get them Xeroxed."

"Doesn't the Police Department have a Xerox machine?"

"Ours doesn't work," Matt said. "So they sent me down to the Roundhouse to have it done. And since I'd never been in there, I figured it would be easier to come in here."

"We'll send the city a bill." She laughed. And then, after a moment, she asked, "Is that what they have you doing? Administration?"

"Sort of."

"I didn't think, with your education, that they'd put you in a prowl car to hand out speeding tickets."

"What they would like to have done was put me in a paddy wagon, excuse me, EPW, but Denny Coughlin has put his two cents in on my behalf."

"You don't sound very happy about that," she said. Irene Craig had known Matthew Payne virtually all of his life, liked him very much, and shared his father's opinion that Matt's becoming a cop ranked high on the list of Dumb Ideas of All Time.

"Ambivalent," he said, as he started to stack the Xeroxed pages. "On one hand, I am, at least theoretically, opposed to the idea of special treatment. On the other hand—proving, I suppose, that I am not nearly as noble as I like to think I am—I like what I'm doing."

"Which is?"

"I'm the gofer for a very nice guy, and a very sharp cop, Staff Inspector Peter Wohl."

"He's the one who had his picture in the paper? The one they put in charge of this new—"

"Special Operations," Matt filled in.

"That sounds interesting."

"It's fascinating."

"I'm glad for you," she said.

Not really, she thought. *I would be a lot happier if he was miserable as a cop; then maybe he'd come to his senses and quit. But at least Denny Coughlin is watching out for him; that's something.*

"I like it," Matt said. "So much I keep waiting for the other shoe to drop."

"Stick around," she said, laughing. "It will. It always does.'"

"Thanks a lot," Matt said, chuckling.

"You want to see your father?"

"No," he said, and when he saw the look on her face, quickly added, "I've got to get back. He's probably busy; and I had breakfast with him this morning."

"Well, I'll tell him you were in."

"If you think you have to."

"You're a scamp," she said. "Okay. I won't tell him. How's the apartment?"

"I can't get used to the quiet," he said.

He had, two weeks before, moved into an attic apartment in a refurbished pre–Civil War building on Rittenhouse Square. His previous legal residence had been a fraternity house on Walnut Street near the University of Pennsylvania campus. Irene Craig knew that he knew his father had "found" the apartment for him, in a building owned by Rittenhouse Properties, Inc., the lower three floors of which were on long-term lease to the Delaware Valley Cancer Society. She wondered if he knew that 80 percent of the stock of Rittenhouse Properties, Inc., was owned by Brewster Cortland Payne II. Now that she thought of it, she decided he didn't.

"Maybe what you need is the patter of little feet to break the quiet," Irene Craig said.

"Don't even *think* things like that!" Matt protested.

When the Xerox machine finally finished, Irene Craig gave him thick rubber bands to bind the four copies together, and then, impulsively, kissed him on the cheek.

"Take care of yourself, sport," she said.

When Matt returned to the Highway Patrol building at Bustleton and Bowler, he stopped first at his car, double-parking the Fury to do so, and put his service revolver and shoulder holster under the driver's seat of his Porsche. Then he drove the Fury into the parking lot.

He gave the keys to Sergeant Frizell, who apparently had had a word with Inspector Wohl about Officer Payne's place in the pecking order of Special Operations.

Frizell handed him a cardboard box full of multipart forms.

"The Inspector said do as many of these as you can today," Frizell sad. "There's a typewriter on a desk in there."

"What are they?" Matt asked.

"The requisition and transfer forms for the cars, and for the extra radios," Frizell explained. "On top is one already filled out; just fill out the others the same way."

They were, Matt soon saw, the "paperwork" without which Good Old Ernie in the radio garage had been, at first, unwilling to do any work. Plus the paperwork for the cars themselves, the ones they had already taken from the motor pool, and blank forms, with the specific data for the particular car to be later filled in, for cars yet to be drawn, as they were actually taken from the motor pool.

The only word to describe the typewriter was "wretched." It was an ancient Underwood. The keys stuck. The platen was so worn that the keys made deep indentations in, or actually punched through, the upper layers of paper and carbon, and whatever the mechanism that controlled the paper feeding was called, that was so worn that Matt had to manually align each line as he typed.

He completed two forms and decided the situation was absurd. He looked at his watch. It was quarter to five.

He went into the other room.

"Sergeant," he said. "I think I know where I can get a better typewriter. Would it be all right if I left now and did these forms there?"

"You mean, at home?"

"Yes, sir."

"I don't give a damn where you type them, Payne, just that they get typed."

"Good night, then."

"Yeah."

Matt took the carton of blank forms and carried it to the Porsche. At this time of day, he decided, he would do better going over to I-95 and taking that downtown, rather than going down Roosevelt Boulevard to North Broad Street. He could, he decided, make better time on I-95. There was not much fun driving a car capable of speeds well over one hundred if you couldn't go any faster than thirty-five.

Two miles down I-95, he glanced in the mirror to see if it was clear to pass a U-Haul van, towing a trailer. It was not. There was a car in the lane beside him. It was painted blue-and-white, and there was a chrome-plated device on its roof containing flashing lights. They were flashing.

He dropped his eyes to the speedometer and saw that he was exceeding the speed limit by fifteen miles per hour. The police car, a *Highway Patrol* car, he realized with horror, pulled abreast of him, and the Highway Patrolman in the passenger seat gestured with his finger for Matt to pull to the side of the superhighway.

"Oh, Jesus!" Matt muttered, as he looked in the mirror and turned on his signal.

He had a flash of insight, of wisdom.

He broke the law. He would take his medicine. He would not mention that he was a fellow Police Officer, in the faint hope that he could beat the ticket. That way, there was a chance that it would not come to Staff Inspector Wohl's attention that on his very first day on the job, he had been arrested for racing down I-95 somewhere between eighty and eighty-five miles per hour.

He stopped and went into the glove compartment for the vehicle registration certificate. The glove compartment was absolutely empty. Matt had a sudden, very clear, mental image of the vehicle registration. It, together with the bill of sale and the title and the other paperwork, was in the upper right-hand drawer of the chest of drawers in his room in the house in Wallingford.

He glanced in the mirror and saw that both Highway Patrolmen had gotten out of the car and were approaching his. He hurriedly dug his wallet from his trousers and got out of the car.

First one, and then three more cars in the outer lane flashed past him, so close and so fast that he was genuinely frightened. He walked to the back of the car and extended his driver's license to one of the Highway Patrolmen.

"I don't seem to have the registration with me," Matt said.

"You were going at least eighty," the patrolman said. "You had it up to eighty-five."

"Guilty," Matt said, wanly.

"You mind if we examine the interior of your car, sir?" the other Highway Patrolman said. Matt turned his head to look at him; he was at the passenger-side window, looking inside.

"No, not at all," Matt said, obligingly. "Help yourself."

He turned to face the Highway Patrolman who had his driver's license.

"My registration is home," Matt said.

"This your address, 3906 Walnut?"

"No, sir," Matt said. "Actually, I just moved. I now live on Rittenhouse Square."

"Look what I got!" the other Highway Patrolman said.

Matt turned to look. The other Highway Patrolman was holding Matt's service revolver and his shoulder holster in his hand.

He didn't get a really good look. He felt himself being suddenly spun around, and felt his feet being kicked out from under him, and then a strong shove against his back. Just in time, he managed to get his hands out in front of him, so that he didn't fall, face first, against the Porsche.

"*Don't* move!" the Highway Patrolman behind him said.

He felt hands moving over his body, around his chest, his waist, between his legs, and then down first one leg and then the other.

"He's got another one!" the Highway Patrolman said, pulling Matt's right trousers leg up, and then jerking the Chief's Special from the ankle holster.

"I can explain this," Matt said.

"Good," the Highway Patrolman said.

Matt felt himself being jerked around again. A hand found his belt and pulled him erect. A handcuff went around his right wrist, and then his right arm was pulled behind him. His left arm was pulled behind him, and he felt the other half of the handcuff snapping in place. Then he was spun around.

"Have you a permit to carried concealed weapons, sir?" the Highway Patrolman said.

"I'm a policeman," Matt said.

"This one's brand new," the second Highway Patrolman said, shaking the cartridges from the Undercover revolver into his palm.

"I just bought it today," Matt said.

"You were saying you're a policeman?" the Highway Patrolman asked.

"That's right," Matt said.

"Where do you work? Who's your Lieutenant?"

"Special Operations," Matt said. "I work for Inspector Wohl."

"Where's that?" the Highway Patrolman asked, just a faint hint of self-doubt creeping into his voice.

"Bustleton and Bowler," Matt said.

"Where's your ID?"

"In my jacket pocket," Matt said.

The Highway Patrolman dipped into the pocket and found the ID.

"Jesus!" he said, then, "Turn around."

Matt felt his wrists being freed.

"What's this?" the second Highway Patrolman said.

"He's a cop," the first one said. "He says he works for Inspector Wohl."

"Why didn't you show us this when we pulled up beside you?" the second asked, more confused than angry.

Matt shrugged helplessly.

"You find anything wrong with the way we handled this?" the first Highway Patrolman asked.

"Excuse me?" Matt asked, confused.

"We stopped an eighty-five-mile-an-hour speeder, and found a weapon concealed under his seat. We asked permission to examine the car. We took necessary and reasonable precautions by restraining a man we found in possession of two concealable firearms. Anything wrong with that?"

Matt shrugged helplessly.

"Isn't that what this is all about? You were checking on us?"

Matt suddenly understood.

"What this is all about is that this is my first day on the job," he said. "And I decided I'd rather pay the ticket than have Inspector Wohl find out about it."

They both looked at him. And both of their faces, by raised eyebrows, registered disbelief.

And then the taller of them, the one who had found the revolver under the seat, laughed, and the other joined in.

"Jesus H. Christ!" he said.

The taller Highway Patrolman, shaking his head and smiling with what Matt perceived to be utter contempt, handed him the Chief's Special and then the cartridges for it. The shorter one looped the shoulder holster harness around Matt's neck. Then, chuckling, they walked back to their car and got in.

By the time Matt got back in his car, they had driven off.

Officer Matthew Payne drove the rest of the way to his apartment more or less scrupulously obeying the speed limit.

It was after the change of watches when Peter Wohl returned to his office. The day-watch Sergeants had gone home; an unfamiliar face of a Highway Patrol Sergeant was behind the desk.

"I'm Peter Wohl," Peter said, walking to the desk with his hand extended.

"Yes, sir, Inspector," the Sergeant said, smiling. "I know who you are. We went through Wheel School together."

Wohl still didn't remember him, and it showed on his face.

"I had hair then," the Sergeant said, "and I was a lot trimmer. Jack Kelvin."

"Oh, hell, sure," Wohl said. "I'm sorry, Jack. I should have remembered you."

"You made a big impression on be back then."

"Good or bad?" Wohl asked.

"At the time I thought it was treason," Kelvin said, smiling. "You spilled your wheel, and I went to help you pick it up, and you said, 'Anybody who rides one of these and likes it is out of his fucking mind.' "

"I said that?"

"Yes, you did," Kelvin said, chuckling, "and you meant it."

"Well, under the circumstances, I'd appreciate it if you didn't go around telling that story."

"Like I said, that was a long time ago, and you'll notice that I am now riding a desk myself. You don't spill many desks."

"I've found that you can get in more trouble riding a desk than you can a wheel," Wohl said. "Did anything turn up on the abduction?"

"No, sir," Kelvin said. "Chief Coughlin called a couple of minutes ago and asked the same thing."

"Did he want me to call him back?"

"No, sir, he didn't. He asked that you call him in the morning."

"Anything else?"

"Sergeant Frizell said to tell you that your driver took the vehicle and radio requisition forms home to fill out," Kelvin said. When Wohl looked at him curiously, Kelvin explained. "Frizell said he didn't like the typewriter here."

Wohl nodded. He understood about the typewriters. It was generally agreed that the only decent typewriters in the Police Department were in the offices of Inspectors, *full* Inspectors, and up.

"He's a nice kid," Wohl said. "Just out of the Academy. He is—was?—how do you say this? Dutch Moffitt was his uncle."

"Oh," Kelvin said. "I heard that Chief Coughlin sent him over, but I didn't get the connections."

"Chief Coughlin also sent over the two Narcotics plainclothesmen who found Gerald Vincent Gallagher," Wohl said. "Until I decide what to do with Payne, I'm going to have him follow them around, and make himself useful in here. He's not really my driver."

"You're entitled to a driver," Kelvin said. "Hell, Captain Moffitt had a driver. It may not have been authorized, but no one said anything to him about it."

"Did Captain Sabara? Have a driver, I mean?"

"No, sir," Kelvin said. "After Captain Moffitt was killed, and Sabara took over, he drove himself."

"Every cop driving a supervisor around is a cop that could be on the streets," Wohl said. "Matt Payne is nowhere near ready to go on the streets."

Kelvin nodded his understanding.

"Jason Washington called. Homicide detective? You know him?"

"Special Operations," Wohl corrected him. "He transferred in today."

"He didn't mention that," Kelvin said. "He called in and asked that you get in touch when you have time to talk to him."

"Where is he?"

"He said he was having dinner in the Old Ale House."

"Call him, please, Jack, and tell him that when he finishes his dinner, I'll be here for the next hour or so."

"Yes, sir," Kelvin said. "Captain Sabara left word that he's going to work the First and Second District roll calls for volunteers, and then go home. Captain Pekach left word that he's going to have dinner and then ride around, and that he'll more than likely be in here sometime tonight."

Wohl nodded. "Payne was supposed to have Xeroxed some stuff for me. You know anything about it?"

"Yes, sir. I left it on your desk. I'd love to know where he found that Xerox machine. The copies are beautiful."

"Knowing Payne, he probably waltzed into the Commissioner's office and used his," Wohl said. He put out his hand again. "It's good to see you, Jack," he said. "And especially behind that desk."

"I'm glad to see you behind your desk, too, Inspector."

He meant that, Wohl decided, flattered. *It wasn't just polishing the apple.*

Wohl went into his office and examined the Xeroxed materials. Kelvin was right, he thought, the copies were beautiful, like those in the Xerox ads on television, not like those to be expected from machines in the Police Department.

He took the original file back out to Sergeant Kelvin and told him to have a Highway Patrol car run it back to Northwest Detectives, and to make sure that it wound up in Lieutenant Spanner's hands, not just dumped on the desk man's desk in the squad room.

Then he sat down and took one of the Xerox copies and started, very carefully, to read through it again.

Fifteen minutes later, he sensed movement and looked up. Jason Washington was at the office door, asking with a gesture of his hand and a raised eyebrow if it was all right for him to come in.

Wohl gestured that it was. Washington did so and then closed the door behind him.

"How was dinner?" Wohl asked.

"All I had was a salad," Washington said. "I have to watch my weight."

"What's on your mind, Jason?"

"Is that the Xerox you said you would get me?"

Wohl nodded, and made a gesture toward it.

Washington took one of the files, then settled himself in an armchair.

"I saw the Flannery girl," he said.

"How did that go?"

"Not very well, as a matter of fact," Washington said. "She wasn't what you could call anxious to talk about it again. Not to anyone, but especially not to a man, and maybe particularly to a black man."

"But?"

"And," Washington said, "I told you Hemmings was a good cop. It was a waste of time. I didn't get anything out of her that he didn't. And then I talked to him. He's pissed, Peter, and I can't say I blame him. Putting me on this job was the same as tell-

ing him either that you didn't think he had done a good job, or that he was capable
of doing one."

"That's not true, and I'm sorry he feels that way."

"How would it look to you, if you were in his shoes?" Washington asked reasonably.

"When I was a new sergeant in Homicide, Jason," Wohl replied, "Matt Lowenstein
took me off a job because I wasn't getting anywhere with it. The wife in Roxborough
who ran herself over with her own car. He put the best man he had on the job, a guy
named Washington."

"I told Hemmings that story," Washington said. "I don't think it helped much."

After a moment, Wohl said, "Thank you, Jason."

Washington ignored that.

"You read that file?"

"I was just about finished reading it for the third time."

"The one time I read it," Washington said, "I thought I saw a pattern. Our doer
is getting bolder and bolder. You see that, something like that, too?"

"Yes, I did."

"If we get the abducted woman back, alive, I'll be surprised."

"Why?"

"That didn't occur to you?" Washington asked.

"Yes, it did, but I want to see if we reached the same conclusion for the same
reasons."

"The reason we don't have a lead, not a damned lead, on this guy is because we
don't have a good description on him, or his van. And the reason we don't is that, until the Flannery thing, he wasn't with the victims more than fifteen, twenty minutes,
and he did what he did where he found them. In the Flannery job, he put her in his
van, but in such a way that it didn't give us any better picture of him than we had
before. He never took that mask off—by the way, it's not a Lone Ranger–type mask;
the Lone Ranger wore one that just covered his eyes."

"I picked up on that," Wohl said.

"That was the one little mistake that Dick Hemmings made, and when I mentioned
it to him, he admitted it right away; said that he'd picked up on that, too, and doesn't
know why he put it in the report the way he did."

"Go on, Jason."

"In the Flannery job, he put her in his van and drove away with her. I think that
convinced him he can take his victims away, and keep them longer. That's what he's
really after, I think, having them in his power. That's more important to him, I think,
than the sexual gratification he's getting; there's been no incident of him reaching or-
gasm except by masturbation."

"I agree," Wohl said, "that he's after the domination; the humiliation is part of that."

"So he now knows he can get away with taking the women away from their
homes; he proved that by taking the Flannery woman to Forbidden Drive. And since
that was so much fun, he took the next victim away, too. Maybe to his house, maybe
someplace else, the country, maybe."

"And the longer he keeps them, the greater the possibility . . . that his mask will
fall off, or something. . . ."

"Or that the victim will look around and see things that would help us to find where
she's been taken," Washington continued. "And this guy is smart, Peter. It is going to oc-

cur to him sooner or later, if it hasn't already, that what he's got on his hands is someone who can lead the cops to him; and that will mean the end of his fun."

Not dramatically, but matter-of-factly, Jason Washington drew his index finger across his throat in a cutting motion.

"And he might find that's even more fun than running around in his birthday suit, wearing a mask, and waving his dong at them," Washington added.

"That's the way I see it," Wohl said. "That's why I wanted you over here, working on it. I want to catch this guy before that happens."

"Dick Hemmings, if you'd have asked him, could have told you the same thing."

"It's done, Jason, you're here. So tell me what we should be doing next."

"Tony Harris has come up with a long list of minor sexual offenders," Washington said. "If I were you, Peter, I'd get him all the help he needs to ring doorbells."

"I don't know where I can get anybody," Wohl said, thinking aloud.

"You better figure out where," Washington said. "That's all we've got right now. Tony's been trying to get a match, in Harrisburg, between the names he's got and people who own any kind of a van. So far, zilch."

"Sabara's got some people coming in," Peter said. "Probably some of them will be here in the morning. I'll put them on it. And maybe I could get some help from Northwest Detectives, maybe even tonight."

"I wouldn't count on that," Washington said. "I think they're glad you've taken this job away from them."

"I didn't take it away from them," Wohl flared. "It was given to me."

"Whatever you say."

"Jason, it's been suggested to me that we might find a psychiatric profile of the doer useful."

"Don't you think we have one?" Washington said, getting to his feet. "Whose suggestion was that? Denny Coughlin's? Or Czernich himself?"

Wohl didn't reply.

"I'm going home," Washington said. "It's been a long day."

"Good night, Jason," Wohl said. "Thanks."

"For what, Peter?" Washington said, and walked out of his office.

Wohl felt a pang of resentment that Washington was going home. So long as Elizabeth J. Woodham, white female, aged thirty-three, of 300 East Mermaid Lane in Roxborough, was missing and presumed to have been abducted by a known sexual offender, it seemed logical that they should be doing something to find her, to get her back alive.

And then he realized that was unfair. If Jason Washington could think of anything else that could be done, he would be doing it.

There was nothing to be done, except wait to see what happened.

And then Wohl thought of something, and reached for the telephone book.

 The apartment under the eaves of what was now the Delaware Valley Cancer Society Building was an afterthought, conceived after most of the building had been renovated.

C. Kenneth Warble, A.I.A, the architect, had met with Brewster C. Payne II of Rittenhouse Properties over luncheon at the Union League on South Broad Street to bring him up to date on the project's progress, and also to explain why a few little things—in particular the installation of an elevator—were going a little over budget.

Almost incidentally, C. Kenneth Warble had mentioned that he felt a little bad, *vis-à-vis* space utilization, about the "garret space," which on his plans, he had appropriated to "storage."

"I was there just before I came here, Brewster," he said. "It's a shame."

"Why a shame?"

"You've heard the story about the man with thinning hair who said he had too much hair to shave, and too little to comb? It's something like that. The garret space is really unsuitable for an apartment, a decent apartment—by which I mean expensive—and too nice for storage."

"Why unsuitable?"

"Well, the ceilings are very low, with no way to raise them, for one thing; by the time I put a kitchen in there, and a bath, which it would obviously have to have, there wouldn't be much room left. A small bedroom, and, I've been thinking, a rather nice, if long and narrow living room, with those nice dormer windows overlooking Rittenhouse Square, *would* be possible."

"But you think it could be rented?"

"If you could find a short bachelor," Warble said.

"That bad?" Brewster Payne chuckled.

"Not really. The ceilings are seven foot nine; three inches shorter than the Code now calls for. But we could get around that because it's a historical renovation."

"How much are we talking about?"

"Then, there's the question of access," Warble said, having just decided that if he was going to turn the garret into an apartment, it would be Brewster C. Payne's wish, rather than his own recommendation. "I'd have to provide some means for the short bachelor to get from the third-floor landing, which is as high as the elevator goes, to the apartment, and I'd have to put in some more soundproofing around the elevator motors—which are in the garret, you see, taking up space."

"How much are we talking about?" Payne repeated.

"The flooring up there is original," Warble went on. "Heart pine, fifteen-eighteen-inch random planks. That would refinish nicely, and could be done with this new urethane varnish, which is really incredibly tough."

"How much, Kenneth?" Payne had asked, mildly annoyed.

"For twelve, fifteen thousand, I could turn it into something really rather nice," Warble said. "You think that would be the way to go?"

"How much could we rent it for?"

"You could probably get three-fifty, four hundred a month for it," Warble said. "There are a lot of people who would be willing to pay for the privilege of being able to drop casually into conversation that they live on Rittenhouse Square."

"I see a number of well-dressed short men walking around town," Brewster C. Payne II said, after a moment. "Statistically, a number of them are bound to be bachelors. Go ahead, Kenneth."

Rental of the apartment had been turned over to a realtor, with final approval of the tenant assumed by Mrs. Irene Craig. There had been a number of applicants, male and female, whom Irene Craig had rejected. The sensitivities of the Delaware Valley Cancer Society had to be considered, and while Irene Craig felt sure they were as broad-minded as anybody, she didn't feel they would take kindly to sharing the building with gentlemen of exquisite grace, or with ladies who were rather vague about their place of employment and who she suspected were practitioners of the oldest profession.

It was, she decided, in Brewster C. Payne II's best interests to wait until the ideal tenant—in Irene's mind's eye, a sixtyish widow who worked in the Franklin Institute—came along. And she waited.

And then Matt Payne had come along, needing a residence inside the city limits to meet a civil service regulation, and about to be evicted from his fraternity house. She called the Director of Administration at the Cancer Society and told him that the apartment had been rented, and that, as he had been previously informed, the two parking spaces in the garage behind the building, which they had until now been permitted to use temporarily, would no longer be available to them.

She assured him that the new tenant was a gentleman whose presence in the building would hardly be noticed, and devoutly hoped that would be the case.

Air-conditioning had also been an afterthought, or more accurately an after-afterthought. Not only was there insufficient capacity in the main unit already installed, but there was no room to install the ductwork that would have been necessary. Two 2.5-ton window units had been installed, one through the side wall, the second in the bedroom in the rear.

The wave of hot muggy air that greeted Matt Payne when he trotted up the narrow stairway from the third floor and unlocked his door told him that he had forgotten to leave either unit on when he had last been home.

He put the carton of requisition forms on the desk in the living room and quickly turned both units on high. The desk, like the IBM typewriter sitting on it, had been "surplus" to the needs of Mawson, Payne, Stockton, McAdoo & Lester. With a great deal of difficulty, four burly movers had been able to maneuver the heavy mahogany desk up the narrow stairs from the third floor, but, short of tearing down a wall, there had been no chance of getting it into the bedroom, as originally planned.

He then stripped off his clothes and took a shower. Despite the valiant efforts of the air conditioners, the apartment was still hot when he had toweled himself dry. If he got dressed now, he would be sweaty again. Officer Charley McFadden had told him, in response to Matt's question as to how he should dress while they sought to locate Mr. Walton Williams, "Nice. Like you are now. He's an arty fag, not the leather and chains kind."

Matt then did what seemed at the moment to be entirely logical. He went into the living room in his birthday suit, sat down behind the IBM typewriter in that condition, and started typing up the forms.

He had been at it for just over an hour when his concentration was distracted by a soft two-toned bonging noise that he recognized only after a moment as his doorbell.

He decided it was his father, who not only had a key to the downstairs, but was a gentleman, who would sound the doorbell rather than just let himself in.

He trotted naked to the door and pulled it open.

It was not his father. It was Amelia Alice Payne, M.D., Fellow of the American College of Psychiatrists, his big sister.

"Jesus Christ, Amy! Wait till I get my goddamned pants on."

"I really hope I'm interrupting something," Amy said as she entered the apartment. She smirked at the sight of her naked brother trotting into his bedroom and then looked around.

Amy Payne was twenty-seven, petite and intense, a wholesome but not quite pretty woman who looked a good deal like her father. She was in fact not related to Matt except in the law. Her mother had been killed in an automobile accident. Six months later, her father had married Matt's widowed mother, and Brewster Payne had subsequently adopted Matthew Mark Moffitt, her infant son. Patricia Moffitt Payne and Matt had been around as far back as Amy could remember.

In Amy's mind, Patricia Moffitt Payne was her mother, and Matt her little brother.

Matt returned to the living room bare-chested and zipping up a pair of khaki pants.

"How'd you get inside?" he asked.

"Dad gave me a key so that I could use the garage," she said. "It also opens the door downstairs, as I just found out."

"Not to the apartment?" he challenged.

"No, not to the apartment," Amy said.

"To what do I owe the honor of your presence?" Matt asked. "You want a beer or a Coke or something?"

"I want to talk to you, Matt."

"Why does that cause me to think I'm not going to like this? The tone of your voice, maybe?"

"I don't care if you like what I have to say or not," she said. "But you're going to listen to me."

"What the hell is the matter with you?"

He looked at the desk, and then at the clock, and then decided he had typed the last form he was going to have to type tonight, and he could thus have a beer.

He walked to the refrigerator and took out a bottle of Heineken. He held it up.

"You want one of these?"

"I don't suppose you would have any white wine in there?"

"Yeah, I do," he said, and took a bottle from the refrigerator door.

"How long has that been in there, I wonder?" she asked.

"You want it or not?" he asked.

She nodded. "Please."

He took a stemmed glass from a cupboard over the sink, filled it nearly full with wine, and handed it to her.

"Make this quick, whatever it is," he said. "I have to work tonight, and between now and nine, I've got to grab a sandwich or something."

She didn't respond to that. Instead she raised her glass toward the mantelpiece of the fireplace, which showed evidence of having recently been bricked in.

"What's this?" she asked. "Your temple of the phallic symbol?"

"What?"

"Firearms are a substitute phallus," she said.

He saw that she was referring to his pistols, both of which he had placed on the wooden mantelpiece.

"Only for people with performance problems," Matt snorted. "I don't have that kind of problem. Not only did I take Psychology 101, too, Amy, but I stayed awake through the parts you missed."

"That's why you have two of them, right?" she replied. "I hope they're not loaded."

"One of them is," he said. "Leave them alone."

"Why two?"

"I bought the little one today; it's easier to conceal," he said. "Is that the purpose of your uninvited visit, to lay some of your psychiatric bullshit on me?"

She turned to face him.

"I had lunch with Mother today," she said. "She worries me."

"What's the matter with Mother?" he asked, concern coming quickly into his voice.

"Why you are, of course," she said. "Don't tell me that hasn't run through your mind."

"Oh, not that again!"

"Yes, that again," she said. "And she has every reason to feel that way. She's had a husband killed, *and* a brother-in-law, and she'd be a fool if she closed her mind to the possibility that could happen to a son, too."

"Did she say anything?"

"Of course not," Amy said. "Mother's not the type to whine."

"We have, I seem to recall," Matt said, "been over this before. My position, I seem to recall, was that I had—there was a much greater chance of my getting myself blown away if I had made it into the Marines. I didn't hear any complaints, I seem to recall, from you about my going in the Marines."

"You had no choice about that," she said. "You do about being a policeman."

"Oh, shit!" he said, disgustedly. "When you get a real complaint about me from Mother, then come to see me, Amy. In the meantime, butt out."

"You refuse to see, don't you, that this entire insane notion of yours to be a policeman is nothing more than an attempt to overcome the psychological castration you underwent when you failed the Marine physical."

"I seem to recall your saying something like that, before, Dr. Strangelove."

"Well, I don't have to be a psychiatrist to know that your being a policeman is tearing Mother up!"

"But your being a shrink makes it easier, right?"

The telephone rang. Matt picked it up.

"Dr. Payne's Looney-Bin, Matt the Castrated speaking."

"Peter Wohl, Matt," his caller identified himself.

Oh, shit! Those two bastards in the highway RPC sure didn't lose any time squealing on me!

And, oh, Jesus, what I just said!

"Yes, sir?"

Amy looked at him curiously. The phrase "yes, sir" was not ordinarily in his vocabulary.

"That was an interesting way to answer your phone," Peter Wohl said.

"Sir," Matt said, lamely. "My sister is here. We were having a little argument."

"Actually, that's what I called you about. You did mean your sister the psychiatrist?"

"Yes, sir."

"Jason Washington was just in to see me. He didn't turn up anything useful interviewing Miss Flannery. I'm sort of clutching at straws. In other words, I was hoping that your offer to talk to your sister was valid."

"Yes, sir, of course. I'm sure she'd be happy to speak with you."

"Who is that?" Amy asked in a loud whisper. Matt held up his hand to silence her, which had the exact opposite reaction. *"Who is that?"* Amy repeated, louder this time.

"I'm talking about now, Matt," Wohl said.

"Yes, sir," Matt said. "Now would be fine."

"I suppose you've eaten?"

"Sir?"

"I asked, have you had dinner?"

"No, sir."

"Well, then, why don't I pick you up, and we'll get a little something to eat, and I can speak with her. Would that be too much of an imposition on such short notice?"

"Not at all, sir."

"You live in the 3800 Block of Walnut, right?"

"No, sir. I've moved. I'm now on Rittenhouse Square, South, in the Delaware Valley Cancer Society Building—"

"I know where it is."

"In the attic, sir. Ring the button that says *'Superintendent'* in the lobby."

"I'll be there in fifteen minutes," Wohl said. "Thank you."

The phone went dead.

"What was all that about? Who were you talking to?"

"That was my boss," Matt said. "He wants to talk to you. I told him about you."

"Tell him to call the office and make an appointment," Amy snapped. "My God, you've got your nerve, Matt!"

"It's important," Matt said.

"Maybe it is to you, Dick Tracy, to polish the boss's apple, but it's not to me. The nerve! I don't believe that you really thought I would go along with this!"

"A lunatic who has already raped, so to speak, a half dozen women, grabbed another one last night, forced her into his van at knifepoint, and hasn't been seen since," Matt said, evenly. "Inspector Wohl thinks you might be able to provide a profile of this splendid fellow, and that might possibly help us to find him."

"Doesn't the Police Department have its own psychologists, psychiatrists?" Amy asked.

"I'm sure they do," Matt said. "But he wants to talk to you. Please, Amy."

She looked at him for a long moment, then shrugged.

"Why did you say, 'raped, so to speak'?"

"Because, so far," Matt said, as evenly, "there has been no vaginal or anal penetration, and the forced fellatio has not resulted in ejaculation."

"You should hear yourself," she said, softly. "How cold-blooded and clinical you sound. Oh, Matt!"

It was, she realized, a wail of anguish at the loss of her little brother's innocence.

"Under these circumstances," she added, as cold-bloodedly as she could manage, "I don't have much choice, do I?"

"Not really," Matt said. "He's going to take us to dinner."

"I can't go anywhere looking like this," she said. "I came here right from the hospital."

"Well, then, we'll go someplace where you won't look out of place," Matt said.

"The bathroom, presumably, is in there?" Amy asked, pointing toward his bedroom.

"Vanity, thy name is woman," Matt quoted sonorously.

"Screw you, Matt," Dr. Amelia Alice Payne replied.

Staff Inspector Peter Wohl was not what Amy Payne expected. She wasn't sure exactly what she had expected—maybe a slightly younger version of Matt's "Uncle Denny" Coughlin—but she had not expected the pleasant, well-dressed young man (she guessed that he was in his early thirties) who came through Matt's apartment door.

"Amy," Matt said, "this is Inspector Wohl. Amy Payne, M.D."

Wohl smiled at her.

"Doctor, I very much appreciate your agreeing to talk to me like this," he said. "I realize what an imposition it is."

"Not at all," Amy said, and hearing her voice was furious with herself; she had practically gushed.

"I've been trying to figure out the best way to do this," Wohl said. "What I would like you to do, if you would be so kind, would be to read the file we have on this man, and then tell me what kind of man he is."

"I understand," Amy said.

He gave her a look she understood in a moment was surprise, even annoyance, that she had interrupted him.

He smiled.

"But that isn't really the sort of thing you want to talk about over dinner. And dinner is certainly necessary. Then there's Matt."

"Sir?" Matt said.

There he goes again with that "Sir" business, Amy thought. *Who does he think this cop is, anyway?*

"What time are you meeting McFadden and Martinez?"

"Nine o'clock, at the FOP," Matt said.

What in the world is the Eff Oh Pee?

"I thought that was it," Wohl said. "So what I propose is that we go to an Italian restaurant I know on Tenth Street, and have dinner. Then I could drop you at the FOP, Matt, and take Dr. Payne to the Roundhouse, and borrow an office there where we could have our talk."

I really loathe spaghetti and meatballs; but what did I expect?

"Sir," Matt said, "why don't you come back here? I mean, she has her car in the garage here."

"Well, I don't know. . . ."

"How would you get in if you gave us your key?" Amy asked.

"I wouldn't give you my key," Matt explained tolerantly. "I would leave the door to the apartment unlocked, and you use your key to get in the building."

"Doctor?" Peter asked, politely.

"Whatever would be best," Amy heard herself saying.

It is absolutely absurd of me to think about being alone in an apartment with a man I hardly know. This is a purely professional situation; he's a policeman and I am a physician. I will do my professional duty, even if that entails pretending I like spaghetti and meatballs. And besides it's important to Matt.

The tailcoated waiter in Ristorante Alfredo bowed over the table, holding out a bottle of wine on a napkin for Peter Wohl's inspection.

"Compliments of the house, sir," he said, speaking in a soft Italian accent. "Will this be satisfactory?"

Wohl glanced at it, then turned to Amy. "That's fine with me. How about you, Doctor? It's sort of an Italian Pinot Noir."

"Fine with me," Amy said. She watched as the waiter uncorked the bottle, showed Wohl the cork, then poured a little in his glass for him to taste.

"That's fine, thank you," Wohl said to the waiter, who proceeded to fill all their glasses.

"I think it will go well with the tournedos Alfredo," the waiter said. "Thank you, sir."

Peter Wohl had explained to both of them that the tournedos Alfredo, which he highly recommended, were sort of an Italian version of steak with a marchand de vin sauce, except there was just a touch more garlic to it.

"You must be a pretty good customer in here, Inspector," Amy said, aware that there was more than a slight tone of bitchiness in her voice.

"I come here fairly often," Wohl replied. "I try not to abuse it, to save it for a suitable occasion."

"Excuse me?"

'Well, my money is no good in here," Wohl said.

"I don't think I understand that," Amy said.

"The Mob owns this place," Wohl said, matter-of-factly. "Specifically a man named Vincenzo Savarese—the license is in someone else's name, but Savarese is behind it—and he has left word that I'm not to get a bill."

"Excuse me," Amy flared, "but isn't that what they call 'being on the take'?"

"My God, Amy!" Matt said, furiously.

"No," Wohl said. " 'Being on the take' means accepting goods or services, or money, in exchange for ignoring criminal activity. Vincenzo Savarese knows that I would like nothing better than to put him behind bars; and that, as a matter of fact, before they dumped this new job in my lap, I was trying very hard to do just that."

"Then why does he pick up your restaurant bills?" Amy asked.

"Who knows? The Mob is weird. They operate as if they were still in Sicily or Naples, with a perverted honor code. He thinks he's a 'man of honor,' and thinks I am, too. He thought Dutch Moffitt was, too. Mrs. Savarese and her sister went to his funeral. The wake, too, I think, and when Dutch, before he went to Highway, was in Organized Crime, he tried very hard to lock Savarese up."

Amy decided she was talking too much, and needed time to consider what she had just heard.

The waiter and two busboys, with great élan, served the tournedos Alfredo and the side dishes. Amy took four bites of the steak, then curiosity got the best of her.

"And it doesn't offend your sense of right and wrong to take free meals from a gangster?" she asked.

"Come on, Amy!" Matt protested again.

"No," Wohl said, making a gesture with his hand toward Matt to show that since he didn't mind the question, Matt should not be upset. "What I will do in the morning is send a memo to Internal Affairs, reporting that I got a free meal here. As far as taking it—why not? Savarese knows he'll get nothing in return, and this is first-class food."

"But you know he's a gangster," Amy argued.

"And he knows I'm a cop, an honest cop," Wohl countered. "Under those circumstances, if it gives both of us pleasure, what's wrong with it?"

Amy Payne could think of no withering counterargument, and was furious. Then doubly furious when she saw Matt smiling smugly at her.

Matt glanced at his watch as the pastry cart was wheeled to the table, then jumped to his feet.

"I better get over to the FOP," he said. "You finish your dinner. I'll catch a cab. Or run."

When he was gone, Wohl said, "He's a very nice young man, soaking wet behind the ears, but very nice."

"I think I should tell you, Inspector," Amy said, "that I'm not thrilled with his choice of career."

"I would be very surprised if you were," Wohl said. "Your mother must really be upset."

Damn it, you weren't supposed to agree with me!

"She is," Amy said. "I had lunch with her today."

"I feel a little sorry for myself, too," Wohl said. "Dennis Coughlin sent him to me, with the unspoken, but very obvious, implication that I am to look after him. I think Coughlin is probably as unhappy as you and your family about his taking the job."

He looked at her, and when she didn't reply, added, "He's twenty-one years old, Doctor Payne. I suspect that he has been very humiliated by having failed the Marine Corps physical. He has decided he wants to be a policeman, and I don't think there's anything anyone can do, or could have done to dissuade him."

I don't need you to explain that to me, damn you again!

"You don't agree?" Wohl asked.

"I suppose that's true," Amy said. "Where's he going tonight? What's the Eff Oh Pee?"

"Fraternal Order of Police," Wohl said. "They have a building on Spring Garden, just off Broad. He's meeting two of my men there. They're going to look for a man we think is connected with a couple of burglaries in Chestnut Hill. I told them to take Matt with them, to give him an idea how things are, on the street."

"Oh," she said.

"That chocolate whateveritis looks good," Wohl said. "Would you like a piece?"

"No, thank you," Amy snipped. "Nothing for me, thank you."

"You don't mind if I do?"

"No, of course not," Amy said.

Damn this man, he has a skin like an elephant, the smug sonofabitch!

Matt got out of the taxi in front of the Fraternal Order of Police Building on Spring Garden Street and looked at his watch. He was five minutes late.

Damn! he thought, and then *Double Damn, either I've got the wrong place, or this place is closed!*

Then, on the right corner of the building, he saw movement, a couple going into a door. He walked to it, and saw there were stairs and went down them. He had just relaxed with the realization that he had found "the bar at the FOP," even if five minutes late, when a large man stepped in front of him.

"This is a private club, fella," he said.

"I'm meeting someone," Matt replied. "Officer McFadden."

The man looked at him dubiously, but after a moment stepped out of his way, and waved him into the room.

Matt wondered how one joined the FOP; he would have to ask.

The room was dark and noisy. There was a dance floor crowded with people and what he thought at first was a band, but quickly realized was a phonograph playing records, very loudly, through enormous speakers. At the far end of the room, he saw a bar, and made his way toward it.

He found Officers McFadden and Martinez standing at the bar, at the right of it.

"Sorry to be late," Matt said.

"We was just starting to wonder where you were," Charley McFadden said. "Talking about you, as a matter of fact."

"You got to learn to be on time," Jesus Martinez said.

"He said he was sorry, Hay-zus," McFadden defended him.

McFadden, Matt saw, was drinking Ortlieb's beer, from the bottle. Martinez had what looked like a glass of water.

"You want a beer, Matt?"

"Please," Matt said. "Ortlieb's."

"Hey, Charley," McFadden called to the bartender. "Give us another round here!"

"Two beers and a glass of water?" the bartender said. "Or is Jesus still working on the one he has, taking it easy?"

"Call him Hay-zus," McFadden said. "He likes that better. Charley, say hello to Matt Payne."

Matt was at the moment distracted by something to his right. A woman leaned up off her barstool, supported herself with one hand on the bar, and threw an empty cigarette package into a plastic garbage can behind the bar. In doing so, her dress top fell open, and her brassiere came into view. Her brassiere was one that Matt had yet to see in the flesh, but had seen in *Playboy, Penthouse,* and other magazines of the type young men buy for the high literary content of their articles and fiction.

It was black, lacy, and instead of the cloth hemispheres of an ordinary brassiere, this one had sort of half hemispheres, on the bottom only, which presented the upper portion of the breast to Matt's view, including the nipple.

Matt found this very interesting, and was grossly embarrassed when the woman glanced his way, saw him looking, said "Hi!" and then returned to her bar stool.

She was old, he thought, at least thirty-five, and she had caught him looking down her dress.

Oh, shit! If she says something . . .

"Matt, say hello to Charley Castel," Charley McFadden repeated.

Matt offered his hand to Charley Castel. "How are you?"

"Matt's out with us in Special Operations," Charley said.

"Is that so?" Charley Castel said.

"He just got out of the Academy," Jesus Martinez offered.

Thanks a lot, pal, Matt thought.

"Is that so?" Charley Castel repeated. "Well, welcome to the job, Matt."

"Aren't you going to introduce me to your friend?" a female voice said in Matt's ear. Out of the corner of his eye, he saw it was the woman who had caught him peering down her dress.

"Yeah, why not?" Charley said, chuckling. "Matt, this is Lorraine Witzell. Lorraine, this is Matt Payne."

"How are you, Matt Payne?" Lorraine said, putting her arm between Matt and Charley to shake his hand, which action served to cause her breast to press against Matt's arm. "Is that short for Matthew, or what?"

"Yes, ma'am," Matt said.

"Yes, ma'am," Jesus Martinez parroted sarcastically.

"You're sweet," Lorraine Witzell said to Matt, looking into his eyes and not letting go of his hand. "Did I hear Charley say you've been assigned to Special Operations?"

"That's right," Matt said.

For an older woman, she's really not too bad-looking. And she either didn't really catch me looking down her dress, or, Jesus, she doesn't care.

"That should be an interesting assignment," Lorraine said.

"We're on the job now, Lorraine," Charley McFadden said. "We was just talking about that."

"You're working plainclothes?" she asked. Matt sensed the question was directed to him, but Charley answered it.

"We're looking for a fag burglar," Charley replied. "Been hitting some rich woman in Chestnut Hill."

"Well, if you're going to work the fag joints," Lorraine said, again directly to Matt, "you better keep your hand you-know-where, and I don't mean on your gun. They're going to love you!"

"What we was talking about," Charley McFadden said, "is maybe splitting up. Hay-zus taking the unmarked car—he don't drink, and it's better that way—and you and me go together."

"Whatever you say, Charley," Matt said.

"You got your car? Mine's a dog."

"I came in a cab," Matt said.

"Oh," Charley said.

Matt saw the look of disappointment on McFadden's face.

"But I don't live far; getting it wouldn't be any trouble."

McFadden's disappointment diminished.

"What I was thinking was that in a car like yours, we could cruise better," McFadden said.

"I understand," Matt said. "You mean it's the sort of car a fag would drive?"

"I didn't say that," McFadden said, embarrassed. "But, no offense, yeah."

"What kind of car do you have?" Lorraine asked.

"A Porsche 911T," Charley answered for him.

"Oh, they're darling!" Lorraine said, clutching Charley's arm high up under the armpit, which also caused her breast to press against his arm again.

Which caused a physical reaction in Matt Payne that he would rather not have had under the circumstances, at this particular point in space and time.

"Where do you live, Payne?" Jesus Martinez asked.

"On Rittenhouse Square," Matt said.

"Figures," Martinez said. "Let's get the hell out of here, somebody's liable to spot that car in the parking lot and start asking questions."

"To which we answer, we were picking up Payne, and you were drinking water," McFadden replied, but Matt saw that he picked up his fresh Ortlieb's and drank half of it.

"Hay-zus is a worrier," Charley said to Matt.

"You better be glad I am," Martinez replied.

Lorraine Witzell pushed between Charley and Matt to sit her glass on the bar, which served to place her rear end against Matt's groin and the physiological phenomenon he would have rather not had manifesting itself at that moment. It didn't seem to bother Lorraine Witzell at all; quite the contrary. She seemed to be backing harder against it.

Matt took a pull at his bottle of Ortlieb's.

"I'm ready," he said, signifying his willingness to leave. "Anytime."

Lorraine Witzell chuckled deep in her throat.

"Well," she said, "if it turns out to be a dull night, come on back. I'll probably be here."

15 At quarter to one, Officer Charley McFadden pulled Matt Payne's Porsche 911T to the curb before a row house on Fitzgerald Street, not far from Methodist Hospital, in South Philadelphia.

"It happens that way sometimes," Charley said to Matt. "Sometimes you can go out and find who you're looking for easy as hell. And other times, it's like this. We'll catch the bastard. Hay-zus will turn up something."

"Yeah," Matt said.

"And you got the fag tour, right?" Charley said. "So it wasn't a complete waste of time, right?"

"It was ... educational," Matt said, just a little thickly.

"And we wasn't in all of them." McFadden laughed. "Maybe half."

"There seem to be more of those places than I would have thought possible," Matt said, pronouncing each syllable carefully.

"You all right to drive?"

"Fine," Matt said.

"You're welcome to sleep on the couch here," Charley offered.

"I'm all right," Matt insisted.

"Well, drive careful, huh? You don't want to fuck up a car like this."

"I'll be careful," Matt said, and got out of the car and walked around the back.

"We'll get the bastard," Charley McFadden repeated. "And what the hell, we were on overtime, right?"

"Right," Matt said. "Good night, Charley. See you in the morning."

He started the engine, returned to South Broad Street, and pointed the nose toward Willy Penn, surveying the city from atop City Hall.

Matt had asked Charley McFadden about "that woman you introduced me to in the FOP" five minutes after they had picked up the Porsche, and were headed into West Philadelphia.

"She works for the district attorney," Charley said. "They call her the shark."

"Why?"

"Well, she likes cops," Charley said. "Young cops in particular. What did she do, grab your joint?"

"No. Nothing like that," Matt said. "I was just curious, that's all."

"I'm surprised," Charley said. "She looked pretty interested, to me."

"She seemed to know a good deal about the police, about police work."

"As much as any cop," Charley had said.

Matt reached City Hall, and drove around it, and up North Broad to Spring Garden and into the FOP parking lot.

The place was still crowded. He made his way to the bar and ordered a scotch and soda. He had a good deal to drink, some of the drinks paid for by either the proprietors of the bars they visited, or put in front of him by the bartender, who had then said, "The tall fellow at the end of the bar," or something like that.

He saw Lorraine Witzell at the far end of the bar, with three men standing around her.

Well, it was dumb coming here in the first place.

And then fingers grazed his neck.

"I was beginning to think you'd found something more interesting to do," Lorraine Witzell said, as she slid onto the bar stool behind, which action caused first one of her knees and then the other to graze his crotch.

"May I buy you a drink?" Matt said, very carefully.

Lorraine Witzell looked at him and smiled.

"You can, but what I think would make a lot more sense, baby, would be for Lorraine to take you home and get some coffee into you. You can take me for a ride in your Porsche some other time. It'll be safe in the parking lot here."

"I'm all right to drive," Matt insisted, somewhat indignantly, as Lorraine led him across the FOP bar and up the stairs to the street.

Peter Wohl walked to his car, and stood outside the door until he saw Dr. Amelia Payne's Buick station wagon come out of the alley beside the Delaware Valley Cancer Society Building and drive past him.

He raised his hand in a wave, but Dr. Payne either did not see it, or ignored it. He shrugged and got in the car, started it up, and reached for the microphone in the glove compartment, realizing only then that was the wrong radio. He put the microphone back, and fumbled around on the seat for the microphone that would give him access to the Highway Band.

He became aware that a car had pulled parallel to him and stopped. He turned to look, and found a pair of Highway Patrolmen looking at him from the front seat of an unmarked Highway car.

He waved and smiled. There was no response from either cop, but the car moved off.

They either didn't recognize me, or they did and aren't in a particularly friendly mood toward the sonofabitch who took Highway away from Good Ol' Mike and gave it to Dave Pekach.

He picked up the microphone, and as he did, smiled.

"Highway One, this is S-Sam One."

"Highway One," Pekach came back immediately. Wohl was not surprised that Pekach was up and riding around. Not only was he new to the job, and conscientious, but Pekach was used to working nights; it would take him a week, maybe longer, to get used to the idea that the Commander of Highway worked the day shift.

"I'm on Rittenhouse Square, David. Where are you? Where could we meet?"

Wohl chuckled. The brake lights on the unmarked Highway car flashed on, and the car slowed momentarily. In what he was sure was an involuntary reflex action, the driver had hit the brakes when he heard the New Boss calling Highway One. He was sure he could read the driver's mind: *I thought that was him. Now what's the bastard up to?*

"I'm on the expressway about a mile from the Manayunk Bridge," Pekach said. "You name it."

"You know where I live?"

"Yes, I do."

"I'll meet you there," Wohl said, and laid the microphone down.

Pekach, in full uniform, complete to motorcyclist's boots and Sam Browne belt festooned with shiny cartridges, was leaning on a Highway blue-and-white on the cobblestones before Wohl's garage apartment when Wohl got there.

I wouldn't be surprised if he was working the expressway with radar for speeders, Wohl thought, and was immediately sorry. That was both unkind and not true. What David Pekach was doing was what he would have done himself in the circumstances, making the point that Highway could expect to find the boss riding around at midnight, and the second, equally important point, that he was not sneaking around in an unmarked car, but in uniform and in a blue-and-white.

Wohl pulled the nose of the LTD up to the garage and got out.

"Let me put this away, David," he called. "And then I'll buy you a beer. Long night?"

"I thought it was a good idea to ride around," Pekach said.

"So do I," Wohl said, as he unlocked the doors and swung them open. "But it's after midnight."

He put the car in the garage, and then touched Pekach's arm as he led him up the stairs to the apartment.

"You seen the papers?" Pekach said.

"No, should I have?"

"Yeah, I think so. I brought you the *Bulletin* and the *Ledger.*"

"Thank you," Wohl said. "It wouldn't take a minute to make coffee."

"I'm coffeed out; beer would be fine."

"Sit," Wohl said, pointing to the couch beneath the oil painting of the voluptuous nude, and went to the refrigerator and came back with two bottles of Schlitz. "Glass?"

"This is fine," Pekach said, "thank you."

"Nothing on Elizabeth Woodham? Wohl asked. "I expect I would have heard. . . ."

David Pekach shook his head.

"Not a damn thing," he said. "I was so frustrated I actually wrote a speeding ticket."

"Really?" Wohl chuckled.

"Sonofabitch came by me at about eighty, as if I wasn't there. I thought maybe he was drunk, so I pulled him over. He was sober. Just in a hurry."

"It's been a long time since I wrote a ticket," Wohl said.

"When he saw he was going to get a ticket," Pekach said, "he got nasty. He said he was surprised a captain would be out getting people for something like speeding when we had a serial rapist and a kidnapped woman on our hands."

"Ouch," Wohl said.

"I felt like belting the sonofabitch," Pekach said. "That was just before you called."

"I had a disturbing session just before I called you," Wohl said. "With a psychiatrist. You've seen that kid hanging around Bustleton & Bowler? Payne?"

"He's Dutch's nephew or something?"

"Yeah. Well, his sister. I let her read the files and asked her for a profile."

"And?"

"Not much that'll help us find him, I'm afraid. But she said—the way she put it was 'slippery slope'—that once somebody like this doer goes over the edge, commits the first act, starts to act out his fantasies, it's a slippery slope."

"Huh," Pekach said.

"Meaning that he's unable to stop, and starts to think of himself as invincible, starts to think, in other words, that he can get away with anything. Worse, that to get the same charge, the same satisfaction, he has to get deeper and deeper into his fantasies."

"Meaning, she doesn't think we're going to get the Woodham woman back alive?"

"No, she doesn't," Peter said. "And worse, that because he's starting to think he's invincible, that he's not going to get caught, that he'll go after somebody else, a new conquest, more quickly than he has before."

"I'm not sure I understand that," Pekach said.

"What she said is that the first time, after he'd done it, he was maybe ashamed and afraid he would get caught. And then when he didn't get caught, he stopped being afraid. And he remembered how much fun it was. So he did it again, got into his fantasies a little deeper, and was a little less frightened, and a lot less ashamed."

"Jesus!"

"What she, Dr. Payne, said was that it 'evolves into frenzy.' "

"She meant he loses control?"

"Yeah."

"You think she knows what she's talking about?"

"I'm afraid she does," Wohl said.

"What can be done that isn't being done?" Pekach asked.

"Tony Harris is working minor sexual offenders," Wohl said. "He thinks this guy may have a misdemeanor arrest or two for exposing himself, soliciting a hooker, you know. Mike has been out recruiting people, and as soon as they start coming in, in the morning, I'm going to put them to work ringing doorbells for Harris."

"If there was a van, any kind of van, in Northwest Philly tonight that got away with not coming to a complete stop, or whose taillights weren't working, you know what I mean, I would be very surprised," Pekach said. "But we just can't stop every goddamned van in town, looking for a hairy white male, no further description available."

"I know," Wohl said.

"I went to the roll call tonight," Pekach said, "and reminded Highway that if we catch this scumbag, it might get the goddamned newspapers, especially the goddamned *Ledger*, off our backs. Not that they wouldn't be trying to catch this scumbag anyway."

"I know," Wohl said.

"Czernich on your back, Peter? Coughlin? The mayor?"

"Not yet," Peter said. "But that's going to happen."

"What do they expect?"

"Results," Wohl said. "I'm wide open to suggestion, David."

"I don't have any, sorry," Pekach said.

"What did you decide after tonight?" Wohl asked.

"Excuse me?"

"What shape is Highway in? Isn't that why you were riding around?"

Pekach met Wohl's eyes for a moment before replying.

"I went in on six calls," he said. "One on 95, one on the expressway, both traffic violations, and the other four all over town, a robbery in progress, two burglaries, man with a gun, that sort of thing. I didn't find a damned thing wrong with anything Highway did."

"Did AID come up with any witnesses in the accident?"

Any accident involving a city-owned vehicle is investigated by the Accident Investigation Division of the Police Department.

"Not a damned one."

"Well, I'll check and make sure they keep trying," Wohl said.

"I intended to do that, Inspector," Pekach said, coldly.

"I didn't mean that, David," Wohl said, evenly, "the way you apparently thought it sounded."

"I also let the word get out that maybe AID could use a little help," Pekach said.

"Meaning exactly what, David?" Wohl asked, his voice now chilly.

Pekach didn't reply; it was obvious he didn't want to.

"Come on, David," Wohl insisted.

Pekach shrugged.

"I wouldn't be surprised," Pekach said, "if a bunch of people in sports jackets and ties went around the neighborhood ringing doorbells. And if one of them turned up a witness, and then, anonymously, as a public-spirited citizen, called AID and gave them the witness's name, what's wrong with that?"

"Off-duty people in sports coats and ties, you mean, of course? Who could easily be mistaken for newspaper reporters or insurance investigators because they never even hinted they might be connected with the Police Department?"

"Of course," Pekach said.

"Then in that case, David," Wohl said, smiling at Pekach, "I would say that the new commander of Highway was already learning that some of the things a commander has to do can't be found in the book."

"I'm sorry I snapped at you before," Pekach said. "I don't know what the hell is the matter with me. Sorry."

"Maybe we're both a little nervous in our new jobs."

"You bet your ass," Pekach agreed, chuckling.

"You want another beer, David?"

"No. This'll do it. Now that I had it, I'm getting sleepy." He got up. "Something will turn up, Peter, it always does," he said.

"I'm afraid of what will," Wohl said. "How long do you think it will take your wife to learn that the Highway Captain doesn't have to work eighteen hours a day?"

"Forever; I don't have a wife," Pekach said. "Or was that to politely tell me not to ride around?"

"It was to politely tell you to knock off the eighteen-hour days," Wohl said.

Pekach looked at him long enough to decide he was getting a straight answer, and gave one in return.

"I think Highway is sort of an honor, Peter. I want to do it right."

"You can do it right on say *twelve* hours a day," Wohl said, smiling.

"Isn't that the pot calling the kettle black?"

"The difference is that you have a kindly, understanding supervisor," Wohl said. "I have Coughlin, Czernich, and Carlucci."

"You may have a point." Pekach chuckled. "Good night, Peter. Thanks for the beer."

"Thanks for the talk," Wohl said. "I wanted to bounce what Dr. Payne said off someone bright."

"I'm very much afraid she's going to be right," Pekach said, and then he added, "Don't read those newspapers tonight. Let them ruin your breakfast, not your sleep."

"That bad?"

"The *Ledger* is really on our ass, yours in particular," Pekach said.

"Now, I'll have to read it," Wohl said, as he walked with Pekach to the door.

Wohl carried the beer bottles to the sink, emptied the inch remaining in his down the drain, and put them both in the garbage can under the sink.

He went to his bedroom, undressed, and then, giving in to curiosity, walked naked into the living room and reclaimed the newspapers.

He spread them out on his bed, and sat down to read them.

There was a photograph of Elizabeth J. Woodham on the front page of the *Ledger,* under the headline: KIDNAPPED SCHOOLTEACHER. Below the picture was a lengthy caption.

Elizabeth J. Woodham, 33, of the 300 block of E. Mermaid Lane in Chestnut Hill, is still missing two days after she was forced at knifepoint into a van and driven away. Her abductor is generally believed to be the serial rapist active in Chestnut Hill.

Inspector Peter Wohl, recently put in charge of a new Special Operations Division, which has assumed responsibility for the kidnapping, was "not available for the press" for comment, and Captain Michael J. Sabara, recently relieved as commander of the Highway Patrol to serve as Wohl's Deputy, refused to answer questions concerning Miss Woodham put to him by a *Ledger* reporter.

Sources believed by the *Ledger* to be reliable, however, have said the police have no clues that might lead them to the abductor, and no description of him beyond that of a "hairy, well-spoken white male." [Further details and photographs on Page B-3. The Police Department's handling of this case is also the subject of today's *Ledger* editorial, page A-7.]

Peter turned to the story, which contained nothing he hadn't seen before, and then to the editorial:

HOUSECLEANING NEEDED,
NOT WHITEWASH

It is frankly outrageous, considering the millions of dollars Philadelphia's taxpayers pour unquestioningly into their police department, that a woman can be taken from her home at knifepoint at all. It is even more outrageous that twenty-four hours after the kidnapping, the police, rather than devoting all of their time and effort to apprehending the individual responsible for the kidnapping, and rescuing a kidnapped schoolteacher, have instead elected to assign many members of the so-called elite Highway Patrol to finding witnesses willing to say that the father of the four-year-old boy killed when a stoplight running Highway Patrol smashed into his car was at fault, not them.

It was unconscionable that Inspector Peter Wohl, a crony of Police Commissioner Czernich, who is the responsible senior police official involved, should make himself "not available" to the press. The people have a right to know how well—or how poorly—their police are protecting them.

Mayor Carlucci should replace Czernich and Wohl with police officers dedicated to protecting the public, and not to whitewashing the Highway Patrol's unjustified, frequent, and well-documented excesses and failures. Anything less is malfeasance in office.

"Oh, *shit,*" Peter Wohl said, tiredly, closing the newspaper. Then he picked up the *Bulletin*. There were two stories about the Woodham abduction. One, a tearjerker, was written by a woman, Cheryl Davies, and chronicled the anguish of Elizabeth J. Woodham's family and friends. She had done her homework, Peter admitted grudgingly. There was a photograph of, and the reactions of, two sixth-graders who had been in her classes.

Mickey O'Hara's story was more or less upbeat. He wrote that Czernich had agreed to transfer to

. . . Staff Inspector Peter Wohl's just-forming new command two of the most highly respected homicide detectives, Jason Washington and Anthony Harris. Wohl, who himself enjoys a wide reputation as an investigator, has turned over the Woodham abduction to Washington and Harris, and is reported to be himself working around the clock on the investigation.

He finished reading Mickey's story, then folded the *Bulletin* closed, too. He exhaled audibly, stood up, and carried the newspapers into the kitchen, intending to put them in the garbage. Then he changed his mind and simply laid them on the counter by the sink.

When he went back into his bedroom, he smashed his right fist into his open palm, grimaced, considered for a moment getting drunk, and wound up with his head pressing against the closed venetian blinds on the window beside his bed.

Without knowing why he did it, he pulled on the cord, and the blinds twisted open, and he could see the Big House thirty yards away.

There were lights in only several of the windows, and he had just decided they were the windows of Two B, Chez Schneider, when there was proof. Naomi Schneider, wearing only her underpants, pranced into view, smiling happily at someone else in the room, and handing him a drink.

Without thinking about it, Peter turned off the lights in his bedroom.

"Peel him a grape, Naomi," Peter said, aloud.

And then he wondered if Mr. Schneider had come home unexpectedly, or whether Naomi had pulled on someone else's dong to lure him into what obviously was her bedroom.

Nice boobs!

And then a wave of chagrin hit him.

"Oh, shit," he said. He closed the blinds quickly, turned the light on, and sat on the bed.

"You're a fucking voyeur, you goddamned pervert! You were really getting turned on watching her boobs flop around like that.

You ought to be ashamed of yourself!

And then he had a second thought, not quite as self-critical: *Or get your ashes hauled, so that you won't get horny, peeking through people's bedroom windows.*

And then he had a third thought, considered it a moment, and then dug the telephone book from where he kept it under his bed.

Amelia Alice Payne, M.D., lived on the tenth floor of the large, luxurious apartment building on the 2600 block of the Parkway, said to be the first of its kind in Philadelphia, and somewhat unimaginatively named the 2601 Parkway.

She got off the elevator, walked twenty yards down the corridor, and let herself into her apartment.

She pushed the door closed with her rear end, turned and fastened the chain, and started to unbutton her blouse. She was tired, both from a long day, and from her long session with Staff Inspector Peter Wohl.

She walked into her living room and slumped into the armchair beside a table, which held the telephone answering device. She snapped it on.

She grunted as she bent to take off her shoes.

There were a number of messages, but none of them were important, or required any action on her part tonight. She had no intention of returning the call of one female patient who announced that she just had to talk to her as soon as possible. Listening to another litany of the faults of the lady's husband would have to wait until tomorrow.

She reset the machine, turned it off, and, carrying her shoes, walked into her bedroom, turning to the drapes and closing them. Open, they had given her a view of downtown Philadelphia, and, to the right, the headlights moving up and down the Schuylkill Expressway.

Amy decided against taking a shower. No one was going to be around to smell her tonight, and it would be better to use the shower as both cleanser and waker-upper in the morning.

She took off her blouse and pushed her skirt off her hips, and jerked the cover of her bed.

She probably had met more offensive men than Peter Wohl in her life, but she couldn't call one to mind at the moment. He represented everything she found offensive in men, except, she thought, that he didn't have either a pencil-line mustache or a pinky ring. But everything else she detested was there, starting with the most advanced (regressive?) case of Male Supremacist Syndrome she had ever encountered.

It was probably his cultural background, she thought. Wohl was certainly German. What was it the Germans said to define their perception of the proper role of females in society, *Kinder, Kirche, und Kuche?* Children, church, and kitchen. He obviously thought that Moses had carried that down from Mount Sinai with the other Commandments.

And he was a cop, the son of a cop. Had he said the grandson of a cop, too? That, obviously, had had a lot to do with what he was, and how he thought.

It wasn't, she thought, that he had implied she was stupid. He had been perfectly willing to pick her mind about this seriously ill man who was raping the women in Northwest Philadelphia. He was willing, as he had proved by *interrogating* her for over three hours after they had gone back to Matt's apartment, to recognize her expertise, and take advantage of it. Men who couldn't fry an egg were always perfectly willing to allow themselves to be fed by the Little Woman.

Peter Wohl, Amy knew, had believed, and had been alarmed by, her announcement that the man he was looking for was rapidly losing what control he had left. He had asked her why she had felt that way, and she had explained, and then he had made her explain her explanations. And in the end, she knew he had accepted everything she had told him.

But he had never let her forget for a moment that he was a great big policeman, charged by God and the City of Philadelphia with protecting the weak and not-too-bright, such as she. He admired her skill and knowledge, Amy thought, the way he would have admired a dog who had been trained to walk on its hind legs. *Isn't that amazing!*

He had actually insisted on walking her to her car and then telling her *"to make sure"* to lock the doors from the inside, *"there were all sorts of people running loose at night."*

And if he had said *"Good Girl"* one more time, she would have thrown something at him.

Which, of course, would only have confirmed his devout belief that women were unstable creatures who needed a great big male to protect them from the world, and from themselves.

She pulled her slip over her head, and unfastened her brassiere and took that off, examining the marks it had left on the lower portion of her breasts.

The telephone rang. She reached down to her bedside table and picked it up.

If it's that hysterical bitch calling again, I'll scream!

"Yes?"

"Dr. Payne?"

"Yes."

I'll be damned, it's him!

"Peter Wohl, Doctor."

"How nice of you to call," Amy said, sarcastically.

"I'm glad I caught you before you got to bed," he said.

"Just barely," she said. "What is it, Inspector?"

Was that a Freudian slip? Amy wondered. She had, quite unintentionally, caught her reflection in the triple mirror of her vanity table. She was, except for her underpants, *bare*. She covered her breasts with her free arm.

"I wanted to say how grateful I am for all the help you gave me, for your time," Peter Wohl said.

That's absurd! What am I modestly concealing? From whom? Mr. High and Mighty is on the telephone; he can't see me.

"You said that earlier," she said.

She pushed her panties off her hips and stepped out of them, found her reflection again, put her free hand on her hip, and thrust it out.

I have nothing whatever to be embarrassed about.

"And I have one more question," he said.

"What?"

"What effect on our doer would seeing a naked woman have? I mean, if he saw one through her window?"

She felt herself flushing.

Why the hell did he ask that?

She looked quickly around the room to see that her own blinds were tightly drawn.

"As opposed to a woman . . . a fully clothed woman," Wohl went on.

"What did you do, Inspector, just see something like that?" Amy asked, sarcastically.

"As a matter of fact, yes," he said, unabashed. "Quite inadvertently."

"I'm sure," Amy said. "But it had no effect on you, right, but you're wondering if it would on . . . a mentally ill man?"

"No," he said. "Actually, it had quite an effect on me. It was rather embarrassing."

Most men would deny that, Amy thought. *How interesting.*

"The nude female, at least a reasonably attractive one," Amy said seriously, and then saw her reflection and almost giggled as she thought, *like me for example,* "has a certain effect on the male. The normal male. A mentally ill male? Let me think." She did, and then went on. "Probably, given a man with mental problems, it would have a more profound effect. I'm not sure what that would be. If he hates women, it might trigger disgust. He might become highly aroused. The disgust might trigger anger, a sense that he thereafter had the right to punish. Innocent nudity, changing clothes, having a bath, might lead him to thinking about the helplessness of the woman."

He grunted.

"Is this of any help to you?"

"Mary Elizabeth Flannery was wearing only her underpants when this scumbag—sorry—when this guy showed up."

"I saw that in the file," Amy said.

"Maybe he drives around looking through windows," Wohl thought aloud, "and when he finds a naked, or partially naked, woman, that turns him on."

"That might have been the trigger early on," Amy said. "I can't really say. But now that I'm almost certain this man is out of control, I don't really know what effect, if any, that would have."

"Ummm," Peter Wohl said, thoughtfully.

"If that's all, Inspector, it's very late."

"Actually," Peter Wohl blurted, "I had something else in mind."

It had, in fact, occurred to him two seconds before.

"Yes?" Amy said, impatiently.

"I really enjoyed our time together," Wohl plunged on, "and I hoped that you might have dinner with me sometime. On a nonprofessional basis."

"Oh, I see," she heard herself saying. "We could run through a long line of gangster-owned restaurants where fellow men of honor get free meals, is that it?"

There was a long pause, long enough for Amy to wonder *what's wrong with me? Why did I say that?*

"I beg your pardon, Doctor. I won't trouble you again."

Oh, God, he's going to hang up!

"Peter—"

There was no reply for a long moment, and then he said, "I'm here."

"I don't know why I said that. I'm sorry."

He didn't reply.

"I would love to have dinner with you," Amy heard herself blurting. "Call me. Tomorrow. I'm glad you called."

"So'm I," Peter Wohl said, happily. "Good night, Amy."

The line went dead.

She looked at herself in the mirror again.

Oh, God, she thought. *It* was *Freudian. Sex is what that was all about!*

16 At five minutes to eight, the nineteen police officers assigned to the day shift of the Fourteenth Police District gathered in the Roll Call Room of the district building at Germantown and Haines streets, and went through the roll call ritual, under the eyes of Captain Charles D. Emerson, the Fourteenth District Commander, a heavyset, gray-haired man of fifty.

The officers formed in ranks, and went through the ritual, obviously based on similar rituals in the armed forces, of inspection in ranks. Trailed by the Sergeant, Captain Emerson marched through the three ranks of men, stopping in front of each to examine his appearance, the length of his hair, whether or not he was closely shaved, and the cleanliness of his weapon, which each officer held up in front of him, with the cylinder open. Several times, perhaps six, Captain Emerson had something to say to an officer: a suggestion that he needed a new shirt, or a shoe shine, or that he was getting a little too fat.

When the Inspection in Ranks was completed, the Sergeant stood before the men and read aloud from several items on a clipboard.

Some of the items he read were purely administrative, and local in nature, dealing with, for example, vacation schedules; and some had come over the police teletype from the Roundhouse with orders that they be read at roll calls. They dealt with such things as the death and funeral arrangements for two retired and one active police officer.

There were some items of a local nature, in particular the report of another burglary of the residence of a Miss Martha Peebles of 606 Glengarry Lane in Chestnut Hill, coupled with instructions that Radio Patrol cars and Emergency Patrol wagons on all shifts were to make a special effort to ride by the Peebles residence as often as possible.

"And we are still looking for Miss Elizabeth Woodham," the Sergeant concluded. "That's at the top of the list. You all have her description, and what description we have of the probable doer and his van. We have to get the lady back. Report anything you come across."

The day shift of the Fourteenth District was then called to attention, and dismissed, and left the roll call room to get in their cars and go on duty.

Captain Charles D. Emerson walked over to Staff Inspector Peter Wohl, who had entered the room just as the roll call started.

"How are you, Peter?" he said, putting out his hand. "Or is this an occasion when I should call you Inspector?"

Staff Inspector Wohl had no authority whatever over the Fourteenth Police District, and both of them knew it. But we *was* a Staff Inspector, and he *was* the new commander of the new Special Operations Division, and no one, including Captain Emerson, had any idea what kind of clout went with the title.

"I hope I didn't get in the way, Charley," Wohl said, shaking Emerson's hand.

"Don't be silly. Distinguished visitors are always welcome at my roll calls."

Wohl chuckled. He knew the roll call ritual had been a bit more formal than usual, because of his presence.

"Bullshit, Charley," Wohl said, smiling at him.

"What can I do for you, Peter?" Emerson smiled back.

"You want the truth?"

"When all else fails, sometimes that helps."

"I'm covering my ass, Charley. This Peebles woman has friends in high places."

"So Commissioner Czernich has led me to believe," Emerson said, dryly. "He's been on the phone to me, too."

"So now both of us can tell him, if he asks, and I think he will, that you and I are coordinating our resources to bring Miss Peebles's burglar to the bar of justice."

Emerson chuckled.

"That's all, Peter?"

"I have the Woodham job. The Northwest rapist. Did you hear?"

"Czernich must like you."

"Czernich, hell. Carlucci."

"Ouch."

"I was hoping . . . maybe something turned up here?"

"I can't think of a thing, Peter. But come on in the office, and we'll call in the watch commander and whoever and kick it around over a cup of coffee."

"Thanks, but no thanks. I've got another roll call to make. Special Operations' first roll call. But call me, or better Jason Washington or Tony Harris—use the Highway Commander's number to get them—if you think of anything, will you?"

"They're working for you?" Emerson asked, surprised.

"Somewhat reluctantly."

"You must have some clout to get them transferred to you."

"I think the word is 'rope,' Charley. As in 'he now has enough rope to hang himself.' "

Captain Emerson's eyebrows rose thoughtfully. He did not offer even a *pro forma* disagreement.

"Say hello to your dad for me when you see him, will you, Peter?" he said.

Fifteen minutes later, Wohl walked into the roll call room at Bustleton and Bowler. He had arrived just in time for the roll call. Captains Pekach and Sabara, and Detectives Washington and Harris, were already in the room, and ultimately, sixteen other police officers came into the room and formed into two ranks.

The sixteen newcomers were a Sergeant, a Corporal, a Detective, and thirteen Police Officers who had reported for duty to the Special Operations Division that morning, and been directed to the roll call room by Sergeant Frizell when they walked in the door.

"Form in ranks," Captain Sabara called, unnecessarily, as the last of the newcomers was doing just that. Then he turned to Wohl, and asked, rather formally. "You want to take this, Inspector?"

"You go ahead, Mike," Wohl said.

Sabara nodded, and moved in front of the formation of policemen.

"Let me have your attention, please," Sabara said. "You all know me, and you probably know Inspector Wohl and Captain Pekach, too, but in case you don't, that's Captain Pekach, the High Commander, and that's the boss. Special Operations now has Highway, in case that wasn't clear to everybody.

"Welcome to Special Operations. I think you'll find it, presuming you can cut the mustard, a good assignment, an interesting job. And we're going to put you right to work.

"You all have read the papers," Sabara said, "and know that a woman named Elizabeth J. Woodham was abducted at knifepoint by a doer we think is the man who has been raping women all over Northwest Philadelphia. Let me tell you, we have damned little to go on.

"Getting Miss Woodham back alive from this critter is the first priority of business for Special Operations. For those of you who don't know them, the two gentlemen standing beside the Inspector are Detectives Washington and Harris. They came to Special Operations from Homicide and the Inspector has put them in charge of the investigation. They report directly to his office, and if they ask you to do something in connection with this investigation, you can take it as if it came from either me or the Inspector himself.

"We have some cars, and we're getting more. They have the J-Band, of course, and they have—or will have, Sergeant Frizell will talk to you about that—the Highway Band and the Detective Band, and when the Roundhouse gets around to assigning one to us, will have a Special Operations Band. From now until we get this lady back, forget about eight-hour shifts."

He paused, looked thoughtful for a moment, then gestured toward Washington.

"Detective Washington will now tell you what we've got, and what we're looking for."

Wohl saw, except on one or two faces, an expression of interest, perhaps even excitement.

There is, he thought, *except in the most jaded, cynical cops, an element of little boy playing cops and robbers, a desire to get involved in something more truly coplike than handing out speeding tickets and settling domestic disputes, in being sent out to catch a bona fide bad guy, to rescue the damsel in distress from the dragon.*

And Mike Sabara has just told them that's what we want them to do, and the proof stands there in the person of Jason Washington. There is still an element of romance in the title "Detective," and an even greater element of romance in the persona of a homicide detective, and Washington is literally a legend among homicide detectives; sort of a real-life Sherlock Holmes. They are in the presence of what they dreamed of being themselves, and maybe still do, and they know it.

Washington spoke for about five minutes, tracing the activities of the serial rapist from the first job, before anyone even thought of that term. He didn't waste any words, but neither, Wohl thought, did he leave anything even possibly important out.

"And since we have, essentially, nothing to go on," Washington concluded, "we have to do it the hard way, ringing doorbells, digging in garbage cans, asking the same questions over and over again. Tony Harris has the only idea that may turn something up that I can think of, so I'll turn this over to him."

Tony Harris, Wohl thought, *does not present anything close to the confident, formidable presence Washington projects. He's a weasel compared to an elephant. No. That's too strong. A mangy lion, the kind you see in the cages of a cheap circus, compared to an elephant. Where the hell does he get his clothes? Steal them from a Salvation Army Depository? Did the Judge really give his ex-wife everything? Or is Tony trying to support two women, and taking the cost out of his clothing budget?*

But almost as soon as Tony started to speak, Wohl saw that the interest of the newcomers—who had almost audibly been wondering *Who the Hell is this guy?* began to perk up. Within a minute or two, they were listening to him with as rapt attention as they had given Washington. *Who the hell is this guy?* had been replaced with *This sonofabitch really knows what he's talking about!*

Tony delivered a concise lecture on sexual deviation and perversity, went from there to the psychology of the flasher, the molester, the voyeur, the patron of prostitutes, and the rapist, and then presented a profile of the man they were looking for that differed from the one Wohl had got from Dr. Amelia Alice Payne only in that he didn't mention "the slippery slope" or "invincibility."

And then he told them what they were looking for, and how he wanted them to look for it: "What I've come up with is a list of minor sexual offenders, white males who have misdemeanor arrests for any of a long list of weird behavior. I'm still working on coming up with names. . . ."

He stopped and looked at Wohl.

"Inspector, I used to work with Bart Cumings in South Detectives," he said, indicating the Sergeant among the newcomers. "Could I have him to work with me on the files?"

"You've got him," Wohl said, smiling at Sergeant Cumings. He saw Officer Matt Payne enter the roll call room, look around, and then head for him.

I'll bet I know what Payne wants, Wohl thought. *And I'll bet Sergeant Cumings will be out of that uniform by tomorrow morning. If he waits that long to get out of it.*

In the Police Department rank structure, the step up from police officer was either to detective or corporal, who received the same pay. There was no such rank as "detective sergeant," so a detective who took and passed the sergeant's examination took the risk of being assigned anywhere in the department where a sergeant was needed, and that most often meant a uniformed assignment. After a detective had been on the job awhile, the prospect of going back in uniform, even as a sergeant, was not attractive. Very few uniformed sergeants got much overtime. Divisional detectives, counting their overtime, always took home more money than captains. Homicide detectives like Tony Harris and Jason Washington, for example, for whom twenty-four-hour days were not at all unusual, took as much money home as a Chief Inspector.

Some detectives, thinking of retirement, which was based on rank, took the Sergeant's exam hoping that when they were promoted they would get lucky and remain assigned to the Detective Division. Wohl felt sure that Sergeant Cumings was one of those who had taken the gamble, and lost, and wound up as a uniformed sergeant someplace that was nowhere as interesting a job as being a detective had been. That explained his volunteering for Special Operations. If he had been a crony of Harris in South Detectives, that meant he had been a pretty good detective.

And if he could work here, in civilian clothes, he would be, Wohl knew, very pleased with the arrangement. He wondered if Cumings would ask permission to wear plainclothes, and decided he probably would not. He was an experienced cop who had learned that if you ask permission to do something, the answer was often no. But if you did the same thing, like working in an investigative job in plainclothes without asking, probably no one would question you.

Wohl decided that whether Cumings asked for permission to work in civilian clothes, or just did it, it would be all right.

"Anyway, what we need you guys to do," Tony Harris went on, "is check these people out. Very quietly. I don't want anybody going where these people work and asking their boss if they think the guy could be the rapist. You work on the presumption of innocence. What you will look for is whether or not he fits the rough description we have—hairy and well spoken. And we look for the van. We've already run these people through Harrisburg for a match with a van and come up with zilch. But maybe his neighbor's got a van, or his brother-in-law, or maybe he gets to bring one home from work. And that's *all* you do! You hit on something, you report it to Washington or me, and now Sergeant Cumings. Unless there's no way you can avoid it, I don't want you talking to these people. You just thin out the list for us. Anybody got any questions about that?"

"You mean, we find this guy, we don't arrest him?" a voice called out.

"Not unless he's got the schoolteacher in the van with him," Harris said, "with her life clearly in danger. Otherwise, you report it, that's all. We're dealing with a real sicko here, and there's no telling what he'll do if he figures he's about to get grabbed."

"Like what, for example, he hasn't already done?" a sarcastic voice called.

Wohl looked quickly to spot the wiseass, but was not successful.

Harris's face showed contempt, not anger, but Wohl suspected there was both, and Harris immediately proved it.

"Okay," Harris said, "since you apparently can't figure it out yourself. We bag this guy, a hairy guy who speaks as if he went past the eighth grade, and who has a van. We even get one or more of the victims to identify him. But we don't have Miss

Woodham, all right? So, if he doesn't figure this out himself, and he's smart, he gets a lawyer and the lawyer says, *'Just keep denying it, Ace. Nobody saw you without your mask, and I'll confuse them when I get them on the stand . . . make them pick you out of a line of naked hairy men wearing masks, or something!'* That's how he would beat the first rapes, unless we can get what we professional detectives call 'evidence.' "

The identity of the wiseass was now clear. At least four of the newcomers had turned around to glower contemptuously at him.

"And we seem to have forgotten Miss Woodham, haven't we?" Harris went on. "Who is the reason we're all out looking for this scumbag in the first place. Now just for the sake of argument, let's say he's got her tied up someplace, like a warehouse or something. Some place we can't connect him to. So our cowboy says, *'Where's the dame?'* and our guy says *'What dame?'* and our cowboy says, *'You know what dame, Miss Woodham,'* and our sicko says, *'Not only did I not piss all over the one lady, I never heard of anybody named Woodham. You got a witness?'* So the latest victim, the one we're trying to find, cowboy, starves or suffocates or goes insane, wherever this scumbag has her tied up. Because once our sicko knows we're onto him, he's not going to go anywhere near the victim. Does that answer your question, smartass?"

Harris handled that perfectly, Wohl thought.

"You think she's still alive?" another newcomer asked, softly.

"We won't know that until we find her," Harris said. "That's all I've got, Captain."

Sabara turned to Wohl.

"Have you got anything, Inspector?"

"Going along with what Harris said, Captain," Wohl said. "About not making the man we're looking for any more disturbed than he is, what would you think about putting as many of these officers as it takes in plainclothes? And in unmarked cars?"

"I'll find out how many unmarked cars there are and set it up, sir," Sabara said.

"If necessary, Mike, take unmarked cars from Highway."

"Yes, sir. Anything else, sir?"

Wohl shook his head and turned to face Matt Payne, who was now standing beside him.

"Inspector, Chief Coughlin called," Matt said, surprising Peter Wohl not at all. "He wants you to call him right away."

"Okay," Wohl said, and walked out of the roll call room toward his office.

As he passed Sergeant Frizell's desk, Wohl told him, "Call Chief Coughlin for me, please."

"Inspector, the Commissioner just called, too, wanting you to get right back to him."

"Get me Chief Coughlin first," Wohl ordered. He walked into his office, sat down, and watched the telephones until one of the buttons began to flash. He picked it up.

"Inspector Wohl," he said.

"Hold one for the Chief," Sergeant Tom Lenihan's voice replied.

"Have you seen the papers, Peter?" Coughlin began, without any preliminaries.

"Yes, sir."

"What's this about you refusing to talk to the press?"

"I wasn't here," Wohl said. "Somebody must have told him I was unavailable."

"That's not what it sounded like in the *Ledger,*" Coughlin said.

"It also said you and I are cronies," Wohl said.

"The Commissioner's upset," Coughlin said.

"He just called here," Wohl said. "As soon as you're through with me, I'm going to return his call."

"What about assigning officers to find witnesses to clear the Highway cop?"

"Guilty," Peter said. "Except that I didn't assign them. They volunteered. Off duty, in civilian clothes. If they turn up a witness, there will be an anonymous telephone call from a public-spirited citizen to AID. It was actually Dave Pekach's idea. I want you to understand that I'm doing the opposite of laying it off on Pekach. If I had thought of it first, I would have done it first. And I'll take full responsibility for doing it."

He heard Coughlin grunt, and there was a pause before Coughlin asked, "Was that smart, under the circumstances?"

"If I could have sent them to find the Woodham woman, I would have," Wohl said.

Matt Payne appeared at his office door. Wohl made a gesture for him to go away, together with a mental note to tell him to learn to knock before he came through a closed door.

"How's that going?" Chief Coughlin asked.

"The first fifteen, maybe sixteen, volunteers just showed up for duty. I turned them all over to Washington and Harris to ring doorbells. That's where I was when you called."

"Maybe, until you get the Woodham woman back, you better put the people who were looking for witnesses to the car wreck to work ringing doorbells, too."

"I will if you tell me to, Chief," Wohl said, "but I'd rather not."

"You want to explain that?"

"Well, for one thing, I think they did all they could, and drew a blank, about finding anyone who saw Mr. McAvoy run the red light."

"Damn," Coughlin said.

"And for another, I don't think having Highway cops going around ringing doorbells is such a good idea. The guy we're looking for is already over the edge. I don't want to spook him."

"You want to go over that again?" Coughlin asked.

Wohl covered the mouthpiece with his hand, and demanded, "What the hell do you want, Payne?"

"Sir, the Commissioner's on Two Six, holding for you," Matt replied.

"Okay," Wohl said, and Matt backed out of the office, closing the door after him.

"Chief, the Commissioner's on the other line. Can I get back to you?"

"Call me when you get something," Coughlin said, impatiently, and then added, "Peter, frankly, I would have a hell of a lot more confidence in the way you're doing things if you had at least been able to keep that Peebles woman from being burgled again."

"I just was talking to Charley Emerson about that—" Wohl said, and then stopped, because Chief Inspector Dennis V. Coughlin had hung up.

He pushed the flashing button on the telephone.

"Good morning, Commissioner," he said, "Sorry to keep you waiting. I was talking to Chief Coughlin."

"Hold on for Commissioner Czernich, please, Inspector Wohl," a female voice Peter did not recognize replied.

"Czernich," the Commissioner snarled a moment later.

"I have Inspector Wohl for you, Commissioner," the woman said.

"It's about time," Czernich said. "Peter?"

"Yes, sir. Sorry to keep you waiting, sir. I was talking to Chief Coughlin."

"You've seen the papers? What's this about you refusing to talk to the press?"

"Sir," Wohl said, "it wasn't quite that way. I wasn't here, and—"

"Lemme have that," a voice said, faintly in the background, and then came over the line full volume. "This is Jerry Carlucci, Peter."

"Good morning, sir," Peter said.

"I know and you know that sonofabitch is after us, Peter," the mayor of the City of Brotherly Love said, "and we both know why, and we both know that no matter what we do, he'll still be trying to cut our throats. But we can't afford to give the sonofabitch any ammunition. You just can't tell the press to go fuck themselves. I thought you were smarter than that."

"Sir, that's not the way it happened," Peter said.

"So tell me," Mayor Carlucci said.

"Sir, I was not in the office. I *was* 'unavailable.' That's it."

"Shit," the mayor said. "What about using Highway to look for witnesses to clear our guy? Is that true?"

"Yes, sir, I did that. But in sports coats and ties. Off-duty volunteers."

"I think I know why you did it," Mayor Carlucci said, "but under the circumstances, was it smart?"

"Sir, I considered it to be the proper thing to do at the time. There was nothing that wasn't already being done to locate Miss Woodham, and I hoped to clear the officers involved of what I considered—consider—to be an unjust accusation."

"You're saying you'd do the same thing again?" Carlucci asked, coldly.

"Yes, sir."

"They find any witnesses for our side?"

"No, sir."

"They still looking?"

"Sir, I have no intention, without orders to the contrary, to tell my men what they can't do when they're off duty and in civilian clothes."

"In other words, fuck Arthur Nelson and his goddamned *Ledger?*"

"No, sir. I frankly think that if we were going to find a witness, they'd have found one by now. But I think, for the morale of Highway, that it's important we keep looking. Or maybe I mean that I don't want Highway to think I threw Officer Hawkins to the wolves because of the *Ledger* editorial."

"Hawkins was the guy driving?"

"Yes, sir. And he says Mr. McAvoy ran the stoplight, and I believe him."

"Goddamn it, I was right," Mayor Carlucci said.

"Sir?"

"When I sent you out there, gave you Special Operations," Mayor Carlucci said.

Peter Wohl could think of no appropriate response to make to that, and so made none.

"I was about to ask where you are with the Woodham job," Mayor Carlucci said.

"Sir, I have turned over all—"

"I said 'was about to ask,' " the mayor said. "Don't interrupt me, Peter."

"Sorry, sir."

"I've been there," the mayor said. "And I know the one thing a commanding officer on the spot does not need is people looking over his shoulder and telling him what they think he should have done. So I won't do that. I'll tell you what I am going to do, Peter. I'm going to issue a statement saying that I have complete faith in the way you're handling things."

"Yes, sir," Peter said.

"But you better catch this sonofabitch, Peter. You know what I'm saying?"

"Yes, sir."

"This sonofabitch is making the Police Department look like the Keystone Cops. The Department can't afford that. I can't afford that. And you, in particular, can't afford that."

"I understand, sir," Peter said.

"I don't want to find myself in the position of having to tell Tad Czernich to relieve you, and making it look like Arthur Nelson and his goddamned *Ledger* were right all the time," Mayor Carlucci said.

"I hope that won't be necessary, sir."

"You need anything, Peter, anything at all?"

"No, sir, I don't think so."

"If you need something, you speak up. Tad Czernich will get it for you."

"Thank you, sir."

"Tell your dad, when you see him, I said hello," the mayor said. "Hang on, Tad wants to say something."

"Peter," Commissioner Czernich said. "I understand Miss Peebles was burgled again last night."

"Yes, sir," Peter said. "I'm working on it."

"Good," Commissioner Czernich said. "Keep me advised."

Then he hung up.

Wohl took the telephone from his ear, looked at the handset, wondered for perhaps the three hundredth time why he did that, and then put it in its cradle. He got up and walked to his office door and pulled it open.

Matt Payne had been put to work collating some kinds of forms.

"Payne?"

"Yes, sir?"

"You look like death warmed over," Wohl said. "Are you sick?"

Payne looked distinctly uncomfortable.

"Sir, I guess I had a little too much to drink last night."

That figures, Wohl thought, *McFadden and Martinez took him to the FOP and initiated him.*

"Where are they?"

"Sir?"

"Where's Sherlock Holmes and the faithful Dr. Watson?"

Matt finally understood that Wohl meant McFadden and Martinez.

"Sir, I don't know," he said.

"Find them," Wohl said. "Tell them as soon as they can fit me into their busy schedule, I want to see them. And find Captain Pekach, too, please, and ask him to come see me."

"Yes, sir."

David Pekach was still in the Seventh District Building. Two minutes later, he was standing in Wohl's doorway waiting for Wohl to raise his eyes from the papers on his desk. Finally, he did.

"Come in, please, David," he said. "You want some coffee?"

Pekach shook his head no, then asked with raised eyebrows if Wohl wanted him to close the door. Wohl nodded that he did.

"I just finished talking to Chief Coughlin and the Commissioner," Wohl said, deciding in that moment not to mention Mayor Jerry Carlucci.

"I thought maybe they would call," David Pekach said, dryly.

"In addition to everything else," Wohl said, "they both seem personally concerned and very upset with me about whatever the hell is going on with this Peebles woman. She was burgled again last night."

"I heard."

"I put your two hotshots, McFadden and Martinez, on the job. They're looking for—"

Pekach's nod of understanding told Wohl that Pekach knew about that, so he stopped. "The way they tackled the job, unless I am very wrong, was to take young Payne out there down to the FOP and get him falling-down drunk."

"I don't know," Pekach said, loyally. "They were always pretty reliable."

"They didn't find the guy—the actor, the boyfriend of the Peebles woman's brother—that I know," Wohl said.

"You want me to talk to them?"

"No. I'll talk to them. I want you to go talk to Miss Peebles."

"What?"

"You go over there right now," Wohl said. "And you ooze sympathy, and do whatever you have to do to convince her that we are very embarrassed that this has happened to her again, and that we are going to take certain steps to make absolutely sure it doesn't happen again."

"What certain steps?"

"We are going to put—call it a stakeout team—on her property from sunset to sunrise."

"You lost me there," Pekach confessed. "Where are you going to get a stakeout team? I mean, my God, if it gets in the paper that you're using manpower to stake out a third-rate burglary site . . ."

"Martinez, McFadden, and Hungover Harry out there," Wohl said. "The wages of sin are death, David. I'm surprised you haven't learned that."

Pekach chuckled. "Okay," he said.

"And you will tell Miss Peebles that a Highway Patrol car will drive past her house not less than once every half hour during the same hours. Then you will tell your shift Lieutenant to set that up, and to tell the guys in the car that they not only are to drive by, but they are to drive into the driveway, making a lot of noise, and slamming the car doors when they get out of the car, so that Miss Peebles, when she looks in curiosity out her window, will see two uniformed officers waving their flashlights around in the bushes."

"That'd spook the guy who's doing this to her," Pekach argued.

"I hope so," Wohl said. "I don't want another burglary at that address on the Overnight Report on the Commissioner's desk tomorrow morning."

"Okay," Pekach said, doubtfully, "you're the boss."

"I'm not going to tell Sherlock Holmes and Dr. Watson this, David," Wohl said. "But I think they're right. I think the doer is the brother's boyfriend. When they're not sitting outside her house, I want them to keep looking for him. Got the picture?"

"Like I said, you're the boss. You're more devious than I would have thought. . . ."

"I'll interpret that as a compliment," Wohl said. "And as devious as I am, I will frankly tell you that the success of this operation will hinge on how well you can charm the lady."

"Then why don't you go charm her?"

"Because I am the commanding officer, and that sort of thing is beneath my dignity," Wohl said, solemnly.

Pekach smiled.

"I'll charm the pants off the lady, boss," he said.

"Figuratively speaking, of course, Captain?"

"I don't know. What does she look like?"

"I don't know," Wohl said.

"Then I don't know about the pants," Pekach said. "I'll let you know how well I do."

"Just the highlights, please, Captain. None of the sordid details."

17 Captain David Pekach was tempted to go see both the Captain of Northwest Detectives and the Captain of the Fourteenth District before going to call on the Peebles woman, but finally decided against it. He knew that his success as the new Highway Captain depended in large measure on how well Highway got along with the Detective Bureau and the various Districts. And he was fully aware that there was a certain resentment toward Highway on the part of the rest of the Department, and especially on the part of detectives and uniformed District cops.

He had seen, several times, and as recently as an hour before, what he thought was the wrong reaction to the *Ledger* editorial calling Highway "the Gestapo." This morning, he had heard a Seventh District uniformed cop call *"Ach-tung!"* when two Highway cops walked into the building, and twice he had actually seen uniformed cops throw a straight-armed salute mockingly at Highway Patrolmen.

It was all done in jest, of course, but David Pekach was enough of an amateur psychologist to know that there is almost always a seed of genuine resentment when a wife zings her husband, or a cop zings another cop. After he had a few words with the cop who had called *"Ach-tung,"* and the two cops who had thrown the Nazi salutes, he didn't think they would do it again. With a little luck, the word would quickly spread that the new Highway Commander had a temper that had best not be turned on.

He understood the resentment toward Highway. Some of it was really unjustified, and could be attributed to simple jealousy. Highway had special uniforms, citywide jurisdiction, and the well-earned reputation of leaving the less pleasant chores of police work, especially domestic disputes, to District cops. Highway RPCs, like all other RPCs, carried fire hydrant wrenches in their trunks. When the water supply ran low, or water pressure dropped, as it did when kids turned on the hydrants to cool off in the summer, the word went out to turn the hydrants off.

David Pekach could never remember having seen a Highway cop with a hydrant wrench in his hand, and he had seen dozens of Highway cars roll blithely past hydrants pouring water into the streets, long after the kids who had turned it on had gone in for supper, or home for the night. That sort of task, and there were others like it—a long list beginning with rescuing cats from trees and going through such things as chasing boisterous kids from storefronts and investigating fender-benders—was considered too menial to merit the attention of the elite Highway Patrol.

The cops who had to perform these chores naturally resented the Highway cops who didn't do their fair share of them, and Highway cops, almost as a rule, managed to let the District cops know that Highway was something special, involved in *real* cop work, while their backward, nonelite brothers had to calm down irate wives and get their uniforms soaked turning off fire hydrants.

So far as the detectives were concerned, it was nearly Holy Writ among them that if Highway reached a crime scene before the detectives did, Highway could be counted on to destroy much of the evidence, usually by stomping on it with their motorcyclists' boots. Lieutenant Pekach of Narcotics had shared that opinion.

One of his goals, now that he had Highway, was to improve relations between Highway and everybody else, and he didn't think a good way to do that would be to visit Northwest Detectives and the Fourteenth District to ask about the Peebles burglaries. They would, quite understandably, resent it. It would be tantamount to coming right out and saying *"since you ordinary cops can't catch the doer in a third-rate burglary, Highway is here to show you how real cops do it!"*

And, David Pekach knew, Peter Wohl had already been to both the Fourteenth District and Northwest Detectives. Wohl could get away with it, if only because he outranked the captains. And Wohl, in Pekach's judgment, was a good cop, and if there had been anything not in the reports, he would have picked up on it and said something.

But Pekach did get out the reports, which he had already read, and he read them again very carefully before getting into his car and driving over to Chestnut Hill.

Number 606 Glengarry Lane turned out to be a very large Victorian house, maybe even a mansion, sitting atop a hill behind a fieldstone-pillar-and-iron-bar fence and a wide expanse of lawn. The fence, whose iron bars were topped with gilded spear tops, ran completely around the property, which Pekach estimated to be at least three, maybe four acres. The house on the adjacent property to the left could be only barely made out, and the one on the right couldn't be seen at all.

Behind the house was a three-car garage that had, Pekach decided, probably started out as a carriage house. The setup, Pekach thought, was much like where Wohl lived, except that the big house behind Wohl's garage apartment had been converted into six luxury apartments. This big house was occupied by only two people, the Peebles woman and her brother, and the brother was reported to be in France.

All three garage doors were open when Pekach drove up the driveway and stopped the car under a covered entrance portal. It was not difficult to imagine a carriage drawn by a matched pair of horses pulling up where the blue-and-white had stopped, and a servant rushing off the porch to assist the Master and his Mistress down the carriage steps.

No servant came out now. Pekach saw a gray-haired black man, wearing a black rubber apron and black rubber boots, washing a Buick station wagon. There was a Mercedes coupe, a new one, and a Cadillac Coupe de Ville in the garage, and a two-year-old Ford sedan parked beside the garage, almost certainly the property of the black guy washing the car.

Pekach went up the stairs and rang the doorbell. He heard a dull bonging inside, and a moment or two later, a gray-haired black female face appeared where a lace curtain over the engraved glass window had been pulled aside. And then the door opened.

"May I help you?" the black woman asked. She was wearing a black uniform dress, and Pekach decided the odds were ten to one she was married to the guy washing the Buick.

"I'm Captain Pekach of the Highway Patrol," David said. "I'd like to see Miss Peebles, please."

"One moment, please," the black woman said. "I'll see if Miss Peebles is at home." She shut the door.

Pekach glanced around.

The way this place is built and laid out, it's an open invitation to a burglar to come in and help himself.

The door opened again a full minute later.

"Miss Peebles will see you," the maid said. "Will you follow me, please?"

Pekach took off his uniform cap, and put his hand to his pigtail, which of course was no longer there.

Inside the door was a large foyer, with an octagonal tile fountain in the center. Closed double doors were on both sides of the foyer, and a wide staircase was directly ahead. There was a stained-glass leaded window portraying, Pekach thought, Saint Whoever-It-Was who slayed the dragon on the stairway landing.

This place looks like a goddamned museum. Or maybe a funeral home.

The maid slid open one of the double doors.

"Here's the policeman, Miss Martha," the maid said, and gestured for him to go through the door.

He found himself in a high-ceilinged room, the walls of which were lined with bookshelves.

"How do you do?" Martha Peebles said.

A fifty-year-old spinster, Pekach instantly decided, looking at Martha Peebles. She was wearing a white, frilly, high-collared, long-sleeved blouse and a dark skirt.

"Miss Peebles, I'm Captain Pekach, commanding officer of the Highway Patrol," David said. "Inspector Wohl asked me to come see you, to tell you how sorry we are about the trouble you've had, and to tell you we're going to do everything humanly possible to keep it from happening again."

Martha Peebles extended her hand.

The cop, as opposed to the man, in Pekach took over. The cop, the trained observer, saw that Martha Peebles was not fifty. She did not have fifty-year-old hands, or fifty-year-old eyes, or fifty-year-old teeth. These were *her* teeth, not caps, and they sat in healthy gums. There were no liver spots on her hands, and there was a fullness of flesh in the hands that fifty-year-olds have lost with passing time. And her neck had not begun to hang. It was even possible that the firm appearance of her breasts was Miss Peebles herself, rather than a well-fitting brassiere.

"How do you do, Captain ... *Pekach,* you said?"

"Yes, ma'am."

Her hand was warm and soft, confirming his revised opinion of her age. She was, he now deduced, maybe thirty-five, no more. She just dressed like an old woman; that had thrown him off. He wondered why the hell she did that.

"You'll forgive me for saying I've heard that before, Captain," Martha Peebles said, taking her hand back and lacing it with the other one on her abdomen. "As recently as yesterday."

"Yes, ma'am, I know," David Pekach said, uncomfortably.

"I am really not a neurotic old maid, imagining all this," she said.

"No one suggested anything like that, Miss Peebles," Pekach said. *Oh, shit! McFadden and Martinez!* "Miss Peebles, did the two officers who were here yesterday say anything at all out of line? Did they insinuate anything like that?"

"No," she said. "I don't recall that they did. But, if I may be frank?"

"Please."

"They did seem a little young to be detectives," she said, "and I got the impression—how should I put this—that they were rather overwhelmed by the house."

"I'm rather overwhelmed with it," David said. "It's magnificent."

"My father loved this house," she said. "You haven't answered my question."

"What question was that, Miss Peebles?" Pekach asked, confused.

"Aren't those two a little young to be detectives? Do they have the requisite experience?"

"Well, actually, Miss Peebles, they aren't detectives," Pekach said.

"They were in civilian clothing," she challenged. "I thought, among policemen, only detectives were permitted to wear civilian clothing."

"No, ma'am," Pekach said. "Some officers work in civilian clothing."

"I didn't know that."

"Yes, ma'am," he said. "When it seems appropriate, that's authorized."

"It seems to me that the more police in uniform the better," she said. "That that would tend to deter crime."

"You have a point," Pekach said. "I can't argue with that. But may I explain the officers who were here yesterday?"

"We're talking about the small Mexican or whatever, and the large, simple Irish boy?"

"Yes, ma'am. Miss Peebles, do you happen to recall hearing about the police officer, Captain Moffitt, who was shot to death recently?"

"Oh, yes, of course. On the television, it said that he was, unless I'm confused somehow, the commanding officer of the Highway Patrol."

"Yes, ma'am, he was," Pekach said.

"Oh, I see. And you're his replacement, so to speak?"

"Yes, ma'am, but that's not what I was driving at."

"Oh?"

"We knew who had shot Captain Moffitt within minutes," Pekach said. "Which meant that eight thousand police officers—the entire Philadelphia Police Department—were looking for him."

"I can certainly understand that," she said.

"Two undercover Narcotics Division officers found him—"

"They threw him under a subway train," she said. "I read that in the *Ledger*. Good for them!"

"That story wasn't true, Miss Peebles," Pekach said, surprised at her reaction. "Actually, the officer involved went much further than he had to capture him alive. He didn't even fire his weapon, for fear that a bullet might hit an innocent bystander."

"He should have shot him dead on the spot," Miss Peebles said, firmly.

David looked at her with surprise showing on his face.

"I read in *Time,*" Martha Peebles said, "that for what it costs to keep one criminal in prison, we could send four people to Harvard."

"Yes, ma'am," Pekach said. "I'm sure that's about right."

"Now, *that's* criminal," she said. "Throwing good money after bad. Money that could be used to benefit society being thrown away keeping criminals in country clubs with bars."

"Yes, ma'am, I have to agree with you."

"I'm sure that people like yourself must find that sort of thing very frustrating," Martha Peebles said.

"Yes, ma'am, sometimes," Pekach agreed.

"I'm going to draw the blind," Martha Peebles announced. "The sun bleaches the carpets."

She went to the window and did so, and the sun silhouetted her body, for all practical purposes making her blouse transparent. David Pekach averted his eyes.

Just a bra, huh? I would have thought she'd have worn a slip. Oh, what the hell, it's hot. But really nice boobs!

She walked back over to him.

"You were saying?" she said.

"Excuse me?"

"There was a point to your talking about the man who shot your predecessor?"

"Oh, yes, ma'am. Miss Peebles, the officer who found Gerald Vincent Gallagher was Officer Charles McFadden."

"Who?"

"Officer McFadden, Miss Peebles. The officer Inspector Wohl sent to see you yesterday. And Officer Martinez is his partner."

"Really?" she replied, genuinely surprised. "Then I certainly have misjudged them, haven't I?"

"I brought that up, Miss Peebles, in the hope you might be convinced that we sent you the best men available."

"Hmmm," she snorted. "That may be so, but they don't seem to be any more effective, do they, than anyone else that's been here?"

"They were working until long after midnight last night, Miss Peebles, looking for Walton Williams—"

"They were looking in the wrong place, then," Martha Peebles said. "They should have been looking here. *He* was here."

Shit, she's right about that!

"Well, actually, we don't know that," David said. "We don't know if whoever was here last night was Mr. Williams. For that matter, we don't even know that Mr. Williams is even connected—"

"Don't be silly," Martha Peebles snapped. "Who else could it be?"

"Literally, anyone."

"Captain, I don't like to think of a total figure for all the things that have been stolen from this house by one of Stephen's 'friends.' I don't know whether he actually pays them to do what—whatever they do—but I do know that almost without exception, they tip themselves with whatever they can stick in their pockets before they go back wherever Stephen finds them."

"I didn't see any record of that, prior to this last sequence of events," Pekach said.

"For the good reason that I never reported it. I find it very painful to have to publicly acknowledge that my brother, the last of the line, is, so to speak, going to *be* the last of the line; and that he's not even very good at that, and has to go out and hire prostitutes."

"Yes, ma'am," David said, genuinely sympathetic.

"Is that the correct word? Or is there another term for males?"

"Same word, ma'am."

"I suppose I would have gone on and on, closing my eyes to what was going on, pretending that I didn't really care about the things that turned up missing . . . but this Williams man shows no sign of stopping this harassment—and that's what it is, more than the value of the items he's stolen—and that proves, it seems to me, that it is he and not any other burglar, who would take as much as he could haul off—"

"You may have a point, Miss Peebles," Pekach said.

"But I am also afraid that he will either steal, or perhaps simply vandalize, for his own perverse reasons, Daddy's gun collection. That would break my heart, if any of that was stolen or vandalized."

Pekach's eyes actually brightened at the word *gun*.

What the hell is going on here? There was not one damned word about guns in any of the reports I read.

"A gun collection?" Pekach asked. "I wonder if you'd be kind enough to show it to me?"

"If you like," she said. "With the understanding that you may look, but not touch."

"Yes, ma'am."

"Well, then, come along." She led him out of the library and up the stairs, past Saint Whatsisname Slaying the Dragon.

"There were some edged pieces," she said.

"Excuse me?"

Pekach had been distracted by the sight of Miss Martha Peebles's rear end as she went up the stairs ahead of him. The thin material of her skirt was drawn tight over her rump. She was apparently not wearing a half slip, for the outline of her underpants was clearly visible. And the kind of underpants she was wearing were . . .

Pekach searched his limited vocabulary in the area and as much in triumph as surprise came up with "bikinis."

Or the lower half of bikinis, whatever the hell they were called. Little tiny goddamned things, which, what there was of them, rode damned low.

Nice ass, too.

"Swords, halberds, some Arabian daggers, that sort of thing," Martha Peebles said, "but they were difficult and time consuming to care for, and Colonel Mawson—do you know Colonel Mawson, Captain?"

"I know who he is, Miss Peebles," Pekach said as she stopped at the head of the stairs and waited for him to catch up with her.

"Colonel Mawson worked out some sort of tax arrangement with the government for me, and I gave them to the Smithsonian Institution," she concluded.

"I see."

She led him down a carpeted corridor, and then stopped so suddenly David Pekach bumped into her.

"Sorry," he said.

She gave him a wan smile, and nodded upward, toward the wall behind him.

"That's Daddy," she said.

It was an oil painting of a tall, mean-looking stout man with a large mustache. He was in hunting clothes, one hand resting on the rack of an elk.

It was a lousy picture, Pekach decided. It looked more like a snapshot.

"I had that done after Daddy passed away," Martha Peebles said. "The artist had to work from a photograph."

"I see," Pekach said. "Very nice."

"The photo had Stephen in it, but I told the artist to leave him out. Stephen hated hunting, and Daddy knew it. I think he probably made him go along to . . . you know, expose him to masculine pursuits. Anyway, I didn't think Stephen belonged in Daddy's picture, so I had the artist leave him out."

"I understand."

Martha Peebles then put her arm deep into a vase sitting on the floor and came out with two keys on a ring. She put one and then the other into locks on a door beside the portrait of her father, and then opened the door, and reached inside to snap a switch. Fluorescent lights flickered to life.

The room, about fifteen feet wide and twenty feet long, was lined with glass-fronted gun racks, except for the bar end, which was a bookcase above a felt-covered table. There were two large, wide, glass-enclosed display cases in the center of the room, plus a leather armchair and matching footstool, and a table on which an old Zenith Trans-Oceanic portable radio sat.

"This is pretty much as it was the day Daddy passed away," Martha Peebles said. "Except that I took out his whiskey."

"How long has your father been dead, Miss Peebles?" Pekach asked, as he walked toward the first display case.

"Daddy passed over three years, two months, and nine days ago," she said, without faltering.

Pekach bent over the display case.

Jesus H. Christ! That's an 1819 J. H. Hall breech action! Mint!

"Do you know anything about these guns, Miss Peebles?" Pekach asked.

She came to him.

"Which one?" she asked and he pointed and she leaned over to look at it, which action caused her blouse to strain over her bosom, giving David Pekach a quick and unintentional glimpse of her undergarments.

Even though Captain Pekach was genuinely interested in having his identification of the weapon he had pointed out as a U.S. Rifle, Model 1819, with a J. H. Hall pivoted chamber breech action confirmed, a certain portion of his attention was diverted to that which he had inadvertently and in absolute innocence glimpsed.

Jesus! Black lace! Who would have ever thought! I wonder if her underpants are black too? Black lace bikinis! Jesus H. Christ!

"That's an Army rifle," Martha Peebles said. "Model of 1819. That particular piece was made in 1821. It's interesting because—"

"It has a J. H. Hall action," Pekach chimed in.

"Yes," she said.

"I've never seen one in such good shape before," David Pekach said. "That looks unfired."

"It's been test fired," Martha said. "It has Z.E.H. stamped on the receiver just beside the flintlock pivot. That's almost certainly Captain Zachary Ellsworth Hampden's stamp. But I don't think it ever left Harper's Ferry Armory for service."

"It's a beautiful piece," Pekach said.

"Are you interested—I was about to ask 'in breech loaders,' but I suppose the first question should be, are you interested in firearms?"

"My mother says that's the reason I never got married," Pekach blurted. "I spend all my money on weapons."

"What kind?"

"Actually, Remington rolling blocks," Pekach said.

"Daddy loved rolling blocks!" Martha Peebles said. "The whole wall case on the left is rolling blocks."

"Really?"

He walked to the cabinet. She caught up with him.

"I don't have anything as good as these," Pekach said. "I've got a sporting rifle something like that piece, but it's worn and pitted. That's mint. They all look mint."

"Daddy said that he regarded himself as their caretaker," Martha Peebles said. "He said it wasn't in him to be a do-gooder, but preserving these symbols of our heritage for later generations gave him great pleasure."

"What a nice way to put it," Pekach said, absolutely sincerely.

"Oh, I'm so sorry Daddy passed over and can't be here now," Martha said. "He so loved showing his guns to people with the knowledge and sensitivity to appreciate them."

Their eyes met. Martha Peebles's face colored and she looked away.

"That was his favorite piece," she said after a moment, pointing.

"What is it? It looks German."

They were looking at a heavily engraved, double-triggered rifle with an elaborately shaped, carved, and engraved wild cherry stock.

"German-American," she said. "It was made in Milwaukee in 1883 by Ludwig Hamner, who immigrated from Bavaria in 1849. He took a Remington rolling block action, barreled it himself, in 32-20, one turn in eighteen inches, and then did all the engraving and carving himself. That's wild cherry."

"I know," Pekach said. "It's beautiful!"

She turned and walked away from him. He saw her bending down to lift the edge of the carpet by the door. She returned with a key and used it to unlock the case. Almost reverently, she took the rifle from its padded pegs and handed it to Pekach.

"I don't think I should touch it," he said. "There's liable to be acid on my fingertips from perspiration."

"I'll wipe it before I put it back, silly," Martha Peebles said. When he still looked doubtful, she said, "I know Daddy would want you to."

He reached to take the gun, and as he did so, his fingers touched hers and she recoiled as if she were being burned, and he almost dropped the rifle.

But he didn't, and when, after an appropriately detailed and appreciative examination of the piece, he handed it back to her, their fingers touched again, and this time she didn't seem to recoil from his touch; quite the contrary.

"So what does Mr. Walton Williams have to say about the burglaries of the Peebles residence?" Staff Inspector Peter Wohl inquired, at almost the same moment Martha Peebles handed Captain David Pekach the 1893 wild cherry–stocked Ludwig Hamner Remington rolling-block Schuetzen rifle.

"We had a little trouble finding him, Inspector," Officer Charley McFadden replied.

"But you did find him?"

"No, sir," McFadden said. "Not really."

"You didn't find him?" Wohl pursued.

"No, sir. Inspector, we was in every other fag bar in Philadelphia, last night."

"Plus the bar in the FOP?" Wohl asked.

"We met Payne there is all, Inspector," McFadden said.

"Oh, I thought maybe you thought you would find Mr. Williams hanging around the FOP."

"No, sir. It was just a place to meet Payne."

"So you had nothing to drink in the FOP?"

"Hay-zus didn't," Charley said.

"Does that mean that you and Payne had a drink? A couple of drinks?"

"We had a couple of beers, yes, sir."

"Payne can't hold his liquor very well, can he?"

"He put it away all right last night, it seemed to me," McFadden said.

"In the FOP, or someplace else?"

"We had to order something besides a soda when we was looking for Williams, sir."

"Hay-zus, too?"

"Hay-zus doesn't drink," McFadden said.

"I thought you just said, or implied, that to look credible in the various bars and clubs in which you sought the elusive Mr. Williams, it was necessary to drink something other than soda."

"I don't know how Hay-zus handles it, sir."

"Weren't you with him?"

"No, sir. We split up. Hay-zus took the plain car, and I took Payne and we looked in different places."

"Using a personal vehicle?"

"Yes, sir."

"Must have been fun," Wohl said. "To judge by the way Payne looks and smells this morning."

"He looked all right to me when we went home," Charley said.

"I'll take your word for that, Officer McFadden," Wohl said. "Far be it from me to suggest that you would consider yourself to be on duty with a bellyful of booze and impaired judgment."

"Yes, sir," McFadden said.

"I have a theory why you were unable to locate Mr. Williams last night," Wohl said. "Would you care to hear it?"

"Yes, sir," McFadden said.

Wohl glared at Jesus Martinez.

"May I infer from your silence that you are not interested in my theory, Officer Martinez?"

"Yes, sir. No, sir. I mean, yes, sir, I'd like to hear your theory."

"Thank you," Wohl said. "My theory is that while you, McFadden, and Payne were running around town boozing it up on what you erroneously believed was going to be the taxpayer's expense, and you, Martinez, were doing—I have no idea what— that Mr. Williams went back to Glengarry Lane and burglarized poor Miss Peebles yet one more time. You did hear about the burglary?"

"Yes, sir," Martinez said. "Just before we came in here."

"Miss Peebles is not going to be burglarized again," Peter Wohl said.

"Yes, sir," they replied in chorus.

"Would either or both of you be interested to know why I am so sure of that?"

"Yes, sir," they chorused again.

"Because, from now until we catch the Peebles burglar, or hell freezes over, whichever comes sooner, between sundown and sunup, one of the three of you is going to be parked somewhere within sight and sound of the Peebles residence."

"Sir," Martinez protested, "he sees somebody in a car, he's not going to hit her house again."

"True," Wohl said. "That's the whole point of the exercise."

"Then how are we going to catch him?" Martinez said.

"I'll leave that up to you," Wohl said. "With the friendly advice that since however you were going about that last night obviously didn't work, that it might be wise to try something else. Are there any questions?"

Both shook their heads no.

Wohl made a gesture with his right hand, which had the fingers balled and the thumb extended. Officers McFadden and Martinez interpreted the gesture to mean that they were dismissed and should leave.

When they were gone, and the door had been closed after them, Captain Michael J. Sabara, who had been sitting quietly on the couch, now quietly applauded.

"Very good, Inspector," he said.

"I used to be a Highway Corporal," Wohl said. "You thought I'd forgotten how to eat a little ass?"

"They're good kids," Sabara said.

"Yes, they are," Wohl said. "And I want to keep them that way. Reining them in a little when they first get here is probably going to prevent me from having to jump on them with both feet a little down the pike."

18 "What we're going to do," Officer Jesus Martinez said, turning to Officer Charles McFadden as they stood at the urinals in the Seventh District POLICE PERSONNEL ONLY men's room, "is give your rich-kid rookie buddy the midnight-to-sunup shift."

"What are you pissed at him for?" Charley McFadden asked.

"You dumb shit! Where do you think Wohl heard that you two were boozing it up last night?"

"We wasn't boozing it up last night," McFadden argued.

"Tell that to Wohl," Martinez said, sarcastically.

"If we make him work from midnight, then who's going to be staking out the house from sunset to midnight? Somebody's going to have to be there."

McFadden's logic was beyond argument, which served to anger Martinez even more.

"That sonofabitch is trouble, Charley," he said, furiously. "And he ain't *never* going to make a cop."

"I think he's all right," McFadden said. "He just don't know what he's doing, is all. He just came on the job, is all."

"You think what you want," Martinez said, zipping up his fly. "Be an asshole. Okay. This is what we'll do: We'll park Richboy outside the house from sunset to midnight. We'll go look for this Walton Williams. Then we'll split the midnight to sunrise. You go first, or me, I don't care."

"That would make him work what—what time is sunset, six? Say six hours, and we would only be working three hours apiece."

"Tough shit," Martinez said. "Look, asshole, Wohl meant it: until we catch this Williams guy, we're going to have to stake out the house from sunset to sunrise. So the thing to do is catch Williams, right? Who can do that better, you and me, or your rookie buddy? Shit, he don't even know where to look, much less what he should do if he should get lucky and fall over him."

Sergeant Ed Frizell raised the same question about the fair division of duty hours when making the stakeout of the Peebles residence official, but bowed to the logic that Officer Payne simply was not qualified to go looking for a suspect on his own. And he authorized three cars, one each for what he had now come to think of as Sherlock Holmes, Dr. Watson, and the Kid. He also independently reached the conclusion that unless Walton Williams was really stupid, or maybe stoned, he would spot the car sitting on Glengarry Lane as a police car, and would not attempt to burglarize the Peebles residence with it there. And that solved the problem of how just-about-wholly inexperienced Matt Payne would deal with the suspect if he encountered him; there would be no suspect to encounter.

At two-fifteen, when Staff Inspector Wohl walked into the office after having had luncheon with Detective Jason Washington at D'Allesandro's Steak Shop, on Henry Avenue, Sergeant Frizell informed him that Captain Henry C. Quaire, the commanding officer of the Homicide Bureau, had called, said it was important, and would Wohl please return his call at his earliest opportunity.

"Get him on the phone, please," Wohl said. Waving at Washington to come along, he went into his office.

One of the buttons on Wohl's phone began to flash the moment he sat down.

"Peter Wohl, Henry," he said. "What's up?"

"I just had a call from the State Trooper barracks in Quakertown, Inspector," Quaire said. "I think they found Miss Woodham."

"Hold it, Henry," Wohl said, and snapped his fingers. When Jason Washington looked at him, Wohl gestured for him to pick up the extension. "Jason's getting on the line."

"I'm on, Captain," Washington said, as, in a conditioned reflex, he took a notebook from his pocket, then a ballpoint pen.

"They—the Trooper barracks in Quakertown, Jason," Quaire went on, "have a mutilated corpse of a white female who meets Miss Woodham's description. Been dead twenty-four to thirty-six hours. They fed it to NCIC and got a hit."

"Shit," Jason Washington said, bitterly.

"Where did they find it?" Wohl asked, taking a pencil from his desk drawer.

"In a summer cottage near a little town called Durham," Quaire said. "The location is . . ."

He paused, and Wohl had a mental image of him looking for a sheet of paper on which he had written down the information.

". . . 1.2 miles down a dirt road to the left, 4.4 miles west of US 611 on US 212."

Jason Washington parroted the specifics back to Quaire.

"That's right," Quaire said.

"They don't have anything on the doer, I suppose?" Washington said.

"They said all they have so far is what I just gave you," Quaire said.

"If they call back," Wohl said, "get it to me right away, will you?"

"Yes, sir," Quaire said, his tone showing annoyance.

That was stupid of me, Wohl thought. *I shouldn't have told Quaire how to do his job.*

"I didn't mean that the way it came out, Henry," Wohl said. "Sorry."

There was a pause, during which, Wohl knew, Henry Quaire was deciding whether to accept the apology.

"The last time we dealt with Quakertown, they were a real pain in the ass, Inspector," Quaire said, finally. "Resented our intrusion into their business. But I know a Trooper Captain in Harrisburg. . . ."

Wohl considered that a moment.

"Let's save him until we need him, Henry," he said. "Maybe we'll be lucky this time."

"Call me if you think I can help," Quaire said.

"Thanks very much, Henry," Wohl said. "I'll keep you advised."

"Good luck," Quaire said, and hung up.

Wohl looked up at Washington.

"I'll get up there just as fast as I can," Washington said. "I'm wondering if I need Tony up there, too."

"Whatever you think," Wohl said.

"Would it be all right if I took the kid with me?" Washington said.

It took Wohl a moment to take his meaning.

"Payne, you mean? Sure. Whatever you need."

"It's in the sticks," Washington explained. "He might be useful to use the phone. . . ."

"You can have whatever you want," Wohl said. "You want a Highway car to go with you?"

"No, the kid ought to be enough," Washington said. "Highway and the Troopers have never been in love. Would you get in touch with Tony and tell him, and let him decide whether he wants to go up there, too?"

"Done."

"Maybe I can get a description of this sonofabitch anyway," Washington said. "Or the van."

"I was afraid we'd get something like this," Wohl said.

"It's not like Christmas finally coming, is it?" Washington said, and walked out of Wohl's office.

Matt Payne was sitting at an ancient, lopsided table against the wall beside Sergeant Ed Frizell's desk, typing forms on a battered Underwood typewriter.

"Come on with me, Payne," Washington said.

Matt looked at him in surprise, and so did Sergeant Ed Frizell.

"Where's he going with you?" Frizell said.

"He's going with me, all right?" Washington said, and took Matt's arm and propelled him toward the door.

"I need him here," Frizell protested.

"Tell Wohl your problem," Washington said, and followed Matt outside.

"You know Route 611? To Doylestown, and then up along the river to Easton?" Washington asked.

"Yes, sir," Matt said.

"You drive," Washington said.

Matt got behind the wheel.

"Take a right," Washington ordered, "and then a left onto Red Lion."

"Yes, sir," Matt said, and started off.

There was a line of cars stopped for a red light at Red Lion Road. Matt started to slow.

"Go around them to the left," Washington ordered. "Be careful!"

And then he reached down and threw a switch. A siren started to howl.

"Try not to kill us," Washington ordered. "But the sooner we get out there, the better. Maybe we can find this sonofabitch before he does it again."

"Where are we going?"

"The State Troopers found Miss Woodham," Washington said. "Mutilated. Dead, of course. In the sticks."

Matt edged into the intersection, saw that it was clear, and went through the stop sign.

My God, I'm actually driving a police car with the siren going, on my way to a murder!

"Are you sure you'd rather not drive, Mr. Washington?" Matt asked.

"You have to start somewhere, Payne. The first time I was driving and my supervisor turned on the light and siren, I was sort of thrilled. I felt like a regular Dick Tracy."

"Yeah," Matt Payne said, almost to himself, as he pulled the LTD to the left and, swerving into and out of the opposing lane, went around a UPS truck and two civilian cars.

Sergeant Ed Frizell stood in Inspector Wohl's doorway and waited until he got off the telephone.

"Sir, am I going to get Payne back? Detective Washington just took him off somewhere, and I have all those—"

"You'll get him back when Washington's through with him. You better find Sherlock Holmes and Dr. Watson and tell them Payne might not be back by the time he's supposed to be at the Peebles residence."

"Yes, sir," Frizell said, disappointed, and started to leave.

"Wait a minute," Wohl said. "There's something else." He had just that moment thought of it.

"Yes, sir."

"Get somebody on the Highway Band and ask them to get me a location on Mickey O'Hara. I mean me, say 'W-William One wants a location on Mickey O'Hara.' "

"He might be hard to find, sir. Wouldn't it be better to put it out on the J-Band? And have everybody looking for him?"

"I think Mickey monitors Highway," Wohl said.

"Can I ask what that's all about, Inspector?"

"Put it down to simple curiosity," Wohl said. "Thank you, Sergeant."

And then, as Frizell closed the door, Wohl thought of something else, and dug out the telephone book.

"Dr. Payne," Amelia Alice Payne's voice came over the line.

"Peter Wohl," he said.

"Oh," she said, and he sensed that her voice was far less professional, more— what? *girlish*—than it had been a moment before.

"I called to break our date," he said.

"I wasn't aware that we had one," she said, coyly.

"We had one for dinner," he said. "*I* remember."

"So do I," she confessed. "I was waiting for you to call."

"The State Police called," he said.

"They found the Woodham woman," Amy said. "Oh, God!"

"They found the mutilated body of a woman who may be Miss Woodham," he said.

"Where?"

"In the sticks. Bucks County. Near the Delaware River. Way up."

"Mutilated? How?"

Now she sounds like a doctor again.

"I don't know that yet," Wohl said. "I just sent a detective up there."

I did not mention Matt Payne, he decided, *because her next question would probably be a challenging "why?"*

"This is another of those times I hate having to say, 'I told you so,' " Amy said.

"It'll take him an hour, an hour and a half to get there and have a quick look. I've been reminded that the State Troopers aren't always as cooperative as they could be.

I may have to go up there myself and wave a little rank around. So that blows our dinner, I'm afraid."

"I'd like to see the body," Amy said.

I know she's a doctor, a shrink, so why did that shock the shit out of me?

"How was she killed?" Amy went on, without waiting for a reply.

"I don't know that, either," Wohl said. "Or even where. All I know is what I told you."

"Where did they find the body?"

"In a summer cottage," he said.

"Maybe if I could look around," Amy said. "Oh, I don't know. I might just be butting in and getting in the way. But you have to find that man, Peter."

"If this body is Miss Woodham," he said.

"Well, what do you think?" she asked, sharply.

"I think it's going to prove to be her," Wohl said. "I have nothing to back up that feeling, of course. It very well could be someone else."

"And thanks but no thanks, huh? Peter, you came to me! I didn't ask to become involved in this."

"Could you get off to go up there with me? Presuming I have to go? In say an hour and a half?"

"I don't want to butt in."

"I'm asking for your help," Wohl said. "Again."

"Yes, I could," she said. "I'll just cancel my appointments, that's all."

"I'll get back to you," he said, "as soon as I hear from Washington."

"From *Washington?*"

"That's the detective's name," Wohl said.

"Oh." She chuckled.

"There's a flock of nice restaurants up there," he said. "We can have dinner in the country, if you'd like."

"Are they run by gangster men of honor, or would you actually have to pay for it?"

"Jesus, you're something," he said. "There goes my other phone. I'll call you."

His caller was an indignant Inspector from the Traffic Division who had wrecked his car, sent someone to get him another from the motor pool, and been informed that Peter Wohl's Special Operations Division had, in the last three days, taken all the available new cars. Peter's explanation that they had drawn what cars the motor pool had elected to give them did not mollify the Inspector from Traffic.

The next call, which came in while the Traffic Inspector was still complaining, was from Mickey O'Hara.

"I understand that you're looking for me," Mickey said. "What's up, Peter?"

"Nothing."

"Bullshit, I heard the call."

"I have no idea what you're talking about," Wohl said. "I thought you had called to demand to know what, if anything, has developed in the Woodham kidnapping."

There was a pause.

"Okay," Mickey said. "What if anything has developed in the Woodham case?"

"Well, since you put that to me as a specific question, which is not the same thing as me volunteering information to one favored representative of the press, I suppose

I am obliged to answer it. The State Police have found a body near Durham, Bucks County, 4.4 miles west of US 611 on US 212, which they feel may be that of Miss Woodham."

"When?"

"They reported the incident to the Philadelphia Police less than an hour ago," Wohl said.

"Anybody else have this?"

"Since no one has come to me, as you did, Mr. O'Hara, with a specific question that I am obliged to answer, I have not mentioned this to anyone outside the Police Department."

"Thanks, Peter," Mickey O'Hara said, "I owe you one."

The line went dead.

Wohl broke the connection with his finger and dialed first Chief Coughlin's number and told him what had happened and what (minus Mickey O'Hara) he had done about it. And then he called Commissioner Czernich and told him the same thing.

Then he called Sergeant Frizell in and told him to have a Highway Patrolman take one of the new cars over to Inspector Paul McGhee in Traffic with the message that he could have the use of it until a car was available to him from the motor pool.

Then he settled down to deal with the mountain of paperwork on his desk until such time as Washington checked in.

A mile the far side of Willow Grove, Jason Washington switched off the siren.

"If this is Miss Woodham," he said. "And we won't know until we get a look at the body—maybe not even then, maybe not until we get her dental records, they didn't say how badly she was mutilated, only that she had been—this may be the first break we've had in this job."

"I don't understand," Matt said. He had been thinking that it was suddenly very quiet in the car, even though the speedometer was nudging eighty.

"Well, maybe somebody saw a van drive in. The site is supposed to be a summer cottage on a dirt road; in other words, not a busy street. People might have noticed. Maybe we can get an identification on the van, at least the color and make. If it's a dirt road, or there's a lawn, or some soft dirt, near the cottage, maybe we can get a cast and match it against the casts on Forbidden Drive—do you know what I'm talking about?"

"Yes, sir," Matt said. "When I Xeroxed the reports, I read them."

"If we get a match on tire casts, that would mean the same vehicle. If we can get a description of the van, that would help. *If* he brought her out here in a van, and *if* the body they have is Miss Woodham. And obviously, he has some connection with the summer cottage. I mean, I don't think he just drove around looking for someplace to take her; he knew where he was taking her. So we start there. Who's the owner? Our guy? If not, who did he rent it to? Does he know a large, hairy, well-spoken white male? Do the neighbors remember seeing anybody, or anything? Hell, we may even get lucky and come up with a name."

Matt wondered if Washington was merely thinking out loud, or whether he was graciously showing him how things were done. The former was more likely; the latter quite flattering.

"I see you got rid of the horse pistol in the shoulder holster," Washington said.

"Yes, sir," Matt said. "I bought a Chief's Special."

"After I told you that, I had some second thoughts," Washington said.

"Sir?"

"What kind of a shot are you?" Washington said.

"Actually, I'm not bad."

"I was afraid of that, too," Washington said. "Listen, I may be just making noise, because the chances that you would have to take that pistol out of its holster—ankle holster?"

"Yes, sir," Matt replied.

"The chances that you will have to take that snub-nose out of its holster range from slim indeed to nonexistent, but there's always an exception, so I want to get this across to you. The effective range, if you're lucky, of that pistol is about as long as this car. If you, excited as you would be if you had to draw it, managed to hit a man-sized target any farther away than seven yards, it would be a miracle."

"Yes, sir," Matt said.

"I don't expect you to believe that," Washington said.

"I believe you," Matt said.

"You believe that *'what ol' Washington says is probably true for other people, but doesn't apply to me. I'm a real pistolero. I shot Expert in the service with a .45.'* "

"Well, I didn't make it into the Marines," Matt said. "But I did shoot Expert with a .45 when I was in the training program."

"Do me a favor, kid?"

"Sure."

"The next time you've got a couple of hours free, go to a pistol range. Not the Academy Range, one of the civilian ones. Colosimo's got a good one. Take that Chief's Special with you and buy a couple of boxes of shells for it. And then shoot at a silhouette with it. Rapid fire. Aim it, if you want to, or just point it—you know what I'm talking about, you know the difference?"

"Yes, sir."

"And then count the holes in the target. If you hit it—anywhere, not just in the head or in the chest—half the time, I would be very surprised."

"You mean I should practice until I'm competent with it?" Matt asked.

"No. That's *not* what I mean. The point I'm trying to make is that Wyatt Earp and John Wayne couldn't shoot a snub-nose more than seven yards, nobody can, and expect to hit what they're shooting at. I want you to convince yourself of that, and remember it, if—and I reiterate—in the very unlikely chance you ever have to use that gun."

"Oh, I think I see what you mean," Matt said.

"I hope so," Washington said. "My own rule of thumb is that if he's too far away to belt in the head with a snub-nose, he's too far away to shoot."

Matt chuckled.

"Where the hell are we?" Washington said. "We should be in Canada by now. Pull in the next gas station and ask for directions."

Route 212, a two-lane, winding road, was fifteen miles from the gas station. They had no trouble finding the dirt road 4.4 miles from the intersection of 611 and 212. There were a dozen cars and vans parked on the shoulder of the road by it, some wearing State Trooper and Bucks County Sheriff's Department regalia, and others the logotypes of radio and television stations.

A sheriff's deputy waved them through on 212, and advanced angrily on the car when Matt turned on the left-turn signals.

"Crime scene," the deputy called when Matt rolled the window down.

"Philadelphia Police," Washington said, showing his badge. "We're expected."

"Wait a minute," the deputy said and walked to a State Trooper car. A very large Corporal in a straw Smokey the Bear hat swaggered over.

"Help you?"

"I hope so," Washington said, smiling. "We're from Homicide in Philadelphia. We think we can help you identify the victim."

"The Lieutenant didn't say anything to me," the Corporal said, doubtfully.

"Well, then, maybe you better ask Major Fisher," Washington said. "He's the one that asked us to come up here."

The Corporal looked even more doubtful.

"Look, can't you get him on the radio?" Washington said. "He said if he wasn't here before we got here, he'd be here soon. He ought to be in radio range."

The Corporal waved them on.

When Matt had the window rolled back up, Washington said, "I guess they have a Major named Fisher. Or Smokey thought that he better not ask."

Matt looked at Washington and laughed.

"You're devious, Mr. Washington," he said, approvingly.

"The first thing a good detective has to be is a bluffer," Washington said. "A good bluffer."

The road wound through a stand of evergreens and around a hill, and then they came to the cabin. It was unpretentious, a small frame structure with a screened-in porch sitting on a plot of land not much larger than the house itself cut into the side of a hill.

There was a yellow CRIME SCENE DO NOT CROSS tape strung around an area fifty yards or so from the house. There was an assortment of vehicles on the shoulders of the road, State Trooper and Sheriff's Department cars; a large van painted in State Trooper colors and bearing the legend STATE POLICE MOBILE CRIME LAB; several unmarked law-enforcement cars, and a shining black funeral home hearse.

"Pull it over anywhere," Washington ordered. "We have just found Major Fisher."

Matt was confused but said nothing. He stopped the car and followed Washington to the Crime Scene tape and ducked under it when Washington did. Washington walked up to an enormous man in a State Police Lieutenant's uniform.

The Lieutenant looked at Washington and broke out in a wide smile.

"Well, I'll be damned, look who escaped from Philadelphia!" he said. "How the hell are you, Jason?"

He shook Washington's hand enthusiastically.

"Lieutenant," Washington said, "say hello to Matt Payne."

"Christ, I thought they would send a bigger keeper than that with you," the Lieutenant said. "I hope you know what kind of lousy company you're in, young man."

"How do you do, sir?" Matt said, politely.

"I'm surprised you got in," the Lieutenant said. "When I got here, there was people all over. The goddamned press. Cops from every dinky little dorf in fifty miles.

People who watch cop shows on television. Jesus! I finally ran them off, and then told the Corporal to let nobody up here."

"I told him I was a personal friend of the legendary Lieutenant Ward," Washington said.

"Well, I'm glad you did, but I don't know why you're here," Ward said.

"If the victim is who we think it is, a Miss Elizabeth Woodham," Washington said, "she was abducted from Philadelphia."

"I heard they got a hit on the NCIC," Lieutenant Ward said. "But I didn't hear what. I was up in the coal regions on an arson job. Can you identify her?"

"From a picture," Washington said, and handed a photograph to Lieutenant Ward.

"Could be," Ward said. "You want to have a look?"

"I'd appreciate it," Washington said.

Ward marched up the flimsy stairs to the cottage, and led them inside. There was a buzzing of flies, and a sweet, sickly smell Matt had never smelled before. He had never seen so many flies in one place before, either. They practically covered what looked like spilled grease on the floor.

Oh, shit, that's not grease. That's blood. But that's too much blood, where did it all come from?

Two men in civilian clothing bent over a large black rubber container, which had handles molded into its sides.

"Hold that a minute," Lieutenant Ward said. "Detective Washington wants a quick look."

One of the men pulled a zipper along the side down for eighteen inches or so, and then folded the rubber material back, in a flap, exposing the head and neck of the corpse.

"Jesus," Jason Washington said, softly, and then he gestured with his hand for the man to uncover the entire body. When the man had the bag unzipped he folded the rubber back.

Officer Matthew Payne took one quick look at the mutilated corpse of Miss Elizabeth Woodham and fainted.

 Officer Matthew Payne returned to consciousness and became aware that he was being half carried and half dragged down the wooden stairs of the summer cottage, between Detective Washington and Lieutenant Ward of the Pennsylvania State Police, who had draped his arms over their shoulders, and had their arms wrapped around his back and waist.

"I'm all right," Matt said, as he tried to find a place to put his feet, aware that he was dizzy, sweat soaked, and as humiliated as he could possibly be.

"Yeah, sure you are," Lieutenant Ward said.

They half dragged and half carried him to the car and lowered him gently into the passenger seat.

"Maybe you better put your head between your knees," Jason Washington said.

"I'm all right," Matt repeated.

"Do what he says, son," Lieutenant Ward said. "The reason you pass out is because the blood leaves your brain."

Matt felt Jason Washington's gentle hand on his head, pushing it downward.

"I did that," Lieutenant Ward said, conversationally, "on Twenty-two, near Harrisburg. A sixteen-wheeler jackknifed and a guy in a sports car went under it. When I got there, his head was on the pavement, looking at me. I went down, and cracked my forehead open on the truck fuel tank. If my sergeant hadn't been riding with me, I don't know what the hell would have happened. They carried me off in the ambulance with the body."

"That better, Matt?" Washington asked.

"Yeah," Matt said, shaking his head and sitting up. His shirt was now clammy against his back.

"He's getting some color back," Lieutenant Ward said. "He'll be all right. Lucky he didn't break anything, the way he went down."

Matt saw the two men carrying the black bag with the obscenity in it down the stairs, averted his eyes, then forced himself to watch.

"Did you get any tire casts," Washington asked, "or did the local gendarmerie drive all over the tracks?"

"Got three good ones," Ward said. "The vehicle was a '69 Ford van, dark maroon, with a door on the side. It has all-weather tires on the back."

"How you know that?"

"I told you, I got casts."

"I mean that it was a '69 Ford?"

"Mailman saw it," Ward said. "Rural carrier. There's a couple of houses farther up the road."

"Bingo," Washington said. "I don't suppose he saw who was driving it?"

"Not driving it," Ward said. "But he saw a large white male out in back."

"That's all, 'large, white male'?"

"He had hair," Ward said.

"Had hair, or was hairy?"

"Wasn't bald," Ward said. "Late twenties, early thirties. The mail carrier lives in that little village down there," he added, jerking his thumb in the direction of the highway. "You want to talk to him?"

"Yes, I do, but what I really want first is a tire cast. Is there a phone in the village?"

"Yeah, sure, there's a store and a post office."

"Are you back among us, Matt?" Washington asked. "Feel up to driving down there and calling the boss?"

"Yes, sir," Matt said.

"Well, then, go call him. Tell him what we have—were you with us when Lieutenant Ward gave us the vehicle description?" He stopped and turned to Ward. "I don't suppose we have a license number?"

"No," Ward said. "Just that it was a Pennsylvania tag. But he saw that the grille was pushed in on the right. What caught the mail carrier's attention was that the van was parked right up by the steps. He thought maybe somebody was moving in."

"I head what Lieutenant Ward said," Matt said. "A '69 dark red Ford with a door on the side."

"*Maroon*, kid," Lieutenant Ward said. "Not red, *maroon*. This ain't whisper down the lane."

"Yes, sir," Matt said, terribly embarrassed. *"Maroon."*

"And a pushed-in, on the right, grille," Washington added, quickly.

"Yes, sir."

"Pennsylvania tag. So tell Inspector Wohl that. Find out if Harris decided to come out here. If he did, tell Wohl that you'll bring the casts in as soon as they're set and dry, and that I'll ride back with Tony. If he's not coming, then I'll do what I can here and go back with you. Or you can take the casts in and come back for me. Ask him how he wants to handle it."

Forty-five minutes later, five miles North of Doylestown on US 611, a Pennsylvania State Trooper turned on his flashing red light, hit the siren switch just long enough to make it growl, and caught the attention of the driver of a Ford LTD that was exceeding the 50 mph speed limit by thirty miles an hour, and which might, or might not, be an unmarked law-enforcement vehicle.

Matt was startled by the growl of the siren, and by the State Trooper car in his rearview mirror. He slowed, and the Trooper pulled abreast and signaled him to pull over. Matt held his badge up to the window, and the Trooper repeated the gesture to pull over.

Matt pulled onto the shoulder and stopped and was out of his car before the Trooper could get out of his. He met him at the fender of the State Police car with his badge and photo ID in his hand.

The Trooper looked at it, and then, doubtfully, at Matt.

"What's the big hurry?" the trooper asked.

"I'm carrying tire casts from the crime scene in Durham to Philadelphia," Matt said. When that didn't seem to impress the trooper very much, he added: "We're trying to get a match. We think the doer is a serial rapist we're looking for."

The trooper walked to the car and looked in the backseat, where the tire casts, padded in newspaper, were strapped to the seat with seat belts.

"I didn't know the Philadelphia cops were interested in that job," the Trooper said, "and I wasn't sure if you were really a cop. I've had two weirdos lately with black-walled tires and antennas that didn't have any radios. And you *were* going like hell."

"Can I go now?"

"I'll take you through Doylestown to the Willow Grove interchange," the Trooper said, and walked back to his car and got in.

There is a stoplight at the intersection of US 611, which at that point is also known as "Old York Road," and Moreland Road in Willow Grove. When Matt stopped for it, the State Trooper by then having left him, his eye fell on the line of cars coming in the opposite direction. The face of the driver of the first car in line was familiar to him. It was that of Inspector Peter Wohl. He raised his hand in sort of a salute. He was sure that Wohl saw him, he was looking right at him, but there was no response. And then Matt saw another familiar face in Wohl's car, that of his sister.

What the hell is she doing with Inspector Wohl?

The light changed. The two cars passed each other. The drivers examined each other, Matt looking at Wohl with curiosity on his face, Wohl looking at Matt with no expression that Matt could read. And Amy Payne didn't look at all.

When he had spoken with Wohl from the pay phone in the little general store in Durham, Wohl had ordered him to bring the tire casts into Philadelphia as soon as they could safely be transported. "Harris is on his way out there, and I'm going out there myself. One or the other of us will see that Washington gets home."

He hadn't mentioned anything about bringing Amy with him. What's that all about? And Harris? I must have passed him on the road. With my luck, when I was being escorted by the Trooper. What would Harris think about that? Or maybe even he drove past when I was stopped for speeding! Oh, Christ, what a fool I'm making of myself!

He had just begun to wallow in the humiliation of having passed out upon seeing his first murder victim when he became aware of the radio, first that W-William One was calling W-William Two Oh One; next that W-William One was Inspector Wohl, and finally that W-William Two Oh One was Washington's—and at the moment, his—call sign.

He grabbed the microphone.

"W-William Two Oh One," he said.

"The crime lab people are waiting for those casts," Wohl's voice said. "So take them right to the Roundhouse; don't bother stopping at Bustleton and Bowler."

"Yes, sir," Matt said.

As he tried to make up his mind the fastest way to get from where he was to the Roundhouse, he turned up the volume on the J-Band.

There came the three beeps of an emergency message, signifying that the message that followed was directed to all radio-equipped vehicles of the Philadelphia Police Department:

Beep Beep Beep.

"All cars stand by unless you have an emergency.

Wanted for investigation for homicide and rape, the driver of a 1969 Ford van, maroon in color, damage to right portion of the front grille, all-weather tires mounted on the rear. Operator is a white male, twenty-five to thirty years of age, may be armed with a knife. Suspect is wanted for questioning in a rape-homicide and should be considered dangerous."

There was a brief pause, then the beeps and the message were repeated.

Jesus, Matt thought, *I'd like to spot that sonofabitch!*

He did not do so, although he very carefully scrutinized all the traffic on Broad Street, and on the Roosevelt Boulevard Extension, and then down the parkway into downtown Philadelphia, looking for a maroon van.

He had difficulty finding a parking space at the Roundhouse, but finally found one. He unstrapped the casts and carried them into the building. A very stout lady with orange hair came rapidly out of the elevator as he prepared to board it, nearly knocking the casts out of his hands.

That, he decided, would not have surprised him at all. It would be the gilding of the lily. If he had dropped and destroyed the casts, he would have spent the rest of his natural life typing up Sergeant Frizell's goddamned multipart forms.

No, he thought, *that's terribly clever, but it's not true. What would have happened if I had carelessly allowed the casts to be broken would be that I would have had to face the question I have been so scrupulously avoiding; whether or not I am, as Amy suggests, simply indulging myself walking around with a gun and a badge, pretending I'm a policeman because I was rejected by the Marines.*

I'm not a policeman. I proved that today, both by the childish pleasure I took rac-

ing through traffic with the siren screaming and then again by passing out like a Girl Scout seeing her first dead rabbit when I saw that poor woman's mutilated body. And just now, again, when I was really looking for a dark red van, so I could catch the bad guy, and earn the cheers and applause of my peers.

What bullshit! *What the hell would I have done if I'd found him?*

Maybe it would have been better in the long run if that fat lady had knocked the casts from my hands; the cops, the real cops, are going to catch this psychopath anyway, and if I had dropped the damned things, I would have been out of the Police Department in the morning, which, logic tells me, ergo sum, *would be better all around.*

Officer Matthew Payne was not at all surprised to be treated as a messenger boy by the officers in the Forensic Laboratory when he gave them the casts, nor when he returned to Bustleton and Bowler to be curtly ordered by a Corporal he had never seen before to get his ass over to the Peebles residence.

"You're late," the Corporal said. "Where the hell have you been?"

"At the Roundhouse," Matt replied.

"Oh, yeah, I heard," the Corporal said. "You have friends in high places, don't you, Payne?"

Matt did not bother to explain that he had been sent to the Roundhouse by Inspector Wohl, and that it had been in connection with police business. The Corporal had just added the final argument in favor of resignation. He did have friends in high places.

Even if I wanted to, even if I had the requisite psychological characteristics necessary in a police officer, which I have proven beyond argument today that I do not, it would be impossible to prove myself a man, uncastrate myself, so to speak, with Uncle Denny Coughlin around, watching over me like a nervous maiden aunt, keeping me from doing what every other rookie gets to do, but rather sending me to a sinecure where, I am sure, the word is out to protect me. And where I am obviously, and with justification, held in contempt by my peers.

I'll complete this tour of duty, because it would not be fair to expect McFadden and Martinez to take my duty in addition to their own, but in the morning, I will type out a short, succinct letter of resignation, and have it delivered out here by messenger.

He took the keys the Corporal had given him in exchange for the keys to Jason Washington's car and drove out to Chestnut Hill.

Charley McFadden had parked his car fifty yards away from the gate to the Peebles residence, on the opposite side of the street. Matt pulled in behind it, got out, and walked up to it.

"I was beginning to wonder if you were going to show up at all," McFadden said, not critically. "Where'd you go with Washington?"

"He went out to Bucks County, where they found the Woodham woman's body," Matt said. "He needed an errand boy."

"Well, all those Homicide guys think they're hotshots," McFadden said, not understanding him. "Don't let it get you down."

"What am I supposed to do here, Charley?"

"This is mostly bullshit," McFadden said. "Most of it is to scare the creep off. Wohl don't want another burglary here on the Overnight Report. And some of it is because he's pissed at me."

"What for?"

"He somehow has the idea I took you out and got you shitfaced last night," Char-ley said. He looked at Matt's face for a reaction, and then went on: "Hay-zus thinks you told Wohl that."

"No," Matt said. "I told Inspector Wohl that *I* got drunk."

"With me?"

"No," Matt said. "And if he formed that impression, I'll see that I correct it."

"Fuck it, don't worry about it," Charley said. "Now, about here. I don't think this asshole will show up again. If he does, he's not stupid, he'll spot your car, and dis-appear. But if he does show up, and he is stupid—in other words, if you see some-body sneaking around the bushes, call for a backup. Don't try to catch him yourself. Highway cars will be riding by here every half hour or so, so what you'll do is sit here and try to stay awake until Hay-zus relieves you at midnight."

"How do I stay awake?"

"You didn't bring a thermos?"

Matt shook his head.

"I should have said something," Charley said. "I'll go get you a couple of contain-ers of black coffee before I leave. Even cold coffee is better than no coffee. Get out of the car every once in a while, and walk around a little. Wave your arms, get the blood circulating. . . ."

"I get the picture," Matt said.

"Every supervisor around is going to be riding past here tonight," McFadden said. "I wouldn't be surprised if Wohl himself came by. So for Christ's sake, don't fall asleep, or your ass will be in a crack."

"Okay," Matt said. "Thanks, Charley."

"Ah, shit," McFadden said, and started his engine. "You want something with the coffee? An egg sandwich, hamburger, something?"

"Hamburger with onions, two of them," Matt said, digging in his pocket for money. "They give me gas. Maybe that'll keep me awake."

Two hamburgers generously dressed with fried and raw onions (Charley McFadden, not knowing Matt's preference, had brought one of each) and two enormous foam containers of coffee, while they produced gas, did not keep Officer Matthew Payne awake on his post.

Neither did half a dozen walks down the street and up the driveway of the Peebles residence. Neither did getting out of the car and waving his arms around and doing deep knee bends.

At five minutes after eleven, while he was, for the tenth or fifteenth time, mentally composing the letter of resignation he would write in the morning, striving for both brevity and avoiding any suggestion that he would entertain any requests to recon-sider, his head dropped forward and he fell asleep.

Five minutes after that, he twisted in his sleep, and slid slowly down on the seat.

Five minutes after that, as Officer McFadden had predicted, a senior supervisor did drive by the Peebles residence. He spotted the car, but paid only cursory attention to it, for he had other things on his mind.

Captain David Pekach thought the odds were about twenty-to-one that he was about to make a complete fool of himself. He was *imagining* that the fingers of Miss Martha Peebles had lingered tenderly and perhaps even suggestively on his when he had damned near dropped the Ludwig Hamner Remington rolling-block Schuetzen, and it was *preposterous* to think that he really saw what he thought he saw in her eyes when she had seen him to the door.

What he was going to do, he decided, as he turned into the Peebles driveway, was simply perform his duty, that given to him by Peter Wohl: to assure the lady that everything that could conceivably be done by the Philadelphia Police Department generally and the Highway Patrol, of which he was the commanding officer, specifically, to protect her property from the depredations of Walton Williams; and to apprehend Mr. Williams; was being done. His presence would be that proof.

The odds are, he thought, that she went to bed long ago, anyway.

But there was a light in the library, and the light over the entrance was on, so he went on the air and reported that Highway One was out of service at 606 Glengarry Lane, checking the Peebles residence.

He walked up the stairs and had his finger out to push the doorbell when the door opened.

"I saw you coming up the drive," Martha Peebles said. "I wasn't sure that you would come."

"Good evening," David Pekach said, unable to choose between "Miss Peebles" and "Martha" and deciding quickly on neither one.

"Please come in," she said.

She was wearing a dressing robe.

Nothing sexy or suggestive or anything like that; it goes from her neck to her ankles. Just what a lady like herself would wear when she was about to go to bed.

"I said I would stop by and check on you," David Pekach said.

"I know," she said.

She started to walk to the stairway, stopped and looked over her shoulder to see if he was following her.

Where the hell is she going?

"And I've ordered cars to check on you regularly," he said.

"I've seen them," she said. "That's why I thought you might not be coming. That you had sent the other cars in your stead."

"If I say I'll do something, I do it," David Pekach said.

"I was almost sure of that, and now that you're here, I'm convinced that you are a man of your word," Martha Peebles said.

They were at the landing before the stained glass window of Saint Whatsisname the Dragon Slayer by then.

"I made a little midnight snack," Martha Peebles said.

"You didn't have to do that."

"I wanted to," she said, and took his arm.

"And there's a plainclothes officer in an unmarked car parked just up the block," David said.

Or I think there is. I didn't see anybody in the goddamned car, now that I think about it.

"I saw him, too," she said. "He's been up the drive four times, waving his flashlight around."

"We're doing our very best to take care of you."

"I wasn't sure if you—if you came, that is—if you could drink on duty, so I made coffee. But there's wine. Or whiskey, too, if you'd rather."

They were on the second floor now, moving down the corridor, away from the gun room.

"Oh, I don't think law and order would come crashing down if I had a glass of wine," David said.

"I'm glad. I put out a port, a rather robust port, that Father always enjoyed."

A door was open. Inside, David saw a small round table with a tablecloth that reached to the floor. There was a tray of sandwiches on it, with the crusts cut off, and a silver coffee set, and beside it was a wine cooler with the neck of a bottle of wine sticking out of it.

Jesus!

And when he stepped inside, he saw that there was an enormous, heavily carved headboard over a bed on which the sheets had been turned down.

Jesus!

"The maiden's bed," Martha Peebles said.

"Excuse me?" David said, not sure that he had heard her correctly.

"The maiden's bed," Martha said. "My bed. I suppose you think that's a bit absurd in this day and age, a maiden my age."

"Not at all." He seemed to have trouble finding his voice.

"I'm thirty-five," Martha said.

"I'm thirty-seven."

"Do you think *I'm* absurd?" Martha Peebles asked.

"No," he said firmly. "Why should I think that?"

"Enticing you, trying to entice you, up here like this?"

"Jesus!"

"Then you do," she said. "I didn't ... it wasn't my intention to embarrass you, David."

"You're not embarrassing me."

"I'll tell you what is absurd," she said. "I never even thought of doing something like this until you came here this afternoon."

"I don't know what to say," David said. "Christ, I've been thinking about you all day ... ever since I almost dropped the Hamner Schuetzen."

"When our hands touched?"

"Yeah, and when you looked at me that way," he said.

"I thought you were looking into my soul," Martha said.

"Jesus!"

"That made you uncomfortable, didn't it?" Martha asked. "For me to say that?"

"I felt the same damned thing!"

"Oh, David!"

He put his arms around her. At first it was awkward, but then they seemed to adjust their bodies to each other, and he kissed the top of her head, then her forehead, and finally her mouth.

"David," Martha said, finally. "Your ... equipment ... the belt and whatever, your badge, is hurting me. If we're going—shouldn't we take our things off?"

David backed away from her and looked down at his badge, then started to take off his Sam Browne belt.

When he glanced at Martha, he saw that she had removed her dressing gown. She hadn't been wearing anything under it.

"Are you disappointed?" she asked.

"You're *beautiful!*"

"Oh, I'm so glad you think so!"

At fifteen minutes to midnight, Officer Jesus Martinez drove down Glengarry Lane in Chestnut Hill, saw the unmarked car parked by the side of the Peebles house, recognized it as one he had ferried from the Academy, and wondered who the hell was in it. Obviously, one of the brass hats, stroking the lady. If there had been anything going on, it would have come over the radio.

He saw Matt Payne's unmarked car and drove past it, made a U-turn, and pulled in beside it. Payne wasn't in the car; maybe he was in the house with the supervisor.

He turned the engine off, and slumped back against the seat waiting for Payne to show up.

When ten minutes passed and he had not, Jesus Martinez got out of his car and walked up to Payne's. Payne knew he was coming. Maybe he had left a note for him on the dashboard or something, saying where he was.

When he saw Matt on the seat, the first thing that occurred to him was that violence had occurred, that maybe he'd run into Walton Williams or something. He was just about to jerk the door open when Matt snored.

The cocksucker's asleep! The cocksucker is really asleep!

This was followed by a wave of righteous indignation approaching blind fury.

The sonofabitch is sleeping when I've been out busting my ass all night looking for the asshole burglar! Before I have to baby-sit this fucking place!

Officer Matthew Payne was a hair's breadth away from being jerked out of the car by his feet when Martinez had one more reaction that infuriated him even more than finding Payne asleep.

The sonofabitch has been getting away with it! While I have been out busting my ass in every tinkerbell saloon in Philadelphia, he has been sleeping and nobody caught him! Highway cars have been going past here every half hour, and nobody caught him—or gave a damn if they did—and every fucking supervisor around, District, Highway, Northwest Detectives, maybe even Wohl and Sabara and that new Sergeant, have ridden by here and nobody noticed!

Officer Martinez stood by the side of Matt's car for a moment, his arms folded angrily across his chest, as he considered the various options open to him to fix the richboy rookie's ass once and for all for this. When the solution came to him, it was simplicity itself.

Now smiling, he took his penknife from his pocket, tested the sharpness of the blade with his thumb, and then knelt by the left front wheel. He sliced into the rubber tire valve where it passed through the tire. There was a piercing whistle of escaping air, which Martinez quickly muffled with his fist.

On the right front and rear wheels, he used his handkerchief to muffle the whistle of air escaping from sliced air valves.

Then he got back in his car and drove off, wearing a smile of satisfaction. The smile grew broader as he thought of the finishing touch. He reached for his microphone.

"W-William Two Eleven, W-William Two Twelve," he said.

"Go," Charley McFadden's voice came back immediately.

"I'm at Broad and Olney, working on something," Martinez said. "I ain't gonna be able to relieve our friend on time. What should I do?"

"I'll go relieve him," Charley replied immediately. "You want to come when you get loose, or do you want me to take the tour?"

"I'll relieve you at three, if that's all right," Martinez said.

"Yeah, fine," McFadden said.

That means I've got to hang around until three, Jesus Martinez thought. *But what the fuck. It's worth it!*

And then he thought that the sonofabitch would probably still be asleep when Charley rode up.

Good, let Charley see for himself what a useless prick Richboy is.

20 Officer Charles McFadden attempted to contact Officer Matthew Payne by radio as he drove to Chestnut Hill. There was no reply, which Charley thought was probably because Payne was walking around, the way he told him to, to keep awake.

But he sensed that something was wrong when he pulled up behind Matt's car and didn't see him. He had had plenty of time to stretch his legs from the time he had called; he should have been back by now. McFadden got cautiously out of his car and walked warily to Matt's.

Then he sensed something was wrong with the car and looked at it and found the four flat tires. McFadden squatted and took his revolver from his ankle holster, then approached the car door, and saw Matt sprawled on the seat.

"Matt!" he called, and then, louder, "Payne!"

Matt sat up, sleepily.

"You dumb fuck!" Charley McFadden exploded. "What in the goddamned hell is wrong with you? If one of the supervisors caught you, you'd be up on charges."

"I guess I fell asleep," Matt said, pushing himself outside the car, and then raising his arms over his head.

"What happened to your tires?" McFadden asked.

"My tires? What about my tires?"

"They're flat," McFadden said. And then he felt rage rise up in him.

That fucking Hay-zus did this! That's what that bullshit was about him working on something at Broad and Olney! He drove up here, and let the air out of Payne's tires!

"They're?" Matt asked. "Plural? As in more than one?"

He knelt beside Charley as Charley, pulling on a valve stem, discovered that someone had slit it with a knife.

Someone, shit! Hay-zus!

"All four of them, asshole!" Charley said. "Somebody caught you sleeping and slit your valve stems open. And I've got a good fucking idea who."

"It doesn't matter, Charley."

"The fuck it *don't!*" McFadden said. "You call for a police wrecker, how you going to explain this? Vandals? You were supposed to be sitting in the car, or close
enough so that you could hear the radio. The guys on the wrecker are going to know
what happened, stupid. It'll be all over Highway and Special Operations, the District,
*'you hear about the asshole was sleeping on a stakeout? Somebody cut his tire
valves.'* "

Matt was touched by Charley's concern. This did not seem to be the appropriate
time to tell him that he was going to resign in the morning. It occurred to him that
he liked Charley McFadden very much, and wondered if some sort of friendship
would be possible after he had resigned.

"Well, now that I've made a jackass of myself, what can be done about it?"

"I'm thinking," Charley said. "There's a Sunoco station at Summit Avenue and
Germantown Pike I think is open all night. I think they fix tires."

"Why don't we just call the police wrecker and let me take my lumps?" Matt
asked.

"Don't be more of an asshole than you already are," Charley said. "We'll jack
your car up, take off two tires at a time, put them in my car, and you get them fixed.
Then the other two."

I have an AAA card, Matt thought, *but this doesn't seem to be an appropriate time
to use it.*

"Come on," Charley said. "Get off the dime! I don't want to have to explain this
to a supervisor."

A supervisor did in fact appear thirty minutes later, by which time Matt had returned from the service station with two repaired tires, and departed with the last two.

"What's going on here?" Captain David Pekach asked. "You need some help?"

"No, sir, another officer's helping me," Charley said. "Payne."

"What the hell happened?"

"There was some roofing nails here, Captain. Got two tires."

"You should have called the police wrecker," David Pekach said. "That's what
they're for."

"This looked like the easiest way to handle it, sir," Charley said.

"Well, if you say so," David Pekach said. "Good night—or is it good morning?—Charley."

"Good night, sir."

"Charley, I'll have a word with Inspector Wohl tomorrow, and see if he won't re-
consider this bullshit stakeout."

"I wish you would, sir."

"Good night, again, Charley," Captain Pekach said. He was in a very good mood.
He was going to check in at Bustleton and Bowler, then go home and change his
clothes, and then come back. Martha had said she completely understood that a man
like himself had to devote a good deal of time to his duty, and that she would make
them breakfast when he came back. Maybe something they could eat in bed, like
strawberries in real whipped cream. Unless he wanted something more substantial.

Jesus!

•   •   •

Matt Payne walked into Bustleton and Bowler thirty minutes later and handed the keys to the car to the same Corporal who had given him hell for being late before he'd gone on the stakeout.

"Where the hell have you been with that car? It's after one."

"Go fuck yourself," Matt said. "Get off my back."

"You can't talk that way to me," the Corporal said.

"Payne!" a voice called. "Is that you?"

"Yeah, who's that?"

"Jason," Washington called. "I'm in here."

"Here" was Wohl's office. Washington was sitting on the couch, typing on a small portable set up on the coffee table.

"Do me a favor?" Washington asked, as he jerked a sheet of paper from the typewriter.

"Sure," Matt said.

"I'm dead on my feet," Washington said, "and you, at least relatively, look bright-eyed and bushy-tailed."

He inserted the piece of paper he had just taken from the typewriter into a large manila envelope and then licked the flap.

"Wohl wants this tonight, at his house," Washington said. "It's a wrap-up of the stuff we did in Bucks County, and what's happening here. You'd think they could find a maroon Ford van, wouldn't you? Well, shit. We'll have addresses on every maroon Ford van in a hundred miles as soon as Motor Vehicles opens in Harrisburg in the morning. Anyway, that's what's in there. He says if there are no lights on, slip it under his door."

"I don't know where he lives," Matt said.

"Chestnut Hill," Washington said. "Norwood Street. In a garage apartment behind a big house in front. You can't miss it. Only garage apartment. I'll show you on the map."

"I can find it," Matt said.

"Thanks, Matt, I appreciate it," Washington said.

"I appreciate . . . today, Mr. Washington," Matt said. "I'll never forget today."

"Hey, it's Jason. I'm a detective, that's all."

"Anyway, thanks," Matt said.

When he was in the Porsche headed for Chestnut Hill, he was glad he had thought to say *"thank you"* to Washington. He would probably never see him again, and thanks were in order. A lesser gentleman would have made merry at the rookie's expense.

He found Norwood Street without trouble. There was a reflective sign out in front with the number on it, and he had no trouble finding the garage apartment behind it, either.

And there was the maroon Ford van that everybody was looking for, parked right under Staff Inspector Peter Wohl's window.

Matt chuckled when he saw it.

That poor sonofabitch is in for a hell of a surprise when he goes tooling down the street tomorrow, and is suddenly surrounded by eight thousand cops, guns drawn, convinced they've caught the rapist.

Matt's attention didn't linger long on the Ford van. There was another motor vehicle parked on the cobblestones he really found fascinating. It was a Buick station wagon, and if the decal on the windshield was what he thought it was, a parking permit for the Rose Tree Hunt Club, then it was the property of Amelia Alice Payne, M.D., which suggested that the saintly Amelia and the respectable Peter Wohl were up to something in the Wohl apartment that they would prefer not to have him know about.

He walked to the station wagon and flashed his light on the decal. It was the Rose Tree decal all right.

There were no lights on in the garage apartment. Wohl and Amy were either conducting a séance, or up to something else.

What the hell, Wohl had no idea I'd bring this envelope. He thought either Jason would, or maybe a Highway car, neither of whom would pay a bit of attention to Amy's car.

What I should do is go up there and beat on the door until I wake him up or at least get his attention. "Hi, there, Inspector! Just Officer Payne running one more safe errand. My, but that lady looks familiar!"

He discarded the notion almost as soon as it formed. Wohl was a good guy, and so, even if he wouldn't want her to hear him say it, was Amy.

He started up the stairs to Wohl's door, intending to slip the envelope under the door. Maybe, later, he would zing Amy with it. That might be fun.

He stopped halfway up the stairs.

I saw movement inside that van.

That makes two things wrong with that van: the grille was damaged. On the right side? Shit, I don't know!

His heart actually jumped, and he felt a little faint.

Oh, bullshit. Your fevered imagination is running away with you. The van probably belongs to the superintendent here. Wohl certainly knows about it, and has checked it out even before we knew we were looking for a maroon Ford.

He stopped for a moment, and then he heard the whine of a starter.

If he's been in there all this time, why is he just starting the engine now?

Matt turned and ran down the stairs, fishing in his pocket for his badge.

What do I say to this character?

"Excuse me, sir. I'm a Police Officer. We're looking for a murderer-rapist. Is there any chance that might be you, sir?"

No. What I am going to wind up saying is, "I'm sorry to have troubled you, sir. We've been having a little trouble around here, and we're checking, just to make sure. Thank you for your cooperation."

He didn't get a chance to say anything. As he got between the Porsche and the van, the van headlights suddenly came on and it came toward him.

Bile filled Matt's mouth as he understood that the man was trying to run him down. He backed up, encountered the rear of the Porsche and scurried up it like a crab, terrified that his leg would be in the way when the van hit the Porsche.

The impact knocked him off the Porsche. He fell to the right, between the car and the garage doors, landing painfully on his rear end, the breath mostly knocked out of him.

He thought: *I'm alive.*

He thought: *Why the hell didn't I wake up Wohl? He would know what to do.*

The van made a sweeping turn, didn't make it, backed up ten feet, and started out the drive.

He thought: *Thank God, he's going and is not going to try to kill me again.*

He thought: *I'm a cop.*

He thought: *I'm scared.*

He pulled the Chief's Special from the ankle holster and got to his feet and ran to the end of the garage building. His leg hurt; he had injured it somehow.

The van was almost up the driveway.

He became aware that he was standing with his feet spread apart, holding the Chief's Special in both hands, pulling the trigger and pulling it again, and that the hammer was falling on the primers of cartridges that had already been fired.

The van was at the main house, seeming to be gathering speed.

Jason told me, "If you can't belt them in the head with a snub-nose, they're out of range."

Shit, shit, shit, shit, I fucked this up, too!

The van reached Norwood Street, crossed the sidewalk, entered the street, kept going, and slammed into a chestnut tree.

A woman began to scream, bloodcurdlingly.

Matt ran up the driveway. His leg was really throbbing now.

What the fuck am I going to do now? The revolver is empty and I don't have any more shells for it.

He reached the van, out of breath, his chest hurting almost as much as his leg. The van was moving, trying to push the tree out of the way, burning rubber. There was the smell of antifreeze sizzling on a hot block.

He went to the front door and jerked it open.

The driver was slumped over the wheel.

There was a sickening bloody white mess on the windshield. A 168-grain lead projectile had penetrated the rear window of the van, and then the rear of the driver's skull, with sufficient remaining energy to cause most of his brain to be expelled through an exit wound in his forehead.

Matt reached inside and shut off the ignition. Then he ran around the front, went to the side door, and pulled it open. There was something on the floor of the van, under a tarpaulin. He jerked the tarpaulin away.

Mrs. Naomi Schneider, naked, her hands bound behind her, looked at him out of wide eyes.

"I'm a police officer," Matt said. "You'll be all right, lady. It's all over."

Naomi started screaming again.

Beep Beep Beep.

Tiny Lewis opened his microphone and said, "Officer needs assistance. Shots fired. 8800 block of Norwood Street. Ambulance Required. Police by telephone."

The first response to the call was from a Fourteenth District RPC. The second was, "M-Mary One in on the shots fired."

The Honorable Jerry Carlucci, Mayor of the City of Philadelphia, was returning to his Chestnut Hill home from a late dinner with friends. M-Mary One was the first car on the scene.

• • •

Staff Inspector Peter Wohl, followed by Amelia Alice Payne, M.D., entered the Rittenhouse Square residence of Officer Matthew Payne. Chief Inspector Dennis V. Coughlin was already there.

"Here's the newspapers. The *Ledger* and the *Bulletin,*" Wohl said. "I bought five of each."

"The *Ledger?* Why did you buy that goddamned rag?" Coughlin asked, surprised and angry.

"I think I'm going to have the *Ledger* story framed," Wohl said.

"What the hell are you talking about?" Coughlin asked as Wohl handed him a copy of the *Ledger.*

There was a photograph of Miss Elizabeth Woodham on the front page, in her college graduation cap and gown, three columns wide, with the caption, "Rapist-Murderer's Latest Victim."

SCHOOLTEACHER
STILL AT LARGE;
PUBLIC CRITICISM OF POLICE
BUBBLING OVER

By Charles E. Whaley
Ledger Staff Reporter

Police Commissioner Thaddeu Czernich confessed tonight that while "everything that can be done is being done" the police have not arrested, or for that matter, even identified, the Northwest Philadelphia rapist-murderer whose latest victim's mutilated body was discovered early today by State Police in Upper Bucks County.

"Our Police Department is a disgrace, and we intend to force the mayor to do something about it," said Dr. C. Charles Fortner, a University of Pennsylvania sociology professor, at a press conference at which he announced the formation of "The Citizen's Committee for Efficient Law Enforcement."

"A recall election would be a last step," Dr. Fortner said, "but not out of the question if the mayor proves unable or unwilling to shake up the Police Department from top to bottom. The people of Philadelphia are entitled to better police protection than they are getting. We will do everything necessary to see that they get it. The kidnapping and brutal murder of Miss Woodham, and the Police Department's nearly incredible ineptness in dealing with the situation, demand immediate action. We are not going to let them forget Miss Woodham as they have forgotten this psychopath's other victims."

Dr. Fortner said that Arthur J. Nelson, publisher of the *Ledger,* has agreed to serve as Vice-Chairman of the committee, and that Nelson and "a number of other prominent citizens" would be with him when the new organization stages its first public protest today. Fortner said that the committee would form before the Police Administration Building at Seventh and Arch streets at noon, and then march to City Hall, where they intend to present their demands to Mayor Jerry Carlucci.

(A related editorial can be found on Page 7-A.)

"If they march," Chief Coughlin said, "I'll get a bass drum, and march right along with them."

Matt was leaning on his desk, sipping at a glass dark with whiskey, looking down at the *Bulletin*'s front page. There was a four-column photograph on it, of Officer Matthew Payne and the Honorable Jerry Carlucci, who had an arm around Matt's shoulder, and who was standing with his jacket open wide enough to reveal that His Honor the Mayor still carried his police revolver. The caption below the picture read, "Mayor Carlucci Embraces 'Handsome Hero' Cop."

When he heard Coughlin speak, he looked over at him.

"What?"

"You read the *Bulletin* first, Matty," Coughlin said. "Then you'll really enjoy the story in the *Ledger.*"

Matt shrugged, and returned to reading the *Bulletin*.

"Mickey O'Hara will do all right by you," Denny Coughlin said. "He told me he thought you'd done a hell of a job. I'll bet that's a very nice story."

"So far it's bullshit," Matt replied.

NORTHWEST SERIAL RAPIST-MURDERER KILLED BY "HANDSOME" SPECIAL OPERATIONS COP AS HE RESCUES KIDNAPPED WOMAN

By Michael J. O'Hara
Bulletin Staff Writer

Officer Matthew Payne, 22, in what Mayor Jerry Carlucci described as an act of "great personal heroism," rescued Mrs. Naomi Schneider, 34, of the 8800 block of Norwood Street in Chestnut Hill, minutes after she had been abducted at knifepoint from her home by a man the mayor said he is positive is the man dubbed the "Northwest Serial Rapist."

The man, tentatively identified as Warren K. Fletcher, 31, of Germantown, had, according to Mrs. Schneider, broken into her luxury apartment as she was preparing for bed. Mrs. Schneider said he was masked and armed with a large butcher knife. She said he forced her to disrobe, then draped her in a blanket and forced her into the rear of his 1969 Ford van and covered her with a tarpaulin.

"The next think I knew," Mrs. Schneider said, "there was shots, and then breaking glass, and then the van crashed. Then this handsome young cop was looking down at me and smiling and telling me everything was all right; he was a police officer."

Moments before Officer Payne shot the kidnapper and believed rapist-murder, according to Mayor Carlucci, the man had attempted to run Payne down with the van, slightly injuring Payne and doing several thousand dollars' worth of damage to Payne's personal automobile.

"Payne then, reluctantly," Mayor Carlucci said, "concluded there was no choice but for him to use deadly force, and proceeded to do so. Mrs. Schneider's life was in grave danger and he knew it. I'm proud of him."

Mayor Carlucci, whose limousine is equipped with police shortwave radios, was en route to his Chestnut Hill home from a Sons of Italy dinner in South Philadelphia when the rescue occurred.

"We were the first car to respond to the 'shots fired' call," the mayor said. "Officer Payne was still helping Mrs. Schneider out of the wrecked van when we got there."

Payne, who is special assistant to Staff Inspector Peter Wohl, commanding officer of the newly formed Special Operations Division, had spent most of the day in Bucks County, where the mutilated body of Miss Elizabeth Woodham, 33, of 300 East Mermaid Lane, Roxborough, had been discovered by State Police in a summer country cottage.

Miss Woodham was abducted from her apartment three days ago by a masked, knife-wielding man. A Bucks County mail carrier had described a man meeting Mr. Warren K. Fletcher's description, and driving a maroon 1969 Ford van identical to the one in which Mrs. Schneider was abducted, as being at a cottage where her body was discovered. Police all over the Delaware Valley were looking for a similar van.

Payne, who had been assigned to work as liaison between ace Homicide detectives Jason Washington and Anthony Harris and Special Operations Division, had gone with Washington to the torture-murder scene in Bucks County.

He spotted the van in the early hours of this morning as he drove to the Chestnut Hill residence of Inspector Wohl to make his report before going off duty.

"He carefully appraised the situation before acting, and decided Mrs. Schneider's very life depended on his acting right then, and alone," Mayor Carlucci said. "She rather clearly owes her life to him. I like to think that Officer Payne is typical of the intelligent, well-educated young officers with which Commissioner Czernich and I intend to staff the Special Operations Division."

Payne, who is a bachelor, recently graduated from the University of Pennsylvania. He declined to answer questions from the press.

"This is going to thrill them in Wallingford," Matt said, when he had finished reading. "When they sit down to read the morning paper."

"Dad already knows," Amy said. "I called him and told him."

"That was smart!" Matt snapped.

"I wanted Dad to know before Mother," Amy said, unrepentant. "Matt, do you want me to give you something . . ."

"I've got it, thanks," he said, picking up his glass. Then he looked around at all of them. "Doesn't anyone but me care that the whole article is bullshit?"

"You've undergone a severe emotional trauma," Amy said.

"Tell me about it," Matt said. "But we were—I was—talking about bullshit."

"I can give you something to help you deal with it," Amy persisted. "Liquor won't help."

"That's what you think," Matt said. "You *are* talking about the bullshit?"

"I'm talking about the shock you've suffered," Amy said.

"I'm talking about bullshit," Matt said. "I damned near killed that peroxide-blond woman," Matt said. "I didn't know she existed until I heard her screaming. I shot that sonofabitch because he tried to run me over. I was not the calm, heroic police officer. I was a terrified and enraged child who had a gun."

"I don't know what you're talking about," she said.

"You're right, Amy," Matt said. "I am not cut out to be a cop."

"You don't want to make a decision like that right now, Matty," Dennis Coughlin said.

"Nobody's listening to me," Matt said. "If there is one thing I learned from this it's that I am not my father's—my blood father's—son."

"Matty!" Dennis Coughlin said.

"I was afraid out there," Matt said. "Terrified. *And* insane."

"That's perfectly understandable under the circumstances," Dennis Coughlin said.

"I almost killed that woman!" Matt said, angrily. "Doesn't anybody understand that?"

"You didn't," Wohl said. "You didn't. You kept her alive."

"Did you know I fell asleep on the job tonight?"

"No."

"Did Washington tell you I fainted when I saw the Woodham body?"

"So what?" Wohl asked.

"Matty," Dennis Coughlin said. "Listen to me."

Matt looked at him.

"I admit, Mickey and the mayor laid it on a little thick," Coughlin said. "That it was, excuse me, Amy, bullshit. But so was the story in the *Ledger*. So you're not a hero. But neither is the Police Department as incompetent as Arthur J. Nelson wants the people to think it is. What he's trying to do to us has nothing to do with the truth about the Police. That's pretty rotten. So the bottom line here is you took this critter down. He's not going to rape or murder anyone else. A lot of single young women around town are going to get to sleep tonight. That's all we try to do on the cops, Matty, try to fix things so people can sleep at night. And if they read in the newspapers that we're all stupid, or on the take, or just can't be trusted . . . Am I getting through to you?"

"I don't know," Matt said.

"And as far as your father—your blood father, as you call him—is concerned. He was my best friend. And I know he would be proud of you. I am. You were scared, but you did what had to be done. And there's something else about your father, Matt. They have his picture and his badge hanging in the lobby of the Roundhouse. He's a hero, an officer who got killed in the line of duty. But—I was his best friend, so I can say this—he didn't do his duty. He let that critter kill him. And before we caught him, he killed three civilians. You didn't let this critter kill you. That psychopath isn't going to get to hurt somebody else. In my book that makes you a better cop than your father. That's the bottom line, Matty. Protecting the public. You think about that."

Matt looked at Coughlin for a moment, then at Wohl, who nodded at him, and then at his sister.

"Matt," Amy said. "Maybe you shouldn't be a cop. But now is not the time for you to make that decision."

"Jesus!" Matt said. "From you?"

There was a knock at the door. Wohl went to it and pulled it open.

Charley McFadden was standing there, a brown bag in his hand.

"What do you want, McFadden?" Wohl asked.

"It's all right, Peter," Chief Coughlin said, "I sent for him."

"I came as quick as I could," McFadden said. "I figured he could use a drink. I didn't know if he had any, so I brung some."

"Come on in, McFadden," Dennis Coughlin said. "We were all just leaving." He looked Amy Payne in the eye. "Officer McFadden, Amy, is the man who was about to apprehend Gerald Vincent Gallagher when he fell beneath the train wheels."

"I wondered who he was," Amy said.

"He's a friend of mine, Amy, all right?" Matt snapped.

"No offense meant," Amy said. She looked at Chief Inspector Coughlin.

"I think you're right, Uncle Denny," she said. "You don't mind if I call you that, do you?"

"I'm flattered, darling."

"You take care of him, Mr. McFadden," Amy said.

"Yeah, sure," Charley McFadden said. "Don't worry about it."

EPILOGUE

Walton Williams was detained three weeks later by officers of the Bureau of Immigration and Naturalization as he attempted to reenter the United States after a vacation in France. He was taken into custody despite the somewhat hysterical protestations of his traveling companion, one Stephen Peebles, that Mr. Williams had not been out of his sight for the past five weeks and could not possibly be the burglar of the home Mr. Peebles shared with his sister.

Following the night Captain David Pekach visited Miss Martha Peebles at her home to assure her that the police were doing everything possible to protect her property from further burglaries, none were ever reported.

When Staff Inspector Peter Wohl reported this happy fact to Chief Inspector Dennis V. Coughlin, he added, with a knowing smile, that this might have something to do with the fact that Captain Pekach and Miss Peebles seemed to have developed a friendship. He said he had heard from an impeccable source, specifically, Lieutenant Bob McGrory of the New Jersey State Police, that Captain Pekach and Miss Peebles had been seen strolling down the Boardwalk in Atlantic City, holding hands, simply enthralled by each other.

Chief Inspector Coughlin smiled back, just as knowingly.

"People who live in glass houses, Peter, my boy, should not toss rocks. I have it from an impeccable source, specifically His Honor the Mayor, that a certain Staff Inspector was seen walking hand in hand down Peacock Alley in the Waldorf-Astoria Hotel in New York, toward the elevators, with a certain female physician, neither of whom were registered there under their own names."

Matthew Payne did not resign from the Police Department.

THE
VICTIM

1 On the train from New York to Philadelphia, Charles read *Time* and Victor read *The Post*. Charles was thirty-three but could have passed for twenty-five. Victor was thirty-five, but his male pattern baldness made him look older. They were both dressed neatly in business suits, with white button-down shirts and rep-striped neckties. Both carried attaché cases. When the steward came around the first time, when they came out of the tunnel into the New Jersey wetlands, Charles ordered a 7-Up but the steward said all they had was Sprite, and Charles smiled and said that would be fine. Victor ordered coffee, black, and when the steward delivered the Sprite and the coffee, he handed him a five-dollar bill and told him to keep the change. Just outside of Trenton, they had another Sprite and another cup of black coffee, and again Charles gave the steward a five-dollar bill and told him to keep the change.

Both Charles and Victor felt a little sorry for someone who had to try to raise a family or whatever on what they paid a steward.

When the conductor announced, "North Philadelphia, North Philadelphia next," Charles opened his attaché case and put *Time* inside and then stood up. He took his Burberry trench coat from the rack and put it on. Then he handed Victor his topcoat and helped him into it. Finally he took their luggage, substantially identical soft carry-on clothing bags from the rack, and laid it across the back of the seat in front of them, which was not occupied.

Then the both of them sat down again as the train moved through Northeast Philadelphia and then slowed as it approached the North Philadelphia station.

Victor looked at his watch, a gold Patek Philipe with a lizard band.

"Three-oh-five," he said. "Right on time."

"I heard that Amtrak finally got their act together," Charles replied.

When the train stopped, Charles and Victor walked to the rear of the car, smiled at the steward, and got off. They walked down a filthy staircase to ground level, and then through an even filthier tunnel and came out in a parking lot just off North Broad Street.

"There it is," Victor said, nodding toward a year-old, 1972 Pontiac sedan. When he had called from New York City, he had been told what kind of car would be waiting for them, and where it would be parked, and where they could find the keys: on top of the left rear tire.

As they walked to the car both Victor and Charles took pigskin gloves from their pockets and put them on. There was no one else in the parking lot, which was nice. Victor squatted and found the keys where he had been told they would be, and unlocked the driver's door. He reached inside and opened the driver's-side rear door and laid his carry-on bag on the seat and closed the door. Then he got behind the wheel, closed the driver's door, and reached over and unlocked the door for Charles.

Charles handed the top of his carry-on bag to Victor, who put it on his lap, and then Charles got in, slid under the lower portion of his carry-on bag, and closed his door. Charles and Victor looked around the parking lot. There was no one in sight.

Charles felt under the seat and grunted. Carefully, so that no one could see what he was doing, he took what he had found under the seat, a shotgun, and laid it on top of the carry-on bag.

He saw that it was a Remington Model 1100 semiautomatic 12-gauge with a ventilated rib. It looked practically new.

Charles pulled the action lever back, checked carefully to make sure it was unloaded, and then let the action slam forward again.

He then felt beneath the seat again and this time came up with a small plastic bag. It held five Winchester Upland shotgun shells.

"Seven and a halfs," he said, annoyance and perhaps contempt in his voice.

"Maybe he couldn't find anything else," Victor said, "or maybe he thinks that a shotgun shell is a shotgun shell."

"More likely he wants to make sure I get close," Charles said. "He doesn't want anything to go wrong with this. I had a phone call just before I left for the airport."

"Saying what?"

"He wanted to be sure I understood that he didn't want anything to go wrong with this. That's why he called me himself."

"What did this guy do, anyway?"

"You heard what I heard. He went in business for himself," Charles said. "Bringing stuff up from Florida and selling it to the niggers."

"You don't believe that, do you?"

"I believe that he probably got involved with the niggers, but I don't think that's the reason we're doing a job on him."

"Then what?"

"I don't want to know."

"What do you think?"

"If Savarese was a younger man, I'd say maybe he caught this guy hiding the salami in the wrong place. It's something personal like that, anyhow. If he had just caught him doing something, business, he shouldn't have been doing, he probably would have taken care of him himself."

"Maybe this guy is related to him or something," Victor said, "and he doesn't want it to get out that he had a job done on him."

"I don't want to know. He told me he went into business for himself with the niggers, that's what I believe. I wouldn't want Savarese to think I didn't believe him, or that I got nosy and started asking questions."

He loaded the shotgun. When it had taken three of the shotshells, it would take no more.

"Damn," Charles said. He worked the action three times, to eject the shells, and then unscrewed the magazine cap and pulled the fore end off. He took a quarter and carefully pried the magazine spring retainer loose. He then raised the butt of the shotgun and shook the weapon until a plastic rod slipped out. This was the magazine plug required by federal law to be installed in shotguns used for hunting wild fowl; it restricted the magazine capacity to three rounds.

Charles then reassembled the shotgun and loaded it again. This time it took all five shells, four in the magazine and one in the chamber. He checked to make sure the safety was on, unzipped his carry-on bag, slid the shotgun inside, closed the zipper, and then put the carry-on bag in the backseat on top of Victor's.

"Okay?" Victor asked.

"Go find a McDonald's," Charles said. "They generally have pay phones outside."

"You want to get a hamburger or something too?"

"If you want," Charles said without much enthusiasm.

Victor drove out of the parking lot, paid the attendant, who looked like he was on something, and drove to North Broad Street, where he turned right.

"You know where you're going?" Charles asked.

"I've been here before," Victor said.

Eight or ten blocks up North Broad Street, Victor found a McDonald's. He carefully locked the car—it looked like a rough neighborhood—and they went in. Charles dropped the plastic bag the shotshells had come in, and the magazine plug, into the garbage container by the door.

"Now that you said it, I'm hungry," Charles said to Victor, and he took off his pigskin gloves. "Get me a Big Mac and a small fries and a 7-Up. If they don't have 7-Up, get me Sprite or whatever. I'll make the call."

He was not on the phone long. He went to Victor and stood beside him and waited, and when their order was served, he carried it to a table while Victor paid for it.

"2184 Delaware Avenue," he said when Victor came to the table. "He's there now. He'll probably be there until half past five. You know where that is?"

"Down by the river. Are we going to do it there?"

"Anywhere we like, except there," Charles said. "The guy on the phone said, 'Not here or near here.' "

"Who was the guy on the phone?"

"It was whoever answered the number Savarese gave me to call. I didn't ask him who he was. He said hello, and I said I was looking for Mr. Smith, and he said Mr. Smith was at 2184 Delaware and would be until probably half past five, and I asked him if he thought I could do my business with him there, and he said, 'Not here or near here,' and I said, 'Thank you' and hung up."

"If it wasn't Savarese, then somebody else knows about this."

"That's not so surprising, if you think about it. He also said, 'Leave the shotgun.' "

"What did he think we were going to do, take it with us?"

"I think he wants to do something with it," Charles said.

"Like what?"

"I don't know," Charles said, then smiled and asked, "Shoot rabbits, maybe?"

"Shit!"

"How are we fixed for time?"

"Take us maybe ten minutes to get there, fifteen tops," Victor said.

"Then we don't have to hurry," Charles said. He looked down at the tray. "I forgot to get napkins."

"Get a handful," Victor said as Charles stood up. "These Big Macs are sloppy."

Officer Joe Magnella, who was twenty-four years old, five feet nine and one half inches tall, dark-haired, and weighed 156 pounds, opened the bathroom door, checked to make sure that neither his mother nor his sister was upstairs, and then ran naked down the upstairs corridor to the back bedroom he shared with his brother, Anthony, who was twenty-one.

He had just showered and shaved and an hour before had come out of Vinny's Barbershop, two blocks away at the corner of Bancroft and Warden streets in South Philadelphia, freshly shorn and reeking of cologne.

The room he had shared with Anthony all of his life was small and dark and crowded. When they had been little kids, their father had bought them bunk beds, and when Joe was twelve or fourteen, he had insisted that the beds be separated and both placed on the floor, because bunk beds were for little kids. They had stayed that way until Joe came home from the Army, when he had restacked them. There was just not enough space in the room to have them side by side on the floor and for a desk too.

The desk was important to Joe. He had bought it ten months before, when he was still in the Police Academy. It was a real desk, not new, but a real office desk, purchased from a used furniture dealer on lower Market Street.

His mother told him he was foolish, that he really didn't need a desk now, that could wait until he and Anne-Marie were married and had set up housekeeping, and even then he wouldn't need one that big or—for that matter—that ugly.

"I already bought and paid for it, Mama, and they won't take it back," he told her.

There was no sense arguing with her. Neither, he decided, was there any point in trying to explain to her why he needed a desk, and a desk just like the one he had bought, a real desk with large, lockable drawers.

He needed a place to study, for one thing, and he didn't intend to do that, as he had all the way through high school, sitting at the dining-room table after supper and sharing it with Anthony from the time Anthony was in the fourth grade at St. Dominic's School.

The Police Academy wasn't school, like South Philly High had been, where it didn't really matter how well you did; the worst thing they could do to you was flunk you and, if it was a required course, make you take it again. The Police Academy was for real. If you flunked, they'd throw you out. He didn't think there was much chance he would flunk out, but what he was after was getting good grades, maybe even being valedictorian. That would go on his record, be considered when he was up for a promotion.

Joe had not been valedictorian of his class at the Police Academy; an enormous Polack who didn't look as if he had the brains to comb his own hair had been. But Joe had ranked fourth (of eighty-four) and he was sure that had been entered on his record.

And he was sure that he had ranked as high as he had because he had studied, and he was sure that he had studied because he had a real desk in his room. If he had tried to study on the dining-room table, it wouldn't have worked. Not only would he have had to share with Anthony, but Catherine and his mother and father would have had the TV on loud in the living room.

And when the guys came around after supper, his old gang, and wanted to go for a beer or a ride, it would have been hard to tell them no. With him studying at the desk upstairs, when the guys came, his mother had told them, "Sorry, Joseph is studying upstairs, and he told me he doesn't want anybody bothering him."

The Army had opened Joe Magnella's eyes to a lot of things, once he'd gotten over the shock of finding himself at Fort Polk, Louisiana. And then 'Nam, once he'd gotten over the shock of being in that godforsaken place, had opened his eyes even more.

He had come to understand that there were two kinds of soldiers. There was the kind that spent all their time bitching and, when they were told to do something, did just enough to keep the corporals and the sergeants off their backs. All they were interested in doing was getting through the day so they could hoist as much beer as they could get their hands on. Or screw some Vietnamese whore. Or smoke grass. Or worse.

The other kind was the kind that Joe Magnella had become. A lot of his good behavior was because of Anne-Marie. They were going to get married as soon as he came home from the Army. She was working at Wanamaker's, in the credit department, and putting money aside every week so they could get some nice furniture. It didn't seem right, at Fort Polk, for him to throw money away at the beer joints when Anne-Marie was saving hers.

So while he didn't take the temperance pledge or anything like that, he didn't do much drinking. There was no temptation to get in trouble with women at Polk, because there just weren't any around. And when he got to 'Nam and they showed him the movies of the venereal diseases you could catch over there, some of them they didn't have a cure for, he believed them and kept his pecker in his pocket for the whole damned time.

How the hell could he go home and marry Anne-Marie, who he knew was a decent girl and was saving herself for marriage, if he caught some kind of incurable VD from a Vietnamese whore?

The first thing he knew, he was a corporal, and then a sergeant, and a lot of the guys who'd gone into the boonies high on grass or coke or something had gone home in body bags.

Joe had liked the Army, at least after he'd gotten to be a sergeant, and had considered staying in. But Anne-Marie said she didn't want to spend their married life moving from one military base to another, so he got out, even though the Army offered him a promotion and a guaranteed thirty-month tour as an instructor at the Infantry School at Fort Benning if he reenlisted.

A week after he got home, he went to the City Administration Building across from City Hall and applied for the cops, and was immediately accepted. He and Anne-Marie decided it would be better to wait to get married until after he graduated from the Police Academy, and then they decided to wait and see if he really liked being a cop, and because her mother said she would really feel better about it if Anne-Marie waited until she was twenty-one.

He really liked being a cop, and Anne-Marie was going to turn twenty-one in two months, and the date was set, and they were already in premarital counseling with Father Frank Pattermo at St. Thomas Aquinas, and in two months and two weeks he could move himself and his desk out of the room and let Anthony finally have it all to himself.

Joe had laid his underwear and uniform out on the lower bunk—Anthony's— before going to take a shower and shave. He pulled on a pair of Jockey shorts and a new T-shirt, and then pinned his badge through the reinforced holes on a short-sleeved uniform shirt, and then put that, his uniform trousers, and a pair of black wool socks on.

He took one of his three pairs of uniform shoes from under the bed and put them on. He had learned about feet and shoes, too, in the Army, that it was better for your feet and your shoes if you always wore wool socks—they soaked up the sweat; nylon socks didn't do that—and never wore the same pair of shoes more than one day at a time, which gave them a chance to dry out.

Some of the cops were now wearing sort of plastic shoes, some new miracle that always looked spit-shined, but Joe had decided they weren't for him. They *were* plastic, which meant that they would make your feet sweaty, wool socks or not. And it wasn't all that much trouble keeping his regular, leather, uniform oxfords shined. If you started out with a good shine on new shoes and broke them in right, it wasn't hard to keep them looking good.

He strapped on his leather equipment belt, which had suspended from it his handcuff case; two pouches, each with six extra rounds for his revolver; the holder for his nightstick; and his holster. His nightstick was on his desk, and he picked that up and put it in the holder and then unlocked the right top drawer of the desk and took out his revolver.

He pushed on the thumb latch and swung the cylinder out of the frame and carefully loaded six 168-grain lead round-nose .38 Special cartridges into it, pushed the cylinder back into the frame, and put the revolver in the holster.

He didn't think much of his revolver. It was a Smith & Wesson Military and Police model with fixed sights and a four-inch barrel, the standard weapon issued to every uniformed officer in the Police Department.

It had been around forever. There were a lot better pistols available, revolvers with adjustable sights, revolvers with more powerful cartridges, like the .357 Magnum. If Joe had his choice, he would have carried a Colt .45 automatic, like he'd carried in the Army in 'Nam after he'd made sergeant. If you shot somebody with a .45, they stayed shot, and from what he'd heard about the .38 Special, that wasn't true.

He'd heard that people had kept coming at cops after they'd been shot two and even three times with a .38 Special. But department regulations said that cops would carry only the weapon they were issued, and that was the Smith & Wesson Military and Police .38 Special, period. No exceptions, and you could get fired if they caught you with anything else.

It probably didn't matter. The firearms instructor at the Police Academy had told them that ninety percent or better of all cops went through their entire careers without once having drawn their pistols and shot at somebody.

Finally Joe Magnella put on his uniform cap and then examined himself in the mirror mounted on the inside of the closet door. Satisfied with what he found, he closed the door and left the bedroom and went downstairs.

"You sure you don't want something to eat before you go to work?" his mother asked, coming out of the kitchen.

"Not hungry, Mama, thank you," Joe said. "And don't wait up. I'll be late."

"You really shouldn't keep Anne-Marie out until all hours. She has to get up early and go to work. And it doesn't look good."

"Mama, I told you, what she does is take a nap when she gets off work. Before I go there. And who cares what it looks like. We're not doing anything wrong. And we're *engaged,* for God's sake."

"It doesn't look right for a young girl to be out all hours, especially during the week."

"I'll see you, Mama," Joe said, and walked out the front door.

His car was parked at the curb, right in front of the house. He had been lucky when he came home last night. Sometimes there was just no place to park on the whole block.

Joe drove a 1973 Ford Mustang, dark green, with only a six-cylinder engine but with air-conditioning and an automatic transmission. He owed thirty-two (of thirty-six) payments of $128.85 to the Philadelphia Savings Fund Society.

The Mustang was one of the few things in life he really wanted to have, and Anne-Marie had understood when they looked at it in the showroom and said, go ahead, make the down payment, it'll be nice to have on the honeymoon, and if you buy a new car and take care of it, it'll be cheaper in the long run than buying a used car and having to pay to have it fixed all the time.

There was bird crap on the hood, on the passenger side, and on the trunk, and he took his handkerchief out and spit on it and wiped the bird crap off. Somebody had told him there was acid in bird crap that ate the paint if you didn't get it off right away.

He opened the hood and checked the oil and the water, and then got in and started it up and drove off, carefully, to avoid scraping the Mustang's bumper against that of the Chevy parked in front of him.

He turned right at the corner and then, when he reached South Broad Street, left, and headed for Center City. He came to City Hall, which sits in the center of the intersection of Broad and Market Streets; drove around it; and headed up North Broad Street. There was no better route from his house to the 23rd District Station, which is at 17th and Montgomery streets.

He found a place to park the Mustang, locked it carefully, and walked a block and a half to the station house and went inside. He was early, but that was on purpose. It was better to be early and have to wait a little for roll call than to take a chance and come in late. He was trying to earn a reputation for reliability.

At five minutes to four he went into the roll-call room and waited for the sergeant to call the eighteen cops on the squad to order and take the roll.

Nothing special happened at roll call. The sergeant who conducted the inspection found nothing wrong with Joe's appearance, neither the cleanliness of his uniform and pistol, nor with the length of his hair. Joe privately thought that some of the cops on the squad were a disgrace to the uniform. Some of them were fat, their uniforms ragged. Some of the cops in the squad had been there for ten years, longer, and wanted nothing more from the Department than to put in their time and retire.

Joe wanted to be something more than a simple police officer. He wasn't sure how far he could go, but there was little doubt in his mind that he could, in time, make at least sergeant and possibly even lieutenant or captain. He was prepared to work for it.

There was nothing special when the sergeant read the announcements. Two cops, both retired, had died, and the sergeant read off where they would be buried from, and when. There had been reported incidents of vandalism on both the Temple University and Girard College campuses, both of which were in the 23rd District. There were reports of cars being stripped on the east side of North Broad Street.

The Special Operations Division was still taking applications from qualified officers for transfers to it. Joe would have liked to have applied, but he didn't have the year's time on the job that was required. He wasn't sure what he would do, presuming they were still looking for volunteers once he had a year on the job.

On one hand, Special Operations, which had been formed only a month before, was an elite unit (not as elite as Highway Patrol, which was *the* elite unit in the Department, but still a *special* unit, and you couldn't even apply for Highway until you had three years on the job), and serving in an elite unit seemed to Joe to be the route to getting promotions. On the other hand, from what he'd heard, Special Operations was pretty damned choosy about who it took; he knew of three cops, two on his squad, who had applied and been turned down.

It would seem to follow then, since Special Operations was so choosy, that it would be full of better-than-average cops. He would be competing against them, rather than against the guys in the 23rd, at least half of whom didn't seem to give a damn if they ever got promoted and seemed perfectly willing to spend their lives riding around the 23rd in an RPC (radio patrol car).

When roll call was over, Joe went out in the parking lot and got in his RPC. It was a battered, two-year-old 1971 Ford. But that, having an RPC, made him think again that it might be smart to stay in the 23rd for a while rather than applying for Special Operations when he had a year on the job.

He had been on the job six months. He was, by a long-established traditional definition, a rookie. Rookies traditionally pull at least a year, sometimes two, working a radio patrol wagon.

RPWs, which are manned by two police officers, serve as a combination ambulance and prisoner transporter. In Philadelphia the police respond to any call for assistance. In other large cities the police pass on requests to assist injured people, or man-lying-on-street calls to some sort of medical service organization, either a hospital ambulance service or an emergency service operated by the Fire Department or some other municipal agency. In Philadelphia, when people are in trouble they call the cops, and if the dispatcher understands that the trouble is a kid with a broken leg or that Grandma fell down the stairs, rather than a crime in progress, he sends a radio patrol wagon.

In addition to the service RPWs provide to the community—and it is a service so expected by Philadelphians that no politician would ever suggest ending it—"wagon duty" serves the police in conditioning new officers to the realities of the job. When a cop in a car arrests somebody, he most often calls for a wagon to haul the doer to the district station. This frees him to resume his patrol and gives the rookies in the wagon a chance to see who was arrested, why, and how.

Joe Magnella had worked an RPW only three months before the sergeant took him off and put him in a car by himself. That was sort of special treatment, and Joe was pretty sure he knew what caused it: It was because he had come home from 'Nam a sergeant with the Combat Infantry Badge.

Captain Steven Haggerman, the 23rd District Commanding Officer, had been a platoon sergeant with the 45th Infantry Division in Korea. Lieutenant George Haskins, the senior of the three lieutenants assigned to the 23rd District, had served in 'Nam as a parachutist and lieutenant with the 187th Regimental Combat Team. Two of the 23rd's sergeants had seen service, either in 'Nam or Korea. An infantry sergeant with the CIB is not regarded as an ordinary rookie by fellow officers who have seen combat.

It was nothing official. It was just the way it was. Army service, particularly in the infantry, was something like on-the-job training for the cops. So when one of the guys on the squad had put his retirement papers in after twenty years and they needed somebody to put in his RPC, the supervisors had talked it over and decided the best guy for the job, the one it seemed to make more sense to move out of wagon duty, was Magnella; he was new on the job but had been an infantry sergeant in Vietnam.

So in that sense, Officer Joe Magnella reasoned as he started up the RPC and drove out of the parking lot, he had already been promoted. He had been on the job only six months, and they had already put him in an RPC by himself, instead of making him work a wagon for a year, eighteen months, two years.

He turned right on Montgomery Avenue, waited for the light on North Broad Street, then crossed it and drove east to 10th Street, where he turned right and began his patrol.

2 When Anthony J. DeZego, a strikingly handsome man of thirty years and who was tall, well built, well dressed, and had a full set of bright white teeth, came out of the warehouse building at 2184 Delaware Avenue just after half past five, Victor and Charles were waiting for him, parked one hundred yards down the street.

DeZego, who was jacketless and tieless, opened the rear door of a light brown 1973 Cadillac Sedan de Ville and took from a hanger a tweed sport coat and shrugged into it. Then, when he got behind the wheel, he retrieved a necktie from where he had left it hanging from the gearshift lever and slipped it around his neck. He slid into the passenger seat, pulled down the mirror on the sun visor, and knotted the tie. Then he slid back behind the wheel, started the engine, and drove off.

Victor put the Pontiac in gear and followed him. "What you said before," Victor said, "I think you were right."

"What did I say before?"

"About him probably fucking somebody he shouldn't have," Victor said. "Those really good-looking guys are always getting in trouble doing that."

"Not all of us," Charles said.

Victor laughed.

Two minutes later he said, "Oh, shit, he's going right downtown."

"Is that a problem?"

"The traffic is a bitch," Victor said.

"Don't lose him."

"If I do, then what? We know where he lives?"

"We do. But I don't want to do it there unless we have to."

Victor did not lose Anthony J. DeZego in traffic. He was a good wheelman. Charles knew of none better, which was one of the reasons he had brought Victor in on this. They had worked together before, too, and Charles had learned that Victor didn't get excited when that was a bad thing to do.

Thirty minutes after they had picked up DeZego—the traffic was that bad—Victor pulled the Cadillac in before the entrance to the Warwick Hotel on South 16th Street in downtown Philadelphia, got out of the car, handed the doorman a bill, and then went into a cocktail lounge at the north end of the hotel.

"A real big shot," Victor said. "Too big to park his car himself."

"I'd like to know where it gets parked," Charles said. "That might be useful."

"I'll see what I can see," Victor said.

"You'll drive around the block, right?"

"Right."

Charles got out of the Pontiac and walked past the door to the cocktail lounge. He saw DeZego slip into a chair by a table right by the entrance, shake hands with three men already sitting there, and jokingly kiss the hand of a long-haired blonde who wasn't wearing a bra.

I hope she was worth it, pal, Charles thought.

The Cadillac de Ville was still in front of the hotel entrance when Charles got there, engine running. But he hadn't walked much farther when, casually glancing over his shoulder, he saw it move away from the curb and then make the first left. A heavily jowled man in a bellboy's uniform was at the wheel.

Charles crossed the street, now walking quickly, to see if he could—if not catch up with it—at least get some idea where it had gone.

Heavy traffic on narrow streets helped him. He actually got ahead of the car and had to stand on a corner, glancing at his watch, until it passed him again. Two short blocks farther down, he saw it turn into a parking garage.

He waited nearby until, a couple of minutes later, the jowly bellboy came out and waddled back toward the hotel. Charles followed him on the other side of the street and, when the bellboy came close to the hotel, timed his pace, crossing the street so that he would be outside the cocktail lounge. He saw the bellboy hand DeZego the keys to the Cadillac, then saw DeZego drop them in the pocket of his jacket.

He walked back to the parking garage and stood near the corner, examining the building carefully. Somewhat surprised, he saw that the pedestrian entrance to the building was via a one-way gate, like those in the subways in New York, a system of rotating gates, ceiling-high that turned only one way, letting people in but not out.

He thought that over, wondering how the system worked, how a pedestrian—or somebody who had just parked his car—got out of the building. Then he saw how it worked. There was a pedestrian exit way down beside the attendant's booth. You had to walk past the attendant to get out. The system, he decided, was designed to reduce theft, at least theft by people who looked like thieves.

He walked to the garage and passed through the one-way gate. Inside was a door. He pushed it open and found two more doors. One had *one* painted on it in huge letters, and the other read, STAIRS. He went through the ONE door and found himself on the ground floor of the garage. The door closed automatically behind him, and there was no way to open it.

DeZego's Cadillac was not on the ground floor. He went up the vehicular ramp to the second floor. DeZego's car wasn't there, either, but he saw that one could enter through the door to the stairwell. He walked up the stairs to the third floor. Same thing. No brown Cadillac but he could get back on the stairs. He found the Caddy on the fourth floor. Then he went back into the stairwell and up another flight of stairs. It turned out to be the last; the top floor was open.

He walked to the edge and looked down, then went into the stairwell again and walked all the way back to the ground floor. The attendant looked up but didn't seem particularly interested in him.

I don't look as if I've just ripped off a stereo, Charles thought.

He walked back to South 16th Street and stood on the corner catty-corner to wait for Victor to come around the block again.

Then he saw the cops. Two of them in an unmarked car parked across the street from the hotel, watching the door to the cocktail lounge.

Were they watching Brother DeZego? Or somebody with him? Or somebody entirely different?

Victor showed up, and when Charles raised his hand and smiled, Victor stopped the Pontiac long enough for Charles to get in.

"The Caddy's in a parking garage," Charles said.

"Penn Services—I saw it," Victor said.

"There," Charles said.

"I also saw two cops," Victor said. "Plainclothes. Detectives. Whatever."

"If they were in plainclothes, how could you tell they were cops?"

"Shit!" Victor chuckled.

"I saw them," Charles said.

"And?"

"And nothing. For all we know, they're the Vice Squad. Or looking for pickpockets. Take a drive for five minutes and then drop me at the garage. Then drive around again and again, until you can find a place to park on the street outside the parking garage. You can pick me up when I'm finished."

"How long is this going to take?"

"However long it takes Lover Boy to leave that bar," Charles said, and then, "How would I get from the garage exit to the airport?"

"I'm driving," Victor said.

"I'm toying with the idea of driving myself in Lover Boy's car," Charles said. "I think I would attract less attention from the attendant if I drove out, instead of carrying the bag."

"Then leave the bag," Victor said.

"I've already walked out of there once," Charles said. "He might remember, especially if I was carrying a bag the second time. I'm not sure what I'll do. Whatever seems best."

"And if you do decide to drive, what do you want me to do?"

"First, you tell me which way I turn to get to the airport," Charles said.

"Left, then the next left, then the next right. That'll put you on South Broad Street. You just stay on it. There'll be signs."

"If you see me drive out, follow me. As soon as you can, without attracting attention, get in front of me and I'll follow you."

"Okay," Victor said.

Victor then doubled back, driving slowly through the heavy traffic until he was close to the Penn Services parking garage. Then he pulled to the curb and Charles got out. He opened the rear door, took out his carry-on bag, held it over his shoulder, and crossed the street to the pedestrian entrance to the garage, where he went through the one-way gate.

There is a basic flaw in my brilliant planning, he thought as he walked up the stairs to the fourth floor. *Lover Boy may send Jowls the Bellboy to fetch his Caddy.*

When he reached the fourth floor, he saw that there were windows from which he more than likely could look down at the street and see who was coming for the car.

If Jowls comes for it, I'll just have to walk down the stairs and get to the hotel be-fore Jowls does, or at least before Lover Boy leaves the bar to get into the car, and follow him wherever he goes next. If the attendant remembers me, so what? Nothing will have happened here, anyway.

Charles took his handkerchief out and wiped the concrete windowsill clean, so that he wouldn't soil his Burberry, and then settled down to wait.

Four young men, one much younger than the other three, each with a revolver con-cealed somewhere under their neat business suits, stood around a filing cabinet in the outer office of the Police Commissioner of the City of Philadelphia, drinking coffee from plastic cups and trying to stay out of the way.

Two of them were sergeants, one was a detective, and one—the young one—was an officer, the lowest rank in the police hierarchy.

Both sergeants and the detective were, despite their relative youth, veteran police officers. One of the sergeants had taken and passed the examination for promotion to lieutenant; the detective had taken and passed the examination for sergeant; and both were waiting for their promotions to take effect. The other sergeant had two months before being promoted from detective. The young man had not been on the job long enough even to be eligible to take the examination for promotion to either corporal or detective, which were comparable ranks, and the first step up from the bottom.

They all had comparable jobs, however. They all worked, as a sort of a police equivalent to a military aide-de-camp, for very senior police supervisors. Their bosses had all been summoned to a meeting with the Commissioner and the Deputy Commis-sioner of Operations, and for the past hour had been sitting around the long, wooden table in the Commissioner's conference room.

Tom Lenihan, the sergeant who was waiting for his promotion to lieutenant to be-come effective, was carried on the books as "driver" to Chief Inspector Dennis V. Coughlin, generally acknowledged to be the most influential of the fourteen Chief In-spectors in the Department, and reliably rumored as about to become a Deputy Commissioner.

Sergeant Stanley M. Lipshultz, who had gone to night school at Temple, had passed the bar exam a week before his promotion to sergeant. He was "driver" to Chief Inspector Robert Fisher, who headed the Special Investigations Division of the Police Department.

Detective Harry McElroy, soon to be a sergeant, was carried on the books as "driver" to Chief Inspector Matt Lowenstein, who was in charge of all the detectives in the Philadelphia Police Department.

Officer Matthew W. Payne, a tall, muscular young man who looked, dressed, and spoke very much like the University of Pennsylvania fraternity man he had been six months before, was carried on the manning charts as Special Assistant to Staff Inspec-tor Peter Wohl, who was Commanding Officer of the newly formed Special Opera-tions Division.

It was highly unusual for a rookie to be assigned anywhere but a district, most often as one of the two officers assigned to a radio patrol wagon, much less to work directly, and in civilian clothes, for a senior supervisor. There were several reasons for

Officer Matthew Payne's out-of-the-ordinary assignment as Special Assistant to Staff Inspector Wohl, but primary among them was that Mayor Jerry Carlucci had so identified his role in the Department to the press.

What Mayor Jerry Carlucci had to say about what went on within the Police Department had about as much effect as if Moses had carried it down from a mountaintop chiseled on stone tablets.

The mayor had spent most of his life as a cop, rising from police officer to police commissioner before running for mayor. He held the not unreasonable views that one, he knew as much about what was good for, or bad for, the Police Department as anybody in it; and two, he was the mayor and as such was charged with the efficient administration of all functions of the city government. It wasn't, as he had told just about all the senior police supervisors at one time or another, that he "was some goddamned politician butting in on something he didn't know anything about."

Officer Payne had been assigned, right out of the Police Academy, to Special Operations before his status as Special Assistant had been made official by Mayor Carlucci, and it could be reasonably argued that that assignment had been blatant nepotism.

The assignment had been arranged by Chief Inspector Coughlin, and there had been a lot of talk about that in the upper echelons of the Department. Officer Payne had grown up calling Chief Inspector Coughlin Uncle Denny, although they were not related by blood or marriage.

Chief Inspector Coughlin had gone through the Police Academy with a young Korean War veteran named John Xavier Moffitt. They had become best friends. As a young sergeant, while answering a silent burglar alarm at a West Philadelphia service station, John X. Moffitt had been shot to death.

Two months later his widow had been delivered of a son. A year after that she had remarried, and her husband had adopted Sergeant Moffitt's son as his own. Denny Coughlin, who had never married, had kept in touch with his best friend's widow and her son over the years, serving as sort of a bridge between the boy and his natural father's family.

The bridge had crossed a stormy chasm. Johnny Moffitt's mother, Gertrude Moffitt, whose late husband had been a retired police captain, was known as Mother Moffitt. She was a devout Irish Catholic and had never forgiven Patricia Sullivan Moffitt, Johnny's widow, for what she considered a sinful betrayal of her heritage. Not only had she married out of the church, to an Episcopalian, a wealthy, socially prominent attorney, but she had abandoned the Holy Mother Church herself and acquiesced to the rearing of her son as a Protestant, and even his education at Philadelphia's Episcopal Academy.

When Mother Moffitt had lost her second son, Captain Richard C. "Dutch" Moffitt, commanding officer of the Highway Patrol, to a stickup vermin's bullet six months before, she had pointedly excluded Patricia Sullivan Moffitt Payne's name from the family list for seating in St. Dominic's Church for Dutch's funeral mass.

The day after Captain Dutch Moffitt had been laid to rest, Matthew W. Payne went to the City Administration Building and joined the Police Department.

Chief Inspector Dennis V. Coughlin had been nearly as unhappy about this as had been Brewster Cortland Payne II, Matt's adoptive father. It was clear to both of them why he had done so. Part of it was because of what had happened to his uncle Dutch, and part of it was because, weeks before he was to enter the Marine Corps as a second lieutenant, they had found something wrong with his eyes disqualifying him for Marine service.

The Marines, in other words, had told him that they had found him wanting as a man. He could prove to himself, and the world, that he was indeed a man by becoming a cop, in the footsteps of his father and uncle.

It was not, in Denny Coughlin's eyes, a very good reason to become a cop. But he and Brewster C. Payne, during a long lunch at the Union League, had decided between them that there was nothing they could, or perhaps even should, do about it. Matt was a bright lad who would soon come to his senses and realize (possibly very soon, when he was still going through the Academy) that he wasn't cut out for a career as a policeman. With his brains and education, he should follow in Brewster C. Payne's footsteps and become a lawyer.

But Matt Payne had not dropped out of the Police Academy, and as graduation grew near, Dennis V. Coughlin thought long and hard about what to do about him. He had never forgotten the night it had been his duty to tell Patricia Sullivan Moffitt that her husband had been shot to death. Now he had no intention of having to tell Patricia Sullivan Moffitt Payne that something had happened on the job to her son.

Shortly before Matt was to graduate from the Police Academy, at the mayor's "suggestion" (which had, of course, the effect of a papal bull), the Police Department organized a new unit, Special Operations. Its purpose was to experiment with new concepts of law enforcement, essentially the flooding of high-crime areas with well-trained policemen equipped with the very latest equipment and technology and tied in with a special arrangement with the district attorney to push the arrested quickly through the criminal-justice system.

Mayor Carlucci, a power in politics far beyond the city limits, had arranged for generous federal grants to pay for most of it.

The mayor had also "suggested" the appointment of Staff Inspector Peter Wohl as commanding officer of Special Operations. Peter Wohl was the youngest of the thirty-odd staff inspectors in the Department. Staff inspectors, who rank immediately above captains and immediately below full inspectors, were generally regarded as super detectives. They handled the more difficult investigations, especially those of political corruption, but they rarely, if ever, were given the responsibility of command.

There was muttering about special treatment and nepotism vis-à-vis Wohl's appointment too. A division the size of the new Special Operations Division, which was to take over Highway Patrol, too, should have had at least an inspector, and probably a chief inspector, as its commander. Wohl, although universally regarded as a good and unusually bright cop, was in his thirties and only a staff inspector. People remembered that when Mayor Carlucci was working his way up through the ranks, his rabbi had been August Wohl, Peter Wohl's father, now a retired chief inspector.

It was also said that Wohl's appointment had more to do with his relationship with Arthur J. Nelson than with anything else. Nelson, who owned the Philadelphia *Ledger* and WGHA-TV, had put all the power of his newspaper and television station against Jerry Carlucci during his campaign for the mayoralty. And it was known that Nelson loathed and detested Wohl, blaming him for making it public knowledge that his son, who had been murdered, was both homosexual and had shared his luxury apartment with a black lover. Right after that had come out, Nelson had had to put his wife in a private psychiatric hospital in Connecticut, and Peter Wohl had made an enemy for life.

Those who knew Jerry Carlucci at all knew that he believed "the enemies of my enemies are my friends."

Denny Coughlin was one of Peter Wohl's admirers. He believed that the real reason Wohl had been given Special Operations was because Jerry Carlucci thought he was the best man for the job, period. He was careful without being timid; innovative without going overboard; and, like Coughlin himself, an absolute straight arrow.

And Denny Coughlin had decided that the safest place to hide young Matt Payne—until he realized that he really shouldn't be a cop—was under Peter Wohl's wing. Wohl didn't think Payne was cut out to be a cop, either. He went to work for Wohl, as sort of a clerk, with additional duties as a gofer. It would be, Denny Coughlin believed, only a matter of time until Matt came to his senses and turned in his resignation.

And then Payne got the Northwest Philadelphia serial rapist. While he was delivering a package of papers to Wohl's apartment in Chestnut Hill late at night, he had spotted, by blind luck, the van everybody was looking for. The driver had tried to run him down. Payne had drawn his pistol and fired at the van, putting a bullet through the brain of the driver. Inside the van was a naked woman, right on the edge of becoming the scumbag's next mutilated victim.

The first car (of twenty) to answer the radio call—"Assist officer, police by phone. Report of shots fired and a hospital case"—was M-Mary One, the mayoral limousine, a black Cadillac. Jerry Carlucci had been headed to his Chestnut Hill home from a Sons of Italy banquet in South Philly and was five blocks away when the call came over the police radio.

By the time the first reporter—Michael J. "Mickey" O'Hara of the Philadelphia *Bulletin,* generally regarded as a friend of the Police Department—arrived at the crime scene, Mayor Carlucci was prepared for him. In the next edition of the *Bulletin* there was a four-column front-page picture of the mayor, his arm around Officer Matt Payne and his suit jacket open just wide enough to remind the voters that even though he was now the mayor, His Honor still rushed to the scene of crimes carrying a snub-nosed revolver on his belt.

In the story that went with the photograph, Officer Payne was described by the mayor as both the Special Assistant to the commanding officer of Special Operations and "the type of well-educated, courageous, highly motivated young police officer Commissioner Czernich is assigning to Special Operations."

Matt Payne, who was perfectly aware that his role in the shooting was far less heroic than painted in the newspapers, had been prepared to be held in at least mild scorn, and possibly even contempt by his new peers, the small corps of "drivers." He had known even before he joined the Department that the "drivers," people like Sergeant Tom Lenihan, who was Denny Coughlin's driver, had been chosen for that duty because they were seen as unusually bright young officers who had proven their ability on the streets and were destined for high ranks.

Working for senior supervisors, drivers were exposed to the responsibilities of senior officers, the responsibilities they, themselves, would assume later in their careers. They had *earned* their jobs, Matt reasoned, where he had been *given* his, and there was bound to be justifiable resentment toward him on their part.

That hadn't happened. He was accepted by them. He thought the most logical explanation of this was that Tom Lenihan had put in a good word for him. Tom obviously thought that Denny Coughlin could walk on water if he wanted to, and could do no wrong, even if that meant special treatment for his old buddy's rookie son.

But that wasn't really the case. Part of it was that it was difficult to dislike Matt Payne. He was a pleasant young man whose respect for the others was clear without being obsequious. But the real reason, which Payne didn't even suspect, was they were actually a little in awe of him. He had found himself in a life-threatening situation—the Northwest Philly serial rapist would have liked nothing better than to run over him with his van—and had handled it perfectly, by blowing the scumbag's brains out.

Only Sergeant Lenihan and Detective McElroy had ever drawn their Service revolvers against a criminal, and even then they had been surrounded by other cops.

The kid had faced a murderous scumbag one-on-one and put the son of a bitch down. He had paid his dues, like the two kids from Narcotics, now also assigned to Special Operations, Charley McFadden and Jesus Martinez, both of whom had gone looking on their own time for the scumbag who'd shot Captain Dutch Moffitt. They had found him, and McFadden had chased him one-on-one down the subway tracks until the scumbag had fried himself on the third rail.

No matter how long they'd been on the job, it wasn't fair to call kids like that rookies; doing what they had done had earned them the right to be called, and considered, cops.

The door to the commissioner's conference room opened, and Chief Inspector Matt Lowenstein—a short, barrel-chested, bald-headed man in the act of lighting a fresh, six-inch-long nearly black cigar—came out. He did not look pleased with the world. He located Detective McElroy in the group of drivers, gestured impatiently for him to come along, and marched out of the outer office without speaking.

"Why do I suspect that Chief Lowenstein lost a battle in there?" Sergeant Tom Lenihan said very softly.

Sergeant Lipshultz chuckled and Officer Payne smiled as Chief Inspectors Dennis V. Coughlin and Robert Fisher and Staff Inspector Wohl came into the outer office.

Coughlin was a large man, immaculately shaved, ruddy-faced, and who took pride in being well dressed. He was wearing a superbly tailored glen-plaid suit. Fisher, a trim and wiry man with a full head of pure white hair, was wearing one of his blue suits. He also had brown suits. He had three or four of each color, essentially identical. No one could ever remember having seen him, for example, in a sport coat or in a checked, plaid, or striped suit.

Matt had heard from both Coughlin and Wohl that Chief Fisher believed that entirely too many police officers were wearing civilian clothing when, in the public interest, they should be in uniform.

Coughlin walked over to the drivers and shook hands with Sergeant Lipshultz.

"How are you, Stanley?" he asked. "You know where I can find a good, cheap lawyer?"

"At your service, Chief," Lipshultz said, smiling.

"Matthew," Coughlin said to Matt Payne.

"Chief," Matt replied.

"Let's go, Tom," Coughlin said to Lenihan. "Chief Lowenstein had a really foul one smoldering in there. I need some clean air."

"We could smell it out here, Chief," Lenihan said, and went out the door to the corridor.

Chief Inspector Fisher nodded at Matt Payne, offered his hand to Coughlin and Wohl, and then walked out of the room. Sergeant Lipshultz hurried after him.

"Say good-bye to the nice people, Matthew," Inspector Wohl said dryly, "and drive me away from here. It's been a *long* afternoon."

"Good-bye, nice people," Matt said obediently to the others, the commissioner's secretary, his driver, and the other administrative staff.

Some chuckled. The commissioner's driver said, "Take it easy, kid."

The commissioner's secretary, an attractive, busty woman in her forties, said, "Come back anytime, Matthew. You're an improvement over most of the people we get in here."

Officer Matt Payne followed Staff Inspector Wohl out of the office and down the corridor toward the elevators.

There was no one else in the elevator. Wohl leaned against the wall and exhaled audibly.

"Christ, that was rough in there," he said.

"What was it all about?"

"Not here," Wohl said.

He pushed himself erect as the door slid open, and walked across the lobby to the rear entrance of the building, stopping just outside to turn and ask, "Where are we?"

Payne pointed. There were four new Ford four-door sedans, one of them two-tone blue, parked together toward the rear of the lot. When they arrived at the roundhouse, Payne had dropped Wohl off at the door and then searched for a place to park.

There were five spaces near the roundhouse reserved for division chiefs and chief inspectors, and one of them was empty, but Matt had learned that the sign didn't mean what it said. What it *really* meant was that the spaces were reserved for chief inspectors who were also division chiefs, and that other chief inspectors could use the spaces if they happened to find one empty. It did not mean that Staff Inspector Wohl, although he was a division chief, had the right to park there.

None of this was written down, of course. But everyone understood the protocol, and Matt had learned that the senior supervisors in the Department were jealous of the prerogatives of their rank. He had parked the unmarked two-tone Ford farther back in the lot, beside the unmarked cars of other senior supervisors who, like Wohl, were not senior enough to be able to use one of the parking spaces closest to the building.

Unmarked new cars were a prerogative of rank too. Senior supervisors, Matt had learned—chief inspectors and inspectors and some staff inspectors—drove spanking new automobiles, turning them over ("When the ashtrays got full," Wohl had said) to captains, who then turned their slightly used cars over to the lieutenants, who turned their cars over to detectives.

When Special Operations had been formed and had needed a lot of cars from the police garage right away, the system had been interrupted, and some full inspectors and captains hadn't gotten new cars when they thought they were entitled to get them, and they had made their indignation known.

When they got to the two-tone Ford and Matt started to get behind the wheel, Wohl said, "I think I'm going to go home. Where's your car?"

"Bustleton and Bowler," Matt said. "I can catch a ride out there."

Special Operations had set up its headquarters in the Highway Patrol headquarters at Bustleton and Bowler streets in Northeast Philadelphia.

"No, I have to stop by the office, anyway. I just didn't know if you had to go out there or not," Wohl said, and got in the passenger seat.

Matt drove to North Broad Street and headed north. They had traveled a dozen blocks in silence when Wohl broke the news. "There are allegations that—I don't have to tell you that you don't talk about this, do I?"

"No, sir."

"There are allegations that certain Narcotics officers have had a little more temptation than they can handle put under their noses and are feeding information to the mob," Wohl said.

"Jesus!"

"Several arrests and confiscations that should have gone smoothly didn't happen," Wohl went on. "Chief Lowenstein told Commissioner Czernich what he thought was happening. Maybe a little prematurely, because he didn't want Czernich to hear it anywhere else. Czernich, either on his own or possibly because he told the mayor and the mayor made the decision, took the investigation away from Chief Lowenstein."

"Who did he give it to?"

"Three guesses," Wohl said dryly.

"Is that why Chief Lowenstein was so sore?"

"Sure. If I were in his shoes, I'd be sore too. It's just about the same thing as telling him he can't be trusted."

"But why to us? Why not Internal Affairs?"

"Why not Organized Crime? Why not put a couple of the staff inspectors on it? Because, I suspect, the mayor is playing detective again. It sounds like him: 'I can have transferred to us anybody I want from Internal Affairs, Narcotics, Vice, or Organized Crime'—theoretically routine transfers. But what they're really for, of course, is to catch the dirty cops—presuming there *are* dirty cops—in Narcotics."

Wohl then fell silent, obviously lost in thought. Matt knew enough about his boss not to bother him. If Wohl wanted him to know something, he would tell him.

Several minutes later Wohl said, "There's something else."

Matt glanced at him and waited for him to go on.

"On Monday morning Special Operations is getting another bright, young, college-educated rookie, by the name of Foster H. Lewis, Jr. You know him?"

Matt thought, then shook his head and said, "Uh-uh, I don't think so."

"His assignment," Wohl said dryly, "is in keeping with the commissioner's policy, which of course has the mayor's enthusiastic support, of staffing Special Operations with bright, young, well-educated officers such as yourself, Officer Payne. Officer Lewis has a bachelor of science degree from Temple. Until very recently he was enrolled at the Temple Medical School."

"The medical school?" Matt asked, surprised.

"It was his father's dream that young Foster become a healer of men," Wohl went on. "Unfortunately young Foster was placed on academic probation last quarter, whereupon he decided that rather than heal men, he would prefer to protect society from malefactors; to march, so to speak, in his father's footsteps. His father just made lieutenant. Lieutenant Foster H. Lewis, Sr. Know him?"

"I don't think so."

"Good cop," Wohl said. "He has something less than a warm, outgoing personality, but he's a good cop. He is about as thrilled that his son has become a policeman as yours is."

Matt chuckled. "Why are we getting him?"

"Because Commissioner Czernich said so," Wohl said. "I told you that. If I were a suspicious man, which, of course, for someone with a warm, outgoing, not to forget trusting, personality like mine is unthinkable, I might suspect that it has something to do with the mayor."

"Doesn't everything?" Matt chuckled again.

"In this case a suspicious man might draw an inference from the fact that Officer Lewis's assignment to Special Operations was announced by the mayor in a speech he gave last night at the Second Abyssinian Baptist Church."

"This is a colored guy?"

"The preferred word, Officer Payne, is black."

"Sorry," Matt said. "What are you going to do with him?"

"I don't know. I was just thinking that there is a silver lining in every black cloud. I'm going to give myself the benefit of the doubt there; no pun was intended, and no racial slur should be inferred. What I was thinking is that young Lewis, unlike the last bright, college-educated rookie I was blessed with, at least knows his way around the Department. He's been working his way through school as a police radio operator. Mike Sabara has been talking about having a special radio net for Highway Patrol and Special Operations. Maybe something to do with that."

When they pulled into the parking lot at Bustleton and Bowler, Matt saw that Captain Mike Sabara's car was in the space reserved for it. Wohl saw it at the same moment. Sabara was Wohl's deputy.

"Captain Sabara's still here. Good. I need to talk to him. You can take off, Matt. I'll see you in the morning."

"Yes, sir," Matt said.

He did not volunteer to hang around. He had learned that if Wohl had a need for him, he would have told him to wait. And he had learned that if he was being sent home, thirty minutes early, it was because Wohl didn't want him around. Wohl had decided that whatever he had to say to Captain Sabara was none of Officer Payne's business.

 Matt Payne walked a block and a half to the Sunoco gas station at which he paid to park his car. Wohl had warned him not to leave it in the street if he couldn't find a spot for it in the police parking lot; playful neighborhood youths loved to draw curving lines on automobile fenders and doors with keys and other sharp objects, taking special pains with nice cars they suspected belonged to policemen.

"Getting a cop's nice car is worth two gold stars to take home to Mommy," Wohl had told him.

Matt got in his car, checked to see that he had enough gas for the night's activities, and then started home, which meant back downtown.

He drove a 1974 silver Porsche 911 Carerra with less than five thousand miles on the odometer. It had been his graduation present, sort of. He had graduated cum laude from the University of Pennsylvania and had expected a car to replace the well-worn Volkswagen bug he had driven since he'd gotten his driver's license at sixteen. But he had not expected a Porsche.

"This is your reward," his father had told him, "for making it to voting age and through college without having required my professional services to get you out of jail, or making me a grandfather before my time."

The Porsche he was driving now was not the one that had surprised him on graduation morning, although it was virtually identical to it.

That car, with 2,107 miles on the speedometer, had suffered a collision, and Matt had come out of that a devout believer that an uninsured-motorist clause was a splendid thing to have in your insurance policy, providing of course that you had access to the services, pro bono familias, of a good lawyer to make the insurance company live up to its implied assurances.

The first car had been struck on the right rear end by a 1970 Ford van. The driver did so intentionally, hoping to squash Matthew Payne between the two and thus permitting himself to carry on with his intentions to carry a Mrs. Naomi Schneider, who was at the time trussed up naked in the back of the van under a tarpaulin, off to a cabin in Bucks County for rape and dismemberment.

He failed to squash Officer Payne, who had jumped out of the way and, a moment later, shot him to death with his off-duty revolver.

The deceased, Matt learned shortly after the Porsche dealer had given him a first rough but chilling estimate of repair costs, had no insurance that a diligent search of Department of Motor Vehicle records in Harrisburg could find.

He next learned the opinion of legal counsel to the Philadelphia Police Department vis-à-vis the outrage perpetrated against his vehicle: Inasmuch as Officer Payne was not on duty at the time of the incident, the Police Department had no responsibility to make good any alleged damages to his personal automobile.

Next came a letter on the crisp, engraved stationery of the First Continental Assurance Company of Hartford, Connecticut. It informed the insured that since he had said nothing whatever on his application for insurance that he was either a police officer or that he intended to use his car in carrying out his police duties; and inasmuch as it had come to their attention that he was actually domiciled in Philadelphia, Pennsylvania, rather than as his application stated, in Wallingford, Pennsylvania; and inasmuch as they would have declined to insure him if any one of the aforementioned facts had come to their attention; they clearly had no obligation in the case at hand.

Furthermore, the letter was to serve as notice that inasmuch as the coverage had been issued based on his misrepresentation of the facts, it was canceled herewith, and a refund of premium would be issued in due course.

He tried to handle the problem himself. He was, after all, no longer a little boy who had to run to Daddy with every little problem but a grown man, a university graduate, and a police officer.

His next learning experience was how insurance companies regarded their potential liability in insuring unmarried males under the age of twenty-five who drove automobiles with 140-mile-per-hour speedometers that were fancied by car thieves and whose previous insurance had been canceled. Five insurance agents as much as laughed at him, and the sixth thought he might be able to get Matt coverage whose premium would have left Matt not quite one hundred dollars a month from his pay to eat, drink, and be merry. At that point he went see Daddy.

The next Monday morning, a letter on crisp, engraved stationery, the letterhead of Mawson, Payne, Stockton, McAdoo & Lester, Philadelphia Savings Fund Society Building, Philadelphia, went out to the general counsel of the First Continental Assurance Company of Hartford, Connecticut. It was signed by J. Dunlop Mawson, senior partner, and began, "My Dear Charley," which was a rather unusual lack of formality for anyone connected with Mawson, Payne, Stockton, McAdoo & Lester.

But Colonel Mawson had quickly come to the point. Mawson, Payne, Stockton, McAdoo & Lester was representing Matthew W. Payne, he said, and it was their intention to sue First Continental Assurance Company for breach of contract, praying the court to award $9,505.07 in real damages and $2 million in punitive damages.

Six days later, possibly because the general counsel of First Continental recalled that when they had been socked with a $3.5 million judgment against the Kiley Elevator Company after a hotel guest had been trapped for eight hours in an elevator, thereby suffering great mental pain and anguish, the plaintiff had been represented by Colonel J. Dunlop Mawson of Mawson, Payne, Stockton, McAdoo & Lester, Matt had both a check for $9,505.07 and a letter stating that First Continental Assurance Company deeply regretted the misunderstanding and that they hoped to keep the favor of his business for many years.

A week later, after the Porsche mechanic told him that after a smash like that, getting the rear quarter panel and knocking the engine off its mounts, cars were never quite right, Matt took delivery of a new one, and the old one was sent off to be dismantled for parts.

It was generally believed by Matt's fellow officers that with a car like that he got laid a lot, so how could he miss?

But this was not the case. When he thought about that, and sometimes he thought a lot about it, he realized that he had spent a lot more time making the beast with two backs when he was still at U of P than he had lately.

He had once thought that if the activity had been charted, the delightful physical-encounters chart would show a gradual increase during his freshman and sophomore years, rising from practically zero to a satisfactory level halfway through his sophomore year. Then the chart would show a plateau lasting through his junior year, then a gradual decline in his senior year. Since his graduation and coming on the job, the chart would show a steep decline, right back to near zero, with one little aberration.

He had encountered a lady at the FOP Bar, off North Broad Street, a divorcée of thirty-five or so who found young policemen fascinating. He did not like to dwell on the aberration on the declining curve.

There were reasons for the decline, of course. In school there seemed to be a pairing off, some of which had resulted in engagements and even marriage. He had never met anyone he wanted to pair with. But there had been a gradual depletion of the pool of availables.

And once he'd graduated and shortly afterward come on the job, he had fallen out of touch with the girls he knew at school and at home.

Tonight, he hoped, the situation might be different. He had met a new girl. He almost had blown that but hadn't. He had heard that God takes care of fools and drunks, and he thought he qualified on both counts.

Her name was Amanda Chase Spencer. She had graduated that year from Bennington. Her family lived in Scarsdale and they had a winter place in Palm Beach. So far he liked Amanda very much, which was rather unusual, for it had been his experience, three times that he could immediately call to mind, that strikingly beautiful blond young women of considerable wealth, impeccable social standing, and, in particular those who went to Bennington, were usually a flaming pain in the ass.

Matt had met Amanda only four days before, at the beginning of what they were now calling "the wedding week." He had not at first been pleased with the prospect. When informed by the bridegroom-to-be that it had been arranged that he serve as escort to Miss Spencer throughout the week, his response had been immediate and succinct: "Fuck you, Chad, no goddamn way!"

Chad was Chadwick T. Nesbitt IV (University of Pennsylvania '73) of Bala-Cynwyd and Camp Lejeune, North Carolina, where he was a second lieutenant, United States Marine Corps Reserve. Matt Payne and Chad Nesbitt had been best friends since they had met, at age seven, at Episcopal Academy. No one was surprised when Chad announced that Matt would be his best man when he married Miss Daphne Elizabeth Browne (Bennington '73) of Merion and Palm Beach.

"I told you," Mr. Payne had firmly told Lieutenant Nesbitt, "the bachelor party and the wedding, and that's it."

"She's Daffy's maid of honor," Chad protested.

"I don't give a damn if she's queen of the nymphomaniacs, no, goddammit, no."

"You don't like girls anymore?"

"Not when more than two or three of them are gathered together for something like this. And I've got a job, you know."

"Tell me about it, Kojak," Chad Nesbitt had replied.

"Chad, I really don't have the time," Matt Payne said. "Even if I wanted to."

"I'm beginning to think you're serious about this, buddy."

"You're goddamn right I'm serious."

"Okay, okay. Tell you what. Show up for the rehearsal and I'll work something out."

"All I have to do is show up sober in a monkey suit and hand you the ring. I don't have to rehearse that."

"It's tails, asshole, you understand that? *Not* a dinner jacket."

"I will dazzle one and all with my sartorial elegance," Payne said.

"If you don't show up for the rehearsal, Daffy's mother will have hysterics."

That was, Matt Payne realized, less a figure of speech than a statement of fact. Mrs. Soames T. Browne was prone to emotional outbursts. Matt still had a clear memory of her shrieking "You dirty little boy" at him the day she discovered him playing doctor with Daphne at age five. And he knew that nothing that had happened since had really changed her opinion of his character. He knew, too, that she had tried to have Chad pick someone else to serve as his best man.

"Okay," Matt Payne had said, giving in. "The rehearsal, the bachelor dinner, and the wedding. But that's it. Deal?"

"Deal," Lieutenant Nesbitt had said, shaking his hand and smiling, then adding, "You rotten son of a bitch."

Matt Payne had been waiting inside the vestibule of St. Mark's Protestant Episcopal Church on Locust Street, between Rittenhouse Square and South Broad Street in central Philadelphia, when the rehearsal party arrived in a convoy of three station wagons, two Mercurys, and a Buick.

Mrs. Soames T. Browne, who was wearing a wide-brimmed hat and a flowing light blue silk dress, briefly offered Matt Payne a hand covered in an elbow-length glove.

"Hello, Matthew. How nice to see you. Be sure to give my love to your mother and father."

"I'll do that, Mrs. Browne," Matt said. "Thank you."

She did not introduce him to the blonde with Daffy.

"Come along, girls," Mrs. Browne said, snatching back her hand and sweeping quickly through the vestibule into the church.

"I'm Matt Payne," Matt said to the blonde, "since Daffy apparently isn't going to introduce us."

"Sorry," Daffy said. "Amanda, Matt. Don't be nice to him; he's being a real prick."

"Who is Daffy Browne and why is she saying all those terrible things about me?"

"You know damn well why," Daffy said.

"Haven't the foggiest," Matt said.

"Well, for one thing, Matt, Amanda won't have a date for the cocktail party after the rehearsal."

"I thought I was going to be her date."

"Chad said you flatly refused," Daffy said.

"He must have been pulling your chain again," Matt said. "He has a strange sense of humor."

"He does not," Daffy said loyally.

"He was suspended from pool privileges at Rose Tree for a year for dropping Tootsie Rolls in the swimming pool," Matt said. "That isn't strange?"

It took Amanda a moment to form in her mind the mental image of Tootsie Rolls floating around a swimming pool, and then she bit her lip to keep from smiling.

"Is that true?" Amanda asked.

"Goddamn you, Matt!" Daffy said, making it clear it was true.

"The mother of the bride made one of her famous running dives into the pool," Matt went on. "Somewhere beneath the surface she opened her eyes and saw one of the Tootsie Rolls. She came out of the pool like a missile from a submarine."

Amanda laughed, a hearty, deep belly laugh. Matt liked it.

"My father wanted to award her a loving cup," Matt said, "inscribed 'to the first Rose Tree matron who has really walked on water,' but my mother wouldn't let him."

"I absolutely refuse to believe that," Daffy Browne said. "Matt, you're disgusting!"

Mrs. Soames T. Browne reappeared.

"Darling, the rector would like a word with you," she said, and led her into the church.

Amanda smiled at Matt Payne.

"You are going to the cocktail party?" she asked.

He nodded. "And the dinner. As a matter of fact, Amanda, whither thou goest, there also shall Payne go. That's from the Song of Solomon, in case you're a heathen and don't know your Bible."

She chuckled and put her hand on his arm. "I'm glad," she said.

"Pay close attention inside," Matt said. "You and I may well be going through some barbarian ritual like this ourselves in the very near future."

She met his eyes for a moment, appraisingly.

"Chad tells me that you've taken a job with the city," she said, smoothly changing the subject.

"Is that what he told you?" Matt asked dryly.

"Was he pulling my chain too?"

"No."

"What do you do?"

"Street cleaning."

"Street cleaning?"

"Right now I'm in training," Matt said. "Studying the theory and history, you see. But one day soon I hope to have my own broom and garbage can on wheels."

"City Sanitation, in other words? Aren't you ever serious?"

"I was serious a moment ago, when I said you should pay close attention to the barbaric ritual."

The only thing that hadn't been just fine with Amanda in the time since he'd met her in the vestibule at St. Mark's was that he hadn't been able to get her alone. There had always been other people around and no way to separate from the group.

He *had* managed to kiss her, twice. The night before last he had tried to kiss her at the Merion Cricket Club, before Madame Browne had hauled her off in the station wagon. She had turned her face at the last second and all he got was a cheek. A very nice cheek, to be sure, but just a cheek. Last night she had not turned her face as she prepared to enter what he thought of as the Barque of the Vestal Virgins to be hauled off from the Rose Tree Hunt Club to the Browne place in Merion.

It had not been a kiss that would go down in the history books to rank with the one Delilah gave Samson before she gave him the haircut, but it had been on the lips, and they were sweet lips indeed, and his heart had jumped startlingly.

Tonight they would be alone. The Brownes were entertaining, especially their out-of-town guests, at cocktails and dinner at the Union League in downtown Philadelphia. It was tacitly admitted to be an old-folks' affair, and the young people could leave after dinner. Amanda liked jazz, another character trait he found appealing. So, they would go listen to jazz. With a little luck the lights would be dim. She probably would let him hold her hand, and possibly permit even other manifestations of affection.

If the gods favored him, after they left the jazz joint she would accept his invitation to see his apartment. There, he wasn't sure what he would do. On one hand, he would cheerfully sacrifice one nut and both ears to get into Amanda's pants, but on the other, she was clearly not the sort of girl from whom one could expect a quick piece of tail. Amanda Spencer was the kind of girl one marched before an altar and promised to be faithful to until death did you part.

Matt Payne was very much aware that he could fuck up the whole relationship by making a crude pass at her. He didn't want to do that.

God only knows what that goddamn Daffy has told her about me. Going back to me talking her out of her pants when we were five.

The residence of Mr. and Mrs. Soames T. Browne in Merion was an adaptation, circa 1890, of an English manor house, circa 1600. The essential differences were that the interior dimensions were larger and there was inside plumbing. But everything else was there: a forest of chimneys, a cobblestone courtyard, enormous stone building blocks, turretlike protrusions, leaded windows, ancient oaks, formal gardens, and an entrance that always reminded Matt of a movie he'd seen starring Errol Flynn as Robin Hood. In the movie, when the heavy oak door had swung slowly open, Errol Flynn had run the door opener through with a sword.

The heavy oak door swung open and an elderly black man in a gray cotton jacket stood there.

"I'm very glad to see you, Matt," the Brownes' butler said.

"Why do you say that, Mr. Ward?" Matt asked. He had known the Brownes' butler, and his wife, all of his life.

"Because the consensus was that you wouldn't show and I'd wind up driving Daffy's friend into town," Ward said. "They're all gone."

"This one's sort of special," Matt confessed.

"It was her and me against everybody else," Ward said. "She insisted on waiting for you."

"Really?" Matt replied, pleased.

"I'll go tell her you're here," Ward said. "There's a fresh pot of coffee in the kitchen, if that interests you."

"No, thank you. I'll just wait."

He watched the elderly man slowly start to ascend the stairs. He had taken only four or five steps when Amanda appeared at the top and started down.

"See?" she said to the butler. "We were right." She looked at Matt. "I saw you drive up. I love the car, but you don't strike me as the Porsche type."

"I can get a gold chain and unbutton my shirt to the navel, if you like," Matt said. She had come up to him by then.

"No, thank you." She chuckled, then surprised him by kissing him on the lips.

"Hot damn!" he said.

"Draw no inferences," she said. "I'm just a naturally friendly person."

When he got behind the wheel and looked at Amanda as she got in beside him, he remembered too late that he had forgotten to hold the door for her.

"I should have held the door for you," he said. "Sorry. My mother says I have the manners of a cossack."

She laughed again, and all of a sudden it occurred to him that their faces were no more than six inches apart—and nothing ventured, nothing gained.

"God, that was nice!" he said a moment later.

"Drive," she said. "Has this thing got a vanity mirror?"

"A what?"

She pulled the visor down and found what she was looking for.

"That's a vanity mirror," she said, and replenished her lipstick. "You've probably got some lipstick on you."

"I will never wash again."

She handed him a tissue.

"Take it off," she ordered, and he complied.

"These are really nice wheels," she said a short while later. "But I bet all the girls tell you that."

"My graduation present," Matt said.

"You already dinged it," Amanda said.

"You mean the cracked turn-signal lens?" he asked, surprised that she had noticed it. "That's nothing. You should have seen what happened to my *first* Porsche. That was totaled."

"Are you putting me on?"

"Not at all. A guy in a van ran into the back and really clobbered it."

"I think I would have killed him."

"As a matter of fact, I did," Matt said. "Took out my trusty five-shooter and blew his brains out."

He heard her inhale. After a moment she said, "You mean six-shooter," and then added, "That wasn't funny. Sometimes, Matt, you don't know where to draw the line."

"Sorry."

"That was the pot calling the kettle black," she said. "I'm sorry, I had no right to say that to you."

"You have blanket authority to say anything you want to me."

He gave in to the temptation and grabbed her hand. When she didn't object and withdraw it, he kissed it. Then she pulled it free.

"Am I going to have trouble with you tonight?"

"No," he said. "We do what you want to do, and nothing else."

"Funny, I thought you were going to offer to show me your etchings."

"I don't have any etchings," he said.

"But you do have an apartment, right?"

"You're supposed to wait until I ask you before you indignantly tell me you're not that kind of girl," Matt said.

She laughed, the genuine laugh Matt had come to like.

"Touché," she said.

"After we escape from this dinner, would you like to see my apartment?"

"I'm not that kind of girl."

"I was afraid of that," he said. "No, that's not true. I knew that. You brought this whole thing up. I'm getting a bum rap."

"Daffy warned me about you," she said. "The best defense is a good offense. Haven't you ever heard that?"

"How did the kiss fit into that strategy?"

"How far is where we're going?" she said, cleverly changing the subject.

"Not far enough. In no more than twenty minutes we'll be there."

A Mercedes-Benz 380 SL convertible with its ragtop up drove onto the fourth floor of the Penn Services Parking Garage. The driver, a young woman, looked forward over the steering wheel, looking for a place to park.

She did not look toward where Charles was standing, behind a round concrete pole at the north end of the building, in a position that both gave him a view of the street down which Anthony J. DeZego would probably come—unless, of course, he sent Jowls the Bellboy to fetch the car—and also shielded him from the view of anyone who came out of the stairwell to get his car.

And she did not find a parking space, as Charles knew she would not; the fourth floor was full.

The Mercedes continued around and went up the vehicular ramp to the roof.

Charles looked out the window again and saw Anthony J. DeZego walking quickly down the street toward the Penn Services Parking Garage from the fourth-floor window. He was alone; there would have been a problem if he had had the blonde-without-a-bra with him.

He looked down at the street and saw Victor, or at least Victor's shoulder, where he was sitting in the Pontiac. It would have been better if he could have caught Victor's attention and signaled him that DeZego was coming; but where Victor was parked, the garage attendant could see him and probably would have remembered having seen some guy across the street in a Pontiac who kept looking up at the garage.

Victor was watching the exit; that was all that counted.

Charles took his pigskin gloves from his pocket and pulled them on. Then he picked up the carry-on bag and walked down the center of the vehicular path toward the stairwell. If another car came or someone walked out of the stairwell, he would be just one more customer leaving the garage.

No one came.

The stairwell was sort of a square of concrete blocks set aside the south side of the building. The door from it was maybe six feet from the wall. Management had generously provided a rubber wedge to keep the door open when necessary. When Charles decided the dame in the Benz had had time to park her car and go down the stairs, he opened the door and propped it open with the wedge.

He had considered doing the job in the stairwell itself but had decided that the stairwell probably would carry the sound of the Remington down to the attendant and make him curious. When he heard footsteps coming up the stairwell, he would kick the wedge loose and let the automatic door-closer do its thing.

Then, when DeZego came onto the fourth floor, and he was sure it was him, he would do the job. With the door closed, the noise would not be funneled downstairs.

He stepped into the shadow of the stairwell wall, unzipped the carry-on, removed the Remington, pushed the safety off, and checked to make sure the red on the little button was visible, that he hadn't by mistake put the safety on. Then he put the Remington under the Burberry trench coat. The pocket had a flap and a slit, so that you could get your hand inside the coat. He held the Remington by the pistol grip straight down against his leg.

He heard footsteps on the stairs.

He dislodged the rubber wedge with his toe, and the door started to close.

He put his ear to the concrete, not really expecting to hear anything. But he was surprised. The stairs were metal, and they sort of rang like a bell. He could hear DeZego coming closer and closer. He waited for the door to open.

It didn't.

There was a moment's silence, and Charles decided that DeZego had reached the landing. The door would open any second.

But then there came the unmistakable sound of footsteps on the metal stairs again. What the fuck?

Lover Boy is going up to the roof. He's daydreaming, or stupid, or something, his Caddy is on *this* floor, not the fucking roof! In a moment he'll come back down.

But he did not.

Charles considered the situation very quickly.

No real problem. There or here. There's nobody on the roof, and if he sees me, he doesn't know me.

He pulled the door open and, as quietly as he could, quickly ran up the stairs to the roof. He pulled the stairwell door open.

Lover Boy was right there, leaning against the concrete blocks of the stairwell, like he was waiting for somebody.

"Long walk up here," Charles said, smiling at him.

"You said it," Anthony J. DeZego said.

Charles walked ten feet past Anthony J. DeZego, turned around suddenly, raised the shotgun to his shoulder, and blew off the top of Anthony J. DeZego's head.

DeZego fell backward against the concrete blocks of the stairwell and slumped to the ground.

There was a sound like a run-over dog.

Charles looked around the roof. In the middle of the vehicular passageway was a young woman, her eyes wide, both of her hands pressed against her mouth, making run-over-dog noises.

Charles raised the Remington and fired. She went down like a rock.

The goddamned broad in the goddamned Mercedes! She didn't go downstairs. She sat there and fixed her fucking hair or something!

Charles went to Anthony J. DeZego's corpse and took the Caddy keys from his pocket.

I better do her again, to make sure she's dead.

There was the sound of tires squealing. Another car was coming up.

And since there's no room on the fourth floor, he'll be coming up here! Damn!

Charles went into the stairwell and down to the fourth floor. He opened the door a crack, saw nothing, and then pushed it open wide enough to get through.

He went to DeZego's Cadillac, unlocked the door, put the Remington on the floor, and got behind the wheel. He started the engine and drove down the vehicular ramp. He stopped at the barrier, put the window down, handed the attendant a five-dollar bill and the claim check, waited for his change, and then for the barrier to be lifted.

Then he drove out onto the street and turned left. He looked in the rearview mirror and saw the Pontiac pull away from the curb and start to follow him.

"Damn, here we are already," Matt Payne said as he turned the Porsche into the Penn Services Parking Garage behind the Bellevue-Stratford Hotel in downtown Philadelphia.

"How time flies," Amanda said, mocking him gently.

He stopped to get a ticket from a dispensing machine and then drove inside. He drove slowly, hoping to find a space on a lower floor. There were none. He searched the second level, and then the third and fourth. They finally emerged on the roof.

Matt stepped hard on the brakes. The Porsche shuddered and skidded to a stop, throwing Amanda against the dashboard.

"My God!" she exclaimed.

"Stay here," Matt Payne ordered firmly.

"What is it?" Amanda asked.

He didn't answer. He got out of the Porsche and ran across the rooftop parking lot. Amanda saw him drop to one knee, and then for the first time saw that a girl was lying facedown, on the roadway between lines of parked cars.

She pushed open her door and got out and ran to him.

"What happened?" Amanda asked.

"I told you to stay in the fucking car!" he said furiously.

She looked at him, shocked as much by the tone of his voice as by the language, and then at the girl on the floor. For the first time she saw there was a pool of blood.

"What happened?" she asked, her voice weak.

"Will you please go get in the goddamned car?" Matt asked.

"Oh, my *God!*" Amanda wailed. "That's *Penny!*"

"You know her?"

"Penny Detweiler," Amanda said. "You must know her. She's one of the bridesmaids."

Matt looked at the girl on the floor. It *was* Penelope Detweiler, Precious Penny to Matt, to her intense annoyance, because that's what her father had once called her in Matt's hearing.

Why didn't I recognize her? I've known her all of my life!

"I'll be damned," he said softly.

"Matt, what *happened* to her?"

"She's been shot," Matt Payne said, and looked at Amanda.

You don't expect to find people you know, especially people like Precious Penny, lying in a pool of blood after somebody's shot them in a garage. Things like that aren't supposed to happen to people like Precious Penny.

He found his voice: "Now, for chrissake, will you go get in the goddamned car!" he ordered furiously.

Amanda looked at him with confusion and hurt in her eyes.

"This just happened," he explained more kindly. "Whoever did it may still be up here."

"Matt, let's get out of here. Let's go find a cop."

"I am a cop, Amanda," Matt Payne said. "Now, for the last fucking time, will you go get in the car? Stay there until I come for you. Lock the doors."

He stooped, bending one knee, and when he stood erect again, there was a snub-nosed revolver in his hand. Amanda ran back to the silver Porsche and locked the doors. When she looked for Matt, she couldn't see him at first, but then she did, and he was holding his gun at the ready, slowly making his way between the parked cars.

I don't believe this is happening. I don't believe Penny Detweiler is lying out there bleeding to death, and I don't believe that Matt Payne is out there with a gun in his hand, a cop looking for whoever shot Penny.

Oh, my God. What if he gets killed?

4 With difficulty, for there is not much room in the passenger compartment of a Porsche 911 Carrera, Amanda Spencer crawled over from the passenger seat to the driver's and turned the ignition key.

There was a scream of tortured starter gears, for the engine was still running. She threw the gearshift lever into reverse, spun the wheels, and turned around, then drove as fast as she dared down the ramps of the parking garage to street level.

She slammed on the brakes and jumped out of the car and ran to the attendant's window.

"Call the police!" she said. "Call the police and get an ambulance."

"Hey, lady, what's going on?"

"Get on that phone and call the police and get an ambulance," Amanda ordered firmly. "Tell them there's been a shooting."

A red light began to flash on one of the control consoles in the radio room of the Philadelphia Police Department.

Foster H. Lewis, Jr., who was sitting slumped in a battered and sagging metal chair, a headset clamped to his head, threw a switch and spoke into his microphone. "Police Emergency," he said.

Foster H. Lewis, Jr., was twenty-three years old, weighed two hundred and twenty-seven pounds, stood six feet three inches tall, and was perhaps inevitably known as Tiny. For more than five years before he had entered the Police Academy, he had worked as a temporary employee in Police Emergency: five years of nights and weekends and during the summers answering calls from excited citizens in trouble and needing help had turned him into a skilled and experienced operator.

He had more or less quit when he entered the Police Academy and was working tonight as a favor to Lieutenant Jack Fitch, who had called him and said he had five people out with some kind of a virus and could he help out.

"This the police?" his caller asked.

"This is Police Emergency," Tiny Lewis said. "May I help you, sir?"

"I'm the attendant at the Penn Services Parking Garage on Fifteenth, behind the Bellevue-Stratford."

"How may I help you, sir?"

"I got a white lady here says there's been a shooting on the roof and somebody got shot and says to send an ambulance."

"Could you put her on the phone, please?"

"I'm in the booth, you know, can't get her in here."

"Please stay on the line, sir," Tiny said.

There are twenty-two police districts in Philadelphia. Without having to consult a map, Tiny Lewis knew that the parking garage behind the Bellevue-Stratford Hotel was in the 9th District, whose headquarters are at 22nd Street and Pennsylvania Avenue.

He checked his console display for the 9th District and saw that an indicator with

914 on it was lit up. The 9 made reference to the District; 14 was the number of a radio patrol car assigned to cover the City Hall area.

Tiny Lewis reached for a small black toggle switch on the console before him and held it down for a full two seconds. A long beep was broadcast on the Central Division radio frequency, alerting all cars in the Central Division, which includes the 9th District, that an important message is about to be broadcast.

"Fifteenth and Walnut, the Penn Services Parking Garage, report of a shooting and a hospital case," Tiny Lewis said into his microphone, and added, "914, 906, 9A."

There was an immediate response: "914 okay."

This was from Officer Archie Hellerman, who had just entered Rittenhouse Square from the west. He then put the microphone down, flipped on the siren and the flashing lights, and began to move as rapidly as he could through the heavy early-evening traffic on the narrow streets toward the Penn Services Parking Garage.

Tiny Lewis began to write the pertinent information on a three-by-five index card. At this stage the incident was officially an "investigation, shooting, and hospital case."

As he reached up to put the card between electrical contacts on a shelf above his console, which would interrupt the current lighting the small bulb behind the 914 block on the display console, three other radio calls came in.

"Radio, EPW 906 in."

"9A okay."

"Highway 4B in on that."

EPW 906 was an emergency patrol van, in this case a battered 1970 Ford, one of the two-man emergency patrol wagons assigned to the 9th District to transport the injured, prisoners, and otherwise assist in law enforcement. If this was not a bullshit call, 906 would carry whoever was shot to a hospital.

The district sergeant, 9A, was assigned to the eastern half of the 9th District.

Highway 4B was a radio patrol car of the Highway Patrol, an elite unit of the Philadelphia Police Department which the the Philadelphia *Ledger* had recently taken to calling Carlucci's Commandos.

As a police captain, the Honorable Jerome H. "Jerry" Carlucci, mayor of the City of Philadelphia, had commanded the Highway Patrol, which had begun, as its name implied, as a special organization to patrol the highways. Even before Captain Jerry Carlucci's reign, Highway Patrol had evolved into something more than motorcycle-mounted cops riding up and down Roosevelt Boulevard and the Schuylkill Expressway handing out speeding tickets. Carlucci, however, had presided over the ultimate transition of a traffic unit into an all-volunteer elite force. Highway had traded most of its motorcycles for two-man patrol cars and had citywide authority. Other Philadelphia police rode alone in patrol cars and patrolled specific areas in specific districts.

Highway Patrol had kept its motorcyclist's special uniforms (crushed crown cap, leather jacket, boots, and Sam Browne belts) and prided itself on being where the action was; in other words, in high-crime areas.

Highway Patrol was either "a highly trained, highly mobile anticrime task force of proven effectiveness" (Mayor Jerry Carlucci in a speech to the Sons of Italy) or "a jackbooted Gestapo" (an editorial in the Philadelphia *Ledger*).

Tiny Lewis had expected prompt responses to his call. EPWs generally were sent in on any call where an injury was reported, a supervisor responded to all major calls, and somebody from Highway Patrol (sometimes four or five cars) always went in on a "shooting and hospital case."

The door buzzer for the radio room went off. One of the uniformed officers on duty walked to it, opened it, smiled, and admitted a tall, immaculately uniformed lieutenant.

He was tall, nearly as tall as Tiny Lewis, but much leaner. He had very black skin and sharp Semitic features. He walked to Tiny Lewis's control console and said, somewhat menacingly, "I didn't expect to find you here. I went to your apartment and they told me where to find you."

"My apartment? Not my 'disgusting hovel'?"

"We have to talk," Lieutenant Lewis said.

"Not now, Pop," Tiny Lewis said. "I'm working a shooting and hospital case." And then he added, "In your district, come to think of it. On the roof of the Penn Services Parking Garage behind the Bellevue-Stratford. Civilian by phone, but I don't think it's bullshit."

"Can we have coffee when you get off?" Lieutenant Lewis asked. "I just heard you're going to Special Operations."

"Strange, I thought you arranged that," Tiny said.

"I told you, I just heard about it."

"Okay, Pop," Tiny said. "I'll meet you downstairs."

Lieutenant Lewis nodded, then walked very quickly out of the radio room.

Officer Archie Hellerman, driving RPC 914, couldn't count how many times he had been summoned to the Penn Services Parking Garage since it had been built seven years before. The attendant had been robbed at least once a month. One attendant, with more guts than brains, had even been shot at when he had refused to hand over the money.

Like most policemen who had been on the same job for years, Archie Hellerman had an encyclopedic knowledge of the buildings in his patrol area. He knew how the Penn Services Parking Garage operated. Incoming cars turned off South 15th Street into the entranceway. Ten yards inside, there was a wooden barrier across the roadway. Taking a ticket from an automatic ticket dispenser activated a mechanism that raised the barrier.

Departing cars left the building at the opposite end of the building, where an attendant in a small, allegedly robbery-proof booth collected the parking ticket, computed the charges, and, when they had been paid, raised another barrier, giving the customer access to the street.

Archie Hellerman in RPC 914 was the first police vehicle to arrive at the crime scene. As he approached the garage, he turned off his siren but left the flashing lights on. He pulled the nose of his Ford blue-and-white onto the exit ramp, which was blocked by a silver Porsche 911 Carrera, and jumped out of the car.

There was a civilian woman, a good-looking young blonde in a fancy dress, standing between the Porsche and the attendant's booth. She was obviously the complainant, the civilian who had reported the shooting.

Just seeing the blonde and her state of excitement was enough to convince Archie that the call was for real. Something serious had gone down.

"What's going on, miss?" Archie Hellerman asked.

"A girl has been shot on the roof. We need an ambulance."

The dying growl of a siren caught Archie's attention. He stepped back on the sidewalk and saw a radio patrol wagon, its warning lights still flashing, pulling up. There was another siren wailing, but that car, almost certainly the Highway car that had radioed in that it was going in on the call, was not yet in sight.

Archie signaled for the wagon to block the entrance ramp and then turned back to the good-looking blonde.

"You want to tell me what happened, please?"

"Well, we drove onto the roof, and my boyfriend saw her lying on the floor—"

"Your boyfriend? Where is he?"

I said "my boyfriend." Why did I say "my boyfriend"?

"He's up there," Amanda Spencer said. "He's a policeman."

"Your boyfriend is a cop?"

Amanda Spencer nodded her head.

Matt Payne is a cop. He really is a cop, as incredible as that seems. He had a gun, and he talked to me like a cop.

The driver of EPW 906, Officer Howard C. Sawyer, a very large twenty-six-year-old who had been dropped from a farm team of the Baltimore Orioles just before joining the Department sixteen months ago, pulled the Ford van onto the entrance ramp and started to get out.

He heard a siren die behind him, then growl again, and turned to look.

"Get that out of there!" the driver of Highway 4B shouted, his head out the window of the antenna-festooned but otherwise unmarked car.

Officer Sawyer backed the van up enough for the Highway Patrol car to get past him. The tires squealed as the car, in low gear, drove inside the building and started up the ramp to the upper floors. Sawyer saw that the driver was a sergeant; and, surprised, he noticed that the other cop was a regular cop, wearing a regular, as opposed to crushed-crown, uniform cap.

At precisely that moment the driver of Highway 4B, Sergeant Nick DeBenedito, who had been a policeman for ten years and a Highway Patrol sergeant for two, had a professional, if somewhat unkind, thought: *Shit, I'm riding with a rookie! And I got a gut feeling that whatever this job is, it's for real.*

Then, as he glanced over at Officer Jesus Martinez, he immediately modified that thought. Martinez, a slight, sharp-featured Latino kid of twenty-four, was, by the ordinary criteria, certainly a rookie. He had been on the job less than two years. But he'd gone right from the Police Academy to a plainclothes assignment with Narcotics.

He'd done very well at that, learning more in the year he'd spent on that assignment about the sordid underside of Philadelphia than a lot of cops learned in a lifetime. And then he'd topped that off helping to catch a scumbag named Gerald Vincent Gallagher, the junkie who had fatally shot Captain Richard F. "Dutch" Moffitt during a failed holdup of the Waikiki Diner on Roosevelt Boulevard.

Every cop in Philadelphia, all eight thousand of them, had been looking for Gerald Vincent Gallagher, especially every cop in Highway. Captain "Dutch" Moffitt had been the Highway commander. But Martinez and his partner, McFadden, had found him, by staking out where they thought he would show up. Martinez and Gallagher had both shown a lot of balls and unusual presence of mind under pressure by chasing the scumbag first through the crowded station and then down the elevated tracks of the subway. They'd had a chance to shoot Gallagher but hadn't fired because they were concerned about where his bullets might land.

McFadden had just about laid his hands on the son of a bitch when Gallagher had slipped and fried himself on the third rail and then gotten himself chopped up under the wheels of a subway train, but that didn't take one little thing away from the way Martinez and McFadden had handled themselves.

Around the bar of the FOP (Fraternal Order of Police), they said they ought to give them two citations, one for finding Gallagher and another for saving the city the cost of trying the son of a bitch.

Once they'd gotten their pictures in the newspapers, of course, that had ruined them for an undercover job in Narcotics. In most other big-city police departments, what they had done would have seen them promoted to detective. But in Philadelphia, all promotions are by examination, and Jesus Martinez had not yet taken it, and Charley McFadden hadn't been on the job long enough even to take it.

That didn't mean the department big shots weren't grateful. They also knew that most young cops who had worked in plainclothes regarded being ordered back into uniform as sort of a demotion, and they didn't want to do that to Martinez and McFadden. "They" included Chief Inspector Dennis V. Coughlin, arguably the most influential of all the chief inspectors.

And at about that time His Honor the Mayor had offered some more of his "suggestions" for the betterment of the Police Department, this one resulting in the establishment of a new division to be called Special Operations, under a young, hotshot staff inspector named Wohl, about whom little was known except some of the old-timers said that his father had been the mayor's rabbi when the mayor was a cop.

The mayor hadn't stopped with that, either. His other "suggestions" had pissed off just about everybody in Highway. He had "suggested" that a newly promoted captain named David Pekach, who had been assigned to Narcotics, be named the new commander of Highway, to replace Captain Dutch Moffitt. Everybody in Highway thought that Dutch Moffitt's deputy, Mike Sabara, who had been on the same captains' promotion list as Pekach, would get the job. Not only that, but Pekach was well-known within Highway as the guy who had bagged the only drug-dirty cop, a sergeant, Highway had ever had.

He had also "suggested" that Captain Sabara be named deputy commander of the new Special Operations Division. And finally, what had really pissed Highway off, he had "suggested" that Highway be placed under the new Special Operations Division. Highway, from its beginnings, had always been special and separate. Now it was going to be under some young clown whose only claim to fame was that he was well connected politically.

It had quickly become common knowledge in Highway that their new boss, Staff Inspector Peter Wohl, not only looked wet behind the ears but was. He was the youngest of the sixteen staff inspectors in the Department. He had spent very little time on the streets as a "real cop," but instead had spent most of his career as an investigator, most recently of corrupt politicians, of which Philadelphia, it was said, had more than its fair share. He had never worn a uniform as a lieutenant or a captain and had zero experience running a district or even a special unit, like Homicide, Intelligence, or even the K-9 Corps.

Five days before, Sergeant DeBenedito had been ordered to report to the commander of Special Operations in Special Operations' temporary headquarters at Bustleton and Bowler streets in Northeast Philadelphia.

Captains Sabara and Pekach were in Staff Inspector Peter Wohl's office when he went in. Mike Sabara was wearing the uniform prescribed for captains not attached to Highway Patrol. It consisted of a white shirt with captain's bars on the collar and blue trousers. He carried a snub-nosed Smith & Wesson .38 Special revolver in a small holster on his belt. DeBenedito had heard that Wohl had told him, to make the point that Sabara was no longer in Highway, that he had his choice of either civilian clothing, or uniform without the distinguishing motorcyclist boots and Sam Browne belt with its row of shiny cartridges.

Captain Pekach was wearing the Highway uniform. The contrast between the two was significant.

Wohl, DeBenedito thought somewhat unkindly, did not even look like a cop. He was a tall, slim young man with light brown hair. He was wearing a blue blazer and gray flannel slacks, a white button-down shirt with a rep-striped necktie. He looked, DeBenedito thought, like some candy-ass lawyer or stockbroker from the Main Line.

He was sitting on a couch with his feet, shod in glistening loafers, resting on a coffee table. When his office had been Dutch Moffitt's office, there had been neither coffee table nor couch in it.

"Well, that was quick," Wohl said. "I just sent for you."

"I just came in, sir," DeBenedito said, shaking hands first with Mike Sabara and then with Pekach.

"Help yourself to coffee," Wohl said, gesturing toward a chrome thermos.

"No, thank you, sir."

"Okay. Right to the point," Wohl had said. "Do you know Officers Jesus Martinez and Charles McFadden?"

"I've seen them around, sir."

"You know *about* them?"

"Yes, sir."

"I'm going to make them probationary Highway Patrolmen," Wohl said.

"I don't know what that means, sir," DeBenedito said.

"That's probably because I just made it up," Wohl confessed cheerfully, with a chuckle. To DeBenedito's surprise, Captain Sabara laughed.

"A probationary Highway Patrolman," Wohl went on, "is a young police officer who has done something outstanding in the course of his regular duties. On the recommendation of his captain, and if he volunteers, he will be temporarily assigned to Highway. For three months he will be paired with a supervisor—a sergeant such as yourself, DeBenedito. . . ."

DeBenedito became aware that Wohl was waiting for a response. "Yes, sir," he said.

"During that three months the probationers will ride either with their sergeant or with a *good* Highway cop. And I mean replacing the second cop in the car, not as excess baggage in the backseat."

"Yes, sir," DeBenedito said.

"And at the end of the three months the supervisor will recommend, in writing, that the probationer be taken into Highway; in other words, go through the Wheel School and the other training or not. With his reasons."

Sergeant DeBenedito did not like what he had heard. When it became apparent to him that Wohl was again waiting for a response, he blurted, "Can you do that, sir?"

"Do you mean, do I have the authority?"

"Yes, sir. I mean, the requirements for getting into Highway are pretty well established. We don't take people with less than four, five years—"

"Didn't," Wohl said, interrupting. "B.W."

" 'B.W.,' sir?"

"Before Wohl," Wohl explained. "And do I have the authority? I don't know. But until someone tells me in writing that I don't, I'm going to presume that I do."

"Yes, sir," DeBenedito said.

"I don't think length of service would be that important a criterion for getting into Highway," Wohl said. "I think doing an outstanding job should carry more weight."

"Sir," DeBenedito said, "with respect, Highway is different."

He saw in the look on Captain Sabara's face that that had been the wrong thing to say.

"Cutting this short," Wohl said, a hint of annoyance in his voice, "based on Captain Sabara's recommendation of you, Sergeant, you are herewith appointed probationary evaluation officer for Officers Jesus Martinez and Charles McFadden, whose probationary period begins today. If you run into any problems, let Captain Pekach know. That will be all. Thank you."

Captain Pekach had followed DeBenedito out of Wohl's office.

"I want to introduce you to Martinez and McFadden," Pekach said. "I told them to wait in the roll call room."

"I guess I said the wrong thing in there, huh?" DeBenedito had asked.

"You're going to have to learn to know what you're talking about before you open your mouth," Pekach had replied. "I don't think you would have told the inspector that Highway was different if you knew he was the youngest sergeant ever in Highway, would you?"

"Jesus, was he?"

"Yeah, he was. He was also the youngest captain the Department has ever had, *is* the youngest staff inspector the Department has ever had, and if he doesn't shoot himself in the foot with Special Operations, stands, I think, a damned good chance to be the youngest full inspector."

"Should I go back in there and apologize?"

"No. Let it go. Peter Wohl doesn't carry a grudge. But if you're looking for advice, don't start this evaluation business with Martinez and McFadden thinking it's a dumb idea it was your bad luck to get stuck with. Give it your best shot."

"Yes, sir," DeBenedito said. "They worked for you in Narcotics, didn't they, Captain?"

"Yeah. And they both did a good job for me. But if you're asking if this was my idea, the answer is no. And if you're asking whether I think either of them can cut the mustard, the answer is, I don't know."

Sergeant Nick DeBenedito, driving with great skill, drove up the ramps until he reached the fourth floor. Then he stopped by the stairwell.

"Martinez," he ordered calmly, "you go up the stairs. I don't think we're still going to find anybody up there, but you never know. If you hear somebody going down the stairs, go and yell down at the district guy." He pointed to the side of the parking garage, where a line of windows were open.

"Got it," Martinez said, then got out of the car and went to the stairwell. DeBenedito saw him take his revolver from his holster and carefully push the stairwell door open and go inside. Then DeBenedito stepped on the accelerator and started up the last ramp to the roof. As he drove, he drew his revolver.

Jesus Martinez listened carefully inside the stairwell for any noise and heard none. Then he went up the stairs, taking them two at a time, until he reached the door opening onto the roof.

He listened there for a moment, heard nothing, and then, standing clear of the door, pushed it open. He quickly glanced around. Sergeant DeBenedito was out of his car. He was holding his revolver in both hands, aiming at someone out of sight.

Christ, Jesus Martinez thought in admiration, *he's already got the son of a bitch on the ground!*

He trotted between the parked cars, staying out of what would be the line of fire if DeBenedito fired his revolver, until he could see who was on the ground.

There was the body of a girl in a fancy dress, lying in a pool of blood, and a man in a tuxedo, lying facedown.

"Put cuffs on him, Martinez," DeBenedito ordered.

The man lying facedown moved his head to look at Jesus Martinez.

"Hay-zus, tell him I'm a cop," Matt Payne said.

"Sergeant," Martinez said, "he's a cop."

DeBenedito looked at him, more for absolute confirmation than in surprise. He started to holster his gun.

"Sorry," he said.

Matt Payne got to his knees.

"Is there a wagon on the way?"

"Martinez, yell down for that wagon to get up here," DeBenedito ordered. Jesus ran to the edge of the roof and did so.

"There's a body, white male, head blown away, over by the stairwell," Payne said, pointing. "I think the doer, doers, were long gone when I drove up here."

"You look familiar," DeBenedito said. "I know you?"

"My name is Payne," Matt said. "I work for Inspector Wohl."

Oh, shit! DeBenedito thought. And then he knew who this guy in the tuxedo was. He was the rookie who had blown the brains of the Northwest Philly serial rapist all over his van.

"What the hell happened here?" Sergeant DeBenedito asked Matt Payne as he dropped to one knee to examine the woman on the floor.

She was unconscious but not dead. When he felt his fingers on her neck, feeling for a heartbeat, she moaned. DeBenedito looked impatiently over his shoulder for the wagon.

If we don't get her to a hospital soon, she will be dead.

"She was on the ground, the floor, when I drove up here," Matt said. "When I saw she was shot, I sent my date down to call it in. Then I found the dead guy."

"Any idea who they are?"

"Her name is Detweiler," Matt said. "Penny—Penelope—Detweiler. I guess she was up here with her car—"

"Brilliant," DeBenedito said sarcastically.

"She was going the same place we were," Matt said. "She's a bridesmaid—"

"A what?"

"A bridesmaid. There's a dinner at the Union League."

"Who is she?"

"I told you. Her name is Detweiler," Matt said, and then finally understood the question. "She lives in Chestnut Hill. Her father is president of Nesfoods."

"But you don't know the other victim?"

"No. I don't think he was with her. He's not wearing a dinner jacket."

"A what?"

"A tuxedo. The dinner is what they call 'black-tie.' "

RPW 902 came onto the roof.

Officer Howard C. Sawyer saw DeBenedito and the victim and quickly and skillfully turned the van around and backed up to them. Officer Thomas Collins, riding shotgun in 902, was out of the wagon before it stopped, first signaling to Sawyer when to stop and then quickly opening the rear door.

"This one's still alive," DeBenedito said. "There's a dead one—" He stopped, thinking, *I don't know if the other one is dead or not; all I have is this rookie's opinion that he's dead.*

"The other one *is* dead, right?" he asked, challenging Matt Payne.

"The top of his head is gone," Matt said.

DeBenedito looked at Officers Sawyer, Collins, Payne, and Martinez.

What I have here is four fucking rookies!

The victim moaned as Sawyer and Collins, as gently as they could, picked her up and slid her onto a stretcher.

The second officer in an RPW, the one said to be "riding shotgun," was officially designated as "the recorder"; he was responsible for handling all the paperwork. According to Department procedure, the recorder in an RPW would ride with the victim in the back of the wagon en route to the hospital to interview her, if possible, and possibly get a "dying declaration," what would be described in court as the last words of the deceased before dying. A dying declaration carried a lot of weight with jurors.

Sergeant DeBenedito didn't think Officer Collins looked bright enough to write down his own laundry list.

He made his decision.

"Take her to Hahneman, that's closest," he ordered, referring to Hahneman Hospital, on just the other side of City Hall on North Broad Street. "Martinez, you get in the back with the girl and see what you can find out. You know about 'dying declarations'?"

"Yeah," Martinez said.

"And you, Payne, take the stairs downstairs and seal off the building. Nobody in or out. Got it?"

"Got it," Matt said, and started for the stairwell.

DeBenedito started for his car, and then changed his mind. He still didn't know for sure if the second victim was really dead.

One look at the body confirmed what Payne had told him. The top of the head was gone. The face, its eyes open and distorted, registered surprise.

On closer inspection the victim looked familiar. After a moment Sergeant DeBenedito was almost positive that the second victim was Anthony J. DeZego, a young, not too bright, Mafia guy known as Tony the Zee.

Now he walked quickly to the Highway car and picked up the microphone.

"Highway 21."

"Highway 21," police radio responded.

"I got a 5292 on the roof of the Penn Services garage," DeBenedito reported. "Notify Homicide. The 9th District RPW is transporting a second victim, female Caucasian, to Hahneman."

DeBenedito glanced around the roof and saw an arrow indicating the location of a public telephone.

"Okay, 21," police radio responded.

DeBenedito tossed the microphone on the seat and trotted toward the telephone, searching his pockets for change.

He dialed a number from memory.

"Homicide."

"This is Sergeant DeBenedito, Highway. I got a 5292 on the roof of the Penn Services Parking Garage behind the Bellevue-Stratford. Top of his head blown off. I think he's a mob guy called Tony the Zee."

"Anthony J. DeZego," the Homicide detective responded. "Interesting."

"There was a second victim. Female Caucasian. Multiple wounds. Looks like a shotgun. Identified as Penelope Detweiler. Her father is president of Nesfoods."

"Jesus!"

"She's being transported to Hahneman."

"This is Lieutenant Natali, Sergeant. We got the 5292 from radio. A couple of detectives are on the way. When they get there, tell them I'm on my way. You're sure it's Tony the Zee?"

"Just about. And the ID on the girl is positive."

"I'm on my way," Lieutenant Natali said, and the phone went dead.

DeBenedito dialed another number.

"Highway, Corporal Ashe."

"Sergeant DeBenedito. Pass it to the lieutenant that I went in on shots fired at the parking garage behind the Bellevue. The dead man is a mob guy, Tony the Zee DeZego. Shotgun took the top of his head off. There's a second victim, white female, transported to Hahneman. Name is Detweiler. Her father is president of Nesfoods."

"I'll get it to Lieutenant Lucci right away, Sergeant," Corporal Ashe said.

Sergeant DeBenedito hung up without saying anything else and went back on the roof to have another look at Tony the Zee.

I wonder who blew this scumbag guinea gangster away? thought Sergeant Vincenzo Nicholas DeBenedito idly. The previous summer he had flown to Italy with his parents to meet most, but not all, of his Neapolitan kinfolk.

Then he thought: *Damn shame that girl had to get in between whatever happened here, on her way, all dressed up, to a party at the Union League.*

And then he had another discomfiting thought: Was *the nice little rich girl from Chestnut Hill just an innocent bystander? Or was she fucking around with Tony the Zee?*

Matt Payne pulled open the door to the stairwell and started down, taking the stairs two and three at a time.

He wanted to see what had happened to Amanda Spencer, and he also desperately needed to relieve his bladder. He had been startled to hear the scream of the tires on the Porsche when she had turned it around and driven off the roof. He had had several thoughts: that she was naturally frightened and logically was therefore getting the hell away from the scene; then he was surprised that she could drive the Porsche, and he modified this last thought to *"drive the Porsche so well"* when he saw her make the turn, then head down the ramp as fast as she could.

Between the third and second floors he startled a very large florid-faced cop wearing the white cap cover of Traffic who was leaning against the cement-block wall. The Traffic cop pushed himself off the wall to block Matt's passage and looked as if he were about to draw his pistol.

"I'm a cop," Matt called. "Payne, Special Operations."

He fished in his pocket and came out with his badge.

"What the hell is going on up there?" the Traffic cop asked.

"A couple of people got shot. With a shotgun. One is dead, and the van is taking a woman to the hospital."

The Traffic cop got out of the way, and Matt ran down the stairs to ground level. He pushed open the door and found himself on 15th Street. Ten yards away, he saw the nose of his Porsche sticking out of the garage and onto the sidewalk. There were a half dozen police cars, marked and unmarked, clustered around the entrance and exit ramps, half up on the sidewalk. A Traffic sergeant was in the narrow street, directing traffic.

When he reached the exit ramp, Amanda was talking to a man with a detective's badge hanging out of the breast pocket of a remarkably ugly plaid sport coat. When she saw him, Amanda walked away from the detective and up to Matt.

"How is she?"

"She's alive," Matt said. "They're taking her to the hospital. We've got to move the Porsche."

As if on cue, the emergency patrol wagon pulled up behind the Porsche and Officer Howard C. Sawyer impatiently sounded the horn. Matt jumped behind the wheel and pulled the Porsche out of the way, onto the sidewalk.

The EPW came off the exit ramp, turned on its siren and flashing lamps, and when the Traffic sergeant, furiously blowing his whistle, stopped the flow of traffic, bounced onto 15th Street, turning left.

When Matt got out of the car, the detective was waiting for him.

"You're the boyfriend?" he asked, and then without waiting for a reply asked, "You found the victim? You're a cop? That's your car?"

Matt looked at Amanda when the detective said the word *boyfriend*. She shrugged her shoulders and looked uncomfortable.

"My name is Payne," Matt said. "Special Operations. That's my car. We saw one of the victims on the ground when we drove onto the roof."

"You're Payne? The guy who blew the rapist away?"

Matt nodded.

"There's a Highway sergeant up there," Matt said. "He sent me to seal the building."

"It's been sealed," the detective said, gesturing up and down the street. "I'm Joe D'Amata, Homicide," he said. "You have any idea what went down?"

"*Two* victims," Matt said. "I found a white male with his head blown off next to the stairwell. Looks like a shotgun." He looked at Amanda. "Did Miss Spencer tell you who the female is?"

"I was about to ask her," the detective said.

"She's Penny Detweiler," Amanda said.

"You know her? You were with her?"

"We know her. We weren't with her. Or not really."

"What the hell does that mean?"

"There's a dinner party. There's a wedding. She was supposed to be at it."

"A dinner party or a wedding?" D'Amata asked impatiently. "Which?"

"A wedding dinner party," Matt said, feeling foolish, and anticipated D'Amata's next question. "At the Union League."

D'Amata looked at Payne. Ordinary cops do not ordinarily go to dinner at the Union League. He remembered what he had heard about this kid. There had been a lot of talk around the Department about him. Rich kid. College boy from Wallingford. But it was also said that his father, a sergeant, had been killed on the job. And there was no question he'd blown away the serial rapist. There had been a picture of him in all the papers, with Mayor Carlucci's arm around him. The critter had tried to run him down with a van, and then the kid had blown the critter's brains out. The critter had had a woman, a naked woman, tied up in the back of the van when it happened. If the kid hadn't caught him when he did, the woman would have been another victim. The critter had tortured and mutilated his previous victim before he'd killed her. A real scumbag loony.

"The Union League," Detective D'Amata said as he wrote it down.

"Her parents are probably there now," Matt Payne said. "Somebody's going to have to tell them what happened."

"You mean, you want to?"

"I don't know how it's done," Matt confessed.

Detective D'Amata looked around, found what he was looking for, and raised his voice: "Lieutenant Lewis?"

Lieutenant Foster H. Lewis, Sr., of the 9th District, who had only moments before arrived at the crime scene, looked around to see who was calling him, and found D'Amata.

"See you a minute, Lieutenant?" D'Amata called.

Lieutenant Lewis walked over.

"Lieutenant, this is Officer Payne, of Special Operations. He and this young lady found the victims."

Lieutenant Lewis looked carefully at Officer Matthew Payne, who was wearing a dinner jacket Lieutenant Lewis would have bet good money was his and hadn't come from a rental agency. He knew a good deal about Officer Matthew W. Payne.

There was a vacancy for a lieutenant in the newly formed Special Operations Division. Lewis had thought—before he'd heard that Foster, Jr., was being assigned there—that it might be a good place for him to broaden his experience and enhance his career. So far all of his experience had been in one district or another.

An old friend of his, a Homicide detective named Jason Washington, had been transferred, over his objections, to Special Operations, and he'd had a long talk with Washington about Special Operations and its youthful commander, Staff Inspector Peter Wohl.

In the course of that conversation the well-publicized heroics of Wohl's special assistant had come up. To Lewis's surprise, Jason Washington had kind words for both men: "Peter Wohl's as smart as a whip and a straight arrow. A little ruthless about getting the job done, not to protect himself. And the kid's all right too. Denny Coughlin dumped him in Wohl's lap; he didn't ask for the job. I think he's got the making of a good cop; the last I heard, it wasn't illegal to be either rich or well connected."

"I'm surprised, Officer Payne," Lieutenant Lewis said, "that Inspector Wohl hasn't told you that it is Departmental procedure for an officer in civilian clothing at a crime scene to display his badge in a prominent place."

Matt looked at him for a moment, then said, "Sorry, sir."

He took the folder holding his badge and photo identification card from his pocket and tried to shove it into the breast pocket of his dinner jacket. It didn't fit. He started to unpin the badge from the leather folder.

I wonder, Lieutenant Lewis thought, *how this young man's father feels about him becoming a policeman? He is probably at least as unenthusiastic about it as I am about that hardheaded, overgrown namesake of mine.*

It is a question of upward and downward social mobility. My son has thrown away a splendid chance at upward mobility, to become a doctor; to make, a few years out of medical school, more money than I will ever make in my lifetime. This young man is turning his back on God alone knows what. Certainly, a partnership in Mawson, Payne, Stockton, McAdoo and Lester. Very possibly a chance to become a senator or a governor. Certainly to make a great deal of money.

I am as baffled by this one as I am by Foster.

"Lieutenant," Detective D'Amata said, "Payne knows one of the victims. The woman." He consulted his notebook. "Her name is Penelope Detweiler. He says her parents are probably at the Union League—"

"Chestnut Hill?" Lieutenant Lewis asked, interrupting. "Those Detweilers, Payne?"

"Yes, sir."

Lieutenant Lewis also knew a good deal about the Detweilers of Chestnut Hill. Four generations ago George Detweiler had gone into partnership with Chadwick Thomas Nesbitt to found what was then called the Nesbitt Potted Meats and Preserved Vegetables Company. It was now Nesfoods International, listed just above the middle of the Fortune 500 companies and still tightly held. C. T. Nesbitt III was chairman of the Executive Committee and H. Richard Detweiler was President and Chief Executive Officer.

C. T. Nesbitt IV was to be married the day after tomorrow by the Episcopal Bishop of Philadelphia at St. Mark's Church. His Honor the Mayor and Mrs. Carlucci had been invited, and there had been a call from a mayor's officer to the 9th District commander, saying the mayor didn't want any problems with traffic or anything else.

Extra officers from the 9th District had been assigned to assist the Traffic Division in handling the flow of traffic. As a traffic problem it would be much like a very large funeral. A large number of people would arrive, more or less singly, at the church. Traffic flow would be impeded as each car (in many cases, a limousine) paused long enough to discharge its passengers and then moved on to find a parking place. After the wedding the problem would grow worse, as the four hundred odd guests left all at once to find their cars or limousines for the ride to the reception at the home of the bride's parents. Only the problem of forming a funeral convoy of cars would be missing.

Additionally there would be a number of plainclothes officers from Civil Affairs and the Detective Division mingling with the guests at the church and at the pre-wedding cocktail party for out-of-town guests in the Bellevue-Stratford Hotel.

Captain J. J. Maloney, the 9th District Commander, had ordered Lieutenant Foster H. Lewis, Sr., to take care of it.

"Has the family of the victim been informed?" Lieutenant Lewis asked.

"No, sir," D'Amata said.

"Sir, I thought maybe I could do that," Payne said.

Lieutenant Lewis thought that over carefully for a moment. It had to be done. Normally it would be the responsibility of the 9th District. But if Payne did it, it would probably be handled with greater tact than if he dispatched an RPC to do it. He considered for a moment going himself, or going with Payne, and decided against it. He also decided that he would not take it upon himself to notify the mayor, although he was sure Jerry Carlucci would want to hear about this. Let Captain J. J. Maloney tell the mayor, or one of the big brass. He would find a phone and call Maloney.

"Very well," Lieutenant Lewis said. "Do so. I don't think I have to tell you to express the regret of the Police Department that something like this has happened, do I?"

"No, sir."

"As I understand the situation, we don't know what happened here, do we?"

"No, sir," Matt Payne said.

"I'm sure that you will not volunteer your opinions, will you, Payne?"

"No, sir."

"And then come back here," Lieutenant Lewis said. "I'm sure Detective D'Amata, and others, will have questions for you."

"Yes, sir."

Lieutenant Lewis turned to Amanda Spencer.

"I didn't get your name, miss," he said.

"Amanda Spencer."

"Are you from Philadelphia, Miss Spencer?"

"Scarsdale," Amanda said, adding, "New York."

"You're in town for the wedding?"

"That's right."

"Where are you staying here?"

"With the Brownes, the bride's family," Amanda answered. "In Merion."

That would be the Soames T. Brownes, Lieutenant Lewis recalled from an extraordinary memory. Soames T. Browne did not have a job. When his picture appeared, for example, in a listing of the board of directors of the Philadelphia Savings Fund Society, the caption under it read "Soames T. Browne, Investments." The Brownes—and for that matter, the Soames—had been investing, successfully, in Philadelphia businesses since Ben Franklin had been running the newspaper there.

There was going to be a lot of pressure on this job, Lewis thought. And a lot of publicity. People like the Nesbitts and the Brownes and the Detweilers took the term *public servant* literally, with emphasis on *servant*. They expected public servants, like the police and the courts, to do what they had been hired to do, and were not at all reluctant to point out where those public servants had failed to perform. When a Detweiler called the mayor, he took the call.

Lieutenant Lewis thought again that Jerry Carlucci had been invited to the wedding and the reception and might even be at the Union League when the Payne kid walked in and told them that Penelope Detweiler had just been shot.

"Ordinarily, Miss Spencer, we'd ask you to come to the Roundhouse—"

"The what?" Amanda asked.

"To the Police Administration Building—"

"The whole building is curved, Amanda," Matt explained.

"—to be interviewed by a Homicide detective," Lieutenant Lewis went on, clearly displeased with Matt's interruption. "But since Officer Payne was with you, possibly Detective D'Amata would be willing to have you come there a little later."

"No problem with that, sir," D'Amata said.

And then, as if to document his prediction that the shooting was going to attract a good deal of attention from the press, an antenna-bedecked Buick Special turned out of the line of traffic and pulled into the exit ramp, and Mr. Michael J. O'Hara got out.

Mickey O'Hara wrote about crime for the Philadelphia *Bulletin*. He was very good at what he did and was regarded by most policemen, including Lieutenant Foster H. Lewis, Sr., as almost a member of the Department. If you told Mickey O'Hara that something was off the record, it stayed that way.

"Hey, Foster," Mickey O'Hara said, "that white shirt looks good on you."

That made reference to Lieutenant Foster's almost brand-new status as a lieutenant. Police supervisors, lieutenants and above, wore white uniform shirts. Sergeants and below wore blue.

"How are you, Mickey?" Lewis said, shaking O'Hara's hand. "Thank you."

"And what are you doing, Matt?" O'Hara said, offering his hand to Officer Payne. "Moonlighting as a waiter?"

"Hey, Mickey," Payne said.

"What's going on?"

"Hold it a second, Mickey," Lewis said. "Miss Spencer, you'll have to make a statement. Payne will tell you about that. And you come back here, Payne, as soon as you do what you have to do."

"Yes, sir. See you, Mickey."

O'Hara waited until Matt Payne had politely loaded Amanda Spencer into the Porsche, gotten behind the wheel, and was fed into the line of traffic by the Traffic sergeant before speaking.

"Nice kid, that boy," he said.

"So I hear," Lieutenant Lewis said.

"What does he have to do before he comes back here?"

"Tell H. Richard Detweiler that his daughter was found lying in a pool of blood on the roof of this place; somebody popped her with a shotgun," Lewis said.

"No shit? Detweiler's daughter? Is she dead?"

"No. Not yet, anyway. They just took her to Hahneman. There's another victim up there. White man. He got his head blown off."

"Robbery?" Mickey O'Hara asked. "With a shotgun? Who is he?"

"We don't know."

"Can I go up there?" Mickey asked.

"I'll go with you," Lewis said, and gestured toward the stairwell.

Between the third and fourth floors of the Penn Services Parking Garage, Lieutenant Lewis and Mr. O'Hara encountered Detective Lawrence Godofski of Homicide coming down the stairs.

Godofski had a plastic bag in his hand. He extended it to Lieutenant Lewis.

"Whaddayasay, Larry?" Mickey O'Hara said.

"How goes it, Mickey?"

The plastic bag contained a leather wallet and a number of cards, driver's license, and credit cards, which apparently had been removed from the wallet.

Lieutenant Lewis examined the driver's license through the clear plastic bag and then handed it to Mickey O'Hara. The driver's license had been issued to Anthony J. DeZego, of a Bouvier Street address in South Philadelphia, an area known as Little Italy.

"I'll be damned," Mickey O'Hara said. "Tony the Zee. He's the body?"

Detective Godofski nodded.

"This is pretty classy for Tony the Zee, getting himself blown away like this," O'Hara said. "The last I heard, he was driving a shrimp-and-oyster reefer truck up from the Gulf Coast."

"Godofski," Lieutenant Lewis said, "have you thought about bringing Organized Crime in on this?"

"Yes, sir. I was about to do just that."

"You find anything else interesting up there?"

Godofski produced another plastic bag, this one holding two fired shotshell cartridges.

"Number seven and a halfs," he said. "Rabbit shells."

"No gun?"

"No shotgun. Tony the Zee had a .38, a Smith and Wesson Undercover, in an ankle holster. I left it there for the lab guys. He never got a chance to use it."

"What the hell has H. Richard Detweiler's daughter got to do with a second-rate guinea gangster like Tony the Zee?" Mickey O'Hara asked rhetorically.

Lieutenant Lewis shrugged and then started up the stairs again.

The Union League of Philadelphia is a stone Victorian building—some say a remarkably ugly one—on the west side of South Broad Street, literally in the shadow of the statue of Billy Penn, which stands atop City Hall at the intersection of Broad and Market streets.

South Broad Street, in front of the Union League, has been designated a NO PARKING AT ANY TIME TOW-AWAY ZONE. Several large signs on the sidewalk advertise this.

Traffic Officer P. J. Ward, who was directing traffic in the middle of South Broad Street, was thus both surprised and annoyed when he saw a silver Porsche 911 pull up in front of the Union League, turn off its lights, and stop. Then a young guy in a monkey suit got out and quickly walked around to the other side to open the door for his girlfriend.

Ward quickly strode over.

"Hey, you! What the hell do you think you're doing?"

The young guy in the monkey suit turned to face him.

"I won't be long," he said. "I'm on the job."

There was a silver-colored badge pinned to his jacket, but Officer Ward decided he wasn't going to take that at what it looked like. There was a good chance, he decided, that when he got a good look at the badge, it would say PRIVATE INVESTIGATOR or OFFICIAL U.S. TAXPAYER, and that the young man in the monkey suit driving the Porsche would turn out to be a wiseass rich kid who thought he could get away with anything.

"Hold it a minute," he said, and trotted onto the sidewalk.

The badge was real. The next question was what was this rich kid driving a Porsche 911 doing with it?

"I'm Payne, Special Operations," the young guy said, and held out his photo ID. Ward saw at a glance that the ID was the real thing.

"What's going on?"

"I have to go in here a minute," Matt said. "I won't be long."

"Don't be," Officer Ward said.

Matt took Amanda's arm and they walked up the stairs to the front door. As they reached the revolving door to the entrance foyer, it was put into motion for them. Matt saw that just inside was a large man, who smelled of retired cop and was functioning more as a genteel bouncer than a doorman.

He had seen the two young people all nicely dressed up and decided they had legitimate business inside.

"Good evening," he said, then saw the badge on the young man's lapel, and surprise registered on his face.

"The Browne dinner?" Matt asked.

"Up the stairs, sir, and to your right," the man at the door said, pointing.

Matt and Amanda started up the stairs. Matt unpinned his badge and put it in his pocket. He would need it again when he went back to the garage, but he didn't want to put it on display here. Then he thought of something else.

"Here," he said, handing the Porsche keys to Amanda.

"What's this for?" she asked.

"Well, I sort of hoped you'd park it for me until I can catch up with you," Matt said. "I really can't leave it parked out in front."

"When are you going to 'catch up with me'?"

"As soon as I can. Sometime tonight you're going to have to make a statement at Homicide."

"I already told that detective everything I know."

"You know that," Matt said. "He doesn't."

She took the keys from him.

"I was about to say," she said, a touch of wonder in her voice, " 'You're not going to just leave me here like this, are you?' But of course you have to, don't you? You're *really* a policeman."

"I'm sorry," Matt said.

"Don't be absurd," Amanda said. "Why should you be sorry? It's just that—you don't look like a cop, I guess."

"What does a cop look like?"

"I didn't mean that the way it came out," she said.

She took his arm and they went the rest of the way up the stairway.

"Wait here, please," Matt said when they came to the double doors leading to the dining room. He stepped inside.

"May I have your invitation, sir?"

"I won't be staying," Matt said as he spotted the head table, and Mr. and Mrs. H. Richard Detweiler, and started for it.

"Hey!" the man who'd asked for the invitation said sharply, and started after him.

Mr. H. Richard Detweiler, who obviously had had a couple of drinks, was engaged in animated conversation with a youthful, trim, freckle-faced woman sitting at his right side. She was considerably older than she looked, Matt knew, for she was Mrs. Brewster Cortland Payne II, and she was his mother.

She smiled at him with her eyes when she saw him approaching the table, then returned her attention to Mr. Detweiler.

"Mr. Detweiler?" Matt said. "Excuse me?"

"Matt, you're interrupting," Patricia Payne said.

The man who had followed Matt across the room came up. "Excuse me, sir, I'll have to see your invitation," he said.

H. Richard Detweiler first focused his eyes on Matt, and then at the man demanding an invitation.

"It's all right," he said. "He's invited. He'd forget his head if it wasn't nailed on."

"Mr. Detweiler, may I see you a moment, please, sir?"

"Matt, for God's sake, can't you see that I'm talking to your mother?"

"Sir, this is important. I'm sorry to interrupt."

"Well, all right, what is it?"

"May I speak to you alone, please?"

"Goddammit, Matt!"

"Matt, what is it?" Patricia Payne asked.

"Mother, please!"

H. Richard Detweiler got to his feet. In the process he knocked over his whiskey glass, swore under his breath, and glowered at Matt.

Matt led him out of the room.

"Now what the devil is going on, Matt?" Detweiler asked impatiently, and then saw Amanda. "How are you, darling?"

"Mr. Detweiler," Matt said, "there's been an incident—"

"Incident? Incident? What kind of an *incident?*"

Brewster C. Payne II came out of the room.

"Penny's been hurt, Mr. Detweiler," Matt said. "She's been taken to Hahneman Hospital."

In a split second H. Richard Detweiler was absolutely sober.

"What, precisely, has happened, Matt?" he asked icily.

"I think it would be a good idea if you went to the hospital, Mr. Detweiler," Matt said.

Detweiler grabbed Matt by the shoulders.

"I asked you a question, Matt," he said. "Answer me, dammit!"

"Penny appears to have been shot, Mr. Detweiler," Matt said.

"Shot?" Detweiler asked incredulously. *"Shot?"*

"Yes, sir. With a shotgun."

"I don't believe this," Detweiler said. "Is she seriously injured?"

"Yes, sir, I think she is."

"How did it happen? Where?"

"On the roof of the parking garage behind the Bellevue," Matt said. "That's about all we know."

" 'All we know'? What about the police?"

"I'm a policeman, Mr. Detweiler," Matt said. "We just don't know yet what happened."

"That's right," Detweiler said, dazed. "Your dad told me you were a policeman— and then there was all the business in the newspapers. My God, Matt, what happened?"

"I don't know, sir."

"Dick, you'd better go to the hospital," Brewster C. Payne said. "I'll get Grace and bring her over there."

"My God, this is unbelievable!" Detweiler said.

"It would probably be quicker if you caught a cab out front," Matt said.

H. Richard Detweiler looked at Matt intently for a moment, then ran down the stairs.

"How did you get involved in this, Matt?" Brewster C. Payne II asked.

"Amanda and I found her— Excuse me. Dad, this is Amanda Spencer. Amanda, this is my father."

"Hello," Amanda said.

"We drove onto the roof of the garage and found her," Matt said. "Amanda called it in. They took her to Hahneman in a wagon."

"How badly is she injured?"

"It was a shotgun, Dad," Matt said.

"Oh, my God! A robbery?"

"We don't know yet," Matt said. "I have to get back over there." He looked at Amanda. "I'll see you . . . later."

"Okay," Amanda said.

Matt ran down the stairs, taking his badge from his pocket and pinning it to his lapel again. The Traffic cop would probably be waiting for him. He reached the door, stopped, and then trotted into the gentlemen's lounge. Concentrating on the business at hand, he didn't notice the young gentleman at the adjoining urinal until he spoke.

"What the *hell* have you pinned to your lapel, Payne?"

Matt turned and saw Kellogg Shaw, who had been a year ahead of him at Episcopal Academy and then had gone on to Princeton.

"What's that sore on the head of your dick, Kellogg?" Matt replied, and then ran out of the men's room, zipping his fly on the run. He glanced over his shoulder and saw Kellogg Shaw exposing himself to the mirror over the sinks.

6 Victor, checking his rearview mirror to make sure that Charles was still behind him, flicked on his right-turn signal and turned into the short-term parking lot at Philadelphia International Airport.

He took a ticket from the dispensing machine, then drove around the lot until he
found two empty parking spaces. A moment after he stopped, Charles pulled the
Cadillac in beside him.

Charles got out of the Cadillac, glanced around the parking lot to make sure that
no one had an idle interest in what they were doing, and then opened the door of the
Pontiac. Quickly he shifted the Remington Model 1100 from the floor of the Cadillac
to the floor of the Pontiac. Victor helped him put it out of sight under the seat.

Charles then took his carry-on from the Cadillac and walked toward the terminal
building. Victor waited until Charles was almost out of sight, then got out of the
Pontiac. He put the keys on top of the left rear tire, then took his carry-on from the
backseat, slammed the doors, checked to make sure they were locked, and then
walked to the terminal.

Victor checked in with TWA, then went to the cocktail lounge. Charles was at the
bar. Victor touched his shoulder and Charles turned.

"Well, look who's here," Charles said.

"Nice to see you. Everything going all right?"

"No problems at all."

"Can I buy you a drink?"

"A quick one. I'm on United 404 in fifteen minutes."

"Lucky you. I've got to hang around here for an hour and a half."

Fifteen minutes later Charles boarded United Airlines Flight 404 for Chicago. An
hour and fifteen minutes after that, Victor boarded TWA Flight 332 for Los Angeles,
with an intermediate stop in St. Louis.

At the entrance to the Penn Services Parking Garage there was a crowd of citizens,
almost all of them well dressed and almost all of them indignant, even furious.

They had been told, or were being told, by uniformed police officers and detectives
that the entire Penn Services Parking Garage had been designated a crime scene and
they could not reclaim their cars, or even go to them, until the investigation of the
scene had been completed. And they had been told, truthfully, that no one could even
estimate how long the investigation of the crime scene would take.

Matt felt sorry for the cops charged with keeping the civilians out. The necessity
to go over the garage with a fine-tooth comb was something understood by everyone
who had ever watched a cops-and-robbers television show. But that was different.

"I'm a law-abiding citizen, and not a holdup man or a murderer or whatever the
hell went on in there. I didn't do anything, and all I want to do is get in my own goddamn car and go home. It's a goddamn outrage to treat law-abiding citizens like this!
How the hell am I supposed to get home?"

When he got to the entrance ramp, Matt saw that it was crowded with police cars.
They had moved off the street, he realized, to do what they could about getting traffic

flowing smoothly again. He decided that the mobile crime lab, and the other technical vehicles, had gone up to the roof.

"Detective D'Amata?" Matt asked the district cop standing in front of the stairwell door.

"On the roof."

Matt went up the stairs two at a time and was a little winded when he finally emerged on the roof. There was a district cop just outside the door, and he took a good look at Matt and his badge but didn't say anything to him.

The mobile crime lab was there, doors open, and three other special vehicles. CRIME SCENE—DO NOT CROSS tape had been strung around the area, the entire half of the roof, and a photographer armed with a 35-mm camera as well as a revolver was shooting pictures of the bloody pool left when the van cops had loaded Penelope Detweiler into their van and hauled her off to Hahneman.

Matt looked around for Detective D'Amata. Before he found him, Lieutenant Foster H. Lewis came up unnoticed behind Matt and touched his arm.

"They want you in homicide, Payne," he said. "Right now."

"Yes, sir," Matt said.

"You know where it is?"

All too well, Matt thought. *When I was questioned by Homicide detectives after I killed the rapist, it had been only after three hours of questioning and a twenty-seven-page statement that someone finally told me it had been a "good" shooting.*

"Yes, sir."

Matt turned and started toward the stairwell. The body of the man who had had half his head blown off was still where Matt had first seen it, slumped against the concrete block wall of the stairwell.

It was horrible, and Matt felt a sense of nausea. He pushed open the stairwell door and started down them. The urge to vomit passed.

And I didn't faint, Matt thought, not without a sense of satisfaction. *When I saw the mutilated body of Miss Elizabeth Woodham, 33, of 300 East Mermaid Lane, Roxborough, I went out like a light and looked like an ass in front of Detective Washington.*

Detective Jason Washington, acknowledged to be the best Homicide detective in the department, had been transferred, over his bitter objections, to the newly formed Special Operations Division. When the state police had found a body in Bucks County meeting the description of Elizabeth Woodham, who had been seen as she was forced into a van, Washington had gone to the country to have a look at it and had taken Matt with him. Not as a fellow police officer, to help with the investigation, but as an errand boy, a gofer. And Matt hadn't even been able to do that; one look at the body and he'd fainted.

Washington, a gentleman (he perfectly met Matt's father's definition of a gentleman: He was never seen in public unshaven, in his undershirt, or with run-down heels; and he never unintentionally said something rude or unkind), hadn't told anyone that Matt had passed out and had gone much further than he had to, trying to make Matt feel better about it.

But the humiliation still burned.

When Matt reached the street, at the entrance ramp a taxi was discharging a passenger with a distracted, I'm-in-a-hurry look on his face. Matt ran to the cab and got in, thinking that if the man getting out had parked his car in the garage, he was about to find something he could talk about when he got home.

"You're not going to believe this, Myrtle, but when I went to get the car from the garage, the goddamn cops wouldn't let me have it. They had some kind of crime in there, and they acted as if I had something to do with it. Can you imagine that? I had to come home in a cab, and I don't have any idea when I can get the car back."

"The Roundhouse," Matt told the cabdriver.

"Where?"

"The Police Department Administration Building at 8th and Race," Matt answered.

"You a cop?" the driver asked doubtfully.

"Yeah."

"I saw the badge," the driver said. "What's going on in there?"

"Nothing much," Matt said.

"I come through here twenty minutes ago, and there was cop cars all over the street."

"It's over now," Matt said.

The cab dropped him at the rear of the administration building. There is a front entrance, overlooking Metropolitan Hospital, but it is normally locked.

At the rear of the building a door opens onto a small foyer. Once inside, a visitor faces a uniformed police officer sitting behind a heavy plate-glass window.

To the right is the central cell room, in effect a holding prison, to which prisoners are brought from the various districts to be booked and to face a magistrate, who sets (or denies) bail. Those prisoners for whom bail is denied, or who can't make it, are moved, males to the Detention Center, females to the House of Correction.

The magistrate's court is a small, somewhat narrow room separated from the corridor leading to the gallery where the public can view arraignment proceedings. This, a dead-end corridor, is walled by large sections of Plexiglas, long fogged by scratches received over the years from family, friends, and lovers, pressing against it to try to get closer to the accused as they are being arraigned.

The arraignment court, as you look down on it from the gallery, has a bench on the left-hand side where the magistrate sits; tables in front of the bench where an assistant district attorney and a public defender sit; and across from them are two police officers, who process the volumes of paperwork that accompanies any arrest. The prisoners are brought up from the basement detention unit via a stairway shaft, which winds around an elevator. All the doors leading into the arraignment court are locked to prevent escape.

To the left is the door leading to the main foyer of the Police Department Administration Building. The door has a solenoid-equipped lock, operated by the police officer behind the window.

Matt went to the door, put his hand on it, and then turned so the cop on duty could see his badge. The lock buzzed, and Matt pushed open the door.

He went inside and walked toward the elevators. On one wall is a display of photographs and police badges of police officers who have been killed in the line of duty. One of the photographs is of Sergeant John Xavier Moffitt, who had been shot down in a West Philadelphia gas station while answering a silent burglar alarm. He had left a wife, six months pregnant with their first child.

Thirteen months after Sergeant Moffitt's death, his widow, Patricia, who had found work as a secretary-trainee with a law firm, met the son of the senior partner as they walked their small children near the Philadelphia Museum on a pleasant Sunday afternoon.

He told her that his wife had been killed eight months before in a traffic accident while returning from their lake house in the Pocono Mountains. Mrs. Patricia Moffitt became the second Mrs. Brewster Cortland Payne II two months after she met Mr. Payne and his children. Shortly thereafter Mr. Payne formally adopted Matthew Mark Moffitt as his son and led his wife through a similar process for his children by his first wife.

"Can I help you?" the cop on duty called to Matt Payne as Matt walked toward the elevators. It was not every day that a young man with a police officer's badge pinned to the silk lapel of a tuxedo walked across the lobby.

"I'm going to Homicide," Matt called back.

"Second floor," the cop said.

Matt nodded and got on the elevator.

The Homicide Division of the Philadelphia Police Department occupies a suite of second-floor rear offices.

Matt pushed the door open and stepped inside. There were half a dozen detectives in the room, all sitting at rather battered desks. None of them looked familiar. There was an office with a frosted glass door, with a sign, CAPTAIN HENRY C. QUAIRE, above it. Matt had met Captain Quaire, but the office was empty.

He walked toward the far end of the room, where there were two men standing beside a single desk that faced the others. Sitting at the desk was a dapper, well-dressed man in civilian clothing whom Matt surmised was the watch officer, the lieutenant in charge.

As he walked across the room he noticed that one of the two "interview rooms" on the corridor side of the room was occupied; a large, blondheaded man in a sleeveless T-shirt was sitting in a metal chair, his left wrist encircled by a handcuff. The other handcuff was fastened to a hole in the chair. The chair itself was bolted to the floor.

He saw Matt looking at him and gave him a look of utter contempt.

As Matt approached the desk at the end of the room the mustached, dark-skinned man sitting at it saw him coming and moved his head slightly. The other two men turned to look at him. Matt saw a brass nameplate on the desk, LIEUTENANT LOUIS NATALI, who Matt surmised was the lieutenant in charge.

"My name is Payne, Lieutenant," Matt said as he reached the desk. "I was told to report here."

No one responded, and Matt was made uncomfortable by the unabashed examination he'd been given by all three men. The examination, he decided, was because of the dinner jacket, but there was something else in the air too.

"He's all yours," Lieutenant Natali said finally.

"Let's find someplace to talk," the smaller of the two detectives said, and gestured vaguely down the room.

There was an unoccupied desk, and Matt headed for it.

"Let's use this," the detective called. Matt stopped and turned and saw that the detective was pointing to the second, empty interview room. That seemed a little odd, but he walked through the door, anyway.

The two detectives followed him inside. One closed the door after them. The other, the one who had suggested the use of the interview room, signaled for Matt to sit in the interviewee's chair.

Matt looked at it with unease. There was a set of handcuffs lying on it, one of the cuffs locked through a hole in the chair.

"Go on, sit down," the detective said, adding, "Payne, my name is Dolan. Sergeant Dolan."

Matt offered his hand. Sergeant Dolan ignored it. Neither did he introduce the other detective.

"Where's your car, Payne?" Sergeant Dolan asked. "Outside? You mind if we have a look in it?"

"What?"

"I asked if you mind if we have a look in your car."

"I don't know where my car is right now," Matt replied. "Sorry. Why are you interested in my car?"

"What do you mean, you don't know where your car is?"

"I mean, I don't know where it is. I loaned it to somebody."

"Somebody? Does somebody have a name?"

"You want to tell me what this is all about?"

"This is an interview. You're a police officer. You should know what an interview is."

"Hey, all I did was find the injured girl and the dead guy."

"What I want to know is two things. What were you doing up there, and where's your car? *Three* things: Why were you so anxious to get your car away from the Penn Services Parking Garage?"

"And I'd like to know why you're asking me all these questions."

"Don't try to hotdog me, Payne, just answer me."

Matt looked at Sergeant Dolan and decided he didn't like him. He remembered two things: that his mother was absolutely right when she said he too often let his mouth run away with him when he was angry or didn't like somebody; and that he was a police officer, and this overbearing son of a bitch was a police *sergeant*. It would be very unwise indeed to tell him to go fuck himself.

"Sorry," Matt said. "Okay, Sergeant. From the top. I went to the top of the garage because I wanted to park my car and there were no empty spots on the lower floors. When I got there, I found Miss Detweiler lying on the floor. Injured. The lady with me—"

"How did you know the Detweiler girl's name? You know her?"

"Yes, I know her."

"Who was the lady with you?"

"Her name is Amanda Spencer."

"And she knows the Detweiler girl too?"

"Yes. I don't know how well."

"How about Anthony J. DeZego? You know him?"

"No. Is that the dead man's name?"

"You sure you don't know him?"

"Absolutely."

• • •

Lieutenant Louis Natali had watched as the two Narcotics detectives led Payne into the interview room and closed the door. He opened a desk drawer and took a long, thin cigar from a box and very carefully lit it. He examined the glowing coal for a moment and then made up his mind. Whatever the hell was going on smelled, and he could not just sit there and ignore it.

He stood up, walked down the room, and entered the room next to the interview room. It was equipped with a two-way mirror and a loudspeaker that permitted watching and listening to interviews being conducted in the interview room.

The mirror fooled no one; any interviewee with more brains than a retarded gnat knew what it was. But it did serve several practical purposes, not the least of which was that it intimidated, to some degree, the interviewees. They didn't know whether or not somebody else was watching. That tended to make them uncomfortable, and that often was valuable.

But the primary value, as Natali saw it, of the two-way mirror and loudspeaker was that it provided the means by which other detectives or Narcotics officers could watch an interview. They could form their own opinion of the responses the interviewee made to the questions, and of his reaction to them. Sometimes a question that should have been asked but had not occurred to them, and they could summon one of the interviewers out of the room and suggest that he go back in and ask it.

And finally, as was happening now, the two-way mirror afforded supervisors the means to watch an interview when they were either curious or did not have absolute faith in the interviewers to conduct the interview, keeping in mind Departmental regulations and the interviewees' rights.

While Lieutenant Natali was happy to cooperate with the Narcotics Division, as he was now, he had no intention of letting Narcotics do anything in a Homicide interview room that he would not permit a Homicide detective to do. And there was something about this guy Dolan that Natali did not like.

"So if you had to guess, Payne, where would say your car is now?" Sergeant Dolan asked.

"Another parking lot somewhere. I just don't know."

"And your girlfriend?"

"I suppose she's back at the Union League having dinner."

"Why don't we go get her?"

"Why can't we wait until the party is over? Detective D'Amata, who was there when Lieutenant Lewis sent me to tell the Detweilers what happened, didn't say anything about getting her over here right away."

"Detective D'Amata has nothing to do with this investigation," Dolan said. "He's Homicide. I'm Narcotics. Let's go get your girlfriend, Payne."

"What the hell is this all about?" Payne asked. Natali saw that he was genuinely surprised and confused to hear that Dolan was from Narcotics. Surprised and confused but not at all alarmed.

"Come on, let's go," Dolan said.

Lieutenant Natali walked out of the small room as the other Narcotics detective came out of the interview room, followed by Payne and then Sergeant Dolan.

Dolan looked at Natali, and it was clear to Natali that he knew he had been watching the interview, and was surprised and annoyed that he had.

"Thank you for your cooperation, Lieutenant," Sergeant Dolan said. "We're going to see if we can find Officer Payne's lady friend and his car, and finish this at Narcotics. I'll see that the both of them get back over here."

Natali nodded but didn't say anything.

He watched as they left the office and then went into Captain Henry C. Quaire's office and closed the door after him. He had called Quaire at home before going to the Penn Services Parking Garage, and Quaire had shown up there ten minutes after he had, and sent him back to the Roundhouse.

He went to the desk and, standing up, dialed a number from memory.

"Radio," Foster H. Lewis, Jr., answered.

"This is Lieutenant Natali, Homicide. Can you get word to W-William One to call me at 555-3343?"

"Hold One, Lieutenant," Foster H. Lewis, Jr., said, and then activated his microphone and threw the switch that would broadcast what he said over the command band.

W-William One was the radio call sign of the commanding officer, Special Operations Division. The private official telephone number of the commanding officer of the Homicide Division was 555-3343.

There were some official considerations—and some ethical and political ones—in what Lieutenant Natali was doing. Viewed in the worst light, Natali was violating Departmental policy by advising the commanding officer of the Special Operations Division that one of his officers was being interviewed by Narcotics officers. That was technically the business of the commanding officer of the Narcotics Division, who would probably confer with Internal Affairs before notifying him.

Ethically he was violating the unspoken rule that a member of one division or bureau kept his nose out of an investigation being conducted by officers of another division or bureau.

Politically he knew he was risking the wrath of the commanding officer of the Narcotics Division, who almost certainly would learn—or guess, which was just as bad— what he was about to do. And it was entirely possible that the commanding officer of the Special Operations Division, who was about as straight a cop as they came, would, rather than being grateful, decide that Natali had no right to break either the official or unofficial rules of conduct.

On the other hand, if he had to make a choice between angering the commanding officer of the Narcotics Division or the commanding officer of Special Operations, it was no contest. For one thing, the commanding officer of Special Operations outranked the Narcotics commanding officer. For another, so far as influence went, the commanding officer of Special Operations won that hands down too. He held his present assignment because the word to give it to him had come straight from Mayor Jerry Carlucci. And he was very well connected through the Department.

Peter Wohl's father was Chief Inspector August Wohl (retired). Despite a lot of sour-grapes gossip, that wasn't the reason Peter Wohl had once been the youngest sergeant in Highway, and was now the youngest staff inspector in the Department, but it hadn't hurt any, either.

But what had really made Louis Natali decide to telephone Staff Inspector Peter Wohl was his realization that not only did he really like him but thought the reverse was true. Peter Wohl would decide he had called as a friend, which happened to be true.

"Sorry, Lieutenant," Foster H. Lewis, Jr., reported, "W-William One doesn't respond. Shall I keep trying?"

"No. Thanks, anyway," Natali said, and hung up.

He left Captain Quaire's office and walked back to his desk and searched through it until he found Peter Wohl's home telephone number. He started to go back to Quaire's office for the privacy it would give him and then decided to hell with it. He sat down and dialed the number.

On the fourth ring there was a click. "This is 555-8251," Wohl's recorded voice announced. "When this thing beeps, you can leave a message."

Natali raised his wrist to look at his watch and waited for the beep.

"Inspector, this is Lieutenant Natali of Homicide. It's five minutes after nine. If you get this message within the next forty-five—"

"I'm here, Lou," Peter Wohl said, interrupting. "What can I do for you?"

"Sorry to bother you at home, Inspector."

"No problem. I'm sitting here trying to decide if I want to go out for a pizza or go to bed hungry."

"Inspector, did you hear about Tony the Zee?"

"No. You are talking about Anthony J. DeZego?"

"Yes, sir. He got himself blown away about an hour and a half ago. Shotgun. On the roof of the Penn Services Parking Garage behind the Bellevue-Stratford. There's some suggestion it's narcotics-related."

"Those who live by the needle die by the needle," Wohl said, mockingly sonorous. "You got the doer?"

"No, sir. Not a clue so far."

"Am I missing something, Lou?" Wohl asked.

"Inspector, Narcotics is interviewing one of your men. He found the body and—"

"They think he's connected. Got a name?"

"Payne," Natali said.

"Payne?" Wohl parroted disbelievingly. "Matthew Payne?"

"Yes, sir. I thought you would like to know."

"Why do they think he was involved?"

"There was another victim, Inspector. A girl. Penelope Detweiler. A 9th District wagon carried her to Hahneman. Payne knew her. And he removed his car from the crime scene right afterward. I think that's what made them suspicious."

There was a moment's silence on the line.

"Where do they have him?"

"They had him here, but they just left. Sergeant Dolan?"

"Don't know him."

"And another guy. Plainclothes or a detective. I don't know him. Dolan said they were going to get Payne's girlfriend and his car—she has the car—and finish the interview at Narcotics."

"Thank you, Lou. I owe you one. How many does that make now?"

Staff Inspector Peter Wohl hung up without waiting for a reply.

Peter Wohl put the telephone back in its cradle and stood up. He had been sprawled, in a light blue cotton bathrobe, on the white leather couch in his living room, dividing his attention between television (a mindless situation comedy but one that featured an actress with a spectacular bosom and a penchant for low-necked blouses) and a well-worn copy of a paperbound book entitled *Wiring Scheme, Jaguar 1950 XK120 Drop-head Coupe.*

Above the couch (which came with two matching armchairs and a plate-glass and chrome coffee table) was a very large oil painting of a voluptuous and, by current standards, somewhat plump, nude lady that had once hung behind the bar of a now defunct men's club in downtown Philadelphia. The service bar of the same club, heavy 1880s mahogany, was installed across the room from the leather furniture and the portrait of the naked, reclining, shyly smiling lady.

The decor clashed, as Peter Wohl ultimately had, with the interior designer who had gotten him the leather, glass, and chrome furniture at her professional discount when she had considered becoming Mrs. Peter Wohl. Dorothea was now a Swarthmore wife, young mother, and fading memory, but he often thought that the white leather had become a permanent part of his life. Not that he liked it. He had found out that the resale value of high-fashion furniture was only a small fraction of its acquisition cost, even if that cost had reflected a forty-percent professional discount.

He turned the television off and went into his bedroom. His apartment had once been the chauffeur's quarters, an apartment built over the slate-roofed, four-car garage behind a turn-of-the-century mansion on Norwood Street in Chestnut Hill. The mansion itself had been converted into luxury apartments.

He went to his closet, hung the bathrobe neatly on a hanger, and took a yellow polo shirt, sky-blue trousers, and a seersucker jacket from the closet. He put the shirt and trousers on, and then a shoulder holster that held a Smith & Wesson .38-caliber Chief's Special five-shot revolver.

Still barefoot, he sat down on his bed and pulled the telephone on the bedside table to him.

"Special Operations, Lieutenant Lucci."

"Peter Wohl, Tony," Wohl said. Lieutenant Lucci was actually the watch officer for the four-to-midnight shift of the Highway Patrol. When Special Operations had been formed, it had moved into the Highway Patrol headquarters at Bustleton and Bowler streets in Northeast Philadelphia. For the time being at least, with Special Operations having nowhere near its authorized strength, Wohl had decided that there was no way (for that matter, no reason) to have the line squad supervisor on duty for the four-to-midnight and midnight-to-eight shift. The Highway watch officer could take those calls.

"Good evening, sir," Lucci said. Two weeks before, Lucci had been a sergeant, assigned as Mayor Jerry Carlucci's driver. Before that he had been a Highway sergeant. Wohl thought he was a nice guy and a good cop, even if his closeness to the mayor was more than a little worrisome.

"What do you know about DeZego getting himself shot, Tony?"

"Blown away, Inspector," Lucci said. "With a shotgun. On the roof of that parking garage behind the Bellevue-Stratford. Nick DeBenedito went in on the call. We were just talking about it."

"Is he there?"

"I think so. You want to talk to him?"

"Please."

Sergeant Nick DeBenedito came on the line thirty seconds later. "Sergeant DeBenedito, sir."

"Tell me what happened with Tony the Zee, DeBenedito."

"Well, I was downtown, and there was a 'shots-fired,' so I went in on it. It was on the roof of the parking garage behind the Bellevue. Inspector, I didn't know he was a cop."

"That who was a cop?"

"Payne. I mean, he was wearing a tuxedo and he had a gun, so I put him down on the floor. As soon as Martinez told me he was a cop, I let him up and said I was sorry."

Peter Wohl smiled at the mental image of Matt Payne lying on the concrete floor of the parking garage in his formal clothes.

"What went down on the roof?"

"Well, the way I understand it, Payne went up there in his car with his girlfriend, saw the first victim—the girl. She was wounded. So he sent his girl downstairs to the attendant's booth to call it in, tried to help the girl, and then he found Tony the Zee. The doer—doers—had a shotgun. They practically took Tony the Zee's head off. Anyway, then we got there. The doers were long gone. I sent Martinez with the wagon to see if he could get a dying declaration—"

"Did she die?"

"No, sir. But Martinez said she was never conscious, either."

"Okay."

"So I hung around until Lieutenant Lewis from the 9th, and then the Homicide detectives, showed up, and then I went to the hospital and got Martinez and we resumed patrol."

"Do you have any reason to think that Payne was involved?"

"Lieutenant," DeBenedito said uncomfortably, "what I saw was a civilian with a gun at a crime scene. How was I supposed to know he was a cop?"

"You did exactly the right thing, Sergeant," Wohl said. "Thank you. Put Lieutenant Lucci back on, will you?"

"Yes, sir?"

"Where's Captain Pekach?"

"Probably at home, sir. He said either he'd be there or in Chestnut Hill. I got the numbers. You want them?"

"No, thank you, Tony, it's not that important. I'm going to Narcotics. If I go someplace else, I'll call in."

"Are we involved in this, Inspector?"

"No. But Narcotics is interviewing a very suspicious character they think is involved. I want to find out what they think they have."

"No kidding? Anybody we know?"

"Officer Payne." Wohl chuckled and hung up.

Captain David Pekach, the recently appointed Highway commander, previously had been assigned to the Narcotics Division. If he had happened to be either at Bustleton and Bowler or on the streets, Wohl would have asked him to meet him at Narcotics, which was located in a onetime public-health center at 4th Street and Girard Avenue, sharing the building with Organized Crime.

But he wasn't working. That meant he was almost certainly in Chestnut Hill with his lady friend, Miss Martha Peebles. Dave Pekach was thirty-two or thirty-three, and Martha Peebles a couple of years older. It was the first romance either had had, and Wohl decided that the problem with Narcotics was not serious enough to interfere with true love.

Lieutenant Anthony Lucci, who knew that Pekach, his immediate superior, had come to Highway from Narcotics, did not know of Pekach's relationship with Miss Martha Peebles. All he knew was that his orders from Captain Pekach had been to keep him informed of anything out of the ordinary.

So far as he was concerned, when Wohl, who was Captain Pekach's immediate superior, announced he was going to Narcotics, to see what they had on Officer Matthew Payne, who, it was common knowledge, had a very powerful rabbi, Chief Inspector Dennis V. Coughlin, and in whom the mayor himself, after the kid had taken down the Northwest Philly serial rapist, had a personal interest, that was something out of the ordinary.

He dialed Pekach's home number and, when there was no answer, dialed the number in Chestnut Hill Pekach had provided.

A very pleasant female voice answered and, when Lucci asked for Captain Pekach, said, "Just one moment, please."

Less clearly, Lieutenant Lucci heard her continue. "It's for you, Precious."

7 When Officer Robert F. Wise saw the Jaguar pull into the Narcotics Division Building parking lot, and into the spot reserved for inspectors, he went quickly from inside the building and intercepted the driver as he was leaving his car.

Officer Wise, who was twenty-five, slightly built, and five feet eight inches tall, had been on the job not quite three years. He had hoped, when just over a year ago he was transferred to Narcotics, he would be able to work his way out of his present duties—which could best be described as making himself useful (and visible in uniform) around the building—and into a job as a plainclothes investigator.

But that hadn't happened. One of the sergeants had been kind enough to tell him that he didn't think it would ever happen. He was too nice a guy, the sergeant said, which Wise understood to mean that he could never pass himself off as a drug peddler. A month before, Wise had applied for transfer to the newly formed Special Operations Division. He hadn't heard anything about the request. In the meantime he was doing the best job he knew how to do.

He had been told to keep his eye on the parking lot behind the building. There had been complaints from various inspectors that when they had come to visit Narcotics, the parking space reserved for visiting inspectors had been occupied by various civilian cars, most of them junks, which they knew damned well were not being driven by inspectors.

The Jaguar that had just pulled up with its nose against the INSPECTORS sign in the parking lot certainly could not be called a junk, but Officer Robert F. Wise doubted that the civilian in the nice, but sporty, clothes was an inspector. Inspectors tended to be fifty years old and wore conservative business suits, not yellow polo shirts, sky-blue pants, and plaid hats.

"Excuse me, sir," Officer Robert F. Wise said, "but you're not allowed to park there."

"Why not?" the young man in the plaid hat asked pleasantly enough.

"Sir, this is a Police Department parking lot."

"You could have fooled me," the young man said, smiling, and gestured toward the other cars in the lot. A good deal of Narcotics work requires that investigators look like people involved in the drug trade. The undercover cars they used, many of them confiscated, reflected this; they were either pimpmobiles or junkers.

"Sir, those are police cars."

"I'm a 369," the young man said.

A police officer in civilian clothes who wishes to identify himself as a cop without producing his badge or identity card says "I'm a 369."

"Well, then," Officer Wise said, "you should know better than to park in an inspector's spot. Move it out of there."

"I'm Inspector Wohl," the young man said, smiling. "Keep up the good work." He started toward the rear door of the Roundhouse.

Two things bothered Officer Wise. For one thing, there were three different kinds of inspectors in the Philadelphia Police Department. There were chief inspectors, who ranked immediately below deputy commissioners. These officers were generally referred to as, and called themselves, Chief. When in uniform, they wore a silver eagle, identical to Army and Marine Corps colonels' eagles, as their insignia of rank.

Next down in the rank hierarchy were inspectors, who, in uniform, wore the same silver oak leaf as Army and Marine Corps lieutenant colonels. And at the bottom were staff inspectors, who wore a golden oak leaf as their insignia. There were not very many staff inspectors (Wise could not remember ever having seen one), but he understood they were sort of super-detectives and handled difficult or delicate investigations.

The guy in the sky-blue pants didn't look to Wise much like a cop, much less a senior officer. He was more than likely a cop, but a wise guy, and no more a chief inspector and/or division chief, and thus entitled to park where he had parked, than Wise was.

"Excuse me, sir, would you mind showing me some identification?"

An unmarked car came into the parking lot at that moment and drove up to them quickly. Wise saw first that it was an unmarked Highway Patrol car. For one thing, it was equipped with more shortwave antennae than ordinary police cars, marked or unmarked, normally carried; and for another, the driver was wearing the crush-crowned uniform cap peculiar to Highway.

Then he saw that the driver was wearing a white shirt, which identified him as at least a lieutenant, and then, when he stopped the car and got out, Wise saw his rank insignia, the twin silver bars of a captain, and then he recognized him. It was Captain David Pekach.

The young guy in the sky-blue pants smiled and said, "You just happened to be in the neighborhood, right? And thought you'd drop by?"

"Lucci called me," Pekach said. "Don't blame him. I told him to call me when something out of the ordinary happened."

"I didn't want to interfere with your love life, Dave. I had visions of you sipping fine wine by candlelight as Miss What's-her-name whispered sweet nothings in your ear," Wohl said.

"What's going on here?" Pekach said. He did not like being teased about Miss Martha Peebles. "Lucci said something about young Payne?"

"Narcotics brought him and his girlfriend here. I don't know why," Wohl said. "That's why I'm here."

"Give me a minute to park the car, Inspector," Captain Pekach said, "and I'll come with you. Or would I be in the way?"

"I didn't send for you, Dave, but I'm glad to see you," Wohl said.

He held out his badge and photo identification to Officer Wise.

"Oh, that's all right, Inspector," Officer Wise said, waving it away. "Sorry to bother you."

Officer Wise decided that his chances of being transferred to Special Operations had just dropped from slim to zero. He had put this encounter all together now. The young guy in the silly cap and sky-blue pants was Peter Wohl, who although "only" a staff inspector, was the Special Operations division commander.

"No bother," Wohl said as Pekach got back in his car and drove it toward a work shed near the gasoline pump.

"Inspector, I'm sorry about this," Officer Wise said.

"Never be sorry for doing your job," Wohl said. "And don't worry, you're not the only one who doesn't think I look like a cop. I get that from my father all the time."

A moment later Captain Pekach walked up to them again.

"They're searching a silver Porsche back there," he said, pointing to the work shed.

"Are they really?" Wohl said. "Dave, while I go ask what they're looking for, why don't you go inside and nose around."

"You going to come in, or should I come back when I find out?"

"I'll come in," Wohl said, and walked to the work shed.

Both doors of the Porsche, and the hoods over the rear engine compartment and the in-front trunk, were open when Wohl walked up to the car. Two Narcotics officers in plainclothes looked up at Wohl. He flashed his badge.

"What are you looking for?" Wohl asked.

"Sergeant Dolan brought it in. He says they probably got rid of it by now but to check, anyway."

"Got rid of what?"

"Probably cocaine," one of the Narcotics cops said.

"You've got a search warrant?"

"No. The owner's a cop. We have permission."

"What makes you think it's dirty?" Wohl asked.

"Sergeant Dolan thinks he—and it—is," the cop replied. "How else would a cop get the dough for a car like this?"

"Maybe he's lucky at cards," Wohl said. "You find anything?"

The cop shook his head no, then said, "Dolan said we probably wouldn't."

Wohl smiled at them and then walked to the Narcotics Building.

He found Officer Matthew Payne, his black bow tie untied and his top collar button open, sitting on one of a row of folding chairs in a room on the first floor.

Payne stood up when he saw Wohl, but Wohl waved him back into his seat and walked down the room to a door marked NO ADMITTANCE and pushed it open.

Captain Pekach and a tall, very thin, bald-headed man in his fifties were inside.

"Inspector," Pekach said, "you know Lieutenant Mikkles, don't you?"

"Sure do," Wohl said. "How are you, Mick?"

Mikkles shook Wohl's hand but didn't say anything.

"Sergeant Dolan's not here," Pekach went on. "He went to the medical examiner's office. They found a plastic bag full of a white crystalline powder on DeZego. He went to check it out."

"Where's the girl?" Wohl asked.

Lieutenant Mikkles pointed to a steel door with INTERVIEW ROOM painted on it.

"You charging her with anything, Mick? Or Officer Payne?"

"We don't have enough to charge either one of them," Mikkles said.

"Just Sergeant Dolan's *feeling* that they're dirty, right?"

"I really don't know much about this, Inspector," Mikkles said.

"They want Officer Payne and the girl at Homicide to make a statement. Would it be all right with you if I took them there?"

"I don't see any problem with that," Lieutenant Mikkles said.

"What about if I asked Captain Pekach to meet with Sergeant Dolan to ask him what he thinks he's got going here? Would you have any problem with that?"

"Sure. Why not?"

Wohl walked to the interview-room door, opened it, went inside, and closed it after him.

Amanda Spencer, sitting in a steel chair that was bolted to the floor, looked at him warily.

He smiled at her.

"Well, *I* don't think you did it," he said.

She smiled, a little hesitantly.

"My name is Peter Wohl," he said. "I'm Matt's boss."

"Hello," she said.

"The people who work in Narcotics spend their lives surrounded by the scum of the earth," Wohl said. "Sometimes—and I suppose it's understandable—they seem to forget that there are some nice people left in the world. What I'm trying to say is that I'm sorry about this, but I understand why it happened."

"They were just doing their jobs, I suppose," Amanda said. "I mean, there was a shooting—"

"Well, I'm relieved that you understand."

"Can I go now?"

"There's bad news and good news about that," Wohl said. "The bad news is that you still have to make a statement at Homicide. That's in the Police Department Administration Building. I'll get you through that as quickly as possible, but it has to be done."

"That's the good news?" she asked almost lightheartedly.

"No. The good news is that you get to ride down there in my car. I drive a Jaguar XK-120. It's a *much* nicer car than that piece of German junk your boyfriend drives."

"I have this strange feeling you're not kidding," Amanda said.

"Do I look like a kidder?"

"Yes, you do," Amanda said, laughing. "What kind of a cop are you, anyway?"

"Depending on who you ask, you can get a very wide range of responses to that question. Are you ready to go?"

"That's the understatement of the year," she said.

He held the door open for her, and she walked out of the interview room.

"Just a moment, please," he said, and walked to Lieutenant Mikkles.

"Your men tell me they found nothing in Officer Payne's car. Is there any reason he can't have it back?"

"No, I don't suppose there is."

"Try 'No, sir,' Mikkles," Captain Pekach said, flaring.

"No, sir," Mikkles said.

"Do you think it would be a good idea, Lieutenant, if you went with Officer Payne to reclaim his car?" Wohl asked evenly.

"Yes, sir. I'll do that."

"Ask him to meet me in Homicide, please. Tell him I'm driving the young lady."

"Yes, sir," Mikkles repeated.

Wohl waited until Mikkles had left the room before speaking to Pekach.

"Run down Sergeant Dolan and find out what he thinks he has," Wohl said. "And then meet us at Homicide. When you're in your car, get word to Lucci where I am."

"Yes, sir."

"And before I forget: On your way out, if that young cop is still out there, talk to him and see if you think he'd be useful to us in Special Operations. He struck me as pretty bright."

It was quarter after eleven before Homicide had finished taking the statements of Officer Matthew Payne and Miss Amanda Spencer, and Captain Pekach had not yet returned from meeting with Sergeant Dolan.

Wohl, who was ninety-five percent convinced that what had happened was that Dolan, for any number of reasons—ranging from a fight with his wife to resentment about a cop wearing formal clothes and driving a Porsche to plain stupidity—had gone off the deep end, but he was reluctant to turn Payne and, for that matter, the girl, loose until he heard from Pekach.

He walked to where they were sitting, on folding chairs against the interior wall.

"Am I the only undernourished person in the room? Did you two get dinner?"

"I'm not especially hungry," Payne said.

"I'm starved," Amanda said. "I haven't had a thing to eat since lunch."

"They serve marvelous hoagies at the 12th Street Market this time of night," Wohl said.

"I just got hungry," Matt Payne said.

"I'd like to know how Penny is," Amanda said.

"I checked a little while ago," Wohl said. "She's listed as 'critical but stable.' "

"What does that mean?"

"That she's hanging on," Wohl said.

"You know where I mean, Matt?" Wohl asked. "In the 12th Street Market?" Matt nodded. "Take Amanda there. I'll meet you. I want to get word to Pekach where we'll be."

In the elevator Amanda said, "He's very nice."

"What was that business about you riding in his car?" Matt asked.

"You're jealous!"

"Oh, bullshit!"

"You are!" she insisted.

"The hell I am."

She smiled at him triumphantly.

"Whatever you say, Officer Payne," she said.

"Thanks for getting us out of there," Matt Payne said to Peter Wohl.

They were sitting at a tiny table in the 12th Street Market, on fragile-looking bent-wire chairs. Three enormous hoagies on paper plates, a pitcher of beer, and three mugs left little room for anything else.

Peter Wohl finished chewing a large mouthful before replying.

"My pleasure," Wohl said.

"How'd you find out?" Matt asked.

"Lieutenant Natali called me. He thought I ought to know."

"Am I in trouble?" Matt Payne asked as he poured a mug half full of beer.

"Why did you take your car away from the crime scene without permission?"

"I didn't know I needed permission. It was blocking the exit ramp. I moved it out of the way of the wagon when they took Penny Detweiler to Hahneman. And then, when I went to the Union League to tell her parents what had happened, I just got in it and drove off. No one said I shouldn't."

"Who told *you* to notify her parents?"

"There was a 9th District lieutenant there. I didn't get his name. Great big black guy. I told him I knew her parents, where they were, and he said it was okay for me to tell them. He saw me get in the car, and he didn't say anything."

"Lewis? Lieutenant Lewis?"

"Yeah. I'm sure that's the name."

"Officer Lewis's father," Wohl said.

"Oh! Oh, yeah. I didn't put that together."

"Okay. Let's take it from the top."

"Jesus, again?"

"Don't be a wiseass with me, Matt. The last I heard, not only am I your commanding officer but also I'm one of the good guys."

"Sorry," Matt said sincerely. "That son of a bitch upset me. The whole thing upset me."

"From the top," Wohl repeated, reaching for the pitcher of beer.

Captain David Pekach walked up just as Matt finished, and a second pitcher of beer was delivered. He took one of the bent-wire chairs from an adjacent table and sat down on it.

"You want a glass? Good beer," Wohl said.

"No, thanks. I'm cutting down. Oh, what the hell!"

He got up and went to the stand and returned with a mug.

"What did you find out?" Wohl asked.

Pekach looked at Payne and Amanda and then at Wohl, his raised eyebrows asking if Wohl wanted him to continue in front of them.

"Go on," Wohl said. "I'm convinced that neither Matt Payne nor Miss Spencer shot Tony the Zee or is into drugs."

"Dolan says the Detweiler girl was," Pekach said.

"My God!" Amanda exclaimed.

"What?" Matt asked incredulously. "That's absurd!"

"No, it's not. Dolan is a good cop," Pekach said, responding more to Peter Wohl's raised eyebrows than to Matt Payne. "I believe him. He says that he was following her, that he has reason to believe she went to the Penn Services Parking Garage to make a buy, and that the shooting was tied in with that. And Tony the Zee had a thousand dollars' worth of coke on him, in a plastic bag."

"Dolan was following her?" Wohl asked thoughtfully. "Where was he during the actual shooting?"

"He said the first he heard of it, he was across the street, watching the entrance and exit, and the other one, who I used to think was a smart cop, was watching the fire exits in the alley."

"Try that again, I'm confused," Wohl said.

"Okay. They followed her to the parking garage. Dolan stayed across the street and watched the entrance and exit ramps. Gerstner, the other Narcotics cop, watched the fire exits on the alley. At least until he heard the sirens and went out on the street to see what was happening. I guess that's when the doers left the building, via the fire escape to the alley."

"So where does Dolan figure Payne ties in?"

"He saw him drive in. Had no idea at first he was a cop but recognized him as someone—him and Miss Spencer—he had seen in the last couple of days. And then he saw him drive his car away from the place later. And apparently figured that's where the drugs—according to him, the Detweiler girl is into cocaine—were."

"That whole scenario is incredible," Matt said.

"No it's not," Wohl said. "If I were the cop on the street, Dolan, that's pretty much how I would see it."

"You don't think I'm into drugs? Or that Amanda is?"

"I didn't say that," Wohl said carefully. "No. I don't think either of you are. But if this Sergeant Dolan has good reason to believe that the Detweiler girl was into drugs, I have no reason to doubt him. And you didn't help matters any by driving away from the crime scene with Miss Spencer."

Matt exhaled audibly.

"Payne went to the Union League," Wohl explained to Pekach, "to tell the Detweiler girl's family what had happened. Lieutenant Lewis, who I suppose was the senior supervisor there then, told him it was okay."

"Dolan didn't mention Lewis," Pekach said.

"Is there a Captain Petcock or something here?" a loud voice interrupted. Matt stopped and turned to the voice. A tall, very skinny, long-haired man in white cook's clothing was holding up a telephone.

"Close." Wohl chuckled. "Go answer the phone, Captain Petcock."

"Yes, sir, Inspector Wall," Pekach said, and got up.

"Miss Spencer—" Wohl began.

"You were calling me Amanda," she said. "Does Miss Spencer mean I'm a suspect again?"

"*Amanda,* did you ever hear anything about the Detweiler girl being into drugs?"

She hesitated a moment before replying. Matt wondered if she was going to defend Penny Detweiler loyally.

"She took diet pills to stay awake to study sometimes," she said finally. "And I suppose she smokes grass—I *know* she smokes grass—I'm about the only one I know who doesn't. But I never heard anything about her and heroin or cocaine or anything else. *Hard* drugs."

"Just out of idle curiosity, why don't you smoke grass?" Wohl asked.

"I tried it once and it made me sick," Amanda said.

"Me too," Wohl said, smiling at the look of surprise on Matt Payne's face.

Captain David Pekach walked back up to the table.

"That was Lucci," he said. "There was just a radio call. M-Mary One wants H-Highway One and W-William One to meet him at Colombia and Clarion."

Curiosity overwhelmed Amanda Spender's normally good manners. "M-Mary One? W-William One? What in the world is that?"

"The mayor is M-Mary One," Wohl explained, somewhat impatiently. "Did Lucci say what the mayor is doing at Colombia and Clarion?"

"They found a 22nd District cop lying in the gutter," Pekach said. "Shot to death."

"Oh, my God!" Amanda said.

Wohl stood up, fished in his pockets, and came up with a set of keys. He handed them to Payne.

"I'll ride with Captain Pekach, Matt. The Jag's on 12th Street. Right across from your car. You bring the Jag there. You know where it is?"

Matt shook his head no.

"Just before you get to Temple University on North Broad, turn right," Captain Pekach said. "Couple of blocks in from North Broad. Colombia and Clarion. You won't have any trouble finding it."

"Yes, sir," Matt said.

"Are you going to be able to get home by yourself all right, Amanda?" Wohl asked.

"Sure. Don't worry about me, I've got Matt's car."

Wohl and Pekach hurried away.

"Is it always like this?" Amanda asked.

"No," Matt said. "It isn't."

He went to the counter and paid the bill. When they got outside to 12th Street, he handed Amanda the keys to the Porsche.

"Wouldn't it be easier if I just got in a cab?" she asked. "Or, how long are you going to be?"

"God knows," he said. "I really don't want to leave the car here. Some street artist would draw his mother's picture with a key on the hood by the time I got back."

"Couldn't I leave it at your apartment, then?" she asked. "Aren't you going to need it?"

"Jesus, would you?" he asked.

"Sure."

"I live on Rittenhouse Square—"

"That's right by the church?"

"Yeah. I live on the top floor of the Delaware Cancer Society Building—"

"Where?" she asked, chuckling.

"You can't miss it. Anyway, there's a parking garage in the back. Just drive in. There's two parking spaces with my name on them. And there's a rent-a-cop on duty. He'll call you a cab."

He started to hand her money. She waved it away.

"Nice girls don't take cab fare," she said. "Haven't you ever heard of women's lib?"

"This has been one hell of a date, hasn't it?" he said.

"It lends an entirely new meaning to the word *memorable,*" Amanda said.

"I'm sorry."

"Don't be an ass," she said, and stretched upward to kiss him.

Whatever her intentions, either to kiss his cheek or, chastely, his lips, it somehow didn't turn out that way. It was not a passionate embrace ending with Amanda semi-swooning in his arms, but when their lips broke contact, there seemed to be some sort of current flowing between them.

"Jesus!" Matt said softly.

She put her hand up and laid it for a moment on his cheek. Then she ran across the street and got in the Porsche.

Matt got in Wohl's Jaguar and drove north to Vine Street, then left to North Broad, and then turned right onto Broad Street. There was not much traffic, and understandably reasoning that he was not going to get ticketed for speeding while driving Inspector Wohl's car to a crime scene, he stepped hard on the gas.

A minute or two later there was the growl of a siren behind him, and he pulled toward the right. An Oldsmobile, its red lights flashing from their concealed position under the grille, raced past him. After a moment he realized that the car belonged to Chief Inspector Dennis V. Coughlin. He wondered if Denny Coughlin, or Sergeant Tom Lenihan, who was driving, had recognized him or Wohl's car or both.

Just south of Temple University he saw that Captain Pekach was right; he would have no trouble finding Colombia and Clarion. There were two RPCs, warning lights flashing, on Broad Street and Colombia, and two uniformed cops in the street.

When he signaled to turn right, one of them emphatically signaled for him to continue up Broad Street. Matt stopped.

"I'm Payne. Special Operations. I'm to meet Inspector Wohl here."

The cop looked at him doubtfully but waved him on.

Clarion is the second street in from Broad. There was barely room for Matt to make it past all the police cars, marked and unmarked, lining both sides of Colombia. There was a black Cadillac limousine nearly blocking the intersection of Clarion and Colombia. Matt had seen it before. It was the mayoral limousine.

Then he saw two familiar faces, Officer Jesus Martinez and the Highway sergeant who had almost made him piss his pants on the roof of the Penn Services Parking Garage by suggesting that the price for moving a fucking muscle would be having his fucking brains blown out, and who had seemed wholly prepared to make good the threat.

They were directing traffic. The sergeant first began—impatiently, even angrily—to gesture for him to turn right, south, on Clarion, and then he apparently recognized Wohl's car, for he signaled him to park it on the sidewalk.

Matt got out of the car and looked around for Wohl. He was standing with Police Commissioner Thaddeus Czernich, Chief Inspector Dennis V. Coughlin, half a dozen uniformed senior supervisors, none of whom looked familiar, two other men in civilian clothing, and His Honor, Mayor Jerry Carlucci.

Twenty feet away, Matt saw Sergeant Tom Lenihan standing with three men Matt supposed were both policemen and probably drivers. He walked over to them.

And then he saw the body. It was in the gutter, facedown, curled up beside a 22nd District RPC. There were a half dozen detectives, or crime-lab technicians, around it, two of them on their hands and knees with powerful, square-bodied searchlights, one of them holding a measuring tape, the others doing something Matt didn't quite understand.

"Hello, Matt," Tom Lenihan said, offering his hand. "I thought that was you in Wohl's Jag."

"Sergeant," Matt said politely.

"This is Matt Payne, Special Operations—" Lenihan said, beginning the introductions, but he stopped when Mayor Carlucci's angry voice filled the street.

"I don't give a good goddamn if Matt Lowenstein, or anyone else, likes it or not," the mayor said. "The way it's going to be, Tad, is that Special Operations is going to take this job and get whatever sons of bitches shot this poor bastard in cold blood. And you're going to see personally that the Department gives Wohl everything he thinks he needs to get the job done. Clear?"

"Yes, sir," Commissioner Czernich said.

"And now, Commissioner, I think that you and I and Chief Coughlin should go express our condolences to Officer Magnella's family, don't you?"

"Yes, sir," Commissioner Czernich and Chief Coughlin said, almost in unison.

The mayor marched toward the small knot of drivers, heading for his limousine. He smiled absently, perhaps automatically, at them, and then spotted Matt Payne. The expression on his face changed. He walked up to Matt.

"Were you at the Union League tonight?"

"I didn't quite make it there, Mr. Mayor," Matt said.

"Yeah, and I know why," the mayor said. He turned to Commissioner Czernich. "And while I'm at it, Tad, I want you to assign Wohl to get to the bottom of what happened to Detweiler's daughter and that mafioso scumbag DeZego on the roof of the parking garage tonight."

Commissioner Czernich looked as if he were about to speak.

"You don't have anything to say about anyone not going to like that, do you, Commissioner?" the mayor asked icily.

"No, sir," Commissioner Czernich said.

"You hear that, Peter?" the mayor called.

"Yes, sir," Peter Wohl replied.

"Keep up the good work, Payne," the mayor said, then walked quickly to his limousine.

 Staff Inspector Peter Wohl walked to where Officer Payne was standing. Matt saw Captain Pekach step out of the shadows and follow him.

"What did the mayor say to you?" Wohl asked.

"He asked me if I'd been at the Union League," Matt replied, "and then he turned and told the Commissioner he wanted us to handle what happened at the Penn Services Parking Garage."

Wohl shook his head.

"I had a strange feeling I should have driven myself up here," Wohl said to Pekach. "Jesus Christ!"

Matt added, chuckling, "And then he told me to keep up the good work."

"I'm beginning to wonder if I can afford you and all your good work, hotshot," Wohl said, and then he saw the look on Matt's face. "Relax. Only kidding."

"You think he might think it over and change his mind?" Captain Pekach asked.

"No. That would mean he made a mistake. We all know the mayor never makes a mistake. Where's Mike?"

"At home."

"And Jason Washington? You know where he is?"

"At the shore. He's got a place outside Atlantic City."

"When's he coming back?"

"Day after tomorrow."

"Get on the radio, Dave. Get word to Mike Sabara to meet me here. And get me a number on Washington. He'll have to come back tomorrow. What about Tony Harris?"

"He's probably at home this time of night."

"Get him over here—now," Wohl ordered. "Have Lucci tell him he and Washington have this job."

"Yes, sir," David Pekach said.

"Where's my car?" Wohl asked Matt.

Matt pointed.

"You might as well go home," Wohl said.

"I don't mind staying," Matt said.

"Go home," Wohl repeated. "I'm going to have enough trouble with Chief Lowenstein the way things are. I don't need his pungent observations about a cop in a tuxedo."

"You're going to stay here?"

"Until Lowenstein shows up and can vent his spleen at me," Wohl said, and then added, "Speaking of the devil . . ."

Everybody followed his glance down Colombia Street, where a black, antenna-festooned car was approaching.

"I think that's Mickey O'Hara, Inspector," Pekach said. "He's driving a Buick these days."

"Yeah, so it is," Wohl said. "But if our Mickey is here, can Chief Lowenstein be far behind?" He looked around the area, then turned to Pekach. "There's enough district cars here. Do we need Sergeant—What's-his-name?—anymore?"

Pekach found what Wohl had seen.

"DeBenedito, Inspector. No."

"Sergeant DeBenedito!" Wohl called.

DeBenedito trotted over.

"Yes, sir?"

"There's no point in you hanging around here, Sergeant," Wohl said. "Take Officer Payne home, and then take it to the barn."

"Yes, sir."

Matt looked at his watch. It was a quarter past one. DeBenedito and Martinez had already worked more than an hour past the end of their shift.

"I can catch the subway, Inspector," he said.

"If the mayor heard that a guy in a dinner jacket got propositioned on the subway, Officer Payne, he would almost certainly give the investigation of that affront to law and order to Special Operations too. Go with the sergeant."

Pekach laughed.

"Good night, Matt," Wohl said. "See you in the morning. Early in the morning."

"Good night, Inspector," Matt said. "Captain."

"Good night, Payne."

Matt got in the back of the Highway RPC.

"Where do you live, Payne?"

"Rittenhouse Square," Officer Jesus Martinez answered for Matt. "In the Delaware Valley Cancer Society Building."

"Yeah, that's right. You guys know each other, don't you?"

Matt knelt on the floor and put his elbows on the top of the front seat.

"What the hell happened here tonight?" he asked as they drove down Colombia to North Broad and then turned left toward downtown.

"A very nice young cop named Joe Magnella got himself shot," DeBenedito said.

"You knew him?" Matt asked.

"He was a second cousin once removed, or a first cousin twice removed, something like that. My mother's sister, Blanche, is married to his uncle. I didn't know him good, but I seen him at weddings and funerals, feast days, like that. Nice kid. Just come back from Veet-Nam. I don't think he was on the job six months. He was about to get married. *Son of a bitch!*"

"What happened?" Matt asked softly.

"Nobody seems to know. He was working an RPC out of the 22nd. He didn't call in or anything, from what I hear. There was a call to Police Emergency, saying there was a cop shot on Clarion Street. Fucker didn't give his name, of course. Martinez and I were on Roosevelt Boulevard, not close, but it was a cop, so we went in on it. By the time we got there, the place was crawling with cops, so we found ourselves directing traffic. Anyway, the kid was in the gutter, dead. Shot at least twice. The door to his car was open, but he hadn't taken his gun out or anything. And he hadn't called in to say he was doing anything out of the ordinary. Some son of a bitch who didn't like cops or whatever just shot him."

"Jesus Christ!" Matt said.

"What was that shit going on between the mayor and them other big shots?" Sergeant DeBenedito asked.

"The mayor assigned the investigation to Special Operations," Matt said.

"Can you guys handle something like that? This is a fucking homicide, isn't it? Pure and simple?"

"When we were looking for the Northwest rapist," Matt said, "Inspector Wohl had two Homicide detectives transferred in. The best. Jason Washington and Tony Harris. If anybody can find the man who shot . . . what was his name . . . ?"

"Magnella, Joseph Magnella," DeBenedito furnished.

". . . Officer Magnella, those two can."

"Washington is that great big black guy?"

"Yeah."

"I seen him around," DeBenedito said. "And I heard about him."

"He's really good," Matt said. "I had the chance to be around him—"

"You're the guy who put down the rapist, ain't you?" DeBenedito asked, and then went on without waiting for an answer. "Martinez told me about that after I put you on the ground in the parking garage. I'm sorry about that. You didn't look like a cop."

"Forget it," Matt said.

"Talk about looking like a cop!" Martinez said. "Did you see the baby-blue pants and the hat on Inspector Wohl? It looked like he was going to play fucking golf or something! Jesus H. Christ!"

"Is he as good as they say he is?" DeBenedito asked. "Or does he just have a lot of pull?"

"Both, I'd say," Matt said. His knees hurt. He pushed himself back onto the seat as DeBenedito drove around City Hall and then up Market Street.

The Highway Patrol pulled to the curb on the south side of Rittenhouse Square as a foot-patrol officer made his way down the sidewalk. He looked on curiously as the cop in the passenger seat jumped out and opened the rear door so that a civilian in a tuxedo could get out. (The inside handles on RPCs are often removed so that people put in the back can't get out before they're supposed to.)

"Good night, Hay-zus," Matt said, and raising his voice, called, "Thanks for the ride, Sergeant."

"Stay off parking garage roofs, Payne," Sergeant DeBenedito called back as Jesus Martinez got back in and slammed the door.

"Good morning," Matt said to the foot-patrol cop.

"Yeah," the cop responded, and then he watched as Matt let himself into the Delaware Valley Cancer Society Building. It was a renovated, turn-of-the-century brownstone. Renovations for a long-term lease as office space to the Cancer Society had been just about completed when the architect told the owner he had found enough space in what had been the attic to make a small apartment.

Matt had found the apartment through his father's secretary and moved in when he'd gone on the job. A month ago he had learned that his father owned the building.

The elevator ended on the floor below the attic. He got out of the elevator, thinking it was a good thing Amanda had been willing to park his car for him before catching a cab to Merion; he would need his car tomorrow, for sure, and then walked up the narrow flight of stairs to the attic apartment.

The lights were on. He didn't remember leaving them on, but that wasn't at all unusual.

He walked to the fireplace, raised his left leg, and detached the Velcro fasteners that held his ankle holster in place on the inside of his leg and took it off. He took the pistol, a five-shot .38 caliber Smith & Wesson Chief's Special, from it. He laid the holster on the fireplace mantel and then wiped off the pistol with a silicone-impregnated cloth.

Jason Washington had told him about doing that; that anytime you touched the metal of a pistol, the body left minute traces of acidic fluid on it. Eventually it would eat away the bluing. Habitually wiping it once a day would preserve the bluing.

He laid the pistol on the mantel and, starting to take off his dinner jacket, turned away from the fireplace.

Amanda Spencer was standing by the elbow-high bookcase that separated the "dining area" from the "kitchen." Both, in Matt's opinion, were too small to be thought of without quotation marks.

"Welcome home," Amanda said.

Matt dismissed the first thought that came to his mind—that Amanda was here because she wanted to make the beast with two backs—as wishful-to-the-nth-degree thinking.

"No rent-a-cop downstairs?" he asked. "I should have told you to look in the outer lobby. They can usually be found there, asleep."

"He was there. He let me in," Amanda said.

"I don't understand," Matt said.

"Either do I," she said. "What happened where you went with Peter Wohl?"

"There was a dead cop," Matt said. "A young one. Now that I think about it, I saw him around the academy. Somebody shot him."

"Why?"

"No one seems to know," Matt said. "Somebody called it in, a dead cop in the gutter. When they got there, there he was."

"How terrible."

"He had been to Vietnam. He was about to get married. He was a relative of Sergeant DeBenedito."

"Who?"

"He was at the garage," Matt said. "And then he was at Colombia and Clarion—where the dead cop was. Wohl had him drive me home."

"Oh."

"Amanda, I'll take you out to Merion. But first, would you mind if I made myself a drink?"

"I helped myself," she said. "I hope that's all right."

"Don't be silly."

He started for the kitchen. As he approached her, Amanda stepped out of the way, making it clear, he thought, that she didn't want to be embraced, or even patted, in the most friendly, big-brotherly manner.

In the kitchen he saw that she had found where he kept his liquor, in a cabinet over the refrigerator; a squat bottle of twenty-four-year-old Scotch, a gift from his father, was on the sink.

He found a glass and put ice in it, and then Scotch, and then tap water. He was stirring it with his finger when Amanda came up behind him and wrapped her arms around him.

"I wanted to be with you tonight," she said softly, her head against his back. "I suppose that makes me sound like a slut."

"Not unless you announce those kind of urges more than, say, twice a week," he said.

Oh, shit, he thought, *you and your fucking runaway mouth! What the* hell *is the matter with you?*

Her arms dropped away from him and he sensed that she had stepped back. He turned around.

"I suppose I deserved that," she said.

"I'm sorry," Matt said. "Jesus Christ, Amanda, I can't tell you how sorry I am I said that."

She looked into his eyes for a long time.

"You'll be the second, all right? I was engaged," she said.

"I know," he said.

"You do?"

"I mean, I know you're not a slut. I have a runaway mouth."

"Yes, you do," she agreed. "We'll have to work on that."

She put her hand to his cheek. He turned his head and kissed it.

When he met her eyes again, she said, "I knew you were going to be trouble for me the first time I laid eyes on you."

"I'm not going to be trouble for you, I promise."

She laughed.

"Oh, yes you are," she said. "So now what, Matthew? You want to show me your etchings now or what?"

"They're in my sleeping-accommodations suite," he said. "That's the small closet to your immediate rear."

"I know," she said. "I looked. Lucky for you I didn't find any hairpins or forgotten lingerie in there."

"You'll be the first," he said.

"You mean in *there*," she said, and when she saw the uncomfortable look on his face, she stood on her toes and kissed him gently on the lips. Then she took his hand and led him into his bedroom.

When Sergeant Nick DeBenedito and Officer Jesus Martinez walked into Highway Patrol headquarters at Bustleton and Bowler, Officer Charley McFadden was sitting on one of the folding metal chairs in the corridor.

Martinez was surprised to see him. He knew that McFadden had spent his four-to-midnight tour riding with a veteran Highway Patrolman named Jack Wyatt. Since he and DeBenedito were more than an hour late coming off shift, he had presumed that Charley would be long gone.

McFadden, a large, pleasant-faced young man of twenty-three, had already changed out of his uniform. He was wearing a knit sport shirt, a cotton jacket with a zipper closing, and blue jeans. When McFadden stood up, the jacket fell open, exposing, on his right, his badge, pinned over his belt, and his revolver. Charley carried his off-duty weapon, a .38-caliber five-shot Smith & Wesson Undercover Special revolver in a "high-rise pancake," a holster reportedly invented by a special agent of the U.S. Secret Service, which suspended the revolver under his right arm, *above* the belt, almost as high as a shoulder holster would have placed it.

Jesus thought Charley looked, except that his hair was combed and he was shaved and the clothes were clean, as he had looked when the two of them were working undercover in Narcotics.

"You still here, McFadden?" Sergeant DeBenedito asked in greeting.

"I thought maybe Hay-zus would want to go to the FOP bar and hoist one," Charley said.

Charley had taken to using the Spanish pronunciation of Martinez's Christian name

because of his mother, a devout Irish Catholic who had been made distinctly uncomfortable by having to refer to her son's partner as Jesus.

"Yeah, why not?" Martinez replied. Actually he did not want to go to the FOP bar
with Charley at all. But he didn't see how he could say no after Charley had hung
around the station for more than an hour waiting for him. "Give me a minute to
change."

He consoled himself with the thought that it was only the decent thing to do. Charley had, after all, volunteered to drive him to work when he learned that Jesus's Ford
was (again) in the muffler shop for squeaking brakes, and then he'd hung around for
more than an hour waiting to drive him home. If he wanted to have a beer, they'd go
get a beer.

Five minutes later he emerged from the locker room in civilian clothing. He wore
a dark blue shirt, even darker blue trousers, and a light brown leather jacket. There
was a fourteen-karat gold-plated chain around his neck, and what the guy in the jewelry store had said was an Inca sun medallion hanging from that. His badge was in
his pocket, and although he, too, carried an Undercover Special, he did so in a shoulder holster. He had tried the pancake and it hadn't worked. His hips weren't wide
enough or something. It always felt like it was about to fall off.

Despite the early-morning hour, the parking lot of the FOP Building, just off North
Broad Street in Central Philadelphia, was almost full. About a quarter of the Police
Department had come off shift at midnight with a thirst. Cops are happiest in the company of other cops, and attracting more customers to the bar at the FOP has never
posed a problem for the officers of the FOP.

Jesus followed Charley down the stairs from the street to the basement bar and was
surprised when Charley took a table against the wall. Charley usually liked to sit at
the bar, which gave him, he said, a better look at the activity, by which he meant the
women.

"Hold the table," Charley ordered, and went to the bar. He returned with two bottles of Ortlieb's and a huge bowl of popcorn. A year or so before, Jesus Martinez had
become interested in nutrition, and was convinced that popcorn, and most of what else
Charley put in his mouth, was not good for you.

"You're going to eat the whole damned bowl?"

"You can have some," Charley said. "I read in the paper that they just found out
that popcorn is just as good for you as wheat germ."

"Really?" Jesus said, and then realized his chain was being pulled.

"Yeah, the article said that they found out that popcorn is almost as good for you
as french fries *without* catsup. No match, of course, for french fries *with* catsup."

"Bullshit!"

"Had you going, didn't I?" Charley asked, pleased with himself.

"Laugh at me all you want. All that garbage you keep putting in your mouth is going to catch up with you sooner or later."

"Tell me about Payne," McFadden said abruptly.

"You heard about that, huh?" Jesus said, chuckling.

"Yeah, I heard about it," McFadden said, on the edge of unpleasantness.

"Well, it was really sort of funny—"

"Funny?" McFadden asked. "You think it's funny?"

"Yeah, Charley, I do. It was sort of funny."

"Well, I think it was shitty, pal!"

"What the hell are you talking about?"

"What are *you* talking about?"

"I'm talking about DeBenedito putting Payne down on the roof of the parking garage in his fancy clothes."

"I didn't hear about that," McFadden said.

"Well, DeBenedito and I went in on the shooting on the roof of the Penn Services Parking Garage. He put me out of the car one floor down, and I went up the stairs. When I got there, he's got your pal Payne down on the floor. *'Tell him I'm a cop, Martinez!'* Payne yells when he sees me. So I did, and DeBenedito let him up. I thought it was funny. If you don't, go fuck yourself."

"I didn't hear about that," Charley repeated, sounding a little confused. "I was talking about *your* pal, Sergeant Dolan, taking Payne and his girlfriend over to Narcotics and searching his car."

"I don't know anything about that," Jesus said.

"Bullshit!"

"I don't. You sure about your facts?"

"Yeah, I'm sure about my facts."

"Well, all I know is that Payne was at the scene, where the cop got shot. He came there driving Inspector Wohl's Jaguar, and then Wohl made us take him home. That's one of the reasons we was an hour late. If Dolan had him over at Narcotics, two things: One, I didn't know about it; and two, he would now be in Central Lockup. Dolan doesn't make mistakes."

"Yeah, I know you think he walks on water."

"He's a goddamned good cop," Martinez said flatly. "Where'd you hear he had something going with Payne?"

"Wyatt and I went by Bustleton and Bowler about ten-thirty, and somebody told him, and he told me."

"You sure he wasn't pulling your chain?"

"Yeah. It was no joke. Dolan had Payne, his girlfriend, and his car, over at Narcotics."

"Then Dolan had something," Martinez said.

"Something he got from you, maybe?" McFadden asked.

"I told you, I never heard about this," Martinez said, and then the implication of what McFadden had said sank in.

"Fuck you, Charley!" he said, flaring, and he stood up so quickly that he bumped against the table, knocking over the beer bottles. "Jesus Christ, what a shitty thing to say!"

"If you didn't do it, then I'm sorry," McFadden said after a moment.

"That's not good enough. Fuck you!"

"You cut off his tire valves!" McFadden said. "Tell me that wasn't a shitty thing to do."

"The son of a bitch was sound asleep on a stakeout," Martinez said. "He deserved that."

"No he didn't. A pal would have woke him up."

"Rich Boy is not my pal," Martinez said. "He doesn't take me riding around in his Porsche like some people I know. All he's doing is *playing* cop."

"He put down the Northwest rapist. That's *playing* cop?"

"You know, and I know, that he just stumbled on that scumbag," Martinez said.

"He put him down! Jesus Christ, Hay-zus!"

"Okay, so he put him down," Martinez admitted grudgingly. "But it wouldn't surprise me at all to find he's stuffing shit up his nose."

"You've got no right to say something like that!"

"You had no right to say what you did about me fingering him to Dolan."

"I said I was sorry."

"Yeah, you said you were sorry," Martinez said. "I'm going home. I've had enough of your bullshit for one night."

"Oh, sit down and drink your beer."

"Fuck you."

"Sit down, Hay-zus."

"Or what?"

"Or I'll sit on *you.*"

Martinez glowered at him angrily for a moment and then smiled.

"You would, too, you fucking, overgrown Mick."

"You bet your ass I would," McFadden said.

Matt woke up and opened his eyes and saw that Amanda was supporting her head on her hand and looking down at him.

"Hi," she said, and bent her head and kissed him.

"Christ, and some people have alarm clocks!"

She laughed.

He looked up at the ceiling, where his bedside clock, a housewarming gift from his sister Amy, projected the time on the ceiling. It was a quarter past five.

"What were you thinking?" he asked.

"Wondering, actually."

"Okay. What were you wondering?"

"Two things."

"What two things?"

"Whether there is anything in your refrigerator besides a jar of olives."

"No," he said. "I haven't been shopping in a week. And what else were you wondering?"

"Whether I'm pregnant," Amanda said.

"Jesus! You're not on the pill?"

"I stopped taking the pill when I broke my engagement. And something like this wasn't supposed to be on the agenda."

"I would be delighted to make an honest woman of you," Matt said.

"Maybe I'll be lucky."

"Not at all, my pleasure."

"That's not what I meant." She giggled and jerked one of the hairs curling around his nipple out.

"Ouch," he said, and reached out for her and pulled her down to him so that she was lying with her face on his chest and her leg thrown over him.

"This is probably not a very smart thing for us to do," she said.

"I disagree absolutely," he said.

"What are the Brownes going to think?" she asked.

"We could tell them we had car trouble. Do you really care what the Brownes think?"

"No," she said, after a moment. "Okay. We'll tell them we had car trouble and not give a damn whether or not they believe us."

He chuckled and tightened his arm around her.

"Are you going to feed me, or what?" she asked.

"I'd rather 'or what,' " he said.

"You're boasting," she said. "Idle promises."

"See for yourself," Matt said.

She raised her head an inch off his chest.

"I'll be damned," she said. "Isn't that amazing?"

There were two Highway cops sitting at the counter of the small restaurant in the Marriott Motel on City Line Avenue when Matt and Amanda walked in.

He didn't recognize either of them and saw nothing like recognition in their eyes, either. Both looked carefully at Amanda and him, however, something Matt ascribed to Amanda's good looks, her low-cut evening dress, and the disparity between that and the tweed sport coat and slacks he had put on to go to work; or all of the above.

He was wrong. As soon as they had sat down in one of the booths, he saw alarm in Amanda's eyes and looked over his shoulder to see what had caused it. Both Highway cops were marching to the booth.

And they were, Matt thought, in their breeches and boots, their Sam Browne belts and leather jackets, intimidating.

"Seen the papers, Payne?" the larger of the two asked.

"No."

"Thought maybe not," the cop said.

How the hell am I going to introduce these guys to Amanda? That's obviously what they want, and I have absolutely no idea what either of their names are.

He was wrong about that too. The second Highway cop carefully laid slightly mussed copies of the *Bulletin*, the *Ledger*, and the *Daily News* on the table and then nodded to Amanda.

"Ma'am," he said. By then the first cop was halfway to the door.

"Hey!" Matt called. Both cops looked at him. "Thank you."

Both waved and then left the diner.

"For a moment there I thought we were going to be arrested again," Amanda said.

"We weren't."

"Call it what you like," she said. "Are they all like that?"

"Like what?"

"So, what's a word? Those two looked like an American version of the Gestapo."

"They're Highway," Matt said. "They're sort of special. Sort of the elite."

"That's what they said about the Gestapo," Amanda said.

"Hey, they're the good guys," Matt said.

"How is it they knew you?"

"I guess they know I work for Inspector Wohl."

"What does Peter Wohl have to do with them?"

"He's their boss, one step removed. He commands Special Operations. Highway is under Special Operations."

A waitress appeared with menus.

"Isn't that awful?" she said, pointing at the front page of the *Daily News*.

Matt looked at it for the first time. Above the headline there was a half-page photo of Anthony J. DeZego slumped against the concrete blocks of the stairwell at the Penn Services Parking Garage.

MAFIA FIGURE MURDERED
SOCIALITE WOUNDED IN
CENTER CITY SHOOTING

"Let me see," Amanda said, and he slid the tabloid across the table to her and turned to the *Ledger*. The story was at the lower right corner of the front page, under a two-column picture of Miss Penelope Detweiler:

NESFOODS HEIRESS SHOT
IN CENTER CITY
POLICE BAFFLED
BY EARLY EVE SHOOTING

By Charles E. Whaley,
Ledger Staff Writer

Phila—Miss Penelope Detweiler, 23, of Chestnut Hill, was seriously wounded, apparently by a shotgun blast, in the Penn Services Parking Garage, on South 15th Street early last evening. She was taken to Hahneman Hospital where she is reported by a hospital spokesperson to be in "serious but stable" condition.

Miss Detweiler, whose father, H. Richard Detweiler, is president of Nesfoods International, was en route to the Union League Club on South Broad Street for a social event when the shooting occurred. A family spokesperson theorized that Miss Detweiler had just parked her car when she found herself in the middle of a "gangland shootout."

Police Captain Henry Quaire refused to comment on the shooting, saying the case is under investigation, but he did confirm that Miss Detweiler had been found lying on the floor of the roof of the garage by Miss Amanda Chase Spencer, of Scarsdale, N.Y., and her escort, as they parked their car. The couple were also guests of Mr. and Mrs. Chadwick T. Nesbitt III at the Union League dinner to honor out-of-town guests for the wedding (tonight) of Miss Daphne Browne of Merion and Lieutenant C. T. Nesbitt IV, USMCR.

"It is absurd to think that Miss Detweiler was anything more than an innocent bystander," the Detweiler family spokesperson said. "It is a sad commentary on life in Philadelphia that something like this could happen."

Matt slid the *Ledger* across the table to Amanda and then became aware that the waitress was still standing there.

"Amanda, would you like to order?"

"I think I lost my appetite," she said.

"You have to eat."

"Can I get a breakfast steak?" she asked.

"Honey, anything your heart desires, we got it," the waitress said.

"They're running a special on me," Matt said. "I'm specially marked down for the occasion."

"Breakfast steak, medium-rare, eggs sunny-side up, toast, tomato juice, and coffee," Amanda said.

"Twice," Matt said. "Thank you."

Matt turned to the *Bulletin*. It used two photographs on the front, placed side by side. One was the same photo the *Ledger* had used of Amanda. The other was of Anthony J. DeZego scowling at the camera from above a board that read PHILA POLICE DEPT and carried his name and the date. Under these the caption gave their names and read, "shooting victims."

MAFIOSO KILLED: SOCIALITE
WOUNDED
IN CENTER CITY
POLICE SEEKING CLUES
IN EARLY EVENING SHOOTING

By Michael J. O'Hara

A shotgun blast to the head killed Anthony J. "Tony the Zee" DeZego, a Philadelphia underworld figure, and a second blast critically wounded Penelope Detweiler, socialite daughter of H. Richard Detweiler, president of Nesfoods International, shortly after seven last night on the roof level of the Penn Services Parking Garage on South 15th Street in downtown Philadelphia.

Miss Detweiler is in "critical but stable" condition at Hahneman Hospital. She was struck by "many" pellets from a shotgun shell, according to a hospital spokesman.

Off-duty Police Officer Matthew M. Payne discovered first Miss Detweiler, lying in a pool of blood, and then DeZego's body when he went to park his car. Payne, who is special assistant to Staff Inspector Peter Wohl, commanding officer of the Police Department's Special Operations Division, last month shot to death Warren K. Fletcher, 31, of Germantown, ending what Mayor Jerry Carlucci termed "the reign of terror of the Northwest serial rapist."

Miss Detweiler, Payne, and Miss Amanda Spencer, of Scarsdale, N.Y., who was with Payne in his silver Porsche, were en route to the Union League Club on South Broad Street to attend a dinner being given for out-of-town wedding guests by C. T. Nesbitt III, Nesfoods International chairman of the board, whose son is to marry Daphne Browne of Merion at seven-thirty tonight at St. Mark's Church, near the site of the shooting.

According to senior police officials, it is most likely that Miss Detweiler was an innocent bystander caught in the middle of a mob exchange of gunfire, but this reporter has learned that police are quietly investigating the possibility that Miss Detweiler knew DeZego, and possibly may have gone to the parking garage to meet him.

In a surprise development last night, Police Commissioner Thaddeus

Czernich announced that responsibility for the investigation of the shooting had been assigned to Staff Inspector Peter Wohl and the Special Operations Division. Such an investigation would normally be conducted by the Homicide Division.

Commissioner Czernich also assigned to Wohl the investigation of the murder of Police Officer Joseph Magnella, who was shot to death last night in North Philadelphia. (See related story, Page 3A.) One theory advanced for this unusual move was the reassignment of ace Homicide Detectives Jason Washington and Anthony J. Harris to Special Operations during the search for the North Philadelphia serial rapist.

"They've got my name in here," Amanda said, "but not yours."

"The *Ledger* never mentions a cop's name unless they can say something nasty about him," Matt said.

"Really?" Amanda said, not sure if he was serious or not. She put her hand on the *Bulletin*. "What does that one say?"

"About the same thing," Matt said.

"Through?" Amanda asked, and slid the *Bulletin* away from Matt's side of the table.

He saw her eyes widen when she got to the place in the story about him. She glanced at him, then finished the story.

"You never told me about that," she said.

"Yes I did," Matt said. "You said if you had a car like mine and somebody dinged it, you'd kill him. And I said somebody did and I had."

The waitress appeared with a stainless-steel coffee pot. Amanda waited until she had poured the coffee and left.

"I thought you were just being a wiseass," she said.

"You should have seen what he did to my car," Matt said. "He was lucky I didn't get really mad."

"Matt, *stop!*"

"Sorry," he said after a moment.

And a moment after that Amanda reached out and caught his hand. They sat that way, holding hands and looking into each other's eyes, until the waitress delivered breakfast.

 There was a fence around the Browne place in Merion, fieldstone posts every twenty-five feet or so with wrought-iron bars between them. The bars were topped with spear points, and as a boy of six or seven Matt had spent all of one afternoon trying to hammer one loose so that he would have a spear to take home.

There was also a gate and a gatehouse, but the gate had never in Matt's memory been closed, and the gatehouse had always been locked and off-limits.

When he turned off the road, the gate was closed, and he had to jump on the brakes to avoid hitting it. And the door to the gatehouse was open. A burly man in a dark suit came out of it and walked to the gate.

A rent-a-cop, Matt decided. *Had he been hired because the Princess of the Castle was getting married? Or did it have something to do with what had happened at the parking garage?*

The rent-a-cop opened the left portion of the gate wide enough to get through and came out to the Porsche.

"May I help you, sir?"

"Would you open the gate, please? Miss Spencer is a guest here."

The rent-a-cop looked carefully at both of them, then smiled, said, "Certainly, sir," and went to the gate and swung both sides open.

Matt saw that a red-and-white-striped tent, large enough for a two-ring circus, had been set up on the lawn in front of the house. There were three large caterer's trucks parked in the driveway. A human chain had been formed to unload folding chairs from one of them and set them up in the tent, and he saw cardboard boxes being unloaded in the same way from a second.

Soames T. Browne, in his shirtsleeves, and the bride-to-be, in shorts and a tattered gray University of Pennsylvania sweatshirt that belonged, Matt decided, to Chad Nesbitt, were standing outside the castle portal when Matt drove up. The rent-a-cop had almost certainly telephoned the house. Matt saw another large man in a business suit standing just inside the open oak door.

"I'll see you later," Matt said, waving at the Brownes with his left hand and touching Amanda's wrist with his right.

Amanda kissed his cheek and opened her door.

Soames T. Browne came around to Matt's side. Matt rolled the window down.

"Morning."

"Daffy said Amanda was probably with you," Browne said. "You should have called, Matt."

"Matt had to work—" Amanda said.

"Sure he did," Daffy snorted.

"—and I waited for him."

"Come in and have some coffee, Matt," Soames T. Browne ordered. "I want a word with you."

"I can't stay long, Mr. Browne."

"It won't take long," Browne said.

Matt turned the ignition off and got out of the car. There was a breakfast room in the house, on the ground floor of one of the turrets, with French windows opening onto the formal garden behind the house. Soames Browne led Matt to it, and then through it to the kitchen, where Mrs. Soames T. Browne, in a flowing negligee, was perched on a stool under a rack of pots and pans with a china mug in her hand.

"Good morning," Matt said.

She looked over him to Amanda.

"We were worried about you, honey," she said.

"I was with Matt," Amanda said.

"That's what we thought; that's why she was worried," Daffy said.

"We should have called. I'm sorry," Matt said.

"We were just going to do something about breakfast," Mrs. Browne said. "Have you eaten?"

"We just had breakfast, thank you," Amanda said.

"I didn't know Matt could cook," Daffy said sweetly.

"Coffee, then?" Mrs. Browne asked.

"Please," Amanda said.

"Do you know how Penny is, Matt?" Soames T. Browne asked.

"As of midnight she was reported to be 'critical but stable,' " Matt said.

"How do you know that?"

"My boss told us," Matt said.

"That was seven hours ago," Soames T. Browne said.

"Would you like me to call and see if there's been any change?"

"Could you?"

"I can try," Matt said. He looked up the number of Hahneman Hospital in the telephone book and then called.

"I'm sorry, sir, we're not permitted to give out that information at this time."

"This is Officer Payne, of the police."

"One moment, please, sir."

The next voice, very deep, precise, that came on-line surprised Matt: "Detective Washington."

"This is Matt Payne, Mr. Washington."

"What can I do for you, Matt?"

"I'm trying to find out how Penelope Detweiler is. They put me through to you."

"For Wohl?"

"For me. She's a friend of mine."

"I heard that. I'll want to talk to you about that later. At six o'clock they changed her from 'critical' to 'serious.' "

"That's better?"

Washington chuckled.

"One step up," he said.

"Thank you," Matt said.

"You at Bustleton and Bowler?"

"No. But I'm headed there."

"When you get there, don't leave until we talk."

"Yes, sir."

"Don't call me sir, Matt. I've told you that."

The phone went dead. Matt hung it up and turned to face the people waiting for him to report.

"As of six this morning they upgraded her condition from 'critical' to 'serious,' " he said.

"Thank God," Soames T. Browne said.

"Mother, I'm sure Penny would want us to go through with the wedding," Daphne Browne said.

"Why did this have to happen *now?*" Mrs. Soames T. Browne said.

Matt started to say, *Damned inconsiderate of old Precious Penny, what?* but stopped himself in time to convert what came out of his mouth to "Damned shame."

Even that got him a dirty look from Amanda.

"What do you think, Matt?" Soames T. Browne said.

"It's none of my business," Matt said.

"Yes it is, you're Chad's best man."

"Chad's on his way to Okinawa," Matt said. "It's not as if you could postpone it for a month or so."

"Right," Daffy Browne said. "I hadn't thought about that. We *can't* postpone it."

"I think Matt is absolutely right, Soames," Mrs. Browne said.

"That's a first," Matt quipped.

"What did you say, Matthew?" Mrs. Browne asked icily.

"I said, you're going to have to excuse me, please. I have to go to work."

"You will be there tonight?" Daffy asked.

"As far as I know."

"I wanted to ask you, Matt, what happened last night," Soames T. Browne said.

"I don't really know, Mr. Browne," Matt said.

And then he walked out of the kitchen. Amanda's eyes found his and for a moment held them.

Peter Wohl leaned forward, pushed the flashing button on one of the two telephones on his office coffee table, picked it up, said "Inspector Wohl" into it and leaned back into a sprawling position on the couch, tucking the phone under his ear.

"Tony Harris, Inspector," his caller said. "You wanted to talk to me?"

"First things first," Wohl said. "You got anything?"

"Not a goddamn thing."

"You need anything?"

"How are you fixed for crystal balls?"

"How many do you want?"

Harris chuckled. "I really can't think of anything special right now, Inspector. This one is going to take a lot of doorbell ringing."

"Well, I can get you the ringers. I had Dave Pekach offer overtime to anybody who wants it."

"I don't have lead fucking one," Harris said.

"You'll find something," Wohl said. "The other reason I asked you to call is that I have sort of a problem."

"How's that?"

"You know a lieutenant named Lewis? Just made it? Used to be a sergeant in the 9th?"

"Black guy? Stiff-backed?"

"That's him."

"Yeah, I know him."

"He has a son. Just got out of the Police Academy."

"Is that so?" Harris said, suspicion evident in his voice.

"He worked his way through college in the radio room," Wohl said.

"You don't say?"

"The commissioner assigned him to Special Operations," Wohl said.

"You want to drop the other shoe, Inspector?"

"I thought he might be useful to you," Wohl said.

"How?"

"Running errands, maybe. He knows his way around the Department."

"Is that it? Or don't you know what else to do with him?"

"Frankly, Tony, a little of both. But I won't force him on you if you don't want him."

Harris hesitated, then said, "If he's going to run errands for me, he'd need wheels."

"Wheels or a car?" Wohl asked innocently.

Harris chuckled. "Wheels" was how Highway referred to their motorcycles.

"I forgot you're now the head wheelman," he said. "A *car*."

"That can be arranged."

"How does he feel about overtime?"

"I think he'd like all you want to give him."

"Plainclothes too," Harris said. "Okay?"

"Okay."

"When do I get him?"

"He's supposed to report here right about now. You get him as soon as I can get him a car and into plainclothes."

"Okay."

"Thanks, Tony."

"Yeah," Harris said, and hung up.

Detective Jason Washington was one of the very few detectives in the Philadelphia Police Department who was not indignant or outraged that the murders of both Officer Joseph Magnella and Tony the Zee DeZego had been taken away from Homicide and given to Special Operations.

While he was not a vain man, neither was Jason Washington plagued with modesty. He knew that it was said that he was the best Homicide detective in the department (and this really meant something, since Homicide detectives were the crème de la crème, so to speak, of the profession, the best detectives, period) and he could not honestly fault this assessment of his ability.

Tony Harris was good, too, he recognized—nearly, but not quite, as good as he was. There were also some people in Intelligence, Organized Crime, Internal Affairs, and even out in the detective districts and among the staff inspectors whom Washington acknowledged to be good detectives; that is to say, detectives at his level. For example, before he had been given Special Operations, Staff Inspector Peter Wohl had earned Washington's approval for his work by putting a series of especially slippery politicians and bureaucrats behind bars.

Jason Washington had, however, been something less than enthusiastic when Wohl had arranged for him (and Tony Harris) to be transferred from Homicide to Special Operations. He had not only let Wohl know that he didn't want the transfer, but also had actually come as close as he ever had to pleading not to be transferred.

There had been several reasons for his reluctance to leave Homicide. For one thing, he liked Homicide. There was also the matter of prestige and money. In Special Operations he would be a Special Operations detective. Since Special Operations hadn't been around long enough to acquire a reputation, that meant it had no reputation at all, and that meant, as opposed to his being a Homicide detective, he would be an ordinary detective. And ordinary detectives, like corporals, were only one step up from the bottom in the police hierarchy.

As far as pay was concerned, Washington's take-home pay in Homicide, because of overtime, was as much as a chief inspector took to the bank every two weeks.

Washington and his wife of twenty-two years had only one child, a girl, who had married young and, to Washington's genuine surprise, well. As a Temple freshman Ellen had caught the eye of a graduate student in mathematics and eloped with him, under the correct assumption that her father would have a really spectacular fit if she announced that she wanted to get married at eighteen. Ellen's husband was now working for Bell Labs, across the river in Jersey, and making more money than Washington would have believed possible for a twenty-six-year-old. Recently they had made him and Martha grandparents.

Mrs. Martha Washington (she often observed that she had nearly not married Jason because of what her name would be once he put the ring on her finger) had worked, from the time Ellen entered first grade, as a commercial artist for an advertising agency. With their two paychecks and Ellen gone, they lived well, with an apartment in a high rise overlooking the Schuylkill River, and another near Atlantic City, overlooking the ocean. Martha drove a Lincoln, and one of his perks as a Homicide detective was an unmarked car of his own, and nothing said about his driving it home every night.

Wohl, who had once been a young detective in Homicide, understood Washington's (and Tony Harris's) concern that a transfer to Special Operations would mean the loss of their Homicide Division perks, perhaps especially the overtime pay. He had assured them that they could have all the overtime they wanted, and their own cars, and would answer only to him and Captain Mike Sabara, his deputy. He had been as good as his word. Better. The cars they had been given were brand-new, instead of the year-old hand-me-downs from inspectors they had had at Homicide.

They had been transferred to Special Operations after the mayor had "suggested" that Special Operations be given responsibility to catch the Northwest Philly serial rapist. After the kid, Matt Payne, had stumbled on that scumbag and put him down, Washington had gone to Wohl and asked about getting transferred back to Homicide.

Wohl had said, "Not yet. Maybe later," explaining that he didn't have any idea what the mayor, or for that matter, Commissioner Thad Czernich, had in mind for Special Operations.

"If the mayor has another of his inspirations for Special Operations, or if Czernich has one, I want you and Tony already here," Wohl had said. "I don't want to have to go through another hassle with Chief Lowenstein over transferring you back again."

Chief Inspector Matt Lowenstein headed the Detective Bureau, which included all the detective divisions, as well as Homicide, Intelligence, Major Crimes, and Juvenile Aid. He was an influential man with a reputation for jealously guarding his preserve.

"What are we going to do, Inspector," Washington had argued, "recover stolen vehicles?"

Wohl had laughed. Department policy required that a detective be assigned to examine any vehicle that had been stolen and then recovered. There were generally two types of recovered stolen vehicles: They were recovered intact, after having been taken for a joyride; or they were recovered as an empty shell, from which all resalable parts had been removed. In either case there was almost never anything that would connect the recovered vehicle with the thief. Investigating recovered vehicles was an exercise in futility and thus ordinarily assigned to the newest, or dumbest, detective in a squad.

"For the time being, I'll talk with Quaire, and see if he'd like you to work on some of the jobs you left behind at Homicide. But I have a gut feeling, Jason, that there will be enough jobs for you here to keep you from getting bored."

And Wohl had been right about that too. Police Commissioner Czernich (Washington had heard even before leaving Atlantic City for Philadelphia where the decision had come from) had decided to give Special Operations the two murder jobs.

And there was no wheel in Special Operations. In Homicide, as in the seven detective divisions, detectives were assigned jobs on a rotational basis as they came in. It was actually a sheet of paper, on which the names of the detectives were listed, but it was called the wheel.

If the mayor hadn't given Wohl the two murders and they had gone instead to Homicide, it was possible, even likely, that the wheel would have seen the jobs given to somebody else. He and Harris, because of the kind of jobs they were, would probably have been called in to "assist," but the jobs probably would have gone to other Homicide detectives. In Special Operations it was a foregone conclusion that these two murder jobs would be assigned to Detectives Washington and Harris.

And they were good jobs. Solving the murder of an on-the-job police officer gave the detective, or detectives, who did so greater satisfaction than any other. And right behind that was being able to get a murder-one indictment against one mafioso for blowing away another.

Jason Washington was beginning to think that his transfer to Special Operations might turn out to be less of a disaster than it had first appeared to be.

He was not surprised when he pulled into the parking lot at Bustleton and Bowler streets to see Peter Wohl's nearly identical Ford in the COMMANDING OFFICER's reserved parking space, although it was only a quarter to eight.

When he walked into the building, the administrative corporal called to him, "The inspector said he wanted to see you the minute you came in."

He smiled and waved and went to Wohl's office.

"Good morning, Inspector," Washington said.

"Morning, Jason," Wohl replied. "Sorry to have to call you back here."

"How am I going to get a tan if you keep me from laying on the beach?" Washington said dryly.

"Get one of those reflector things," Wohl replied, straight-faced, "and sit in the parking lot during your lunch hour. Now that you mention it, you do look a little pale."

Jason Washington's skin was jet black.

They smiled at each other for a moment, and then Wohl said, "Harris was at Colombia Street—"

"I talked to Tony this morning," Washington said, interrupting him.

"Okay," Wohl said. "Did I mention last night that a Narcotics sergeant named Dolan thought Matt Payne was involved at the parking garage?"

"Tony told me," Washington said.

Then that, Wohl thought a little angrily, must be all over the Department.

"Well, I don't think he's dirty, but he did find the girl, and DeZego's body. If you want to talk to him, he should be here any minute."

"He called the hospital while I was there," Washington said. "I told him I'd see him here."

"You were at the hospital?" Wohl asked.

Washington nodded.

"I don't know why I got out of bed so early to talk to you," Wohl said.

"Early to bed, early to rise, et cetera, et cetera," Washington said. "You going to need Payne this morning, Inspector?"

"Not if you want him for anything. If I have to say this, Jason, just tell me what you think you need."

"I thought I'd take him to Hahneman and then to the parking garage," Washington said. "I didn't get in to see the girl. That needed permission of a doctor who won't be in until eight."

Wohl's eyebrows rose questioningly.

"They're giving me the runaround," Washington went on. "I didn't push it. Incidentally, they've got a couple of Wachenhut Security guys down there guarding her room. One of them is a retired sergeant from Northwest detectives."

"I'm not surprised. The victim, according to the paper—have you seen the papers?"

Washington nodded.

"Is the Nesfoods Heiress," Wohl concluded.

"Which is something I should keep in mind, right?" Washington laughed.

"Right," Wohl said. "There's coffee, Jason, while you're waiting for Payne."

"Thank you," Washington said, and went to the coffee-brewing machine.

Wohl picked up one of the telephones on his desk.

"When Officer Payne comes in, don't let him get away," he said, and then, "Okay. Tell him to wait." He turned to Washington. "Payne's outside."

"I think he might get some answers I couldn't," Washington said. "Is that all right with you?"

There was a just perceptible hesitation before Wohl replied, "Like I said, whatever you want, Jason."

"You know what I'm asking," Washington said.

"Yeah. I think we have to give him the benefit of the doubt until proven otherwise. I think he knows he's a cop."

"Yeah, so do I. And I really think he might be useful. I don't have a hell of a lot of experience with Nesfood Heiresses."

"Don't let them worry you," Wohl said. "Dave Pekach seems to do very well with heiresses."

"How about that?" Washington laughed. "Is that as serious as I hear?"

"Take a look at his watch," Wohl said. "He had a birthday."

"What's he got?"

"A gold Omega with about nine dials," Wohl said. "It does everything but chime. Maybe it does that too."

"Well, good for him," Washington said. He put down his coffee cup and stood up and shot his cuffs.

"I'll keep you up-to-date," he said. "Thanks for the coffee."

"Let me know if I can help," Wohl said.

"I will. Count on it," Washington said.

He walked out of Peter Wohl's office. Matt Payne was leaning over the desk of Wohl's administrative sergeant.

"Still have your driver's license, Matthew?" Washington said.

"Yes, sir."

"The next time you say 'Yes, sir' to me, I will spill something greasy on that very nice sport coat," Washington said. "Come on, hotshot, take me for a drive." He saw the look on Matt's face and added, "I fixed it with the boss."

"Frankly," H. Russell Dotson, M.D., a short, plump man in a faintly striped dark blue suit that Jason Washington thought was very nice, indeed, said, "I'm very reluctant to permit you to see Miss Detweiler—"

"I understand your concern, Doctor," Washington said. "May I say two things?"
Dotson nodded impatiently.

"Time is often critically important in cases like this—"

"I know why you think you should see her," Dr. Dotson interrupted. If the interruption annoyed Washington, it didn't show on his face or in his voice.

"And we really do understand your concern about unduly upsetting your patient, and with that in mind I arranged for Officer Payne to come with me and actually speak with Miss Detweiler. Officer Payne is a close friend—"

"So that *is* who you are! Matt Payne, right? Brewster Payne's boy?"

"Yes, sir," Matt said politely.

"I thought I recognized you. And you're a policeman?"

"Yes, sir."

"That's a new one on me," Dr. Dotson said. "Since when?"

"Since right after graduation, Dr. Dotson," Matt said.

"Well, you understand my concern, Matt. I don't want anything to upset Penny. She's been severely traumatized. Physically and psychologically. For a while there, frankly, I thought we might lose her."

"She's going to be all right now?"

"Well, I don't think she's going to die," Dr. Dotson said. "But she's still very weak. We had her in the operating room for over two hours."

"I understand, sir," Matt said.

"I'm going in there with you," Dr. Dotson said. "And I want you to keep looking at me. When I indicate that I want you to leave the room, I want you to leave right then. Understood? Agreed?"

"Yes, of course, sir."

"Very well, then."

If it had been Dr. Dotson's intention to discreetly keep Jason Washington out of Penelope Detweiler's room, he failed. By the time the doctor turned to close the door, Washington was inside the room, already leaning against the wall, as if to signal that while he had no intention of intruding, neither did he intend to leave.

Penny Detweiler's appearance shocked Matt Payne. The head of her bed was raised slightly, so that she could watch television. Her face and throat and what he could see of her chest were, where the skin was not covered with bandages and exposed sutures, black and blue, as if she had been severely beaten. Patches of hair had been been shaved from the front of her head, and there were bandages and exposed sutures there too. Transparent tubing fed liquid into her right arm from two bottles suspended at the head of the bed.

"Now that the beauticians are through with you, are you ready for the photographer?" Matt asked.

"I made them give me a mirror," she said. "Aren't I ghastly?"

"I cannot tell a lie. You look like hell," Matt said. "How do you feel?"

"As bad as I look," she said, and then, "Matt, what are *you* doing here? And how did you get in?"

"I'm a cop, Penny."

"Oh, that's right. I heard that. I don't really believe it. Why did you do something like that?"

"I didn't want to be a lawyer," Matt said. He saw that Dr. Dotson, who had been tense, had now relaxed somewhat.

She laughed and winced.

"It hurts," she said. "Don't make me laugh."

"What the hell happened, Penny?"

"I don't know," she said. "I was walking to the stairwell. You know where this happened to me?"

"We found you. Amanda Spencer and me. When we drove on the roof, you were on the floor. Amanda called the cops."

"You did? I don't remember seeing you."

"You were unconscious," Matt said.

"I guess I won't be able to make it to the wedding, will I?" she asked, and then added, "What are they going to do about the wedding?"

"I saw Daffy—and the Brownes—before I came here. They asked me what I thought about that, and since it was none of my business, I told them."

She giggled, then winced again.

"I told you, don't make me laugh," she said. "Every time I move my—chest—it hurts."

"Sorry."

"What did you tell them?"

"That Chad is in the Marines and that they couldn't postpone it."

"And?"

"I don't know, but I think everything's going ahead as planned."

"Just because this happened to me is no reason to ruin everybody else's fun," Penny said.

"I still don't know what happened to you," Matt said.

"I don't really know," Penny said.

"You don't remember anything?"

"I remember getting out of my car and walking toward the stairwell. And then the roof fell in on me. I remember, sort of, being in a truck—not an ambulance, a truck—and I think there was a cop in there with me. But that's all."

"There's no roof over the roof," Matt said.

"You know what I mean. It was like something ran into me. Hit me hard."

"You didn't see anyone up there?"

"No."

"Nothing at all?"

"There was nobody up there but me," she said firmly.

"Does the name Tony DeZego mean anything to you?"

"No. Who?"

"Tony. Tony DeZego."

"No," she said, "should it?"

"No reason it should."

"Who is he?"

"A guinea gangster," Matt said.

"A what?"

"An Italian-American with alleged ties to organized crime," Matt said dryly.

"Why are you asking me about him?"

"Well, he was up there too," Matt said. "On the roof of the garage. Somebody blew the top of his head off with a shotgun."

"My God!"

"No great loss to society," Matt said. "He wasn't even a good gangster. Just a cheap thug with ambition. A small-time drug dealer, from what I hear."

"I think that's about enough of a visit, Matt," Dr. Dotson said. "Penny needs rest. And her parents are on their way."

Matt touched her arm.

"I'll bring you a piece of the wedding cake," he said. "Try to behave yourself."

"I don't have any choice, do I?" she said.

In the corridor outside, Dr. Dotson laid a hand on Matt's arm.

"I can't imagine why you told her about that gangster," he said.

"I thought she'd be interested," Matt said.

"Thank you very much, Dr. Dotson," Jason Washington said. "I very much appreciate your cooperation."

"She's lying," Matt said when Washington got in the passenger seat beside him.

"She is? About what?"

"About knowing DeZego."

"Really? What makes you think so?"

"Jesus, didn't you see her eyes when I called him a 'guinea gangster'?"

"You're a regular little Sherlock Holmes, aren't you?" Washington asked.

Matt looked at him, the hurt showing in his eyes.

"If I did that wrong in there, I'm sorry," he said. "If you didn't think I could handle it, you should have told me what to ask and how to ask it. I did the best I could."

"As a matter of fact, hotshot," Washington said, "I couldn't have done it any better myself. I would have phrased the questions a little differently, probably, because I don't know the lady as well as you do, but that wasn't at all bad. One of the most difficult calls to make in an interview like that, with a subject like that, is when to let them know you know they're lying. That wasn't the time."

"I didn't think so, either," Matt said, and then smiled, almost shyly, at Washington.

"Let's go to the parking garage," Washington said.

As they drove around City Hall, Matt said, "I'd like to know for sure if she's taking dope. Do you suppose they took blood when she got to the hospital? That could be tested?"

"I'm sure they did," Washington said. "But as a matter of law, not to mention ethics, the hospital could not make the results of that test known to the police. It would be considered, in essence, an illegal search or seizure, as well as a violation of the patient's privacy. Her rights against compulsory incrimination would also be involved."

"Oh," Matt said.

"Your friend is a habitual user of cocaine," Washington went on, "using it in quantities that make it probable that she is on the edges of addiction to it."

Matt looked at him in surprise.

"One of the most important assets a detective can have, Officer Payne," Washington replied dryly, "is the acquaintance of a number of people who feel in his debt. Apropos of nothing whatever, I once spoke to a judge prior to his sentencing of a young man for vehicular theft. I told the judge that I thought probation would probably suffice to keep the malefactor on the straight and narrow, and that I was acquainted with his mother, a decent, divorced woman who worked as a registered nurse at Hahneman Hospital."

"Nice," Matt said.

"I suppose you know the difference between ignorance and stupidity?"

"I think so." Matt chuckled.

"A good detective never forgets he's ignorant. He knows very, very little about what's going on. So that means a good detective is always looking for something, or someone, that can reduce the totality of his ignorance."

"Okay," Matt said with another chuckle. "So where does that leave us, now that we know she's using cocaine and knew DeZego?"

"I don't have a clue—witticism intended—why either of them got shot," Washington said. "There's a lot of homicide involved with narcotics, but what it usually boils down to is simple armed robbery. Somebody wants either the drugs or the money and uses a gun to take them. The Detweiler girl had nearly seven hundred dollars in her purse; Tony the Zee had a quantity of coke—say five hundred dollars' worth, at least. Since they still had the money and the drugs, I think we can reasonably presume that robbery wasn't the basic cause of the shooting."

They were at the Penn Services Parking Garage. When Matt started to pull onto the entrance ramp, Washington told him to park on the street. Just in time Matt stopped himself from protesting that there was no parking on 15th Street.

Washington did not enter the building. He walked to the alley at one end, then circled the building as far as he could, until he encountered a chain-link fence. He stood looking at the fence and up at the building for a moment, then he retraced his steps to the front and walked onto the entrance ramp. Then he walked up the ramp to the first floor.

Three quarters of the way down the parking area, Matt saw a uniformed cop, and a moment later yellow CRIME SCENE—DO NOT CROSS tape surrounding a Dodge sedan.

"What's that?" he asked, curiosity overwhelming his solemn, silent vow to keep his eyes open and his mouth shut.

"It was a hit on the NCIC when they ran the plates," Washington said. "Reported stolen in Drexel Hill."

The National Crime Information Center was an FBI-run computer system. Detectives (at one time there had been sixteen Homicide detectives in the Penn Services garage) had fed the computer the license numbers of every car in the garage at the time of the shooting. NCIC had returned every bit of information it had on any of them. The Dodge had been entered into the computer as stolen.

"Good morning," Washington said to the uniformed cop. "The lab get to this yet?"

"They were here real early this morning," the cop said. "I think there's still a couple of them upstairs."

Washington nodded. He walked around the car and then looked into the front and back seats. Then he started up the ramp to the upper floors.

"It'll probably turn out the Dodge has nothing to do with the shooting," he said to Matt. "But we'll check it out, just to be sure."

The ramp to the roof was blocked by another uniformed cop and a cross of crime-scene tape, but when Matt and Washington walked on it, Matt saw there was only a Police Lab truck and three cars—a Mercedes convertible, roof up; a blue-and-white; and an unmarked car—on the whole floor.

He could see a body form outlined in white, where Penny Detweiler had been when he had driven on the roof and where he had found the body of Anthony J. DeZego. It seemed pretty clear that the Mercedes was Penny's car.

But where was DeZego's?

A hollow-eyed man came out of the unmarked car, smiled at Washington, and offered his hand.

"You are your usually natty self this morning, Jason, I see," he said.

"Is that a touch of jealousy I detect, Lieutenant?" Washington replied. "You know Matt Payne? Matt, this is Lieutenant Jack Potter, the mad genius of Forensics."

"No. But what do they say? 'He is preceded by his reputation'? How are you, Payne?"

"How do you do, sir?"

"Anything?" Washington asked.

"Not much. We picked up some shotshell pellets and two wads, either from off the floor or picked out of the concrete. No more shell casings. Which means that the shooter knew what he was doing; or that he had only two shells, which suggests it was double-barrel, as opposed to an autoloader; or all of the above."

"Anything in the girl's car?"

"Uh-uh. No bags of anything," Lieutenant Potter replied. "Haven't had a chance either to run the prints or analyze what the vacuum cleaner picked up."

"I'd love to find a clear print of Mr. DeZego inside the Mercedes," Washington said.

"If there's a match, you'll be the first to know," Potter said.

"Can you release the Mercedes?" Washington asked. Potter's eyebrows rose in question. "I thought it might be a nice gesture on our part if Officer Payne and I returned the car to the Detweiler home."

"Why not?" Potter replied. "What about the Dodge? There was nothing out of the ordinary there."

"You've got the name and address of the owner?"

Potter nodded.

"Let me have it. I'll have someone check him out. I think we can take the tape down, anyway."

Potter grunted.

"Which raises the question, of course, of Mr. DeZego's car," Washington said. "Do you suppose he walked up here?"

"Or he came up here with the shooter and they left without him," Potter said.

"Or his car is parked on the street," Washington said. "Or *was* parked on the street and may be in the impound yard now."

"I'll check on that for you, if you like," Potter said.

"Matt," Washington said, "find a phone. Call Organized Crime and see if they know what kind of a car Anthony J. DeZego drove. Then call Traffic and see if they impounded a car like that and, if so, where they impounded it. Maybe we'll get lucky."

"Right," Matt replied.

"And if that doesn't work, call Police Radio and have them see if they can locate the car and get back to me, if they can."

"Right," Matt said.

Washington turned to Potter.

"You have any idea where the shooter was standing?"

"Let me show you," Potter said as Matt walked to the telephone.

10 Mrs. Charles McFadden, Sr., a plump, gray-haired woman of forty-five, was watching television in the living room of her home, a row house on Fitzgerald Street not far from Methodist Hospital in South Philadelphia, when the telephone rang.

Not without effort, and sighing, she pushed herself out of the upholstered chair and went to the telephone, which had been installed on a small shelf mounted on the wall in the corridor leading from the front door past the stairs to the kitchen.

"Hello?"

"Can I reach Officer McFadden on this number?" a male voice inquired.

"You can," she said. "But he's got his own phone. Did you try that?"

"Yes, ma'am. There was no answer."

Come to think of it, Agnes McFadden thought, *I didn't hear it ring.*

"Just a minute," she said, and then: "Who did you say is calling?"

"This is Sergeant Henderson, ma'am, of the Highway Patrol. Is this Mrs. McFadden?"

"Senior," she said. "I'm his mother."

"Yes, ma'am."

"I'll get him," she said. "Just a moment."

She put the handset carefully beside the base and then went upstairs. Charley's room was at the rear. When he had first gone on the job—working Narcotics under-cover, which had pleased his mother not at all, the way he went around looking like a bum and working all hours at night—he had had his own telephone line installed.

Then, as happy as a kid with a new toy train, he had found a little black box in Radio Shack that permitted the switching on and off of the telephone ringer. It was a great idea, but what happened was that after he turned off the ringer, he forgot to turn it back on, which meant that either he didn't get calls at all, or the caller, as now, had the number of the phone downstairs, and she or his father had to climb the stairs and tell him he had a call.

She knocked at his door and, when there was no answer, pushed it open. Charley was lying facedown on the bed in his Jockey shorts, his arms and legs spread, snoring softly. That told her that he'd stopped off for a couple (to judge by the sour smell, a whole hell of a lot more than a couple) of beers when he got off work last night.

She called his name and touched his shoulder. Then she put both hands on his shoulders and bounced him up and down. He slept like the dead. Always had.

Finally he half turned and raised his head.

"What the hell, Ma!" Charley said.

"Don't you swear at me!"

"What do you want, Ma?"

"There's some sergeant on the phone."

Still half asleep, Charley found his telephone, picked it up, heard the dial tone, and looked at her in confusion.

"Downstairs," she said. "You and your telephone switch!"

He got out of bed with surprising alacrity and ran down the corridor. She heard the thumping and creaking of the stairs as he took them two at a time.

"McFadden," he said to the telephone.

"Sergeant Henderson, out at Bustleton and Bowler."

"Yes, sir?"

"You heard about Officer Magnella being shot last night?"

"Yeah."

"We're trying to put as many men on it as we can. Any reason you can't do some overtime? Specifically, any reason you can't come in at noon instead of four?"

"I'll be there."

Sergeant Henderson hung up.

Charley had two immediate thoughts as he put the phone in its cradle: *Jesus, what time is it?* and, an instant later, *Jesus, I feel like death warmed over. I've got to start cutting it short at the FOP.*

"What was that all about?" his mother asked from the foot of the stairs, and then, without waiting for a reply, "Put some clothes on. This isn't a nudist colony."

"I gotta go to work. You hear about the cop who got shot?"

"It was on the TV. What's that got to do with you?"

"They're still trying to catch who did it."

Mrs. Agnes McFadden had been the only person in the neighborhood who had not been thrilled when her son had been called a police hero for his role in putting the killer of Captain Dutch Moffitt of the Highway Patrol out of circulation. She reasoned that if Gerald Vincent Gallagher was indeed a murderer, then obviously he could have done harm to her only son.

"I thought you were in training to be a Highway Patrolman."

Charley McFadden had done nothing to correct his mother's misperception that Highway Patrol was primarily charged with removing speeding and/or drunk drivers from the streets.

"I am," he said. "It's overtime. I gotta go."

"I'll make you something to eat," she said.

"No time, Ma. Thanks, anyway."

"You have to eat."

"I'll get something after I report in."

He went up the stairs and to his bedroom and found his watch. It was quarter to ten. He had declined breakfast because he knew it would be accompanied by comments about his drinking, his late hours, and probably, since she had heard about Magnella getting himself shot, by reopening the subject of his being a cop at all.

But since he had announced he had to leave right away, he would have to leave right away, and even if he took his time getting something to eat and going by the dry cleaners to drop off and pick up a uniform, he still would have an hour or more to kill before he could sign in.

He took his time taking a shower, steeling himself several times for the shock turning off the hot water would mean, hoping that the cold would clear his mind, and then he shaved with care.

He didn't need a haircut, although getting one would have killed some time.

Fuck it, he decided finally. *I'll just go get something to eat and go out to Bustleton and Bowler and just hang around until noon.*

His mother was standing by the door when he came down the stairs, demanding her ritual kiss and delivering her ritual order for him to be careful.

He noticed two things when he got to the street: first, that the right front wheel of his Volkswagen was on the curb, which confirmed he had had a couple of beers more than he probably should have had at the FOP; and, second, that the redhead with the cute little ass he had noticed several times around the neighborhood was coming out of the McCarthys', across the street and two houses down.

He smiled at her shyly and, when she smiled back, equally shyly, gave her a little wave. She didn't wave back. Just smiled. But that was a step in the right direction, he decided. Tomorrow morning he would ask around and see who she was. He could not ask his mother. She would know, of course; she knew when anybody in the neighborhood burped, but if he asked her about the girl, the next thing he knew, she would be trying to pair him off with her.

Charley knew that his mother devoutly believed that what he needed in his life was a nice, decent Catholic girl. If the redhead with the cute little ass had anything to do with the McCarthys, she met that definition. Mrs. McCarthy was a Mass-every-morning Catholic, and Mr. McCarthy was a big deal in the Knights of Columbus.

Still, it was worth looking into.

He got into the Volkswagen, started it up, and drove around the block, eventually turning onto South Broad Street, heading north. And there was the redhead, obviously waiting for a bus.

Impulsively he pulled to the curb and stopped. First he started to lean across the seat and roll the window down, and then he decided it would be better to get out of the car. He did so, and leaned on the roof and smiled at her. He was suddenly absolutely sure that he was about to make a real horse's ass out of himself.

"You looking for a ride?" he blurted.

"I'm waiting for a bus," the redhead said.

"I didn't mean that the way it sounded," Charley said.

"How did you mean it?" the redhead said.

"Look," he said somewhat desperately, "I'm Charley McFadden—"

"I know who you are," she said. "My uncle Bob and your father are friends."

"Yeah," he said.

"You don't remember me, do you?" she said.

"Yeah, sure I do."

"No you don't." She laughed. "I used to come here when I was a kid."

His mind was blank. "Look, I'm headed across town. Can I give you a ride?"

"I'm going to Temple," she said. "You going anywhere near there?"

"Right past it," he said.

"Then yes, thank you, I would like a ride," she said.

"Great," Charley said.

She walked to the car and got in. When he got behind the wheel and glanced at her, she had her hand out.

"Margaret McCarthy," she said. "Bob McCarthy is my uncle, my father's brother."

"I'm pleased to meet you," Charley said.

He turned the key, which resulted in a grinding of the starter gears, as the engine was already running. He winced.

"So what are you doing at Temple?" he asked a moment or so later.

"Going for my B.S. in nursing."

"Your what?"

"I'm already an RN," she said. "So I came here to get a degree. Bachelor of Science, in Nursing. I live in Baltimore."

"Oh," Charley said, digesting that. "How long will that take?"

"About eighteen months," she said. "I'm carrying a heavy load."

"Oh."

What the hell did she mean by that?

"I'm a cop," he said.

She giggled.

"I would never have guessed," she said.

"Oh, Christ!" he said.

"Uncle Bob sent us the clippings from the newspaper," Margaret McCarthy said, "when you caught that murderer."

"Really?"

"My father said he thought you would wind up on the other side of the bars," she said, laughing. And then she added, "Oh, I shouldn't have said that."

"It's all right," he said.

"You put a golf ball through his windshield," she said. "Do you remember that? Playing stickball?"

"Yeah," Charley said, remembering. "My old man beat hell out of me."

"So, do you like being a policeman?"

"I liked it better when I was plainclothes," he said. "But, yeah, I like it all right."

"I don't know what that means," she said.

"I used to work undercover Narcotics," Charley said. "Sort of like a detective."

"That was in the newspapers," she said.

"Yeah, well, after that, getting your picture in the newspapers, the drug people knew who I was. So that was the end of Narcotics for me."

"You liked that?"

"I liked Narcotics, yeah," Charley said.

"What are you doing now?"

"What I want to do is be a detective," Charley said. "So what I'm really doing now is killing time until I can take the examination."

"How are you 'killing time'?"

"Well, they transferred us, me and my partner, Hay-zus Martinez—"

"Hay-zus?"

"That's the way the Latin people say Jesus," Charley explained.

"Oh," she said.

"They transferred us to Special Operations," Charley said, "which is new. And then they made us probationary Highway Patrolmen. Which means if we don't screw up, after six months we get to be Highway Patrolmen."

"Is that something special?"

"They think it is. Like I said, I'd rather be a detective."

"I should think that after what you did, they'd want to make you a detective," Margaret McCarthy said.

"It don't work that way. You have to take the examination."

"Oh," she said.

I'm going to ask her if she wants to go to a movie or something. Maybe dinner and *a movie.*

He had difficulty framing in his mind the right way to pose the question, the result of that being that they rode in silence almost to the Temple campus without his saying a word.

Then he was surprised to hear himself say, "Right in there, two blocks down, is where Magnella got himself shot."

"You mean the police officer who was murdered?" Margaret asked, and when Charley nodded, she went on. "My uncle Bob and his father are friends. They're in the Knights of Columbus together."

"Yeah. That's why I'm going to work now. They called up and asked me to come in early to work on that."

"Like a detective, you mean?"

"Yeah, well, sort of."

"That should be very rewarding," Margaret McCarthy said. "Working on something like that."

"Yeah," he said. "Look, you want to catch a movie, have dinner or something?"

"A movie or dinner sounds nice," she said. "I'm not so sure about something."

"I'll call you," he said. "Okay?"

"Sure," she said. "I'd like that. I get out at the next corner."

"How about in the morning?" Charley asked.

"You want to go to the movies in the morning?"

"Christ, I'm on the four-to-twelve," he said. "How are we going to . . ."

"We could have coffee or something in the mornings," she said. "My first classes aren't until eleven."

He pulled to the curb and smiled at her. She smiled back.

A horn blew impatiently behind him.

Charley, at the last moment, did not shout, "Blow it out your ass, asshole!" at the horn blower. Instead he got out of the Volkswagen and stood on the curb with Margaret McCarthy for a moment.

"I have to go, Charley," she said. "I'll be late."

"Yeah," he said. "I'll call you."

"Call me," she said.

They shook hands. Margaret walked onto the campus.

Charley glowered at the horn blower, who was now smiling nervously, and then got in the Volkswagen and drove off. He remembered that he had not dropped off his dirty uniform at the dry cleaner. It didn't seem to matter. He felt better right now than he could remember feeling in a long time.

Things were looking up. Even things at work were looking up. It didn't make sense that they would call him, and probably Hay-zus, too, to go through that probationary bullshit and pay them overtime. The odds were that Captain Pekach was going to put them back on the street, doing what he knew they already knew how to do: grabbing scumbags.

"Is Inspector Wohl in his office?" the heavyset, balding man with a black, six-inch-long handmade long filler Costa Rican cigar clamped between his teeth demanded.

"I believe he is, sir," Sergeant Edward Frizell said politely as he picked up his telephone. "I'll see if he's free, sir."

By the time he had the telephone to his ear, Chief Inspector Matt Lowenstein was inside Staff Inspector Peter Wohl's office at the headquarters of the Special Operations Division at Bustleton and Bowler streets.

Peter Wohl was not at his desk. He was sitting on his couch, his feet up on his coffee table. When he saw Lowenstein come through the door, he started to get up.

"Good morning, Chief," he said.

Lowenstein closed the door.

"I came to apologize," he said. "For what I said last night."

"No apology necessary, Chief."

"I didn't mean what I said, Peter, I was just pissed off."

"You had a right to be," Wohl said. "I would have been."

"At the dago I did. Do. Not at you. God*damn* him! If he wanted to run the Police Department, why didn't he just stay as commissioner?"

"Because when he was commissioner, the mayor could tell him how to run the Department. Now he answers only to God and the voters."

"I'm not so sure how much input he'd take from God," Lowenstein said. "The last I heard, God was never a captain in Highway."

Wohl chuckled. "Would you like some coffee?" he asked.

"Yes, I would, thank you," Lowenstein said.

When Wohl handed him the cup, Lowenstein said, "I want you to know that before I came out here, I called Homicide and Organized Crime and Narcotics and told them that I completely agreed with Czernich's decision and that they were to give cooperation with you their highest priority. Goddamn lie, of course, about me agreeing, but it wasn't your fault, and I want the people who shot that young cop. As far as the DeZego job goes, frankly you're welcome to that one. I don't want the Detweilers mad at me."

"Thanks a lot, Chief," Wohl said.

"What's this I hear that one of your guys is dirty?"

"No. I don't think so. The Narcotics sergeant went off the deep end."

"Is that so?"

"The cop he suspected of being dirty is Matt Payne."

"Dutch Moffitt's nephew? I thought that he was working for you."

"He is. Payne drove into the parking lot shortly after the Detweiler girl. The Narcotics sergeant was watching her. Right afterward Payne drove away, which the sergeant thought was suspicious. Payne drives a Porsche, which is the kind of a car a successful drug dealer would drive. And then, when the Narcotics guy found out Payne was a cop, he really put his nose in high gear."

"But he's clean?"

"Payne parked his car there because he was also headed for the Union League, and the reason he drove the car away was because the 9th District lieutenant, Foster Lewis . . . ?"

"I know him. Just made lieutenant. Good cop."

". . . on the scene sent him to tell the Detweiler family, at the Union League."

"Payne drives a Porsche?"

Wohl nodded.

"Nice to have a rich father."

"Obviously."

"I heard Denny Coughlin put him in your lap."

"Chief Coughlin and the gentleman with an interest in the Police Department we were discussing earlier," Wohl said. "After Payne shot the rapist the mayor told the newspapers that Payne is my special assistant, so I decided Payne *is* my special assistant."

"Good thinking," Lowenstein said, chuckling.

"I also got Foster H. Lewis, Jr., this morning," Wohl said.

"Lewis's son is a cop?"

"Just got out of the Academy."

"Why did they send him here?"

"Just a routine assignment of a new police officer that the mayor just happened to announce in a speech at the First Abyssinian Baptist Church."

"Oh, I see." Lowenstein grunted. "The Afro-American voters. There's two sides to being the mayor's fair-haired boy, aren't there?"

"Chief," Wohl said solemnly, "I have no idea what you're talking about."

"The hell you don't," Lowenstein growled. "What are you going to do with the Lewis boy?"

"I gave him to Tony Harris, as a gofer. Harris has Lewis, and Jason Washington just borrowed Payne."

"To do what?"

"Whatever Jason tells him to. I think Washington likes him. I think they may have the same tailor."

"Well, you better hope Harris and Washington get lucky," Lowenstein said. "Your salami is on the chopping block with these two jobs, Peter."

"Chief, that thought *has* run through my mind," Wohl said.

Chief Lowenstein, who had not finished delivering his assessment of the situation, glowered at Peter Wohl for cutting him short and then went on.

"When the Payne kid got lucky and put down the serial rapist, that only made Arthur Nelson and his goddamn *Ledger* pause for breath. It did not shut him up. Now he's got two things: drug-related gang warfare in the center city with a nice little rich girl lying in a pool of blood as a result of it; and a cop shot down in cold blood, the cops not having a clue who did it. Nelson would make a case against the Department, and Carlucci, if the doers were already in Central Lockup. With the doers still running around loose—"

"I know," Wohl said.

"I don't think you do, Peter," Lowenstein said as he hauled himself to his feet. "I was sitting at my kitchen table this morning wondering if I had the balls to come out here and apologize to you when Carlucci made up my mind for me."

"I'm sorry?" Wohl asked, confused.

Chief Lowenstein examined the glowing end of his cigar for a moment and then met Wohl's eyes.

"The dago called me at the house," he said. "He said he wanted me to come out here this morning and see how things were going. He said that he'd told Lucci to call him at least once a day, but that 'too much was at stake here to leave something like this to someone like Lucci.' "

"Jesus Christ!" Wohl said bitterly. "If he didn't think I could do the job, why did he give it to me?"

"Because if you do the job, *he* looks good. And if you don't, *you* look bad. They call that smart politics, Peter."

"Yeah," Wohl said.

"I think I can expect at least a daily call from the dago, Peter, asking me how I think you're handling this. I wouldn't worry about that. I don't want these jobs back, so all he's going to get from me is an expression of confidence in you, and the way you're doing things. On the other hand, whatever else I may think of him, your Lieutenant Lucci *is* smart enough to know which side of the bread has the butter—no telling what he's liable to tell the dago."

"Christ, my father warned me about crap like this. I didn't believe him."

"Give my regards to your dad, Peter," Lowenstein said. "I always have admired him."

Wohl stared at the phone on his coffee table for a moment. When he finally raised his eyes, Lowenstein was gone.

Lieutenant Foster H. Lewis, Sr., who was wearing a light blue cotton bathrobe over his underwear, had just offered, aloud, although he was alone in the apartment, his somewhat less than flattering opinion of morning television programming and the even more appallingly stupid people who watched it, himself included, when the chimes sounded.

He went to the door and opened it.

"Good morning, sir," the uniformed policeman standing there said, "would you like to take a raffle ticket on a slightly used 1948 Buick?"

"What did you do, Foster, lose your key?"

He looks good in that uniform, even if I wish he weren't wearing it.

"So that I wouldn't lose it, I put it somewhere safe," Tiny Lewis said. "One of these days I'll remember where."

"I just made some coffee. You want some?"

"Please, Dad."

"What are you doing here?"

"I've got to get a suit," Tiny said. "Mom said she put them in a cedar bag."

"Probably in your room," Foster Lewis, Sr., said. "Am I permitted to ask why you need a suit?"

"Certainly," Tiny said. He followed his father into the kitchen and took a china mug from a cabinet.

"Well?" Foster Lewis asked.

"Well, what? Oh, do you want to know why I need a suit?"

"I asked. Where were you when I asked?"

"You asked if you were permitted to ask, and I said, 'Certainly,' but you didn't actually ask."

"Wiseass." His father chuckled. "There's a piece of cake in the refrigerator."

"Thank you," Tiny said, and helped himself to the cake.

"You know a Homicide—ex-Homicide—detective named Harris? Tony Harris?"

"Yeah. Not well. But he's supposed to be good."

"You are now looking, sir, at his official errand runner," Tiny said.

"What does that mean?"

"I suppose it means that if he says 'Go fetch,' I go fetch, happily wagging my tail."

"If you're being clever, stop it," his father said. "Tell me what's going on."

"Well, I was told to report to a Captain Sabara at Highway. When I got there, he wasn't, but Inspector Wohl called me into his office—"

"You saw him?" Foster Lewis, Sr., asked.

"Yeah. Nice guy. *Sharp* dude. *Nice* threads."

I was on the job, Lieutenant Foster H. Lewis thought, *for two or three years before I ever saw an inspector up close.*

"Go on."

"Well, he said that Harris has the Magnella job, and that he needed a second pair of hands. He said it would involve a lot of overtime, and if I had any problem with that to say so; he didn't want any complaints later. So I told him the more overtime the better, and I asked him what I would be doing. He said—that's where I got that— that if Harris said 'Go fetch,' I was to wag my tail and go fetch. He said the detail would last only until Harris got whoever shot Magnella, but it would be good experience for me."

"That's it?"

"Well, he gave me a speech about what not to do with the car—"

"What car?"

"A '71 Ford. Good shape."

"You have a Department car?"

"Yeah. Unmarked, naturally," Tiny said just a little smugly.

"My God!"

"What's wrong?"

Lieutenant Foster H. Lewis, Sr., thought, *When I got out of the Academy, I was assigned to the 26th District. A potbellied Polack sergeant named Grotski went out of his way to make it plain he didn't think there was any place in the Department for niggers and then handed me over to Bromley T. Wesley, a South Carolina redneck who had come north to work in the shipyards during the Second World War and had joined the cops because he didn't want to go back home to Tobacco Road.*

I walked a beat with Bromley for a year. When he went into a candy store for a Coke or something, he made me wait outside. For six months he never used my name. I was either "Hey, You!" or worse, "Hey, Boy!" I was told that if I turned out okay, maybe after a year or so, I could work my way up to a wagon. The son of a bitch made it plain he thought all black people were born retarded.

Bromley T. Wesley was an ignorant bigot with a sixth-grade education, but he was a cop. He knew the streets and he knew people, and he taught me about them. Between Wesley and what I learned on the wagon, when I went out in an RPC by myself for the first time I was a cop.

What the hell is Peter Wohl thinking of, putting this rookie in civilian clothes instead of in a wagon, at least?

"Nothing, I suppose," Lieutenant Lewis said. "It's a little unusual, that's all. Eat your cake."

11 The normally open gate of the Detweiler estate in Chestnut Hill, like the gate at the Browne place in Merion, was now both closed and guarded by rent-a-cops.

When Matt pulled the nose of Penelope Detweiler's Mercedes against the gate, one of them, a burly man in a blue suit, came through a small gate within the gate and looked down at Matt.

"May I help you, sir?"

"We're returning Miss Detweiler's car," Matt said.

" 'We,' sir?"

"I'm a cop," Matt said, and jerked his thumb toward Jason Washington, who was following him in the unmarked Ford. "And so is he."

"You expected?"

"No."

"I'll have to call, sir."

"Tell them it's Matt Payne."

The rent-a-cop looked at him strangely and then said, "Matt Payne. Yes, sir."

He went back through the small gate, entered the gate house, and emerged a moment later to swing the left half of the double gate open. He waved Matt through.

H. Richard Detweiler, himself, answered the door. He had a drink in his hand.

"Boy, that was quick!" he said. "Come in, Matt."

"Sir?"

"I just this second got off the phone with Czernich," Detweiler said. "Penny was worried about her car, so I called him and asked about it, and he said he'd have it sent out here."

"I think we probably were on our way when you called him, Mr. Detweiler," Matt said. "Mr. Detweiler, this is Detective Washington."

"I was just talking about you too," Detweiler said, offering Washington his hand. "Thad Czernich told me you're the best detective in the Department."

"Far be it from me to question the commissioner's judgment," Washington said. "How do you do, Mr. Detweiler?"

Detweiler chuckled. "Oh, about as well as any father would be after just seeing a daughter who looks like the star of a horror movie."

"We saw Miss Detweiler earlier this morning," Washington said.

"So she said. That was kind of you, Matt. And you, too, Mr. Washington."

"I think you'll be surprised to see how quickly that discoloration goes away, Mr. Detweiler," Washington said.

"I hope," Detweiler said. "I needed a drink when I got back here. I'd offer you one, but I know—"

"That would be very nice, thank you," Washington said.

"Oh, you can take a drink on duty?" Detweiler asked. "Fine. I always feel depraved drinking alone. Let's go in the bar."

He led them to a small room off the kitchen.

"This is supposed to be the serving pantry," he said, motioning them to take stools set against a narrow counter under and above the glass-fronted cupboards. The cupboards held canned goods, and there was an array of bottles on the counter.

"I'm not exactly sure what a butler's pantry is supposed to be for," Detweiler went on, reaching for a bottle of gin. "My grandfather copied this place from a house in England, so it came with a butler's pantry. Anyway, what *we* serve here is liquor. Help yourself."

"Matt, if you would splash a little of that Johnny Walker Black in a glass, and a *little* water, and *one* ice cube?" Washington said.

"You sound like a man who appreciates good Scotch and knows how to drink it," Detweiler said.

"I try," Washington said.

Matt made two drinks to Washington's specifications, handed him one, and raised his own.

"To Penny's recovery," he said.

"Hear, hear," Washington said.

"Penny," Detweiler said, his voice breaking. "God*damn* whoever did that to her!"

"I'm sure He will," Washington said, "but we would like to get our licks in on him before he gets to the Pearly Gates."

Detweiler looked at him, smiling.

"Good thinking," he said.

The telephone on the counter buzzed; one of the four lights on it lit up. Detweiler made no move to answer it.

"Have you found out anything, Mr. Washington? What's going on?"

"Well, frankly, Mr. Detweiler, we don't have much to go on. The theory I'm working under is that Miss Detweiler was simply in the wrong place at the wrong time—"

"Is there another theory? Theories?"

"Well, I've been doing this long enough to know the hazards of reaching premature conclusions—" Washington said.

"Goddamn," Detweiler said, angrily grabbing for the phone, which had continued to buzz, "we keep six in help here, and whenever the phone rings, they *all* disappear." He put the handset to his ear and snarled, "Yes?"

There was a pause.

"This is Dick Detweiler, Commissioner. I wish I could get people as efficient as yours. No sooner had I put down the phone than Matt Payne and Detective Washington drove up with my daughter's car. I'm impressed with the service."

There was an inaudible reply to this, then Detweiler said, "Thank you very much, Commissioner." He extended the phone to Washington. "He wants to talk to you."

"Yes, sir."

"Watch yourself out there, Washington. And when you leave, call me and let me know how it went."

The phone went dead in Washington's ear.

"Yes, of course, Commissioner," Washington said after a pause that sounded longer than it was. "Thank you very much, sir. Good-bye, sir."

He handed the telephone to Detweiler.

"The commissioner asked me to impress upon you, Mr. Detweiler, that the Department is doing everything humanly possible to get to the bottom of this, to find whoever did this to your daughter. He said that I was to regard this case as my first priority."

"Thank you," Detweiler said. "That's very good of him."

"We were talking, a moment ago, about other theories," Washington said. "I think one of the possibilities we should consider is robbery."

"Robbery?"

Washington nodded.

"Ranging from a simple, that is to say, unplanned, mugging, some thug lurking in the parking garage for whoever might come his way to someone who knew about the dinner party in the Union League—"

"How would someone know about that?" Detweiler said, interrupting.

"I'm sure it was in the society columns of the newspapers," Washington went on. "That might explain the shotgun."

"Excuse me?"

"Muggers are rarely armed with anything more than a knife. A *professional* thief, for lack of a better word, who went to the Penn Services Parking Garage knowing that there would be a number of well-to-do people using it at that time, would be more likely to take a shotgun with him. Not intending to shoot anyone but for its psychological effect."

"Yes," Detweiler said.

"And his plans could have gone astray, and he found himself having to use it."

"Yes, I see," Detweiler said.

"Was your daughter wearing any valuable jewelry, Mr. Detweiler?"

"I don't think so," Detweiler said. "She doesn't have any. Some pearls. All girls have pearls. But nothing really valuable." He looked at Matt and grinned. "Matt hasn't seen fit to offer her an engagement ring yet. . . ."

"A brooch? A pin of some sort?" Washington said, pursuing the matter.

"She has a pin, a brooch"—he gestured at his chest to show where a female would wear such an ornament—"from my wife's mother. She could have been wearing that. It has some rubies or whatever, in a band of—what do they call those little diamonds?—chips?"

"I believe so," Washington said.

"She could have been wearing that," Detweiler said.

"There was no such pin in her personal effects," Washington said. "Do you happen to know where she kept it?"

"In her room, I suppose," Detweiler said. "Do you think we should check to see if it's there?"

"I think we should," Washington said.

Detweiler led them up a narrow flight of stairs from the serving pantry to the second floor and then into Penelope's bedroom. There was a Moroccan leather jewelry case, sort of a miniature chest of drawers, on a vanity table. Detweiler went to it and searched through it and found nothing.

"It's not here," he said. "But let me check with my wife. She needed a lay-down when we came back from the hospital."

Washington nodded sympathetically.

"I hate to disturb her," he said.

"Nonsense, she'd want to help," Detweiler said, and walked out of the room.

Washington immediately picked up a wastebasket beside the vanity table and dumped the contents on the floor. He squatted and flicked through with his fingers, picking up a couple of items and putting them in his pocket. Then, very quickly, he was erect again.

"Fix that," he ordered, and moved toward a double mirrored-door closet. Matt set the wastebasket upright and began to replace what Washington had dumped on the floor.

When he was finished, he turned to see what Washington was doing. He was methodically patting down the clothing hanging in the closet, dipping his hands in every pocket. Matt saw him stuffing small items—including what, at quick glance, appeared to be some sort of plastic vial—in his pocket.

And then Mrs. H. Richard Detweiler appeared in the doorway, just a moment after Washington had slid closed the mirrored door.

"I think this is what you were looking for," she said, holding up a gold brooch.

"Hello, Mrs. Detweiler," Matt said. "Mrs. Detweiler, this is Detective Washington."

"I'm Grace Detweiler. How do you do?" she said, flashing a quick smile. Then she turned to Matt. "I don't know what to think about you. It's natural to see you here, under these absolutely horrible circumstances, but not as a policeman. I really don't quite know what to make of that."

"We're trying to find out what happened to Penny," Matt said.

"You're driving your mother to distraction, you know," she said. "I can't fathom your behavior."

"Grace," H. Richard Detweiler said, "that's none of your business."

"Yes it is," she snapped. "Patricia is one of my dearest friends, and I've known Matt since he was in diapers."

"Matt's no longer a child," Detweiler said. "He can make his own decisions about what he wants to do with his life."

"Why am I not surprised you'd say something like that?" she replied. "Well, all right then, Mr. Policeman, what do you think happened to Penny?"

"Right now we think she was just in the wrong place at the wrong time," Matt said.

"How can parking your car in a public garage be the wrong place?" she snapped.

"We think she was probably an innocent bystander," Matt said.

"*Probably?* What do you mean, 'probably'? What other explanation could there possibly be?"

"Ma'am, we try to check out everything," Washington said. "That's why we were interested in the jewelry."

"Penny doesn't have any good jewelry," she said.

"They didn't know that until they asked," Detweiler said. "Ease off, Grace." Washington gave him a grateful look.

"Mrs. Detweiler, what about money?" Washington asked.

"What about it?"

"Did Miss Detweiler habitually carry large amounts of cash?"

"No," she said, "she didn't. It's not safe to carry cash, or anything else of value, in your purse these days."

"Yes, ma'am, I'm afraid you're right about that," Washington agreed. "You would say, then, that it's probable she didn't have more than a hundred dollars in her purse?"

"I would be very surprised if she had more than—actually, as much as—fifty dollars. She had credit cards, of course."

"There were seven or eight of those in her purse," Washington said. "They weren't stolen."

"Well, this pretty much shoots down your professional-thief theory, then, doesn't it, Mr. Washington?" H. Richard Detweiler said.

"Yes, sir. It certainly looks that way, doesn't it? We're back to Matt's theory that Miss Detweiler was an innocent bystander."

"Does that mean that whoever did this to my daughter is going to get away with it?" Grace Detweiler asked unpleasantly.

"No, ma'am," Washington said. "I think we'll find whoever did it."

"I called Jeanne Browne, Matt," Grace Detweiler said, "and told her that there is absolutely no reason to let what happened to Penny interfere with Daffy and Chad's wedding."

"I was out there this morning," Matt replied. "They were worried about it. What to do, I mean."

"Well, as I say, Mr. Detweiler and I have agreed that this should not interfere with the wedding in any way. Are we going to see you there?"

"I'll be holding Chad up," Matt said.

"Nice to have met you, Mr. Washington," she said, and marched out of the room.

"She didn't mean to jump on you that way, Matt," H. Richard Detweiler said. "She's naturally upset."

"Yes, sir," Matt said.

"Thank you very much for your cooperation, Mr. Detweiler," Washington said.

"Thank you, Mr. Washington," Detweiler said. "And you, too, Matt."

In the car Washington asked, even before they'd passed through the gate, "What's going on this afternoon? With the wedding party?"

"I don't know what you're asking," Matt confessed.

"If you weren't out Sherlock Holmesing with me, where would you be?"

Pushing a typewriter outside Wohl's office, Matt thought, then, *That's not what he's asking.*

"With Chad Nesbitt," Matt said.

"The bridegroom?"

"Yeah."

"That's what I hoped," Washington said. "Where's that gorgeous new car of yours?"

"Bustleton and Bowler."

Washington reached for the microphone, then flicked a switch.

"W-William Three," he said into the mike. "I need a Highway car to meet me at City Line and Monument."

"W-William Three, this is Highway Twenty. I'm westbound on the Schuylkill Expressway at City Line."

"Highway Twenty, meet me at City Line and Monument."

"Twenty, 'kay."

Washington put down the microphone and turned to Matt. "They'll give you a ride to get your car," he said. "What I'm hoping is that your peers will not be struck dumb when they remember you're a cop. You just might pick up something. Go through the whole business. What is that again?"

"Not much. Just the wedding itself and the reception."

"The bachelor party was last night?"

"Yeah. I missed it."

"Pity. It might have been interesting."

Washington shifted around on the seat, taking out the stuff he had removed from Penelope Detweiler's wastebasket and clothing pockets and handing it to Matt. There were half a dozen matchbooks, several crumpled pieces of paper, several tissues with what could have been spots of dried blood on them, and the small plastic vial.

"What do you think is in the vial?"

"I wouldn't be surprised if what was in the vial was cocaine," Washington said. "I'll drop it by the lab and find out. The tissues indicate she might have been injecting heroin."

Washington saw the look of mingled surprise and confusion on Matt's face and went on: "Heroin users will often dab the needle mark with tissues. Thus the blood spots. Cocaine is usually snorted or smoked, but some experienced junkies sometimes mix cocaine with their heroin and then inject it. They call it a speedball. The cocaine provides an immediate euphoria, a rush, lasting maybe fifteen, twenty, twenty-five minutes. Then the heroin kicks in, as a depressant, and brings the user down from the high into a mellow low lasting for several hours. Very powerful, very dangerous."

"Jesus," Matt said, visibly upset. Then he asked, "Is it evidence? I mean, we didn't have a search warrant or probable cause."

"No. Moot point. No Assistant DA in his right mind is going to try to indict Penelope Detweiler for simple possession."

"Her mother said she probably didn't have fifty dollars in cash; she really had seven hundred and change."

"Her mother told us the truth, as far as she knew it. I don't think she knows that her daughter is doing cocaine. But that does suggest, since Penelope uses coke and didn't have any but had a lot of money, that she was shopping for some, doesn't it?"

"From DeZego?"

"We don't know that, but—"

"Somebody was trying to rip DeZego off, and/or his customer?"

"But why the shotgun? Why kill him?" Washington replied. "Any of that stuff ring a bell?"

"Gin-mill matchbooks," Matt said. "From saloons where Penny and her kind drink."

"They all familiar?"

"This one's new to me," Matt said, holding up a large matchbook with a flocked purple cover and the legend INDULGENCES stamped in silver.

Washington glanced at it.

"New to me too," he said. "Is there an address?"

"Not outside," Matt said. He opened it. "There's a phone number, printed inside."

"I'll check that out," Washington said. "Anything else?"

Matt examined the other matchbooks.

"Phone number in this one, handwritten."

Matt unfolded the crumpled pieces of paper.

"This one has a printed number: four eight two. Looks like something from the factory. There's another phone number in one of the others, and the last one is the same as the first."

"Call in to Special Operations every hour or so. When I get addresses, I'll pass them on to you. If you come up with something, pass it on. Leave a phone number, so if something interesting turns up I think you should know, I can call you." He paused and smiled. "I'll say I'm the Porsche service department."

"Clever," Matt said, chuckling.

"Yes, I sometimes think so," Washington said. "The evidence is overwhelming."

A Highway Patrol car was waiting at City Line and Monument when Jason Washington and Matt Payne got there. Washington stopped on the pedestrian crosswalk and Matt got out. Matt walked to the Highway car, opened the back door, and got in.

"Hi," he said. "I need a ride to Bustleton and Bowler."

"What the hell are we supposed to be, a fucking taxi?" asked the driver, a burly cop with an acne-scarred face.

"I thought you were *supposed* to be the Gestapo," Matt said.

Oh, shit, there goes the automatic, out-of-control mouth again.

The Highway cop in the passenger seat, a lean, sharp-featured man with cold blue eyes, turned and put his arm on the back of the seat and looked at Matt. Then he smiled. It did not make him look much warmer.

"He can't be in the Gestapo, Payne," he said. "You have to be able to read and write to be in the Gestapo."

"Fuck you too," the driver said.

"You in a hurry or what?" the other one asked. "We was about to get coffee when we got the call."

"Coffee sounds like a fine idea," Matt said.

"Why don't we go to the Marriott on City Line?" he said to the driver, and then turned back to Matt. "Is that Washington as good as people say?"

"I was just thinking about that," Matt said. "Yeah. He's good. Very good. He not only knows what questions to ask, but how to ask them. A master psychologist."

"He better be a master something," the driver said. "They don't have shit on who shot the cop, much less the mob guy."

"Instead of going off shift," the cop with the cold blue eyes said, "we're doing four hours of overtime."

"I heard about that," Matt said. Peter Wohl had told him how it worked: While detectives rang doorbells and talked to people—conducted "neighborhood interviews"—Highway cops would cover the area, stopping people on the street and in cars, both looking for information and hoping to find someone with contraband—drugs, for example, or stolen property. If they did, the people caught would be given a chance to cooperate, in other words provide information. If they did, the contraband might get lost down the gutter or even dropped on the sidewalk where it could be recovered.

If they didn't have any information to offer, they would be arrested for the violation. By the time their trial came up, they might work hard on coming up with something the police could use, knowing that if they did and the Highway cops told one of the ADAs (assistant district attorneys) of their cooperation, he would be inclined to drop the charges.

Anyone caught in the area with an unlicensed pistol would be taken into Homicide for further questioning.

They pulled into the parking lot of the Marriott on City Line Avenue and went into the restaurant and sat at the counter. Matt sensed that they immediately had become the center of attention—much, if not most, of it nervous.

He remembered Amanda's reaction to the Highway cops in the diner at breakfast.

There is something menacing about the Highway Patrol. Is that bad? Any cop in uniform is a symbol of authority; that's why there is a badge, which, if you think about it, is descended from the coat of arms of a feudal lord and means about the same thing: I am in the service of authority. The badge says, "I am here to enforce the law, the purpose of which is to protect you. If you are obeying the law, you have nothing to fear from me. But, malefactor, watch out!"

Given that, isn't the very presence of these two, in their leather jackets and boots and rows of shiny cartridges, a deterrent to crime and thus of benefit to society? No stickup man in his right mind would try to rob this place with these two in here.

On the other hand, if some third-rate amateur came in here and saw only Officer Matthew Payne, in plainclothes, with his pistol cleverly concealed and his badge in his pocket, he would figure it was safe to help himself to what's in the cash register, using what force he considered necessary and appropriate.

A little fear of law enforcers, ergo sum, *is not necessarily a bad thing.*

There was almost immediate substantiation of Officer Payne's philosophic ruminations. The proprietor, wrapped in a grease-spotted white apron, came out from the kitchen smiling. He shook hands with both Highway Patrolmen.

"How about a cheese steak?" he asked. "I just finished slicing—"

"No, thanks," the Highway cop with the cold blue eyes said. "Just coffee."

The driver said, "Thanks, anyway. Next time."

The proprietor, Matt saw, was genuinely disappointed.

He's genuinely pleased to see the Gestapo and sorry he can't show his appreciation for what they do for him; allow him, so to speak, his constitutional right to the pursuit of happiness.

"You hungry, Payne?" the blue-eyed cop asked, then saw the look of surprise in the proprietor's eyes and added, "He might not look it, but he's a cop."

"Actually," the driver said, "he's a pretty good cop. Dave, say hello to Matt Payne. He's the guy who took down the Northwest Philly rapist."

"No *shit?*" the proprietor said, and grabbed Matt's hand. "I'm really happy to meet you. Jesus Christ, I . . . can't I get you something more than a lousy cup of coffee?"

"Coffee's fine, thank you," Matt said.

"Well, then, you got to promise to come back when you have an appetite, for chrissake. My pleasure."

"Thank you, I will," Matt said.

I'm sorry he brought that up, Matt thought. And then, *Don't be a hypocrite. No, you're not. You love it.*

There was a good deal of resentment in Highway about Staff Inspector Peter Wohl's having named Officers Jesus Martinez and Charles McFadden as "probationary Highway Patrolmen."

It was not directed toward Martinez or McFadden. It wasn't their fault. But it was almost universally perceived as a diminution of what being Highway meant. An absolute minimum of three years, most often four or five or even longer, in a district before transfer to Highway. Then Wheel School, where motorcycling skills were taught, and then a year or so patrolling I-95 and the Schuylkill Expressway, and only then, finally, being assigned to a Highway RPC and sent out to high-crime areas citywide.

Martinez had been on the job less than two years, and McFadden even less, and here they were riding around with Sergeant DeBenedito on probation, and unless he could really find something wrong with them, when they finished, they would go to Wheel School and be in Highway.

The resentment was directed primarily at Inspector Wohl, but some went toward Captain Sabara (who really should have told Wohl what a dumb idea it was, and talked him out of it) and Captain Pekach (ditto, but what can you expect from a guy who used to wear a pigtail when he was in Narcotics?).

A problem arose when Officers Martinez and McFadden reported, four hours early, for overtime duty in connection with the investigation of the murder of Officer Magnella. Written instructions, later updated, had come down from Captain Pekach's office concerning the probationary periods of Officers McFadden and Martinez. Among other things, they stated, in writing, that the probationary officers would ride with either Sergeant DeBenedito or with Highway officers on a list attached and with no one else.

Captain Pekach, who, it was suspected, was not overly enthusiastic about Inspector Wohl's brainstorm, was nevertheless determined to see that it was carried out as well as it could be. He was not going to see Martinez and McFadden turned into passengers in Highway RPCs. He spread the word that it was to be a learning experience for them, watching the best Highway cops on the job.

The list of officers who would take the probationers with them had been drawn up by Sergeant DeBenedito, approved by Captain Pekach and then by Captain Sabara. The officers on it were experienced, intelligent, and a cut above their peers.

The same qualities that had gotten them on the probationary officer supervisor's list were the qualities that had seen them assigned to ring doorbells and otherwise assist Detective Tony Harris in the investigation of the murder of Officer Magnella.

When Officers Martinez and McFadden reported, four hours early, for overtime work, Sergeant DeBenedito was not around. Inspector Wohl had learned that DeBenedito was related to Officer Magnella, had relieved him of his regular duties, and told him to do what he could for Magnella's family, both personally and as the official representative of Highway and Special Operations.

Neither was anyone on the list of Highway cops authorized to supervise the probationers available.

So what to do with Martinez and McFadden?

The first thought of Sergeant William "Big Bill" Henderson was to find something useful for them to do around Bustleton and Bowler. There was always paperwork to catch up with, and housekeeping chores. They could take care of that while *real* Highway cops went about their normal duties. He proposed this to Lieutenant Lucci.

Lieutenant Lucci had been a Highway sergeant under Mike Sabara before he had gone off to be the mayor's driver. He clearly remembered, from painful personal experience, that when Mike Sabara said something, he grew very annoyed when later he learned that only the letter, and not the spirit, of his orders had been followed. And he had been present when Captain Sabara had said, "I don't want these two riding around as passengers or shoved off somewhere in a corner."

The problem was presented to Captain David Pekach. It annoyed him. For one thing, it struck him as the sort of question that a sergeant should be able to decide on his own, without involving his lieutenant and the commanding officer. For another, Officers Martinez and McFadden had worked for him in Narcotics, and it was his judgment that they were pretty good cops who had learned more working undercover about what it takes to be a good cop in their brief careers than most cops, including some in Highway, learned in ten years.

"For chrissake, Luke!" he said, his Polish temper bubbling over slightly. "If you really need me to make this momentous decision, I will. Put them in a goddamn car and have them hand out goddamn speeding tickets on the goddamn Schuylkill Expressway!"

Almost immediately, after Lucci had fled his office, he regretted having lost his temper. What he should have done, he realized—what really would have been the most efficient utilization of available manpower resources—was to order the two of them back into civilian clothes and given them to Tony Harris. And if that had offended the prima donnas of Highway, fuck them.

But it was too late for that now that he had lost his temper and ordered the first thing that came into his mind. A commanding officer who is always changing his orders is correctly perceived by his subordinates to be someone who isn't sure what he's doing.

Lieutenant Lucci relayed the commanding officer's decision vis-à-vis Officers Martinez and McFadden to Sergeant Big Bill Henderson, who relayed it, via a ten-minute pep talk, to Martinez and McFadden.

Following a review of the applicable motor vehicle codes of the Commonwealth of Pennsylvania and the City and County of Philadelphia, he explained, in some detail, the intricacies of filling out the citation form.

Then he turned philosophical, trying to make them understand that because of the personnel shortage caused by the murder of Officer Magnella, they were being given a special opportunity to show their stuff. He could not remember, he told them (honestly) any other time when two untrained officers had been sent out by themselves in a Highway car. If they performed well, he told them, it certainly would reflect well on the report Sergeant DeBenedito would ultimately write on them. And he made the point that they should feel no embarrassment, or reluctance, to call for assistance or advice anytime they encountered a situation they weren't quite sure how to handle.

Officers Martinez and McFadden heard him out politely, then left the building and got in the Highway RPC.

"Do you believe that shit?" Jesus Martinez said.

"If I'd have known they were going to have us handing out speeding tickets, I'd have told them to stick their overtime up their ass," Charley McFadden said.

 Matt dropped change into the pay phone at the gas station where he parked his car near Special Operations, got a dial tone, and dialed a number from memory.

"Hello?"

The voice of the bridegroom-to-be did not seem to be bubbling over with joyous anticipation or anything else.

"It's not too late to change your mind," Matt said. "I believe that's known as leaving the bride at the altar."

"Where the fuck have you been? Where are you?"

"I just got off work," Matt said. "I'm at Bustleton and Bowler."

"I was getting worried."

"I can't imagine why."

"Can you get a couple of suitcases in that car of yours?"

"Sure."

"Then come get me," Chad Nesbitt ordered. "You can take me by Daffy's with my bags and then to the hotel."

"Oh, thank you! Thank you!" Matt said emotionally, but he said it to a dead telephone. Chad Nesbitt had hung up.

Second Lieutenant Chadwick T. Nesbitt IV, USMCR, was waiting under the field-stone portico of the Nesbitt mansion in Bala-Cynwyd when Matt got there. He was in uniform, freshly shaved, and sitting astride a life-size stone lion. Two identical canvas suitcases with his name, rank, and serial number stenciled on them sat beside the lion. A transparent bag held a Marine dress uniform, and there was a box that presumably held the brimmed uniform cap, and another that obviously held Chad's Marine officer's sword.

He held a stemmed glass filled with red liquid in his hand. Another glass, topped with a paper napkin, was balanced on one of the suitcases.

"It took you long enough," he greeted Matt when Matt got out of the car and walked up to him.

"Fuck you."

"Well, fuck you too. Now you don't get no Bloody Mary."

"Is that what that is?" Matt replied, picking up the glass. "Thank you, I don't mind if I do."

They smiled at each other.

"You must have had a good time last night," Matt said. "You look like the finest example of the mortician's art."

"Speaking of that, where the hell were you?"

"Fighting crime, where do you think?"

" 'Fighting crime'? Is that what you call it? Daffy said you were shacked up with What's-her-name Stevens."

"Her name is Amanda and we weren't shacked up."

"Methinks thou dost protest too much," Chad said. "Madame Browne is, of course, morally outraged at you."

"So what else is new?"

"I think I'll have another of these to give me courage to face the traffic, and then you can take us over there, and then to the hotel."

"I thought you weren't supposed to see the bride before the wedding."

"All I'm going to do is drop my bags off. Then we go to the hotel and get a little something to quiet my nerves."

"You're already—or maybe still—bombed," Matt said. "I don't want to have to carry you into the church."

"You have always been something of a prig, Payne. Have I ever told you that?"

"Often," Matt said, putting the Bloody Mary down and picking up the suitcases. "Jesus, what the hell have you got in here?"

"Just the chains and whips and handcuffs and other stuff one takes on one's bridal trip," Chad said. "Plus, of course, what every Marine second lieutenant takes with him when going off to battle the forces of Communism in far-off Okinawa."

"The sword and dress blues too?"

"I'll change into the blues at the hotel, and then out of them at Daffy's after the wedding. We don't use swords no more, you know, to battle the forces of Communism."

Matt set the suitcases on the cobblestone driveway and opened the hatch.

"Get in," he said, then, "What are your travel plans, by the way?"

"We're going into New York tonight and flying to the West Coast tomorrow."

"You're not coming back here?"

"I hope to come back, of course, but if you were asking 'after the wedding and before going overseas,' no."

He swung his leg off the stone lion, picked up Matt's Bloody Mary glass, and walked to the car.

"If you were to open the door for me, I think I could get in without spilling any of this on your pristine upholstery," he said.

Matt closed the hatch and opened the door for him. He took his Bloody Mary from him, drained it, and set the glass on the step.

When he straightened, Mrs. Chadwick T. Nesbitt III was standing there.

"I'm not at all sure that's a very good idea, Matt," she said, and then walked around him to the car.

"He insisted, Mother," Chad said. "He said he didn't think he could get through the ceremony without the assistance of a little belt."

"Well, don't let him give you any more," she said. "Have you got everything?"

"Yes, Mother."

"You're sure?"

"Yes, Mother."

"Well, then, I guess we'll see you at St. Mark's."

"God willing, and if the creek don't rise," Chad said, and slammed his door shut.

Matt walked around to the driver's side of the Porsche.

"Matt . . ." Chad's mother said.

"Yes, ma'am."

"Just . . . behave, the two of you."

"We will," Matt said.

He got behind the wheel, made a U-turn, and started down the drive to the gate.

Mrs. Nesbitt waved. Chad waved back.

"Mother, I think, is aware that she may be watching her firstborn leave the family manse for the last time," Chad said. "That somewhat discomfiting thought has occurred to me."

Matt didn't know what to say.

"If I asked you politely, would you give me a straight answer to a straight question?" Chad asked.

Matt sensed that Chad was serious. "Sure," he said.

"What does it feel like to kill somebody?"

"Jesus!"

"At the moment your experience in that area exceeds mine," Chad said, "although, to be sure, I am sure the Marine Corps plans to correct that situation as quickly as possible."

"I haven't had nightmares or done a lot of soul-searching about it," Matt said. "Nothing like that. The man I shot was a certified scumbag—"

"Interesting word," Chad said, interrupting. "Meaning, I take it, someone who has as much value as a used rubber?"

"I really don't know what it means. It's . . . cop talk. A very unpleasant individual. The same day I shot him, earlier that day I saw what he did to a woman he abducted. He raped her, tortured her, mutilated her, and then killed her. I suppose that's part of the equation. I knew that he was no fucking good."

"In other words, you were pleased that you had killed him?"

"When I saw him, he tried to run me over. He totaled my car. The only emotion I had was fear and anger. He was trying to kill me. I had a gun, so I killed him."

"Courage is defined as presence of mind under stress," Chad said.

"Then, *ergo sum,* courage was not involved in what I did," Matt said. "He had a woman in the van, another one he had abducted. It was just blind fucking luck that I didn't hit her when I was shooting at him. If I had had *'presence of mind,'* I wouldn't have shot at him at all."

"The newspapers made quite a hero of you," Chad said thoughtfully. "The Old Man sent them all to me."

"That was all bullshit," Matt said.

"Fuck you. *I'm* impressed."

"You never were very smart."

"So tell me, Sherlock, who popped Penny Detweiler?"

"We're still looking," Matt said.

"Let me give you a clue," Chad said. "Daffy said Penny knew that Eye-talian."

"Daffy told you that?"

"Surprised?"

"No," Matt said. "She tell you anything else?"

"No. Just that she knew Penny had been seeing him."

" 'Seeing,' as opposed to 'buying cocaine from'?"

"Penny's into cocaine?"

"A small voice just told me I shouldn't be talking to you about this."

"Just between thee, me, and this empty Bloody Mary glass?"

"To go absolutely no further than that, Chad, yeah. Penny has a problem with cocaine. But she doesn't know that we know, and I want to keep it that way."

"What she said was 'seeing,' " Chad said, "as in getting fucked by. She didn't say anything about dope. Are you sure about that? *Penny Detweiler?*"

"Yeah, we're sure, Chad."

" '*We're* sure,' huh? I think I liked things better when 'we' meant you and me and Daffy and Penny, and the cops were . . . well, the goddamn cops."

"I'm sorry we got into this," Matt said. "Do you suppose you could forget we did?"

"Consider it forgotten," Chad said. "But one more question?"

"You can *ask* it."

"You ever take any of that shit?"

"No."

"You never even smoked grass?"

"No."

"Me, either. But I'm beginning to suspect that it's us two Boy Scouts alone in the world."

Soames T. Browne, whom they found wandering around among the catering staff on his lawn, insisted they have a little nip with him, which turned into three before they could get away.

"You know, I really think he likes me," Chad said when they were finally back in the Porsche.

"You're taking Daffy off his hands," Matt said. "He should be overwhelmed with gratitude."

"Fuck you, Matt."

"He will be considerably less fond of you, of course, if you show up at the church shit-faced."

"Don't worry about me, buddy," Chad said confidently.

Matt dropped Chad and his sword and dress blues and uniform cap box off at the Bellevue-Stratford Hotel on South Broad Street, then drove to his apartment on Rittenhouse Square, several blocks away. The idea was that he would pick up his tails and carry them to the hotel and change there in the suite of rooms the Nesbitts had taken for Chad's out-of-town ushers.

But he decided that he would rather not do that, as it would really be easier to change in his apartment. He called Special Operations on the rent-a-cop's telephone. Jason Washington was not there, so he left word for him that he had confirmation that Penelope Detweiler knew Anthony J. DeZego and that he would be, for the next couple of hours, at the Bellevue-Stratford.

Then he walked back to the Bellevue-Stratford Hotel.

The Nesbitts had rented two large adjoining suites on the seventh floor for Chad's out-of-town guests. The Brownes had done the same thing for Daffy's friends, putting the girls up in a series of rooms on the fifth floor. It was inevitable that they should find each other, and there was a party just getting started when he got there. The official pre-wedding party, in a ballroom on the mezzanine floor, would not start for an hour.

He had been in the room less than five minutes when one of Chad's Marine Corps buddies answered the telephone, then stood on a coffee table, holding up the phone, and bellowed, *"At ease!"*

When he had everyone's attention, some of it shocked, he politely inquired, "Is there a Mr. Matthew Payne in the house?"

"Here," Matt said, and went and took the phone, certain that it would be Jason Washington. It was not.

"Matt, if he comes to the church drunk," Daffy Browne said, "I'll never speak to you again as long as I live."

"Would you be willing to put that in writing?"

"Oh, Matt, *please!*"

"I'll do my best, Daffy," Matt said.

"Try to remember this is the most important day in our *lives*," Daffy said.

"Right."

"He listens to you, Matt, you know he does."

He was looking at Chad Nesbitt. Chad had a Bloody Mary in his hand.

Bullshit, he listens to me!

"Relax, Daphne," he said. "I'll get him to the church on time."

Daffy was not amused. She hung up. Matt put the telephone down and walked over to Chad.

"That was the bride-to-be," he said. "She wants you sober for the wedding."

"Well, one doesn't always get what one wishes, does one?"

"Come on, Chad. You get pissed and I'm the villain."

"Who's going to get pissed?"

Matt decided he was wasting his breath.

If he wants to drink, he will drink. He does not listen to me. If he gets pissed, Daffy will be pissed off with me, and that means that I will not be able to get her alone and ask her, between old pals, what she knows about Penny and Tony the Zee. Shit!

A gentle hand brushed his back.

"I thought maybe you'd be here," Amanda said.

She was so close that he could smell her perfume. She was wearing a skirt and a crisp white blouse.

Jesus, she's beautiful!

"Hi," he said.

"I understand that this disreputable character has been keeping you out all night," Chad said to Amanda.

Amanda walked away without replying, or even showing that she had heard him. Matt walked after her. She headed for the door; he caught up with her there.

"Where are you going?" he asked.

"If you're having a good time," she said, "by all means stay."

He followed her into the corridor and to the elevator.

"I heard all that," she said. "You did everything you could be expected to do."

"Tell Daffy," he said.

"I intend to," Amanda said.

That pleased him very much.

"There's a couple of bars right here in the hotel," he said as they stepped onto the elevator.

"No bars, thank you," she said.

"Okay. Then how about Professor Payne's famous walking tour of downtown Philadelphia until it's time for the cocktail party?"

"No cocktail party for me, thank you just the same."

"Then where would you like to go? What would you like to do?"

She looked up at him with mischief, and something else, in her eyes.

"Really?" he asked after a moment.

"Really," she said.

Somehow their hands touched and then grasped, and holding hands, they walked out of the elevator and through the lobby and then to the apartment over the Delaware Valley Cancer Society on Rittenhouse Square.

At five minutes to five Lieutenant Tony Lucci knocked at Staff Inspector Peter Wohl's office door, waited to be told to come in, and then announced, "Everyone's here, Inspector."

"Ask them to come in, please, Tony," Wohl said. He was sitting on the front edge of his desk. Chief Inspector Dennis V. Coughlin and his driver, Sergeant Tom Lenihan, who had come to Bustleton and Bowler ten minutes before, were sitting on the couch.

"Harris has the Lewis kid with him, Inspector. Him too?"

"Why not?"

I recognize your dilemma, Tony, my boy. His Honor the Mayor has told you to keep your eye on things, or words to that effect. And now, with, so to speak, a conference at the highest levels of this little fiefdom about to take place behind a closed door without you, you don't quite know how to handle it. Are you going to ask if I want you in here? If you do that, it would be tantamount to admitting that you are functioning as the mayor's little birdie. Or are you going, so to speak, to put your ear to the keyhole? Desperately hoping, of course, that I won't catch you at it.

"Yes, sir," Lucci said.

Captains Mike Sabara and David Pekach, Detectives Jason Washington and Tony Harris, and Officer Foster H. Lewis, Jr., filed into the office.

Lieutenant Lucci stood in the open door, almost visibly hoping that he would be told to come in.

"Chief," Wohl said, "do you know Officer Lewis?"

"How are you?" Coughlin said, offering his hand. "I know your dad."

Wohl looked at Lucci in the door, his eyebrows raised in question. Lucci quickly closed the door.

"For reasons I can't imagine, Officer Lewis is known as Tiny," Wohl said. "He's been helping Tony."

There were chuckles and Coughlin said, "Good experience for you, son."

"Tiny, would you ask Lucci to come in here?" Wohl said.

Coughlin looked at Wohl curiously as Tiny went to the door.

Lucci appeared in a moment.

"Tony, get yourself a pad and sit in on this, please," Wohl said. Lucci disappeared for a moment, then returned with a stenographer's notebook and three pencils in his hand.

"Tony, I want you to make note of anything you think the mayor would like to know. I know he's interested in what we're doing, and you're obviously the best person to tell him. From now on I want you to stay in close touch with him, so that he's up-to-date on what's happening."

"Yes, sir," Lucci said, now very confused.

Coughlin's and Wohl's eyes met for a moment; Wohl thought he saw both amusement and approval in Coughlin's eyes.

This is either proof of my general, all-around brilliance in How to Deal with the Honorable Jerry Carlucci, or one more proof of the adage that when rape is inevitable, the thing to do is relax and enjoy it.

"From now until we can clear these jobs—Officer Magnella, Anthony J. DeZego, and Penelope Detweiler," Wohl began, "I think we should have a meeting like this every day. At this time of day, probably, but that can be changed if need be. And I think we should start by hearing what Tony has."

"I've got zilch," Tony Harris said.

"That's encouraging," Coughlin said sarcastically.

"Officer Magnella, on routine patrol in the 22nd District," Harris said, "was shot by the side of his RPC near the intersection of Colombia and Clarion between eleven-ten and eleven twenty-five. We know the time because he met with his sergeant at eleven-ten, and the call from the civilian that a cop had been shot came at eleven twenty-five. The medical examiner has determined that the cause of death is trauma caused by five .22-caliber—.22 Long Rifle, specifically—lead bullets, four in the chest, and one in the upper left leg.

"Officer Magnella did not, *did not,* get on the radio to report that he was doing anything at all. When he met with his sergeant, he did not indicate to him that anything at all was out of the ordinary. In fact, he commented that it had been an unusually quiet night. Neither his sergeant, nor his lieutenant, was aware of him taking any kind of a special interest in anything in his patrol area. *Nobody* in the 22nd had any idea that he was onto something special. There have been no reports of any special animosity toward him specifically, or the 22nd generally.

"There are *no* known witnesses, except, of course, the civilian who called Emergency and reported him down. That civilian is not identified and has not come forward. Obviously he—the tape suggests it was a male, probably white and probably around forty—doesn't want to get involved.

"No one in the neighborhood heard anything unusual, including shots. A .22 doesn't make a hell of a lot of noise.

"Everything I have been able to turn up suggests that Magnella was a straight arrow. He didn't gamble; he hardly drank; he was about to get married to a girl from his neighborhood; he was a churchgoer; he didn't drink—I said that, didn't I? Anyway, there's nothing to suggest that the shooting was connected to anything in his personal life—"

"What's your gut feeling, Tony?" Chief Coughlin asked, interrupting.

"Chief, what I think is he saw something, a couple of kids, a drunk, a hooker, nothing he considered really threatening. And he stopped the car and got out and they—or maybe even *she*—shot him."

"Why?" Coughlin asked.

Harris shrugged and held his hands up in a gesture of helplessness.

"So where are you now, Tony?" Coughlin asked.

"Going over it all again. There are some people in the neighborhood we haven't talked to yet. We're going to talk to people who work in the neighborhood. We're going to check everybody Magnella ever arrested. We're going to talk to his family again, and people in his neighborhood—"

"You need anything?" Coughlin asked.

That's my question, Wohl thought. *But Coughlin wanted to ask it so that when Tony says, "Can't think of anything," he can say, "Well, if there's anything at all you need, speak up." And Lucci will report that to the mayor, that Chief Coughlin is staying on top of things.*

"Can't think of anything, Chief," Tony Harris said.

"Well, if there's anything you need, anything at all, speak up," Coughlin said.

"You getting everything you need from Homicide?" Wohl asked.

"Yeah, sure," Harris said. "Lou Natali even called me up and asked if there was anything he could do. Said Chief Lowenstein told him to."

"I'm sure that it's just a matter of time, Tony," Coughlin said.

"Jason?" Wohl asked.

"Nothing. Well, not quite nothing. We found out the Detweiler girl uses cocaine, and we found out she knew DeZego, so that's where we're headed."

"You're sure about that?" Coughlin asked. "Detweiler's daughter is using cocaine?"

"I'm sure about that," Washington said evenly.

"Jesus!" Coughlin said. "And she knew DeZego?"

"I got that just a couple of minutes ago when I came in," Washington said. "Matt Payne left a message."

"I thought he was working with you. I mean, why isn't he here?" Coughlin asked.

"He's at the wedding. I thought he might hear something. He did. I wouldn't be surprised if he heard a little more at the reception."

"I thought you were working on the scenario that the Detweiler girl was just an innocent bystander," Coughlin said.

"That was before we found out she's using cocaine and knew DeZego."

"Any other explanation could turn into a can of worms, Jason," Coughlin said.

"I'm getting a gut feeling, Chief, that what happened on the roof was that somebody wanted to pop DeZego. I have no idea why. But if that holds up, if DeZego getting popped wasn't connected, in other words, with cocaine or robbery—but had something to do with the mob is what I'm trying to say—then the Detweiler girl could very easily really be an innocent bystander."

"Yeah," Coughlin said thoughtfully, adding, "It could very well be something like that."

You'd like that, wouldn't you, Chief? Wohl thought, somewhat unpleasantly. *That would eliminate that can of worms you're talking about.*

"I'm going to see Jim Osgood when I leave here," Washington said. "Maybe he'll have something."

Lieutenant James H. Osgood, of the Organized Crime Division, was the department expert on the internal workings of the mob (actually, *mobs*) and the personal lives of their members.

"You waited until now to get into that?" Coughlin asked. It was a reprimand.

"I was over there at eight this morning, Chief," Washington said, "before I went to Hahneman to see the girl. Osgood was in New York. He got back, was supposed to get back, at five."

"If anyone would have a line on something like that, it would be Osgood," Chief Coughlin said somewhat lamely.

"Chief," Wohl asked, "am I under any sort of budgetary restrictions about overtime?"

"Absolutely not!" Coughlin said emphatically. "You spend whatever you think is necessary, Peter, on overtime or anything else."

I hope you wrote that down, Lucci. I'm sure that Chief Coughlin really wants that on the record, for the mayor to know that he personally authorized me to spend whatever I think is necessary on overtime or anything else. The son of a bitch is covering his ass *while he hangs me out in the wind.*

"Anybody else got anything?" Wohl asked.

Heads shook. "No."

"Chief, have you got anything else?" Wohl asked.

"No. I'm going to get out of here and let you and your people get on with it," Coughlin said.

He got out of the couch, shook hands with everyone in the room, and left.

"I think this is where, as your commanding officer, I am expected to say something inspiring," Wohl said.

They all looked at him.

" 'Something inspiring,' " Wohl said. "Get the hell out of here. I'll see you tomorrow."

When they had all gone, Wohl closed the door after them and then sat on the edge of his desk again and pulled the phone to him.

"Yes?" a gruff voice asked.

"Buy you a beer?"

"Come to supper."

"I don't want to, Dad," Wohl said.

"Oh," Chief Inspector August Wohl (retired) said. "Downey's, Front and South, in half an hour?"

"Fine. Thanks."

 Captain David Pekach was relieved when the meeting in Wohl's office broke up so quickly. Under the circumstances it could have gone on for hours.

Both he and Mike Sabara followed Lieutenant Lucci to his desk, where Sabara told Lucci he would either be at home or at St. Sebastian's Church; Lucci had both numbers. Pekach told him that he would be at either of the two numbers he had given Lucci, and from half past seven at the Ristorante Alfredo downtown. He wrote the number down and gave it to Lucci.

Lucci and Sabara exchanged smiles.

"Big date, Dave, huh?" Sabara asked.

"I'm taking a lady friend to dinner, all right?" Pekach snapped. "Is there anything wrong with that?"

"Wow!" Sabara said. "What did I do? Strike a raw nerve?"

Pekach glared at him, then walked toward the door to the parking lot.

"Nice watch, Dave," Sabara called after him.

Pekach turned and gave him the finger, then stormed out of the building. Sabara and Lucci grinned at each other.

"What was that about the watch?" Lucci asked.

"His *'lady friend'* gave him a watch for his birthday," Sabara said. "An Omega. Gold. With all the dials. What do you call it, a chronometer?"

"Chrono*graph,"* Lucci said. "Gold, huh?"

"Gold," Sabara confirmed.

"Why's he so sensitive about her?" Lucci asked, deciding at the last moment not to tell Captain Sabara that he had heard Captain Pekach's lady friend call him Precious when he had called him at her house.

"I don't know," Sabara replied. "I've seen her. She's not at all bad-looking. Nothing for him to be ashamed of."

She was Miss Martha Ellen Peebles, a female Caucasian thirty-four years and six months old, weighing 121 pounds and standing five feet four inches tall.

Miss Peebles resided alone, in a turn-of-the-century mansion at 606 Glengarry Lane in Chestnut Hill. There was a live-in couple—a chauffeur-butler-majordomo and a housekeeper-cook—who were in turn helped by a constantly changing staff of maids and groundskeepers, most often nieces and nephews of the live-in couple, who kept the place up.

The house had been built by Alexander F. Peebles, who owned, among other things, what the *Wall Street Journal* estimated was eleven percent of the nation's anthracite coal reserves. Mr. Peebles had one son, Alexander, Jr., who in turn had two children, Martha, and her brother Stephen, four years younger.

Mrs. Alexander Peebles, Jr., had died of cancer when Martha was twelve and Stephen eight. Alexander Peebles decided on the night that God finally put his wife out of her misery that his daughter was an extraordinarily good creature. Martha, who was entitled to being comforted by him on the loss of her mother, had instead come to him, in his gun-room sanctuary, where he was wallowing in Scotch-soaked self-pity, and comforted him. He was not to worry, Martha had told him; she would take care of him from now on.

Mr. Peebles never remarried and devoted the remaining eighteen years of his life to his quest for grouse in Scotland, big game in Africa, trophy sheep in the Rocky Mountains, and his collection of pre-1900 American firearms.

Since Martha truly believed she was taking care of him, her father didn't think it right to leave her at home in the company of a governess or some other domestic, so he engaged a tutor-companion for her and took her along on his hunting trips.

Their adoration was mutual. Martha thought her father was perfect in all respects. He thought she embodied all the desirable feminine traits of beauty and gentility. Her reaction to learning, while they were shooting Cape Buffalo in what was then still the Belgian Congo, that Miss Douglass, her tutor-companion, was sharing his cot was, he thought, simply splendid. One simply didn't expect that sort of sympathetic, sophisticated understanding from a sixteen-year-old girl. And by then she was as good a shot as most men he knew. What more could a father expect of a daughter?

Alexander Peebles, Jr.'s, relationship with his son was nowhere near so idyllic. The boy had always been delicate. That was probably genetic, he decided, inherited from his mother's side of the family. Her father had died young, he recalled, and her two brothers looked like librarians.

The several times he had tried to include Stephen, when he turned sixteen, in hunting trips had been disasters. When Stephen had finally managed to hit a deer-for-the-safari-pot in Tanganyika, he had looked down at the carcass and wept. The next year, after an absolutely splendid day of shooting driven pheasant on the Gladstone estate in Scotland, when their host had asked him what he thought of pheasant shooting, Stephen had replied, "Frankly I think it's disgusting slaughter."

When Alex Peebles had told his son that his remark had embarrassed him and Martha, Stephen had replied, "Tit for tat, Father. *I* am grossly embarrassed having a father who brings a whore along on a trip with his children."

Alex Peebles, furious at his defiant attitude and at his characterization of Karen Cayworth (who really had had several roles in motion pictures before giving up her acting career to become his secretary) as a whore, had slapped his son, intending only that, not a dislocated jaw.

Predictably, Martha had stood by her father and gone with Stephen to the hospital and then ridden with him on the train to London and put him on the plane home. She had then returned to Scotland. But the damage had been done, of course. Lord Gladstone was polite but distant, and Alex Peebles knew that it would be a long time before he was asked to shoot the estate again.

Five months after that, a month before he was to graduate, Stephen was expelled from Groton for what the headmaster called "the practice of unnatural vice."

From then on, until his death of a heart attack in the Rockies at fifty-six, Alex Peebles had as little to do with his son as possible. He put him on an allowance and gave him to understand that he was not welcome in the house on Glengarry Lane when his father was at home.

Martha, predictably, urged him to forgive and forget, but he could not find it in himself to do so. He relented to the point of offering, via Martha, to arrange for whatever psychiatric treatment was necessary to cure him of his sexual deviance. Stephen, as predictably, refused, and so far as Alex Peebles was concerned, that was that.

Alex Peebles's last will and testament was a very brief document. It left all of his worldly possessions, of whatever kind and wherever located, to his beloved daughter, Martha, of whom he was as proud as he was ashamed of his son, to whom, consequently, he was leaving nothing.

It did occur to Alex Peebles that Martha, being the warmhearted, generous, indeed Christian young woman that she was, would certainly continue to provide some sort of financial support for her brother. Stephen would not end up in the gutter.

It never entered Alex Peebles's mind that Martha, once the to-be-expected grief passed, would have trouble getting on with her own life. She was not at all bad-looking, and a damn good companion, and he was, after all, leaving her both a great deal of money and a law firm, Mawson, Payne, Stockton, McAdoo & Lester, which he felt sure would manage her affairs as well, and as honestly, as they could.

Equally important—perhaps even more so—Martha was highly intelligent, well read, and levelheaded. Somewhere down the pike a man would enter her life. It was not unreasonable to hope that she would name her firstborn son after her father, Alexander Peebles Whatever.

He erred. Matha Peebles was devastated by the death of her father, and her perception of herself as a thirty-year-old woman literally all alone in the world, rather than passing, grew worse.

A self-appointed delegation of her mother's family pressed her soon after the will was probated to share her inheritance with her brother. Stephen's "peculiarities," they argued, were not his fault and probably should be laid at his father's feet. His treatment of his son, they said, was barbaric.

When she refused to do that, deciding it would constitute disobedience, literally, of her father's last will and testament, she understood that she was more than likely closing the door on any relationship she might have developed with them. That prediction soon proved to be true.

She came to understand that while she had a large number of acquaintances, she had very few, almost no, friends. There were overtures of friendship, to be sure. Some of them were genuine, but she quickly understood that she had virtually nothing in common with other well-to-do women in Philadelphia except money. She hadn't been in any school long enough to make a lifelong best friend, and felt that it was too late to try to do so now.

There was some attention from men, but she suspected that much of it was because they knew (from a rather nasty lawsuit Stephen had undertaken and lost, to break his father's will) that she alone owned Tamaqua Mining and everything else. And none of the suitors, if that word fit, really interested her.

The hunting was gone too. It was not the sort of thing a single woman could do by herself, even if she had wanted to, and without her father she had no interest in going.

She forced herself to take an interest in the business, going so far as to spend three months in Tamaqua and Hazleton, and taking courses in both mineralogy and finance at the University of Pennsylvania. Taking the courses became an end in itself. It passed the time, got her out of the house every day, and posed a challenge to her when an essay was required or an examination was to be taken.

Three years after their father died, she allowed Stephen to move back into the house. Or didn't throw him out when he moved back in without asking. She didn't want to fight with him, the court suit had been a terrible experience, she was lonely, and they could at least take some meals together.

But that didn't work, either. Stephen's young friends proved to be difficult. They didn't like him; she saw that. They were selling themselves to him. There wasn't much difference, she came to think, between her father's "secretaries" and Stephen's young men. While there probably was not an actual cash payment in either case, there were gifts and surprises that amounted to the same thing.

And when the gifts and surprises were not judged to be adequate by Stephen's young men, there were either terrible scenes or the theft of things they saw in the house. That came to a head with a handsome young man named William Walton, who said he was an actor.

She went to Stephen and told him she was sure that his friend, William Walton, was stealing things, and Stephen told her, almost hysterically, that she didn't know what she was talking about. When she insisted that she knew precisely what she was talking about, he said some very cruel things to her. She told Stephen that the next time something turned up missing, she was going to the police.

It did and she did, and the police came and did nothing. When Stephen heard about her calling the police, there was another scene, ending when she told him he had two days to find someplace else to live.

Stephen had moved out the next day. She had come down the stairs as he was putting his suitcases out and he had seen her.

"I'm sorry it's come to this, Stephen," she said.

He had looked up at her with hate in his eyes.

"Get fucked!" he had shouted. "You crazy goddamn bitch, get fucked! That's what you need, a good fuck!"

He's beside himself, she decided, *because I told him to get out and because he knows that I was right, that his William Walton doesn't really like him for himself and really is stealing things. As long as he could pretend he wasn't stealing things, he could pretend that William Walton liked him for himself.*

She had turned and gone back upstairs and into the gun room and wept. The gun room had been her father's favorite place, and now it was hers.

What Stephen had said, "Get fucked," now bothered her. Not the words but what they meant.

Why haven't *I been fucked? I am probably the only thirty-four-year-old virgin in the world, with the possible exception of cloistered nuns. The most likely possibility is that I am not so attractive to men so as to make them really try to overcome what is my quite natural maidenly reticence. Another possibility, of course, is that my natural maidenly reticence has been reinforced by the fact that I have encountered very few (unmarried) men who I thought I would like to have do that to me. Or is it "with" me?*

And there is another possibility, rather disgusting to think of, and that is that I am really like Stephen, a deviate, a latent Lesbian. Otherwise, wouldn't I have had by now some of that overwhelming hunger, to be fucked, so to speak, that all the heroines in the novels are always experiencing? Or, come to think of it, some women I know have practically boasted about? Why don't *my pants get wet when some man touches my arm—or paws my breast?*

Realizing that she was slipping into depression, which, of late, had meant that she would drink more than was good for her, she resolved to fight it.

She took out a bottle of the port her father had liked so much and taught her to appreciate, and drank two glasses of it, and not a drop more, and then left the gun room, carefully locking it after her.

In the next two days there were more thefts of bric-a-brac and other valuables, and she called the police again, and again they did nothing.

So she got in her car and drove downtown to see Colonel J. Dunlop Mawson, one of the senior partners in the law firm of Mawson, Payne, Stockton, McAdoo & Lester in the Philadelphia Savings Fund Society Building. Colonel Mawson wasn't there, but another senior partner, Brewster C. Payne, of whom, she remembered, her father had spoken admiringly, saw her.

She told him what was going on, of the thefts and the break-ins, and how the po-

lice had been absolutely useless. He tried to talk her into moving out of the house until the police could get to the bottom of what was happening. She told him she had
no intention of being run out of her own house.

He told her that Colonel Mawson and Police Commissioner Czernich were great
friends, and that as soon as Colonel Mawson returned to the office, he would tell him
of their conversation and that he felt sure Colonel Mawson would get some action
from the police.

The very same day, late in the afternoon, Harriet Evans, the gentle black woman
who—with her husband—had been helping them run the house as long as Martha
could remember, came upstairs and said, "Miss Martha, there's another policeman to
see you. This one's a captain."

Miss Martha Peebles received Captain David Pekach, commanding officer of the
Highway Patrol, in the upstairs sitting room. She explained the problem all over again
to him, including her suspicion that Stephen's "actor" friend was the culprit. He assured her that the entire resources of the Highway Patrol would from that moment
guarantee the inviolability of her property.

Somehow in conversation it came out that Captain Pekach was not a married man.
And she mentioned her father's weapons, and he expressed interest, and, somewhat
reluctantly, she took him to the gun room.

When he showed particular interest in one piece, she identified it for him: "That
is a U.S. rifle, that is to say, a military rifle, Model of 1819—"

"With a J. H. Hall action," Captain Pekach interrupted.

"Oh, do you know weapons?"

"And stamped with the initials of the proving inspector," he went on. "Z. E. H."

"Zachary Ellsworth—" Martha began to explain.

"Hampden," Captain Pekach concluded as their eyes met. "Captain, Ordnance
Corps, later Deputy Chief of Ordnance."

"He was born in Allentown, you know," Martha said.

"No. I didn't know."

"There are some other pieces you might find interesting, Captain," Martha said, "if
I'm not taking you away from something more important."

He looked at his watch.

"I'm running late now," he said.

"I understand," she said.

"But perhaps some other time?"

"If you like."

He gestured around the gun room.

"I could happily spend the next two years in here," he said.

He means that. He does want to come back!

"Well, perhaps when you get off duty," she said.

He looked pained.

"Miss Peebles, I'm commanding officer of the Highway Patrol. We're trying very
hard to find the man the newspapers are calling the Northwest Philadelphia serial
rapist."

"Yes, I read the papers."

"I want to speak to the men coming off their shifts, to see if they may have come
up with something. That will keep me busy, I'm afraid, until twelve-thirty or so."

"I understand," she said. Then she heard herself say, actually shamelessly and brazenly lie, "Captain, I'm a night person. I rarely go to bed until the wee hours. I'm sure if you drove past here at one, or even two, there would be lights on."

"Well, I had planned to check on your property before going home," he said. "I've stationed officers nearby."

"Well, then, by all means, if you see a light, come in. I'll give you a cup of coffee."

After five minutes past one that morning Martha Peebles could no longer think of herself as the world's oldest virgin, except for cloistered nuns, perhaps.

And her father, she thought, would have approved of David, once he had gotten to know him. They were very much alike in many ways. Not superficially. Inside.

Martha knew from the very beginning, which she placed as the moment, post-coitus, that he had reached out to her and rolled her over onto him, so that she lay with her face against the hair on his chest, listening to the beat of his heart, feeling the firm muscles of his leg against hers, that David was the man she had been waiting for—without of course knowing it—all her life.

Captain David Pekach drove directly from the meeting in Staff Inspector Peter Wohl's office at Bustleton and Bowler to 606 Glengarry Lane in Chestnut Hill. He parked his unmarked car in one of the four garage stalls in what had been the carriage house behind the house, then walked back down the drive to the entrance portico.

The door opened as he got there.

"Good evening, Captain," Evans, the black guy, greeted him. He was wearing a gray cotton jacket and a black bow tie.

"What do you say, Evans?"

"Miss Martha said to say that if you would like to change, she will be with you in a moment."

"We're going to dinner," Pekach said.

"So I understand, sir. Can I get you a drink, Captain? Or a glass of beer?"

"A beer would be fine, thank you," Pekach said.

"I'll bring it right up, sir," Evans said, smiling.

Martha had told David that Evans "adores you, and so does Harriet," and Evans was always pleasant enough, but there was something about him—and about his wife—living in the house and knowing about him and Martha that made Pekach uncomfortable.

Pekach climbed the wide curving stairs and went down the corridor to "his room." That was a little game they were playing. The story was that because he lived to hell-and-gone on the other side of Philadelphia, he sometimes "stayed over." When he "stayed over," he stayed in a guest room, which just happened to have a connecting door to Martha's bedroom.

Every time he "stayed over," which was more the rule than the exception, either he or Martha carefully mussed the sheets on the bed in the guest room, sometimes by even bouncing up and down on them. And every morning either Harriet or one of the nieces made up the guest-room bed and everyone pretended that was where he had slept.

When he went in the guest room, there was clothing, not his, on what—because he didn't know the proper term—he called the clotheshorse. It was a mahogany device designed to hold a jacket and trousers. There was a narrow shelf behind the jacket hanger, intended, he supposed, to hold your wallet and change and watch. He had never seen any clothing on it and had never used it. He hung his uniforms and clothes in an enormous wardrobe.

When he opened the wardrobe to change into civilian clothing, there was another surprise. He had expected to find his dark blue suit and his new gray flannel suit (Martha bought it for him at Brooks Brothers, and he hated to remember what it had cost). The wardrobe was now nearly full of men's clothing, but neither his dark blue suit nor his new gray flannel suit was among them.

"What the hell?" he muttered, confused. He turned from the wardrobe. Both Evans (bearing a tray with a bottle of beer and a pilsner glass) and Martha were entering the room.

Martha was wearing a black dress and a double string of pearls long enough to reach her bosom.

My God, she's good-looking!

"Oh, damn, you haven't tried it on yet!" Martha said.

"Tried what on?"

"That, of course, silly," she said, and pointed at the clothing on the clotheshorse.

"That's not mine," he said.

"Yes and no, Precious," Martha said. "Try it on."

She took the coat—he saw now that it was a blue blazer with brass buttons.

"Honey," he said, "I told you I don't want you buying me any more clothes."

"And I haven't," she said. "Have I, Evans?"

"No, Captain, she hasn't."

There was nothing to do but put the jacket on. It was double-breasted and it fit.

"Perfect," Evans said.

"Look at the buttons," Martha said. He looked. The brass buttons were the official brass buttons of the Police Department of the City of Philadelphia.

"Thank Evans for that," Martha said. "You have no idea how much trouble he had getting his hands on those."

"Where did the coat come from?"

"Tiller and Whyde, I think," Martha said.

"That's right, Miss Martha," Evans confirmed.

"What the hell is that?"

"Daddy's tailor—one of them—in London," Martha said. "Precious, you look wonderful in it!"

"This is your father's?" he asked. The notion made him slightly uncomfortable, quite aside from considerations of Martha getting him clothes.

"No, it's yours. *Now* it's yours."

"I suggested to Miss Martha, Captain," Evans said, "that you and Mr. Alex were just about the same size, and all his clothes were here, just waiting to feed the moths."

"So we checked, and Evans was right, and all we had to do was take the trousers in a half inch, and an inch off the jacket sleeves, and of course find your policeman's buttons. Evans knows this marvelous Italian tailor on Chestnut Street, so all you have to do is say 'Thank you, Evans.' "

"*All* of those clothes?" Pekach said, pointing to the wardrobe.

"Mr. Alex always dressed very well," Evans said.

Captain David Pekach came very close to saying *Oh, shit, I don't want your father's goddamn clothes.*

But he didn't. He saw a look of genuine pleasure at having done something nice on Evans's face, and then he looked at Martha and saw how happy her eyes were.

"Thank you, Evans," Captain Pekach said.

"My pleasure, Captain. I'm just glad the sizes worked out; that you were just a little smaller than Mr. Alex, rather than the other way around."

"It worked out fine, thank you, Evans."

Evans smiled and left the room.

"I don't know what I'm going to do with you," Pekach said to Martha.

She met his eyes and smiled. "Oh, you'll think of something."

Martha walked to where Evans had left the beer, poured some skillfully in the glass, and handed it to Pekach.

"I love it when I can do something nice for you, my Precious," she said.

He kissed her gently, tasting her lipstick.

"I better take a shower," he said.

She came into the bathroom, as she often did, and watched him shave. She had told him she liked to do that, to feel his cheeks when he had just finished shaving.

When they went downstairs, Evans had brought her Mercedes coupe around to the portico from the garage, and was holding the door open for her. Pekach got behind the wheel and glanced at her to make sure she had her seat belt fastened. There was a flash of thigh and of the lace at the hem of her black slip.

For a woman who didn't know the first fucking thing about sex, he thought for perhaps the fiftieth time, *she really knows how to pick underwear that turns me on.*

He put the Mercedes in gear, drove down the drive to Glengarry Lane, and idly decided that the best route downtown would be the Schuylkill Expressway.

Just north of the Zoological Gardens, Martha asked if they had caught whoever had shot the policeman.

"No. And we don't have a clue," Pekach said. "Just before I came ... to your place"—he'd almost said "home"—"we had a meeting, and Tony Harris, who's running the job, and is a damn good cop, said all he knows to do is go back over what he already has."

"You almost said 'home,' " Martha said, "didn't you?"

He looked at her and was surprised to find they were holding hands.

"Slip of the tongue," he said.

"Nice slip, I like it."

"You too."

"I beg your pardon?"

"I like your slip," he said.

"Oh," she said. "Thank you."

She raised his hand to her mouth and kissed it.

There was the howl of a siren. He looked in the rearview mirror and saw a Highway car behind him and dropped his eyes to the large round speedometer of the Mercedes. The indicator was pointing just beyond seventy.

"Shit," he said, freed his hand, and moved into the right lane.

The Highway car pulled up beside him. The police officer in the passenger seat gestured imperiously for him to pull to the curb, the gesture turning into a friendly wave as Officer Jesus Martinez, a stricken look on his face, recognized the commanding officer of the Highway Patrol. The Highway car suddenly slowed and fell behind.

"I hate that," Pekach said. "Getting caught by my own men."

"Then you shouldn't speed, Precious." Martha laughed. "You should see your face!"

"It's this damn car," Pekach said. "They don't know it. If we were in my car, that wouldn't have happened."

"Then you should drive this car more, so they get to know it."

"I couldn't drive your car to work," he said.

"Why not?"

"Because it's yours."

"Let me give it to you, then."

"Martha, goddammit, stop!"

"We've been over this before," she said. "It makes me happy to give you things."

"It's not right," he said.

"I love you and I can easily afford it, so what's wrong with it?"

"It's not right," he repeated.

"Sorry," Martha said.

"Honey, you always giving me things . . ." He searched for the words. "It makes me feel less than a man."

"That's absurd," she said. "Look at yourself! As young as you are, being a captain. Commanding Officer of Highway. You're worried about being a man?"

He didn't reply.

"And that's not the only manly thing you do very well," Martha said. She leaned over and put her tongue in his ear and groped him.

"Jesus, honey!"

"You must be getting tired of me," Martha teased. "I remember when you used to like that."

"I'm not tired of you, baby," he said. "I could never get tired of you."

"So then let me give you the car."

"Will you ever quit?"

"Probably not," she said, and caught his hand and held it against her cheek. Then she asked, "Where are we going? Not that it matters."

"Ristorante Alfredo," he said, trying to pronounce it in Italian.

"I hear that's very nice."

"Peter Wohl says it is," Pekach said. "I asked him for a good place to go, and he said Ristorante Alfredo is very nice."

"You like him, don't you?"

"He's a good boss. He doesn't *act* much like a cop, but from his reputation and from what I've seen, he's a hell of a cop."

What Peter Wohl had said specifically were that there were two nice things about Ristorante Alfredo. First, that the food and atmosphere were first-class; and second, that the management had the charming habit of picking up the tab.

"The Mob owns it, I guess you know," Wohl had said. "They get some sort of perverse pleasure out of buying captains and up their meals. You're a captain now, Dave. Enjoy. Rank hath its privileges. I try to make them happy at least once a month."

Dave Pekach had made reservations for dinner at Ristorante Alfredo because of what Wohl had said about the food and atmosphere. He wasn't sure that Wohl wasn't pulling his leg about having the check grabbed. If that happened, fine, but he wasn't counting on it. He even sort of hoped they wouldn't. It was important somehow that he take Martha someplace that she would enjoy, preferably expensive.

There was a young Italian guy (a *real* Italian, to judge by the way he mangled the language) in a tuxedo behind a sort of stand-up desk in the lobby of Ristorante Alfredo. When Pekach said his name was Pekach and that he had made reservations, the guy almost pissed his pants unlatching a velvet rope and bowing them past it to a table in a far corner of the room.

Dave saw other diners in the elegantly furnished room looking at Martha in her black dress and pearls, and the way she walked, and he was proud of her.

The Italian guy in the tuxedo held Martha's chair for her and said he hoped the table was satisfactory, and then he snapped his fingers and two other guys appeared, a busboy and a guy in a short red jacket with what looked like a silver spoon on a gold chain around his neck. The busboy had a bottle wrapped in a towel in a silver bucket on legs.

The guy with the spoon around his neck unwrapped the towel so that Dave could see that what he had was a bottle of French champagne.

"Compliments of the house, Captain Pekach," the Italian guy said. "I hope is satisfactory."

"Oh, Moet is always satisfactory," Martha said, smiling.

"You permit?" the Italian guy said, and unwrapped the wire, popped the cork, and poured about a quarter of an inch in Pekach's glass.

I'm supposed to sip that, to make sure it's not sour or something, Dave remembered, and did so.

"Very nice," he said.

"I am so happy," the Italian guy said, and poured Martha and then Pekach each a glassful.

"I leave you to enjoy wine," the Italian guy said. "In time I will recommend."

"To us," Martha said, raising her glass.

"Yeah," Dave Pekach said.

A waiter appeared a minute or so later and delivered menus.

And a minute or so after that the Italian guy came back.

"Captain Pekach, you will excuse. Mr. Baltazari would be so happy to have a minute of your time," he said, and gestured across the room to the far corner where two men sat at a corner table. When they saw him looking, they both gave a little wave.

Dave Pekach decided the younger one, a swarthy-skinned man with hair elaborately combed forward to conceal male pattern baldness, must be Baltazari, whom he had never heard of. The other man, older, in a gray suit, he knew by sight. On a cork bulletin board in the Intelligence Division, his photograph was pinned to the top of the Organized Crime organizational chart. The Philadelphia *Daily News* ritually referred to him as "Mob Boss Vincenzo Savarese."

Jesus Christ, what's all this? What's he want to do, say hello?

The Italian guy was already tugging at Dave Pekach's chair.

"Excuse me, honey?"

"Of course," Martha said.

Dave walked across the room.

"Good evening, Captain Pekach," Baltazari said. "Welcome to Ristorante Alfredo. Please sit down."

He waved his hand and a waiter appeared. He turned over a champagne glass and poured and then disappeared. Then Baltazari got up and disappeared.

"I won't take you long from the company of that charming lady," Vincenzo Savarese said. "But when I heard you were in the restaurant, I didn't want to miss the opportunity to thank you."

"Excuse me?"

"You were exceedingly understanding and gracious to my granddaughter, Captain, and I wanted you to know how grateful I am."

"I don't know what you're talking about," Dave Pekach said honestly.

"Last June—defying, I have to say, the orders of her parents—my granddaughter went out with a very foolish young man and found herself in the hands of the police."

Pekach shook his head, signifying that he was still in the dark as he searched his memory.

"It was very late at night in North Philadelphia, where Old York Road cuts into North Broad?"

Pekach continued to shake his head no.

"There was a chase by the police. The boy wrecked the car?" Savarese continued.

Dave suddenly remembered. He had been on the way home from his Cousin Stanley's wedding in Bethlehem. He had passed the scene of a wreck and had seen a Narcotics team and their car and, curious, stopped. What it was, was a minor incident, a carful of kids who had bought some marijuana, been caught at it, and had run.

There had been four kids, the driver and another boy, and two girls, both of them clean-cut, nice-looking, both scared out of their minds, in the back of a district RPC, which was about to transport them to Central Lockup. He had felt sorry for the girls and didn't want to subject them to the horrors of going through Central Lockup. So, after making sure the district cops had their names, he had turned them loose, sending them home in a cab.

"I remember," he said.

"My granddaughter said that you were gracious and understanding," Savarese said. "Far more, I suspect, than were her mother and father. I don't think she will be doing anything like that ever again."

"She seemed to be a very nice young woman," Pekach said. "We all stub our toes from time to time."

"I simply wanted to say that I will never forget your kindness and am very grateful," Savarese said, and then stood up and put out his hand. "If there is ever anything I can do for you, Captain . . ."

"Forget it. I was just doing my job."

Savarese smiled at him and walked across the restaurant to the door. The Italian in the tuxedo stood there waiting for him, holding his hat and coat.

Pekach shrugged and started back toward Martha.

Baltazari intercepted him.

"I think you dropped these, Captain," he said, and handed Pekach a book of matches.

"No, I don't think so," Pekach said.

"I'm sure you did," Baltazari said.

Pekach examined the matchbook. It was a Ristorante Alfredo matchbook. It was open, and a name and address was written inside it. The name didn't ring a bell.

"Mr. Savarese's friends are always grateful when someone does him, or his family, a courtesy, Captain Pekach," Baltazari said. "Now go and enjoy your meal."

Pekach put the matches in his pocket.

The young Italian was at his table.

"If I may suggest—"

"What was that all about?"

Dave shrugged. He smiled at her. "You may suggest," he said to the young Italian.

Martha's knee found Dave's under the table.

"I think you like our Tournedos Alfredo very much," the young Italian said.

"I love tournedos," Martha said.

Dave Pekach had no idea what a tournedo was.

"Sounds fine," he said.

Martha's knee pressed a little harder against his.

"And before, some clams with Sauce Venezia?"

"Fine," Dave said.

14 Certain enforcement and investigation jobs in Narcotics, Vice, and elsewhere require the use, in plainclothes, of young policemen who don't look like policemen, or even act like policemen, and whose faces are unknown to the criminals they are after. The only source of such personnel is the pool of young police officers fresh out of the Police Academy.

There are certain drawbacks to the assignment of such young and, by definition, inexperienced officers to undercover jobs. While they are working undercover, they require as much supervision as they can be given, because of their inexperience. But the very nature of undercover work makes close supervision difficult at best, and often impossible. Most of the time an undercover cop is on his own, literally responsible for his own fate.

Some young undercover cops can't handle the stress and ask to be relieved. Some are relieved because of their inability to do what is asked of them, either because of a psychological inability to act as anything but what they are—nice young men—or, along the same line, their inability to learn to think like the criminals they are after.

But some rookies fresh from the Academy take to undercover work like ducks to water. The work is sometimes what they dreamed it would be like—conditioned by cops-and-robbers movies and television series—when they got to be cops: putting the collar on really bad guys, often accompanied by some sort of sanctioned violence, knocking down doors, or apprehending the suspect by running the son of a bitch down and slamming his scumbag ass against a wall.

There are rarely—although this is changing—either the gun battles or high-speed chases of movies and television, but there *is* danger and the excitement that comes with that, plus a genuine feeling of accomplishment when the assistant district attorney reviews their investigation and their arrest and decides it is worth the taxpayers' money and his time to bring the accused before the bar of justice, and, with a little luck, see the scumbag son of a bitch sent away for, say, twenty to life.

Officers Charles McFadden and Jesus Martinez had been good, perhaps even very good, undercover police officers working in the area of narcotics. Officer McFadden, very soon after he went to work, learned that he had a rather uncanny ability to get purveyors of controlled substances to trust him. Officer Martinez, who shared with Officer McFadden a set of values imparted by loving parents and the teachings of the Roman Catholic church, took great pride in his work.

He had a Latin temperament, which had at first caused him to grow excited or angry—or both—during an arrest. He had noticed early on that when he was excited or angry or both, more often than not the scumbags they had against the wall some-where seemed far more afraid of him than they did of Officer McFadden, although Charley was six inches taller and outweighed him by nearly ninety pounds.

As Charley had honed the skills that caused the bad guys to trust him and help dig their own graves, Hay-zus worked on what he thought of as his practice of psycho-logical warfare against the criminal element. During the last nine months or year of his undercover Narcotics assignment, he was seldom nearly as excited or angry as those he was arresting thought he was. And he had picked up certain little theatrical embellishments, for example, sticking the barrel of his revolver up an arrestee's nose or excitedly encouraging Charley, knowing that he was incapable of such a thing, to "Shoot the cocksucker, Charley. We can plant a gun on him."

Either or both techniques, and some others that he had learned, often produced a degree of cooperation from those arrested that was often very helpful in securing con-victions and in implicating others involved in criminal activities.

Both Martinez and McFadden knew they had been good, perhaps even very good, undercover cops, and they both knew they had not been relieved of their undercover Narcotics assignments because of anything *wrong* they had done, but quite the re-verse: They had bagged the junkie scumbag who had shot Captain Dutch Moffitt of Highway. That had gotten their pictures in the newspapers and destroyed their effec-tiveness on the street.

They would have happily forgone their celebrity if they had been allowed to keep working undercover Narcotics, but that, of course, was impossible.

A grateful Police Department hierarchy had sent them to Highway Patrol, where they were offered, presuming satisfactory probationary performance, appointment as *real* Highway Patrolmen much earlier on in their police careers than they could have normally expected.

Big fucking deal!

Maybe that shit about getting to wear boots and a Sam Browne belt and a cap with the top crushed down would appeal to some asshole who had spent four years in a dis-trict, keeping the neighborhood kids from getting run over on the way home from school, and turning off fire hydrants in the summer, and getting fucking cats out of fucking trees, and that kind of shit, but it did not seem so to either Hay-zus or Charley.

They had gone one-on-one (or two-on-two) with some really nasty critters in some very difficult situations, had come out on top, and thought themselves, not entirely without justification, to be just as experienced, just as good *real* cops, as anybody they'd met in Highway.

They were smart enough, of course, to smile and sound grateful for the opportunity they had been offered. While Highway wasn't undercover Narcotics, neither was it a district, where they would have spent their time breaking up major hubcap-theft rings, settling domestic arguments, and watching the weeds grow.

There was soon going be another examination for detective, and they were both determined to pass it. Once they were detectives, they had agreed, they could apply for—and more important probably get, because they had caught Gerald Vincent Gallagher, Esquire—something interesting, Major Crimes, maybe, but if not Major Crimes, then maybe Intelligence or even Homicide.

In the meantime they understood that the smart thing for them to do was keep smiling, keep their noses clean, keep studying for the detective exam, do what they were told to do, and act like they liked it.

As their first tour enforcing the Motor Vehicle Code on the Schuylkill Expressway very slowly passed, however, they found this harder and harder to do.

Only two interesting things had happened since they began their patrol. First, of course, was making asses of themselves by turning the lights and the siren on and then pulling alongside Captain Pekach and that rich broad from Chestnut Hill he was fucking and signaling him to pull over.

Captain Pekach probably wouldn't say anything. He was a good guy, and before he made captain they had worked for him when he was a lieutenant in Narcotics, but that sure hadn't made them look smart.

And an hour after that a northbound Buick had clipped a Ford Pinto in the ass, spinning him around and over into the southbound lane, where he got hit by a Dodge station wagon, which spun him back into his original lane. Nobody got hurt bad, but there wasn't much left of the Pinto, and the Buick had a smashed-in grille from hitting the Pinto and a smashed-in quarter-panel where the Pinto had been knocked back into it by the Dodge. The insurance companies were going to have a hard time sorting out who had done what to whom on that one. It had been forty-five minutes before they'd gotten that straightened out, before the ambulance had carried the guy in the Pinto and his girlfriend off to the hospital and the wreckers had hauled the wrecked cars off.

Sergeant William "Big Bill" Henderson had shown up at the crash site about five minutes after they'd called it in, even before the ambulance got there. He clearly got his rocks off working accidents.

First he called for another Highway car, and then he took over from Charley McFadden, who by then had a bandage on the forehead of the guy in the Pinto where he'd whacked his head on the door and had him and his girlfriend calmed down and sitting in the back of the RPC.

He sent Charley down the expressway to help Hay-zus direct traffic around the wreck. And then once the other Highway car and then the ambulance and the wreckers showed up, he really started to supervise. He told the ambulance guys to put the guy in the Pinto in the ambulance, which wasn't really all that hard to figure out, since he was the only one bleeding. Then he told the wrecker guys how to haul away the Pinto and the Buick. He even got his whistle out and directed traffic while that was going on.

Sergeant Henderson, in other words, confirmed the opinion (asshole, blowhard) Officers McFadden and Martinez had formed of him when he delivered his little pep talk at Bustleton and Bowler before sending them on patrol.

Neither Charley nor Hay-zus had liked standing in the middle of the expressway, directing traffic. They had especially disliked it after the southbound lane had been cleared, and four hundred and twenty assholes had passed them going fifty miles an hour two feet away while gawking at the crumpled Pinto and the other cars.

It had to be done, of course; otherwise the assholes would have tried to drive right over the Dodge before they got that out of the way. Both privately wondered if the Highway guys got used to having two tons of automobile whiz past them—*whoosh, whoosh, whoosh, whoosh*—two feet away at fifty miles an hour, or if they were scared by it.

But directing traffic did temper their enthusiasm to enforce rigidly the Motor Vehicle Code insofar as it applied to permitted vehicular speeds. There were several things wrong with stopping a guy who was going five or ten miles over the posted speed limit but doing nothing else wrong.

First, there was something not quite right about handing a guy a ticket for doing something you knew you had done yourself. Then there was the fine; and there were a lot of points against your record in Harrisburg for a moving violation and so many points and you lost your license. And finally, the goddamn insurance companies found out you had a speeding ticket and they raised your premiums.

If a guy was going maybe seventy where the limit was fifty-five, or he was weaving in and out of traffic or tailgating some guy so close that he couldn't stop, that was something else: Ticket the son of a bitch and get him off the road before he hurt somebody.

That made the other things wrong with handing out tickets worthwhile. You never knew, when you pulled some guy to the side of the road to write him a ticket, what you were going to find. Ninety times out of a hundred it would be some guy who would be extra polite, admit he was going a little over the limit, and maybe mention he had a cousin who was an associate member of the FOP and hope you would just warn him.

Four times out of a hundred it would be some asshole who denied doing what you had caught him doing; said he was a personal friend of the mayor (and maybe was); or that kind of crap. And maybe one time in a hundred, one time in two hundred, when you pulled a car to the side and walked up to it, it was stolen, and the driver tried to back over you; or the driver was drunk and belligerent and would hit you with a tire iron when you leaned over and asked to see his license and registration. Or the driver was carrying something he shouldn't be carrying, something that would send him away for a long time, unless he could either bribe, or shoot, the cop who had stopped him.

And one hundred times out of one hundred, when you pulled a guy over on the Schuylkill Expressway, when you bent over and asked him for his license and registration, two-ton automobiles went fifty-five miles per hour two feet off your ass—*whoosh, whoosh, whoosh, whoosh.*

At five minutes past nine, heading north on the Schuylkill Expressway, Officers McFadden and Martinez spotted a motorist in distress, pulled to the side of the southbound lane.

"The time of day, prevailing weather conditions, the traffic flow, and other considerations will determine how much assistance you may render to a motorist in distress," Sergeant Big Bill Henderson had lectured them, "your primary consideration to be the removal or reduction of a hazard to the public, and secondly to maintain an unimpaired flow of traffic."

"In other words, Sergeant," McFadden had replied, "we don't have to change a tire for some guy unless it looks as if he's going to get his ass run over changing it himself?"

Officer Charles McFadden had a pleasant, youthfully innocent face, which caused Sergeant Henderson to decide, after glowering at him for a moment, that he wasn't being a wiseass.

"Yeah, that's about it," Sergeant Henderson said.

Officer Martinez, who was then driving, slowed so as to give them a better look at the motorist in distress. It was a two-year-old Cadillac Sedan de Ville. Apparently it had suffered a flat tire.

The motorist in distress was in the act of tightening the wheel bolts when he saw the Highway Patrol car. He stood up, quickly threw the other tire and wheel in the trunk, and finally the hubcap.

"Marvin just fixed his flat in time," Officer McFadden said. "Otherwise we would have had to help the son of a bitch."

Marvin P. Lanier, a short, stocky, thirty-five-year-old black male, was known to Officers Martinez and McFadden from their assignment to Narcotics. He made his living as a professional gambler. He wasn't very good at that, however, and was often forced to augment his professional gambler's income, or lack of it, in other ways. He worked as a model's agent sometimes, arranging to provide lonely businessmen with the company of a model in their hotel rooms.

And sometimes, when business was really bad, he went into the messenger business, driving to New York or Washington, D.C., to pick up small packages for business acquaintances of his in Philadelphia.

Narcotics had been turned on to Marvin P. Lanier by Vice, which said they had reason to believe Marvin was running coke from New York to North Philly.

Officers McFadden and Martinez had placed the suspect under surveillance and determined the rough schedule and route of his messenger service. At four o'clock one Tuesday morning, sixty seconds after he came off the Tacony-Palmyra Bridge, which is not on the most direct route from New York City to North Philadelphia, they stopped his car and searched it and found one plastic-wrapped package of a white substance they believed to be cocaine, weighing approximately two pounds and known in the trade as a Key (from kilogram).

The search and seizure, conducted as it was without a warrant—which they couldn't get because they didn't have enough to convince a judge that there was "reasonable cause to suspect" Mr. Lanier of any wrongdoing—was, of course, illegal. Any evidence so seized would not be admissible in a court of law. Both Officers Martinez and McFadden and Mr. Lanier knew this.

On the other hand, if the excited and angry Hispanic Narcotics officer who had jammed the barrel of his revolver up Mr. Lanier's nostril and called him a "slimy nigger cocksucker" went through with his suggestion to "just pour that fucking shit down the sewer," Mr. Lanier knew that he would be in great difficulty with the business associates who had engaged him to run a little errand for them.

If he had been arrested, the cocaine, illegally seized or not, would be forfeited. It would be regarded as a routine cost of doing business. But if the fucking spick slit it open and poured it down the sewer, his business associates were very likely to believe that he had diverted at least twenty thousand dollars' worth of their property to his own purposes, and that the Narcs putting it down the sewer was a bullshit story. Who would throw twenty big ones' worth of coke down a sewer? That was as much as a fucking cop made in a fucking year!

A deal was struck. Mr. Lanier was permitted to go on his way with the Key, it being understood that within the next two weeks Mr. Lanier would come up with information that would lead Officers Martinez and McFadden to at least twice that much coke, and those in possession of it.

Mr. Lanier thought of himself as an honorable man and lived up to his end of the bargain. Officers Martinez and McFadden rationalized the somewhat questionable legality of turning Mr. Lanier and the Key of coke loose because it ultimately resulted in both the confiscation of three Keys and the arrest and conviction of three dopers who they otherwise wouldn't have known about. Plus, of course, they had scared the shit out of Marvin P. Lanier. It would be some time before he worked up the balls to go back into the messenger business.

They had not, in the three months after their encounter with Mr. Lanier, before they had been transferred from Narcotics, unduly pressed him for additional information. They viewed him as a long-term asset, and asking too much of him would have been like killing the goose who laid the golden egg. It would not have been to their advantage if Mr. Lanier had become suspected by those in the drug trade and removed from circulation.

"Do you think he spotted us?" Hay-zus asked. By then he had brought the RPC almost to a halt, and was looking for a spot in the flow of southbound traffic into which he could make a U-turn.

"He spotted the Highway car," McFadden replied. "But he was so busy shagging ass out of there, I don't think he saw it was you and me."

Hay-zus found a spot and, tires screaming, moved into it.

"Why do you think Marvin was so nervous?" Charley asked excitedly. "Shit, stop!"

"What for?" Hay-zus asked, slowing, although he was afraid he would lose Marvin in traffic.

"Marvin forgot his jack," Charley said. "Somebody's liable to run into it. And besides, I think we should give it back to him."

Hay-zus saw the large Cadillac jack where Marvin had left it. He turned on the flashing lights and, checking the rearview mirror first, slammed on the brakes.

Charley was out of the car and back in it, clutching the jack, in ten seconds.

"Marvin will probably be very grateful to get his jack back," he said as Hay-zus wound up the RPC. "And besides, if Big Bill wants to know how come we left the expressway, we can tell him we were trying to return a citizen's property to him."

"We got no probable cause," Hay-zus said.

"All we're going to ask him is what he heard about Officer Magnella. And/or that guinea gangster, what's his name?"

"DeZego," Hay-zus furnished.

"I guess he spotted us," Charley McFadden said. The proof of that was that Marvin's Cadillac was in the left lane, traveling at no more than forty-six miles per hour in a fifty-mile-per-hour zone.

"What do we do?" Hay-zus asked.

"Get right on his ass and stay there. Let the cocksucker sweat a little. We can stop him when he gets off the expressway."

Mr. Lanier left the Schuylkill Expressway via the Zoological Gardens exit ramp.

"Pull him over now?"

"Let's see where he's going," Charley said. "If he's dirty, he'll try to lose us. If he's not, he'll probably go home. He lives on 48th near Haverford, and he's headed that way."

"Why follow the fucker home?"

"So we can let his neighbors see how friendly he is with the Highway Patrol," Charley said. "That ought to raise his standing in the community."

"You can be a real prick sometimes, Charley," Hay-zus said admiringly.

Scrupulously obeying all traffic regulations, and driving with all the care of a school-bus driver, Mr. Lanier drove to his residence just off Haverford Avenue on North 48th Street. As the RPC turned onto 48th, Charley bumped the siren and turned the flashing lights on.

Mr. Lanier got out of his car and smiled uneasily at the RPC, which pulled in behind him.

"He didn't run," Hay-zus said.

"He's nervous," Charley said as he retrieved the jack and opened the door. "Hello there, Marvin," he called cheerfully and loudly. "You forgot your jack, Marvin."

Marvin P. Lanier looked at McFadden and Martinez, finally recognizing them, and then suspiciously at the jack.

Charley thrust it into his hands.

"I guess I did," Marvin said. "Thanks a lot."

No one moved for a full sixty seconds, although Mr. Lanier did glance nervously several times at the spick Narc who had once shoved the barrel of his revolver up his nostril.

"How come you guys are in uniform?" Mr. Lanier finally asked.

"What's that to you, shitface?" Officer Martinez said with a snarl.

"Aren't you going to put your jack in the trunk, Marvin?" Officer McFadden asked, ignoring him.

Mr. Lanier put his hand on the rear door of his Cadillac.

"I'm running a little late," he said. "I think I'll just put it in the backseat for now."

"You don't want to do that, Marvin," Officer McFadden said. "You'd get grease and shit all over the carpet. Why don't you put it in the trunk?"

"I don't think I want to do that," Mr. Lanier said.

"Who gives a flying fuck what you want, asshole?" Officer Martinez inquired.

"Why are you guys on my ass?" Mr. Lanier inquired.

"You know fucking well why!" Officer Martinez, now visibly angry, flared. "Now open the fucking trunk!"

Mr. Lanier opened the trunk of his vehicle, Officers Martinez and McFadden standing on either side of him as he did so.

"Well, what have we here?" Officer McFadden asked, leaning over and picking up a Remington Model 870 12-gauge pump-action shotgun with a short barrel.

"Marvin must be a deer hunter," Officer Martinez said. "You a deer hunter, Marvin?" he asked.

"Yeah," Mr. Lanier said without much conviction.

"You got a license for this, of course?" Officer McFadden asked, although he was fully aware that not only was such a license not required; there was no such thing as a license to possess a shotgun, as there was for possession of a pistol. Neither did it violate any laws for a citizen like Mr. Lanier, who had not been convicted of a felony and was not, at the moment, under indictment or a fugitive from justice to transport such a weapon unloaded and not immediately available, such as in a locked trunk.

"No," Mr. Lanier said resignedly, confirming Officer McFadden's suspicion that Mr. Lanier was not fully conversant with the applicable law.

"Goddamn, Marvin, what are we going to do with you?" Officer McFadden asked almost sadly.

"What're you doing with the shotgun, Marvin?" Officer Martinez snarled again.

"I just had it, you know?"

"You been picking up coke in Harlem again, Marvin?" Officer McFadden asked sadly, as if he were very disappointed. "And the shotgun was a little protection?"

"Maybe," Officer Martinez said, getting a little excited, "if we wasn't right on your ass all the time so you couldn't get to that shotgun, you would have used it on us? Is that what you were doing with that fucking shotgun, you slimy nigger asshole?"

"No!" Mr. Lanier stated emphatically.

"You used that shotgun on Tony the Zee DeZego, didn't you, Marvin?" Officer McFadden suddenly accused.

"No!" Mr. Lanier proclaimed. "Honest to God! Some other guinea shot that motherfucker!"

"Bullshit!" Officer Martinez said, spinning Mr. Lanier around, pushing him against his Cadillac, kicking his feet apart and patting him down.

"I was in Baltimore with my sister when that happened," Mr. Lanier said. "I drove my mother down. My sister had another kid."

Officer Martinez held up a small plastic bag full of red-and-yellow capsules.

"Look what Marvin had in his pocket," he said.

"You got a prescription for these, Marvin?" Officer McFadden asked. "I'd hate to think you were using these without a prescription."

"You're not going to bust me for a couple of lousy uppers," Mr. Lanier said without much conviction.

"We're going to arrest you for the murder of Tony the Zee," McFadden said. "You have the right to remain silent—"

"I told you, I didn't have nothing to do with that. Some *guinea* shot him!"

"Which guinea?" Officer McFadden asked.

"I don't know his name," Mr. Lanier said.

Officers McFadden and Martinez exchanged glances.

They had worked together long enough that their minds ran in similar channels. Both had independently decided that Marvin had probably not shot Tony the Zee. There was no connection, and if there had been, the detectives or somebody would have picked up on it by now. It was possible, however, that Marvin had heard something in his social circles, concerning who had blown away Tony the Zee, that had not yet come to the attention of the detectives.

They knew they had nothing on Mr. Lanier. He had broken no law by having an unloaded shotgun in his trunk. The search of his person that had come up with the bag of uppers had been illegal.

"Maybe he's telling the truth," Officer McFadden said.

"This shit wouldn't know the truth if it hit him in the ass," Officer Martinez replied. "Let's take the son of a bitch down to the Roundhouse and let Homicide work him over."

"I swear to Christ, I was in Baltimore with my mother when that motherfucker got himself shot!"

"Who told you some guinea did it?" McFadden asked.

"I don't remember," Mr. Lanier said.

"Yeah, you don't remember because you just made that up!" Officer Martinez said. There followed a full sixty seconds of silence.

"Marvin, if we turn you loose on the shotgun and the uppers, do you think you could remember who told you a guinea shot Tony the Zee?" Officer McFadden finally asked. "Or get me the name of the guinea he said shot him?"

"You are not going to turn this cocksucker loose?" Officer Martinez asked incredulously.

"He ain't lied to us so far," Officer McFadden replied.

"That's right," Mr. Lanier said righteously. "I been straight with you guys."

"I think we ought to give Marvin the benefit of the doubt," Officer McFadden said. Officer Martinez snorted.

"But if we do, what about the shotgun and the uppers?" McFadden asked.

"What uppers?" Mr. Lanier said. "What shotgun?"

"What are you saying, Marvin?" Officer McFadden asked.

"Suppose the uppers just went down the sewer?" Mr. Lanier asked.

"And the shotgun? What are we supposed to do with the shotgun?"

"You mean that shotgun we just found laying in the gutter? That shotgun? I never saw it before. I guess you would do what you ordinarily do when you find a shotgun someplace. Turn it in to lost and found or whatever."

"What do you think, Hay-zus?" Officer McFadden asked.

"I think we ought to run the son of a bitch in, is what I think," Officer Martinez said, and then added, "But I owe you one, Charley. If you want to trust the son of a bitch, I'll go along."

Officer McFadden hesitated a moment and then said, "Okay, Marvin. You got it. You paid your phone bill? Still got the same number?"

"Yes."

"Be home at four tomorrow afternoon. Have something to tell me when I call you."

"I'll try."

"You better do more than try, you cocksucker. You better have something!" Officer Martinez said.

He picked up the shotgun and walked to the RPC and put it under the front seat.

"Marvin, I'm trusting you," McFadden said seriously. "Don't let me down."

Then he walked to the RPC and got in.

"We didn't ask him about Magnella," Hay-zus said as he turned right on Haverford Avenue and headed back toward the Schuylkill Expressway.

"I think he was telling the truth," Charley said. "About what he heard, I mean, about some guinea popping Tony the Zee. I wanted to stay with that."

"I think his sister had a baby too," Hay-zus said. "But we should have asked him about Magnella, anyway."

"So we didn't," Charley said. "So what do we do with what we got?"

"You mean the shotgun?"

"I mean, who do we tell what he said about who shot DeZego?"

"Shit, I didn't even think about that. Big Bill will have a shit fit and have our ass if we tell him what we done."

Sergeant Big Bill Henderson, in his little pep talk, had made it clear that, except in cases of hot pursuit, or in responding to an officer-needs-assistance call, they were not to leave their assigned patrol route; in other words, since they were not *real* Highway Patrolmen, they could not, as *real* Highway cops could, respond to any call that sounded interesting, or head for any area of their choosing where things might be interesting.

"Well, we can't just sit on it," Charley said.

"Captain Pekach," Hay-zus said thoughtfully after a moment.

"He's not on duty and he's not at home. We saw him and the rich lady, remember?"

"In the morning," Hay-zus said. "We'll ask to see him first thing in the morning."

"He's liable to be pissed. You think about that?"

"Well, you said it, we can't just sit on what Marvin told us."

"Maybe we could just tell Washington."

"And he tells somebody what we told him, like Big Bill, or even the inspector? It's gotta be Captain Pekach."

Charley's silence meant agreement.

A moment later Charley asked, "What about the shotgun?"

"We run it through the NCIC computer to see if it's hot."

"And if it is?"

"Then we turn it in."

"And burn Marvin? Which means we have to explain how we got it."

"Maybe it ain't hot."

"Then what?"

"Then I'll flip you for it," Hay-zus said. "I always wanted a shotgun like that."

15 Amanda Spencer was a little drunk. Matt Payne's usual reaction to drunken—even half-drunk—women was that they had all the appeal of a run-over dog, but again, Amanda was proving herself to be the exception to the rule. He thought she was sort of cute. Her eyes were bright, and she was very intent.

And, Jesus Christ, she was beautiful!

She was still wearing the off-the-shoulder blue gown she and Daffy's other brides-maids had worn at Saint Mark's. He found the curvature of the exposed portion of her upper bosom absolutely fascinating. During the ceremony his mind had wandered from what the bishop of Philadelphia was saying about the institution of marriage to recalling in some detail the other absolutely fascinating aspects of Amanda's anatomy, in particular the delightful formation of her tail.

The ceremony had gone off without a hitch. Although Chad Nesbitt had been as tight as a tick, his condition hadn't been all that apparent, and except for one burp and one incident of flatulence that had caused some smiles and a titter or two, the exchange of vows had been appropriately solemn and even rather touching: Matt had happened to glance at Daffy while the bishop was asking her if she was willing to forsake all others until death did them part, and she actually had tears in her eyes as she looked at Chad.

Outside Saint Mark's afterward, however, his plans to kiss Amanda tenderly and as quickly as possible were sent awry by Lieutenant Foster H. Lewis, Sr., of the 9th District, who had been outside the church, seen Matt, and beckoned him over.

"Excuse me, please, Amanda," he said, and touched her arm, and she had smiled at him, and he'd walked over to Lieutenant Lewis.

"Yes, sir?"

"Are you on duty, Payne?"

"No, sir."

Lieutenant Lewis had examined him for a moment, nodded his head, and walked away.

By then Amanda had been shepherded into one of the limousines and driven off to the Browne estate in Merion. He had known that it was highly unlikely that Amanda would have gone back to his apartment with him before they went to the house for the reception, but it had not been entirely beyond the realm of possibility.

Matt had to drive out to the Brownes' place by himself.

But once there he had found her right away, by one of the bars, with a champagne glass in her hand that she, with what he thought was entirely delightful intimacy, had held up to his lips.

Chad had searched him out, by then more visibly pissed, and extracted a solemn vow that if something happened to him in the service, Matt would look after Daffy.

There had been an enormous wedding cake. Chad had used his Marine officer's sword to cut it. From the way he withdrew it from the scabbard and nearly stabbed his new bride in the belly with it, Matt suspected that it was no more than the third time the sword had been out of its scabbard.

An hour after that the bride and groom, through a hail of rice and bird seed, had gotten in a limousine and driven off.

And now, an hour after that, he and Amanda were dancing.

The vertical manifestation of a horizontal desire, he thought, delightfully aware of the pressure of Amanda's bosom against his abdomen, the brushing of his thighs against hers.

"I watched you during the wedding," Amanda said against his chest.

He pulled back and looked down at her and smiled.

"I saw your gun," she said.

"How could you do that?" he asked, surprised. "It's in an ankle holster."

"Figuratively speaking," she said, pronouncing the words very carefully.

"Oh," he said with a chuckle.

"Shipboard romance," she said.

"I beg your pardon?"

"You know about shipboard romances, presumably?" Amanda asked.

"No," he said.

"People fall in love on a ship very quickly," she said.

"Okay," he said.

"Because they are in a strange environment and there is an element of danger," Amanda said.

"You have made a study of this, I gather?"

"The romance fades when the ship docks," Amanda said, "and people see things as they really are."

"So we won't get on a ship," Matt said. "A small sailboat, maybe. But no ship. Or if we do, we'll just never make port. Like the *Flying Dutchman.*"

"They grow up, so to speak," Amanda went on. "See things for what they really are."

"You said that," he said.

"Or," she said significantly, "one of them does."

"Meaning what?" There was something in what was going on that made him uncomfortable.

"When are you going to stop playing policeman and get on with your life is what I'm wondering," she said, putting her face against his shirt again.

"I don't think I'm 'playing' policeman," he said.

"You don't *know* that you're playing policeman," she said. "That's what I meant when I said *one* of them grows up."

"I don't think I like this conversation," Matt said. "Why don't we talk about something pleasant, like what are we going to do next weekend?"

"I'm *serious,* Matt."

"So'm I. So what's your point?"

"I know why you became a policeman," she said.

"You do?"

"Because you couldn't get in the Marines with Chad and had to prove you were a man."

"You have been talking to Daffy, I see," he said.

"Well, now you've done that. You became a cop and you shot a man. You have nothing else to prove. So why are you still a cop?"

"I like being a cop."

"That's what I mean," she said.

She stopped dancing, freed herself from his arms, and looked up at him.

"The ship has docked," she said.

"Meaning what?"

"Meaning I'm sorry I started this conversation," she said, "but I *had* to."

"I don't know what the hell you're talking about!"

"Yes you do!" she said, and Matt saw that she was on the edge of tears.

"What's wrong with me being a cop?" Matt asked softly.

"If you don't know, I certainly can't tell you."

"Jesus!"

"I'm tired," she said. "And a little drunk. I'm going to bed."

"It's early," he protested.

She walked away with a little wave.

"Call you in the morning before you go?"

There was no reply to that, either.

"Shit," Matt said aloud.

Thirty minutes later, just as Matt had decided she wasn't coming back out of the house, and as he had indicated to the bartender that he would like another Scotch and soda, easy on the soda, his father touched his arm and announced, "I've been looking for you."

I am about to get hell, Matt decided. *The party is just about over, and I have not danced with my mother. Actually I haven't done much about my mother at all except wave at her. And to judge by the look on his face, he is really pissed. Or disappointed in me, which is even worse than his being pissed at me.*

"My bad manners are showing again, are they?" Matt asked.

"Are you sober?" Brewster C. Payne asked evenly enough.

"So far," Matt said.

"Come with me, please, Matt," his father said. "There's no putting this off, I'm afraid."

"No putting what off?"

"Leave your drink," his father said. "You won't be needing it."

They walked out of the tent and around it and up the lawn to the house. His father led him into the butler's pantry, where he had been early that morning with Soames T. Browne.

H. Richard Detweiler was sitting on one of the high stools. When he saw Matt, he got off it and looked at Matt with both hurt and anger in his eyes.

"Would you like a drink, Matt?" Detweiler asked.

"He's already had enough to drink," Brewster C. Payne answered for him, and then turned to Matt. "Matt, you are quoted as saying that Penny has a problem with drugs, specifically cocaine."

"Quoted by whom?" Matt said.

"Did you say that? Something like that?" his father pursued.

"Jesus Christ!" Matt said.

"Yes, or no, for God's sake, Matt!" H. Richard Detweiler said angrily.

"Goddamn him!" Matt said.

"So it's true," Detweiler said. "What right did you think you had to say something filthy like that about Penny?"

"Mr. Detweiler, I'm a policeman," Matt said.

"Until about an hour ago I was under the impression that you were a friend of Penny's first, and a policeman incidentally," he said.

"Oh, Matt," Matt's father said.

"I think of myself as a friend of Penny's, Mr. Detweiler," Matt said. "We're trying very hard to find out who shot her and why."

"And the way to do that is spread . . . something like this around?"

"I didn't spread it around, Mr. Detweiler. I talked to Chad about Penny—"

"Obviously," Detweiler said icily.

"And in confidence I told him what we had learned about Penny—about Penny and cocaine."

"Not thinking, of course, that Chad would tell Daffy, and Daffy would tell her mother, and that it would soon be common gossip?" Brewster Payne said coldly.

"And that's all it is, isn't it?" H. Richard Detweiler said angrily, disgustedly. "Gossip? Filthy supposition with nothing to support it but your wild imagination? What were you trying to do, Matt, impress Chad with all the inside knowledge you have, now that you're a cop?"

"Where did you hear this, Matt? From that detective? The black man?" his father asked.

"Mr. Detweiler," Matt said, "I can't tell you how sorry I am you learned it the way you have, but the truth is that Penny is into cocaine. From what I understand, she is on the edge of being addicted to it."

"That's utter nonsense!" Detweiler flared. "Don't you think her mother and I would know if she had a problem along those lines?"

"No, sir, I don't think you would. You *don't,* Mr. Detweiler."

"I asked you the source of your information, Matt," his father said.

"I'm sorry, I can't tell you that," Matt said. "But the source is absolutely reliable."

"You mean you *won't* tell us," Detweiler said. "Did it occur to you that if there was any semblance of truth to this that Dr. Dotson would have been aware of it and brought it to my attention?"

"I can't believe that Dr. Dotson is not aware of it," Matt said. "Mr. Detweiler, I don't pretend to know anything about medical ethics—"

"Medical ethics or any other kind, obviously," Detweiler snapped.

"But Penny is twenty-one, an adult, and it seems to me that Penny wouldn't want you to know."

"Russell Dotson has been our family doctor for—for all of Penny's life and then some. Good God, Matt, he's a friend. He's outside right now. If he knew, *suspected,* something like that, he would tell me."

"I can't speak for Dr. Dotson, Mr. Detweiler," Matt said.

"Maybe we should ask him to come in here," Detweiler said. "I think I will. Let the two of you look each other in the eye."

"I wish you wouldn't do that, Mr. Detweiler," Matt said.

"I'll bet you do!"

"Dick, Matt may have a point," Brewster C. Payne said. "There is the question of doctor-patient confidentiality."

"Whose side are you on?" Detweiler snapped.

"Yours. Penny's. Matt's," Brewster C. Payne said.

Detweiler glowered at him for a moment, then turned to Matt. "How long did you say you have been aware of this situation?"

"Since I saw Penny in the hospital this morning," Matt said after having to think a moment.

Christ, was that only this morning?

"In other words, when you and that detective came to the house, you knew, or thought you knew, that Penny was a drug addict?"

"Yes, sir."

"In other words, then, when I allowed you, because I thought you were trying to find out who shot Penny, to paw through her drawers, you and that black detective were actually looking for evidence to support your notion that Penny's taking drugs?"

"No, sir," Matt said. "That's not so."

"Yes, it is, goddamn you! You took advantage of our friendship! That's despicable!"

"Dick, take it easy!" Brewster C. Payne said.

"You better get him out of here before I beat him up," H. Richard Detweiler said.

"Mr. Detweiler—" Matt said.

"Get out of my sight, goddamn you! I never want to see your face again!"

"You can believe this or not, Mr. Detweiler, but we're trying to help Penny," Matt said.

Detweiler stepped menacingly toward Matt.

"God*damn* you!"

Oh, Christ, I don't want to hit him! Matt thought.

His father stepped between them and kept them apart. He motioned with his head for Matt to leave.

Matt felt sick to his stomach. He fled the house and after some difficulty found his car. It was blocked in by several limousines, and he had to find their chauffeurs and get them to move them.

As he started down the drive he saw his father, obviously waiting for him. There was a temptation to pretend he didn't see him, but at the last moment he braked sharply and stopped and rolled down the window.

"You had better be sure of your facts," Brewster C. Payne said, leaning down to the window. "Dick Detweiler is looking for Dr. Dotson right now."

"And if Dotson won't tell him, then what?"

"All I'm saying is that you had better be sure of your facts," his father said.

"There seems to be some doubt in your mind, Dad," Matt said.

"I know that you don't have very much experience as a policeman," his father said. "If you had, you wouldn't have run off at the mouth about any of this to Chad. A lot of damage has been done."

"To whom, Dad?" Matt's mouth ran away with him. "To Penny? Or to your cozy relationship with Nesfoods International?"

"That," Brewster C. Payne said calmly, "was a despicable thing for you to say."

"You think so?" Matt said, his mouth now completely out of control. "Then try this on for size: Our information, as we cops are prone to say, is that Penny Detweiler was not only a coke junkie but was fucking that guinea gangster who got himself blown away. Nice girl, our precious Penny."

Brewster C. Payne looked at Matt intently for a moment, then straightened, turned, and started to walk back to the house.

Matt drove down the driveway and, after one of the rent-a-cops had carefully examined him and the car, was passed out the gate.

A hundred yards down the road he pulled the car to the curb, got out, and took several deep breaths. The technique, alleged to constrain the urge to become nauseous, didn't work.

Matt took Lancaster Avenue, which is U.S. Highway 30, into Philadelphia, driving slowly, trying to think of some way he could explain, in the morning, his runaway mouth to Jason Washington. Then it occurred to him that he had to tell Peter Wohl, not Washington, and he had to tell him tonight, not wait until morning.

The worst possible, and thus the most likely, scenario was that the trouble I am going to cause for having confided, like a fourteen-year-old—which, it may be reasonably argued, I am, intellectually speaking—in Chad Nesbitt is going to start tonight.

Mr. Detweiler will find Dr. Dotson. Dr. Dotson will either deny outright, or downplay,
Penny's coke problem. Mr. Detweiler will then naturally construe Brewster C. Payne's
best legal advice, to cool it, as being based on Brewster C. Payne's paternal loyalty
to his son, Boy Cop, Ye Olde Blabbermouth. He will then express his displeasure, his
outrage, to the nearest official ear he can find. Which will be that of His Honor
Mayor Jerry Carlucci, last seen in the striped tent on his lawn.

There was a cheese-steak joint at 49th and Lancaster. He pulled the Porsche to the
curb and walked across Lancaster to it. There was a 19th District RPC at the curb,
and two cops at the counter drinking coffee.

The cops looked at him with unabashed curiosity, reminding him that he was wearing formal evening wear.

Be not concerned, Officers. While my unbelievable stupidity has just brought down
upon the Police Department generally, and on two of its best, who have been both
holding my hand to keep me out of trouble, and have so foolishly placed an entirely
unjustified faith in my common sense, the completely justified wrath of a very power-
ful man, what you have here is not some rich kid in a monkey suit who will disturb
the peace of this establishment, but, incroyable, one of you, a police officer, complete
to gun, badge, and out in the Porsche, handcuffs and everything.

Matt walked to a pay phone mounted on the wall and fished change from his
pocket. He had just received a dial tone when his eye fell on a stack on newspapers,
apparently just delivered, on the counter. It was the *Ledger*. At first glance there
seemed to be a three-column photograph of His Honor Mayor Jerry Carlucci just
about in the act of either punching or choking someone.

Curiosity overwhelmed Matt. He hung the phone up and went to the counter. On
closer examination the photograph on the front page of the *Philadelphia Ledger* was
indeed of the mayor, and he did indeed look as if he were about to either choke someone or punch him out. The caption, simply "The Honorable Jerry Carlucci, mayor of
the City of Philadelphia," provided no explanation.

The explanation came in the story below the picture.

SOCIALITES MARRY UNDER
HEAVY POLICE GUARD:
HEIRESS' SHOOTING
CONTINUES
TO BAFFLE POLICE

By Charles E. Whaley,
Ledger Staff Writer

Phila—The wedding of socialites Daphne Elizabeth Brown and Chadwick T.
Nesbitt IV went on as scheduled at 7:30 P.M. at St. Mark's Church last evening,
minus one bridesmaid, and with a heavy force of police and private security
personnel evident at the church.

Penelope Detweiler, 23, whose father, H. Richard Detweiler, is president of
Nesfoods International and who was to have been a bridesmaid, instead lay in
Hahneman Hospital after having suffered multiple shotgun wounds at the hands
of an unknown assailant in a downtown parking garage the previous day.

As the Right Reverend Wesley Framingham Kerr, Protestant Episcopal

Bishop of Philadelphia, united in marriage the daughter of financier Soames T. Browne and the son of Nesfoods International Chairman, C.T. Nesbitt III, police and private detectives scattered among the socially prominent guests in the church nervously scanned them and the church itself in a manner that reminded this reporter of Secret Service agents guarding the president.

It was reported that the police were present at the orders of Philadelphia Mayor Jerry Carlucci, himself a guest, who is reported to be grossly embarrassed both that Miss Detweiler was shot in what appears to have been a Mafia-connected incident, and that the Special Operations Division of the Philadelphia Police Department, which was organized with his enthusiastic support, and which he personally charged with solving the crime, has been so far unable to identify any suspects in the shooting. The presence of private detectives at the church, reportedly from Wachenhut Security, Inc., was taken by some as an indication that the Browne and Nesbitt families had little faith in the Philadelphia Police Department to protect them and their guests.

Mayor Carlucci, outside the church, refused to discuss that issue with this reporter, and a scuffle ensued during which a *Ledger* photographer was knocked to the ground and his camera damaged.

(See related stories, "No Clues" and "Gangland War Victim," p.3a.)

"Oh, Jesus!" Matt said aloud.

His Honor must know about this. That's going to have put him in a lovely frame of mind so that when Mr. Detweiler says, "Jerry, old pal, let me tell you about this blabbermouth cop of yours," he will be understanding and forgiving.

He turned to page 3a and read the other stories.

"NO CLUES" SAY POLICE IN POLICEMAN'S MURDER; FUNERAL OF SLAIN OFFICER SCHEDULED FOR TODAY

By Mary Ann Wiggins
Ledger Staff Writer

Police Officer Joseph Magnella will be buried at three this afternoon, following a Mass of Requiem to be celebrated by John Cardinal McQuire, Archbishop of Philadelphia, at Saint Dominic's Church. Interment will be in the church cemetery, traditional last resting place for Roman Catholic police officers slain in the line of duty.

Officer Magnella, 24, of a Warden Street address in South Philadelphia, was found shot to death beside his 23rd Police District patrol car near Colombia and Clarion Streets just before midnight two nights ago.

A Vietnam veteran, he was unmarried and made his home with his parents. He had been on the police force less than a year and was engaged to be married.

Police Captain Michael J. Sabara, deputy commander of the Special Operations Division of the Police Department, which has been charged by Mayor

Jerry Carlucci with solving his murder, admitted that so far the police "don't have a clue" as to who shot Magnella or why.

Mayor Jerry Carlucci, who was interviewed briefly as he left the Stanley Rocco & Sons Funeral Home, where he had gone to pay his respects, seemed visibly embarrassed at the inability of the police to quickly solve what he called "the brutal, cold-blooded murder of a fine young officer." He refused to discuss with this reporter the murder of Anthony J. DeZego, an alleged organized crime figure, and the wounding of socialite Penelope Detweiler, which occurred the same night Officer Magnella was shot to death.

Several thousand police officers, both fellow Philadelphia officers and police from as far away as New York City and Washington, D.C., are expected to participate in the final rites for Officer Magnella.

GANGLAND WAR VICTIM WAS "GOOD SON, HUSBAND AND FATHER" SAYS MOTHER OF ANTHONY J. DEZEGO

By Tony Schuyler,
Ledger Staff Writer

Anthony J. DeZego, who met his death on the roof of the Penn Services Parking Garage two nights ago, his head shattered by a shotgun blast, was described on the eve of his funeral as a "good son, husband and father" by his mother, Mrs. Christiana DeZego.

DeZego, 34, was a truck driver for Gulf Sea Food Transport at the time of his death in what police suspect was a gangland killing. Police Captain Michael J. Sabara, Deputy Commander of Special Operations, which is investigating the early evening murder, refused to comment on DeZego's alleged ties to organized crime but said the shooting was "not unlike a Mafia assassination." He said that DeZego had a criminal record dating back to his teens and had only recently been released from probation.

His most recent brush with the law, according to Captain Sabara, had been a conviction for "possession with intent to distribute controlled substances."

DeZego had recently purchased for his family (a wife and two sons) a home four doors down from that of his mother in South Philadelphia. His late-model Cadillac, found abandoned by police at Philadelphia International Airport the morning after the shooting, was returned to his family yesterday.

Salvatore B. Mariano, DeZego's brother-in-law and president of Gulf Sea Food Transport, said that DeZego was "a reliable employee and would be missed at work." He refused to speculate on how DeZego could afford a new home and a Cadillac on ordinary truck driver's wages and dismissed as "nonsense" that DeZego had ties to organized crime.

DeZego will be buried at three P.M. this afternoon, following a Requiem Mass at St. Teresa of Avalone Roman Catholic Church.

The investigation into his murder is "proceeding well," according to Captain

Sabara, who declined to offer any further details. He confirmed that the investigation is being conducted by ace homicide detective Jason Washington.

"Nothing would please us more than to see Mr. DeZego's murderer face the full penalty of the law," Sabara said.

"You want to *buy* that newspaper, Mac? Or did you think you was in a library?" a counterman with sideburns down to his chin line demanded.

"I want to buy it," Matt said. "Sorry."

He laid a dollar bill on the counter and turned back to the telephone and dialed Peter Wohl's home number.

After the fourth ring there was a click. "This is 555-8251," Wohl's recorded voice announced. "When this thing beeps, you can leave a message."

"Inspector, this is Matt Payne. I have to talk to you just as soon as possible—"

"This soon enough?" Wohl's cheerful voice interrupted.

Matt was startled.

"Have you seen the papers? The *Ledger?*"

"No. But I'll bet you called me to tell me about them," Wohl said dryly.

"There's a picture of the mayor on the front page. About to punch a photographer. And several bullshit stories putting him and us down."

"I'd like to see them," Wohl said. "Is *that* why you called me at quarter to one?"

"No, sir. Sir, I've fucked up."

"Another run-in with Sergeant Dolan?"

"No, sir. It's something else."

"Where are you?"

"At 49th and Lancaster. At a pay phone."

"If you don't think—which, *ergo sum,* you've called, so you don't—this will wait until morning, come over here. Bring the *Ledger* with you."

"Yes, sir, I'll be right there."

When he went outside, one of the two cops who had been at the counter was on the sidewalk. The other one was across the street, by the Porsche. Matt walked back across Lancaster Avenue.

"Nice car," the cop said.

"Thank you."

"You been drinking?"

"I had a couple of drinks," Matt said.

"Wedding, huh?"

"Yes, sir."

"Well, you always take a couple of drinks at a wedding, don't you? And you made it across the street in a straight line," the cop said.

"Yes, sir."

"You open to a little friendly advice?"

"Sure."

"Dressed up like that, driving a car like this, this time of night, with a couple of drinks in you, maybe stopping in a neighborhood like this isn't such a good idea. You know what I mean?"

"I think so," Matt said. "Yes. I know what you mean."

"Good night, sir," the cop said. "Drive careful."

He walked back across Lancaster Avenue, got in the 19th District RPC, and drove off.

He had no idea I'm cop. Obviously I don't look like a cop. Or act like one. But I know that, don't I, that I don't act like a cop?

As Matt swung wide to turn off Norwood Street in Chestnut Hill and to enter into the driveway that led to Peter Wohl's apartment, the Porsche's headlights swept across a massive chestnut tree and he thought he could see a faint scarring of the bark.

He thought: *I killed a man there.*

Warren K. Fletcher, 34, of Germantown, his brain already turned to pulp by a 168-grain round-nosed lead bullet fired from Officer Matt Payne's .38-caliber Chief's Special snub-nosed revolver, a naked civilian tied up with lamp cord under a tarpaulin in the back of his van, had crashed the van into that chestnut tree, ending what Michael J. O'Hara had called, in the *Philadelphia Bulletin,* "The Northwest Philadelphia Serial Rapist's Reign of Terror."

Matt recalled Chad asking him what it was like to have killed a man. And he remembered what he had replied: "I haven't had nightmares or done a lot of soul-searching about it. Nothing like that."

It was true, of course, but he suddenly understood why he had said that: It hadn't bothered him because it was unreal. It hadn't happened. Or it had happened to somebody else. Or in a movie. It was beyond credibility that Matthew M. Payne, of Wallingford and Episcopal Academy, former treasurer of Delta Phi Omicron at, and graduate of, the University of Pennsylvania, had been given a badge and a gun by the City of Philadelphia and had actually taken that gun from its holster and killed somebody with it.

He drove down the driveway. There was a Buick Limited parked in front of one of Peter Wohl's two garages. There was nothing on the car to suggest that it was a Department car, and he wondered who it belonged to.

He got out of the Porsche and climbed the stairs to Wohl's door and knocked.

A silver-haired, stocky man in his sixties, jacketless, his tie pulled down, wearing braces, opened the door.

"You must be Matt Payne," he said, offering one hand. The other held a squat whiskey glass. "I'm Augie Wohl. Peter's taking a leak. Come on in."

Matt knew that Peter Wohl's father was Chief Inspector August Wohl, retired, but he had never met him. He was an imposing man, Matt thought, just starting to show the signs of age. He was also, Matt realized, half in the bag.

"How do you do, sir?" Matt said.

"Let me fix you a little something," Chief Wohl said. "What's your pleasure?"

"I'm not sure that I should," Matt said.

"Oh, hell, have one. You're among friends."

"A little Scotch, then, please," Matt said.

He followed Wohl's father across the room to Wohl's bar. It was covered with takeout buckets from a Chinese restaurant. Chief Wohl reached over the bar, came up with a fifth of Johnnie Walker and a glass, and poured the glass half full. He added ice cubes from a plastic freezer tray and handed it to him.

"Dilute it yourself," he said cheerfully. "There's soda and water."

"Thank you," Matt said.

Peter Wohl, in the act of closing his zipper, came out of his bedroom.

"What we have here is obviously the best-dressed newspaper boy in Philadelphia," he said. "Have you and Dad introduced yourselves?"

He's not feeling much pain, either, Matt decided.

"Yes, sir."

"And I see he's been plying you with booze," Wohl went on. "So let me see what *The Ledger* has to say, and then you can tell me how you fucked up."

Matt handed him the newspaper, which Wohl spread out on the bar, and then read, his father looking over his shoulder.

"It could be worse," Chief Wohl said. "I think Nelson is being very careful. Nesfoods takes a lot of tomato soup ads in his newspapers."

"So how did you fuck up, Matt?" Peter Wohl asked.

Matt told him about his confrontation with H. Richard Detweiler, fighting, he thought successfully, the temptation to offer any kind of an excuse for his inexcusable stupidity.

"You're sure, son," Chief Wohl asked, "that Detweiler's girl has a drug problem?"

"If Washington has the nurse in Hahneman, Dad—" Peter Wohl said.

"Yeah, sure," Chief Wohl said. "What about the girl's relationship with DeZego? How reliable do you think that information is?"

"It's secondhand," Matt said. "It could just be gossip."

"You didn't tell her father about that, anyhow, did you, Matt?" Peter Wohl asked.

"No, sir, I didn't," Matt said. But that triggered the memory of his having told his father. And, shamed again, he felt morally obliged to add that encounter to everything else.

"Well, fortunately for you," Chief Wohl said, looking at Matt, "Jerry tried to belt the photographer. Or did he belt him? Or just try?"

"The paper said 'a scuffle ensued,' " Peter Wohl said.

"It was more than that," Chief Wohl said, went to the bar and read, somewhat triumphantly from the newspaper story: ". . . 'a scuffle ensued during which a *Ledger* photographer was knocked to the ground and his camera damaged.' Don't you watch television? A cop is supposed to *get the facts."*

" 'Just the facts, ma'am.' " Peter Wohl chuckled, mimicking Sergeant Friday on *Dragnet.*

"Carlucci is going to be far more upset about that picture being on every other breakfast table in Philadelphia, son," Chief Wohl said, "than about you telling Detweiler his daughter has a drug problem."

"That was pretty goddamn dumb," Peter Wohl said.

"Yes, sir, I know it was. And I'm sorry as hell," Matt said.

"He was talking about Jerry Carlucci," Chief Wohl said.

"But the shoe fits," Peter Wohl said, "so put it on."

Matt glanced at him. There was a smile on Peter Wohl's face.

He's not furious, or even contemptuous, Matt realized, very surprised. *He doesn't even seem very annoyed. It's as if he expected this sort of stupid behavior from a rookie. Or maybe from a college boy.*

"Jerry never learned when not to use his fists," Chief Wohl said, then chuckled.

"My God, the gorilla suit!" He laughed. "You ever tell Matt about Carlucci and the gorilla suit?"

Wohl, chuckling, shook his head.

"You tell him," he said, and walked to the bar.

"Well, this was ten, maybe twelve years ago," Chief Wohl began. "Jerry had Highway. I had Uniformed Patrol. Highway was under Uniformed Patrol then. I kept getting these complaints from everybody, the DA's office, a couple of judges, Civil Liberties, everybody, that Highway was taking guys to Bustleton and Bowler and working them over before they took them to Central Lockup. So I called Jerry in and read the riot act to him. I was serious, and he knew I was serious. I told him that the first time I could prove that he, or anybody in Highway, was working people over at Bustleton and Bowler, he would be in Traffic the next morning, blowing a whistle at Broad and Market . . ." He paused, glancing over his shoulder. "If you're making one of those for Matt, my glass has a hole in it too."

"None for me, thanks," Matt said about two seconds before Peter Wohl handed him a fresh drink.

"Ssh," Peter Wohl said, "you're interrupting the old man."

"So he stopped for a while," Chief Wohl went on. "Maybe for a week. Then I started hearing about it again. So I went to the sergeant in Central Lockup. I was serious about this and told him the next time they got a prisoner from Highway that looked like he'd been worked over, I wanted to hear about it right then. So, sure enough, two or three nights later, about eleven o'clock at night, I get this call from Central Lockup."

Peter Wohl handed his father a drink.

He looked at it, and then at Matt.

"Don't worry about getting home, son," he said. "I'll drive you myself."

"The hell you will." Peter Wohl laughed. "He stays here and you're getting driven home. The one thing I don't need is either or both of you running into a bus."

"You're not suggesting that I'm drunk, are you?"

"It's not a suggestion at all," Wohl said. "It's one of those facts you were talking about before." He went to the telephone and dialed a number.

"This is Inspector Wohl," he said. "Would you put out the word to have the nearest Highway car meet me at my house, please?"

"I'm not sure I like that," Chief Wohl said.

"I would rather have you pissed at me than Mother, okay?" Wohl said. "Finish the gorilla story."

"Where was I?"

"You got a call from Central Lockup," Peter furnished.

"Yeah. Right. So what happened, Matt, was that I got in my car and went down there. They had a bum, a real wiseass, in one of the cells, and somebody in Highway had really worked him over. Swollen lips. Black eye. The works. And I knew Jerry Carlucci had been out at Bustleton and Bowler. So I thought I had him. So I went into the cell with this guy and asked him what had happened. 'Nothing happened,' he said. So I asked him where he got the cut lip and the shiner. And he said, 'From a gorilla.' And I said 'Bullshit' and he said a gorilla beat him up, and if I didn't like it, go fuck myself. And I asked, where did the gorilla beat him up, and he said 'Bustleton and

Bowler' and I said there weren't any gorillas at Bustleton and Bowler, and he said 'The hell there wasn't, one of them came into the detention cell there and kicked the shit out of me.' "

Peter Wohl laughed out loud. "True story, Matt," he said.

"Well," Chief Wohl went on, "like I said, Matt, this guy was a real wiseass, and I knew I was wasting my breath. If Carlucci had beat him up, he wasn't going to tell me. So I went home. About a week later a piece of paper crossed my desk. It was a court order for the release of evidence in a truck heist before trial. You know what I mean, son?"

"Matt," Peter Wohl said, "sometimes a court will order the release of stolen property to its owners before the case comes to trial, if they can prove undue hardship, that sort of thing."

"Yes, sir," Matt said.

"The evidence was described as 'theatrical costumes and accessories.' Highway had the evidence. I didn't pay much attention to it at the time, but the same afternoon, I was out at Bustleton and Bowler, and I was a little curious. So I asked the sergeant where the theatrical costumes were—I was asking, in other words, if they had been returned to the owners yet. The sergeant said, 'Everything but the gorilla suit's out in the storeroom. Captain Carlucci's got the gorilla suit.' "

He put his glass down and laughed so hard, his eyes watered.

"That goddamn Jerry Carlucci had actually put the gorilla suit on, gone into the holding cell, and worked the bum over. And the bum, who had his reputation to think of, was not going to go to court and complain he'd been assaulted by a guy in a gorilla suit. Oh, Jesus, Jerry was one hell of a cop!"

There were the sounds of footsteps on the stairs outside, and then a rap at the door. Wohl went to it and opened it. Sergeant Big Bill Henderson stood there.

"Not that I'm not glad to see you, Sergeant," Wohl said, "but I guess I should have asked for a two-man car."

"What's the problem, Inspector?"

"There's no problem at all, Sergeant," Chief Wohl said. "My son has got the cockamamie idea that I'm too drunk to drive."

"Hello, Chief," Big Bill said. "Nice to see you again, sir."

"I was just telling Matt Payne about Jerry Carlucci and the gorilla suit," Chief Wohl said. "You ever hear that story?"

"No, sir," Big Bill said. "You can tell me on the way home. Inspector, I'll have a car pick up mine and meet me at the chief's house. Okay?"

"Fine," Wohl said. "Or we could wait for a two-man car."

"No, I'll take the chief. I want to hear about the gorilla suit." He winked at Peter Wohl.

Peter Wohl found his father's coat and helped him into it. Matt saw for the first time that Chief Wohl had a pistol.

I guess once a cop, always a cop.

"You tell Mother going to Groverman's Bar was your idea, Dad?" Peter said.

"I can handle your mother, don't you worry about that," Chief Wohl said. He walked over to Matt and shook his hand. "Nice to meet you, son. I probably shouldn't tell you this, but Peter thinks you're going to make a hell of a cop."

"I said 'in twenty years or so' is what I said," Peter Wohl said.

Chief Wohl and Sergeant Henderson left.

Wohl walked past Matt, into his bedroom, and returned in a moment carrying sheets and blankets and a pillow. He tossed them at Matt.

"Make up the couch. Go to bed. Do not snore. Leave quietly in the morning. You are still working with Jason?"

"Yes, sir. I'm to meet him at the Roundhouse at eight."

"Try not to breathe on him," Wohl said. "I would hate for him to get the idea that you've been out till all hours drinking."

"Yes, sir. Good night, sir."

At his bedroom door Peter Wohl turned. "When you hear the gorilla suit story again, and you will, remember that the first time you heard it, you heard it from the source," he said.

"Yes, sir."

"Good night, Matt," Wohl said, and closed the door.

Matt undressed to his underwear. The last thing he took off was his ankle holster. He laid it on the table beside his tuxedo trousers.

My gun, he thought. *The tool of the policeman's trade. Chief Wohl still carries his. And Chief Wohl thinks I'm a cop. A rookie, maybe, but a cop. He wouldn't have told that story to a civilian, about the mayor when he was a cop, putting on a gorilla suit and knocking some wiseass around. I wouldn't tell it to my father; he's a civilian and wouldn't understand. And Chief Wohl wasn't kidding when he said that Inspector Wohl told him he thought I could make a good cop.*

Matt Payne went to sleep feeling much happier than when he had walked in the door.

16 Matt Payne's bladder woke him with a call to immediate action at half past five. It posed something of a problem. There was only one toilet in Peter Wohl's apartment, off his bedroom. It was either try to use that without waking Wohl or going outside and relieving himself against the wall of the garage, something that struck him as disgusting to do, but he knew he could not make it to the nearest open diner or hamburger joint.

When he stood up, the decision-making process resolved itself. A sharp pain told him he could not wait until he got outside.

On tiptoe he marched past Wohl, who was sleeping on his stomach with his head under a pillow. He carefully closed the door to the bathroom, raised the lid, and tried to accomplish what had to be done as quietly as possible. He had just congratulated himself on his skill doing that and begun to hope that he could tiptoe back out of Wohl's room undiscovered when the toilet, having been flushed, began to refill the tank. It sounded like Niagara Falls.

Finally it stopped, with a groan like a wounded elephant. Matt opened the door and looked. Wohl did not appear to have moved. Matt tiptoed past the foot of Wohl's bed and made it almost to the door.

"Good *morning*, Officer Payne," Wohl said from under his pillow. "You're up with the goddamn roosters, I see."

"Sorry," Matt said.

He closed Wohl's door, dressed quickly, left the apartment as quietly as he could, and drove to Rittenhouse Square. He went directly to the refrigerator, took out a half gallon of milk, and filled a large glass. It was sour.

Holding his nose, he poured it down the drain, then leaned against the sink.

The red light on his telephone answering machine was flashing.

"Why did you leave?" Amanda's voice inquired metallically. *Because, after telling me the cruise ship had docked, you went to bed.* "I hope I didn't run you off." *Perish the thought!* "Call me." *Now? It's quarter after six in the morning!*

This was followed by electronic beeping noises that indicated that half a dozen callers had declined Matt's recorded invitation to leave their number so he could get back to them. Then a familiar, deep, well-modulated voice: "This is Jason, Matt. I've got to do something first thing in the morning. Don't bother to come to the Round-house. I'll either see you at Bustleton and Bowler around nine, or I'll call you there."

Another series, five this time, of electronic beeping noises, indicating that many callers had not elected to leave a recorded message, and then Amanda's recorded voice, sounding as if she were torn between sorrow and indignation, demanded, "Where the hell are you? I've called you every half hour for hours. Call me!"

Matt looked at his watch.

It is now 6:18 A.M. I will shower and shave and see if I can eliminate the source of the rumbling in my belly, and then dress, and by then it will be close to 7:00 A.M., and I will call you then, because I really don't want to talk to Mrs. Soames T. Browne at 6:18 A.M.

At 7:02 A.M. Matt called the residence of Mr. and Mrs. Soames T. Browne and asked for Miss Spencer. Mrs. Soames T. Browne came on the line. Mrs. Browne told him that five minutes before, Amanda had gotten into her car and driven home, and that if he wanted her opinion, his behavior in the last couple of days had been despicable. She said she had no idea what he'd said or done to Amanda to make her cry that way and didn't want to know, but obviously he was still as cavalier about other people's feelings as he had always been. She told him she had not been surprised that he had thought it amusing to try to get Chad drunk before the wedding, but she really had been surprised to learn that he had been spreading scurrilous stories about poor Penny Detweiler to one and all, with the poor girl lying at death's door in the hospital.

And then she terminated the conversation without the customary closing salutation.

"Oh, shit!" Matt said to a dead telephone.

He put on his necktie, slipped his revolver into his ankle holster, and left the apartment. He went to his favorite restaurant, Archie's, on 16th Street, where he had the *specialité de la maison,* a chili dog with onions and two bottles of root beer, for his breakfast.

Then he got in the Porsche and headed for Bustleton and Bowler. He was almost there when he noticed that a thumb-sized glob of chili had eluded the bun and come to rest on his necktie and shirt.

Jason Washington had been glad when the computer came along, not so much for all the myriad benefits it had brought to industry, academia, and general all-around record-keeping, but rather because it gave him something to sort of explain the workings of the brain.

He had been fascinated for years with the subconscious deductive capabilities of the brain, going way back to his freshman year in high school, where he found, to his delight, that he could solve simple algebraic equations in his head. He had often had no idea why he had written answers to certain examination questions, only that they had been the right answers. He had sailed through freshman algebra with an A. When he got to sophomore algebra, not having taken the time to memorize the various theories offered in freshman algebra, he got in trouble, but he never forgot the joy he had experienced the year before when the brain, without any effort at all on his part, had supplied the answers to problems he didn't really understand.

He had first theorized that the brain was something like a muscle; the more you flexed it, the better it worked. That seemed logical, and he carried that around a long time, even after he became a policeman. He had really wanted to become a detective and had studied hard to prepare for the detective's examination. When he took the examination, he remembered things he was surprised that he had ever learned. That tended to support the brain-is-a-muscle theory, but he suspected that there was more to it than that.

He saw comptometers on various bureaucrats' desks, watched them in operation, and thought that possibly the brain was sort of a supercomptometer, but that (and its predecessor, the abacus) seemed too crude and too slow for a good comparison.

Then came the computer. Not only did the computer never forget anything it was told, but it had the capability to sort through all the data it had been fed, and do so with the speed of light. The computer was a brain, he concluded. More accurately the brain was a computer, a supercomputer, better than anything at MIT, capable of sorting through vast amounts of data and coming up with the answer you were looking for.

Some of its capabilities vis-à-vis police work were immediately apparent. If you fed everyone's license-plate number into it, and the other data about a car, and queried the computer, it would obligingly come up with absolutely correct listings of addresses, names, makes, anything you wanted to know.

Jason Washington had gone to an electronics store and bought a simple computer and, instead of watching television, had learned to program it in BASIC. He had written a program that allowed him to balance his checkbook. There had been a difference of a couple of pennies between what his computer said he had in his account and what the bank's computer said he had. He went over his program and then challenged the bank, not caring about the three cents but curious why two computers would disagree. He didn't get anywhere with the First Philadelphia Savings Fund Society, but a long-haired kid at the electronics store, a fellow customer, had taught him about anomalies.

As the kid explained it, it was a freak, where sometimes two and two added up to four point one, because something in either the data or the equation wasn't quite right.

By then Jason had been a detective for a long time, was already working in Homicide, and had learned that when you were working a tough job, what you looked for was something that didn't add up. An anomaly. That had a more professional ring to it than "something smells."

And he had learned something else, and that was that the brain never stopped working. It was always going through its data bank if you let it, sifting and sifting and sifting, looking through its data for anomalies. And he had learned that sometimes he could, so to speak, turn the computer on. If he went to sleep thinking about a problem, sometimes, even frequently, the brain would go on searching the data bank while he was asleep. When he woke up, rarely was there the solution to the problem. Far more often there was another question. There was no answer, the brain seemed to announce, because something is either missing or wrong. Then, wide awake, all you had to do was think about that and try to determine what was missing and/or what was wrong.

Jason Washington had gone to sleep watching the NBC evening news on television while he was going over in his mind the sequence of events leading to the death, at the hands of person or persons unknown, of Anthony J. DeZego.

Mr. DeZego had spent the day at work, at Gulf Seafood Transport, 2184 Delaware Avenue, which fact was substantiated not only by his brother-in-law, Mr. Salvatore B. Mariano, another guinea gangster scumbag, but by four of his coworkers whom Jason Washington believed were telling the truth.

Mr. DeZego had then driven to the Warwick Hotel in downtown Philadelphia in his nearly new Cadillac. That fact was substantiated by the doorman, whom Washington believed, who said that Mr. DeZego had handed him a ten spot and told him to take care of the car. The car had then been parked in the Penn Services Parking Garage, fourth floor, by Lewis T. Oppen, Jr., a bellboy, who had done the car parking, left the parking stub, as directed, on the dashboard, and then delivered the keys to Mr. DeZego in the hotel cocktail lounge.

Mr. DeZego had later walked to the Penn Services Parking Garage and gone to the roof, where someone had blown the top of his head off, before or after popping Miss Penelope Detweiler, who had more than likely gone there to meet Mr. DeZego.

There was additional confirmation of this sequence of events by Sergeant Dolan and Officer What's-his-name of Narcotics, who had staked out the Warwick. They even had photographs of Mr. DeZego arriving at the Warwick, in the bar at the Warwick, and walking to, and into, the Penn Services Parking Garage.

Mr. DeZego's car had been driven by somebody to the airport. Probably by the doer. Doers. Why?

"Wake up, Jason, dammit!" Mrs. Martha Washington had interrupted the data-sorting function of his subconscious brain. "You toss and turn all night if I let you sleep in that chair!"

"You act like I've done something wrong," Jason said indignantly.

His brain said, *There is an anomaly in what Dolan told me.*

"Run around the room or something," Martha Washington said. "Just don't lay there like a beached whale. When you snore, you sound like—I don't know what."

Jason went into the kitchen.

I will just go see Sergeant Dolan in the morning. But I can't take the kid with me. Dolan thinks Matt is dealing coke.

He poured coffee in a mug, then dialed Matt's number and told his answering machine not to meet him at the Roundhouse but to go to Bustleton and Bowler instead.

At nine-fifteen he went to bed, at the somewhat pointed suggestion of his wife.

He went to sleep feeding questions to the computer.

Where is the anomaly? I know *it's there.*

Officers Jesus Martinez and Charles McFadden, in uniform, came to their feet when Captain David Pekach walked into the building at Bustleton and Bowler.

"Good morning," Pekach said.

"Sir, can we talk to you?" McFadden asked.

I know what that's about, I'll bet, Pekach thought. *They were not thrilled by their twelve-hour tour yesterday riding up and down the Schuylkill Expressway. They want to do something important, be real cops, and they do not think handing out speeding tickets meets that criteria.*

Then he had an unpleasant thought: *Do they think that because they caught me speeding, they have an edge?*

"Is this important?" he asked somewhat coldly.

"I don't know," McFadden said. "Maybe not."

"Have you spoken to your sergeant about it?"

"We'd really like to talk to you, sir," Jesus Martinez said.

Pekach resisted the urge to tell them to go through their sergeant. They were good cops. They had done a good job for him. He owed them that much.

"I've got to see the inspector," he said. "Hang around, if you like. If I can find a minute, we'll talk."

"Yes, sir," Martinez said.

"Thank you," McFadden said.

Pekach walked to Peter Wohl's door. It was open, and Wohl saw him and waved him in.

"Good morning, Inspector," Pekach said.

"That's open to debate," Wohl said. "Have I ever told you the distilled essence of my police experience, Dave? Never drink with cops."

"You've been drinking with cops?"

"Two cops. My father and Payne."

Pekach chuckled. "What's that, the odd couple?"

"I went to cry on the old man's shoulder, and that led us first to Groverman's Bar and then to my place, and then Payne showed up to cry on my shoulder. I sent the old man home with Sergeant Henderson and made Payne sleep on my couch."

"What was Payne's problem?"

"He let his mouth run away with him, told the Nesbitt kid, the one who was married, the Marine . . . ?"

Pekach nodded.

". . . that we know the Detweiler girl was using coke. And he told the bride, and she told her mother, and her mother told H. Richard Detweiler, who is highly pissed that we could suspect his daughter of such a thing, and the last time Payne saw him, he was looking for the mayor to express his outrage."

"Is he going to be trouble?"

"Probably," Wohl said, "but Payne looked so down in the mouth about it that I didn't have the heart to jump all over him. You may find this hard to believe, David, but when I was young, I ran off at the mouth once or twice myself."

"No!" Pekach said in mock shock.

"True." Wohl chuckled. "How was your evening? How was Ristorante Alfredo? You go there?"

"Yeah. I want to talk to you about that," Pekach said, and handed Wohl the matchbook he had been given in the restaurant.

"There's a name inside. Marvin Lanier. Is that supposed to mean something to me?"

"I got that from Vincenzo Savarese," Dave replied.

Wohl looked at him with interest in his eyes.

"Not from Savarese himself," Pekach went on carefully, "but from the greaseball, Baltazari, who runs it for him. But he made it plain it had come from Savarese."

"Ricco Baltazari gave you this?" Wohl asked.

There was a rap on the doorjamb.

"Busy?" Captain Mike Sabara asked when he had Wohl's attention.

"Come on in, Mike, I want you to hear this," Wohl said. As Sabara entered the office Wohl tossed the matchbook to him. "Dave got that from Vincenzo Savarese at the Ristorante Alfredo." When Sabara, after examining it, looked at him curiously, Wohl pointed to Pekach.

"Okay," Pekach said. "From the top. Almost as soon as we got in the place, the headwaiter came to the table and said Baltazari would like a word with me. He was sitting at a table across the room with Savarese."

"They knew you were going to be there, didn't they?" Wohl said thoughtfully. "You made a reservation, right?"

"I had a reservation," Pekach said. "So I went to the table, and as soon as I got there, Baltazari left me alone with Savarese. Savarese told me he wanted to thank me for something I did for his granddaughter."

"Huh?" Sabara asked.

"A couple of months ago, when I was still in Narcotics, I was coming home late one night and stopped when I thought I saw a drug bust. Big bust. Four kids caught buying some marijuana. But they ran and there was a chase, and the kid wrecked his old man's car, so they were headed for Central Lockup. I looked at them, felt sorry for the girls, didn't want them to have to go through Central Lockup, and sent them home in a cab."

"And one of the girls was *Savarese's* granddaughter?" Sabara asked. "We got any unsolved broken arms, legs, and head assaults on the books? We could probably pin that on Savarese. You don't give grass to his granddaughter unless you've got a death wish."

Wohl chuckled. "He'd beat it. Temporary insanity."

"I didn't know who she was and had forgotten about it until Savarese brought it up."

Pekach nodded and went on. "He gave me some bullshit about my graciousness and understanding—"

"*I* always thought you were gracious and understanding, Dave," Wohl said.

"—and said he would never forget it, et cetera, and said if there was ever anything he could do for me—"

"And he probably meant it too," Sabara said. "Anybody you want knocked off, Dave? Your neighbors playing their TV too late at night, anything like that?"

"Shit, Mike!" Pekach exploded.

"Sorry," Sabara said, not sounding overwhelmed with remorse.

"What I thought he was doing was letting me know he'd grab the tab for dinner. But on my way back to the table Baltazari handed me that matchbook and said I dropped them, and I said no, and he said he was sure, so I kept them."

"You see the name inside?" Wohl asked.

"Yeah. It didn't mean anything to me. Baltazari gave me the same line of greaser bullshit, something about 'Mr. Savarese's friends always being grateful when somebody does him a favor.' What I think he said was 'him or his family a courtesy.' By then I was beginning to wish I'd tossed the little bitch in the can."

"No you didn't." Wohl chuckled. "You really are gracious and understanding, Dave."

Pekach glared at him.

"That wasn't a knife," Wohl said.

"So, anyway, when I got home, I called Records and got a make on this guy. Sort of a make. Black male. He's supposed to be a gambler, but what he really is, is a pimp. He runs an escort service."

"Marvin P. Lanier," Sabara said, reading the name inside the matchbook. "I never heard of him."

"Misterioso," Wohl said.

"I figured I better tell you about it," Pekach said.

"Yeah," Wohl said thoughtfully. "Neither of them gave any hint why they gave you this guy's name?"

"Nope," Pekach said.

One of the phones on Wohl's desk rang. Wohl was in his customary position, on the couch with his feet up on the coffee table. Pekach, who was leaning on Wohl's desk, looked at him questioningly. Wohl nodded. Pekach picked up the phone.

"Captain Pekach," he said, and listened, and then covered the mouthpiece with his hand. "There's a Homicide detective out there. Wants to see you, me, or Dave. You want me to take it?"

"Bring him in," Wohl said.

"Send him in, Sergeant," Pekach said to the phone, and put it back in its cradle. He went to the door and pulled it open.

Detective Joseph D'Amata walked in.

"Hey, D'Amata," Wohl called. "How are you?"

"Good morning, Inspector," D'Amata said. "Am I interrupting anything?"

"Captain Pekach was just telling Captain Sabara and me about his dinner last night," Wohl said. "What can we do for Homicide?"

"You hear about the pimp who got himself blown away last night?"

"I haven't read the overnights," Wohl said.

"Black guy," D'Amata said. "Lived on 48th near Haverford."

"His name wouldn't be Marvin P. Lanier, would it?" Wohl asked.

"Yes, sir, that's it," D'Amata said, obviously pleased. "I sort of hoped there'd be something for me here."

"I don't think I follow that," Wohl said.

"I got the idea, Inspector, that you—that is, Highway—knows something about this guy."

"Why would you think that?"

"You knew the name," D'Amata said, just a little defensively.

"That's all?"

"Sir, an hour before somebody shot this guy there was a Highway car in front of his house. With him. Outside the crime scene, I mean."

"You're sure about that?"

"Yes, sir. Half a dozen people in the neighborhood saw it."

"Dave?" Wohl asked.

Pekach threw up his hands in a helpless gesture, making it clear that he knew nothing about a Highway involvement.

"Fascinating," Wohl said. "More *misterioso*."

"Sir?" D'Amata asked, confused.

"Detective D'Amata," Wohl said, "why don't you help yourself to a cup of coffee and then have a chair while Captain Pekach goes and finds out what Highway had to do with Mr. Lanier last night?"

"Inspector, this is the first I've heard anything about this," Pekach said.

"So I gathered," Wohl said sarcastically.

Pekach left the office.

"How did Mr. Lanier meet his untimely demise, D'Amata?"

"Somebody popped him five times with a .38," D'Amata said. "In his bed."

"That would suggest that somebody didn't like him very much," Wohl said. "Any ideas who that might be?"

D'Amata shook his head.

"Have you learned anything that might suggest Mr. Lanier was connected with the mob?"

"He was a *pimp*, Inspector," D'Amata said.

"Then let me ask you this: Off the top of your head, would you say that Mr. Lanier was popped, in a crime of passion, so to speak, by one of his ladies, or by somebody who knew what he was doing?"

D'Amata thought that over briefly. "He took two in the head and three in the chest."

"Suggesting?"

"I don't know. Some of those whores are tough enough. A whore could have done it."

"Have you any particular lady in mind?"

"I asked Vice"—he paused and chuckled—"to round up the usual suspects. Actually for a list of girls who worked for him, or did."

Wohl chuckled and then asked, "Whose gun?"

"We don't have that yet," D'Amata said. "Those are interesting questions you're asking, Inspector."

"Just letting my mind wander," Wohl said. "Try this one: Can you think of any reason that Mr. Lanier's name would be known to Mr. Vincenzo Savarese?"

"Jesus!" D'Amata said. "Was it?"

"Let *your* mind wander," Wohl said.

"He could have owed the mob some money," D'Amata said. "He liked to pass himself off as a gambler. The mob likes to get paid."

"That would get him a broken leg, not five well-placed shots, and from someone with whom Mr. Savarese would be only faintly acquainted," Wohl said.

"Yeah," D'Amata said thoughtfully.

"What would that leave? Drugs?" Wohl asked.

There was not time for D'Amata to consider that, much less offer an answer. Pekach came back in the office.

"There's nothing in the records about a Highway car being anywhere near 48th and Haverford last night," he said.

"You sure?" D'Amata challenged, surprised.

"Yeah, I'm sure," Pekach said sharply. "Are you?"

"Captain," D'Amata said, "I got the same story from four different people. There was a Highway car there."

There was a knock at the door.

"Not now!" Wohl called.

There came another knock.

"Open the door, Dave," Wohl said coldly.

Pekach opened the door.

Officers Jesus Martinez and Charles McFadden stood there, looking more than a little uncomfortable.

"Didn't you hear me say not now?" Wohl said. "How many times do I have to—"

"Inspector," Charley McFadden blurted, "we heard Captain Pekach asking—"

"Goddammit, we're busy," Pekach flared. "The Inspector said not now. And whatever's on your mind, go through your sergeant!"

"That was us," Charley said. "At 48th and Haverford. With Marvin Lanier." He looked at Pekach. "That's what we wanted to see you about, Captain."

"Officer McFadden," Wohl said, "please come in, and bring Officer Martinez with you."

They came into the office.

"You have heard, I gather, that Mr. Lanier was shot to death last night?" Wohl asked.

"Just now, sir," Hay-zus said.

"Before we get started, this is Detective D'Amata of Homicide," Wohl said. "Joe, these two are Jesus Martinez and Charley McFadden, who before they became probationary Highway Patrolmen worked for Captain Pekach when they were all in Narcotics."

"I know who they are," D'Amata said.

"What is your connection with Mr. Lanier?" Wohl asked.

Charley McFadden looked at Hay-zus, then at Wohl, then at Pekach.

"What we wanted to tell Captain Pekach was that Marvin told us another guinea shot Tony the Zee," he blurted.

"Fascinating," Wohl said.

"What I want to know is what you were doing with Lanier when you were supposed to be patrolling the Schuylkill Expressway," Captain Pekach said.

"Isn't that fairly obvious, Dave?" Wohl said sarcastically. "Officers McFadden and Martinez decided that since no one else has any idea who shot Mr. DeZego and Miss Detweiler, it was clearly their duty to solve those crimes themselves, even if that meant leaving their assigned patrol area, which we, not having the proper respect for their ability as supercops—they are, after all, former undercover Narcs—had so foolishly given them."

I said that, he thought, *because I'm pissed at what they did and wanted to both let them know I'm pissed, and to humiliate them. Having done that, I now realize that I am very likely to be humiliated myself. I have a gut feeling these two are at least going to be part of the solution.*

"I used to be a Homicide detective," Wohl said. "Let me see if I still remember how. McFadden—first of all, what was your relationship to Marvin Lanier?"

"He was one of our snitches. When we were in Narcotics."

"Then I think we'll start with that," Wohl said. "Let me begin this by telling you I want the truth, the whole truth, and nothing but the truth. Leave nothing out. You are already so deeply in trouble that nothing you admit can get you in any deeper. You understand that?"

The two mumbled "Yes, sir."

"Okay. Martinez, tell me how you turned Marvin Lanier into a snitch."

Wohl was convinced that the story was related truthfully and in whole. He didn't particularly like hearing that they had turned Lanier loose with a kilogram of cocaine—and could tell from the look on his face that Dave Pekach, who had been their lieutenant, was very embarrassed by it—but it convinced him both that McFadden and Martinez were going to tell the whole truth and that they had turned Lanier into a good snitch, defined as one that was more terrified of the cops who were using him than of the people on whom he was snitching.

He noticed, too, that neither Sabara, Pekach, nor D'Amata had added their questions to his. On the part of D'Amata, that might have been the deference of a detective to a staff inspector—he didn't think so—but on the parts of Sabara and Pekach, who were not awed by his rank, it very well could be that they could think of nothing to ask that he hadn't asked.

Christ, maybe what I should have done was just stay in Homicide. I'm not all that bad at being a detective. And by now I probably would have made a pretty good Homicide detective. And all I would have to do is worry about bagging people, not about how pissed the mayor is going to be because one of my people ran off at the mouth.

"So when Marvin wanted to put his jack in the backseat instead of his trunk," Hay-zus said, "we knew there was something in the trunk he didn't want us to see. So there was. A shotgun."

"A shotgun?" Joe D'Amata asked. It was the first time he had spoken. "A Remington 12 Model 1100, 12-gauge?"

"A Model 870," Martinez said. "Not the 1100. A pump gun."

"Is there an 1100 involved?" Wohl asked.

"There was an 1100 under his bed," D'Amata said. "I've got it out in my car."

"And you say there was an 870 in his trunk?" Wohl asked Martinez.

"Yes, sir."

"Where is it?"

"Outside in my car."

"You took it away from him? Why?"

"On what authority?" Pekach demanded. Wohl made a calm-down sign to him with his hand.

"He didn't know it was legal," McFadden said.

"So you just decided to take it away from him? That's theft," Wohl said.

"We wanted something on him," McFadden protested. "We was going to turn it in."

Bullshit!

"That's when he told us another guinea shot Tony DeZego," Hay-zus said. "I don't know if that's so or not, but Marvin believed it."

"He didn't offer a name?" Wohl asked.

"We told him to come up with one by four this afternoon," McFadden said.

"And you think he would have come up with a name?"

"If he could have, he would have. Yes, sir."

Wohl looked at Mike Sabara.

"Do you know where Washington is?"

"No, sir. But Payne's outside. They're working together, aren't they?"

"See if either of them is still there," Wohl ordered.

Pekach went to the door and a moment later returned with Matt Payne.

"Do you know where Washington is?"

"No, sir. He told me he would either see me here or phone."

"Find him," Wohl ordered. "Tell him I want to see him as soon as I can."

"Yes, sir," Matt said, and left the room.

Wohl looked at Joe D'Amata.

"You know where this is going, don't you?" he asked.

"Sir, you're thinking there's a connection to the DeZego shooting?"

"Right. And since Special Operations has that job, I've got to call Chief Lowenstein and tell him I want the Lanier job—and that means you, too, Joe, of course—as part of that."

"He's not going to like that," Sabara said.

"If you're sure about that, Mike, you call him," Wohl said, and let Sabara wait ten seconds before he reached for the telephone himself.

To Peter Wohl's genuine surprise Chief Lowenstein agreed to have D'Amata work the Lanier job under Special Operations supervision with absolutely no argument.

"I don't believe that," he said when he hung up. "All he said was that you're a good man, D'Amata, and if there is anything else I need, all I have to do is ask for it."

"Well, how do you want me to handle it?" D'Amata asked.

"Very simply, ask Washington how he wants it handled. Aside from one wild one, I am about out of ideas."

"Wild idea?"

"I want to send the two shotguns to the lab. I have a wild idea that one of them is the one that popped DeZego."

"Yeah," D'Amata said thoughtfully, "could be."

"Do you two clowns think you could take the shotguns to the lab and tell them I need to know, as soon as possible, if the shells we have were ejected from either of them, without getting in any more trouble?"

"Yes, sir," Martinez and McFadden said in unison, and then McFadden asked, "You want us to come back here, sir?"

"No," Wohl said. "You're working four to twelve, right?"

"Yes, sir. Twelve to twelve with the overtime."

"I haven't made up my mind what to do with you," Wohl said. "Let your sergeant know where you're going to be, in case Washington or somebody wants to talk to you, and then report for duty at four. Maybe by then Captain Pekach can find somebody to sit on the both of you. Separately, I mean. Together you're dangerous."

"Yes, sir," they chorused.

"Dave," Wohl said, turning to Pekach, "as soon as D'Amata gets Sherlock Holmes and his partner the shotgun, tell D'Amata what happened in the Ristorante Alfredo," Wohl ordered.

"Yes, sir."

The door opened. Matt Payne put his head in.

"Can't find Washington, sir. He doesn't answer the radio, and he's not at home."

"What I told you to do, Payne, is find him. Not report that you can't. Get in a car and go look for him. The next time I hear from you, I want it to be when you tell me Detective Washington is on his way here."

"Yes, sir," Matt said, and quickly closed the door again.

The telephone rang. Obviously his calls were being held. So the ring indicated that this call was too important to hold.

"Inspector Wohl," he said, answering it himself.

"Dennis Coughlin, Peter."

"Good morning, Chief."

"We're due in the mayor's office at 10:15. You, Matt Lowenstein, and me."

"Yes, sir."

"He's mad, Peter. I guess you know."

"Yes, sir."

The phone went dead.

Well, that explains Chief Lowenstein's inexplicable spirit of enthusiastic cooperation. He knew we were all going to have a little chat with the mayor. He can now go on in there and truthfully say that this very morning, when I asked for it, he gave one more of his brighter detectives and asked if there was anything else he could do for me.

17 Detective Jason Washington did not like Sergeant Patrick J. Dolan, and he was reasonably convinced the reverse was true.

Specifically, as Washington drove his freshly waxed and polished, practically brand-new unmarked car into the parking lot behind the former district station house that was now the headquarters for both the Narcotics and Intelligence Divisions at 4th and Girard and parked it beside one of the dozen or more battered, ancient, and filthy Narcotics unmarked cars, he thought, *I will have to keep in mind that Dolan thinks I'm a slick nigger. It would be better for me if he thought I was a plain old, that is to say, mentally retarded nigger, but he is just smart enough to know that isn't so. He knows that Affirmative Action does not go so far as to put mentally retarded niggers to work as Homicide detectives.*

I will also have to remember that in his own way Dolan is a pretty good cop, that is to say, that a certain degree of intelligence does indeed flicker behind that profanely loudmouthed mick exterior. He is not really as stupid as I would like to think he is, notwithstanding that really stupid business of hauling Matt Payne over here in the belief that he was dealing drugs.

Most important, I will have to remember that what Dolan hasn't told me—and there is something he hasn't told me—is because he doesn't even know he saw it. The dumb mick has tunnel vision. He was looking for a drug bust and saw two rich kids, one driving a Mercedes and one driving a Porsche, and he was so anxious to put them in the bag, what was important to him, a good drug bust, that he just didn't see Murder One going down.

Inside the building, Washington found Sergeant Patrick J. Dolan in the office of Lieutenant Mick Mikkles.

"Good morning, sir," Jason Washington said politely. "And thank you, Sergeant, for making yourself available."

"I'm due in court in an hour," Sergeant Dolan said. "What's on your mind, Washington?"

"I need a little help, Sergeant," Washington said. "I'm getting nowhere with the DeZego job."

"You probably won't," Dolan said. "You want to know what I think?"

"Yes, I really do."

"It was a mob hit. Pure and simple. DeZego broke the rules and they put him out of the game. It's just that simple. You're Homicide. You tell me how many mob hits ever wind up in court."

"Very, very few of them."

"Fucking right! You don't mind me telling you that you're spinning your wheels on this job, Washington?"

"Sergeant, I think you're absolutely right," Washington said. "But because of the Detweiler girl—"

"She's a junkie. I told you that."

"She's also H. Richard Detweiler's daughter," Washington said, "and so the mayor wants to know who did the shooting. If she wasn't involved—"

"I get the picture," Dolan interrupted. "So you go through the motions, right?"

"Exactly."

"So you came back here and *interviewed* me again. And I told you exactly the same thing I told you the first time, all right? So now we're finished, right?"

"I'd really like to go over it all again," Washington said.

"Jesus fucking Christ, Washington," Dolan said. He looked at his watch. "I *told* you, I'm due in fucking court in *fifty-five* minutes. I gotta go over my notes."

He really wants to get rid of me. And I don't think it has a damn thing to do with him being due in court.

"The mayor's on Inspector Wohl's back, so he's on mine. I really—"

"Fuck Inspector Wohl! That's your problem."

"Hey, Pat," Lieutenant Mikkles said, "take it easy!"

"You're thinking that if Wohl hadn't come here and turned his driver loose, you could have gotten something, right?"

"Yeah, that's exactly what I think."

"Well, then you know my problem with Wohl," Washington said.

"No, I don't know your problem with Wohl," Dolan said.

"You don't think I wanted to leave Homicide to go work for him, do you?"

Dolan considered that for a moment.

"Yeah, I heard about that. You and Tony Harris, right?"

"Right. Wohl's got a lot of clout, Sergeant. He generally gets what he wants."

That last remark was for you, Lieutenant Mikkles, to feed your understandable concern that if this doesn't go well, your face will be in the breeze when the shit hits the fan.

"Maybe from you," Dolan said.

"Pat," Lieutenant Mikkles said, "give him fifteen minutes. Go through the motions. You know how it is."

Dolan looked at Mikkles, his face indicating that he thought he had been betrayed. Mikkles nodded at him.

"Fifteen minutes," he said. "You'll still have time to make court."

"Okay," Sergeant Dolan said. "Fifteen minutes. Okay?"

"We'll just go through the motions," Washington said.

"Okay. Start."

"Those pictures you took handy?"

"What the hell do you need those for? I already showed them to you."

Why doesn't he want me to look at the pictures?

"Who knows? Maybe if we look at them again, we'll see something we missed."

"Like what?"

"I don't know."

"I don't know where the hell they are."

I am onto something!

"Maybe your partner has them?" Washington asked.

"Nah, they're probably in the goddamn file. I'll look," Dolan said, and left the room.

"Washington," Lieutenant Mikkles said, "Dolan is a good man."

"Yes, sir, I know."

"But he comes equipped with a standard Irish temper. I would consider it a favor if you could forget that 'Fuck Inspector Wohl' remark."

"I didn't hear anybody say anything like that, Lieutenant."

"I owe you one," Lieutenant Mikkles said.

"Forget it," Washington said.

Sergeant Dolan came back in the office with a handful of five-by-seven photographs.

"Here's the fucking photographs," he said, handing them to Washington. "What do you want to know?"

Washington looked through the photographs, then sorted them so they would be sequential.

They showed Anthony J. DeZego getting out of his car in front of the Hotel Warwick; handing the doorman money; walking toward the hotel cocktail lounge; inside the cocktail lounge (four shots, including one of the bellboy giving him the car keys); leaving the cocktail lounge; walking toward the garage; and, the last shot, entering the garage.

"This is in the right sequence? This all of them?" Washington asked, handing the stack of photographs to Dolan.

"What do you mean, is this all of them?" Dolan snapped. "Yeah, it's all of them." He flipped through them quickly and said, "Yeah, that's the order I took them in."

Anomaly! Anomaly! Anomaly!

"Sergeant, I'd like a set of these pictures for my report," Washington said. "The negatives, I guess, are in the photo lab?"

"The guy that runs the lab is a pal of mine," Dolan said. "I'll give him a ring and have him run you off a set."

"Thank you," Washington said. "Looking at them again, does anything new come to your mind?"

"Not a fucking thing," Dolan said firmly.

"Well, we tried," Washington said.

"Is that all?"

"Unless you can think of something."

"Not a fucking thing. If I think of something, I'll give you a call."

"I'd really appreciate that," Washington said.

"And like I said, I'll call my friend in the photo lab and have him run off a set of prints for you."

"Thank you," Washington said.

Jason Washington parked his unmarked car in the parking lot behind the Roundhouse at 7th and Race and walked purposefully toward the building.

There are four anomalies vis-à-vis Sergeant Dolan and his photographs.

One, Dolan had told me that he and his partner had been trailing the Detweiler girl and had trailed her to the parking garage. There were no photographs of Penelope Detweiler; they were all of Anthony J. DeZego. Why?

Two, there were no photographs of Matt Payne and his girlfriend in the Porsche. If he thought Matt was dealing drugs, there should have been.

Three, there were only thirteen photographs in the stack Dolan showed me. Thirty-five-millimeter film comes in twenty-four- and thirty-six-exposure rolls. Ordinarily almost every frame on a roll of film is exposed, and ordinarily every exposed frame on a roll is printed. And since it is better to have too many photographs than too few, it seemed likely that Dolan would have taken far more than thirteen photographs during the time he had been watching DeZego. Probably a roll at the hotel, and then a fresh one, starting from the moment DeZego left the hotel. Probably a thirty-six-exposure roll, so he wouldn't run out at the wrong time. That's what I would have done.

Four, he suddenly turned obliging at the end. He would call a pal in the photo lab and have his pal make a set of prints and send them to me. Had he suddenly joined the Urban League and vowed to lean over backward in the interests of racial harmony and/or interdepartmental cooperation? Or did he want to control what pictures the lab sent me to include in my report?

Three guys were on duty in the photo lab. One of them seemed less than overjoyed to see Detective Jason Washington. Washington consequently headed straight for him.

"Morning!" he said cheerfully.

"I just this minute got off the phone," the lab guy, a corporal, said. "With Dolan, I mean."

"Good," Washington said. "Then you know why I'm here."

"I'll get to it as soon as I can," the corporal said. "You want to come by about two, or do you want I should send them to you?"

"I want them now," Washington heard himself say. "Didn't Sergeant Dolan tell you that?"

"What do you mean, 'now'?"

"Like, I'll wait," Washington said.

"It don't work that way, Washington, you know that. Other people are in line ahead of you."

"No," Washington said. "I'm at the head of line."

"The fuck you are!"

"Well, you can either take my word for that or we can call Inspector Wohl and he'll tell you I'm at the head of the line."

"Wohl don't run the photo lab," the corporal said.

This Irish bastard is sweating too. What the hell have I found here?

"Well, you tell him that."

"What I am going to do is find the lieutenant and ask him what to do about your coming in here like Jesus Christ Almighty. Who the fuck do you think you are, anyway?"

"Let's go see him together," Washington said.

"I'll go see him," the corporal said. *"You* read the fucking sign." He pointed to the sign: AUTHORIZED PERSONNEL ONLY IN THE LAB.

"I'm surprised," Jason Washington said as he ducked inside the counter, "that an experienced, well-educated police officer such as yourself hasn't learned that there is an exception to every rule."

"You lost your fucking mind or what, Washington?"

That's entirely possible. But the essence of my professional experience as a police officer is that there are times when you should go with a gut feeling. And this is one of those times. I have a gut feeling that if I let you out of my sight, that roll, or rolls, of film are going to turn up missing.

What the hell *are these two up to?*

The corporal turned surprisingly docile when they were actually standing before the lieutenant's desk. His indignation vanished.

"Sir," he said, "Detective Washington has an unusual request that I thought you should handle."

"Hello, Jason," the lieutenant said. "Long time no see. How are things out in the country? Do you miss the big city?"

"I would hate to think the lieutenant was making fun of our happy home at Bustleton and Bowler," Washington said. "Where the deer and the antelope play."

"Who, me?" the lieutenant chuckled. "What can we do for you?"

"I'm working the DeZego job," Washington said.

"So I heard."

"Sergeant Dolan of Narcotics shot a roll of film. I need prints this time yesterday."

"You got the negatives?" the lieutenant asked the corporal, who nodded. "You got it, Jason. Anything else?"

"I want to take the negatives with me."

After only a second's hesitation the lieutenant said, "Sign a receipt and they're yours."

"And I may want some blown up specially," Washington said. "Could I go in the darkroom with him?"

"Sure. That's it?"

Since your face reflected a certain attitude of unease when you heard that I want to go into the darkroom with you, Corporal, and that I'm taking the negatives with

*me, I will go into the darkroom with you and I will take the negatives with me. What
the* hell *is it with these photographs?*

"Yes, sir. Thank you very much."

"Anytime, Jason. That's what we're here for."

The corporal became the spirit of cooperation, to the point of offering Washington
a rubber apron once they entered the darkroom.

If I were a suspicious man, Washington thought, *or a cynic, I might think that he
has considered the way the wind is blowing, and also that if anything is amiss, he
didn't do it, or at least can't blamed for it, and has now decided that Dolan can swing
in the wind all by himself.*

There was only one roll of film, a thirty-six-exposure roll.

"Hold it up to the light," the corporal said. "Or, if you'd like, I can make you a
contact sheet. Take only a minute."

"A what?"

"A print of every negative in negative size on a piece of eight-by-ten."

"Why don't you just feed the roll through the enlarger?" Washington asked.

Jason Washington was not exactly a stranger to the mysteries of a darkroom. Years
before, he had even fooled around with souping and printing his own 35-mm black-
and-white film. That had ended when Martha said the chemicals made the apartment
smell like a sewage-treatment station and had to go. He had no trouble "reading" a
negative projected through an enlarger, although the blacks came out white, and vice
versa.

The first negative projected through the enlarger showed Anthony J. DeZego
emerging from his Cadillac in front of the Warwick Hotel. The second showed him
handing money to the doorman. The third showed him walking toward the door to the
hotel cocktail lounge. The fourth showed him inside the cocktail lounge; the view partially blocked by a pedestrian, a neatly dressed man carrying an attaché case who was
looking through the plate-glass window into the cocktail lounge. That photograph had
not been in the stack of five-by-sevens Sergeant Dolan had shown him.

Next came an image of DeZego inside the bar, the pedestrian having moved on
down the street. Then there were two images of DeZego's car as the bellboy walked
toward it and got in it. The pedestrian was in one of the two, casually glancing at the
car. He was not in the second photograph. Dolan had shown him a print of the bell-
man and the car, less the pedestrian.

What's with the pedestrian?

The next image was of DeZego's Cadillac making a left turn. And the one after
that was of the pedestrian crossing the street in the same direction. Dolan's stack of
prints hadn't included that one, either.

Is that guy following DeZego's car? Who the hell is he?

The next shot showed the chubby bellboy walking back to the hotel, apparently after having parked DeZego's Cadillac. Two frames later the pedestrian with the attaché
case showed up again. Then came a shot of the bellboy giving DeZego his car keys,
and then, no longer surprising Jason Washington, the pedestrian came walking down
the sidewalk again.

"Go back toward the beginning of the roll, please," Jason Washington said. "The
third or fourth frame, I think."

"Sure," the corporal said cooperatively.

The image of the well-dressed pedestrian with the attaché case looking into the Warwick Hotel cocktail lounge appeared.

"Print that one, please," Washington said.

"Five-by-seven all right?"

"Yeah, sure," Washington said, and then immediately changed his mind. "No, make it an eight-by-ten. And you better make three copies."

"Three eight-by-tens," the corporal said. "No problem."

Sergeant Patrick J. Dolan is an experienced investigator. If he didn't spot the guy with the attaché case, my name is Jerry Carlucci. Who the hell is he, and why didn't Dolan want me to see his picture?

Even in a well-equipped photographic laboratory with all the necessary equipment to print, develop, and then dry photographs, it takes some time to prepare thirty-six eight-by-ten enlargements. It was 10:10 when Detective Jason Washington, carrying three large manila envelopes each containing a set of the dozen photographs Sergeant Dolan had taken, but not either included in his report or shown to Washington, came out of the Police Administration Building.

He got in his car and drove the half dozen blocks to Philadelphia's City Hall, then parked his car in the inner courtyard with its nose against a sign reading RESERVED FOR INSPECTORS.

As he got out of the car he saw that he had parked beside a car familiar to him, that of Staff Inspector Peter Wohl. He checked the license plate to be sure. Wohl, obviously, was somewhere inside City Hall.

Peter will want to know about this, Jason Washington thought immediately. *But even if I could find him in here, what the hell could I tell him I have? It's probably a good thing I didn't bump into him.*

He then visited inside City Hall and began to prowl the cavernous corridors outside its many courtrooms, looking for Sergeant Patrick J. Dolan.

"You have your special assistant with you, Inspector?" Mayor Jerry Carlucci asked, by way of greeting, Staff Inspector Peter Wohl.

"No, sir," Peter Wohl replied.

"Where is he?"

"He's working with Detective Washington, sir."

"That's a shame," the mayor said. "I had hoped to see him."

"I didn't know that, sir."

"Didn't you, Inspector? Or were you thinking, maybe, 'He's a nice kid and I'll keep him out of the line of fire'?"

"I didn't know you wanted to see him, Mr. Mayor," Peter said.

"But now that you do, do you have any idea what I would have liked to have said to him, if given the opportunity?"

"I think he already heard that, Mr. Mayor, from me. Last night," Peter said.

"So you know he has diarrhea of the mouth?"

"I used those very words, Mr. Mayor, when I *counseled* him last night," Peter said.

Carlucci glowered at Wohl for a moment and then laughed. "You *counseled* him, did you, Peter?"

"Yes, sir."

"I don't know why the hell I'm laughing," the mayor said. "That was pretty goddamn embarrassing at the Browne place. Dick Detweiler was goddamn near hysterical. Christ, he *was* hysterical."

"Mr. Mayor," Chief Inspector Dennis V. Coughlin said, "I think any father naturally would be upset to learn that his daughter was involved with narcotics."

"Particularly if he heard it thirdhand, the way Detweiler did," the mayor said icily, "instead of, for example, from a senior police official directly."

"Yes, sir," Coughlin said.

His Honor the Mayor was not through.

"Maybe an *Irish* police official," Carlucci said. "The Irish are supposed to be good at politics. An Irishman could have told Detweiler about his daughter with a little Irish—what is it you call your bullshit, Denny, the kind you just tried to lay on me?—blarney."

"Sir," Wohl said, "it could have been worse."

"How the hell could it have been worse?" the mayor snapped. "Do you have any idea how much Detweiler contributed to my last campaign? Or phrased another way, how *little* he, and his friends, will contribute to my next campaign unless we put away, for a long time—and more importantly, soon—whoever popped his daughter?"

"We have information that Miss Detweiler was involved with Tony the Zee, Mr. Mayor. He may not know that. Payne didn't tell him."

The mayor looked him, his eyebrows raised in incredulity.

"Oh, *shit!*" he said. "How good is your information?"

"My source is Payne. He got it from the Nesbitt boy—the Marine?—who got it from the Browne girl," Wohl said.

"Then it's just a matter of time until Detweiler learns that too," the mayor said.

"Even if that's true, Mr. Mayor," Dennis Coughlin said, "I don't see how he could hold that against you."

The mayor snapped his head toward Coughlin and glowered at him a moment. "I hope that's more of your fucking blarney, Denny. I would hate to think that I have a chief inspector who is so fucking dumb, he believes what he just said."

"Jerry, for chrissake," Chief Inspector Matt Lowenstein said. It was the first time he had spoken. "Denny's on your side. We all are."

Carlucci glared at him, then looked as if he were going to say something but didn't.

"I really don't see, Jerry," Coughlin said reasonably, "how he could hold his daughter's problems against you."

"Okay," Carlucci said, his tone as reasonable, "I'll tell you how. We have a man who has just learned his daughter is into hard drugs. And, according to Peter, here, is about to learn that she has been running around with a guinea gangster. What's your information, Peter? What does 'involved with' mean? That she's been fucking him?"

"Yes, sir. Payne seemed pretty sure it was more than a casual acquaintance."

"Okay. So what we have here is a guy who is a pillar of the community. His *wife* is a pillar of the community. They have done everything they could for their precious daughter. They have sent her to the right schools and the right churches and seen that she associates with the right kind of people—like young Payne, for example. And all of a sudden she gets herself popped with a shotgun, and then it comes out that she's a junkie and fucking a guinea gangster. How can that be? It's certainly not *her* fault, and it's certainly not *their* fault. So it has to be society's fault. And who is responsible for society? Who is supposed to put gangsters and drug dealers in jail? Why, the *police* are. That's why we *have* police. If the *police* had done their job, there would be no drugs on the street, and if the *police* had done their job, that low-life guinea gangster would have been put in jail and would not have been getting in precious Penny's pants. That's what Detweiler called his daughter last night, by the way: 'precious Penny.' Is any of this getting through to you, Denny?"

"Yeah, sure," Coughlin said resignedly. "It's not fair, but that's the way it is."

"Nothing personal, Denny, but that's the first intelligent thing you've said so far this morning," the mayor said. He let that sink in a moment, then turned to Peter Wohl. "What I told Detweiler last night—not knowing, of course, that his precious Penny was fucking DeZego—was that we were close to finding the man who had shot her. How much more of an asshole is that going to make me look like, Peter?"

"We may be onto something," Wohl said carefully.

"Christ, I hope so. What?"

"Dave Pekach had dinner with his girlfriend—"

"The Peebles woman? That one?"

"Yes, sir."

"I'm going off on a tangent," the mayor said. "What about that? Is that going to embarrass the Department?"

"No. I don't think so," Wohl said. "Unless a police captain acting like a teenager in love for the first time is embarrassing."

The mayor was not amused. "She has friends in very high places," he said coldly. "Do you think maybe you should drop a hint that he had better treat her right?"

"I don't think that's necessary, Mr. Mayor," Wohl said. "Dave Pekach is really a decent guy. And they're really in love."

The mayor considered that dubiously for a moment but finally said, "If you say so, Peter, okay. But what we don't need is any more rich people pissed off at the Department than we already have. Arthur J. Nelson and Dick Detweiler is enough already. So he had dinner with her . . ."

"At Ristorante Alfredo," Wohl went on. "He had made reservations. When he got there, Vincenzo Savarese was there. He gave him— I'm cutting corners here."

"You're doing fine," the mayor said.

"A little speech about being grateful for a favor Dave had done for him—nothing dirty there, just Dave being nice to a girl he didn't know was Savarese's granddaughter. You want to hear about that?"

"Not unless it's important."

"Savarese said thank you for the favor, and then Ricco Baltazari gave Dave a matchbook, said Dave dropped it. Inside was a name and address. Black guy named Marvin P. Lanier. Small-time. Says he's a gambler. Actually he's a pimp. And according to two of Dave's undercover cops—Martinez and McFadden, the two who caught the junkie who killed Dutch Moffitt—Lanier sometimes transports cocaine from Harlem."

"You've lost me," the mayor said. "What's a nigger pimp got to do with precious Penny Detweiler?"

"Last night Martinez and McFadden saw Lanier. They had been using him as a snitch. Lanier told them, quote, a guinea shot Tony the Zee, unquote."

"He had a name?" the mayor asked.

"He was supposed to come up with one by four o'clock this afternoon," Wohl said.

"You think he will?"

"Lanier got popped last night. Five shots with a .38," Wohl said. "Do you know Joe D'Amata of Homicide?"

"Yeah."

"He got the job. Because there was a Highway car seen at the crime scene, he came out to Bustleton and Bowler first thing this morning to see what we had on Lanier."

"Which was?"

"Nothing. Martinez and McFadden were in the car. Working on their own."

"I'm having a little trouble following all this, Peter," the mayor said, almost apologetically.

"When McFadden and Martinez saw Lanier, they took a shotgun away from him. Joe D'Amata said Lanier had a shotgun under his bed. So I thought maybe there was a tie-in—"

"How?"

"Savarese pointed us to this guy. DeZego was popped with a shotgun. Lanier had two. Lanier gets killed."

"What about the shotgun? Shotguns?"

"I sent them to the lab."

"And?"

"I can call. They may not be through yet."

"Call."

Less than a minute later Wohl replaced one of the mayor's three telephones in its cradle.

"Forensics," Wohl announced, "says that the shotgun-shell cases found on the roof of the Penn Services Parking Garage were almost certainly, based on the marks made by the ejector, fired from the Remington Model 1100 shotgun D'Amata found under Lanier's bed."

"Bingo," Dennis V. Coughlin said.

"You're saying the pimp shot DeZego?" the mayor asked.

"I think Savarese wants *us* to think Lanier shot DeZego," Matt Lowenstein said.

"Why?" the mayor asked.

"Who the hell knows?" Lowenstein said.

"Check with Organized Crime," the mayor said. "See if they can come up with any reason the mob would want DeZego dead."

"They're working on that, Jerry," Lowenstein said. "I asked them the day after DeZego got popped; they said they'd already been asked to check by Jason Washington."

If there was a rebuke in Lowenstein's reply, the mayor seemed not to have noticed.

"Washington working on this dead-pimp angle?" Carlucci asked.

"No, sir," Wohl replied. "Chief Lowenstein loaned me D'Amata. I was going to have him work with Washington. But when I couldn't find him, I put Tony Harris on it."

"Why can't you find Washington?"

"I don't know where he is," Wohl said, and then heard his words. "I didn't mean that, sir, the way it came out. He's working on the street somewhere, and when I got the word to come here, he hadn't reported in yet. I've got Payne looking for him. For all I know, he's probably already found him."

"Tony Harris is working on the Officer Magnella job, right?" the mayor asked. "So you turn him off that to put him on this?"

"We're getting nowhere on the Magnella job, Mr. Mayor," Peter Wohl said. "That one's going to take time. I wanted a good Homicide detective at the Lanier scene while it was still hot."

"Meaning you don't think Joe D'Amata is a good Homicide detective?" Lowenstein snapped.

"If I didn't think Joe was as good as he is, I wouldn't have asked you for him, Chief," Wohl replied. "Maybe that was a bad choice of words. What I meant was that I wanted Harris and D'Amata, now that we know we're looking for something beside the doer of a pimp shooting, to take another look at the crime scene as soon as possible."

"I don't like that," the mayor said thoughtfully.

"Sir?" Peter asked.

"Shit, I didn't mean *that* the way it came out. I wouldn't tell you how to do your job, Peter. What I meant was what you said about the Magnella job, that it's going to take time. We can't afford that. You can't let people get away with shooting a cop. You have to catch him—them—quick. And in a good, tight, all-the-i's-dotted, all-the-t's-crossed arrest."

"Yes, sir, I know. But Harris told me all he knows how to do is go back to the beginning. There's nothing new to run down."

"Lowenstein giving you all the help you need?"

"Chief Lowenstein has been very helpful, sir. I couldn't ask for anything more," Wohl said.

"Denny, you paying attention?" the mayor asked.

"Sir?"

"Peter knows what's the right thing to say to make friends and influence people. You ought to watch him, learn from him."

"Oh, fuck you, Jerry," Coughlin said when he realized that the real target of Carlucci's barb was Wohl, and that he was being teased.

"Make that, 'oh, fuck you, Mr. Mayor,' sir," Carlucci said, chuckling. Then his voice grew serious. "Okay. Thanks for coming in. If it wasn't for what Peter said about the Magnella job, I'd say I feel a lot better than I felt before. Jesus, I'd like to hang the DeZego job on Savarese, or even on one of his scumbags."

Coughlin stood up and shook the mayor's hand when it was offered. Lowenstein followed him past the mayor's desk, and then past Wohl.

The mayor hung on to Wohl's hand, signaling that he wanted Wohl to remain behind.

"Yes, sir?"

"I spoke to your dad last night," the mayor said.

"Last night?" Peter asked, surprised.

"This morning. Very early this morning. He told me he had been talking to you and that you led him to believe your salami was on the chopping block with all this, and you thought that was unfair."

"I— We had a couple of drinks at Groverman's."

"So he said."

"I'm sorry he called you, Mr. Mayor."

"How could you have stopped him? What I told him, Peter, was that you were absolutely right. Your salami is on the chopping block, and it isn't fair. I also told him that if you come out of this smelling like a rose, you stand a good chance to be the youngest full inspector in the Department."

"Jesus," Wohl said.

"My salami's in jeopardy, Peter, not only yours. I'm going to look like a fucking fool if Special Operations drops the ball on all this. If I don't look like a fucking fool when this is all over, then you get taken care of. Take my meaning?"

"Yes, sir."

"Give my regards to your mother, Peter," Mayor Carlucci said, and walked Peter to his office door.

Charley McFadden was almost home before he realized there was a silver lining in the dark cloud of being on Inspector Wohl's shit list. And that was a dark cloud indeed. If Wohl was pissed at them, that meant Captains Sabara and Pekach were also pissed at them, and that meant that Sergeant Big Bill Henderson would conclude that hunting season was now open on him and Hay-zus. Christ only knew what *that* son of a bitch would do to them now.

There was a good possibility that he and Hay-zus would wind up in a district somewhere, maybe even in a goddamn wagon. McFadden really didn't want to be a Highway Patrolman, but he wanted to be an ordinary, turn-off-the-fire-hydrants, guard-a-school-crossing cop even less.

And if Wohl did send them to a district, it would probably go on their records that they had been Probationary Highway Patrolmen and flunked, or whatever it would be called. Busted probation. *Shit!*

The silver lining appeared when he turned onto his street and started looking for a place to park the Volkswagen. His eyes fell on the home of Mr. Robert McCarthy, and his mind's eye recalled the red hair and blue eyes and absolutely perfect little ass of Mr. McCarthy's niece, Margaret McCarthy, R.N.

And he had all fucking day off, until say, three, which would give him an hour to get back in uniform and drive out to Bustleton and Bowler.

He found a place to park—for once—almost right in front of his house and ran up the stairs and inside.

"What are you doing home?" his mother asked.

"Got something to do, Ma," he called as he went up the stairs.

He took his uniform off and hung it carefully in the closet. Then he dressed with great care: a new white shirt with buttons on the collar, like he had seen Matt Payne wear; a dark brown sport coat; slightly lighter brown slacks; black loafers with a flap and little tassels in front, also seen on Matt Payne; and a necktie with stripes like both Inspector Wohl and Payne wore. He was so concerned with his appearance that he forgot his gun and had to take the jacket off and put on his shoulder holster.

Then it occurred to him that although he had shaved before going out to Bustleton and Bowler, that was a couple of hours ago, and a little more after-shave wouldn't hurt anything; girls were supposed to like it, so he generously splashed Brut on his face and neck before leaving his room.

"Where are you going all dressed up?" his mother asked, and then sniffed suspiciously. "What's that I smell? Perfume?"

"It's after-shave lotion, Ma."

"I'd hate to tell you what it smells like," she said.

And then he was out the door.

He walked purposefully toward Broad Street until he was certain his mother, sure to be peering from behind the lace curtain on the door, couldn't see him anymore, and then he cut across the street and went back to the McCarthy house, where he quickly climbed the steps and rang the bell, hoping it would be answered before his mother made one of her regularly scheduled, every-five-minutes inspections of the neighborhood.

Mr. McCarthy, wearing a suit, opened the door.

"Hello, Charley, what can I do for you?"

"Is Margaret around?"

"We're going to pay our respects to the Magnellas," Mr. McCarthy said.

"Oh," Charley said.

"You been over there yet?"

"No."

"You want to go with us?"

"Yeah," Charley said.

"I thought maybe that's what you had in mind," Mr. McCarthy said. "You're all dressed up."

"Yeah," Charley said.

"Goddamn shame," Mr. McCarthy said.

"Hello, Charley," Margaret McCarthy said. "You going with us?"

She was wearing a suit with a white blouse and a little round hat.

Jesus Christ, that's a good-looking woman!

"I wanted to pay my respects," Charley said.

"You might as well ride with us," Mr. McCarthy said.

The ride to Stanley Rocco and Sons, Funeral Directors, was pleasant until they got there. That is to say, he got to ride in the backseat with Margaret and he could smell her—an entirely delightful sensation—even over his after-shave. He could even see the lace at the hem of her slip, which triggered his imagination.

But then, when Mr. McCarthy had parked the Ford and Margaret had climbed out and he had in a gentlemanly manner averted his eyes from the unintentional display of lower limbs and he got out, he saw that the place was crowded with cops, in uniform and out.

"Jesus, wait a minute," he said to Margaret.

He took out his wallet and sighed with relief when he found a narrow strip of black elasticized material. He had put it in there after the funeral of Captain Dutch Moffitt, intending to put it in a drawer when he got home.

Thank God I forgot!

"What is that?" Margaret asked.

"A mourning stripe," Charley said. "You cut up a hatband."

"Oh," she said, obviously not understanding.

"When there's a dead cop, you wear it across your badge," he explained as he worked the band across his. "I almost forgot."

He started to pin the badge to his lapel.

"You got it on crooked," Margaret said. "Let me."

He could see her scalp where her hair was parted as she pinned the badge on correctly.

She looked up at him and met his eyes and smiled, and his heart jumped.

"There," she said.

"Thanks," he said.

They caught up with Mr. and Mrs. McCarthy and walked to the funeral home.

There was a book for people to write their names in on a stand just inside the door. It was just about full.

He wrote "Officer Charles McFadden, Badge 8774, Special Operations" under the name of some captain he didn't know from the 3rd District.

Officer Joseph Magnella was in an open casket, surrounded by flowers. They were burying him in his uniform, Charley saw. There were two cops from his district, wearing white gloves, standing at each end of the casket, and there was an American flag on a pole behind each of them.

In his turn Charley followed Mr. and Mrs. McCarthy and Margaret to the prie-dieu and dropped to his knees. He made the sign of the cross and, with part of his mind, offered the prayers a Roman Catholic does in such circumstances. They came to him automatically, and although his lips moved, he didn't hear them.

He was thinking, *Christ, they put face powder and lipstick on him.*

I wonder if they will take the badge off before they close the casket, or whether they'll bury him with it.

The last time I saw him, he was still in the gutter with somebody's coat over his face and shoulders.

Holy Mary, Mother of God, don't let that happen to me!

And the word is, they're not even close to finding the scumbags who did this to him!

I'd like to find those cocksuckers! They wouldn't look as good in their coffins as this poor bastard does!

As he had approached the coffin he had noticed the Magnella family, plus the girlfriend, sitting in the first row of chairs. When he rose from the prie-dieu, they were all standing up. Mr. Magnella was embracing Mr. McCarthy, and Mrs. McCarthy was patting Mrs. Magnella. The girlfriend looked as if somebody had punched her in the stomach; Margaret was smiling at her uncomfortably.

"Al," Mr. McCarthy said when Charley approached, "this is Charley McFadden, from the neighborhood."

"I'm real sorry this happened," Charley said as Mr. Magnella shook his hand.

"You knew my Joe?"

"No. I seen him around, though."

"It was nice of you to come."

"I wanted to pay my respects."

"This is Joe's mother."

"Mrs. Magnella, I'm real sorry for you."

"Thank you for coming."

"I was Joe's fiancée," the girlfriend said.

"I'm real sorry."

"We were going to get married in two months."

"I'm really sorry for you."

"Thank you for coming."

"I'm Joe's brother."

"I'm really sorry this happened."

"Thank you for coming."

"Bob," Mr. Magnella said to Mr. McCarthy, "go in the room on the other side and fix yourself and Officer McFadden a drink."

"Thank you, Al," Mr. McCarthy said. "I might just do that."

Margaret put her hand on Charley's arm, and they followed Mr. and Mrs. McCarthy across the room to a smaller room, where a knot of men were gathered around a table on which sat a dozen bottles of whiskey.

Margaret opened her purse and wiped her eyes with a handkerchief.

"Seagram's all right for you, Charley?" Mr. McCarthy asked.

"Fine," Charley said.

As he put the glass to his mouth the soft murmur of voices died out. Curious, he turned to see what was going on.

Mrs. Magnella had entered the room. She looked like she was headed right for him.

She was. Her son and husband were on her heels, looking worried.

"I know who you are," Mrs. Magnella said to Charley McFadden. "I seen your picture in the papers. You're the cop who caught the junkie and pushed him under the subway, right?"

That wasn't what happened. I was chasing the son of a bitch and he fell!

"Uh!" Charley said.

"I want you to find the people who did this to my Joseph and push them under the subway!"

"Mama," Officer Magnella's brother said. "Come on, Mama!"

"I want them dead! I want them dead!"

"Come on, Mama! Pop, where's Father Loretto?"

"I'm here," a silver-haired priest said. "Elena, what's the matter?"

"I want them dead! I want them dead!"

"It's going to be all right, Elena," the priest said. "Come with me, we'll talk."

"I'm sorry about this," Officer Magnella's brother said to Officer McFadden as the priest led Officer Magnella's mother away.

"It's all right, don't worry about it," Charley said.

Margaret McCarthy looked at Charley McFadden and saw that it wasn't all right. Without thinking what she was doing, she put her hand out to his face, and when he looked at her, she stood on her tiptoes and kissed him.

18 Officer Matthew Payne was feeling a little sorry for himself. He had been given an impossible task—how the hell was he supposed to find one man in a city the size of Philadelphia?—and Peter Wohl had made it plain that he expected him to accomplish it: No excuses, please. Just do it.

When he had tried looking for Jason Washington in all the places he could think, starting with his home, and then going to the Roundhouse and over to the parking garage and even to Hahneman Hospital, he went back to the Roundhouse, on the admittedly somewhat flimsy reasoning that Washington had told him to meet him in Homicide in the Roundhouse before he left word on the answering machine not to meet him there.

Washington was not in Homicide and had not been there.

It occurred to Matt that very possibly Washington had finished doing whatever he was doing and had gone, as he said he would, out to Bustleton and Bowler. If Washington *was* at Bustleton and Bowler, where he said he would be, and Officer Payne was downtown at the Roundhouse looking for him, Officer Payne was going to look like a goddamn fool.

Which, in the final analysis, was probably a just evaluation.

He called Bustleton and Bowler.

"Special Operations, Sergeant Anderson."

"This is Payne, Sergeant. Is Detective Washington around there someplace?"

"No. He called in and wanted to talk to you. He said he told you to wait for him here."

"Did he say where he was?"

"No. He just said if I saw you, I was to sit on you."

"Okay."

"Wait a minute. He said that he would be at City Hall."

"Thank you very much," Matt said.

He hung up, rode the elevator down from Homicide, and ran out of the building into the parking lot, where a white-capped Traffic officer was in the process of putting an illegal-parking citation under the Porsche's windshield wiper.

"Could I change your mind about doing that if I told you I was on the job?" Matt asked.

The Traffic cop, who was old enough to be Matt's father, looked at him dubiously.

"You're a 369?"

Matt nodded.

"Where?"

"Special Operations," Matt said.

The Traffic cop, shaking his head, removed the citation.

"What did you guys do?" he asked, nodding at the Porsche. "Confiscate that from a drug dealer?"

This is not the time to tell Daddy that I chopped down the cherry tree.

"Yeah," Matt said. "Nice, huh?"

The Traffic cop shook his head resignedly and walked off without another word.

Matt drove to City Hall and parked the Porsche in an area reserved FOR POLICE VEHICLES ONLY.

I would not be at all surprised, the way things are going today, that when I come out of here, to find a cop, maybe that same cop, putting another ticket on me here.

He went inside the building and trotted up the stairs to the second floor. Thirty seconds after that he spotted Detective Jason Washington walking toward him. From the look on Washington's face, Matt could tell he was not overcome with joy to see him.

"What are you doing here?" Washington asked in greeting.

"Inspector Wohl sent me to find you," Matt said. "He wants to see you right away."

"Keep looking," Washington said. "You didn't find me yet."

"Okay," Matt said, with only a moment's hesitation. "I didn't."

"In ten minutes, give or take, you will find me in the ground-floor stairwell, on the southeast corner of the building."

"Yes, sir," Matt said.

"It's important, Matt," Washington said. "Trust me."

"Certainly."

Wait a minute! If my intention is to put Dolan off-balance, the kid can help. Dolan doesn't like him.

"I don't have time to explain this, even if I were sure I could," Washington said. "But I just changed my mind. I want you to come with me. I'm looking for your friend, Sergeant Dolan."

Matt's face registered surprise.

"I don't want you to open your mouth, understand?"

"Yes, sir."

"You any kind of an actor?"

"I don't know."

"Let us suppose that I have caught your friend Dolan doing something he shouldn't have," Washington said, "and I told you. Do you think you could work up a smug, self-satisfied look? So that Dolan would think you know he's in trouble and are very pleased about it?"

"If that son of a bitch is in trouble, I wouldn't have to do very much acting," Matt said.

"Just keep your mouth shut," Washington said. "I mean that. If I blow this, we could both be in trouble."

"Okay," Matt said.

"And there, obviously at the intervention of a benign deity," Washington said softly, "is the son of a bitch."

Matt looked over his shoulder. Sergeant Dolan was coming down the crowded corridor. At the moment Matt looked, Dolan spotted them. He did not look very happy about it.

"Sergeant Dolan," Washington called out, "may I see you a moment, please?"

He walked over to him with Matt at his heels.

"What's on your mind, Washington?" Sergeant Dolan asked.

Washington turned to Matt and handed him two of the three large manila envelopes.

"Give one to Chief Lowenstein and the other one to Chief Coughlin," he said.

"Yes, sir."

"But I'd suggest you stick around, Matt, until we have Sergeant Dolan's explanation."

"Yes, sir."

"You know Officer Payne, don't you, Sergeant? He's Inspector Wohl's special assistant."

"Yeah, I know him. Whaddaya say, Payne?"

Matt nodded at Sergeant Dolan.

"Sorry to bother you again, Sergeant," Washington said. "But I've come up with some more photographs. I'd like to show them to you."

He handed Dolan the third envelope. Dolan opened it. His face showed that what he considered the worst possible scenario had begun to play.

"So?" he said with transparent belligerence.

"I was hoping you could tell me who those two gentlemen are," Washington said.

"Haven't the faintest fucking idea. They was just on the street."

"I was wondering why those photographs weren't included in your report, or in the photographs you showed me."

"They wasn't important."

"You wouldn't want to even guess who those two gentlemen are?"

"No, I wouldn't," Dolan said.

"Let's stop the crap, Dolan," Washington said. "This has gone too far."

"Fuck you, Washington," Dolan said, his bravado transparent.

"Payne, get on the phone and tell Inspector Wohl that Sergeant Dolan is being uncooperative," Washington said. "And ask him to please let me know whether he wants to take it from here or whether I should take this directly to Chief Lowenstein. I'll wait here with Sergeant Dolan."

"Yes, sir," Matt said.

"Washington, can I talk to you private?" Dolan asked. "It's not what you think it is."

"How do you know what I think it is?"

"It's dumb but it's not dirty," Dolan said, "is what I mean."

Detective Washington's face registered suspicion and distaste.

"Come on, Washington," Sergeant Dolan said, "I've got as much time on the job as you do. I told you this isn't dirty."

"But you don't want Payne to hear it, right?" Washington said. "So you tell me about it, and later it's your word against mine?"

"That's not it at all," Dolan said.

"Then what is it?"

"Well, okay, then. But not here in the fucking corridor."

Washington let him sweat fifteen seconds, which seemed to be much longer, and then he said, "Okay, Dolan. I know you're a good cop. You and I will find someplace to talk. Alone. And Payne will wait here until we're finished."

Dolan nodded. He looked at Matt Payne. "Nothing personal, Payne."

Matt nodded.

Washington took Dolan's arm and they walked down the wide, high-ceilinged corridor. Washington opened a door, looked inside, and then held it wide for Dolan to precede him.

Matt waited where he had been told to wait for three or four minutes, and then curiosity got the better of him and he walked down the corridor. Through a very dirty pane of glass he saw Washington and Dolan in an empty courtroom. They were standing beside one of the large, ornately carved tables provided for counsel during trial.

Matt walked back down the corridor to where he had been told to wait.

A minute later Washington and Dolan came out of the courtroom. Dolan walked toward Matt. Washington beckoned for Matt to follow him and then walked quickly in the other direction, toward the staircase. Dolan avoided looking at Matt as he passed him. Matt thought he looked sick.

Washington didn't wait for Matt to catch up with him. On the stair landing Matt looked down and saw Washington going down the stairs two at a time. He ran after him and caught up with him in the courtyard. By then Washington was in his car, and had taken the microphone from the glove compartment.

"W-William One, W-William Seven," Washington said.

"W-William One."

"Inspector, I'm at City Hall. Can I meet you somewhere?"

"I'm headed for Bustleton and Bowler. Did Payne find you?"

"Yeah. But I would rather talk to you before you get to the office."

"Okay. I'm at Broad and 66th Avenue at the Oak Lane Diner. I'll wait for you there."

"On my way. Thank you," Washington said, and put the microphone away. He looked at Payne. "You ever read *Through the Looking Glass?*"

Matt nodded.

"Profound book, although I understand he wrote it stoned on cocaine. Things really are more Curiouser than you would believe. If I lose you in traffic, Wohl's waiting for us in the Oak Lane Diner at Broad and 66th Avenue."

He pulled the door closed and started the engine.

Matt ran across the interior courtyard to the Porsche. There was an illegal parking citation under the windshield wiper.

He didn't see Washington in traffic, but when he got to the Oak Lane Diner, Washington's car was parked beside Wohl's. When he went inside, a waitress was delivering three cups of coffee to a booth table, on which Washington was spreading out the eight-by-ten photographs he had shown Sergeant Dolan.

Wohl looked up.

"Mr. Payne, well-known tracer of lost detectives," he said, "sit." He slid over to make room.

Washington was smiling.

"Okay, I give up," Wohl said. "What am I looking at?"

Matt looked at the photographs. A neatly dressed man carrying an attaché case and looking in the window of the cocktail lounge of the Warwick Hotel. A bald-headed man driving a Pontiac. The first man getting into the Pontiac. There were a dozen variations.

"Your FBI at work," Washington said.

"What?"

"They were apparently—what's the word they use, surveilling?—surveilling Mr. DeZego."

"Where'd these come from?"

"Sergeant Dolan."

"Why haven't we seen them before?"

"You're not going to believe this," Washington said.

"Try me."

"Sergeant Dolan does not like the FBI."

"So what? I'm not all that in love with them myself," Wohl said.

"So he decided to zing them," Washington said.

"What does that mean?"

"He wanted to make them squirm, to let them know that their surveillance was not as discreet as they like to think it is."

"You've lost me."

"He sent the FBI office pictures of themselves at work," Washington said. "In a plain brown envelope."

"Jesus Christ, that's childish!" Wohl said disgustedly.

"I would tend to agree," Washington said.

"Didn't he know Homicide would want to talk to these guys?" Wohl asked, and then, before there could be a reply, he thought of something else: "And the goddamn FBI! They must have known what went down. Why didn't they come forward?"

"Far be it from me to cast aspersions on our federal cousins," Washington said dryly, "but it has sometimes been alleged that the FBI doesn't like to waste its time dealing with the local authorities—unless, of course, they can steal the arrest and get their pictures in the newspapers."

"I'll be a son of a bitch!" Wohl said furiously.

"Can I say something to you as a friend, Inspector?" Washington asked.

"Sure," Wohl said. "I just can't *believe* this shit! God damn those arrogant bastards! DeZego was murdered! Assassinated! And the fucking FBI can't be bothered with it!"

"Peter, go by the book," Washington said.

"Meaning?"

"There is a departmental regulation that says any contact with federal agencies will be conducted through the Office of Extradepartmental Affairs. There's a captain in the Roundhouse—"

"Duffy," Wohl said. "Jack Duffy."

"Right. Go through Duffy."

Wohl looked at Washington for a long moment, his jaws working.

"When you're angry, Peter," Washington said, "you really give the word a whole new meaning. You get *angry*. And you *stay* angry."

A faint smile appeared on Wohl's face.

"You remember, huh, Jason?"

"I'm one of the few people who knows that it's not true you have never lost your temper," Washington said.

"Now Sherlock Holmes knows too," Wohl said, nodding at Matt Payne. "He tell you about the pimp?"

"No."

"What pimp?" Matt asked.

"That's right," Wohl said. "You don't know, either, do you?"

"No, sir."

Wohl related the whole sequence of events leading up to the death of Marvin Lanier.

"So what I think you should do, Jason," he concluded, "is get on the radio and get in touch with Tony Harris, and see what, if anything, they—he and D'Amata—have come up with. And then tell Tony I saw the mayor this morning, and he wants the Magnella shooting solved. I wish he'd get back on that."

"You saw the mayor? I saw your car at City Hall."

"Just a friendly little chat, to assure me of his absolute faith in me," Wohl said dryly.

"Yes, sir," Washington said. "You want me to take Payne with me? Or have you got something for him to do?"

Wohl gathered the photographs together, stacked them neatly, and put them back in the envelope. "Payne, you go out to Bustleton and Bowler, driving slowly and carefully, obeying all the speed limits. When you get there, telephone Captain John J. Duffy at the Roundhouse and tell him that I would be grateful for an appointment at his earliest convenience."

"Yes, sir."

"And then contact me and tell me when Captain Duffy will be able to see me."

"Where will you be, Inspector?"

"Around," Wohl said. "Around."

"Come on, Peter!" Washington said.

"You made your point, Jason. Leave it," Wohl said. He bumped hips with Matt, signaling he wanted to get up, then picked up the envelope with the photographs. When Matt was standing in the aisle, Wohl dropped money on the table and started to walk away. Then he turned. "Good job, Jason, coming up with the photographs. Thank you."

"Just don't do something with them that will make me regret it," Washington said.

"I told you to leave it, Jason!" Wohl said, icily furious. Then he walked out of the Oak Lane Diner and got in his car. Neither Jason Washington nor Matt Payne was surprised to see him head back downtown rather than toward Bustleton and Bowler. The Philadelphia office of the Federal Bureau of Investigation was downtown.

"Until a moment ago," Washington said, "there was an element of humor in this. Now it's not at all funny."

"So he tells the FBI what he thinks of them. So what?"

Washington looked at him, as if surprised that Matt could ask such a stupid question.

"I really don't understand," Matt said.

"The FBI doesn't like criticism," he explained. "Especially in a case like this, where it's justified. So instead of admitting they acted like horses' asses, they will come up with a good reason why they didn't happen to mention to us that they had men on DeZego. 'A continuing investigation' is one phrase they use; 'classified national security matters' is another one. And they go to Commissioner Czernich and say, 'We thought we had an agreement that whenever one of your people wants something from us, he would go through Captain Duffy's Office of Extradepartmental Affairs. Your man Wohl was just in here making all kinds of wild accusations and behaving in a most unprofessional manner.' "

"But they were wrong," Matt protested.

"We don't like to admit it, but we need the FBI, use it a lot. The NCIC is an FBI operation. They have the best forensic laboratories in the world. They sometimes tip us off to things. They pass out spaces at the FBI Academy. You get an FBI expert to testify in court, the jury believes him if he announces the moon is made of green cheese. The bottom line is that we need them as much, maybe more, than they need us. For another example, the FBI was 'consulted' before we got the federal grant to set up Special Operations. If they had said—even suggested—that we wouldn't use the money wisely, we wouldn't have gotten it. So we try to maintain the best possible relationship with the FBI."

"And Wohl doesn't know that?"

"Wohl's angry. He has every right to be. He doesn't get that way very often, but when he does—"

"Shit," Matt said.

"Let's just hope he cools off a little before he storms through the door and tells the SAC what he thinks of him and the other assholes," Washington said.

"The what?"

"SAC, special agent in charge," Washington explained, translating. "There are also AACs, three of them, which stands for assistant agent in charge. But as pissed as Peter is, he's going to see the head man, not one of the underlings."

He slid off the seat and stood up.

"If you hear anything, let me know, and vice versa," he said.

"If that goddamn Dolan hadn't gotten clever—"

"Don't be too hard on him," Washington said. "I think one of the reasons Peter Wohl is so angry is that he knows that if he had a chance to take pictures of a couple of FBI clowns on a surveillance, he would have mailed them to their office too. I've pulled their chain once or twice myself. There's something in their anointed-by-the-Almighty demeanor that brings that sort of thing out in most cops."

He smiled at Matt and then walked out of the diner. Matt got in the Porsche and turned right onto North Broad Street. A minute or two later he glanced at the passenger seat and saw that he still had the two envelopes with duplicate sets of photographs Washington had given him in City Hall.

He felt sure that the order to "give one to Chief Lowenstein and the other to Chief Coughlin" Washington had given him was intended only to unnerve Sergeant Dolan.

Since the pictures were of two goddamn FBI agents, they really had no value at all.

A moment later he had a second thought: *Or did they?*

Two blocks farther up North Broad Street, in violation of the Motor Vehicle Code of the City of Philadelphia, Officer Matthew Payne dropped the Porsche 911 into second gear, pushed the accelerator to the floor, and made a U-turn, narrowly averting a collision with a United Parcel truck, whose driver shook his fist at him and made an obscene comment.

"May I help you, sir?" the receptionist in the FBI office asked.

"I'd like to see Mr. Davis, please," Peter Wohl said.

"May I ask in connection with what, sir?"

"I'd rather discuss that with Mr. Davis," Wohl said. "I'm Inspector Wohl of the Philadelphia Police."

"One moment, sir. I'll see if Special Agent Davis is free."

She pushed a button on her state-of-the-art office telephone switching system, spoke softly into it, and then announced, "I'm sorry, sir, but Special Agent Davis is in conference. Can anyone else help you? Perhaps one of the assistant special agents in charge?"

"No, I don't think so. Were you speaking with Mr. Davis or his secretary?"

She did not elect to respond verbally to that presumptuous question; she just smiled benignly at him.

"Please get Mr. Davis on the line and tell him that Inspector Wohl is out here and needs to see him immediately," Peter said.

She pushed another button.

"I'm sorry to bother you, sir, but there's a Philadelphia policeman out here, a gentleman named Wohl, who insists that he has to see you." She listened a moment and then said, "Yes, sir."

Then she smiled at Peter Wohl.

"Someone will come for you shortly. Won't you have a seat? May I get you a cup of coffee?"

"Thank you," Peter said. "No coffee, thank you just the same."

He sat down on a couch in front of a coffee table on which was a glossy brochure with a four-color illustration of the seal of the Federal Bureau of Investigation and the legend, YOUR FBI in silver lettering. He did not pick it up, thinking that he knew all he wanted to know about the Federal Bureau of Investigation.

Ten minutes later a door opened and a neatly dressed young man who did not look unlike Officer Matthew W. Payne came out, walked over to him, smiled, and offered his hand.

"I'm Special Agent Foster, Inspector. Special Agent in Charge Davis will see you now. If you'll come with me?"

Wohl followed him down a corridor lined with frosted glass walls toward the corner of the building. There waited another female, obviously Davis's secretary.

"Oh, I'm so sorry, Inspector," she said. "Washington's on the line. I'm afraid it will be another minute or two. Can I offer you coffee?"

"No, thank you," Peter said.

There was another couch and another coffee table. On this one was a four-color brochure with a photograph of a building on it and the legend, THE J. EDGAR HOOVER FBI BUILDING. Wohl didn't pick this one up to pass the time, either.

Five minutes later Wohl saw Davis's secretary pick up the receiver, listen, and then replace it.

"Special Agent Davis will see you now, Inspector," she said, then walked to Davis's door and held it open for him.

The FBI provided Special Agent in Charge Walter Davis, as the man in charge of its Philadelphia office, with all the accoutrements of a senior federal bureaucrat. There was a large, glistening desk with matching credenza and a highbacked chair upholstered in dark red leather. There was a carpet on the floor; another couch and coffee table; a wall full of photographs and plaques; and a large FBI seal. There were two flags against the curtains. It was a corner office with a nice view.

Walter Davis was a tall, well-built man in his forties. His gray hair was impeccably barbered, and he wore a faint gray plaid suit, a stiffly starched white shirt, a rep-striped necktie, and highly polished black wing-tip shoes.

He walked from behind his desk, a warm smile on his face, as Peter Wohl entered his office.

"How are you, Peter?" he asked. "I'm really sorry to have had to make you wait this way. But you know how it is."

"Hello, Walter," Wohl said.

"Janet, get the Inspector and I cups of coffee, will you, please?" He looked at Wohl. "Black, right? Don't dilute the flavor of good coffee?"

"Right. Black."

"So how have you been, Peter? Long time no see. How's this Special Operations thing coming along?"

"It's coming along all right," Peter said. "We're really just getting organized."

"Well, you've been getting some very favorable publicity, at least."

"How's that?"

"Well, when your man—how shall I put it—*abruptly terminated* the career of the serial rapist, the publicity you got out of that was certainly better than being stuck in the eye with a sharp stick."

"I suppose it was," Wohl said.

"Nice-looking kid too," Davis said. "I'm tempted to try to steal him away from you."

You would, too, you smooth, genial son of a bitch!

"Make him an offer," Peter Wohl said.

"Only kidding, Peter, only kidding," Special Agent in Charge Davis said.

"I never know with you," Wohl said.

Davis's secretary appeared with a tray holding two cups of coffee and a plate of chocolate-chip cookies.

"Try the cookies, Peter," Davis said. "It is my means of teaching the young the value of a dollar."

"Excuse me?"

"My daughter makes them. No cookies, no allowance."

"Very clever," Wohl said, and picked up a cookie.

"So what can the FBI do for you, Peter?"

"The nice-looking kid we're talking about is at this moment setting up an appointment for me with Jack Duffy. When Duffy can see me, I'm going to ask him to arrange an appointment with you, for me. So I am here unofficially, okay?"

"Officially, unofficially, you're always welcome here, Peter, you know that," Davis said, smiling, but Wohl was sure he saw a flicker of wariness in Davis's eyes.

"Thank you," Wohl said. "You've heard, probably, about the shooting of Anthony J. DeZego?"

"Only what I read in the papers," Davis said, "and what Tom Tyler, my AAC for criminal matters, mentioned *en passant*. I understand that Mr. DeZego got himself shot. With a shotgun. That's what you're talking about?"

As if you didn't know, you son of a bitch!

"On the roof of the Penn Services Parking Garage, behind the Bellevue-Stratford. DeZego was killed—with a shotgun. It took the top of his head off—"

"Why can't I work up many tears of remorse?" Davis asked.

"And a young woman, a socialite, named Penelope Detweiler, was wounded."

"Heiress, the paper said, to the Nesfoods money."

"Right. What we're looking for are witnesses."

"And you think the FBI can help?"

"You tell me," Peter said, and got up and walked to Davis's desk and handed him the manila envelope.

"What's this?" he asked.

"I was hoping that you could tell me, Walter," Wohl said.

Davis opened the envelope and took out the photographs and went through them one at a time.

"These were taken here, weren't they? That is the Hotel Warwick?"

"And the Penn Services Parking Garage," Wohl said.

"I have no idea what the significance of this is, Peter," Davis said, looking up at Wohl and smiling. "But I have seen these before. This morning, as a matter of fact. Did you, or one of your people, send us a set?"

"None of my people did," Wohl said.

"Well, someone did. Without, of course, a cover letter. We didn't know what the hell they were supposed to be."

"You don't know who those men are?" Wohl asked.

"Haven't a clue."

I'll be a son of a bitch! He's telling the truth!

"Where did you come by these, Peter? If you don't mind my asking?"

"We had plainclothes Narcotics officers on DeZego," Wohl said. "One of them had a camera."

"But they didn't see the shooting itself?"

Wohl shook his head.

"That sometimes happens, I suppose," Davis said. "God, I wish I had known where these pictures had come from, Peter. I mean, when the other set came over the threshold."

"Why?"

"Well, I finally decided—my criminal affairs AAC and I did—that someone was trying to tell us something and that we'd really have to check it out. So we went through the routine. Sent copies to Washington and to every FBI office. Real pain in the ass. It's not like the old days, of course, when we would have to make a copy negative, then all those prints, and then mail them. Now we can wire photographs, of course. They're not as clear as a glossy print but they're usable. The trouble is, they tie up the lines. A lot of the smaller offices don't have dedicated phone lines, you see, which means the Bureau has to absorb all those long-distance charges."

"Well, Walter," Wohl said, "you have my word on it. I'll locate whoever sent those photos over here without an explanation and make sure that it never happens again."

"I'd appreciate that, Peter," Davis said. "We try to be as cooperative as we can, and you know we do. But we need a little help."

"I'm sorry to have wasted your time with this," Peter said.

"Don't be silly," Davis said, getting up and putting his hand out. "I know the pressures you're under. Don't be a stranger, Peter. Let's have lunch sometime."

"Love to," Wohl said. "One thing, Walter. You said those pictures have already been passed around. Do you think you'll get a make?"

"Who knows? If we do, I'll give Jack Duffy a call straight off."

"Thank you for seeing me," Peter said. "I know you're a very busy man."

"Goes with the territory," Special Agent in Charge Davis said.

"I'm sorry, sir," the rent-a-cop sitting in front of Penelope Detweiler's room in Hahneman Hospital said as he rose to his feet and stood in Matt Payne's way. "You can't go in there."

"Why not?" Matt asked.

"Because I say so," the rent-a-cop said.

"I'm a cop," Matt said.

He felt a little uneasy making that announcement. The rent-a-cop was almost surely a retired policeman. He remembered hearing Washington say that one of the rent-a-cops the Detweilers had hired was a retired Northwest Detectives sergeant. He suspected he was talking to him.

"And I've been hired by the Detweiler family to keep people away from Miss Detweiler without Mr. or Mrs. Detweiler's say-so."

"You've got two options," Matt said, hoping his voice sounded more confident than he felt. "You either get out of the way, or I'll get on the phone and four guys from Highway will carry you out of the way."

"There's a very sick girl in there," the rent-a-cop said.

"I know that," Matt said. "What's it going to be?"

"I could lose my job letting you in."

"You don't have any choice," Matt said. "If I have to call for help, I'll charge you with interfering with a police officer. That *will* cost you your job."

The rent-a-cop moved to the side and out of the way, watched Matt enter the room, and then walked quickly down the corridor to the nurses' station, where, without asking, he picked up a telephone and dialed a number.

"Ready for water polo?" Matt said to Penelope Detweiler.

Christ, she looks even worse than the last time I saw her.

"Hello, Matt," Penelope said, managing a smile.

"You feel as awful as you look?" he asked. "One might suppose that you have been out consuming intoxicants and cavorting with the natives in the Tenderloin."

"I really feel shitty," she said. "Matt, if I asked you for a *real* favor, would you do it?"

"Probably not," he said.

"That was pretty quick," she said, hurt. "I'm serious, Matt. I really need a favor."

"I really wouldn't know where to get any, Penny. Your supplier's dead, you know."

"What's that supposed to mean?" she snapped.

He handed her one of the manila envelopes of photographs.

"What's this?"

"Open it. Have a look. The jig, as they say, is up."

"I thought you were my friend, that I could at least count on you."

"You can, Penny."

"Then do me the favor. I'll give you a phone number, Matt. And all you would have to do is meet the guy someplace."

"You're not listening," he said. "Bullshit time is over, Penny. Look at the photographs."

"You're a son of a bitch, you always have been. A son of a bitch and a shit. I hate you."

"I like you too," Matt said. "Look at the goddamn pictures."

"I don't want to look at any goddamn pictures. What are they of, anyway?"

She slid the stack of photographs out of the envelope.

"Oh, Jesus," she said, her voice quavering.

"Got your attention now, have I?"

"Have you got him in jail?"

"In jail"? What the hell does that mean? Why should we have the FBI guys in jail?

"Looks familiar, does he?"

"He's the man who shot me, who killed Tony," Penelope Detweiler said. "I'll never forget him—that face—as long as I live."

Jesus H. Christ! What the hell is she talking about? What am I into?

"We know all about you and Tony, Penny," Matt said. "As I said, you can stop the bullshit."

"Who is this man? Why did he kill Tony?"

"Who knows?" Matt blurted.

"He won't tell you?"

"He's being difficult," Matt said. "I don't think he believes that you're alive. If he had killed you, there would be no witnesses."

I don't know what the fuck I'm doing. I'm just saying the first thing that pops into my mind. Jesus Christ, why did I do this? I'm going to fuck the whole thing up!

"I'll testify. I saw him. I saw him shoot Tony, and then he shot me."

"Why didn't you tell us before?"

"I couldn't hurt my father that way," Penelope said, making it clear she considered her reply to be self-evident. "My God, Matt, he thinks I'm still his little girl."

"And all the while you've been fucking Tony DeZego, right?"

"That's a shitty thing to say. We were in love. That was just like you, Matt. Always thinking the nastiest thing and then saying it in the nastiest possible way."

"Tony the Zee had a wife and two kids," Matt said. "Little boys."

He couldn't tell from the look in her eyes if this was news to her or not.

"I don't believe that," she said.

"I told you, precious Penny, bullshit time is over. You were running around with a third-rate guinea gangster, a *married* guinea gangster with two kids. Who was supplying you with cocaine."

"He really was married?" she asked.

Matt nodded.

"I didn't know that," she said. "But it wouldn't have mattered. We were in love."

"Then I feel sorry for you," Matt said. "I really do."

"Does Daddy know about Tony?"

"Not yet. He knows about the coke. But he'll have to find out about DeZego."

"Yes, I suppose he will," she said calmly. "If I'm going to testify against this man, and I will, it will just have to come out, and Daddy and Mommy will just have to adjust to it."

She looked at him and smiled.

Jesus Christ, he thought, *she's stoned.*

He saw that her pupils were dilated.

Has she been getting that shit in here? In a hospital?

She's on cloud nine. I think the technical term is "euphoric." She didn't even react when I called DeZego a guinea gangster, or when I told her he's married and has two kids. The first should have enraged her, and the second should have . . . caused a much greater reaction than it did. She didn't deny it when I said DeZego was sup-

plying her with cocaine, and she didn't seem at all upset when I told her I know her father knows about the cocaine and will inevitably learn about her and DeZego.

Ergo sum, Sherlock Holmes, she doesn't give a damn about things that are important, and is therefore, almost by definition, stoned.

It could be, come to think of it, that she is stoned on something legitimate, something they gave her for the pain. Or possibly that Dr. Dotson gave her a maintenance dose, having decided that this is not the time or place to detoxify her, either because of her condition or because he'd rather do that someplace where a lot of questions would not be asked.

So where are you now, hotshot? What do you do now?

"Penny, are you absolutely sure that the man in those photographs is the one who shot you?"

"I told you I was," she said.

"And you are prepared to testify in court about that?"

"Yes, of course," she said.

"Well, what happens now, Penny," Matt explained—*I don't know what the hell happens now*—"is that I will ask you to make a statement on the back of one of the photographs."

"What?"

"Quote, 'Having been sworn, I declare that the individual pictured in this photograph is the individual who, on the roof of the Penn Services Parking Garage, shot Mr. Anthony J. DeZego and me with a shotgun,' unquote. And then you sign it and I sign it. And then soon, Detective Washington will come back here and take a full statement."

" 'Killed,' " Penelope Detweiler said. "Not just 'shot,' 'killed.' "

"Right."

"You write it down and I'll sign it," Penny said agreeably.

"It has to be in your handwriting," Matt said. He rolled the bedside tray in place over Penny, selected one of the photographs, and showed it to her. "This him?"

"Yes, that's the man."

He spotted a Gideon Bible on the lower shelf of her bedside table and held it out to her. She put her hand on it.

"Do you swear to tell the truth, the whole truth and nothing but the truth?"

"I do," Penny said solemnly.

He handed her a ballpoint pen.

"Write," he said.

"Say that again," Penny said.

He dictated essentially what he had said before, and she wrote it on the back of the photograph.

"Sign it," he ordered. She did, and looked at him, he thought, like a little girl who expected her teacher to give her a Gold Star to Take Home to Mommy.

He pulled the bedside tray away from the bed, read what she had written, and then wrote, "Witnessed by Officer Matthew Payne, Badge 3676, Special Operations Division," and the time and date.

And now what?

"Penny, as I said before, someone will be back, probably Detective Washington and a stenographer, and they will take a full statement."

"All right," she said obligingly.

"And I have to go now, to get things rolling."

"All right. Come and see me again, Matt."

He smiled at her and left the room.

Dr. Dotson, the rent-a-cop, and two hospital private security men in policelike uniforms were coming down the corridor.

"I don't know who you think you are, Matt," Dotson said furiously, "or what you think you're doing, but you have absolutely no right to go in Penny's room without my permission and that of the Detweilers."

"I'm finished, Dr. Dotson," Matt said.

"See that he leaves the hospital. He is not to be let back in," Dotson said. "And don't you think, Matt, that this is the end of this."

19   "Inspector Wohl's office, Captain Sabara," Sabara said, answering one of the telephones on Wohl's desk.

"This is Commissioner Czernich, Sabara. Let me talk to Wohl."

"Commissioner, I'm sorry, the inspector's not here at the moment. May I take a message? Or have him get back to you?"

"Where is he?"

"Sir, I'm afraid I don't know. We expect him to check in momentarily."

"Yeah, well, he doesn't answer his radio, and you don't know where he is, right?"

"No, sir. I'm afraid I don't know where he is at this moment."

"Have him call me the moment you see him," Commissioner Czernich said, and hung up.

"I wonder what that's all about," Sabara said to Captain David Pekach as he put the phone in its cradle. "That was Czernich, and he's obviously pissed about something. You don't know where the boss is?"

"The last I heard, he was on his way to the mayor's office."

"I felt like a fool, having to tell Czernich I don't know where he is."

"What's Czernich pissed about?"

"I don't know, but he's pissed. Really pissed."

Pekach got up from his upholstered chair and went to the Operations sergeant.

"Have you got any idea where Inspector Wohl might be?"

"Right at this moment he's on his way to see the commissioner," the sergeant said.

"How do you know that?"

"It was on the radio. There was a call for W-William One, and the inspector answered and they told him to report to the commissioner right away, and he acknowledged."

"Thank you," Pekach said. He went back in the office and told Sabara what he had learned.

Staff Inspector Peter Wohl arrived at Special Operations an hour and five minutes later. He found Officer Matthew W. Payne waiting for him in the corridor outside the Operations office.

"I'd like to see you right away, sir," Matt said.

"Have you called Captain Duffy?"

"No, sir. Something came up," Matt said, and picked up the manila envelope containing the photographs.

"So I understand," Wohl said. "Come in the office."

Sabara and Pekach got to their feet as Wohl entered his office.

"We've been trying to reach you, Inspec—" Sabara said.

"I had my radio turned off," Wohl interrupted.

"The commissioner wants you to call him right away."

"How long ago was that?"

"About an hour ago, sir," Pekach said. He looked at his watch. "An hour and five minutes ago."

"I've seen him since then," Wohl said. "I just came from the Roundhouse." He turned to look at Payne. "We were discussing you, Officer Payne, the commissioner and I. Or rather the commissioner was discussing you, and I just sat there looking like a goddamn fool."

Pekach and Sabara started for the door.

"Stay. You might as well hear this," Wohl said. "I understand you have been at Hahneman Hospital. Is that so?"

"Yes, sir," Matt said.

"I seem to recall having told you to come here and call Captain Duffy for me."

"Yes, sir, you did."

"Did anyone else tell you to go to Hahneman Hospital?"

"Inspector," Matt said, handing him the photograph on which Penelope Detweiler had written her statement. "Would you please look at this?"

"Did anyone tell you to go to Hahneman Hospital?" Wohl repeated icily.

"Those two guys weren't from the FBI," Matt said.

"Answer me," Wohl said.

"No, sir."

"Then why the *hell* did you go to Hahneman Hospital?"

"Sir, would you please look at the back of the picture?"

Wohl turned it over and read it.

"You're a regular little Sherlock Holmes, aren't you?" Wohl said. He handed the photograph to Sabara, who examined it with Pekach leaning over his shoulder.

"She positively identifies that man as the guy who shot her and DeZego."

"And now all we have to do is find this guy, bring him in front of a jury, convict his ass, send him off to the electric chair, and Special Operations generally and Officer Matthew Payne specifically will come across as supercops, and to the cheers of the crowd we will skip happily off into the sunset, is that what you're thinking?"

"Sir," Matt said doggedly, "she positively identified that man as the man who shot her."

"You did have a chance to buy uniforms before you came out here to Special Operations, I hope?"

"Yes, sir. I've got my uniforms."

"Good. You're going to need them. By verbal direction of the police commissioner, written confirmation to follow, Officer Payne, you are reassigned to the 12th District, effective immediately. I doubt very much if you will be assigned plainclothes duties. You are also officially advised that a complaint, making several allegations against you involving your visit to Miss Detweiler at Hahneman Hospital today, has been made by a Dr. Dotson and officials of Hahneman Hospital. It has been referred to Internal Affairs for investigation. No doubt shortly you will be hearing from them."

"Peter, for chrissake, you're not listening to me!" Matt said. "She positively identified the shooter!"

"It's Inspector Wohl to you, Officer Payne," Wohl said.

"Sorry," Matt said.

"Matt, for chrissake!" Wohl said exasperatedly. "Let me explain all this to you. One, the chances of us catching these two, or either one of them, range from slim to none. On the way out here I stopped at Organized Crime and Intelligence. Neither of them are known by sight to anyone in Organized Crime or Intelligence—"

"You knew they weren't FBI guys?" Matt blurted, surprised.

"I have the word of the Special Agent in Charge about that," Wohl said. "They are not FBI agents. I have a gut feeling they are Mob hit men. Good ones. Imported, God only knows why, to blow DeZego away. Professionals, so to speak. We don't know where they came from. We can't charge them with murder or anything—unlawful flight or anything else, on the basis of some photographs that show them standing on a street."

"Penelope Detweiler swore that one of them is the guy who shot her and DeZego."

"Let's talk about Miss Detweiler," Wohl said. "She is a known user of narcotics, for one thing, and for another, she is Miss Penelope Detweiler, whose father's lawyers—your father, for example—will counsel her. They will advise her—and they probably should, I'm a little fuzzy about the ethics here—on the problems inherent in bringing these two scumbags before a grand jury for an indictment, much less before a jury. If I were her lawyer, I would advise her to tell the grand jury that she's really a little confused about what actually happened that day."

"Why would a lawyer tell her that?" Matt asked softly.

"Because, again presuming we can find these two, which I doubt, and presuming we could get an indictment—it isn't really true that any district attorney who can spell his own name can get an indictment anytime he wants to—and get him before a jury, then your friend Miss Detweiler would be subject to cross-examination. It would come out that she is addicted to certain narcotics, which would discredit her testimony, and it would come out that she was, tactfully phrased, romantically involved with Mr. DeZego. The press would have a certain interest in this trial. If I were her lawyer, I would suggest to her that testifying would be quite a strain on her and on her family."

"Oh, shit," Matt said. "I really fucked this up, didn't I?"

"Yeah, and good intentions don't count," Wohl said. "What counts, I'm afraid, is that Commissioner Czernich believes, more than likely correctly, that H. Richard Detweiler is going to be furious when he hears about your little escapade and is going to make his displeasure known to the mayor. When the mayor calls him, the commissioner will now be able to say that he's taken care of the matter. You have been relieved out here and assigned to duties appropriate to your experience. In other words, in a district, in uniform, and more than likely in a wagon."

"Oh, Christ, I'm sorry."

"So am I, Matt," Wohl said gently. "But what you did was stupid. For what it's worth, you probably should have gone to a district like anybody else fresh from the Academy."

"Hell, I'll just resign," Matt said.

"You think you're too good to ride around in a wagon?" Wohl asked.

"No," Matt said, "not at all. That's what I expected to do when I got out of the Academy. Denny Coughlin made sure I understood what to expect. I mean, under these circumstances. I have fucked up by the numbers, and they'll know that at the 12th. I think it would be best all around, that's all, if I just folded my tent and silently stole away."

"Today's Thursday," Wohl said. "I'll call the captain of the 12th and tell him you will either report for duty on Monday or resign by then. Think it over, over the weekend."

"You don't think I should resign?"

"I don't think you should resign right now, today," Wohl said. "I think you would have made a pretty good cop. I think you were given too great an opportunity to fuck up. But you did fuck up, and you're going to have to make your mind up whether or not you want to take your lumps."

Matt looked at him.

"That's all, Officer Payne," Wohl said. "You can go."

When Payne had left and closed the door behind him, Wohl went to his coffee machine and poured himself a cup of coffee.

"Fuck it," he said suddenly, angrily. He opened a filing cabinet drawer and took out a bottle of bourbon and liberally laced the coffee with it.

"If anybody wants any of that, help yourself," he said.

"Inspector," Captain Sabara said, "I didn't want to open my mouth, but a lot of what happened just now went right over my head."

Wohl looked at him as if confused.

"Oh, that's right," he said. "You guys don't know about the FBI agents, do you?"

Both shook their heads.

He told them.

"So what Payne was really doing at Hahneman Hospital was less playing at detective than trying to get my chestnuts out of the fire," he concluded. "The poor bastard waited for me out there, in that pathetic innocence, really thinking that now that he had solved this shooting, it would get me off the hook for making an ass of myself with the FBI."

"Shit," Pekach said.

"If I was him, I'd quit," Wohl said. "But if he doesn't, I'll—I don't know how— try to get the word around the 12th that he's really a good kid."

"I know Harry Feldman over there," Sabara said.

"He's the captain?"

"Yeah. I'll have a word with him," Sabara said.

"Thanks. Not surprising me at all, it seems to have turned out that Payne's new boss hates my ass. Do you think Czernich knew that?"

"I know a couple of guys in the 12th," Pekach said. "I'll talk to them."

"What do you think is going to happen about the FBI?" Sabara asked.

"If Duffy doesn't know about the photographs yet, or of me going down there out of channels, he will shortly," Wohl said. "And from there, how long will it take him to walk down the corridor from his office to Czernich's?"

"Give Czernich Dolan," Sabara said. "That wasn't your fault."

"I might have done the same thing," Wohl said. "Those two looked like your standard, neatly dressed, shiny-shoes 'Look at me, Ma, I'm a G-man' FBI agents, just begging for the needle. I won't give Czernich Dolan. What he did was dumb, but not dumb enough to lose his pension over it, and that's what Czernich's reaction would be. Anyway, all Czernich is interested in doing is covering his ass in front of the mayor. I'm on his list now, so just let him add the photographs to everything else I've done wrong or shown a lack of judgment doing."

"Dolan won't do anything like that again, Peter," Pekach said.

"You're not defending the son of a bitch, Dave, are you?" Sabara asked.

"I should have added 'when I'm through with him,' " Pekach said.

"Well, what's done is done," Sabara said. "Let's go get some lunch."

"I've got to meet someone for lunch," Pekach said.

"Is that what they call a nooner, Dave?" Wohl asked mischievously. Then he saw the look on Pekach's face. "Sorry, I shouldn't have said that."

Pekach's face showed the apology was inadequate.

"What that is, Dave," Wohl said, "is a combination of a bad day and a bad case of jealousy. But I was out of line, and I'm sorry."

"I already forgot it," Pekach said. Both his face and his tone of voice made it clear that was far short of the truth.

"I'll buy lunch," Captain Mike Sabara said, "providing it doesn't go over two ninety-five."

Wohl chuckled. "Thanks, Mike, I really hate to pass that up, but I've got plans too. Maybe it would be a good idea if you hung around here until either Dave or I get back."

"You got it," Sabara said. "I'll send out for something. You want to tell me where you're going?"

"If you need me, put it on the radio," Wohl said. He looked at Dave Pekach. "If you're still sore, Dave, I'm still sorry."

"I just don't like people talking that way about her," Pekach blurted. "It's not like what everybody thinks."

"What everybody thinks, Dave, is that you have a nice girl," Wohl said. "If anybody thought different, you wouldn't get teased."

"That's right, Dave," Sabara agreed solemnly.

Pekach looked intently at each of them. He smiled, shrugged, and walked out of the room.

When he was out of earshot, Sabara said, "But you were right, that's what you call it, a nooner."

"Captain Sabara, for a Sunday school teacher, you're a dirty old man," Wohl said. "I should be back in an hour. If something important comes up, put it on the radio."

"Yes, sir," Sabara said.

Martha Peebles was on the lawn, armed with the largest hedge clippers Dave Pekach had ever seen—they looked like two of King Arthur's swords or something stuck together—when he drove into the drive. She waved it at him when she saw him.

He parked the car in the garage, where it wouldn't attract too much attention, and walked toward the house. She met him under the portico.

"Hello, Precious," she said. "What's the matter?"

"Nothing," he said. "What are you going to do with that thing?"

She pointed the clippers in the general direction of his crotch and opened and closed it. Both of his hands dropped to protect the area.

"Oh, come on," she said. "You know I wouldn't want to hurt that."

"I don't know," he said. "I hope not."

"Something is wrong," she said. "I can tell. Something happen at Bustleton and Bowler?"

"Nothing that anybody can do anything about," Pekach said.

"Well," she said, taking his arm. "You can tell me all about it over lunch. I made French onion soup. Made it. Not from one of those packet things. And a salad. With Roquefort dressing."

"Sounds good," he said.

"And there's *nobody* in the house," she said. "Which I just happen to mention *en passant* and not to give you any ideas."

"I always wonder when I eat this stuff," Jason Washington said as he skillfully picked up a piece of Peking Beef with chopsticks and dipped it in a mixture of mustard and plum preserves, "if they really eat it in Peking, or whether it was invented here by some Chinaman who figured Americans will eat anything."

"It's good," Peter Wohl said.

"They use a lot of monosodium glutamate," Washington said. "To bring the taste out. It doesn't bother me, but it gets to Martha. She thought she was having a heart attack—angina pectoris."

"Really?"

"Pain in the pectoral muscles," Washington explained, and pointed to his pectorals.

"She went to the doctor and told him that whenever she had Chinese food, she had angina pectoris. He said, in that case, don't eat Chinese food. And then, when she calmed down, he told her that making diagnoses was his business, and about the monosodium glutamate."

"I didn't know that," Wohl said, "about monosodium glutamate."

In his good time, Wohl thought, *Jason will get around to telling me what's on his mind. He didn't ask if I was free for lunch because he didn't want to eat Peking Beef alone.*

"I feel really bad about Matt Payne," Washington said. "If I had any idea he was going to see that Detweiler girl, I would have stopped him."

So that's what's on his mind.

"I know that," Wohl said. "He went over there to help me."

"He thinks you're really something special," Washington said.

"He thinks you make Sherlock Holmes look like a mental retard," Wohl replied.

"If I was Matthew M. Payne and they put me back in uniform and in a 12th District wagon or handed me a wrench and told me to go around and turn off fire hydrants, I would quit."

"I think he probably will."

"We need young cops like that, Peter," Washington said.

"So?"

"I have a few favors owed me," Washington said. "How sore would you be if I called them in?"

"You'd be wasting them," Wohl said. "Czernich decided the way to cover his ass was to jump on the kid before the mayor told him to. He knew that would piss off a lot of people. Denny Coughlin, for one. If Coughlin goes to the mayor, and I really hope he doesn't, it would make the mayor choose between him and Czernich. I'm not sure how that would go. And while I agree, I would hate to see Matt resign, and I would *really* hate to see Denny Coughlin retire. I'd like to see Coughlin as commissioner."

"So you're saying, just let the kid go, right? 'For the good of the Department'?"

"Pekach and Sabara say they know people in the 12th. They'll put in a good word for him."

"You won't?"

"Feldman is the captain. When I was working as a staff inspector, I put his brother-in-law away."

"Christ, I forgot that. Lieutenant in Traffic? Extortion? They gave him five to fifteen?"

Wohl nodded. "I really don't think Captain Feldman would be receptive to anything kind I would have to say about Matt Payne."

"Interesting, isn't it, that Czernich sent Payne to the 12th?"

Wohl grunted.

"You think I could talk to Payne, tell him to hang in?"

"I wish you would. I think you might tip the scales."

"Okay," Jason Washington said, nodding his head. And then he changed the subject: "So what's the real story about DeZego and the pimp getting hit?"

"It's your job, you tell me," Wohl said.

"You haven't been thinking about it? That something smells with Savarese pointing Pekach at the pimp? Doing it himself?"

"I've been thinking that it smells," Wohl replied.

"Intelligence has a guy, I guess you know, in the Savarese family."

Wohl nodded.

"I talked to him about an hour ago," Jason Washington said.

"Intelligence know you did that?"

"Intelligence doesn't even know I know who he is," Washington said. "He tells me that the word in the family is that Tony the Zee ripped off the pimp, the pimp popped him, and Savarese ordered the pimp hit. I even got a name for the doer, not that it would do us any good."

"One of Savarese's thugs?"

"One of his bodyguards. Gian-Carlo Rosselli, also known as Charley Russell."

"Who has eight people ready to swear he was in Atlantic City taking the sun with his wife and kids?"

Washington nodded.

"Tony the Zee ripped off the pimp?" Wohl asked. "How?"

"Drugs, what else?" Washington replied.

"You don't sound as if you believe that," Wohl said.

"I think that's what Savarese wants the family to think," Washington said.

"Why, do you think?"

"I think Savarese had DeZego hit, and doesn't want the family to know about it."

"Why?"

"Why did he have him hit? Couple of possibilities. Maybe Tony went in business for himself driving the shrimp up from the Gulf Coast. That would be enough. Tony the Zee was ambitious but not too smart. He might have figured, who would ever know if he brought a kilo of cocaine for himself back up here in his suitcase."

"Interesting," Wohl said.

"He was also quite a swordsman," Washington went on, "who could have played hide-the-salami with somebody's wife. They take the honor of their women seriously; adultery is a mortal sin."

"Wouldn't Savarese have made an example of him, if that was the case?"

"Not necessarily," Washington said. "Maybe the lady was important to him. Her reputation. Her honor. He might have ordered him hit to remove temptation. It didn't have to be a wife. It could have been a daughter—I mean, unmarried daughter. If it came out that Tony had *dishonored* somebody's daughter, she would have a hell of a time finding a respectable husband. These people are very big, Peter, on respectability."

Wohl chuckled.

"You never heard of honor among thieves?" Washington asked innocently.

They both laughed.

"Why the hell are we laughing?" Wohl asked.

"Everyone laughs at quaint native customs," Washington said, and then added, "Or both of the above. Bottom line: For one or more reasons we'll probably never find out, Savarese decided Tony the Zee had to go; he didn't want his family to know that he had ordered the hit, for one or more reasons we'll probably never find out, either; imported those two guys in the photos Dolan took to do the hit; and then had Gian-Carlo Rosselli, aka Charley Russell, hit Lanier, conveniently leaving the shotgun the imported shooters had used on Tony at the crime scene; and finally, pointed us at the pimp. We would then naturally assume that Lanier had gotten popped for having popped Tony DeZego and tell Mickey O'Hara and the other police reporters, which would lend credence to Savarese's innocence. He almost got away with it. He would have, if it hadn't been for Dolan's snapshots and those two Highway cops hassling the pimp and coming up with another shotgun."

Wohl exhaled audibly.

"One flaw in your analysis," he said finally. Washington looked at him curiously. "You said, 'He almost got away with it,' " Wohl went on. "He did get away with it. What the hell have we got, Jason? We don't know who the professional hit men are, and we're not likely to find out. And if we did find them, we don't have anything on them. The only witness we have is a socialite junkie whose testimony would be useless even if we got her on the stand. And we can't hang the Lanier murder on Rosselli, or Russell, or whatever he calls himself. So the bastard did get away with it. Goddamn, that makes me mad!"

"You win some and you lose some," Washington said, "that being my profound philosophical observation for the day."

"On top of which we look like the Keystone Kops in the newspapers and, for the cherry on top of the cake, have managed to antagonize H. Richard Detweiler, Esquire. Christ only knows what that's going to cost us down the pike. *Damn!*"

"What I was going to suggest, Peter," Washington said softly, "presuming you agreed with what I thought, is that I have a talk with Mickey O'Hara."

"About what?"

"Mickey doesn't like those guineas any more than I do. He could do one of those 'highly placed police official speaking on condition of anonymity' pieces."

"Saying what?"

"Saying the truth. That Tony the Zee was hit for reasons known only to the mob, and that What's-his-name the pimp, Lanier, didn't do it. That would at least embarrass Savarese."

Wohl sat for a long moment with his lips pursed, tapping the balls of his fingers together.

"No," he said finally. "There are other ways to embarrass Mr. Savarese."

"You want to tell me how?"

"You sure you want to know?"

Washington considered that a moment.

"Yeah, I want to know," he said. "Maybe I can help."

"So what you were telling me before," Martha said to Dave, interrupting herself to reach down on the bed and pull a sheet modestly over her, "is that although it's really not Inspector Wohl's fault, he looks very bad?"

"Goddamn shame. He's a hell of a cop. I really admire him."

"And those gangsters are just going to get away with shooting the other gangster?"

"That happens all the time," Pekach said. "It's not like in the movies." He tucked his shirt in his trousers and pulled up his zipper. "Even if we somehow found those two, they would have alibis. They'll never wind up in court, is what I mean."

"I don't know what you mean."

"Sometimes some things happen," Pekach said.

"Precious, what in the world are you talking about?"

"Nothing," he said. "What makes Wohl look bad is the shot cop. We don't have a damn thing on that. And that's bad. It makes the Department look incompetent, stupid, if we can't get people who murder cops in cold blood. And it makes Peter Wohl look bad, because the mayor gave him the job."

"I understand," she said. "And there's nothing that he can do?"

"There's nothing anybody can do that isn't already being done. Unless we can find somebody who saw something—"

"What about offering a reward? Don't you do that?"

"Rewards come from people who are injured," Dave explained. "I mean, somebody knocks off the manager of an A&P supermarket, A&P would offer a reward. The Department doesn't have money for something like that, and even if there was a reward, we'd look silly, wouldn't we, offering it? It would be the same thing as admitting that we can't do the job the taxpayers are paying us to do."

"*I* don't think so," Martha said.

He finished dressing and examined himself in the mirror.

His pants are baggy in the seat, Martha thought. *And that shirt doesn't fit the way it should. I wonder if that Italian tailor Evans has found on Chestnut Street could make him up something a little better? He has a marvelous physique, and it just doesn't show. Daddy always said that clothes make the man. I never really knew what he meant before.*

Pekach walked to the bed and leaned down and kissed Martha gently on the lips.

"Gotta go, baby," he said.

"Would you like to ride out to New Hope and have dinner along the canal?" Martha asked. "You always like that. It would cheer you up. Or I could have Evans get some steaks?"

"Uh," Pekach said, "baby, Mike Sabara and I thought that we'd try to get Wohl to go out for a couple of drinks after work."

"I thought Captain Sabara wasn't much of a drinking man," Martha said, and then: "Oh, I see. Of course. Can you come over later?"

"I think I might be able to squeeze that into my busy schedule," Pekach said, and kissed her again.

When he left the bedroom, Martha got out of bed and went to the window and watched the driveway until she saw Pekach's unmarked car go down it and through the gate.

She leaned against the window frame thoughtfully for a moment, then caught her reflection in the mirrors of her vanity table.

"Well," she said aloud, not sounding entirely displeased, "aren't *you* the naked hussy, Martha Peebles?"

And then walked back to the bed, sat down on it, fished out a leather-bound telephone book, and looked up a number.

Brewster Cortland Payne, Esquire, saw that one of the lights on one of the two telephones on his desk was flashing. He wondered how long it had been flashing. He had been in deep concentration, and lately that had meant that the Benjamin Franklin Bridge, visible from his windows on a high floor of the Philadelphia Savings Fund Society Building, could have tumbled into the Delaware without his noticing the splash.

It probably means that when I'm free, Irene has something she thinks I should hear, he thought. *Otherwise, she would have made it ring. Well, I'm not free, but I'm curious.*

As he reached for the telephone it rang.

"Yes, ma'am?" he asked cheerfully.

"Mr. and Mrs. Detweiler are here, Mr. Payne," his secretary of twenty-odd years, Mrs. Irene Craig, said.

Good God, both of them?

"Ask them to please come in," Payne said immediately. He quickly closed the manila folders on his desk and slid them into a drawer. He had no idea what the Detweilers wanted, but there was no chance whatever that they just happened to be in the neighborhood and had just popped in.

The door opened.

"Mr. and Mrs. Detweiler, Mr. Payne," Irene announced.

Detweiler's face was stiff. His smile was uneasy.

"Unexpected pleasure, Grace," Payne said, kissing her cheek as he offered his hand to Detweiler. "Come on in."

"May I get you some coffee?" Irene asked.

"I'd much rather have a drink, if that's possible," Detweiler said.

"The one thing you don't need is another drink," Grace Detweiler said.

"I could use a little nip myself," Payne lied smoothly. "I'll fix them, Irene. Grace, will you have something?"

"Nothing, thanks."

"We just came from the hospital," Detweiler announced.

"Sit down, Dick," Payne said. "You're obviously upset."

"Jesus H. Christ, am I upset!" Detweiler said. He went to the wall of windows looking down toward the Delaware River and leaned on one of the floor-to-wall panes with both hands.

Payne quickly made him a drink, walked to him, and handed it to him.

"Thank you," Detweiler said idly, and took a pull at the drink. He looked into Payne's face. "I'm not sure if I'm here because you're my friend or because you're my lawyer."

"They are not mutually exclusive," Payne said. "Now what seems to be the problem?"

"If five days ago anyone had asked me if I could think of anything worse than having my daughter turn up as a drug addict, I couldn't have imagined anything worse," Grace Detweiler said.

"Penny is not a drug addict," H. Richard Detweiler said.

"If you persist in that self-deception, Dick," Grace said angrily, "you will be compounding the problem, not trying to solve it."

"She has a *problem*," Detweiler said. "That's all."

"And the name of that problem, goddamn you, is addiction," Grace Detweiler said furiously. "Denying it, goddammit, is not going to make it go away!"

H. Richard Detweiler looked at his wife until he cringed under her angry eyes.

"All right," he said very softly. "Addicted. Penny is addicted."

Grace nodded and then turned to Brewster C. Payne. "You're not even a little curious, Brewster, about what could be worse than Penny being a cocaine addict?"

"I presumed you were about to tell me," Payne said.

"How about getting rubbed out by the Mob? Does that strike you as being worse?"

"I don't know what you're talking about," Payne said.

"Officer Matthew Payne of the Philadelphia Police Department marched into Penny's room a while ago—past, incidentally, the private detective Dick hired to keep people out of her room—and showed Penny some photographs. Penny, who is not, to put it kindly, in full possession of her faculties, identified the man in the photographs as the man who had shot her and that Italian gangster. And then she proceeded to confess to him that she had been involved with him. With the gangster, I mean. In love with him, to put a point on it."

"Oh, God!" Payne said.

"And he got her to sign a statement," H. Richard Detweiler said, "Penny is now determined to go to court and point a finger at the man and see him sent to the electric chair. She thinks it will be just like Perry Mason on television. With Uncle Brewster doing what Raymond Burr did."

"What kind of a statement did she sign?"

"We don't know," Grace said. "Matt didn't give her a copy. A *statement.*"

"I'd have to see it," Payne said, as if to himself.

"I think I should tell you that Dotson has filed a complaint against Matt with the Police Department," H. Richard Detweiler said.

"For what?"

"Who knows? What Matt did was wrong," Detweiler said. "I think he said, criminal trespass and violation of Penny's civil rights. Does that change anything between us, Brewster?"

"If you're filing a complaint, it would," Payne said. "Are you?"

"That sounds like an ultimatum," Detweiler said. "If I press charges, I should find another lawyer."

"It sounded like a question to me," Grace Detweiler said. "The answer to which is no, we're not. Of course we're not. I'd like to file a complaint against Dotson. He knew that Penny was taking drugs. He should have told us."

"We don't know he knew," Detweiler said.

"God, you're such an ass!" Grace said. "Of course he knew." She turned to Brewster Payne. "Don't you think?"

"Penny's over twenty-one. An adult. Legally her medical problems are none of your business," Payne said. "But yes, Grace, I would think he knew."

"Right," Grace said. "Of course he did. The bastard!"

"If there are charges against Matt—a complaint doesn't always result in charges— but if there are and he comes to me, I'll defend him," Payne said. "Actually, if he doesn't come to me, I'll go to him. One helps one's children when they are in trouble. I am unable to believe that he meant Penny harm."

"Neither am I," Grace said. "I wish I could say the same thing for Penny's father."

"I'll speak to Dotson," Detweiler said. "About dropping his charges. I don't blame Matt. I blame that colored detective; he probably set Matt up to do what he did."

"What Matt did *wasn't* wrong, Dick," Grace said. "Can't you get that through your head? What he was trying to do was catch the man who shot Penny."

"Dick, I think Matt would want to accept responsibility for whatever he did. He's not a child any longer, either," Payne said.

"I'll speak to Dotson," Detweiler said. "About the charges, I mean."

"As sick as this sounds," Grace Detweiler went on, "I think Penny rather likes the idea of standing up in public and announcing that she was the true love of this gangster's life. The idea that since they tried to kill her once so there would be no witness suggests they would do so again never entered her mind."

"Off the top of my head, I don't think that a statement taken under the circumstances you describe—"

"What do you mean, 'off the top of your head'?" H. Richard Detweiler asked coldly.

"Dick, I'm not a criminal lawyer," Brewster C. Payne said.

"Oh, great! We come here to see how we can keep our daughter from getting shot—again—by the Mob, and you tell me 'Sorry, that's not my specialty.' My God, Brewster!"

"Settle down, Dick," Payne said. "You came to the right place."

He walked to his door.

"Irene, would you ask Colonel Mawson to drop whatever he's doing and come in here, please?"

"Mawson?" Detweiler said. "I never have liked that son of a bitch. I never understood why you two are partners."

"Dunlop Mawson is reputed to be—in my judgment *is*—the best criminal lawyer in Philadelphia. But if you think he's a son of a bitch, Dick—"

"For God's sake," Grace said sharply, "let's hear what he has to say."

Colonel J. Dunlop Mawson (the title making reference to his service as a lieutenant colonel, Judge Advocate Generals' Corps, U.S. Army Reserve, during the Korean War) appeared in Brewster C. Payne's office a minute later.

"I believe you know the Detweilers, don't you, Dunlop?" Payne asked.

"Yes, of course," Mawson said. "I've heard, of course, about your daughter. May I say how sorry I am and ask how she is?"

"Penny is addicted to cocaine," Grace Detweiler said. "How does that strike you?"

"I'm very sorry to hear that," Colonel Mawson said.

"There is a place in Hartford," Grace said, "that's supposed to be the best in the country. The Institute for Living, something like that—"

"Institute *of* Living," Payne said. "I know of it. It has a fine reputation."

"Anyway, she's going there," Grace Detweiler said.

"I had a hell of a time getting her in," H. Richard Detweiler said.

" '*I*'?" Grace Detweiler snapped, icily sarcastic.

"Really?" Payne asked quickly. He had seen Grace Detweiler in moods like this before.

"There's a waiting list, can you believe that? They told Dotson on the phone that it would be at least three weeks, possibly longer, before they'd take her."

"Well, that's unfortunate, but—" Colonel Mawson said.

"*We* got her in," Detweiler said. "*We* had to call Arthur Nelson—"

"Arthur Nelson?" Payne interrupted. "Why him?"

Arthur J. Nelson, Chairman of the Board of Daye-Nelson Publications, one of which was the Philadelphia *Ledger,* was not among Brewster C. Payne's favorite people.

"Well, he had his wife in there, you know," Grace Detweiler answered for her husband. "She had a breakdown, you know, when that sordid business about her son came out. Arthur put her in there."

"Yes, now that you mention it, I remember that," Payne said. "Was he helpful?"

"Very helpful," H. Richard Detweiler said.

"Dick, you're such an ass," Grace said. "He was not!"

"He said he would do everything he could to minimize unfortunate publicity," H. Richard Detweiler said. "And he gave us Charley Gilmer's name."

"Charley Gilmer?" Payne asked.

"President of Connecticut General Commercial Assurance. He's on the board of directors, trustees, whatever, of that place."

"Whose name, if you were thinking clearly," Grace Detweiler said, "you should have thought of yourself. We've known the Gilmers for years."

H. Richard Detweiler ignored his wife's comment.

"It was not very pleasant," H. Richard Detweiler said, "having to call a man I have known for years to tell him that my daughter has a drug problem and I need his help to get her into a mental institution."

"Is that all you're worried about, your precious reputation?" Grace Detweiler snarled. "Dick, you make me sick!"

"I don't give a good goddamn about my reputation—or yours, either, for that matter. I'm concerned for our daughter, goddamn you!"

"If you were really concerned, you'd leave the booze alone!"

"Both of you, shut up!" Brewster C. Payne said sharply. Neither was used to being talked to in those words or that manner and looked at him with genuine surprise.

"Penny is the problem here. Let's deal with that," Payne said. "Unless you came here for an arena, instead of for my advice."

"I'm upset," H. Richard Detweiler said.

"And I'm not?" Grace snapped.

"Grace, shut up," Payne said. "Both of you, shut up."

They both glowered at him for a moment, the silence broken when Grace Detweiler walked to the bar and poured an inch and a half of Scotch in the bottom of a glass.

She turned from the bar, leaned against the bookcase, took a swallow of the whiskey, and looked at both of the men.

"Okay, let's deal with the problem," she said.

"We're sending Penny up there tomorrow, Colonel Mawson," Detweiler said, "to the Institute of Living, in an ambulance. It's a six-week program, beginning with detoxification and then followed by counseling."

"They know how to deal with the problem," Mawson replied. "It's an illness. It can be cured."

"That's *not* the goddamn problem!" Grace flared. "We're talking about Penny and the *goddamn gangsters!"*

"Excuse me?" Colonel H. Dunlop Mawson asked.

"Let me fill you in, Dunlop," Payne said, and explained the statement Matt had taken and Penny's determination to testify against the man whom she had seen shoot Anthony J. DeZego.

Colonel Mawson immediately put many of the Detweilers' concerns to rest. He told them that no assistant district attorney more than six weeks out of law school would go into court with a witness who had a "medical history of chemical abuse."

The statement taken by Matt Payne, in any event, he said, was of virtually no validity, taken as it was from a witness he knew was not in full possession of her mental faculties, and not even taking into consideration that he had completely ignored all the legal t's that had to be crossed, and i's dotted, in connection with taking a statement.

"And I think, Mr. Detweiler," Colonel Mawson concluded, "that there is even a very good chance that we can get the statement your daughter signed back from the police. If we can, then it will be as if she'd never signed it, as if it had never existed."

"How are you going to get it back?"

"Commissioner Czernich is a reasonable man," Colonel Mawson said. "He's a friend of mine. And by a fortunate happenstance, at the moment he owes me one."

"He owes you one what?" Grace Detweiler demanded.

Brewster C. Payne was glad she had asked the question. He didn't like what Mawson had just said, and would have asked precisely the same question himself.

"A favor," Mawson said, a trifle smugly. "A scratch of my back in return, so to speak."

"What kind of a scratch, Dunlop?" Payne asked, a hint of ice in his voice.

"Just minutes before I came in here," Mawson said, "I was speaking with Commissioner Czernich on the telephone. I was speaking on behalf of one of our clients, a public-spirited citizeness who wishes to remain anonymous."

"The point?" Payne said, and now there was ice in his voice.

"The lady feels the entire thread of our society is threatened by the unsolved murder of Officer Whatsisname, the young Italian cop who was shot out by Temple. So she is providing, through me, anonymously, a reward of ten thousand dollars for information leading to the arrest and successful prosecution of the perpetrators. Commissioner Czernich seemed overwhelmed by her public-spirited generosity. I really think I'm in a position to ask him for a little favor in return."

"Well, that's splendid," H. Richard Detweiler said. "That would take an enormous burden from my shoulders."

"What do we do about the newspapers?" Grace Detweiler asked. "Have you any influence with them, Colonel?"

"Very little, I'm afraid."

"Arthur Nelson will do what he can, I'm sure, and that should take care of that," H. Richard Detweiler said.

"I don't trust Arthur J. Nelson," Grace said.

"Don't be absurd, Grace," H. Richard Detweiler said. "He seemed to understand the problem, and was obviously sympathetic."

"Brewster, will you please tell this horse's ass I'm married to that even if Nelson never printed the name Detweiler again in the *Ledger*, there are three other newspapers in Philadelphia that will?"

"He implied that he would have a word with the others," H. Richard Detweiler said. "We take a lot of advertising in those newspapers. We're entitled to a little consideration."

"Oh, Richard," Grace said, disgusted, "you can be such an ass! If Nelson has influence with the other newspapers, how is it that he couldn't keep them from printing every last sordid detail of his son's homosexual love life?"

Detweiler looked at Payne.

"I'm afraid Grace is right," Payne said.

"You can't talk to them? Mentioning idly in passing how much money Nesfoods spends with them every year?"

"I'd be wasting my breath," Payne said. "The only way to deal with the press is to stay away from it."

"You're a lot of help," Detweiler said. "I just can't believe there is nothing that can be done."

"Unfortunately there *is* nothing that can be done. Except, of course, to reiterate, to stay away from the press. Say nothing."

"Just a moment, Brewster," Colonel Mawson said. "If I might say something?"

"Go ahead," Grace said.

"The way to counter bad publicity is with good publicity," Mawson said. "Don't you agree?"

"Get to the point," Grace Detweiler said.

He did.

20 Matt Payne was watching television determinedly. PBS was showing a British-made documentary of the plight of Australian aborigines in contemporary society, a subject in which he had little or no genuine interest. But if he did not watch television, he had reasoned, he would get drunk, which did not at the moment have the appeal it sometimes did, and which, moreover, he suspected was precisely the thing he should not do at the moment, under the circumstances.

He had disconnected his telephone. He did not want to talk to either his father, Officer Charles McFadden, Amanda Spencer, Captain Michael J. Sabara, or Chief Inspector Dennis V. Coughlin, all of whom had called and left messages that they would try again later.

All he wanted to do was sit there and watch the aborigines jumping around Boy Scout campfires in their loincloths and bitching, sounding like brown, fuzzy-haired Oxford dons, about the way they were treated.

His uniform was hanging from the fireplace mantelpiece. He had taken it from the plastic mothproof bag and hung it there so he could look at it. He had considered actually putting it on and examining himself in the mirror, and decided against that as unnecessary. He could imagine what he would look like in it as Officer Payne of the 12th Police District.

If there was one thing that could be said about the uniform specified for officers of the Philadelphia Police Department, it did not have quite the class or the élan of the uniform prescribed for second lieutenants of the United States Marine Corps.

He had actually said, earlier on, "Damn my eyes," which sounded like a line from a Charles Laughton movie. But if it wasn't for his goddamn eyes, he would now be on his way to Okinawa and none of this business with the cops would have happened.

He would have gone to Chad and Daffy's wedding as a Marine officer and met Amanda, and they would have had their shipboard romance, as she called it, in much the same way. And things probably would have turned out much the same way, except that what had happened between them in the apartment would have happened in a hotel room or something, for if he had gone into the Marines, *ergo,* he would not have gotten the apartment.

But he had not gone into the Marines. He had gone into the cops and as a result of that had proven beyond any reasonable doubt that he was a world-class asshole with a naïveté that boggled the imagination, spectacular delusions of his own cleverness, and a really incredible talent for getting other people—goddamn *good* people, Washington and Wohl, plus of course his father—in trouble because of all of the above. Not to mention embarrassing Uncle Denny Coughlin.

And now, having sinned, he was expected to do penance. He had not told Wohl the truth, the whole truth, and nothing but the truth about whether he thought he was too good to ride around in an RPW hauling drunks off to holding cells and fat ladies off to the hospital. He didn't want to do it. Was that the same as thinking he was too good to do it?

Presuming, of course, that he could swallow his pride and show up at the 12th District on Monday, preceded by his reputation as the wiseass college kid who had been sent there in disgrace, what did he have to look forward to?

Two years of hauling the aforementioned fat lady down the stairs and into the wagon and then off to the hospital, perhaps punctuated, after a while, when they learned that within reason I could be trusted with exciting assignments, like guarding school crossings and maybe even—dare I hope?—filling in for some guy on vacation or something and actually getting to go on patrol in my RPC.

Then I will be eligible to take the examination for detective or corporal. Detective, of course. I don't want to be a corporal. And I will pass that. I will even study to do well on it, and I will pass it, and then what?

Do I want to ride shotgun in a wagon for two years to do that?

Amanda would, with justification, decide I was rather odd to elect to ride shotgun on a wagon. Amanda does not wish to be married to a guy who rides shotgun on a wagon. Can one blame Amanda? One cannot.

There was a rustling, and then a harsher noise, almost metallic.

The building is empty. I carefully locked the door to my stairs; therefore it cannot be anything human rustling around my door. Perhaps the raven Mr. Poe spoke of, about to quote "Nevermore" to me, as in "Nevermore, Matthew Payne, will you be the hotshot, hotshit special assistant to Inspector Wohl."

It's a rat, that's what it is. That's all I need, a fucking rat!

"You really ought to get dead-bolt locks for those doors," a vaguely familiar voice said.

Matt, startled, jumped to his feet.

Chief Inspector August Wohl, retired, was standing just inside the door, putting something back in his wallet.

"How the hell did you get in?" Matt blurted.

"I'll show you about doors sometime. Like I said, you really should get dead-bolt locks."

"What can I do for you, Mr. Wohl?"

"You could offer me a drink," he said. "I would accept. It's a long climb up here. And call me Chief, if you don't mind. It has a certain ring to it."

Matt walked into the kitchen and got out the bottle of Scotch his father had given him.

"Well, I'm glad to see there's some left," Chief Wohl said.

"Sir?"

"I really expected to find you passed out on the floor," Chief Wohl said. "That's why I let myself in. People who drink alone can get in a lot of trouble."

"I'm already in a lot of trouble," Matt said.

"So I understand."

"Water all right?"

"Just a touch. That's very nice whiskey."

"How'd you know I was here?"

"Your car's downstairs. There's lights on. There was movement I could see—

shadows—from the street. It had to be either you or a burglar. I'm glad it was you. I'm too old to chase burglars."

Matt chuckled.

"Why'd you come?" he asked.

"I wanted to talk to you, but I'll be damned if I will while drinking alone."

"I'm not so sure that drinking is what I need to be doing just now."

"And the pain of feeling sorry for yourself is sharper when you're stone sober, right? And you like that?"

"What the hell," Matt said, and poured himself a drink.

"I see you have your uniform out," Chief Wohl said. "Does that mean you're going to report to the 12th on Monday?"

"It means I'm thinking about it," Matt said.

"Which side is winning?"

"The side that's wondering if I can find anybody interested in buying a nearly new set of uniforms, size forty regular," Matt said.

"You going to ask me if I want to sit down?" Chief Wohl said.

"Oh! Sorry. Please sit down."

"Thank you," Chief Wohl said. He sat in Matt's chair and put his feet up on the footstool. Matt sat on the window ledge.

"I told Peter that I think he's wrong about you needing the experience you'll get—if you decide to go over there on Monday—at the 12th," Chief Wohl said. "Incidentally, Peter feels lousy about the way that happened. I want you to understand that. It was out of his hands. That's one of the reasons I came here, to make sure you understood that."

"I thought it probably was," Matt said. "I mean the commissioner's decision."

"Reaction, not decision," Chief Wohl said. "There's a difference. When you decide something, you consider the facts and make a choice. When you react, it's different. Reactions are emotional."

"I'm not sure I follow you."

"Right or wrong wasn't on Czernich's agenda. What he saw was that Jerry Carlucci was going to be pissed off at Peter because of your little escapade with the Detweiler girl. He wanted to get himself out of the line of fire. He *reacted*. By jumping on you before Carlucci said anything, he was proving, he thinks, to Jerry Carlucci, that he's one of the good guys."

Matt took a pull at his drink.

"You're not going to learn anything," Chief Wohl said, "if you decide to go over there on Monday, hauling fat ladies with broken legs downstairs—"

Matt laughed.

"I say something funny?" Chief Wohl snapped.

"I'm sorry," Matt said. "But I was thinking in exactly those terms—hauling fat ladies—when I was thinking about what I would be doing in the 12th."

"As I was saying, you won't learn anything hauling fat ladies except how to haul fat ladies. The idea of putting rookies on jobs like that is to give them experience. You've already had your experience."

"Do you mean because I shot the serial rapist?" Matt asked.

"No. As a matter of fact, I didn't even think about that," Chief Wohl said. "No, not that. That was something else. What I meant was the price of going off half-cocked before you think through what's liable to happen if you do what seems like such a great idea. The price of doing something dumb is what I mean."

"It's obviously expensive," Matt said. "I lose my job. I get my boss in trouble. I get to haul fat ladies. And because I was dumb, the scumbags who shot the other scumbag and Penny Detweiler get away with it. That really makes me mad. No, not mad. Ashamed of myself."

He became aware that Chief Wohl was looking at him with an entirely different look on his face.

"Chief, did I say something wrong?" Matt asked.

"No," Chief Wohl replied. "No, not at all. Can I have another one of these?"

"Certainly."

When Matt was at the sink, Chief Wohl got up and followed him.

"They may not get away with it," he said. "I have just decided that if I tell you something, it won't go any further. Am I right?"

"Do you think, after the trouble I've caused, that I am any judge of my reliability?"

"I think you can judge whether or not you can keep your mouth shut, *particularly* since you have just learned how you can get other people in trouble."

"Yes, sir," Matt said after a moment. "I can keep my mouth shut."

Chief Wohl met his eyes for a moment and then nodded.

"There is a set of rules involving the Mob and the police. Nobody talks about them, but they're there. I won't tell you how I know this, but Vincenzo Savarese got word to Jerry Carlucci that the Mob—Mobs, there's a couple of them—had nothing to do with the shooting of that Italian cop . . . what was his name?"

"Magnella. Joseph Magnella," Matt furnished.

"We believe him. The reason he told us that is not because he gives a damn about a dead cop but because he doesn't want us looking for the doer, doers, in the Mob. We might come across something else he doesn't want us to know. Since we're taking him at his word, that means we can devote the resources to looking elsewhere. You with me?"

"Yes, sir."

"Okay. The DeZego hit is different. Ordinarily we really don't spend a lot of time worrying about the Mob killing each other. If we can catch the doer, fine. But we know that we seldom do catch the doers, so we go through the motions and let it drop. The DeZego hit is different."

"Because of Penny Detweiler?"

"No. Well, maybe a little. But that's not what I'm talking about. The one thing the Mob does not do is point the finger at some other Mob guy and say he's the doer, go lock him up. That violates their Sicilian Code of Honor, telling the police anything about some other mafioso. If a Mob guy is hit, it's one of two ways. It was, by their standards, a justified hit, and that's the end of it. Or it was unjustified and they put out a contract on the guy who did it. This was different. They pointed us, with that matchbook Savarese gave Dave Pekach, at the pimp."

"He was black."

"More important," Chief Wohl said, a tone of impatience in his voice, "he didn't do it."

"Yeah," Matt said, chagrined. "Maybe they wanted him—the pimp, I mean—killed for some other reason."

"Could well be, but that's not the point. The point is that Savarese tried to play games with us. Two things with that. One, we wonder why. Two, more important, that breaks the rules. He lied to us. We can't have that."

"So what happens?"

"The first thing we think is that if he lied to us about the pimp, he's probably lying to us about not knowing who killed the Italian cop. So that means we can't trust him."

"So you start looking around the Mob for who killed DeZego and who killed Magnella."

"Yeah," Chief Wohl said. "But before we do that, to make sure that he knows we haven't broken our end of the arrangement, we let him know we know he broke the rules first."

"How?"

Chief Wohl told him. And as he was explaining what was going to happen—in fact, had *already* happened, thirty minutes before, just after ten P.M., just before Chief Inspector Wohl, retired, had shown up at the apartment—a question arose in Matt's mind that he knew he could never raise: whether the chief had been a spectator or a participant.

When Mr. Vincenzo Savarese's Lincoln pulled to the curb in front of the Ristorante Alfredo right on time to pick up Mr. Savarese following his dinner and convey him to his residence, a police officer almost immediately came around the corner, walked up to the car, and tapped his knuckles on the window.

When the window came down, Officer Foster H. Lewis, Jr., politely said, "Excuse me, sir, this is a no-parking, no-standing zone. You'll have to move along."

"We're just picking somebody up," Mr. Pietro Cassandro, who was driving the Lincoln, said.

"I'm sorry, sir, this is a no-standing zone," Officer Lewis said.

"For chrissake, we'll only be two minutes," Mr. Gian-Carlo Rosselli, who was in the front seat beside Mr. Cassandro, said.

Officer Lewis removed his booklet of citations from his hip pocket.

"May I see your driver's license and registration, please, sir? I'm afraid that I will have to issue a citation."

"We're moving, we're moving," Mr. Cassandro said as he rolled up the window and put the car in gear.

"Just drive around the block," Mr. Rosselli said.

"Arrogant fucking nigger—put them in a uniform and they really think they're hot shit."

"That was a *big* nigger. Did you see the size of that son of a bitch?"

"I didn't want to have Mr. S. coming out of the place and finding jumbo Sambo standing there. If there's anything he hates worse than a nigger, it's a nigger cop."

There was more fucking trouble with the fucking cops going around the block. There was something wrong with the sewer or something, and there was a cop standing in the middle of the street with his hand up. And they couldn't back up and go around, either, because another car, an old Jaguar convertible, was behind them. They took five minutes minimum, and the result was that when they went all the way around the block, Mr. S. was standing on the curb looking nervous. He didn't like to wait around on curbs.

"Sorry, Mr. S.," Mr. Cassandro said. "We had trouble with a cop."

"What kind of trouble with a cop?"

"Fresh nigger cop, just proving he had a badge," Mr. Cassandro said.

"I don't like trouble with cops," Mr. Savarese said.

"It wasn't his fault, Mr. S.," Mr. Rosselli said.

"I don't want to hear about it. I don't like trouble with cops."

Mr. Savarese's Lincoln turned south on South Broad Street.

Mr. Cassandro became aware that the car behind, the stupid bastard, had his bright lights on. He reached up and flicked the little lever under the mirror, which deflected the beam of light, and he could see the car behind him.

"There's a fucking cop behind us," Mr. Cassandro said.

"I don't like trouble with cops," Mr. Savarese said. "Don't give him any excuse for anything."

"Maybe he's just there, like coincidental," Mr. Rosselli said.

"Yeah, probably," Mr. Cassandro said.

Six blocks down South Broad Street, the police car was still behind the Lincoln, which was now traveling thirty-two miles per hour in a thirty-five-mile-per-hour zone.

"Is the cop still back there?" Mr. Savarese asked.

"Yeah, he is, Mr. S.," Mr. Cassandro said.

"I wonder what the fuck he wants," Mr. Rosselli asked.

"I don't like trouble with cops," Mr. Savarese said. "Have we got a bad taillight or something?"

"I don't think so, Mr. S.," Mr. Cassandro said.

Three blocks farther south, the flashing lights on the roof of the police car turned on, and there was the whoop of its siren.

"Shit," Mr. Cassandro said.

"You must have done something wrong," Mr. Savarese said.

"I been going thirty-two miles an hour," Mr. Cassandro said.

"You sure it's a cop?" Mr. Savarese said as they pulled up to the curb.

"It's that gigantic nigger that gave us the trouble before," Mr. Rosselli said.

"Jesus," Mr. Savarese said.

Officer Lewis walked up to the car and flashed his flashlight at Mr. Cassandro, Mr. Rosselli, and Mr. Savarese in turn.

"Is something wrong, Officer?" Mr. Cassandro said.

"May I have your driver's license and registration, please?" Tiny Lewis asked.

"Yeah, sure. You gonna tell me what I did wrong?"

"You were weaving as you drove down the street," Officer Lewis said.

"No I wasn't!" Mr. Cassandro said.

"Have you been drinking, sir?"

"Not a goddamn drop," Mr. Cassandro said. "What is this shit?"

"Shut your mouth," Mr. Savarese said sharply to Mr. Cassandro.

Officer Lewis flashed his light at Mr. Savarese.

"Oh, you're Mr. Savarese, aren't you?"

After a discernible pause Mr. Savarese said, "Yes, my name is Savarese."

"You left something behind you in the restaurant, Mr. Savarese," Officer Lewis said.

"I did? I don't recall—"

"Here it is, sir," Tiny Lewis said, and handed Mr. Savarese a large manila envelope.

"Please try to drive in a straight line," Tiny Lewis said. "Good night."

He walked back to his car and turned off the flashing lights.

"What did he give you?" Mr. Rosselli asked.

"Feels like photographs," Mr. Savarese replied.

"Of who?"

"There's two of them, Mr. S.," Mr. Rosselli said. "I adjusted the rearview mirror. I can see good."

"Two of who?"

"Two cop cars. The other's got a lieutenant or something in it. Another nigger."

"Get me out of here," Mr. Savarese said.

"You got it, Mr. S.," Mr. Cassandro said.

Officer Tiny Lewis watched until the Lincoln was out of sight, then drove to a diner on South 16th Street. Lieutenant Foster H. Lewis, Sr., drove his car into the parking lot immediately afterward.

A very large police officer, obviously Irish, about forty years of age, came out of the diner.

"Thank you," Lieutenant Lewis said to him.

"Don't talk to me, I haven't seen you once on this shift," the officer said, and got in the car Officer Lewis had been driving and drove away.

Officer Lewis got in the car with his father.

"You going to tell me what that was all about?"

"What *what* was all about?"

"Thanks a lot, Pop."

"You did that rather well for a rookie who's never spent sixty seconds on the street," Lieutenant Lewis said.

"Runs in the family."

"Maybe."

"You're really not going to tell me what that was all about?"

"What *what* was all about?"

The next day, Friday, Officer Matthew W. Payne was stopped twice by law-enforcement authorities while operating a motor vehicle.

The first instance took place on the Hutchinson River Parkway, north of the Borough of Manhattan, some twelve miles south of Scarsdale.

An enormous New York State trooper, wearing a Smoky the Bear hat, sat in his car and waited until he had received acknowledgment of his radio call that he had stopped a 1973 Porsche 911, Pennsylvania tag GHC-4048, for exceeding the posted limit of fifty miles an hour by twenty miles per hour. Then he got out of the car and cautiously approached the driver's window.

Nice-looking kid, he thought. But twenty miles over the limit is just too much.

And then he saw something on the floorboard. His entire demeanor changed. He flicked the top of his holster off and put his hand on the butt of his revolver.

"Put your hands out the window where I can see both of them," he ordered in a no-nonsense voice.

"What?"

"Do what I say, pal!"

Both hands came out the window.

"There's a pistol on your floorboard. You got a permit for it?"

"I'm a cop," Matt said. "I wondered what the hell you were up to. You scared the hell out of me."

"You got a badge?"

"I've got photo ID in my jacket pocket."

"Let's see it. Move slowly. You know the routine."

Matt produced his identification.

"You normally drive around with your pistol on the floorboard?"

"It's in an ankle holster. It rubs your leg if it's on a long time."

"I never tried one," the state trooper said. "I always thought I would kick my leg or something, and the gun would go flying across a room."

"No. They work. They just rub your leg, is all."

"You working?"

"I cannot tell a lie, I'm on my way to see my girl."

"This is yours?" the state trooper asked incredulously, gesturing at the Porsche.

"We take them away from drug dealers," Matt said.

"You work Narcotics?"

"Until Monday I work in something called Special Operations."

"Nice work."

"Yeah. It was. Monday I go back in uniform."

"Into each life some rain must fall," the state trooper said. "Take it easy."

"I will."

"I mean that. Take it easy. I clocked you at seventy-one."

"Sorry," Matt said. "I wasn't thinking. I'll watch it."

"My sergeant is a prick. He would ticket Mother Teresa."

"I have a lieutenant like that," Matt said.

The state trooper returned to his car, tooted the horn, and resumed his patrol.

It wasn't that I wasn't thinking. I was thinking. And what I was thinking was the closer I get to Scarsdale, to Amanda, the worse of an idea it seems. This is not the time to see her. She would not understand anything I have to say to her. And the reason for that is that I have nothing to say to her. Nothing that makes any sense, even to me.

Shit!

He put the Porsche in gear, reentered the flow of traffic, and at the next intersection turned around and headed for Philadelphia.

The second time Matt Payne attracted the attention of police officers charged with enforcement of the Motor Vehicle Code on the public highways took place several hours later, on Interstate 95, just inside the city limits of the City of Philadelphia.

"Jesus Christ!" he said aloud as he pulled to the side of the road, "this is really my day."

He glanced at the floorboard. His revolver and holster were safely out of sight. Two Highway Patrol officers approached the car.

"You're a cop?" one asked.

"You're Payne, right?"

"Guilty," Matt said.

"You better come back to the car with us," one of them said. "They're looking for you."

"Really?"

We have changed our minds about you, Payne. You are really an all-around splendid fellow, and we have decided that instead of sending you to the 12th, we are going to make you a chief inspector.

What the hell could it be?

If they've really been looking for me, then it's serious. Christ! Mother? Dad? One of the kids?

He leaned on the Highway car so he could listen.

"Highway 19. We have located Officer Payne. We're on I-95, near the Cottman Avenue exit."

"Wait one, Highway 19," radio replied.

"I really like your wheels, Payne," one of the Highway guys said.

"Thanks," Matt said.

"Highway 19, escort Officer Payne to City Hall. They are waiting for him in the mayor's office."

"This is 19, 'kay," the Highway guy on the radio said, and then turned to Matt. "What the hell is that all about?"

"I wish to hell I knew."

"Christ, if we had the lights and siren on that," the other one said, pointing at Matt's Porsche, "we could set a record between here and City Hall."

"We'll go ahead," the other one said, chuckling. "You can catch up, right?"

"I'll try," Matt said.

The Highway car was moving with its flashing lights on and the siren howling by the time Matt got back behind the wheel of the Porsche, but he had no trouble catching up with it.

Peter Wohl was waiting for him in the courtyard of City Hall.

"Well, you don't look hung over. Pull your necktie up."

"What's going on?"

"You ever hear that God takes care of fools and drunks? Just smile and keep your mouth shut. For once."

"Before we get this press conference started here," the Honorable Jerry Carlucci, mayor of the City of Philadelphia, said, "let's make sure everybody knows who everybody is. You all know Chief Lowenstein and Chief Coughlin, I know. Chief Coughlin's standing in for Commissioner Czernich, who's tied up and couldn't be with us, although he would have liked to. I'm sure most of you know the two who just came in: Inspector Peter Wohl, who commands Special Operations; and Officer Matt Payne, who is the Inspector's special assistant and who most of you will remember as the splendid young officer who . . . removed the threat to Philadelphia posed by the Northwest serial rapist. And standing beside me is a gentleman I'm sure most of you know and who is the reason I asked you to come here this afternoon. I would be very surprised if anyone here doesn't recognize Mr. H. Richard Detweiler, president of Nesfoods International, but in case . . . ladies and gentlemen, Mr. H. Richard Detweiler."

Detweiler and Carlucci shook hands, which seemed to sort of surprise Mr. Detweiler, who then moved to a lectern.

"Thank you, ladies and gentlemen, for coming here this afternoon," he said, reading it from a typewritten statement. "I am sure that most of you are aware of the tragedy that struck my family recently, with my daughter very nearly killed not six blocks from here.

"I am not here to talk about my daughter but about the Police Department. I am somewhat ashamed to admit that before my daughter was shot and nearly killed, I never paid much attention to the police. They were simply there. But my experience with them since my daughter was injured, an innocent bystander in what seems to be an incident of gangland warfare, has taught me how devoted to the safety and welfare of us all they are.

"Something even more shocking than the senseless shooting of my daughter has occurred in our city. I refer to the cold-blooded murder of Officer Joseph Magnella. That brutal, vicious act, the slaying of a police officer, poses a real, present, and absolutely intolerable danger to the entire fabric of our society, a threat we simply cannot tolerate.

"It came to my attention that one citizen, who wishes to remain anonymous, was thinking along the same lines. More important, she was prepared to do something about it. She was prepared to offer a reward for information leading to the arrest and conviction of those responsible for the brutal murder of Officer Magnella. The reward she offered was in the amount of ten thousand dollars. My wife and I have decided to offer an equal amount for the same purpose. I have a check here with me.

"I call upon—"

He stopped and fished in his pocket and came up with a check, which he handed to Mayor Carlucci, who shook his hand while flashbulbs popped.

That forgotten little detail out of the way, Detweiler continued. "I call upon my fellow citizens of Philadelphia to assist with the investigation of the murder of Officer Magnella. The police would prefer information, but if you have no information, certainly you can afford a dollar or two, whatever amount, to add to the reward fund and to demonstrate to the police that the people are behind them. Thank you very much."

Matt felt a tug at his arm. Wohl pulled him off the stage and out of the room.

"You are only partially forgiven," he said. "That whole ambience would be ruined if Detweiler tried to choke you. I know he'd love to."

"What does 'partially' mean?"

"What do you think it means?"

"I don't know."

"Put your uniform back in the mothball bag," Wohl said. "And forget the 12th."

"Thank you."

"Don't thank me. That came from the mayor."

"In other words, you'd rather not have me."

"I didn't say that," Wohl said. "Don't put words in my mouth."

Matt looked at him.

"My father thinks you'll make a pretty good cop," Wohl said. "Okay? Who am I to question his judgment?"

"Thank you," Matt said.

Two weeks and two days later, Staff Inspector Peter Wohl received a call from Walter J. Davis, Special Agent in Charge, of the Philadelphia office of the Federal Bureau of Investigation.

Mr. Davis told him that he had received word from the assistant special agent in charge (Criminal Affairs) of the Chicago, Illinois, office of the FBI that one Charles Francis Gregory, who was almost certainly the man in the photographs Wohl had shown him, had been found in the trunk of his automobile in Cicero, Illinois, having suffered seven large-caliber pistol wounds to the head and chest, probably from a Colt Government Model .45 ACP pistol.

Special Agent in Charge Davis said, unofficially, that the Chicago FBI believed Mr. Gregory to be a hit man and that the word was that Mr. Gregory had been shot because he had botched a job he had been hired to do.

"We've got to get together for lunch, Peter," Special Agent in Charge Davis said.

"We really should," Inspector Wohl replied. "Call me."